THE SUMMER GIRL

CW 01091319

ALSO BY ELLE KENNEDY

Good Girl Complex
Bad Girl Reputation

THE
SUMMER
GIRL

An Avalon Bay Novel

Elle Kennedy

ST. MARTIN'S
GRIFFIN
NEW YORK

First published in the United States by St. Martin's Griffin, an imprint of St. Martin's Publishing Group

THE SUMMER GIRL. Copyright © 2023 by Elle Kennedy. All rights reserved. Printed in the United States of America. For information, address St. Martin's Publishing Group, 120 Broadway, New York, NY 10271.

www.stmartins.com

Designed by Steven Seighman

Library of Congress Cataloging-in-Publication Data

Names: Kennedy, Elle, author.
Title: The summer girl / Elle Kennedy.
Description: First edition. | New York : St. Martin's Griffin, 2023. |
    Series: Avalon Bay ; 3
Identifiers: LCCN 2023009381 | ISBN 9781250863874 (trade paperback) |
    ISBN 9781250863881 (ebook)
Subjects: LCGFT: Romance fiction. | Novels.
Classification: LCC PS3611.E55857 S86 2023 | DDC 813/.6—dc23/
    eng/20230227
LC record available at https://lccn.loc.gov/2023009381

Our books may be purchased in bulk for promotional, educational, or business use. Please contact your local bookseller or the Macmillan Corporate and Premium Sales Department at 1-800-221-7945, extension 5442, or by email at MacmillanSpecialMarkets@macmillan.com.

First Edition: 2023

10 9 8 7 6 5 4

THE SUMMER GIRL

CHAPTER 1

CASSIE

July

"I don't think we should hook up anymore."

Oh my God.

No.

No no no no no.

See, this is why parties should be banned. I'm not even joking. We need to go back to the prohibition days, except we outlaw social events instead of alcohol. It's the only way to avoid this level of embarrassment. Or rather, secondhand embarrassment, because *I'm* not even the one getting dumped.

That honor is bestowed upon the guy with the deep, playful voice, who hasn't caught up to the fact that his dumper is dead serious. "Is this some weird sort of foreplay? I don't get it, but, sure, I'm down."

The girl's voice is flat, lined with dry humor. "I'm being serious."

She pauses for a long beat, during which I consider whether I can make a run for it without the couple noticing.

No more than ten feet away from them, I'm sitting against a driftwood log, concealed by shadows. But a clean getaway is difficult because they chose to break up in the worst possible location—

right where the beach grass thins and the dunes flatten into a stretch of packed sand. My mind has been *Mission: Impossible*-ing escape routes since The Dumping commenced. The couple is facing the dark ocean, which means if I attempt to take the beach route back to the party, they'll see me. But if I try to sneak behind them, they'll hear me. Have you ever tried walking silently in beach grass? You might as well attach a bell around your neck.

My only option is to remain hidden until it's over. The conversation *and* the relationship. Because while nobody wants to get dumped, having it happen in front of an audience is a hundred times worse, so I'm officially trapped here. Held hostage by social etiquette.

Of *all* the times to wander away from the bonfire and look at the stupid stars.

"I think this has run its course," the dumper says.

I can't tell what either of them look like. They're mere shadows. A tall shadow and a shorter one. I think the short one has long hair; I glimpse wispy strands blowing in the night breeze.

From the other end of the beach, the hum of voices, laughter, and faint hip-hop music travels along the water, triggering the desperate urge to be back at the party. I don't know a single person there, yet I don't think I've ever longed for the company of total strangers more than I do in this moment. The party is at some local named Luke's house. I was supposed to meet my friend Joy, who bailed at the last second. I was literally getting out of my car when her text popped up; otherwise, I would've just stayed home. But I figured, hey, I'm already here. Might as well mingle, maybe meet some people.

I should've hopped right back in the car and escaped when I had the chance.

The guy is finally catching on that this isn't a joke. "Wait, really? I thought we were still having a good time."

"Honestly? Not so much lately."

Ouch. Sorry, bro.

"Oh, don't look at me like that. I don't mean the sex. That's always good. But we've been doing this friends-with-benefits arrangement for almost a year now. Yeah, it's been on and off, but I think the longer we keep it up, the greater the risk that one of us catches feelings. We said from the start that we didn't want anything serious, remember?"

"Yeah, I remember."

The tall shadow lifts a hand and drags it through his hair. Either that, or he's petting a tiny cat that's sitting atop his head.

I truly can't see a damn thing out here.

"I'm not interested in getting into a relationship anytime soon," she adds. "I don't want a boyfriend."

There's a pause. "What about Wyatt?"

"What about him? Like I keep telling him, he and I are just friends. And I just want to be alone for a while." She chuckles. "Look, we both know you'll have no trouble finding a new friend with bennies, Tate. And if you want more than that, you'll have no trouble finding a girlfriend either. It's just not going to be me."

Double ouch.

I appreciate her candor, though. She's not wasting any time. Not leading this guy around by the nose. I mean, it does sound like this was more of a casual FWB situationship, but that might actually be the worst kind of breakup. Being friends with the person before the sexy stuff and wanting to remain friends *after* it? That's a tricky needle to thread.

I haven't been officially dumped before—that would require being in an actual relationship—but if I were to ever be the recipient of a breakup speech, I'd want it to sound like this one. Quick and to the point. Just snuff out the candle so there's not even a glimmer of light left. It's over. Move on.

Granted, I say that now. But considering I bawl at those courier commercials where the lonely grandmother receives a holiday card from her grandkids, I'd probably collapse in a pool of tears at my dumper's feet and then promptly check myself into a posh wellness facility for melancholia.

"Okay. Cool." He chuckles too, albeit wryly. "I guess that's that, then."

"That's that," she echoes. "Are we good?"

"Of course. We've known each other since we were thirteen. We're not going to stop talking just because we've stopped banging."

"I'm holding you to that," she warns.

Finally, blessedly, miraculously—they're done. The interaction ends. Her flip-flops smack loudly against the sand as she walks away, taking the beach route toward the party.

One down.

One to go.

To my dismay, the guy moves closer to the water, where he proceeds to stand like a statue, staring out. The new position places him closer to a shard of moonlight, providing a better view of him. He's tall. Muscular. Wearing board shorts and a T-shirt, although I can't tell what color they are because it's too dark. I think his hair might be blond. And he's got a great butt. I don't tend to notice butts—didn't think I was a butt girl, in fact—but this one really draws the eye.

With his back to me, this is my chance to creep away. I slowly rise to my feet and wipe my clammy hands on the front of my denim shorts. Man, I hadn't realized how wrought with tension I was. My palms only get sweaty before a first kiss and a particularly harrowing situation. Aka every conversation with my mother. Ergo, my palms are perpetually damp.

I take a deep breath, and then a small step.

Relief flutters through me when the guy doesn't turn my way.

Yes. I can totally do this. Hell, I only need to make it to that dune ten feet away. If he notices me after that, I can pretend I came from the grass. Oh sorry! Just taking a walk, didn't see you there!

Escape is within reach. I can taste it. So, of course, I make it about five feet before my phone decides to thwart my efforts by loudly alerting an incoming text.

And then another one.

And another one.

The guy spins around, startled.

"Hey." His deep, suspicious voice travels toward me in the night breeze. "Where the hell d'you come from?"

I feel my cheeks heat up. I'm grateful it's too dark for him to see the blush. "I'm sorry," I blurt out. "I, um . . ." My brain scrambles for a suitable reason for my presence. It fails. "I didn't hear a single second of your breakup, I swear."

Oh, fucking hell. Brilliant, Cassandra.

That gets me a faint laugh. "Not a single second, huh?"

"Nope, not a one. Seriously, I can assure you I most certainly did *not* just sit here and listen to you get dumped." My mouth has run away from me. It's in charge. It's the captain now. Another thing that happens when I'm nervous: I tend to babble. "For what it's worth, you handled it well. I mean, you didn't drop to your knees and cling to her legs and beg her not to go. So I'm grateful for that. Spared us both more embarrassment, you know? It's almost as if you knew I was trapped behind that log over there."

"Trust me, if I knew you were sitting there, I would've upped the sadness factor by like two hundred percent. Thrown in some tears, maybe cursed at the heavens and bemoaned my poor broken heart."

He saunters closer, and when I get a better look at his face, my heart instantly speeds up. Holy shit, he's gorgeous. What on earth was that girl thinking letting him get away?

I sweep my gaze over his classically handsome features. I wish I could discern what color his eyes are, but it's too dark out here. I was right about the blond hair, though, so I assume he has light-colored eyes. Blue. Maybe green. In those board shorts and slightly rumpled tee, he looks like the quintessential beach boy.

"And why would you have done that?" I ask.

"You know, just to make you extra uncomfortable. As punishment for your eavesdropping."

"*Involuntary* eavesdropping."

"That's what they all say." His mouth curves into a mischievous smile, which I think might be his default expression. He tips his head thoughtfully. "But you know what, I'll let it slide. I can never hold a grudge against a cute girl."

My cheeks get hotter.

Oh my God.

He thinks I'm cute?

I mean, I did select tonight's outfit with the end goal being cuteness. Short shorts that give my legs a deceptively longer look, paired with a tight tank top. Black, because that's the only color with the ability to make my boobs appear smaller. In light colors, they're bouncing around like two uncontained beach balls, even with a super supportive bra.

I realize his gaze hasn't once drifted to my chest, though. Or if it has, he's done it so smoothly and discreetly that I hadn't noticed. His eyes remain fixed on my face, and for a moment I'm tongue-tied. I see attractive guys back in Boston all the time. My college campus is practically crawling with them. But something about this one is making me wobbly in the knees.

Before I can think of a witty response to his *cute girl* remark—or any response at all, really—my phone dings again. I glance down. Another text from Peyton. Followed by another one.

"Someone's popular," he teases.

"Um, yeah. I mean, no. It's just my friend." I grit my teeth. "She's one of those annoying people who send, like, ten one-line messages instead of a single paragraph, so they just keep popping up and the phone dings over and over again until you want to smash it over their head. I hate that—don't you hate that?"

His jaw drops. "*Yes*," he says, with such sincerity I have to grin. He shakes his head. "I fucking *hate* that."

"Right?"

A final ding sounds, bringing us to a total of six Peyton messages.

When I skim the notifications, I'm once again thankful to be in the dark, because I'm certain my face is even redder.

Peyton: *How's the party?*
Peyton: *Any cute guys?*
Peyton: *Who are we going to fling with?*
Peyton: *Try to snap some pictures of the candidates!*
Peyton: *I really want to be part of this process.*
Peyton: *I wish I was there!*

I want to say that Peyton is joking. Alas, she is not. My main purpose for coming to the party tonight was to find a worthy candidate for my summer fling.

It's been a while since I spent an entire summer in Avalon Bay, but I still remember watching various friends over the years fall headfirst into summer romances. Those passionate, giddy, exhilarating love affairs where you can't keep your hands off each other and everything feels so urgent and intense because you know it's only temporary. Every moment is precious because come September, it's goodbye. I'd been so jealous of those girls, longing for a summertime love of my own, but it was hard to focus on boys and romance when my family was in constant turmoil.

After my parents divorced when I was eleven, Mom and I continued returning for the summers, at least at first. Mom's side of the family, the Tanners, has a long history with Avalon Bay. My grandparents own a beach house in the more affluent part of town, and they expected us to make the yearly trip to visit them. Back then, Mom and Dad were still putting on the cordial pretense for my sake. Once Dad remarried, however, all bets were off. Mom's anger and disdain toward him was out in the open now, and vice versa, which made coming back to the Bay an exercise in psychological warfare.

Fortunately, Mom remarried shortly after and announced we would no longer be spending our summers in the South Carolina beach town where I'd been born and raised. I can't say I wasn't relieved. It meant that when I did come back to visit, I could see Dad in peace and enjoy myself. Of course, then I'd return to Boston where Mom would interrogate me and demand to know every word my father uttered about her. Which was annoying and unfair, but still better than being trapped in the same town with both of them.

"Are you going to text her back?"

The guy's voice jolts me from my thoughts. "Oh. No. I'll answer her later."

I hastily tuck the phone into my back pocket. If I thought hearing him get dumped had been uncomfortable, it's nothing compared to the mortification I'd feel if he saw Peyton's message thread.

He watches me for a moment. "I'm Tate," he finally says.

I hesitate. "Cassie."

"Are you here for the summer?"

I nod. "I'm staying with my grandmother—she has a house over on the south end. But I actually grew up in Avalon Bay."

"You did?"

"Uh-huh. I moved to Boston with my mom after my parents' divorce, but my dad still lives here, so I basically became a summer girl. Well, maybe not an official summer girl, since I usually only come back for a week or two every July. Except this year I'm staying till after Labor Day, so I guess I'm a real summer girl now."

Stop babbling! I order myself.

"What about you?" I ask, desperate to take the focus off me and the fact that I must've used the phrase *summer girl* about four million times in one sentence.

"The opposite of you. I moved to the Bay at the start of junior high. Before that we lived in Georgia. St. Simon's Island." Tate sounds a bit glum. "I envy the Boston thing, to be honest. I kind of wish we moved to a city instead of trading one beach town for another. Do you go to school up there?"

"Yes. I go to Briar University."

"An Ivy girl, huh?"

We fall into step with each other, headed in the direction of the party. It's not a discussed course of action, just instinctive.

"I'm going into my senior year," I add.

"Cool. What are you studying?"

"English Lit." I glance over wryly. "I know. Totally useless unless I want to be a teacher."

"Do you want to be a teacher?"

"Nope."

He grins, and I catch a glimpse of straight white teeth in the moonlight. His smile is perfection. A girl could get lost in it.

I force myself to look forward, shoving my hands in my pockets as we walk. "You know what pisses me off, Tate?"

"What pisses you off, Cassie?" I can still feel him smiling at me.

"Everyone says you find yourself when you're in college, right? But from what I've seen, it's just a bunch of lame parties and all-night study sessions and listening to some blowhard drone on and on in a lecture hall. And meanwhile you sit there pretending you enjoyed the boring-ass book you were assigned to read, when in reality it's more enjoyable watching water boil than reading most classic literature. There—I said it. The classics suck, okay? And college is boring."

Tate chuckles. "Maybe you're not going to the right parties."

He's right. I'm not. Because I've never, ever attended a party where I've spoken at length with a guy who looks like Tate.

As we near the bonfire, our path is now clearly illuminated. Music continues to blast, a slow reggae song that has several couples wrapped around each other, moving to the sultry beat. The crowd seems to be comprised entirely of locals. At least, if there's anyone here from the country club, I don't recognize them. The summer set doesn't typically socialize with the year-round folks. Joy thinks the only reason she was invited tonight was because that Luke guy was hoping to hook up. "Those local boys get a kick out of seducing the rich girls," she'd laughed over lunch earlier.

Not that I would know. I've never been seduced by a local. I also don't consider myself a *rich girl*, although I suppose I am one. My mother's side of the family has money. A fair amount of it. But I'll always view myself as the girl who grew up on Sycamore Way, in a cozy house in the suburbs not far from this section of the Bay.

With the light of the bonfire making it easier to see each other, Tate eyes the ponytail I'm fiddling with and lets out a groan. "You're a ginger," he accuses, his eyes twinkling. They're a light blue, just as I suspected.

"Don't paint me with that ginger brush," I protest. "I'm a *copper*."

"That's not a real thing."

"I'm a copper," I insist. I grip my ponytail and hold it closer to his face. "See? Dark red. It's practically brown!"

"Mmm-hmm. Keep telling yourself that, ginger."

He seems distracted now. His gaze drifts across the fire and my gaze follows, coming to rest on a girl with bright red hair. A true ginger. Unlike me, who is a *copper,* thank you very much.

The ginger is chatting with two other young women, and all three are drop-dead gorgeous. Shiny hair and pretty faces. Skimpy clothes. And they've got those perfect beach bodies that trigger a pang of insecurity in me. I've always wondered what it's like to have normal proportions. It's probably awesome.

Tate's expression grows pained for a moment before he wrenches his eyes off the girl.

Understanding dawns on me. "Oh my God. Is that her? The dumper?"

He slides out a laugh. "It wasn't a dumping. And we're still friends—that's not going to change. She just caught me off guard, is all. I'm usually the one who ends those types of things."

"Do you want me to go beat her up for you?" I offer.

Pursing his lips, he assesses my frame. I'm five-three and kind of scrawny. Slender, except for my huge chest. Really, my boobs are probably more effective weapons than my fists.

"Nah," he answers, lips twitching. "I don't think I'd feel right being responsible for your death."

"That's really sweet."

He snorts.

"Tate!" someone calls, and we both turn toward the shout.

A very tall guy with a reddish beard stands nearby, holding up a joint. He waves it enticingly at Tate and arches a brow. An invitation. Tate nods at the guy, indicating with his hand that he'll be right there.

"Why are there so many redheads here?" I demand. "Is this a convention?"

"You tell me. These are your people, after all."

I growl at him, and he just laughs again. I like the sound of his laughter.

"Want me to introduce you around?" Tate offers.

Hesitation grips me. I'm torn. On one hand, it would be fun to stay and hang out. But the redheaded girl is watching us now, a slightly bemused look on her gorgeous face. In fact, *a lot* of eyes are on us, I realize. I get the feeling a guy like Tate invites this kind of attention, and I suddenly wish we were still shrouded in the darkness of the beach, just he and I. I hate being the center of attention. And I can't imagine how much nervous babbling I'll do with each new person I meet.

So I shake my head and say, "Actually, I'm heading out. Got somewhere else to be."

He grins. "Fine. Be that way, Ms. Popular."

Hardly. The only place I'm going after this is home. But it's probably better to let him believe I'm fluttering from party to party on Friday nights like some elusive social butterfly. Peyton would approve of that plan. *Always leave 'em wanting more* is my best friend's motto.

"You're here till September, you said?"

"Yup," I say lightly.

"Cool. Then I'm sure we'll see each other around."

"Yeah, maybe."

Shit. That sounded far too noncommittal. What I *should* have said is something coy and flirty, like, *I hope so . . .* and then asked for his number. I inwardly smack myself, scrambling for a way to fix the error, but it's too late. Tate is already sauntering off toward his friends.

If they look back, it's a good sign. That's what Peyton always says.

Swallowing hard, I stare at his retreating back, his long stride making tracks in the sand.

And then.

He looks back.

I breathe in relief and offer him an awkward wave before turning away. My heart's beating fast as I head up the grassy path toward the road, where I parked my grandmother's Land Rover. I pull my phone out of my pocket just as another text lights up the screen.

Peyton: *So??? Have we found the lucky guy?*

I bite my lip and glance back in the direction of the party.

Yes.

Yes, I think we have.

CHAPTER 2

CASSIE

I find my grandmother in the kitchen the next morning, pulling a muffin pan out of the oven. She moves it to the cooling rack on the counter, next to the three other trays already sitting there.

"Morning, dear. Pick your poison," Grandma chirps, glancing at me over her shoulder. "We've got banana nut, bran, carrot, and the blueberry just came out so it needs some time to cool."

No doubt she's been up since 7 A.M. baking up a storm. For a woman in her seventies, she's still remarkably spry. Which is funny, because on the outside she appears so fragile. She's got a slender build, delicate hands, and her skin is thinning in her old age so you can always see bluish veins rippling beneath it.

And yet Lydia Tanner is a force of nature. She and my grandpa Wally ran a hotel for fifty years. They bought the beachfront lot for a song in the late sixties, after Grandpa was injured in Vietnam and discharged from the military. Even wilder is that they were my age when they built the Beacon Hotel from the ground up. I can't imagine building and then operating a hotel at twenty, especially one as grand as the Beacon. And up until two years ago, the waterfront property was my grandparents' pride and joy.

But then Grandpa passed, and the hotel was nearly gutted by the last hurricane to ravage the coast. It wasn't the first time the

Beacon fell victim to a storm—it's happened twice before—but unlike the previous times, nobody in the family wanted to renovate and restore it this time. Grandma was too old and tired to do the job herself, especially without Grandpa Wally by her side, and I know she's secretly disappointed none of her kids chose to take up that mantle. But my mom and her siblings weren't interested in salvaging the Beacon, so Grandma finally made the decision to sell. Not just the hotel, but her house too.

The house sale closes in two months, and the Beacon is being reopened in September under its new ownership, which is why we're back. Grandma wanted to spend one last summer in Avalon Bay before she moves up north to be closer to her kids and grandkids.

"How was the party?" she asks as she settles into a chair at the kitchen table.

"It was okay." I shrug. "I didn't really know anyone there."

"Who was hosting it?"

"Some guy named Luke. He's a sailing instructor at the club. That's how Joy met him. And speaking of Joy, she didn't even show up! She invites me to a party and then deserts me. I felt like a random interloper."

Grandma smiles. "Sometimes that's more fun. Going someplace where nobody knows you . . ." She arches a thin eyebrow. "It can be exciting to reinvent yourself and play a role for the night."

I grimace. "Please don't tell me you and Grandpa used to meet at hotel bars back in the day and pretend to be other people in some weird role-play to spice up the marriage."

"All right, dear. I won't tell you that."

Her brown eyes sparkle, giving her a youthful air. It's funny, Grandma comes off as so elegant and unapproachable in public. Always dressed like she stepped off a yacht, sporting these preppy

little outfits more suited for posh Nantucket than laid-back Avalon Bay. I swear she owns a thousand Hermès scarves. Yet when
she's around family the icy exterior melts and she's the warmest
woman you'll ever meet. I love hanging out with her. And she's
hilarious. Sometimes she'll drop a dirty joke out of nowhere at a
big family dinner. It's jarring when spoken in her delicate southern
accent, and it puts us all in hysterics. My mother hates it. Then
again, my mother doesn't have a sense of humor. Never has.

"Did you make any new friends?" Grandma prompts.

"No. But that's okay. I'll see Joy while in town, and Peyton
might come visit for a week or two in August." I wander over to
the baking trays and study the muffin selections. "I still wish I
didn't let you talk me out of getting a job this summer."

Grandma plucks off a small piece of her bran muffin. As long
as I've known her, her breakfast has consisted of a muffin and a
cup of tea. That's probably how she's maintained her figure all
these years.

"Cass, sweetheart, if you'd gotten a job, well, then you wouldn't
be able to have breakfast with me, would you?"

"That's a good point." I select a banana nut muffin and grab a
small glass plate from the cupboard, then join her at the table. A
little walnut falls off my muffin, and I pop it into my mouth. "So
what are we doing today?"

"I thought we'd go into town and browse some of the new
shops that have opened up? Levi Hartley has taken it upon himself to revamp the entire boardwalk. His construction company
has been making its way through all the establishments hurt by
the hurricane, fixing them up one by one. There's a very nice hat
shop I passed the other day that I wouldn't mind visiting."

Only Grandma Lydia would want to go to a *hat* shop. The only
hat I've ever worn is the Briar U baseball cap they handed out at
freshman orientation, and that's because they forced us to put them

on in order to swear fealty to our new school. I think it's somewhere in the back of my closet now.

"Hat shopping. I can't wait."

She snorts softly.

"And I need to find a present for the girls' birthday, so I wouldn't mind peeking into a couple of those kid stores. Oh! Any chance we can pop into the hotel too? I really want to see what they did inside."

"So do I," Grandma says, a slight frown touching her lips. "The young woman who bought it—Mackenzie Cabot—promised she would preserve your grandfather's and my intent for the property, maintain its charm and character. She sent me the drawings of the upgrades they'd be doing, along with pictures of her progress. They indeed showed her commitment to restoring everything as close to the original as possible. But I haven't received an update since early June."

Her concern is evident. I know that was Grandma's biggest fear—the Beacon becoming completely unrecognizable. The hotel was her legacy. It survived three hurricanes, was lovingly rebuilt by my grandparents twice. They put everything they had into it. Their blood, sweat, and tears. Their love. And it irks me, just a bit, that not a single one of their four children fought to keep it in the family.

My two uncles, Will and Max, live in Boston with their wives, and they each have three young kids. Both were adamant they weren't going to relocate to the South to renovate a hotel they didn't care about. Aunt Jacqueline and her husband, Charlie, have a house in Connecticut, three kids, and zero interest in dipping their toes in the hospitality industry. And then there's Mom, who has a full social calendar in Boston and is busy spending her ex-husband's money, which at this point is out of pure spite because she went into the marriage independently wealthy; the Tanners are worth millions. But my former stepdad Stuart made the mistake of being the one to ask for a divorce, and my mother is nothing if not petty.

I scarf down the rest of my muffin before hopping out of my chair.

"Okay, if we're going into town, let me change into something a little more presentable," I say, gesturing to my ratty shorts and loose T-shirt. "I can't be going hat shopping in this." I aim a pointed glare at Grandma's impeccably pressed chinos, sleeveless shirt, and striped silk scarf. "Especially next to you. Like, jeez, lady. You look like you're going to a luncheon with a Kennedy."

She chuckles. "Have you forgotten my most important rule of life, dear? *Always leave the house dressed as if you're going to—*"

"*—be murdered,*" I finish, rolling my eyes. "Oh, I remember."

I tell ya, Grandma can get dark sometimes. But it's good advice. I think about it often, in fact. One time I accidentally left my dorm wearing my must-do-laundry panties, the neon-orange ones with the huge hole in the crotch. When I realized it, I almost broke out in hives at the thought that if I were to be killed today, the coroner would undress me on that metal slab and my crotch hole would be the first thing they saw. I'd be the only blushing dead body in the morgue.

Upstairs, I find a pink sundress and slip it on, then braid my hair. My phone rings as I'm slapping an elastic band around the end of the braid. It's Peyton. I didn't call her back when I got home last night, but I did send an intentionally cryptic text I knew would drive her nuts.

"Who is he?" she demands when I put her on speakerphone. "Tell me everything."

"Nothing to tell." I wander over to the vanity table and examine my chin. I feel a zit coming on, but my reflection says otherwise. "I met a hot guy, turned down his invitation to hang out with him at the party, and went home instead."

"Cassandra." Peyton is aghast.

"I know."

"What the hell is wrong with you? The *whole point* of going last night was to meet a dude! And you found one! And you said he's hot?"

"Hottest guy I've ever seen," I moan.

"Then why did you leave?" Her confusion might as well be an accusation.

"I chickened out," I confess. "He was too intimidating! And you should've seen the girls he was with—they were these perfect, tall, fit goddesses. With perfectly proportioned boobs . . . unlike someone you know."

"Oh my God, Cass. Stop. You know how I feel about you beating up on yourself."

"Yeah, yeah, you want to punch me in the face. I can't help it, though. Seriously, those girls were gorgeous."

"And so are you." A frazzled sound echoes over the speaker. "You know, I really hate your mother."

"What does my mother have to do with this?" I snicker.

"Are you kidding me? I've been to your house. I hear how she talks to you. I was actually speaking to my mom about it the other day, and she was saying all that hurtful shit is bound to affect your self-esteem."

"Why are you speaking to your mom about me?" I demand, embarrassment climbing up my throat.

Having a best friend whose mother is a clinical psychologist is definitely a pain in the ass sometimes. I've known Peyton since we were eleven—we met not long after Mom and I moved to Boston—and Peyton's mother would constantly pry into my psyche when I was a kid. She always tried getting me to talk about my parents' divorce, how it made me feel, how my mother's criticism affected me. Blah, blah, and blah. I don't need a shrink to tell me there's a direct correlation between my insecurities and my mother's verbal attacks. Or that my mother is a raging bitch. I know it all too well.

On the rare occasions Dad and I have spoken about her, he's admitted that Mom has always skewed more toward *me me me* on the altruism scale. But the divorce really twisted something inside her. Made her worse. It certainly didn't help that he remarried within a year and a half and now has two other daughters.

"Mom thinks we need to silence your inner critic. Aka your mother's horrible voice in your head."

"I shut my inner critic up all the time. Silver lining, remember?" Because while my grandmother's life rule is to make sure you get murdered in your Sunday best, mine has always been to look on the bright side. Find the silver lining in every situation, because the alternative—wallowing in the darkness—is bound to destroy you.

"Of course, Little Miss Sunshine," Peyton says mockingly. "Always looking for the silver lining—how could I forget?" Her voice takes on a note of challenge. "Okay, fine. So tell me, what's the silver lining in letting Hottie slip away?"

I mull it over. "He's too hot," I finally answer.

Laughter bursts out of the phone. "That would be the reason *not* to let him slip away." She makes a loud buzzing sound. "Try again."

"No, that's really it," I insist. "Imagine if the first guy I ever sleep with is at *that* level of hotness? It'll spoil all future men for me! I'll expect every man who comes afterward to be a perfect ten, and when nobody measures up I'm just going to be devastated."

"You're impossible. Did you get his number at least?"

"No, I told you, I ran away like a nervous babbling bunny."

She lets out a loud, heavy sigh. "This is unacceptable to me, Cassandra Elise."

"My deepest apologies, Peyton Marie."

"If you see him again, you're asking him out, understood?" My best friend has snapped into totalitarian mode. "No babbling. No excuses. Promise me you'll ask him out next time you see him."

"I will. I promise," I say lightly, but only because I'm confident I'll never see him again.

Joke's on me, though.

The moment Grandma and I step outside five minutes later, I find none other than Tate standing in our driveway.

CHAPTER 3

TATE

It takes a second to realize the cute redhead on the porch is the same one from the party last night. She was right—her hair is more copper than ginger. I guess the bonfire made it appear lighter. My gaze then darts to her chest, just a quick peek to confirm I hadn't fallen into some teenage-boy fantasy yesterday. But nope, didn't dream it. Her rack is objectively spectacular. Sue me for noticing. I'm a man. I always notice a great rack.

She's wearing a short sundress that falls mid-thigh and clashes with the red-painted toenails poking out of her strappy sandals. And she's staring at me as if she's not quite sure what to make of my presence.

"Mr. Bartlett, what brings you here this morning?"

My gaze shifts to the older woman next to Cassie. "Morning, Mrs. Tanner." I flash an easy smile that my friends tell me could disarm a dictator. Not that Lydia Tanner is a dictator. She's a perfectly nice lady, based on the interactions we've had when I was housesitting the place next door. This is my fourth summer staying at Gil and Shirley Jackson's luxury waterfront property. I've been looking forward to it for weeks.

"Just wanted to stop by and let you know I'm watching the Jackson place again for the summer," I tell her. "So if you see lights on at random hours, or, you know, handsome guys walking around in the nude, don't be alarmed . . . and feel free to keep looking." I wink.

Cassie snorts out a sarcastic laugh.

"Cassandra," Lydia chides. "Let the boy think he's charming us."

"Think?" I mock good-naturedly. "You know you love me, Mrs. Tanner."

"As I told you last year, you can call me Lydia. This is my granddaughter, Cassandra."

"Cassie," she corrects.

"Actually, we met last night," I inform Lydia. "Ran into each other at a party. How's it going, ginger?"

"Do not call me that." Cassie glowers at me.

Lydia turns to her granddaughter. "Well, there you go, dear. We were just discussing your lack of friend options, and look, now you'll have a friend right next door. And he's already given you an amusing nickname! This is wonderful." She reaches out and pats Cassie on the arm, as if placating a distressed puppy.

Cassie's cheeks redden. "You are the worst," she grumbles at her grandmother.

Chuckling, Lydia descends the steps of the wraparound porch. "I'll go start the car."

"She said that on purpose just to embarrass me," Cassie mutters. She narrows her eyes at me. "I have friends."

I blink innocently. "Sure sounds like it."

"*I have friends,*" she insists, a growl coming from the back of her throat.

I choke down a laugh. Fuck, she's cute. Like, ridiculously cute. I have a thing for chicks with freckles. And ones who blush when I smile at them.

"Does that mean you don't want to be my friend?" I ask, eyeing Cassie in amusement.

"Friendship is a huge commitment. We should probably just

stick to being neighbors. But you're in luck, because that means we can do lots of fun neighborly things." She pauses. "I'm not quite sure what. Maybe stand at two windows that face each other and use flashlights to send Morse code messages?"

"Is that what you think neighbors do?"

"I don't know. My dorm window looks out at a brick wall, so nobody's sending any covert messages to me, unless you count the drunk frat boy who always gets lost on his way to Greek Row and stumbles around shouting that the moon isn't real. And I'm not friends with any of the neighbors at Mom's house in Boston. Not that you and I are friends. I mean, I don't even know you. We're total strangers. Although, I *did* see you get dumped, which was equally upsetting for both of us, and that kind of shared humiliation leads to a forced kind of intimacy that nobody should ever have to experience—" She cuts herself off. "You know what? I'm just gonna go. Grandma and I are going into town. Goodbye, Tate."

My lips twitch in a difficult attempt to suppress a grin. "Uh-huh. Cool. See you later, neighbor."

She huffs, and my smile springs loose as I watch her march off. My gaze lowers, resting briefly on her ass. Damn, a great rack *and* a great ass. She's on the shorter side, though. I've always been drawn to taller girls. At six-one, I don't want to break my neck bending down to kiss someone. Cassie's five-two, five-three tops, but something about the set of her shoulders and the way she walks gives her more stature. And she's funny. A little strange. But funny. I was already looking forward to these next eight weeks at the Jackson house. Having Cassie next door for the summer is the icing on an already delicious cake.

The white Range Rover heads for the end of the circular driveway with Mrs. Tanner behind the wheel. I watch it disappear, then head next door. Because the homes on this stretch of the waterfront are situated on a slope, there isn't a lot of space between the houses, at least not on the street-facing side, which means you're always seeing your neighbors. But the high, westerly location also means spectacular views of Avalon Bay, and unparalleled sunsets.

The Jackson house took a few hits in the last storm, but Gil instantly hired a contractor to fix it up and a landscaper to haul out all the fallen trees and debris. All that remains now are the moss-draped oaks and other mature trees that have stood strong and proud for decades. The property is loaded with charm. It blows me away every time I stay here.

I step through the graceful white columns onto the covered porch and let myself in through the front door. Inside, I give the immaculate main floor a long once-over. I always get paranoid housesitting this place, afraid of breaking something priceless or spilling beer all over their expensive rugs. I wander into the chef's kitchen toward the longest island I've ever seen. My fingertips skim sleek oak, painted a nautical blue. The housekeeper, Mary, was here yesterday, so everything is clean and dust-free. The smell of lemon and pine mingles with the familiar salty scent wafting in from the back doors. The first thing I did when I got here was open the three sets of French doors that make up the entire rear wall of the living room. My mood is always a thousand times better when I can smell the ocean.

My phone buzzes and I pull it out of my pocket to see a message from my mother.

Mom: *All settled in?*

I tap out a quick response.

Me: *Yup. Unpacked and ready for two months of freedom. You guys were really cramping my style.*

Mom: *Yes, I'm sure all that home cooking was a real drag.*

Me: *Shit. Fine. I'll miss that part. But Gil added a Fountain Lightning to his private fleet, so I think that might make up for all the greasy takeout I'll be eating.*

Mom: *I'll drop off some frozen lasagnas. Grease poisoning is no joke.*

Me: *How are my children? Do they miss me?*

Mom: *Well . . . Fudge just took a four-hour nap, and Polly just ate a bug. So I'm gonna say . . . no?*

Me: *Nah, sounds like coping mechanisms for missing me. You should let them sleep in your bed while I'm gone so they don't feel lonely.*

Mom: *Sure won't!*

I grin at the phone. My parents are sadists who refuse to let our family dogs sleep in their bed. I'll never understand it.

Me: *Anyway, I gotta go. I'll message you tomorrow.*

Mom: *Love you.*

Me: *Love you too.*

I don't care if it makes me the biggest loser on the planet, but sometimes I think my mom is my best friend. Hands down, she's the coolest chick I know. And I tell her nearly everything. I mean, sure, I keep my sex life to myself, but there's very little else I won't confide in Mom about. Dad, too. In fact, I think he might also be my best friend.

Christ, maybe I *am* a huge loser.

Leaving my phone on the counter, I amble toward the French doors and peer outside. Beyond the stone dining patio, grill, and outdoor fireplace is a short wooden staircase leading to the upper deck. Beyond *that* is the path that takes you to the lower deck and the Jacksons' long, private dock, complete with an electric boat lift and a covered pierhead. I focus my gaze on the end of the dock, admiring the two boats currently moored there. Gil's prized Hallberg-Rassy, the *Surely Perfect,* is moored at the yacht club marina, but he keeps his high-performance powerboat and Boston Whaler Sport Fisherman at the house for the season.

A shiver runs through me as I gawk at the red-and-white powerboat. The Lightning. Christ, I'd kill to take her out, but she's ludicrously expensive and I'd never dream of asking Gil if I could use her.

I seriously envy this man's life. A real estate developer who's worth millions, Gil owns several properties around the globe and pretty much an entire fleet of boats. He and Shirley are spending the next two months in New Zealand, where they're looking to add another house to their portfolio. And, knowing Gil, another sailboat. Lucky assholes. Their life sounds like pure heaven to me—sailing around the world, exploring new places . . .

The sailing part, in particular, is what really gets my blood going. Being a part-time sailing instructor at the club doesn't feel like enough to me; for years I've longed to be out on the water full-time, but that's simply not feasible, not when I also need to put in the hours at Bartlett Marine, the family business. Don't get me wrong, it's not a bad gig. And it's always astonishing to see how much money people are willing to drop on their boats. But still, I'd rather be *on* a boat than hand over her keys to somebody else.

Since I have the day off—and Gil's permission to use the Whaler and the Sea-Doos—I grab my phone from the kitchen counter. The weather's perfect for a day on the water, and I scroll through my message threads trying to decide which one of my boys to text.

I'm pretty sure Danny, a fellow instructor at the club, is working today.

Luke should be home, but I have a feeling he'll be too hung-over from the party last night. When I left around 2 A.M., he was still doing tequila shots with our friends Steph and Heidi.

I'd ask my buddy Wyatt, our local tattoo artist, but things are kind of weird between us. Not on my account, though. I was just going about my business, hanging out with Alana here and there, when Wyatt broke up with his longtime girlfriend and suddenly decided he had a thing for Alana too. Next thing I know, I'm in a love triangle I never wanted to be part of, over a woman who doesn't actually want either one of us.

I text Luke first, who responds without mincing words.

Luke: *Bro, I'm so hungover. If I go out on the water I'll puke all over your ugly face.*

I try Evan Hartley next, though I'm pretty sure he told me last night that he and his brother Cooper were at one of their construction sites today. I message him anyway, because he's the twin more likely to shirk his responsibilities and go day-drinking on a boat with me.

Evan: *Can't. We're so fucking behind on this stupid job.*

Damn. Guess I'm on my own today.

Evan: *But we're grabbing beers with Danny later. Rip Tide. Around 7. You in?*

I quickly shoot off a response.

Me: *I'm down. See you there.*

CHAPTER 4

CASSIE

"Do you think a six-year-old would like this?" I hold up a red T-shirt that features a purple unicorn riding a surfboard. "What are kids into these days? I have no idea what's age appropriate."

My grandmother's laughter echoes between us. "And I do? I just turned seventy-four, dear. When I was six years old, dinosaurs still roamed the earth."

I snort. "Seventy-four is not old. And you don't look it anyway."

I put the shirt back on the rack. I feel like the colors are too loud. When I saw the girls at Easter, they were both clad in pale pastels. Hmmm. But that could have just been an Easter thing. I know my stepmother, Nia, likes to dress them up for holidays. When I visited this past Christmas, they were in matching red dresses and cute mistletoe headbands.

Ugh. This is way too hard, which only highlights how little I know my half sisters. But I suppose that's bound to be the result when their mother makes sure I spend as little time as possible with them. Hell, I bet if it were up to her, I wouldn't even be joining them for the birthday celebrations next month. Poor Nia. She was probably secretly furious when her twin girls were born on my birthday. And, God, the irony of that . . . Dad's new daughters born on the same day as his old one, effectively erasing me from his life and—

Silver lining! the voice in my head shouts before I sink any deeper.

Right. I draw an even breath. The silver lining of sharing a birthday with my sisters . . . One party instead of two. Consolidation is always a plus.

"I don't know." My gaze conducts another sweep of the rack of children's clothing. "Maybe we can go to the board game store instead? The one next to the smoothie place?" Shopping for this gift has become surprisingly daunting.

Grandma and I exit the store and step into the oppressive July heat. I forgot how hot it gets down here in the summer. And what a total madhouse the main strip becomes. But I'm unbothered by both the sweltering air and the crowds. Avalon Bay isn't just the quintessential beach town with its boardwalk, tourist shops, and annual carnival—it's my home. I was born here. All my childhood memories are tied to this town. I could be gone for fifty years and that sense of familiarity, of belonging, would still be right here when I returned.

"When are you seeing your father?" Grandma asks as we head down the sidewalk. The air is so hot and humid that the pavement beneath our feet is practically hissing from the heat.

"Friday," I answer. "I'm going over there for dinner. And then Saturday evening we might take the girls out somewhere. Maybe mini golf."

"That will be fun. He wasn't able to see you this weekend?"

Although there's no judgment in her voice, I can't help but come to Dad's defense. "The girls had a whole bunch of birthday parties to attend. I guess their entire social circle is a bunch of July babies."

And he couldn't step away for an hour or so and take you to lunch? Dinner?

Do the girls not have a mother who can watch them for a while?

Isn't their bedtime eight o'clock?

All valid questions if she'd asked, but Grandma has more tact than that and knows my relationship with Dad is complicated.

In all honesty, I'm used to being an afterthought to him. For years now he's made a concerted effort to avoid being alone with me if he can help it, grasping on to any opportunity to ensure Nia and the twins are there to serve as a buffer. I'm sure he knows I notice, but he doesn't acknowledge what he's doing and neither do I. And so it just keeps growing between us, this mountain of words I can't say to him. It started off as a tiny little word hill and now it's a peak of unspoken proportions. Thick with emotion and riddled with obstacles. Little accusations I'll never say out loud.

Why didn't you fight for custody?

Why didn't you want me?

"Are you looking forward to seeing your sisters?"

I push the bleak thoughts away and paste on a sunny smile for Grandma. "I'm always excited to see the twins. They're so cute."

"Are they still fluent in French?" she asks curiously.

"Yup. Fluent in French and English." My stepmother is Haitian and grew up speaking French, so she was adamant that her kids know her native tongue. It's fun watching Roxanne and Monique converse in French. Sometimes, it's Roxy speaking French and Mo answering in English, or vice versa, which makes for some hilarious one-sided conversations. I really do adore my sisters. I wish I got to spend more time with them.

Grandma seems to be slowing down, so I match my gait to hers. "You okay?" I ask.

We've been shopping for two hours. Not the longest time, but it's also a hundred degrees out and she's dressed in silk from head to toe. I'm surprised her clothing isn't plastered to her body. I would be a sweaty mess. But Grandma is perpetually put-together, even when baking under the sun.

"I am feeling the heat," she admits. She uncurls the scarf from around her neck and uses a pale hand to fan the exposed flesh. The sun continues to beat down on us. She's wearing a wide-brimmed hat, but I'm hat-free despite our visit to the hat shop.

"Let's just hit the board game place and then head home," I suggest.

She nods. "That's a good idea."

We're nearing the smoothie shop when a traitor appears at the storefront window. Joy taps on the window and waves at me. She holds up a finger to signal she'll be one second.

"Oh, Joy's coming out," I tell my grandmother.

I take her arm and move away from the sidewalk to let a group of pedestrians pass. It's a never-ending stream of people, Avalon Bay at its prime tourist peak. Families, couples, and groups of rowdy teens are already swarming the streets and filling the beach, and with the carnival having just been set up at the end of the board-walk, it's going to be even more packed in the coming weeks. I really missed this place.

Joy exits the shop sucking on the straw of her smoothie. She's wearing a white minidress that complements her dark complex-ion, wedge sandals, and oversized sunglasses. Gucci, her go-to designer.

"I'm so glad I bumped into you," she chirps, brown eyes shin-ing happily. "I was literally about to text and see if you wanted to go out tonight."

I mock glare at her. "Why? So you can bail on me again?"

She groans repentantly. "Argh, I know, I'm so sorry about last night."

"What the hell was that about? You twist my arm into going to some townie's party and then don't even show?" I grumble.

"I'm sorry," she says again, but her tone is breezier now, her re-morse all but gone. Joy's been flighty for as long as I've known her, and she doesn't waste much time groveling. Once she apologizes for a sin, she moves on from it with lightning speed. "I left the club and was going home to change for the party, just like I texted, but then I pulled into the drive to find Isaiah waiting on my doorstep."

Isaiah is the guy she's been on and off with since we were sixteen. Last time she and I spoke, though, she swore she was done with that. I *tsk* with disappointment. "Please don't tell me you got back together with him."

"No, no. He was just dropping off a box of stuff I left at his place. And there were some photos in there that I'd printed out, so we started going through them, and one thing led to another and—cover your ears, Mrs. Tanner—we fucked."

My grandmother barks out a laugh. "It's lovely to see you too, Joy," Grandma says, before reaching over to lightly pat my arm. "Cass, why don't I drive back to the house and Joy can take over as your shopping companion?"

"Are you sure?" My brow creases. "You're okay driving on your own?"

"I drove us here," she reminds me, offering that dignified one-raised-eyebrow look that translates to *don't question your elders, dear*.

I question her anyway. "Yes, but you said you were feeling the heat. What if you have sunstroke—"

"I'll be fine. Go. You girls have fun. Sounds like you have a lot to chat about." Eyes twinkling, Grandma leaves us to our own devices.

I watch her go, and her strong gait and straight shoulders ease my concerns. Sometimes it's hard to remember what a tough broad she is when it looks like the merest breeze could knock her over.

"So what are we buying?" Joy asks.

"I wanted to pop into the board game store to find something for Roxy and Mo's birthdays."

"Wow, Nia's letting you see her precious progeny on their special day?"

"Be nice."

"Nah, that's your job. You're the nice one. I'm the raging bitch in this friendship, remember? That's why we make a good team."

It's an interesting friendship, I'll give her that. Whereas I met Peyton when I moved to Boston, I've known Joy since we were five. She was a summer girl, her family coming down from Manhattan every year to spend June till August in the Bay. We were inseparable as kids, but eventually drifted apart, not reconnecting until I was sixteen and visiting my dad for a few weeks. My sisters were barely two at that point, so Dad had his hands full and very little time for me. I ended up spending most of the vacation hanging out by the country club pool, where I bumped into Joy one morning and the friendship got a reboot.

"Yeah, and where was my teammate last night?" I demand. "I still can't believe you ditched me. I didn't know a single person there." Which isn't surprising, considering I could probably count the number of townies I know by name on one hand.

The summer kids don't usually socialize with the locals. They travel in different circles, spending most of their time on expensive family yachts or at the country club, where I anticipate passing the bulk of my time this summer. In my future I predict a lot of lying around on lounge chairs and checking out all the hot preppy boys.

Don't get me wrong, I'm not one of those rich girls who refuses to work. I've had part-time jobs since I was sixteen and just spent the last three years of college working as a barista. My work ethic comes solely from my father. Dad, who didn't come from a filthy-rich family like Mom, always hammered the importance of good, honest work into my head. Grandma, however, refuses to let me get a job while I'm in the Bay this summer, determined to force daily quality time on me. I'm certainly not complaining, though. I prefer Grandma's company to most.

"I heard it was a good time," Joy says as we fall into step with each other. She sips her smoothie. "The guy who invited me— Luke? He texted earlier asking why I didn't show. Poor boy was devastated." She grins. "I totally would've hooked up with him too. He's cute. But stupid Isaiah. I just can't stay away from that asshole."

"It's a real problem," I agree solemnly.

"You didn't talk to anyone at all?" she pushes. "Not even the infamous Hartley twins? I think one of them was there."

Okay, so I can name *those* locals. I'm pretty sure everyone, local and summer kid alike, has heard of the Hartleys. The two sinfully hot twins who used to raise hell around town. There was one rumor going around back in the day about a stolen goat, a stolen police car, and a joyride around the Bay that ended with one of the twins in the hospital for a concussion. But that sounds too ludicrous to be true. The tales of their numerous hookups, particularly with the Garnet College girls who arrive every September . . . well, those rumors I tend to believe.

"I didn't see them," I say, searching my memory. I vaguely remember a tall dude with dark hair and tattoos, but, really, that could have been anyone. "I did talk to one guy, though."

"Ahh! Yes! That's my girl. Who?"

"Tate." I try to recall what Grandma called him this morning. Mr. . . . "Bartlett. Tate Bartlett?"

Joy's jaw falls open. "Really? Oh, I know *all* about him."

"You do?" I'm surprised. Like I said, aside from the occasional illicit tryst, summer kids and locals aren't too socially compatible.

"Oh yeah, he hooked up with my sister last summer."

"No! Shut up! Louisa?" For the sheer life of me, I cannot envision Joy's older sister hooking up with anybody, let alone Tate.

Louisa is as prim and proper as they come. I always assumed she was waiting for marriage. "What about her chastity belt?"

My friend snorts. "Someone found the key, and his name was Tate Bartlett. He's an instructor at the yacht club, like that Luke guy. They're friends."

I still can't wrap my head around Louisa and Tate. "How did that even happen? Him and Louisa."

"She was feeling adventurous last year. Remember she was going through her awful platinum-blond phase? I texted you a pic of it."

I nod gravely. "That did not look good."

"No, it didn't." Joy twists the smoothie straw around with her fingers. "So, anyway, they met at the club, he asked her out, and they hooked up. Just third base, I think. Because, you know, it's my sister. But I'm told he's a major playboy."

Not exactly a shock. Guys that good-looking usually have their pick of women.

Hearing he's a player, though, does dull some of the Tate shine. "So he's got a rep for being a sleaze?"

"Actually, it's the opposite. Like, this man hooks up more than a celebrity, yet you won't hear a bad word about him. Everyone who knows him or who's been with him gets all starry-eyed when you bring him up. Starts gushing about how sweet and wonderful he is. And great in bed, of course."

"Of course," I echo, rolling my eyes. Inside, I'm a bit relieved to hear he doesn't have a slimy reputation.

"How did you meet him? What did you talk about?" She links her arm through mine. "I want all the details."

We spend the next hour in town, where I strike out on the girls' birthday presents. I realize I'm going to have to ask Dad for suggestions, which feels like defeat. Joy drops me off at home and we make plans to return to the boardwalk later to catch some live music. She leaves me with the promise that she'll grab me at eight and absolutely, one hundred percent *not* bail on me this time.

At home, I pass the rest of the day reading by the pool and texting with Peyton, then eat dinner with Grandma on the back deck overlooking the quiet bay. I offer to play cards with her afterward, but she wants to turn in early, so we part ways at the top of the staircase, Grandma heading to her room and me ducking into mine.

I always stay in the same room when I visit. Decorated in shades of white and yellow, the bedroom is spacious and airy, with hardwood flooring, a private en suite bath, and a big bay window with a built-in reading bench. Other than the antique desk and armoire, the main piece of furniture is the huge four-post bed that I toss my phone onto.

I need to take a shower, wash my hair, and find something cute to wear into town tonight. Operation Fling may have hit a snag last night, but if I'm serious about finding myself a passionate summer affair—and I am—then it's time to kick that plan into gear.

Ideally, my super-hot and apparently very-open-to-hookups neighbor would be the one to have a fling with, but I've already had two opportunities to make a move, or at least ask for his number, and I've blown it both times. Therefore, putting all my eggs in the Tate basket probably isn't a smart move. I need to be open to meeting other guys. Broadening my fling horizons.

And no better time to start than tonight.

I pull the elastic off and begin undoing my braid, wandering toward the window to preemptively close the curtains before my shower.

Then I freeze. My fingers go motionless, my half-undone braid forgotten.

From my window, I have a clear view of the house next door.

And the window next door. The one that faces mine. And since the two houses are separated by mere yards, and there aren't any trees on the side path that cuts between the homes, I am provided with a clear, unobstructed, perfect, glorious view of Tate as he undresses in the bedroom across the way.

My breath lodges in my throat.

He's facing away from me, and I practically drool while I watch the sinewy muscles of his back ripple as he tosses his shirt aside. His shoulders are broad, arms well-sculpted. He reaches for the waistband of his swim trunks.

His shorts drop to the floor and I almost choke on my tongue.

Holy fuck. I knew he had a nice butt, but seeing it in all its bare glory is . . . otherworldly. I can't take my eyes off it. I feel like a total perv, and I know if the situation was reversed and he was watching me change from his window, I'd be reporting him to the cops. But I'm frozen in place, unable to tear my gaze away.

Turn away, Cassandra.

Turn away.

Stop it.

My mouth has gone completely dry. His body is spectacular. Hard planes and lean muscles and long, tanned limbs all joining together to form one outrageously sexy specimen of a man. I'm breathing hard now. Heart pounding. Tate drags one hand through hair that appears a bit windblown, wandering around the room as if in search of something. Completely naked. Completely oblivious to the fact that his next-door neighbor is ogling him.

Then he turns toward the window.

And he's not so oblivious anymore.

He's visibly startled when our eyes lock. His brow furrows. Lips part, just slightly. I catch one brief glimpse of the full-frontal experience before I spin on my heel and dart away from the window. My heart rate is officially in cardiac arrest territory. He *caught* me looking. What the hell do I do now? What if he reports me or tells my grandmother—

My phone lights up.

"Oh my God," I moan out loud.

I can barely walk over to the bed, that's how weak my legs feel. My hand trembles as I reach for the phone. I grab it and dive into the bathroom, as far away from that damned window as possible.

On the screen, someone is trying to AirDrop me a note.

Tate B.

With a shaky finger I hit *accept,* and the note pops up.

I think we need to talk about this. —Tate

Underneath the message is his phone number.

I'm mortified. But I'm also not dumb enough to think we can sweep this under the rug and pretend I wasn't watching him undress. And while I'm normally the type of person who runs screaming from all confrontations, this needs to be dealt with ASAP. Otherwise we're in for a long, awkward summer.

I click on Tate's number to pull up a new message thread.

Me: *I AM SO SO SORRY. I swear I wasn't spying on you. I was just standing at my window when you walked by and started stripping.*
Tate: *Uh-huh. I'm sure that's exactly what happened.*
Me: *It's true! I only saw you naked for like three seconds, max.*

There's a short beat.

Tate: *Did you enjoy the show?*
Me: *Ew. No.*

Ew no?

What the hell is wrong with me? *This* is why I'm single. Someone tries to flirt with me, and I respond with *ew no*. Clearly I have issues.

Me: *I mean, I barely saw anything.*
Tate: *Come back to the window.*

My pulse quickens again.

Me: *No.*
Tate: *Just come back. I promise I'm not standing here with my hand on my dick or something creepy.*

Wary, I exit the bathroom. As promised, Tate is not being creepy. He's at the window, a towel wrapped around his waist, a phone in his hand. When he sees me, he gives a cheeky smile and raises his other hand. He's holding a flashlight.

I narrow my eyes, which prompts him to start typing one-handed.

Tate: *What's Morse code for "peeping Tom"?*
Me: *OMG stop. I'm already embarrassed enough.*

It occurs to me that instead of texting, we could just open our respective windows and call out to each other. Then again, sound travels on the water and I don't want my grandmother hearing a second of this conversation.

Tate: *Look. Cassie. I'll be honest. You saw my ass. I think it's only fair that I see yours.*

THE SUMMER GIRL • 41

I squawk in outrage. He can't hear it, but he must know I made some sort of indignant sound because he grins widely.

Me: *Absolutely not.*
Tate: *One cheek?*
Me: *No!*
Tate: *Fine. You drive a hard bargain. I'll settle for your tits.*

I know he's joking. And I think if anyone else had said that to me they'd come off as a total perv. But there's just something about this guy's good looks and dazzling smile. No part of him gives off perverted vibes.

Still, I can't reward him for that kind of talk. Don't want to set a precedent or anything. So I walk to the window while typing a final message.

Me: *You'll just have to use your imagination.*

Then I close the curtains.

CHAPTER 5

TATE

My dad calls when I'm on my way to meet the boys at the Rip Tide. The Bluetooth kicks in and I answer with a quick, "Hey, Dad, what's up?" Since I've got the top down on the Jeep, I ease up on the gas, driving slower so the wind doesn't drown out his voice.

"Can you do me a solid tomorrow, kid?"

I can't help rolling my eyes. I'm twenty-three and he still calls me *kid*. Meanwhile, if anyone is a kid, it's Gavin Bartlett. My dad is basically an overgrown boy, so full of energy and life it honestly gets overwhelming sometimes. He was a big baseball hero back in Georgia, so I grew up hearing from everyone on the island how awesome my father was. Then we moved to Avalon Bay, a place where he didn't know a soul, and within a year he had the entire bay singing his praises too. Everywhere he goes, people love him. He's just one of those universally likable dudes. Doesn't possess a shred of arrogance. Always puts his family first. He's humble. Hilarious. And other than his occasional grumbling when I was a teenager about me not being interested in following in his athletic footsteps, he's a pretty great dad. Luckily, our shared love of the water made up for my disinterest in baseball, so we still had plenty to bond over.

"Depends," I tell him, since I know better than to blindly agree to favors. "What's up?"

"Can you come into work tomorrow morning for a couple hours? I want to take your mom to Starfish Cove."

"What's the occasion?"

"Does there need to be one? A man can't take his wife on a spontaneous Sunday picnic? It's romantic!"

"Dude. I don't want to think about my parents making out at a romantic picnic, please and thank you."

"Making out? We're going to third base at least, kid."

I make a loud gagging noise, mostly for his benefit. Truthfully, there are worse things in this world than having parents who are still madly in love after twenty-five years of marriage.

I'm one of the rare members of my friend group whose family is wholly, disgustingly normal. I'm an only child, so I never had to deal with any of that sibling rivalry shit. Mom loves to garden and Dad still plays baseball with a men's league in town. When people ask me why I'm so laid-back and take everything in stride, it's because, well, I haven't encountered many hardships in my life. The closest thing to turmoil we experienced as a family was a brief rough period when we moved from St. Simon's to Avalon Bay. The stress of the move, combined with Dad changing careers, caused some arguing between my parents, a bit of friction around the house. And then it passed.

I've been lucky, I guess.

"Sure, I can do that," I relent. As much as I hate the idea of working two jobs tomorrow—morning at the dealership and then afternoon at the yacht club—I know Mom would enjoy a picnic at Starfish Cove. And I'm one of those assholes who likes making my parents happy.

"Thanks, kid. I owe you one. Oh, and keep an eye out for a man named Alfred. Or Albert? Can't remember. Anyway, he's coming in around nine to look at the fifty-foot Beneteau that Sam Powell just brought in."

"What? Sam's selling the Beneteau?" I ask in dismay.

"Already did. We closed the deal on Friday."

"Shit, really? Didn't he just do a refit in 2019? And he spent a chunk on that new teak deck, no?"

"That's why he's selling now—the refit upped the value. This is the time to sell."

"But Sam loves that boat."

"Loves his kid more. And she got into Harvard. Gotta pay for that Ivy League tuition somehow, right?"

"That's rough."

We chat for a few more minutes before hanging up. As I turn left onto the main road leading downtown, my mind is still on Sam Powell parting with his beloved sailboat. Man, I never want to be in the position where I need to choose between my kid and my boat. Not that I have either one of those yet, but my goal is to at least start working toward securing the latter. I could probably buy a used forty-foot Bristol, maybe even a Beneteau Oceanis in the next couple years if I'm able to save more money.

After that, well, ideally I'd be sailing her around the world, although that's more a dream than a goal. A pipe dream, at that, because there's no way I can just fuck off for months on end. Dad already has it all planned out—he wants to retire early, and once he does, I'll be taking over Bartlett Marine, selling other people their dream boats rather than sailing my own. And while I can't deny the dealership turns a serious profit, it hasn't exactly been my lifelong dream to run it.

Main Street is already packed with cars, not an open space to be found. I end up having to pull into one of the gravel beach-access lots and hoof it half a mile to the Rip Tide, where I find my friends gathered around a high-top table near the stage. Our buddy Jordy and his reggae band play this venue most weekends, but they're not here tonight. In their place is a metal outfit with a lead singer who's scream-singing unintelligible lyrics as I sidle up to the boys.

Cooper, clad in a black T-shirt and ripped jeans, is sipping on a beer and wincing at the ungodly noises coming from the stage. His other half is nowhere to be found, and by that I mean Evan, his twin. Mackenzie would be his *better* half, the chick who got Cooper to smile more times in the last year than in all the years I've known him combined. Genuine smiles, too, and not the cocky smirks he'd flash right before we used to fuck shit up.

Chase is next to Coop, engrossed with his phone, while Danny listens to the band with a pained expression.

"These guys are awful," I say, wondering who the hell decided to book them. The singer is now making strange breathing noises while the two guitarists whisper into their microphones. "Why are they whispering now?"

"Is he saying *my skull is weeping*?" Cooper demands, wrinkling his brow.

"No. It's *my soul is sleeping*," Danny tells him.

"It's both," Chase says without looking up from his phone. "My skull is weeping/my soul is sleeping. Those are the lyrics."

"Deep," I say dryly, and my own skull nearly weeps with relief when the song—if you could call it that—ends, and the singer—if you could call him that—announces they're taking a ten-minute break.

"Oh thank fuck," Danny breathes.

My peripheral vision catches the blur of a waitress, and I twist around to signal her before she can disappear. "Becca," I call, because everyone knows everyone in this town.

"Tate! Hey! What can I get ya?"

"Could I trouble you for a Good Boy?" I ask, naming one of our locally brewed beers.

"You got it. A Good Boy for a good boy." She winks and hurries off.

Cooper sighs. "Between you and my brother, I don't think there's a waitress in town who hasn't seen your dicks."

"And?" I counter, grinning. "Are waitresses off-limits now?"

"Only if you break their hearts. I don't need anyone spitting in our drinks."

"Ha, talk to your brother then. I've never had a hookup end on anything other than good terms. Can't say the same for Evan. And speaking of Evan—where is he? Wasn't it his idea to come here tonight?"

"Yup." Cooper rolls his eyes. "But then he got the better idea of locking Genevieve in their bedroom after we got home from work, and nobody's seen him since."

I have to laugh. Evan had been itching to get back together with Genevieve West since she moved back to the Bay after a year away in Charleston. Not only did he win her back, but they're now engaged. Good for Evan, though. He's loved the girl since the eighth grade, for fuck's sake. He deserves the win.

"I can't believe they're actually getting married," Chase says, shaking his head.

"It's wild," I concur.

"I hear you're next," Danny pipes up, elbowing me in the arm. "When do you plan on proposing to Alana?"

I pretend to think it over. "I'm gonna have to go with . . . never. I don't think I've met anyone less interested in marriage than Alana. Besides, that's not happening anymore."

Coop glances over, intrigued. "No?"

"No more friends with benefits," I tell him, shrugging. "We're back to being regular old friends."

Danny hoots. "She dump you?"

"Dumping would imply being in a relationship, and we definitely weren't in one."

"Did you break the news to Steph yet?" Cooper snickers. "I think the girls had a bet going that you would fall in love with Alana. Pretty sure Steph staked her life savings on yes."

"Love?" I raise a brow. "Dude, I can't be held responsible for Steph's irresponsible gambling choices. Has she *met* me?"

What the hell is love, anyway? It's one of those words that gets thrown around so haphazardly, like grains of rice at a wedding. *I love this. I love that. Love you. Love you too.* I've experienced platonic love, sure. I love my family, my friends. But romantic love? The kind of love that runs so deep you feel the other person in your soul? My only real relationship was with a girl I dated in high school for a year. We had a good time together. The sex was phenomenal. But was I in love with her?

When it boils down to it, I suspect it was just lust. Same as the rest of my encounters with the opposite sex. The string of hook-ups, the flings . . . love didn't play a role in any of those, and that includes my arrangement with Alana.

"Yo. Tate." A coaster nails me in the forehead.

I blink back to reality and hear the boys chortling. "What the hell was that?" I growl, rubbing my forehead.

"You literally zoned out for ten minutes," Danny informs me.

"Ten minutes?" I challenge.

"Okay, maybe, like, ten seconds, but still. Becca dropped off your beer and you didn't even say thanks."

Oh shit. I look over my shoulder, but Becca is already serving another table. I reach for my Good Boy and take a sip, just as the flinch-inducing shriek of microphone feedback fills the bar.

"No," Danny blurts out. "Fuck, no. They're back."

Unenthused, the four of us turn toward the stage, where the

band has indeed returned. They waste no time bursting into a song that starts with an inexplicable surf riff that's completely incongruous to the plaintive wails leaving the lead singer's mouth.

"Yeah, no," Cooper says. He slams his bottle down and glances at me. "Chug that beer so we can get the hell out of here. I can't listen to this all night."

"Joe's has half-price shots tonight," Chase says, already sliding off his stool. "I vote we go there."

Danny frowns when he notices I'm not drinking. "Didn't you hear the man? Chug," he orders, pointing to my bottle. "My ears are rebelling, bro."

"Fine." I grimace, then tip my head back and drain about two-thirds of my Good Boy before calling it quits.

While the band continues to assault the eardrums of the Rip Tide's patrons, my friends and I bail, hurriedly climbing the narrow staircase up to the street. We emerge into the night a moment later, the balmy heat warming my face. It's just as noisy out here on the main strip, but I prefer loud voices, raucous laughter, and faint carnival noises to the torture chamber we left behind.

We've made it about three steps down the sidewalk when a familiar face enters my line of sight.

Well, look at that. My new temporary neighbor. She's with a friend, a tall chick with flat-ironed hair and flawless skin. Both girls wear short dresses, although the friend's is much tighter than Cassie's.

"Seriously, ginger?" I call out, grinning. "You've been in town, what, less than a week and somehow I've run into you eighty-nine times already? If I didn't know any better, I'd think you were stalking me."

Cassie's jaw drops. "I am not. And stop calling me *ginger*. I told you I'm not a ginger, I'm a copper." She crosses her arms as if to emphasize her outrage, but all it does is emphasize her chest, pressing her tits together in a seriously appealing way.

Fuck. That rack. I can't handle it. It doesn't go unmissed by the others, either. Even Cooper, who has a girlfriend with whom he's nauseatingly smitten, briefly flicks his dark eyes toward Cassie's chest. She notices the attention, because her faces flushes and her arms drop to her sides.

The friend looks highly amused. "Don't deny it, Cass." She winks at me. "We totally followed you here."

"We did not," Cassie insists, poking her friend in the side. Then she gestures to the door of the Rip Tide. "We're just here to see the band."

"Oh, you don't want to do that," I warn. "Trust me. They're total shit."

"Aw, no, really?" Her expression conveys disappointment. "This is one of the only places that's featuring a live band tonight. Why are they shit? What kind of music is it?"

Cooper snorts. "Fucked if I know."

Danny thinks it over. "All right. If I had to pin down a genre, I'd say it was, like . . . rockabilly surf emo metal."

My gaze swivels to him. "Dude. That's actually pretty fucking accurate."

Cassie and her friend make identical faces, scrunching up their noses. "That sounds awful," Cassie complains.

"I think Sharkey's has a band playing tonight," Chase says helpfully.

The friend shakes her head. "Yeah, we can't go there," she answers, pouting. "It's the one place we always get carded."

Cooper spins toward me. "Bro, we're making friends with underage girls now?" He sighs.

"Hey. I'm twenty-one," protests the friend. She jabs a French-tipped fingernail at Cassie. "She's the one holding us back."

"Gee, thanks," Cassie says, her voice dry.

"But don't you worry," the friend assures Cooper, clearly having set her sights on him. "Cassie's birthday is next month, so she and I will be happy to meet you two"—that bossy fingernail snaps the air between me and Coop—"at Sharkey's once my girl is legal. How does that sound? One month from now. Eight o'clock. Sharkey's. It's a date."

"Joy," Cassie chides. She looks back at me. "She's just joking."

I raise a brow. "So it's not your birthday next month?"

"No, it is. That's not the part she's joking about. We're not going on a double date, I promise."

"I would've been up for a double date," Danny proclaims with a sad moan, pretending to be wounded. "But *I* wasn't invited."

"I'm gay, so I don't care," Chase tells the women.

Cooper lets out another snort.

"Anyway, it was nice seeing you again," Cassie tells me, already edging away. She glances at my friends. "I'm Cassie, by the way. This is Joy. And I'm not a stalker, no matter what your stupid friend says. I've never stalked anyone in my life. Well, unless you count that one week in high school when I kept refreshing this guy's Facebook page hoping his relationship status would change because I heard he and his girlfriend were having problems, but that's more cyberstalking, I guess, and I'm not sure that actually counts—" She stops abruptly when she realizes she's babbling.

Openly grinning, Joy doesn't come to her friend's aid. I suspect she's used to Cassie's blabbering, and I kind of love that she doesn't jump in and rescue her. Just lets her dig that hole deeper.

"Tate," I introduce myself to Joy, and she smirks in a way that tells me she knows who I am. Reputation precedes me, I guess. I introduce the others, ending with Cooper, and it turns out both girls know exactly who he is too.

"You're one of the bad-boy twins," Joy says with barely disguised glee.

He offers a faint smile. "Everything you've heard about us is a lie."

"Excellent," she says, flashing a sassy smile. "Because I heard you have a girlfriend. Now that I know you don't . . ."

I smother a laugh. She's got him there.

"Okay, that one is true," he amends, laughing softly.

"He's very much spoken for," I confirm. "Living happily ever after and building a hotel empire with his girl."

"Oh, right," Joy exclaims. "I heard about that." She looks at Cassie. "His girlfriend is the new owner of the Beacon."

That captures Cassie's interest. She instantly focuses on Cooper. "Your girlfriend is the one who bought the Beacon?"

He nods. "We've spent the past year restoring the place. The grand reopening is in September."

"I know. That's why I'm here. My grandmother was the seller. The Beacon was in my family for more than fifty years before she sold."

Coop is startled. "No shit? Lydia Tanner is your grandmother?"

"She is," Cassie confirms. "I'm staying with her for the summer. We sold her house here, too. It closes in October and then she's moving up north to be near family. My whole family is coming to the reopening. Grandma's really excited for it."

"Damn, don't tell my girlfriend that." Coop grins. "Mac is stressing so hard about it. She doesn't want to let your grandmother down."

"I'm sure she won't. Honestly, Grandma is just happy the new owner is dedicated to preserving her original vision for the place."

"We did our best," he says, his tone sincere. And now that he's realized these chicks are more than just thirsty boardwalk tourists looking to hook up, he's a lot more amenable to their plight. "Go to Big Molly's instead of Sharkey's," he advises. "They've got a band tonight too, and I have it on good authority the bartender there isn't above serving a cocktail or two to a twenty-year-old." He winks. "Tell Jesse that Coop says hi."

"Thanks for the tip," Cassie says, flashing a grateful smile.

Danny steps in, clearly bored with all the chitchat. "All right, ladies. Nice running into you, but we've got some alcohol to consume, fellas."

We say goodbye and part ways, moving in opposite directions. From behind me I hear Cassie tell Joy she needs to use the restroom before they hit Big Molly's. "I'll wait out here" is Joy's faint response, and the guys and I are almost a block away when I hear high heels on the pavement.

"Tate," a voice hisses. "Wait."

I look over my shoulder to find Joy barreling our way, heels clicking and slinky red dress swirling around her toned thighs.

"Interesting," Cooper murmurs, clearly amused.

"One second," I tell the boys. I break off from the group and meet Joy about ten feet away.

She's breathless from running in heels. "I gotta be quick," she blurts out. "Before Cass comes out."

Shit. Is she hitting on me? I hope not, because that feels kind of shady, doing it behind Cassie's back like that.

But she surprises me by asking, "What do you think of Cassie?"

I furrow my brow. "In what way?"

"In all ways. Think she's cute?"

"Smoking hot," I correct, a grin springing up.

Joy brightens. "Oh. Perfect. That was easy. And you're okay with all the nervous babbling?"

"In what way?" I echo. "What do you mean by okay with it? What's happening right now?" I feel stupid. Sometimes it feels like women are speaking an entirely different language from me.

My mom does it all the time, carrying on these conversations she must have started in her head, because I have no clue what she's saying, and Dad and I will constantly lock gazes over her head, like, *what the fuck?*

"Listen," Joy says in a serious tone. "Cass and I are fling shopping."

"I'm sorry, what?"

"Well, *she's* fling shopping. I may or may not be back together with my selfish ass of an ex Isaiah, but that's a whole other drama." She waves a manicured hand. "Anyway, Cassie's looking for a summer fling, and I think you'd be the perfect candidate."

I'm having trouble containing my amusement, biting my lip to keep from laughing. "Is that so?"

"Oh, it's so. But she's never going to ask you out, so I've taken it upon myself to intervene. Especially after I saw you two interact. It seemed like, I don't know, there was a little banter happening? From where I was standing, it looked like you might be interested in . . . dot dot dot . . ."

"I might," I say slowly. "I mean, I'm always up for . . . dot dot dot . . ."

She beams at me. "Excellent. Then I'm giving you her number."

I offer a smug look. "Already have it."

Her jaw drops. "Seriously? That sneaky little . . ." She shakes her head. "Well, okay then. That was supposed to be my role in this whole transaction. You know, putting the idea out there in the universe, that if you were to be into her, she might be into you too. I'm the sexual communications facilitator."

"Of course. Because that's a real job." I tip my head. "Are we at the part where you hand me the note that says *Do you like Cassie?* and I have to check the yes or no box?"

"Oh, honey, we're in the era of dick pics and *u up?* texts," she replies, rolling her eyes. "You can figure it out from here."

CHAPTER 6

CASSIE

On Thursday morning, Grandma and I finally get that tour of the Beacon Hotel, an experience that is paradoxically like stepping into a time capsule while also taking a time machine into the future. Mackenzie Cabot chose an aesthetic that somehow managed to preserve the original look of the Beacon while modernizing it. It's amazing to see. She knocked down walls I never would've thought of knocking down, brightening the main building with natural light and adding a dozen more ocean-view rooms.

Even with all the changes, I'm still overcome with nostalgia. Everything I see triggers a new memory. In the lobby, as we ascend the grand staircase, I run my fingertips along the intricately carved banister and remember hearing Grandpa Wally boast, *See this banister, kiddo? I sanded it all by myself. And your grandma, she helped me paint it.*

When Mackenzie shows us how she managed to replicate many of the old brass fixtures in the bathrooms, Grandpa Wally's excited voice is in my head, explaining, *These nifty towel hooks? They were specifically designed for passenger ships. Ocean liners. Grandma saw them in a nautical magazine and said,* Wallace, we need these for the Beacon!

His memory was so sharp, every detail etched into his brain.

That's probably what made it all the more heartbreaking when he started to forget everything in his later years. It was devastating to watch. He forgot our names first, the grandchildren. Then his own kids—my mom, her sister and brothers. Even Uncle Will, who'd been Grandpa's firstborn and favorite, was eventually lost to the jumbled sea that had become Grandpa's brain. And then, finally, he no longer recognized Grandma when she came to visit, and that's when we knew it was over. Mentally, he was gone. Physically, it took another year for his body to catch up. Sometimes I think the dementia was worse than his actual death.

Mackenzie radiates pride as she takes us around, pointing out various upgrades. They redid the electrical. All new plumbing. Installed two elevators. Constructed an addition in the back, moving the restaurant so that half of it is now an outdoor patio that overlooks the sprawling pool grounds. We visit the spa, which is no longer housed on the third floor, but in a newly built adjoining building connected to the hotel via winding palm-lined paths, with a gorgeous white stone fountain in the center of the main path.

Whoa. This chick has sunk a lot of money into this. And she's so young. Mackenzie can't be older than twenty-two or twenty-three, yet somehow she owns a beachfront hotel in South Carolina. I think I know who I want to be when I grow up.

"You did a stunning job," Grandma Lydia tells the young woman. "Simply exquisite." My grandmother can be hard to read when she's in public, but right now there's no mistaking her pleasure, the deep glow of approval in her eyes.

Mackenzie releases a breath heavy with relief. "You have no idea how happy I am to hear that. I swear, every design change I made, I was so conscious of trying to stay true to your original vision."

"You did, dear. This is . . ." Grandma looks around. We've ended our tour in the small café off the lobby. It used to be the gift shop, but Mackenzie moved that to another wing. "It's perfect."

A broad smile fills Mackenzie's face. "Thank you. I'm so thrilled you like it." She gestures behind us. "Can I get you two a coffee or anything?" she offers. Technically, the hotel isn't open yet, but she told us the café has been up and running the past few weeks to accommodate the workers who are still making finishing touches on the place.

"A tea would be wonderful," Grandma tells her.

"I'll take a coffee," I say. "Cream, no sugar. Thanks."

Mackenzie nods and goes to the counter, where she exchanges words with the barista, a man in a navy-blue polo with THE BEACON stitched in gold thread over the left breast.

"This is amazing," I whisper to Grandma as I lead her to a table outside.

The café offers a small patio with a smattering of tables. To our right is a white-painted staircase that leads down to a wide veranda with handmade rocking chairs, a cozy spot to sit and watch the waves.

Grandma adjusts her sunhat to better secure it to her head. She's always been incredibly protective of her skin. *Sun damage is no joke, Cassandra,* I grew up hearing. It's the one thing she and my mom agree on; Mom's always harping about sunscreen and hats too. Although in my mother's case, it's less about getting cancer and more about maintaining youthful-looking skin. Appearance trumps everything in my mother's world.

"Mackenzie is cool," I admit, sitting down. "Oh, and I met her boyfriend on the boardwalk this weekend."

"Is that so?"

"Yeah. Joy and I ran into Tate. The guy who's housesitting next door. He was with some of his friends, and one of them was Mackenzie's boyfriend, Cooper."

Grandma looks pleased. "That's wonderful you're making friends."

"I mean, I wouldn't say I'm making friends. I spoke to our neighbor on the boardwalk and consequently met his friends. That's about it." I chuckle at her. "Stop trying to force friendships on me. I'm good. I have Joy."

"I know, but it would be nice if you could find yourself a nice big group to spend time with this summer." She takes on a far-away tone. "When I was younger, all the young people in the Bay socialized together. There were about fifteen, twenty of us. We would take the boats out and spend hours on the water, or the girls would lie on the beach watching all the oiled-up boys play sports." She chuckles. "There might have been plenty of alcohol involved too."

I snicker, trying to picture my grandmother in a tiny bikini and oversized hat, cruising the Bay with a bunch of rowdy teenagers. But it's impossible. Whenever I try to imagine Grandma at my age, my brain can't compute. Same goes for my mother. It's even harder to imagine her as young and carefree. I refuse to believe Mom was ever anything other than a haughty, designer-clad woman in her midforties.

As if on cue, my phone buzzes. Mom has the unsettling habit of always calling just as I'm thinking about her.

"Ugh. It's Mom. I have to take this." I glimpse Mackenzie heading toward us with a tray of beverages, so I stand up. "I'll be right back."

Grandma nods. "Tell her I said hello. Take your time."

In the quiet lobby, I answer the call. "Hey, Mom," I say, and then I brace myself. You never know which side of my mother's personality you're going to get on any given day. But I'm an old pro at dealing with her now, always prepared for whatever attack she throws my way. Sometimes, it's instant criticism, or a huffy demand to explain why I committed one perceived crime or another. Other times she starts off sweet, complimentary even, encouraging you to lower your guard, and then bang! Goes in for the kill.

But I'm not a naïve little girl anymore. I know all my mother's tricks and what tactic is required to deal with each one.

So when she says, "I'm hurt, sweetie! Why has it been three days since I've heard your lovely voice?" in that light, teasing tone, I know it's a trap. She's not hurt, she's pissed. And she's not teasing, which means I can't counter with a joking response.

"I'm sorry," I tell her, with just the proper amount of grovel in my voice. Too apologetic and she becomes suspicious. "You're right. I should have called sooner. It's been chaotic here."

My strategy works. Nothing elates my mother more than hearing those two words: *You're right*.

"I suppose your grandmother is keeping you very busy," she says, which is her way of "forgiving" me for my sin.

And although it's clearly an opening to shift the blame from me to her own mother, I'm not going to throw Grandma under the bus.

"Not really. We went shopping on the weekend, but mostly I've been catching up with Joy. How's Boston?"

"The whole city? What kind of question is that?"

I smother a sigh and quickly switch tacks, letting out a fake laugh. "Ha, ha, you're right, that was a stupid question. I'm so dumb sometimes. I just meant, how are you doing? Are you enjoying the city or are you looking forward to coming down—"

Abort!

I rue the question the second it slips out. Shit, maybe I'm off my game.

Sometimes it's so hard to forget you're not dealing with a normal human. Narcissists are a whole other breed.

Her bitterness practically permeates the line. "There is nothing I'd like to do less than spend time in that town." She snorts humorlessly. "But we owe a duty to our family."

It infuriates her that she can't back out, I know that. But my two uncles and my aunt committed to making the trip to say goodbye to the Beacon, and if there's one thing my mother can't allow, it's looking like the bad guy.

The ingratitude, though, is kind of incredible. The Beacon belonged to our family for decades. It's the reason for all that wealth my mother sure enjoys taking advantage of. The least she can do is give it a proper farewell. It's the Tanner family's final hurrah. Like giving away a treasured ship and watching the new owners christen it with a champagne bottle before they sail away forever.

"I'm actually at the hotel right now," I say, hoping to mollify her with one of her favorite topics: money. "The new owner poured buckets of money into it, and it has absolutely paid off. It's gorgeous. I swear, you're going to love it. We just finished the tour of the spa—all the products there were custom-made in Italy. An exclusive brand just for the Beacon."

That piques her interest. "Well, that sounds promising!"

"Right?" Then, although I'd rather gnaw my own tongue off than speak the words, I know the script and force myself to speak it. "We should do a mother/daughter spa day," I suggest, injecting as much fake enthusiasm into my voice as possible.

The silver lining when talking to narcissists is they assume everyone adores them and is dying to spend time with them, which means they rarely stop to wonder if you're being disingenuous. In their minds, *of course* we want to hang out with them. Because they're perfect and remarkable and a credit to all of humanity.

The worst part is, most people don't see through their bullshit. At least not at first. I can't even count how many times over the years I'd been told how wonderful my mother is. Or accused of being "too sensitive." Of reading too much into her veiled—and sometimes not at all veiled—barbs. *Oh, that Cassie, so insecure that she imagines disparaging subtext with every word.*

Eventually, though, most people see the light. I still remember the first time Peyton had her epiphany after my mother took us out to dinner during a sleepover. We were thirteen and, wide-eyed and shaking her head, she announced, "I just realized—your mom is a real bitch."

There is nothing more liberating than having your traumatic experiences validated like that.

"What a lovely idea!" Mom says in response to my suggestion. "Also, I just thought of it, but while you're there you should ask for a tour of the fitness center too."

My jaw tightens. I know where this is going.

"Yeah, we peeked into it," I answer carefully. "It's attached to the spa, but it's closed off because none of the equipment has been delivered yet."

"You should use the gym at the club, then. I saw on Joy's Instagram that she's been going there every morning. She's looking very fit these days."

I smother an inward scream. I hate that Mom follows my friends on social media. Joy even has a private account, but she confessed she would've felt like an asshole if she hadn't accepted my mother's request.

"Maybe she can give you some fitness tips," Mom adds, because no conversation with my mother is complete without her advising me on all the ways I can better myself.

"Yeah, I'll ask her," I say obediently.

"Oh, and speaking of Instagram, I was on your page this morning too and saw the picture you posted. The one of you in the pink top and denim shorts? Those shorts were adorable!"

I wait for the next sniper's bullet.

"But the top . . . you know I mean well when I say this, but maybe you should consider taking the photo down. That cropped style isn't the most flattering on you, Cass. With your proportions, you know. Oh! We should also go shopping when I'm here, how does that sound? Maybe drive into Charleston?"

"Sounds great! I'd love that, actually. I always appreciate your opinion."

There's a short beat, and I know that in her judgmental, self-absorbed brain, she's wondering, *was that sarcasm?*

But that would be too detrimental to her ego, so rather than question me, she does her trademark subject switcheroo. "Have you seen your father yet? And his nurse?"

I hold the phone away from my ear for a second and scream silent obscenities at it, making faces at the screen.

As is my luck, a passing man in work boots and a tool belt enters the lobby at that moment. He looks startled by my antics at first, then barks out a laugh before walking on.

I bring the phone back to my ear. "Not yet. I'm seeing them tomorrow for dinner."

"He's waited an entire week to see his child?" she says indignantly. "That's selfish, even for Clayton."

You wrote the book on selfish, lady.

Although for once, she's not entirely wrong. I've been thinking the same thing since I arrived in Avalon Bay. So what if the twins go to day camp and Dad and Nia have work? They still eat dinner together every weeknight, do they not? Is it that difficult to invite me to join them?

On the other hand, when her husband's bitter ex-wife refers to her as his *nurse*, maybe it's understandable Nia doesn't want that bitter woman's daughter around her house. The nurse comments grate on me too, especially since it's total nonsense. Nia was never Dad's nurse. She was his physical therapist after he got in a car accident not long after his and Mom's divorce. He required surgery for a torn bicep, and Nia was in charge of his rehab. That's how they met and fell in love.

"Mom, I gotta go," I say, done with this entire conversation. "Grandma's waiting for me to drive her home." In reality, Grandma's deep in conversation with Mackenzie, the two of them leaning forward, animated about whatever they're discussing.

"All right, sweetie. I'll see you next month."

"Can't wait."

I'm exhausted when I return to the table. Talking to Mom really does feel like I've just fought a war. Grandma eyes me with a flicker of concern. "Is everything all right?"

"All good," I lie. Because that's what I do. I plaster on sunny smiles and pretend the attacks on my appearance, my father, my entire life have zero effect on me.

"I was just telling your grandmother there's a bonfire tonight at my place," Mackenzie says, giving me a warm smile. "Having a few friends over. If you'd like to join?"

My first instinct is to beg off and say thank you but I'm busy. I'm so awkward around strangers. But then it occurs to me that Mackenzie's boyfriend is friends with Tate. Which means Tate might be there. Which means maybe I can work up the nerve to . . . to what?

Ask him out, I guess.

Proposition him.

Rip my clothes off and order him to rock my world.

Okay, maybe not the last one. But I've been back in town for a week now, and Tate is the only guy I've met who makes my heart pound. I feel like I'd regret it if I didn't at least *try* to stop babbling and ask him to hang out. And I suppose there's no better time than tonight.

CHAPTER 7

CASSIE

The Hartley twins live in a Low Country–style beach house with a huge front porch and not a neighbor in sight. It isn't at all like my grandparents' house, which was built in the last couple decades and has a more modern feel. This is a house that's been in someone's family for a hundred years. Old, rambling, and oozing charm, a testament to time and the elements. The roof looks new, however, and the covered porch has clearly been painted recently, hinting that the residents are in the process of upgrading.

The front door creaks loudly when Mackenzie opens it to let me in. "Hey!" She looks delighted to see me. "You made it!"

"Thanks for having me." I awkwardly fiddle with the belt loops of my denim shorts. Despite my mother's negging earlier, I'm wearing a cropped T-shirt that shows a sliver of midriff, and black flip-flops that Mackenzie tells me to leave on.

"We're going out back," she says, leading me through the living room and country-style kitchen toward a set of glass sliding doors.

Out back is a massive deck that overlooks the ocean, with a winding, wooden staircase that goes down to the sand. The view alone is worth a million dollars, and my eyebrows soar as we step onto the deck.

"Whoa," I remark. "That view is *sick*. I'm surprised developers haven't tried to snatch this place up. Build a little condo community or something."

"Oh, they've tried, but we're never selling," Cooper Hartley says, appearing behind us. He steps out of the kitchen, shirtless, barefoot, and clad in red swim trunks. He's sporting two full sleeves of tattoos and rock-hard abs, and I get a little starry-eyed just looking at him.

Then I blink and a second Cooper appears to my left from the rickety stairs. Also shirtless, except this Cooper is wet, as if he'd just come from the ocean. His tall, muscular body drips seawater all over the deck floor as he strides up.

"Oh wow." I glance at Cooper, then his twin. "You guys really are identical."

"Nah," the twin says. "I'm way better looking."

"Bullshit," Cooper argues.

Rolling her eyes, Mackenzie introduces me to Evan, Cooper's twin, who flashes a sexy grin before disappearing into the house.

"Come on," she says, touching my arm. "Everyone's already on the beach."

We head down to the sand, where several loungers and Adirondack chairs are arranged in a haphazard circle around the fire pit. The fire's not yet lit since the sun hasn't set, and it's still so hot out that a bonfire feels almost redundant.

On one of the loungers, a platinum blonde sits in the lap of a guy who, even sitting down, looks massive. Six-five at least, with huge muscular arms that could probably bench-press everyone here. A gorgeous brunette in a black string bikini is sprawled on the neighboring lounger, scrolling on her phone, while another girl with a high ponytail and dusky complexion stands at a plastic table laden with drinks, pouring liquor into a tall plastic cup.

Mackenzie quickly runs through some more introductions.

Table girl is Steph. The couple on the chair are Heidi and her boyfriend, Jay. The brunette is Jay's sister, Genevieve, who also happens to be Evan Hartley's fiancée.

That startles me. "You guys are engaged?"

"Sure are," Genevieve answers. She narrows her eyes at me in a challenge. "And don't give me that *you're too young* BS. I hear it from my brothers on a daily basis."

"You're too young," her brother grumbles as if on cue.

"I wasn't going to say that," I assure her. "It's just so rare to find people who want to get married in their early twenties."

"Well, I mean, we gotta tie that knot ASAP if we're going to start pumping out kids. We've decided we want at least six. Isn't that right, Hartley?" she calls up at the deck.

Evan appears at the railing above us. "Seven," he calls back. "That's my lucky number."

"Do you want a drink?" Mackenzie heads over to the table, where I greet Steph with a tentative smile.

"Here, let me make you what I'm having," Steph says, reaching for another plastic cup. "I'm experimenting with a new recipe. I picked up some of that vanilla-flavored vodka and I'm mixing it with raspberry lemonade. It's either going to be vomit-inducingly sweet or the most delicious thing you've ever tasted."

"Can't wait to find out," I say with a snicker.

As I wait for her to mix the drink, I glance toward the deck, where the twins are laughing about something at the railing. I guess Tate isn't here. Neither is the redhead from the party last week, I note. Alana. For some reason that triggers a tiny prickle of jealousy. What if they're both gone because they're hooking up again?

I ignore the tight knot in my belly and accept the drink Steph hands me. I'm thirsty, so I take a big gulp and it isn't until after I've swallowed that I realize what I'm in for. The liquid burns a fiery path to my stomach and induces a bout of coughing.

"Too sweet?" she frets.

I gape at her. My eyes water as I let out a final cough. "I can barely taste the lemonade," I squawk. "This is, like, ninety percent vodka."

Steph grins. "So?"

"So I wasn't expecting that. Jeez. Warn a girl next time."

We rejoin the others around the unlit fire pit. Steph settles in one of the chairs, while Mackenzie and I share a lounger. I take a teeny sip of my potent cocktail. This time I anticipate the vodka burn and make a conscious decision to pace myself. One cup of this stuff is liable to get me sloppy drunk.

Mackenzie and her friends aren't much older than me, yet for some reason I feel like a kid next to them. Maybe it's because they're all so gorgeous. Genevieve is basically a supermodel—long legs, toned body slick with tanning oil, sunglasses resting on her pert nose. Beside me, Mackenzie looks like she stepped off a yacht, a striped T-shirt hanging off one tanned shoulder and dark hair loose and cascading down her back.

Mackenzie glances at Genevieve. "Gen, so Cassie is Lydia Tanner's granddaughter."

"Oh, are you?" Gen exclaims. "I was *obsessed* with your grandmother when I was a teenager."

"Really?" I laugh.

"Oh yeah. I used to see her around town all the time in those big sunglasses and silk scarves. She always wore a scarf, even in the summer."

"She still does. It's her trademark."

"She was the most elegant woman I'd ever seen in my life," Gen says wistfully. "I wanted to be her when I grew up, and it was my dream to work for her at the Beacon one day. Joke's on me. Now I'm stuck working for this one." She jerks a thumb at Mackenzie, but her sparkling eyes tell me she's joking.

"You work at the Beacon?" I ask.

"I will be when we open in September. I'm going to be the general manager."

"Wow. That's a lot of responsibility," I tell her. "I remember our old manager, this British guy. James De Vries. Grandma flew him in from London, after poaching him from some five-star hotel near Buckingham Palace. He always wore this navy-blue blazer with a gold—"

"—bowtie," Genevieve finishes, snickering loudly. "Oh, I remember the man. Remember him, Heidi? Mr. De Vries?"

"Oh my God. Yes." Heidi's laugh is a bit evil. "We used to hop the fence into the pool area and try to steal people's cabanas, and De Vries would appear out of fucking nowhere."

"And every time," Gen picks up the story, "every damn time he'd greet us with this bland smile and politely ask if we were guests of his fine establishment, even though he clearly knew we were a bunch of delinquent teenagers breaking the rules."

"He never chased us out, though," Steph pipes up. "Dude was classy. He'd escort us out through the front doors, then watch us leave while giving one of those stiff Queen of England waves, all distinguished like."

I laugh, totally picturing what they're describing. James was the epitome of a well-mannered Brit.

"Meanwhile," Genevieve says to me, snorting in amusement, "you were probably there legally, sunbathing poolside and watching us being marched past your lounge chair."

"Actually, we never stayed at the hotel," I admit. "Before my parents got divorced, we lived in a house on Sycamore. And after that, we stayed at Grandma's house whenever we were in town for a visit. I would've killed to spend an entire summer at the Beacon."

"Well, you're in luck," Mackenzie says cheerfully, "because you now have a room there for life. Free of charge."

"No way," I protest. "I could never accept that offer."

"Seriously? *I* can," Genevieve declares. "I totally want the free room." She shouts up at the deck again. "Hey, Evan, we have a permanent suite at the hotel."

"Nice," he shouts back.

"Oh," Mackenzie says suddenly, glancing at me. "I forgot, I wanted to ask you something."

"Yeah?" I shift self-consciously and take another sip of my vodka lemonade, aka vodka and a teaspoon of lemonade. I'm already feeling the alcohol, my blood buzzing from it.

"Beach Games is next month," she says. "You've heard of it, right?"

"Yeah, of course. It's a tradition."

Beach Games is an annual event in Avalon Bay, where teams representing local businesses compete in, well, beach games. It's a two-day affair, and I think there're gift certificates and trophies in it for the winners, but most of the competitors do it for the glory. The honor of being dubbed *Best Business on the Bay.*

Last time I attended a Beach Games celebration was a few years ago, right before freshman year of college. I went with my dad, and we had a blast watching the various activities. The tug-of-war event that year got real ugly. I remember the old ladies from the bakery brutally heckling the dudes from the mechanic shop. I believe the phrase *You're going down, motherfuckers* was uttered more than once. Afterward, Dad and I got ice cream and walked along the boardwalk. It was nice. Maybe he'll want to go again this year.

"We missed out last year," Mackenzie says, "but now that the Beacon is back in business we need to put together a team. Your grandmother and I were talking about it this morning and she mentioned nobody in your family ever competed in the Games. She thought you might like joining us on Team Beacon."

"Me?" I say, startled.

She nods. "You'd be our fourth. Right now it's me, Gen, and our activities director, Zale."

"I'm sorry—Zale?" Genevieve's brother guffaws. "That's gotta be a fake name."

"It's not," Gen says with a grin. "I questioned it too, so he showed me his birth certificate."

"Those can be forged," Jay insists.

"Zale is hilarious," Mackenzie tells me. "You'll love him."

I'm still trying to wrap my head around the offer. "You really want me to be your fourth? Did my grandmother force you into this?" I ask suspiciously.

"Not at all. Like I said, she just mentioned it's something you might enjoy."

Apparently Grandma's going to foist a friend group on me come hell or high water. It's baffling. I mean, seriously. Why does she believe I'm an antisocial loser? I don't know what signals I'm giving off to make her think I'm some tragic shut-in, but I might need to have a talk with the lady.

"All right. Then, sure," I relent, because even if it *was* my grandmother's idea, it does sound like fun. "I'm down for Beach Games."

"How are your sandcastle-building skills?" Gen demands.

I mull it over. "Above par?"

She nods, pleased. "I'll take it. Mac and I have a little wager going with the twins."

"You mean the *winners*," comes Evan's smug voice, and he's projecting some serious swagger as he descends the deck steps. Scampering at his feet is an eager golden retriever with a bright orange ball in its mouth.

Evan hurls the ball down the beach and the dog takes off like a rocket, paws kicking up sand.

"You haven't won a damn thing yet," Gen retorts.

"But we will." He offers a broad smile. "Aka you will lose. Badly, and with no mercy from us."

Laughing, I glance between them. "What are the stakes?"

"Well, I'm glad you asked, Cassie," Evan says solemnly. "*When* we win, my beautiful fiancée here, along with my brother's okay-looking girlfriend—"

Mackenzie gives him the finger.

"—will be serving us a home-cooked dinner . . ."

"That's not so bad," I tell the girls.

But Evan isn't finished. ". . . in French maid uniforms."

I bite back a laugh. The others do not display such tact. Jay, Heidi, and Steph are doubled over, practically howling.

"Nah," Gen argues. "When *we* win, my smartass fiancé here, along with his obnoxious brother, will proudly be holding up signs advertising the Beacon Hotel on the boardwalk . . ."

"That's not bad," I say to Evan.

". . . in neon-pink G-strings."

I sigh.

"Yeah, no. Never gonna happen," Cooper announces as he joins the group. He's put on a shirt and is holding a beer.

Someone else follows him down the steps, and my heart skips when I realize it's Tate. He's wearing a white T-shirt, khaki shorts, and a pair of aviator sunglasses. For some reason his hair always looks a little windblown, pushed away from his face to emphasize his cheekbones. He's so good-looking it makes my throat run dry. I try to remedy that by gulping my drink, remembering only at the last second that it's basically pure vodka.

My coughing draws Tate's attention. An easy smile curves his lips. "Ginger," he drawls. "I didn't know you were going to be here tonight."

I respond with a self-conscious shrug. "Uh, yeah. Mackenzie invited me. And stop calling me *ginger*."

"I will when your hair is no longer ginger."

"It's copper," I growl.

"You two know each other?" Mac's wary green eyes shift from me to Tate.

"We're neighbors," I explain.

"Just for the summer," Tate adds. He grabs one of the Adirondack chairs and drags it closer to our lounger.

"Oh right. You're housesitting for the Jacksons," Evan pipes up. "Fuck, I love that house. Remember the rager we threw there a couple summers ago?"

Tate makes a sardonic noise. "Oh, you mean the night you did body shots off Gen's ass on the custom-made hand-carved coffee table Shirley Jackson had specially shipped from Denmark?"

Evan's eyes glimmer as he winks at his fiancée. "That was a good night."

Genevieve's eyes are equally ablaze. "Such a good night," she echoes, and the two exchange a sultry look loaded with so much heat I have to turn away. They might as well be having sex in front of everybody—that's how potent their chemistry is.

"Yeah, well, there won't be any repeat performances of that," Tate warns his friends. "I had to pay for an army of cleaners to come deal with the mess you guys left behind. Never again." He sips his beer, watching me over the lip of the bottle. "Has Mac given you a tour of the hotel yet?"

"Did that today," I confirm.

"And Cassie just agreed to join our team for Beach Games," Gen tells him.

"Oh yeah?" He cocks his head at me. "That officially makes us archenemies, then."

"You're competing?" I demand.

"Of course. Someone's got to represent the yacht club. Plus, this is the twins' first year competing, and I never miss an opportunity to kick their asses at something."

"Is your uncle going to be on your team?" Steph asks the Hartleys. "Because I'd pay to see that."

"We asked him, but he said no way in hell," Cooper says. "So we're using our foreman, Alex, and this guy Spencer who's on the crew." From his chair across the pit from us, he flashes a cocky smile at his girlfriend. "Be prepared to get murdered, princess."

She presses one hand to her heart. "You're so romantic."

Cooper just chuckles.

The rest of the evening flies by, much to my surprise. But the conversation is lively and the various personalities are so entertaining that three hours pass before I know it. I'm having a great time. Mac's cool. Gen's hilarious. Heidi's kind of bitchy, but after a while you get used to it. At some point Steph plants a fresh cup of vodka lemonade in my hand, while Evan and Cooper, who are literally identical from head to toe, start arguing about which one of them is better looking. And the entire time, I'm shooting sidelong looks at Tate and wondering how it's possible for someone to be so hot. Like, criminally hot. Every now and then my gaze flicks toward his abdomen, because whenever he runs a hand through his hair, the bottom of his shirt shifts upward and I catch a flash of his abs.

God, I just want to lick him.

Annnd the second vodka lemonade has officially gone to my head.

In fact, my knees are a bit wobbly as I stand up and head for the drinks table. I rummage around in one of the mini coolers in search of water. I need to hydrate. My mind is too foggy with thoughts of Tate's abs.

"Hey, neighbor."

I jump at the sound of his deep voice. I didn't even notice him come up beside me, but here he is, less than two feet away, a hint of a smile on his face.

"Sorry, didn't mean to startle you," he says. He brings his beer to his lips, taking a long swig. "You having a good time?"

Before I can answer, Steph shouts, "There she is!"

"Finally! Bitch, where've you been?" Heidi now.

I turn to check out the newcomer, faltering when I realize it's Alana. She saunters up to the group, bright red hair loose around her shoulders, eyes gleaming from the light of the fire that Cooper lit about an hour ago. I don't miss the way her gaze flicks toward me and Tate before focusing on her friends.

Gulping down some water, I move away from the table. Tate follows along beside me.

"Should I go introduce myself?" I ask, giving a discreet nod in Alana's direction. I feel like I should, but she's chatting with her friends and, what, I'm going to interrupt them just to say, *Hello, my name is Cassandra, what's your name,* like some awkward fool?

"Nah," Tate says to my relief. "She'll make her way over here eventually."

"Or she'll avoid you because she thinks you're pining over her."

He rolls his eyes. "I'm not pining. And she knows me better than that."

"So you're over it?"

"I'm over it," he confirms.

"Come on, you must still be a *little* into it," I push, sneaking another peek at Alana. "She's gorgeous."

"The view's not bad," he agrees, nodding. "But neither is *this* view." He slowly rakes his gaze down my body. Not even trying to hide the fact that he's checking me out.

A part of me is now like, *fuck,* because I'd debated this crop top earlier and now I'm doing it again. Not only does it cling to my boobs, but it shows a lot more skin than I'm used to.

But another part of me really, really enjoys having those appreciative blue eyes on me.

"You're staring," I accuse.

"Yes." He takes another sip of his beer. I wonder if he's drunk. His eyes have a hazy shine to them that tells me he might be. But he's not slurring or stumbling.

Still, I say, "You're drunk."

"No. Just buzzed." He shrugs, a lazy smile tugging on the corners of his mouth. "I feel good. You look good. Life's good right now, Cass."

I laugh. And then, because they've gone dry all of a sudden, I lick my lips.

He doesn't miss that. "Fuck." He groans softly.

My forehead creases. "What?"

"You licked your lips."

"Yeah, and? They were dry. So I licked them and now they're moist—oh my God, what a horrible word. *Moist*. Isn't it horrible?" I shake my head in dismay. "I'm sorry I said the word *moist*."

Tate chokes out a noise. A cross between a laugh and a sigh. "Man, I swear, it's like you go out of your way to kill a mood."

"What mood?" I ask, and my lips are suddenly bone-dry again. "Was there a mood?"

His shoulders quake with laughter. "Yes, Cassie, there was a mood. We were having a moment."

I blink. "We were?"

"Well, *I* thought so." Now he sounds exasperated. "In case you didn't notice, I was about to kiss you."

CHAPTER 8

TATE

"Seriously?" Cassie stares at me with narrowed eyes, as if she can't possibly fathom why I would be interested in kissing her.

"Seriously," I say, fighting a laugh. This chick is such a confusing puzzle to me. She must know she's gorgeous, right? Unless she's lived her entire life without looking in a mirror or seeing herself naked, I can't imagine she's unaware of her appeal.

"You said you were about to . . . Does that mean now you're not going to?" The groove in her forehead deepens.

"That's up to you." I lift a brow. "Do you want me to?"

She hesitates, and once again I'm thrown for a loop. Her friend Joy seemed real confident last weekend when she cornered me on the street and informed me that Cassie was down for a summer hookup. If I hadn't been swamped at work, I would've called Cassie earlier in the week. Tonight was my first opportunity to be social. In fact, I was planning on asking her to hang out this weekend, but that was before she hesitated at the thought of kissing me.

Maybe her friend was just fucking with me.

My gaze rests on her lips. Goddamn, she's licking them again. She has no idea what that does to me.

"Or do you want to keep dissecting the word *moist*?" I prompt.

She gives a weak laugh. "No. I'm sorry. I'm just . . . I'm not good at this stuff. Like, I'm standing here with the hottest guy I've ever seen and he just told me he wants to kiss me, and my first instinct is to interrogate him because I'm so awkward when it comes to—" She cuts herself off, as I'm noticing she's prone to do when she catches herself babbling.

Then she shocks the hell out of me. On an impatient groan, she mumbles, "Screw it," and the next thing I know, her soft lips are pressed against mine.

Christ. *Yes.*

My surprise quickly turns to hunger, a jolt of heat going right to my dick when Cassie's tongue finds mine and she makes a tiny whimpering sound. Nothing gets me harder than a really good kiss. Sure, I love the feel of a woman's mouth on my cock. The sensation of sliding in and out of a hot, tight pussy. But nothing beats a kiss. Especially one of those kisses where your mouths melt together, tongues teasing while your hands drift downward to find a firm, supple ass in your palms.

Cassie moans when I squeeze her ass over her shorts. Her lower body shifts closer, straining against my groin. She tastes like vodka and raspberries and feels like absolute heaven. I drive the kiss deeper, groaning against her lips, completely forgetting my surroundings until a voice shouts my name.

"Tate!"

Cassie and I jerk apart. I glance over my shoulder to find Mackenzie waving at me from the deck. There's no mistaking her slight frown.

"I need your help carrying some beer cases," she calls out.

Bullshit. Ten feet away, she's got Jay West, a dude who can lift a mountain, not to mention her own boyfriend who works construction. And she's targeting me for help-me-carry-something duty?

Cabot's cockblocking me and it's intentional.

But regardless of Mac's motives, she's succeeded in ruining the moment. Cassie is hastily taking a step back, shoving errant strands of hair behind her ear. Her cheeks are flushed. A moment ago, that was because she was turned on. Now it's from her visible embarrassment that all eyes are on us.

"Uh. Yeah." My voice sounds like gravel. I clear my throat. "Hold that thought. I'll be back in a minute."

As I turn away, I do some discreet rearranging beneath my shorts. Damn, that kiss got me rock hard. My pulse is still racing, too. On my way to the deck, I catch Alana watching me. I nod in greeting, and she rolls her eyes as I walk past her. It's funny. Any other girl would probably display at least a trace of jealousy at watching a former fling make out with someone else, but Alana's expression is wholly indifferent.

I didn't kiss Cassie to make Alana jealous, though. It's been a while since I met someone who makes me laugh as much as Cassie does. And she's goddamn edible. That body does something to me. Turns me on something fierce. Alana was the furthest thing from my mind just now. The moment Cassie's friend told me she was in the market for a summer hookup, my dick got on board faster than you can say *hell yeah*.

On the deck, Mackenzie fixes a bemused look on me but doesn't speak as she gestures for me to follow her.

Annoyed, I trail after her. "What the fuck was that?"

"What?" She spares me a glance before stalking forward again, crossing the living room toward the front door.

"What do you mean, *what*? I was clearly indisposed," I grouse.

"Yeah, I noticed." Her tone is unapologetic, which confirms my suspicion she broke up that kiss on purpose. Yet I'm still oblivious as to why.

Mac and I aren't joined at the hip or anything, but I thought we were good friends. And I've always thought she was cool, especially for a rich girl. Around here we call them clones, but while the women I encounter at the country club literally came off a clone conveyer belt, with their stuck-up personalities and yoga instructors on retainer, it didn't take long to realize Mackenzie Cabot was one of a kind. I'm starting to wonder if us locals might be rushing to judgment when it comes to clones, because Cassie doesn't fit that mold either. Her family is loaded, but she's one of the most down-to-earth people I've ever met.

It isn't until we step into the twins' garage that Mac makes her reasons known. "Why do you have to make a move on everything with a pulse?" she asks with a sigh.

I blink. Flabbergasted. "I don't," I protest.

"Bullshit. Every time a new girl comes around, it takes all of five seconds before you're sticking your tongue down her throat."

My surprise gives way to indignation. I don't know where this is coming from, and I don't like it.

"Were you trying to get Alana's attention or something?"

"Not in the slightest," I reply, which startles her. I roll my eyes at her reaction. "Come on, Mac. We both know Alana and I were just killing time. We were just bored." I shrug. "I like Cassie, so I kissed her. Big deal."

"I like Cassie too. And what if it is a big deal?"

"What do you mean?"

"I mean, she's really sweet. I don't want to see her get hurt."

I swallow my irritation. Why must women always jump directly to the worst-case scenario? And why do they always assume one measly kiss will lead to a trip to the altar? Like, damn. Slow down, ladies. Sometimes we kiss because it feels good.

"I don't plan on hurting her," I answer with a frown. "I like her. And all we did was make out."

"Then maybe you should leave it at that. Just be her friend."

I bristle. "You in charge of my dick now, Mac?"

"No, but . . ." She pauses, then voices a sheepish confession. "This morning when her grandmother and I had a moment alone at the Beacon, Lydia asked me to watch out for her. I don't know . . . I guess I'm a bit worried. You're the king of hookups. Which is fine," she adds hastily. "No judgment. That's probably why your arrangement with Alana worked so well. Neither of you have ever been interested in relationships. But Cassie is one hundred percent girlfriend material—you get that, right? She seems a lot more serious than your usual type."

I feel a deep groove form in my forehead. She's not entirely wrong. Cassie *is* different. Sweeter, as Mac had said. And not as confident or outwardly experienced as women I've been with in the past.

"I just figured I'd point all this out before things out there got . . . un-take-back-able."

I draw a troubled breath. The more I'm thinking with my upstairs head, the more I'm realizing Mac's cockblocking might have been for the best.

"Unless you're in the market for a girlfriend now, which I don't think you are. I mean, you just spent months seeing Alana, who we both know is the safest choice for someone actively *not* looking to settle down. She'd be the first person to say she's not interested in a commitment. She's constantly referring to herself as emotionally unavailable."

I go silent. In all honesty, I never gave much thought to why I spent so much time with Alana. But my gut tells me Mac isn't completely off-base. For as long as I've known her, Alana has been aloof, untouchable. The woman locks her emotions behind a steel wall. I never had any illusions about breaking down that wall.

"Anyway, I'll stop meddling now. But I made a promise to Lydia, and I just wanted to make sure you're going into this with your eyes wide open."

"Noted."

"Okay, good." She heads for the door, adding over her shoulder, "Oh, and I do need you to bring out a couple cases of beer."

"Yes, Mom."

I'm grumbling under my breath as I cross the garage toward the drinks fridge. Despite my lingering aggravation, I can't quite bring myself to hate on Mac for interrupting. Now that the buzz is wearing off and my head is clearing, it's easy to see the mistake I almost made.

Hooking up with Cassie is a disaster waiting to happen. First off, we're neighbors. What if we sleep together and things go south? I'd still have to live next door to her until September, and that could get mighty awkward.

And then there's the fact that I like her a hell of a lot. She's fun to talk to, and I can envision us building a genuine friendship this summer. To some people that might seem more like a perk than a disadvantage, but I know how fragile male/female friendships can be. After Cooper and Heidi hooked up a couple years ago, their friendship almost didn't recover. Yes, Alana was my friend when we started sleeping together, but like Mac said, Alana isn't Cassie.

I'm not sure whether Cassie can keep things casual. Sure, one conversation could clear all that up—but that's based on the assumption she's being honest with herself. In my experience, plenty of women *say* they're down for no-strings sex. And maybe they mean it in the moment. Maybe they think they'll be okay keeping it strictly physical. But more often than not, the strings form before you can blink, and suddenly you're accused of being a selfish prick. It's a frequent occurrence for my more promiscuous friends, but to me it only happened once.

Last year of high school, I slept with a cute girl on the yearbook committee, not realizing that one—she was a virgin, and two—

she'd had a crush on me for years. Lindsey assured me she just wanted a hookup before she left for college. Next thing I know, I have her entire friend group screaming at me in the school corridor accusing me of breaking her heart and ruining her life. To this day, I feel goddamn awful about it. I never meant to hurt Lindsey, but I'd made it clear I didn't want a relationship.

Well, I still don't want that relationship, and I really don't want to hurt Cassie either.

Sometimes, having a good friend in your life is more rewarding than a few nights of hot, sweaty sex.

Except Cassie has other ideas. When I return, she's standing by the water, her back to the fire. She hears my footsteps and turns toward me, a soft smile curving her lips.

Man, she's pretty. She took her hair out of its ponytail, and the copper-colored strands are loose around her shoulders, once again appearing bright orange in the firelight.

"Hey," she says.

"Hey. Sorry about that."

"No worries."

"So . . ." I step closer but maintain a few feet of distance.

She notices, because her eyes drop to the gaping space between us. "So . . ." she mimics. She bites her bottom lip and studies me for a moment.

Damn it. I don't know if I should bring up the kiss and let her know it can't happen again, or just pretend it never happened. I shove my hands in my pockets, shifting in discomfort. I'm still trying to decide what to say when Cassie beats me to it.

"Will you fling me?" she blurts out.

I blink. "Sorry, what?" I blink again. "You want me to throw you? Like, into the water?"

At that, she bursts out laughing. "No! Why would I want you to throw me into the water?"

I snicker. "I don't know! It's a crazy request. That's why I clarified."

Still giggling, she offers her own clarification. "I'm asking if you want to have a fling with me. A summer fling."

Shit.

She went there.

And here her pal Joy thought Cassie would never have the balls to ask me.

I sort of wish she hadn't found the courage. Because I'm about to look like a total asshole by saying no to a hookup ten minutes after I made a move on her. If that's not liable to give a woman whiplash, I don't know what will.

"Uh. Cass." I scrub a hand over my forehead then drag it through my hair. I'm stalling. But that means I'm also prolonging the agony and that's even worse. I let out a breath and say, "So, listen, I was actually just thinking that I . . . well, that I was sort of glad for the interruption."

"Oh." Her eyes instantly go shuttered, but not before I catch a flash of hurt.

"It's good we got interrupted before things went any further, you know? I like you, and I think you're awesome, but I'm not sure it's a good idea for us to get involved. Like, sexually." Christ, this is torture. "It's better if we keep things platonic."

"Okay." She studies me for a moment, her expression unreadable. "Can I ask why?"

I shrug lamely. "I just don't think it's a good idea, especially with you being next door. I'm going to be busy this summer. I work two jobs, you know? I won't have a lot of free time to spend with you, and even if we agreed to no expectations, that never actually pans out. This kind of arrangement always leads to conflict, and, honestly, I like you too much to screw up this friendship thing we've got going—"

"All right, I get it," she cuts in. "It's cool."

"Are you sure?" I still can't gauge her expression.

"Yeah, it's fine. This town is full of suitable candidates for a fling, right?"

"Right," I say, nodding in relief. "And you're smoking hot. You'll have no trouble finding someone. I can help you scope out potential candidates if you want."

Seriously?! shouts the incredulous voice in my head.

I wish you could un-say words the way some platforms let you un-send messages, but nope. I said what I said and there's no taking it back.

Man. I basically friend-zoned her and now I'm offering to be her *wingman*? Way to twist the knife in deeper. I'm a fucking asshole.

Clearly, she agrees, because she eyes me in disbelief before letting out a sarcastic laugh. "Um, yeah . . . I don't know about that." Rolling her eyes, she steps away from the water's edge. "Come on, friend, let's go back to the party. I desperately need another drink."

CHAPTER 9

CASSIE

Freshman year of college, I was plagued by a recurring anxiety dream. The damn thing tortured my sleeping brain at least once a week and it always went the same way. I'm staring at a small suitcase; behind it, there's an entire wall with stacks and stacks of test answer booklets. Those thin, lined notebooks the profs hand out when you write exams. My task? I need to put the notebooks in the suitcase. All of them. I must make them all fit, no matter what. It is imperative they fit.

And somehow, by some miracle, I manage to jam all the booklets into the suitcase. The anxiety would then lift, my subconscious breathing a sigh of relief, and I'd think, *Thank God, I've done it.*

All good, right?

No. I then cart the suitcase into my English Lit lecture hall, where I need to give a presentation on a Brontë book. Not one written by Charlotte or Emily, but Anne. The lesser-known Brontë. I haven't read the book—and yet *that's* not what I'm stressed about? Go figure. Despite that, I nail the presentation.

All good, right?

No. Now I'm supposed to hand the suitcase to my professor. I pick it up and carry it toward him, and just as I reach the center of the room, the overstuffed case bursts open and its contents spill out. Except, for some inexplicable reason, all the notebooks are gone.

They've been replaced with naked pictures of me.

Now the entire floor of the lecture hall is covered in eight-by-ten photographs of my bare boobs and ass and lady bits. A sea of nudes.

And then I wake up.

I don't know what that says about my psyche—or what I was watching on TV the first time I dreamed it—but that nightmare became imbedded in my subconsciousness like a rusty nail. I could expect it every week like clockwork, and I'd wake up every time feeling the burn of humiliation and a potent rush of insecurity.

I can honestly say that what I felt last night was a hundred times worse.

I have never propositioned a guy in my life.

And I never intend to do it again.

Because rejection is a bitch. It's soul-sucking. Confidence-crushing. I cannot erase from my mind that uneasy look on Tate's face. The flicker of panic in his eyes when I suggested a fling. The way he fidgeted when he told me he just wants to be friends.

Brutal.

Fucking brutal.

If I'd had a shovel on me, I would've dug a huge hole in the ground, gotten into it, and buried myself alive. Knowing my luck, though, the afterlife would end up being that nightmare lecture hall full of my nudes.

Now, I'm forced to repeat the whole story to Peyton, whose voice blares out of the car speakers as I drive over to my dad's house for dinner.

"There's no way it was the kiss," Peyton insists.

She's responding to the suspicion I'd just voiced: that Tate had kissed me, almost threw up in his mouth, and promptly decided he could never do it again.

"What other explanation is there?" I counter. "One minute we're making out. Then he leaves for a few minutes and when he comes back, he tells me he wants to be platonic. That absolutely means he hated the kiss."

"Not necessarily." She pauses. "But if we were to play that theory out . . . were there any signs he didn't like it? Did he try to pull away at any point?"

"No," I groan. "If anything, he just came closer! And I swear he was hard. I felt him against my leg."

"Hmmm. Okay?" She mulls it over. "Maybe he was drunker than you thought?"

"Gee, thanks, Peyton. So what you're saying is, a man needs to be completely wasted to kiss me?"

"That's not what I'm saying! *But.* Maybe he was drunk when he kissed you, and we both know people do impulsive things when they're drinking, right? So hooking up could've seemed like a good idea to him in the moment, but then he sobered up a bit and everything he said afterward wasn't some elaborate excuse. He really *does* want to do his own thing this summer and not hook up with anyone. And he really *does* think you're awesome, is attracted to you, but doesn't want to do anything to jeopardize the friendship. All of those things can be true at once."

She's right. But the bottom line remains the same: I propositioned Tate Bartlett and he said no.

"Honestly, it's probably for the better. Remember my silver lining? Don't spoil all subsequent prospects by flinging with a guy that's too attractive. I shouldn't have let myself forget that." I purse my lips. "What I need to do is find myself, like, a seven. Maybe a six."

"You are *not* flinging with a six." She is utterly aghast. "Over my dead body. I'm willing to compromise and settle halfway between a six and a ten—Tate's a ten, right?"

"Oh yeah," I say miserably.

"Fine, then we're aiming for an eight. Go out with Joy tomorrow to try to meet someone else and send pics so I can verify his eight-ness."

"We'll see. I might need to nurse this rejection for a little while first." I turn onto Sycamore Way and slow down. "Anyway, just got to my dad's. I'll text you later."

"All right. Love you, babe," she chirps before disconnecting.

It's so strange returning to my childhood home when I don't even have my own bedroom there anymore. The twins usurped it because it's larger than the other option, which Dad and Nia use as a guest room now. That's where I sleep when I come to visit, ensuring my old house never quite feels like home anymore. Also, Nia redecorated the entire place not long after she moved in. Where my mom's design eye lends itself to grays, creams, and whites and modern furnishings, Nia is all about bright colors. She loves mismatched furniture, pieces that offer a cozy rather than museum-like feel. I can't deny I like Nia's décor better.

I also can't deny it stings that Dad's new daughters sleep in my room.

Excited shrieks greet me in the front hall. Two dark-haired tornadoes spiral toward me, and then two sets of arms curl around my legs like greedy tentacles.

"Cassie!"

They're both screaming my name as if they didn't just see me in the spring. Honestly, it's great for my ego. I give them an enthusiastic bear hug, but Monique is hopping around, so excited to see me, that she loses her footing and ends up teetering out of the three-way hug, falling to the floor onto her butt. Her sister Roxanne starts hooting with laughter.

I tug Mo to her feet. "Hey, squirts," I say. "How's life?"

"Life. Is. Awful," announces Roxy, the ringleader of the two. Both my sisters possess sweet, lovable temperaments, but Roxanne is definitely bossier, always speaking in a more authoritative tone. She's the elder by two minutes and takes that role very seriously. Even if she didn't have that tiny birthmark on her left cheekbone that allows me to tell them apart, I'd know Roxy just based on her tone of voice.

"And why is it awful?" I ask, fighting a smile.

"You tell her," Mo says, as if Roxy wasn't going to do it anyway.

"Mama won't get us a turtle."

I stare at them. "A turtle?"

"Yes!" Roxy huffs loudly. "They *promised* we could have a turtle when we turned six and now we're turning six and there's no turtle."

"There's no turtle!" Monique echoes.

They're wearing identical looks of outrage, and since their features are identical to begin with, their thunderous expressions give off some serious *redrum* vibes, a la *The Shining*.

"Like, a pet turtle?" I'm still perplexed. "Wait a second. You guys are campaigning for a pet and you chose a *turtle*? Man, I would've killed for a dog growing up."

"We don't care for dogs," Roxy says, sniffing. "They're waaay too much work."

"And we'd have to pick up *poo,*" Mo adds. "That is so gross."

"*So* gross." Roxy peers up at me, her brown eyes twinkling impishly. "Did you know the French word for poo is *merde*?"

I smother a laugh. I'm pretty sure the correct translation is *shit*. Either way there's something hilarious about hearing the word *merde* exit the mouth of a six-year-old.

The most delicious smells float out of the kitchen, so I wander toward it with the twins scampering at my heels. Neither Dad nor Nia is anywhere to be found, but I notice there's something baking in the oven, and several pots and pans simmering on the stove.

The big, airy kitchen was the first room Nia renovated when she moved in, changing the tiled floor to hardwood, painting the white cabinets a bright eggshell blue. She replaced the marble island for a cedar one, claiming she didn't like the way marble feels beneath her hands. She told Dad the counters were cold and unfeeling and made her sad. I didn't know counters could have that much of an impact on a person, but I suppose she's not wrong. Mom's aesthetic did lean toward cold and unfeeling.

Beyond the kitchen is the sunroom, which also doubles as the dining room, its entire wall of windows overlooking the spacious backyard. I peer into it, but it's empty.

"Where are the folks?" I ask, just as footsteps thud behind us.

"There's my girl!" Dad appears in the kitchen doorway, wearing khakis and a flannel shirt. "All my girls!" he adds, noticing the twins who are still bouncing around me. "C'mere, Cass. Give your old man a hug."

I go over and let him envelop me with his arms. Dad's not a tall man, but he's stocky and has some bulk, so his hugs always make you feel safe and warm.

His eyes shine behind his wire-rimmed glasses when he releases me. "Sorry I didn't get to see you this week. Just been busy around here."

"No worries. You know I love spending time with Grandma."

"Well, I'm glad you're here tonight. And I know you're excited to spend the summer with Lydia, but we were hoping you'd come stay here too."

"Yes!" Roxy says happily, throwing her arms around my legs again. "Then you can tell us bedtime stories every night."

"Every single night!" Mo gives an enthusiastic nod.

"I want one now," Roxy begs. "I wanna know what happens to Kit!"

"Me too!"

The request makes me smile. It's become sort of a tradition that I read the girls a bedtime story whenever I'm here, but these last couple years I've been entertaining them with an ongoing original tale. I pulled it out of my ass one time when we couldn't pick a book they both agreed on, and before I knew it I'd created an entire imaginary world for them, in which a little girl named McKenna finds a dragon egg in her backyard and proceeds to raise a pet dragon she names Kit, without anyone in her family catching on.

"What do you say?" Dad presses. "Can you swing a longer visit this summer? Stay for a week? Or maybe a weekend here and there?" he trails off, a bit uncertain.

"Definitely," I assure him. "Nia's okay with that?"

"Of course she is. She loves having you here."

Doubtful. But I never voice my suspicions about Nia's level of enthusiasm toward me, especially not to Dad. Peyton's psychiatrist mother would call it a coping mechanism, and I suppose it is. Whether I'm talking to my mom or my dad, I always put on that bright, sunny show. It's not just because I hate conflict—I've been burned too many times in the past with Dad shutting down. The brunt of it happened right after the divorce, whenever I tried talking to him about my feelings. He didn't even fight for joint custody of me, for Pete's sake. He let Mom have it all. And I never got answers for that, only uncomfortable silences and stilted smiles as he changed the subject.

As the memories surface before I can stop them, I swallow the lump clogging my throat and then take a breath, firmly banishing the resentment to that place inside of me where all the dark thoughts go.

My father is a good guy, he truly is. I know he loves me. But sometimes it feels like he wanted to wash his hands of everything after the divorce. He wanted zero reminders of my mother, and, unfortunately, I was the biggest reminder of all. Hence, I became collateral damage.

And to Nia, I'm a reminder of her husband's bitchy ex-wife, which is why her smile seems forced and her hug lacks warmth when she greets me a few minutes later.

"Cassandra," she says, her dark eyes guarded. "It's so good to see you."

"Good to see you too. Can I help with dinner?"

"*Non, non.*" She still has a noticeable French accent despite all her years living in the US. "Why don't you go sit at the table and catch up with your father and sisters? I have it handled."

"Are you sure?"

"Yes."

She's practically shoving me out of the kitchen. Not exactly the actions of a woman who's desperate to spend time with her stepdaughter.

In the sunroom, Dad and I settle at the dining table while the twins wander around us, running their little fingers over the backs of all the chairs. Those two can't sit still to save their lives.

"We told Cassie about the turtle," Roxy informs Dad.

He's clearly fighting a smile. "Oh, did you now? Why am I not surprised?" He glances at me. "The girls have alerted every single human they've encountered this past month to their desperate need for a turtle."

"Because we need a turtle!" Roxy complains.

"And it's not fair," Mo chimes in.

I arch a brow at Dad. "Just out of curiosity, why are we anti-turtle?"

"We're not," he answers, shrugging. "But pets are a lot of work.

We're not convinced the girls are grown up enough to handle all the responsibility that comes with it."

"Yes, we are!" they both shriek, and stomp their feet, basically proving the point he's trying to make.

Dad and I wince. "Indoor voices," he chides. "And we're going to table this turtle discussion for now, all right? Your mama and I said no turtle. We can revisit it next year."

Their faces collapse.

Knowing that tears are imminent, Dad snaps into action. He glances around the table with an exaggerated look of dismay and proceeds to do that thing I've seen him do a thousand times before, where he pretends there's a critical task that needs undertaking. Usually it's a pretty impressive trick, but tonight he's reaching.

"Oh no!" he exclaims. "We only put out the red napkins. We also need the white ones!"

"Oh, do we?" I say innocently.

He shoots me a look. "Yes, Cassandra. You know this. We must always dine with both red and white," he says poetically, laying it on thick. "To go with the wine."

I choke down a laugh. "Right. How could I forget that."

"We'll get them!" Roxy offers, just as Dad had intended for her to do. The girls are in that phase where they must be involved in *all* household matters.

"I'll help!" Mo chimes in.

"Oh wonderful. Thanks, girls." His tone oozes gratitude, as if he didn't just con them into doing his bidding.

The moment the sliding door closes, I stare at my father. "One: That was really smooth."

"Thank you."

"Two: You realize next to a goldfish, a turtle is the easiest pet you can have, right? And those things never die, so there's no risk of you flushing it down the toilet and replacing it with a thousand other goldfish like you did with mine."

Dad chortles. "Man, you were a clueless kid, Cass. I think we were on Rocky Fifteen before you figured it out?"

"Why would my child brain ever immediately go to *my fish died, so my parents drowned his corpse and keep replacing him with impostors*?" I glare in accusation. "Parents who do that are sociopaths."

"Sure, come talk to me when you have kids and your hamster accidentally gets eaten by a red-tailed hawk. Would you rather your child live in ignorance and love an impostor hamster, or do you plan on sharing all the gory details? And I'm talking *gory*."

"Oh my God, Dad, did that happen to you? Did a hawk eat your hamster?"

"Yes." He sounds glum. "And Grandpa Lou sat me down and gave me a play-by-play of his death. I'm sure if he'd taken pictures of the carnage, he would've showed them to me."

I bust out laughing. Oh man. Dad's father was the greatest. It honestly sucks that I lost both my grandfathers within a couple years of each other. But at least my grandmothers are still alive and kicking.

"Can I tell you a secret?" Dad says. His gaze flicks toward the kitchen. "I wouldn't mind getting a turtle. I think they're cool. But Nia isn't having it. She insists they're a lot more work than we think."

"Maybe there's a certain breed that's easier to own than others," I point out. "Did you even research it?"

"No."

"Did Nia?"

"I don't think so. She just shot down the idea point-blank. Told the girls we'll talk about it next year." Dad purses his lips for a moment. Mulling. "You think I should get them one?"

"Not necessarily. But I don't think it hurts researching the pros and cons." Crap. This isn't going to endear me in Nia's eyes. She already doesn't like me. But I feel like I owe it to my sisters to advocate for their dreams of turtle ownership. "I mean, it can't hurt, right? The least you can do is go to a pet store and talk to someone about it."

"Yeah. I suppose we could do that." One corner of his mouth quirks up, and then his eyes start twinkling. "Whatcha doing tomorrow morning?"

"Um." I offer a pointed look. "Potential turtle shopping?"

"Damn right."

We both snicker, exchanging secretive smiles when Nia and the twins return and we all settle around the table for dinner. It makes me feel like a little kid again, sharing a secret with my father. It's rare to have these bonding opportunities with him, where we're truly connecting without the heavy pall of my mother or Nia hanging over us. Those rare times when it's just us, me and him. The way it used to be when I was a child and he was my dad. When he didn't have two other kids, or two different wives who both can't stand to be around me.

I cling to those moments, because they're so few and far between.

CHAPTER 10

CASSIE

"I can't believe we're doing this," Dad whispers the next morning.

"I can't believe you're wearing a disguise," I respond in a normal speaking volume, for there is absolutely no reason for us to be whispering.

"I told you, Nia's friend works at the bakery over there," Dad protests, nodding toward a storefront on the other end of the strip mall. He glowers. "Chandra. One of the nosy PTA moms. I don't want her to notice me."

"Dad. You're wearing a hot-pink adventure hat with a purple string. She is absolutely going to notice you. In fact, you had a better chance of her not caring what your face looks like *without* the hat. Now she's going to *want* to see your face in order to understand what sort of person would ever choose to wear that hat."

"All I'm hearing is, you love my hat."

"That's not what I'm saying at all."

He just grins. We're a few feet from the entrance of the pet store when he says, "The girls loved seeing you last night, by the way. They were going on and on over breakfast about that bedtime story you told them, the one about the purple dragon? You need to start writing some of those down, Cass. I bet if you compiled all the stories in one file, you could have an entire—"

I suddenly gasp.

"What? What is it?" he demands, looking around in a panic. "Have we been compromised?"

"Oh my God, no. Dad, the baker lady doesn't give a shit about you." I'm practically bouncing with glee. "But you just gave me the best idea for the girls' birthday present. I can take one of the Kit 'n McKenna stories and create a children's book for them. I'm sure I could find a place to print a hardcover version of it." I pause. "I just wish I could draw. It would be cool to have illustrations to go with the story."

My mind snaps into troubleshooting mode, scanning through every person I've ever met in my life while I try to recall if they possess any artistic talent.

Robb! I remember in triumph. Robb Sheffield was my step-brother for five years during Mom's marriage to his dad, Stuart. He was always doodling in his sketchpad when we watched TV together, mostly drawing fantasy-type stuff, like freaky-looking monsters and warriors with deadly weapons. He works in video-game design now, creating the kind of imagery that's a lot grislier than a tale of a little girl and a purple dragon, but maybe he'd be willing to do me this favor.

"That's a terrific idea," Dad tells me. "The girls would love that. And if the final product turns out well, you should try to sell it."

"What do you mean? Like, self-publish a children's book?"

"Or submit it to a publishing house."

My brow furrows. "Really?"

"Sure. Why not? Aren't you majoring in literature?" he teases.

"Yes, but . . . I mean, I never really thought about going into a creative field. I only picked English Lit because I couldn't think of anything better to major in."

Truth be told, I have no clue what career path to take after graduation. So many people just *know*. They have that one skill, that one field they've always been passionate about. I'm not one of those people. I was hoping by the time graduation rolled around, I'd have landed on something, anything, but I'm going into my senior year and remain completely stumped as to what job I'll end up in.

"Could I even make a career out of that?" I ask, chewing on my lip. "It's just a bunch of silly bedtime stories for my sisters. It's not like I've been writing forever."

"Do you need to have been writing forever to start doing it now?"

"I guess not." I glare at him. "Ugh. You've given me a bunch of stuff to think about now."

"God forbid my daughter thinks!" Snorting, he reaches for the door handle. "Ready to turtle down?"

"Please don't ever say that."

When we enter the store, Dad pushes the pink hat off his head so it's dangling at his back by its purple string. He looks like a lost adventurer who stopped to ask for directions. We find ourselves surrounded by rows and rows of tanks, each housing various aquatic creatures.

I approach a fish tank full of fat orange goldfish and raise a brow. "I had no idea goldfish could get this big. If you tried to flush one of these guys, you'd clog the toilet."

"Welcome to AquaPets," a bored voice says from behind us. "Can I help you find something? You looking for a goldfish?"

A teenager in a store uniform sidles up to us. His name tag reads JOEL, and he's got shoulder-length black hair, acne-riddled skin, and he reeks of pot. The skunky odor practically radiates from his pores.

"We're considering buying a turtle for my six-year-old daughters," Dad explains. "But we're hoping for some more information before we commit."

"Yeah, yeah, that's cool," Joel says. The kid is clearly stoned. "I can help you with that. I've got three loggerheads at home. Those little dudes are rad."

"Loggerheads?" I echo.

"Loggerhead musk turtle," he says briskly, and, stoned or not, we discover the kid knows his stuff. For the next twenty minutes, he dumps an obscene amount of information on us, ushering us from tank to tank while spitting out reptilian facts.

"These guys? Smallest species of turtle you're allowed to keep in captivity. So if you got limited space, this is your dude. And they're so cute, man. Like, look." Leaning closer to the glass, he proceeds to make cooing noises at the spotted turtle. "You doing okay in there, Marshall? I named him Marshall. After Eminem."

I press my lips together. "Cool."

"The problem is, Marshall can't swim too good. See? That's why his water isn't very deep. And let's be honest—he's kind of a dick. The spotted ones get cranky sometimes. You want a social one, I'll show you my man Jay-Z. He's what we call a Reeve's turtle. Come. You'll love him."

Dad and I exchange a look that loosely translates to *why is this happening to us?*

But we're committed now, so we follow Joel the Turtle Whisperer to see his man Jay-Z.

"Best thing about this breed is they like being stroked," he tells us, so animated I'm having a hard time reconciling him with the pothead who greeted us at the door. "Most turtles don't enjoy being handled. It's stressful for them, you know? But if you're patient with him, Jay-Z might let you hold him sometimes."

He stares longingly at the tank. "The downside is," he says, and his expression collapses, "they've got a shorter life expectancy. Fifteen years, maybe twenty? If you're looking for a little dude who'll live longer, I'd go with the common musk. We're talking a ripe old age of fifty years. Just don't handle them roughly. They're feisty, man. If they feel threatened, they skunk you out."

"Skunk you out?" Dad echoes blankly. He looks as over-whelmed as I feel. Who knew turtle ownership was so intensive?

"Yeah, like, they release a foul odor. It stinks." Joel guffaws. "We call 'em *stinkpots*."

I don't ask who *we* is, but I'm definitely curious.

"They're not strong swimmers either," he adds. "But they've got pretty basic care requirements compared to other breeds."

"Wow," I say. "This is a lot of information."

So much, in fact, that eventually Dad and I beg off and tell Joel we need to think about it. Then we make our escape and step outside, breathing in the non-marijuana-infused air.

Dad sags against the concrete wall separating AquaPets from the pool equipment shop next door. He heaves a massive sigh of relief. "That was . . ."

"Intense," I supply.

"Very." He pulls his glasses off and cleans them with the hem of his T-shirt before popping them back on his face. "Thoughts?"

I join him at the wall, shoving my hands in the pockets of my denim shorts. "That Keanu Reeves turtle sounded promising."

Dad snickers. "Really? I'm leaning toward the musk."

"But Keanu Reeves has a shorter life expectancy," I argue. "Do you seriously want a pet that lives for fifty years?"

"What do I care? I'll probably be dead."

"Don't say that."

"Come on, there's no way I'll be alive to experience that turtle's entire life."

"But the musks don't like it when you touch them. They lose their shit and skunk you out, remember? Meanwhile, we were told on the good authority of Joel the Pothead that Keanu Reeves enjoys being stroked."

"Ahem."

Dad and I jump in surprise. Our heads swivel in the direction of the throat clearing, and at this point I'm not even surprised when I lay eyes on Tate. Since I arrived in Avalon Bay, it seems like everywhere I go, Tate Bartlett is there.

"Hi," he says in amusement, giving a nonchalant wave.

"You know," I say solemnly, "I long for the days of yore when I turned my head and didn't always find you standing there in front of me." It's meant to be a joke, but it then occurs to me that after last night's mortifying exchange, he might think I'm being serious. So I quickly add, "Kidding. But really, why are you here?"

He gestures toward a storefront on the other side of the parking lot. "I work at the boat dealership. Saw you from the window and came over to say hi—a decision I deeply regret because I'm not sure I want to know why you're discussing Keanu Reeves's love of handjobs and how you stumbled upon that information."

I can't stop the laugh that pops out. "You know what, not even going to explain it. I'm going to let it haunt you forever." I notice my father sporting a questioning expression, and gesture toward Tate. "Dad, this is Tate. He's housesitting the place next door to Grandma's."

Tate extends a hand. "Nice to meet you, Mr. Tanner."

Dad blanches.

"Oh no, no," I hastily intervene. "He's not a Tanner. My mom's side is the Tanners."

"Clayton Soul," Dad corrects, stepping forward to shake Tate's hand.

"Soul?" Tate turns to me in surprise. "Your name is Cassie Soul?"

"Yeah." I frown. "Is that bad?"

"Bad? Try bad-*ass*. That's a solid name."

"I guess? I never really thought that much about it. It's just my name."

There's a long beat during which we both start fidgeting with random sections of our clothing. I toy with the hem of my tank top. Tate pretends to pick at some lint on his shirt sleeve. Damn it. Things are awkward between us now. I knew this would happen.

"Turtles!" I blurt out.

Tate startles. "What?"

"Um, my sisters demanded a pet turtle for their birthday. That's why we're here. Doing some research. But it sounds like turtles are kind of jerks."

"Nah," he disagrees. "They're the easiest of pets. I had one when I was a kid and all it did was laze around in his tank all day. They pretty much entertain themselves." He shrugs. "My dogs, on the other hand . . . needy as fuck. Dogs require attention pretty much twenty-four-seven."

Dad chuckles. "You're making a good case for turtles."

"I'm telling you, they're great."

Another silence falls.

Tate fiddles with his other sleeve. I play with a frayed thread on my shorts. It's unbearable. This is what rejection does to people.

"Bye!" I blurt out.

Tate blinks at the sudden dismissal. "Oh. All right. Bye."

"I mean, we have to go now," I amend lamely. "So, ah, good-bye. See you around."

"Sure." His forehead creases. "See you around."

I practically drag Dad to the car, where I hurl myself into the passenger seat and pretend not to see Tate walking past the windshield on his way back to work.

"So," Dad says cheerfully, "do we have a crush on that boy, or is this how you interact with all your peers? Because I remember you used to be a lot less . . . weird."

"That was weird, wasn't it?" I moan. "Do you think he noticed?"

"Yes."

"Damn it." My face is on fire, and I refuse to look in the side mirror because I'm certain I'm redder than a lobster. "He and I are just friends." I pause. "I think." Pause again. "It's complicated."

"It always is." Dad suddenly jolts in his seat before reaching into his pocket to retrieve his buzzing phone. He checks the screen and balks. "Son of a bitch."

"What is it?" I ask immediately, concern washing over me.

Without a word, he hands over the phone to show me the text from Nia.

Nia: *Chandra said she just saw you at a pet store. Explain yourself!*

My eyebrows greet my hairline. "Wow. Fuckin' Chandra did us dirty."

"Did I not tell you?" Dad grumbles. Sighing, he starts the engine and puts the car in drive. "Time to go home and face the music."

* * *

Later that night, I walk up to my window just as a familiar figure enters my line of vision. It's becoming routine now. Grabbing something from my room? Tate's doing the same. Getting ready for bed? Tate's doing the same. This time, we're both reaching to close the curtains, almost in perfect sync. We stop, look at each other, then start to laugh. He disappears for a moment and returns holding his phone.

A message pops up on mine.

Tate: *Are we good?*

I stifle a sigh. I guess I knew that was coming. I meet his eyes briefly, then type a response.

Me: *Yeah, we're fine.*
Tate: *You sure? Because you were babbling more than usual when I saw you this morning.*

I don't have an excuse for that, so I just repeat myself.

Me: *We're fine.*
Tate: *I know last night was kind of awkward and I'm sorry about that. I really didn't want to embarrass you or anything. But I do think we're better as friends.*
Me: *OMG you're embarrassing me NOW by talking about it. We're cool, I promise. And we are friends, okay?*
Tate: *Yeah?*
Me: *Yeah.*
Tate: *Good.*

Rather than end the conversation there, he remains at the window, still typing, and I do my best not to stare at his bare chest. His abs look like they were chiseled out of stone and his pecs are stupidly defined and—damn it. I'm failing at not staring. I swear, would it kill him to throw on a shirt? He rarely wears shirts when he's inside the house. Doesn't he ever get cold? Here, we've always got the AC blasting. I'm wearing a sweater right now, for Pete's sake.

Tate: *I'm still waiting for deets on that Keanu Reeves handjob . . .*

I grin at the phone. Really? That's what took him so long to type? I wonder how many messages he deleted before he settled on that one.

Me: *I'm taking it to the grave.*
Tate: *You're a cruel woman, ginger.*
Me: *Copper!*
Tate: *It's really cute you actually believe that. What are you up to this weekend?*
Me: *I'm spending the day at the club tomorrow with Joy. We're going guy shopping.*
Tate: *You realize if any man said something like that he'd be labeled as the biggest douchebag in the Bay?*
Me: *Double standards, you gotta love them!*
Tate: *Sure don't!*
Me: *What are your plans this weekend?*
Tate: *Working, working, and working. Tomorrow I'm at the club too. Teaching a beginner dinghies class for kids. If I run into you, I'll make sure to say hi. You know, just to make it awkward again.*
Me: *Perfect. I'll pencil you in.*

At least we can joke about it.

CHAPTER 11

CASSIE

"Okay, don't kill me. But I like him. He's funny." Joy reaches across her lounger and hands me back my phone. I showed her last night's text exchange with Tate with the goal of highlighting how embarrassing it was. Instead, she goes and declares her love for the guy who rejected me.

Not that I disagree with her assessment.

"He *is* funny," I sigh. "And I like him too."

As the memory of his rejection pricks at my skin, I order myself to conduct a silver-lining check. Shockingly, I land on something genuine.

"You know what, though? Maybe it's a good thing he turned me down. I can see myself catching feelings," I admit.

Joy gives me a somber look. "Oh boy. Yeah. That's no good. You can't fall for your summer fling. Well, unless you plan on moving to Avalon Bay and living happily ever after with a local."

I muse on that for a moment. "I don't know if I could live here. I enjoy the energy of the city. The Bay is nice to visit, but I think I prefer a faster pace."

"Exactly. I wouldn't live here full-time either," Joy says, leaning back in her chair. She readjusts her sunglasses and gazes up at the cloudless sky. It's a perfect day for sunbathing. "And from what I've seen, the townies don't tend to leave this place. If you fell for the guy, you'd be stuck here forever."

"There you go," I say wryly. "One more item in the plus column for getting friend-zoned."

Joy smiles. "For what it's worth, it sounds like he really does like you and want to hang out with you. Maybe being friend-zoned isn't the end of the world."

"Maybe not," I agree, and while I half mean it this time, it doesn't exactly change my current situation. I'm still left in the same fling-less predicament.

I want my fling, damn it. I was genuinely looking forward to finding someone to spend the next couple of months with. Finally experiencing that summer romance I've always envied my friends for. I'd hoped to go into my final year of college with a fresh dose of confidence and some experience under my belt. My entire collegiate dating experience consists of the six months I spent with a guy in junior year, Mike. He was funny and interesting, but we didn't sleep together because I wasn't ready, and eventually he got bored of third base and bailed. This year I want a relationship that actually lasts, one that's chock-full of passion and chemistry. I'm craving passion.

"We should pick you up someone at the bachelor auction," Joy suggests while applying some moisturizing lip balm. She always complains that the sun dries out her lips.

"Are they seriously still doing that?"

"Oh yeah. You should go check out the events desk. I peeked at the calendar when I got here to see what's coming up this summer, and I swear there are *so* many events."

"Like what?" From the table sandwiched between our chairs, I grab the aerosol can of sunscreen and spray some on my legs. Either my sunglasses are warping the colors around me, or I'm starting to burn a little. I lift my shades and wince. Yup, burning.

I can practically hear Grandma's voice in my head lecturing me for not consistently reapplying my sunscreen.

"We just missed the regatta—that was last week. Next weekend is the charity gala, which features the bachelor auction. First week of August is the golf tournament. Beach Games at the end of the month."

"Did I tell you I'm competing this year? Mackenzie Cabot asked me to join Team Beacon."

"That sounds like my worst nightmare," Joy informs me. I'm not surprised, seeing as how she's the least athletic person I know.

"Nah, it'll be fun. And then the grand reopening of the Beacon is the weekend after that," I remind her. That's the only event I'm truly excited about, although I know it'll be bittersweet. "Grandma and I will be at the charity thing this weekend. She likes bidding in the silent auction. She's giving me some cash to bid with since it's for a good cause, but I doubt I'll attend the bachelor event. It's always a bunch of old dudes with very noticeable hair plugs."

She laughs. "Nuh-uh, last year there were some young'uns in the mix." She waggles her eyebrows at me. "Including your best friend Tate."

"Really?" I ignore the way my heart skips a beat. "You think he signed up again?"

"No idea. But I vote we check it out regardless. Maybe we'll find you a cute guy to fling with."

"Wasn't that today's goal?"

"Well, yeah, but I haven't seen any suitable candidates yet. Have you?"

"No," I say glumly.

She slides up in her chair, readjusting her sunglasses. "Let's take another look."

Weekends at the Manor are always busy, so the pool area is packed, every single lounger occupied. We had to reserve ours in advance, and Joy had grumbled up a storm when she was informed there were no available cabanas to book for the day. Her family usually reserves one for three full months, but this year her parents opted out because her mom got a promotion at work and will be spending the bulk of the summer in Manhattan.

"Oooh," she suddenly says. "I got one. Eleven o'clock, end of the bar."

I pop my sunglasses back on to make it less obvious that we're staring. The guy she's homed in on does look promising. Average height, dark hair, chiseled profile. He's decked out in shorts, a green polo, and brown Sperrys. When he turns slightly, angling away from us, my gaze lowers to his butt, because apparently I'm a butt girl now. It's decent. And he's at least an eight, which ought to satisfy Peyton.

"I sure could use a refill of this piña colada," Joy says. With a grin, she waves her empty glass around.

"You're really going to make me go up there? Haven't we established I'm terrible at asking guys out?"

"Who's asking him out? Just go and talk to him. See if you like him. Then you can decide if you even want to ask him out. You always make yourself needlessly anxious by assuming the outcome."

Good point. I do tend to jump the gun a lot, assuming every cute guy I speak to is my potential boyfriend when really it's just a person to say hello to.

"Fine." With a brisk nod, I slide off the striped towel draped over my chair and get to my feet. I don't bother with my shorts, just slip into my flip-flops and saunter across the pool deck. There are women here walking around in string bikinis; my one-piece is hardly scandalous. It's high-cut and does show quite a lot of thigh, but it supports my boobs well, a rare feat for a Cassie Soul bathing suit.

When I approach, the guy is sitting on a stool laughing at something the bartender just said. The second bartender, a curly-haired woman with a deep tan, greets me with a smile. "What can I do you for?"

"Two piña coladas, please. Virgin." I blush at the word, but it sounds less dorky than *nonalcoholic*. Joy and I decided against day drinking today, even though I'd probably be served here. Most of the bars in the country club turn the other way when it comes to underage clientele, provided their families are rich enough. And my family passes the wealth test, apparently.

The sound of my voice catches the guy's attention. He gives me a sidelong look.

I crack a half smile, one of those teeny quirks of the lips that says I acknowledge his presence.

He smiles back.

And as always, his eyes drop to my chest. The curse of owning double Ds.

His gaze lingers, and now I feel self-conscious standing there in nothing but a bathing suit and pink flip-flops. There's nowhere for me to hide. No clothing to burrow under. His perusal doesn't feel overly creepy, only a glimmer of appreciation, but I'm still relieved when he raises his eyes.

"Hey," he says easily. "I'm Ben."

"Cassie."

"Are you new here?" He flashes another smile, a tad bashful. "You must be, 'cause I thought I knew all the pretty members in this club."

"Uh, no. I'm not new. I'm here a lot. I mean, I don't visit for the whole summer often, but I have been here before."

The bartender approaches with an apologetic look. "It'll just be a few more minutes. We ran out of coconut milk. Someone's running over to grab a fresh case from the restaurant bar."

"That's fine. I can wait." I glance over my shoulder to find Joy watching us intently. Grinning impishly, she gives a little wave.

"Sit," Ben urges, gesturing to the stool beside him. "Take a load off."

We chat for a while, the coconut milk taking longer than a few minutes to arrive. Ben tells me he's originally from New York but goes to Yale. He's in his first year of law school and loving it. His family recently bought a vacation home in the Bay and this is his second summer here. When I tell him my grandparents were the previous owners of the Beacon Hotel and built it from the ground up, he's suitably impressed. He's got a bland sort of humor but the conversation flows easily, and when two piña coladas are finally slid in front of me, I decide I don't want the conversation to end yet.

I lean toward an approaching waitress and ask, "Do you mind dropping this drink off to my friend? I don't want it to get all melty." I point across the pool deck at Joy's lounger. "She's the one in the red bikini."

"No problem," the blonde chirps, taking the tall glass, which is already dripping with condensation. Before she steps away, she gives me a warning look. Or at least I think it's a warning? I'm not entirely sure.

When I wrinkle my forehead, her head moves, almost imperceptibly, toward my companion, who's checking something on his phone. Is she warning me away from Ben? I must be misreading the look, but she hurries off before I can figure it out.

A few minutes later, I figure it out.

"You want to get out of here?" he suggests with a devilish gleam in his eyes, twisting his body so that our knees are now touching.

I shift in my seat, easing my knee away. "And go where?" I ask uneasily.

"My family booked a cabana here for the summer. We can hang out there. Lots of privacy . . ." He raises an enticing brow.

"Oh. No, it's fine. Let's just stay out here." I lift my drink and take a sip. "I'm good."

"Really? 'Cause I think you'd feel a lot better if we had some privacy."

It's funny how fast they transform from cool guy I'm talking to, to *run, girl, run*.

"Yeah, no. Like I said, I'm good. But my friend's probably getting bored sitting there all alone. I think I'll head back." I start to slide off the stool.

Ben stops me by reaching out and placing a hand on my bare thigh.

Instantly, my cheeks are scorching and my palms feel damp. This stupid bathing suit. Why didn't I put my shorts on?

Clenching my teeth, I shove his hand off and say, "Don't."

"What?" he protests. "I thought we were getting along." When he notices my dark expression, he leans closer. Lowers his voice. "Look, I'm going to be honest. I think you're hot. From the second you walked up here, I've been fantasizing about pulling that bathing suit off you and feasting my eyes on those tits. They're gorgeous."

My eyes become hot, stinging wildly, which is stupid because there's no reason for me to cry. I've been objectified before, and I'll be objectified again. That's just the reality of it. And yet shame clamps around my throat, squeezing my windpipe so tight I have a hard time choking out words.

Luckily, someone else does it for me.

"She said no."

Tate appears behind us. He's wearing his club uniform, khaki shorts and a white polo with the name of the club embroidered in gold, Tate's name stitched beneath it. His hair is tousled, probably from being out on the water all morning.

Relief trickles through me as I meet Tate's hard blue eyes.

"Uh, yeah, get lost, Bartlett," Ben says snidely, which tells me the two of them are already acquainted. "This is a private conversation."

"I don't think I'm the one Cassie would like to see go." Tate tips his head toward me. "Isn't that right, Cass?"

I finally find my voice. "That's right."

A scowl darkens Ben's face. "Are you fucking serious right now? *You're* the one who came over here, smiled at me, sat down beside me. And I'm the bad guy? Clearly you started this."

"And I'm about to finish it if you don't leave," Tate snaps. "Seriously, dude. I'm getting sick of having to pry you off women who clearly don't want you around."

"Fuck off." But he does get up. Ben throws a hundred-dollar bill on the bar and then stalks off without a backward look. Asshole.

"Thanks," I tell Tate, letting out the breath I'd been holding.

"You okay?"

"I'm fine. He didn't do anything, really. Just put his hand on my leg and told me how much he loves my boobs." I shrug, my tone flat. "They always love my boobs."

"Don't do that," Tate says softly.

"Do what?"

"Try to make light of it. Look, yes, men enjoy a nice rack. But that doesn't give them the right to objectify you or make you feel uncomfortable. Or to lay a fucking hand on you."

I chew the inside of my cheek. The truth is, I have a very complicated relationship with my breasts. When I was younger, they made me so self-conscious, which led to some seriously bad posture thanks to my attempts to make them appear smaller by hunching. Eventually I grew to accept my chest, although I'm still not entirely comfortable that it tends to be the first thing

THE SUMMER GIRL • 113

most people notice about me. It's embarrassing. I mean, I get it—humans are visual creatures. It's hard not to stare when someone has huge tits. Sometimes I even like showing mine off, wearing a tight top or a sexy dress. But Tate is right. Being objectified isn't a joke. I shouldn't make light of it, no matter how immune I've gotten over the years.

"You're right. That wasn't okay." I release another breath. "He seemed really cool at the beginning."

"I know. I've seen him pull the Mr. Charming act all summer. Usually he keeps it going for at least a few dates, though. I think you caught him when he was drunker than usual. The lowered inhibitions make it harder to hide the sleaze."

"He didn't seem that drunk," I start, but then remember the waitress's warning look. She'd probably been serving him all afternoon. Both bartenders had seemed well acquainted with him too. I pick up my drink and chug the rest of it. "Oh well. Another fling bites the dust."

"Nah, ginger, you don't want that loser. There are a million better candidates."

I roll my eyes. "Is this the part where you offer to be my wingman again?"

"You know what? Yes. Let's do this shit." He flashes that dimpled smile.

"Do what?" I find myself laughing. It's amazing how fast he's able to cheer me up. I'm not even thinking about creepy Ben anymore.

"Let's go out tomorrow night," Tate urges. "I'm done at the dealership at five and then having dinner with my mom, but I can come grab you afterward. We'll hit Joe's Beach Bar. It's got a balanced combo of locals and your crowd."

"My crowd?"

"Yeah, the clones. The rich folks. There'll be a good variety at

Joe's. I'll help you scope out the candidates. I know practically everyone in town, so I can tell you which ones to stay away from."

"Really. You're going to help me find a fling." I remain reluctant. "I don't know."

"Come on, what do you have to lose?"

My dignity.

My self-esteem.

"I don't know," I say again.

"C'mon.

"Ugh . . ."

"C'mon."

"Are you just going to keep pestering me until I agree?"

"Pretty much." His dimples make another appearance. "C'mon."

"Oh my God. Fine."

* * *

And that's how the following night I find myself waiting outside Joe's Beach Bar while Tate searches for a parking spot. The boardwalk is packed, even on a Monday night. And Joe's is situated in a prime location, its beachfront patio a major draw for the tourist crowd. Six steps off the patio and literally you're on the sand. I've always liked this place. The food is great. Super laid-back atmosphere.

"Ready?" Tate saunters up the sidewalk toward me.

"How far away did you have to park?"

"Not too bad. Beach access lot near the Soapery."

We step to the door as a group of loud, drunk young men are exiting, one of them stumbling into us before offering a slurred apology. Tate reaches out to steady me, which places his hand at the small of my back. And since I'm wearing a cropped tee, his palm meets my bare skin.

A hot shiver runs through me.

"You okay?" he says.

"Good." I swallow. Wishing my pulse still didn't careen whenever we accidentally touch.

But Tate made it clear he's not interested in flinging with me, and since I'd really like to find a cute guy to spend the summer with, I can either mope around during my remaining six weeks in the Bay and moon over Tate Bartlett—or I can try to meet someone who's equally cool.

As a woman who's trained herself to forever focus on the positive, I do what I always do and paste on a cheerful smile. "All right, Bartlett. The game's afoot."

"The game is gonna end in spectacular defeat if you keep using phrases like *the game's afoot*." He rolls his eyes. "Let's get us some drinks, Sherlock."

We order a couple of beers and migrate toward a standing table against the wall, which offers a view of the entire bar, including the patio. Sipping my beer, I scope out the room. Tate's doing the same.

"How about him?" he suggests. Gives a discreet nod to our right.

I follow his gaze to a dark-haired guy with a lean frame and an attractive face. Sadly, his good looks are eclipsed by his unfortunate choice of arm ink.

"Absolutely not," I retort.

"Is it the tattoo?"

"Of course it's the tattoo. I'm not sure I want to date someone who loves tacos so much they permanently etch one into their flesh. Imagine how often we'd have to eat tacos for dinner?" I shake my head. "No way."

Tate stares at me.

"What?"

His lips twitch with unrestrained laughter. "Cassie. Baby. Sweetie. I'm pretty sure that's not the kind of taco he's looking to commemorate."

"What do you mean? What else—" I gasp. "Oh. Ew. No." I glare at him. "Really? And you think *he's* a viable option?"

"Why not? Means he does oral . . ."

"Thank you, next."

"So picky. Won't even consider a man who wants to worship your taco."

I burst out laughing. He doubles over half a second later and then we're both in hysterics. Damn it, why do I have such a good time with this guy? You wouldn't expect Tate to be so funny. With his perpetually tousled hair and lazy smiles, that trace of a Georgia accent thrown into the mix, he gives off a slacker, surfer-boy vibe, when he's the total opposite of that. Tate is intelligent, hard-working. And I think it speaks volumes that every single person who knows him genuinely likes him. Not many people can say that.

"How about him?" I nod toward a cute guy by the dartboards.

The bar features an entire wall exclusively for darts. It's basically a huge wooden board riddled with so many dents, holes, and puncture marks it's clear many a projectile has been hurled at it by intoxicated hands. The guy I point out is in the process of aiming. He grips his dart, forehead lined with intensity, when his friend sidles up to him and breaks his concentration. The guy swivels his head and snaps something. The friend, taken aback, holds up both hands and backs away like he just confronted a territorial lion.

"Are you kidding me?" Tate says. "Mr. Angry over there?"

"He wasn't angry when I first noticed him," I protest.

"Well, he is now and that's a red flag. It's fucking darts. Nobody gets that invested in darts."

He's right. I can't date someone who's so passionate about *darts* they nearly bite someone's head off for interrupting.

Or is that too picky?

"Am I being too picky?" I ask in dismay.

"No. I mean, yes. *Must hate darts* is picky. But I also know those overcompetitive blowhard types. They're not fun to be around." He shrugs. "And they tend to be selfish in bed."

"Really? Had sex with a lot of overcompetitive men, have ya?"

"No, but I'm friends with a lot of girls. They spill the tea."

"I cannot believe you just used that expression."

"Why? It's legit."

I rib him with my elbow. "Maybe you're the one who needs pickup help if that's the kind of lingo you're dropping around the ladies."

"Trust me, I do just fine."

I have no doubt.

We spend the next little while people-watching and joking around. Despite his assurance that Joe's draws a diverse crowd, there aren't many prospects here for me. Mostly drunk tourists or couples. Tate goes to grab us another round of beers, and I take the opportunity to check my phone. My message thread with Peyton contains her customary one-line format.

Peyton: *How's it going?*
Peyton: *Is your wingman any good?*
Peyton: *Did we find somebody?*
Peyton: *They better not be a six.*
Peyton: *Well?*

Would it kill her to send one paragraph? I have an impossible time trying to locate the silver lining in Peyton's aggravating texting style.

Along with Peyton's messages, I find a response from my former stepbrother to my illustration request.

Robb: *Sorry for the delay! Was trying to figure out if I could squeeze it in. I just wrapped up a project at work ahead of schedule, so I'm in! Send me the story and I can come up with some concepts this week.*

Yes! The children's book is a go. I give a mental fist pump. My sisters are going to love me forever.

Before I can reply to Robb, a shadow falls over the table. I look up . . . and then up . . . and up. Because the guy who's wandered up is a literal giant. He must be six-six, maybe even taller.

A hesitant smile touches his lips. He's got a sweet-looking face. "Hey," he says. "A pretty girl like you shouldn't be sitting all alone." Then he winces. "Shit. I'm sorry. That's a terrible line."

I can't help but laugh. "I mean, it's not the most original, but it does the job."

"Mind if I join you? My friend kind of ditched me." He gestures toward a booth across the room, where a young couple is eating each other's faces off. And I'm pretty sure she has her hand down his pants. They're either going to be kicked out any second, or soon the entire bar will witness an enthusiastic bout of public sex.

"Wow," I remark. "They're really going at it."

"Yeah. I know. He does this every weekend." The giant makes a face. "He's the worst person to go out with."

"And yet you keep doing it every weekend . . ."

"Maybe I'm hoping one day I'll find a cute girl to keep me company."

"Nice. That line was much better."

"Thank God." He gives a tentative smile and rests one forearm on the table. "I'm Landon."

"Cassie."

"It's nice to meet you, Cassie."

His shyness is slowly melting away, so of course my wingman chooses precisely that moment to return with our beers.

Landon takes one look at Tate and instantly goes on guard. "Oh. I'm sorry. I didn't know you were with someone."

"No, no, we're not together," I say. "This is my friend Tate."

"I'm her wingman," Tate supplies.

Landon laughs, but the sound is laced with discomfort. "That's, um, cool."

Tate flicks up an eyebrow. "I'm also her gatekeeper."

"You are not." I turn to reassure Landon. "He's not, I swear."

"Of course I am. I'm not letting my friend leave here with anyone unless I know their intentions." Tate crosses his arms in some macho posturing move that makes me roll my eyes. "So." He pins Landon with a stern stare-down. "Please state your intentions."

"Oh my God," I groan. "Just ignore him."

"I'm serious. Intentions. State 'em. I'm waiting."

Landon shifts awkwardly, and he's so big that he can't help jarring the table. I'm surprised the liquid in our bottles doesn't start rippling like in Jurassic Park when the T. rex walks up. With an uncertain expression, he finally pieces together a response.

"Um. I don't know. I thought I'd buy her a drink. Is that okay? I think she's cute, and, um . . ." I don't know if it's the word *cute* that causes him to lower his eyes to my boobs, or if he's simply trying to avoid Tate's death glare and it's pure coincidence where his gaze lands.

Either way, it earns him a warning growl from Tate. "Eyes on me." He points two fingers at his own eyes as if to punctuate that.

"I'm sorry." Landon's panicking. "I . . ." He takes a step away. "You know what? I think my friend's calling me."

Nobody is calling him, but my poor sweet giant has apparently decided that watching his friend grope some chick is better than being subjected to Tate's outrageous interrogation.

"Cockblock," I accuse, scowling at my wingman.

"Nah. Trust me, that's not our guy."

"Why not?"

"He kept apologizing for everything. And he was too nervous."

I object to the latter. "Nervous can be endearing."

Tate is quick to disagree. "He asked if it was okay to buy you a drink. Is that really what we want? No. We want someone who's proactive. Someone with confidence. Dude over there is the kind of guy who asks for permission to hold your hand." He pauses. "If you were only allowed to use one word to describe what you want from your fling this summer, what would it be?"

"Passion," I answer without thinking, and immediately regret that decision.

The air between us shifts, growing thicker, headier. Or maybe it's only happening on my end. Maybe I'm only imagining that his lips are slightly parted, that his blue eyes suddenly appear darker, loaded with heat. There's no way those eyes are smoldering at me right now.

"Passion," he echoes, his voice a bit raspy. I swear I see him gulp. Then he clears his throat and shrugs. "Are you telling me you think *that* guy actually fits the passion bill?"

"No," I admit.

"Then I've done my wingman duty."

We finish our second beers and order a third round, eventually drifting over to the dartboard wall to play a couple of games. After Tate beats me for a second time, the guys next to us, a pair of brothers visiting from New York, challenge us to a game. Two on two. I'm downright terrible, but luckily my counterpart is equally atrocious. Tate and *his* counterpart are stupidly good, hitting bullseye after bullseye while the other guy and I glumly watch our teammates outshoot us. At this point, we're completely inconsequential to the outcome of the game. Those two are basically battling it out alone.

"We suck," the guy informs me. They introduced themselves earlier. I can't remember his brother's name, but his name is Aaron. He's tall and lean, with bright brown eyes, a great smile, and not a single pink taco tattoo.

"Oh, big time," I agree.

Tate scores another bullseye, prompting Aaron's brother to rub his forehead and marvel, "Damn, bro. You're like some darts whiz kid. How often do you play?"

"Hardly ever," Tate replies proudly. "I was born with this gift."

I snicker from our spot on the sidelines, prompting Tate to turn and flash me a grin.

"How long have you two been together?" Aaron asks.

"Oh, we're not together," I reply, and I don't miss the flicker of interest in his eyes. He really is cute. And I'm definitely picking up on some chemistry between us while we've been chatting.

Once he knows Tate and I aren't a couple, Aaron gets even flirtier. After three beers, I'm feeling loose and relaxed, and find myself flirting back with very minimal nervous babbling. It's going well, at least until Aaron's brother takes a bathroom break and Tate comes over and interrupts us. He looks Aaron up and down, then shifts his gaze to me and lifts a brow, as if to ask, *Do we like this guy?*

I nod slightly, then curse myself for it because Tate views that as permission to interrogate.

"All right," he says cheerfully, planting himself in front of Aaron. "Let's hear it. What are your intentions with my friend?"

A faint grin appears on Aaron's face. He dons a thoughtful look. Goes quiet for several seconds. "Hmmm. Alright. Tough question. At the moment, I'm torn between inviting her to accompany me to the carnival tomorrow night—or, and hear me out, asking her to partner up for a darts tournament, except instead of playing to see who's best, we'd be vying for the title of America's Worst."

Tate nods his approval. "Two solid options. Okay. Permission granted. Carry on." He claps Aaron on the shoulder and wanders off.

"Well?" Aaron says, directing that appealing smile my way. "You, me, and a carnival? Tomorrow night?"

"Sure," I say shyly. "I'd love to."

CHAPTER 12

TATE

Tuesday is a slow day at Bartlett Marine, so Dad and I spend half the morning looking at boat porn. He's hoping to replace our ancient thirty-seven-foot Hatteras with a newer model, maybe one with built-in GPS and a few more bells and whistles. But while I keep trying to steer him toward more practical options, Dad keeps clicking on shit that in no way meets our criteria.

"Dude," I chastise. "We don't need a high-performance speed-boat."

"Everyone needs a high-performance speedboat."

"Well, yeah." I sigh. "But we're looking for something suitable for deep-sea fishing, remember?"

"I know, but . . ." Dad groans happily. "Look at this one, kid. Check out the design of her V-bottom hull . . . aw, man, she's so sexy I can't take it."

A dry laugh echoes from the door. We both look up to see Mom standing there. We were so engrossed with the computer screen we didn't even hear her come in.

"What's her model number?" Mom asks.

I snicker. Most people would hear *she's so sexy I can't take it* and assume we're ogling photos of women. "What makes you think we're not looking at human porn?" I challenge.

"Because I know you boys better than that." She strides toward us, an oversized wicker tote slung over her shoulder. With her yellow dress, flip-flops, and blond hair in a ponytail, she could easily pass for one of the college girls who'll be swarming the Bay in September.

"Hi, sweetie." She plants a kiss on my cheek.

"Hey, Mom."

She turns to greet Dad, except when her lips near his cheek he pulls a sly switcheroo and plants his mouth on hers instead. I glimpse a slip of tongue, and cringe.

"You guys are repulsive," I say, pretending to gag.

I don't really mean it, though. Because all that stuff Mackenzie said last week about me never showing much interest in girlfriends? I suspect my parents' relationship has a lot to do with that. When you grow up witnessing that sort of love, you start to believe that's how all relationships are supposed to feel. And then you wait. You hold out for that feeling. It's obscure, impossible to describe, but you know it exists. *I* know it exists because I see it with my folks.

I've been with many women, fucked a lot of them, dated a few, but I've yet to experience a deep connection with anyone. It might be cheesy and embarrassing and I'd never say it out loud, but I think I'm waiting for that feeling. And unless I feel it, there's no point falling into a relationship with anyone.

Dad says he knew Mom was the one the moment he met her. She tells it a little differently, always teasing him that *technically* they met in high school and clearly he had no clue she was the one, otherwise they would've been dating back then. Dad was a big baseball star, dated cheerleaders and didn't know Mom existed, according to her. After graduation, he left Georgia for St. Louis to play in the minors, while Mom stayed in St. Simon's and started dating an accountant named Brad. A year into his ball career, Dad

got injured and returned to the island, where he quickly recon-
nected with an old cheerleader flame. Which means they were
both otherwise involved when they bumped into each other in the
grocery store one afternoon. Despite that, Dad claims he took one
look at her and knew he was going to marry her.

Mom ditched Brad, Dad ditched the cheerleader, and they've
been blissfully married for twenty-five years.

Dad calls it their origin story. He gets a kick out of telling it.
But Mom . . . it's weird. Sometimes when she talks about it, she
still wears this odd expression of disbelief. As if she can't fathom
how Gavin Bartlett could have chosen *her,* Gemma McCleary,
over some cheerleader he dated in high school. I don't get why
she's so stumped. Of course he chose her. Mom's the coolest person I know.

With a curious expression, she peers closer at the computer
screen, then lifts her head to narrow her eyes at Dad. "You can't
fish in that, Gavin."

"But isn't she beautiful?"

"Can you fish in her?"

"Well, no, but—"

"Then she's ugly," Mom declares. "Utterly hideous."

Dad pouts. "Spoilsport." He leans back in his rolling chair.
"What brings you here, darlin'?"

"I took a half day at work today, so I decided to drop off some
lunch for my boys."

She reaches into her bag and pulls out a pair of sandwiches
wrapped in foil. They're *man-sized,* as she calls it. Meaning each
sandwich is about the size of a shoebox.

"The vegetable garden is growing out of control, so I'm trying to use everything I can from it. Picked some fresh tomatoes,
lettuce, peppers. And I grabbed some of that deli meat from the
butcher in town. The roast ham you like."

Dad's eyes light up. "Oh man, yes. Thanks, Gem."

"How are my children?" I ask Mom. "You're not sending me enough pics of them."

"Because I have more pressing matters to attend to than taking pictures of your dogs, sweetheart. You know, like go to work every day?"

"The kids are great," Dad assures me. "Polly killed a rabbit last week and brought us its severed head as a token of her love."

I guffaw.

"And Fudge got into the pantry yesterday and ate half a box of cookies, so he was farting all night. Around ten he was in a dead sleep and ripped one out so loud he woke himself up. Got so freaked out he was barking for a solid five minutes."

Now I can't stop laughing. "Shit, I can't believe I missed that."

Leaning against the side of the desk, Mom glances at Dad and nods toward me. "Did you ask him yet?"

I eye them both. "Ask me what?"

"No, I didn't get a chance to yet," he tells her. "Got distracted looking at boat pics." He spins around in his chair, hands propped behind his neck. "It's a big ask, but we were hoping you could do us a favor, kid. You know how we planned to take a trip in the fall?"

I nod. "A week in California."

"Right. Well, we're hoping to be gone a little longer than a week. We figured if we're already on the west coast, we should make a real holiday out of it. Add Hawaii to the itinerary."

"Hawaii!" Mom claps excitedly.

I rise from my chair and head for the water cooler to pour myself a cup. "So how long would you be gone?"

"If you're on board, it'd be a month," Dad says. "Your contract with the club is done in September, right?"

"Yeah." I don't teach sailing during the off season, working only from April to September. After that, I switch over to full-time shifts at the dealership. But I've never run the place on my own before. It's always Dad and me, so the responsibilities are split fairly evenly. Working solo for a month means much longer hours.

On the other hand, it also means much bigger paychecks. I could put all that extra money toward buying my own sailboat.

"I think I could manage it," I say slowly.

"Thanks, sweetie." Mom comes up and gives me a quick hug, resting her chin on my shoulder. "We really appreciate it."

"Told you we could count on him," Dad says with a pleased smile. "Family always takes care of family, right, kid?"

"Yup."

* * *

The rest of the workday flies by after Mom leaves. Around one o'clock we deal with a rush of tourists coming in to inquire about boat rentals, which we also provide. Dad and I are so busy we don't even have a chance to eat our sandwiches. I scarf mine down in the Jeep on the way home later.

As always, I conduct a quick visual sweep of the Jackson house when I walk in, just to make sure nothing bad happened when I was at work. No wild animals finding their way in, or greedy hooligans getting the bright idea to rob us. All is good, and I head upstairs to change into sweats.

My plan for the night is lazing on the couch and watching mindless TV, because tomorrow's going to be busy. Working with Dad till four, then speeding over to the yacht club to teach a five o'clock safety class to a group of teenagers who're hoping to get the certification required for them to compete in single-handed dinghy racing. I love that the Manor sponsors junior programs for young sailors—I found them so valuable when I was their age. I do wish we offered club races to prepare kids for national events, but at least they're able to compete at our sister club in Charleston.

I've just pulled a pair of gray sweatpants up my hips when I glimpse a flash of movement next door. It's messed up, this strange synchronization Cassie and I have going on. As she passes her window, I narrow my eyes, frown, then grab my phone to text her.

Me: *You're wearing pink to your carnival date? No.*
Cassie: *Why not??*
Me: *Because you'll get lost in a sea of cotton candy. You won't stand out.*
Cassie: *But I look cute in pink.*

I can't argue with that. As it happens, she looks cute in everything, but I keep that observation to myself. I insisted I only wanted to be friends. Telling her how hot she is would only send mixed signals and confuse us both. And to be honest, I'm enjoying the hell out of this friendship. Hanging out with Cassie feels so damn natural. We have fun together, and there's no pressure on my end to be on top of my game. I can be stupid and say whatever nonsense comes to mind, and, like a good friend, Cassie just laughs and doesn't judge.

At the window, Cassie toys with the edge of her side braid, clearly mulling it over. She types another message.

Cassie: *Okay. Stand by.*

The curtains shut. But I don't think she realizes they're kind of sheer, especially when the bedroom light is on. The gauzy white material does very little to conceal the silhouette of the pinup girl next door.

Don't look.

Too late.

Heat streaks through my bloodstream and settles in my balls, drawing them up tight. Oh fuck. I never knew a silhouette could turn me on so much. My throat is dryer than sawdust as I watch Cassie's delectable shape move around the room. She disappears for a moment. In the walk-in closet, I think. Then she's back and my dick weeps with joy. I'm semi-hard and unable to stop myself from staring. She's in profile now. Her arms raise as she slips a garment over her head. The move makes her chest jut out, offering a perfect side-boob view.

Sweet Jesus.

She's incredible.

Gulping rapidly, I wrest my pervy eyes away from her and make a mental note to jerk off next time before even *thinking* about stepping foot in my bedroom. It appears I need to curb all temptation before indulging in future window time.

The drapes part, and she reappears, clad in a white sundress. Instead of a bra, she's wearing a bikini top, or at least I think that's what those thin straps belong to. The pink strings peek out of her bodice, climbing up her collarbone to wind around her neck. The dress itself is knee-length, with a skirt that flutters around as she gives a little twirl before texting me.

Cassie: *Now hear me out. Yes, I threw in a splash of pink with the bikini top. But that's because I think it's smart to color-coordinate with the cotton candy. We'll complement each other.*

Me: *I'll allow it.*

Cassie: *Do we like?*

She does another twirl and I pretend the glimpse of bare thigh doesn't do all sorts of things to my body.

I give her a thumbs-up, then type, *Go get 'em, tiger.*

* * *

Around midnight, I finally admit defeat and accept I can't sleep. It has nothing to do with the fact that I haven't heard a car engine next door or noticed her bedroom light flick on. She's still out with that Aaron dude, clearly. Good for her. She deserves to have fun. My inability to fall into slumber is not Cassie-related at all. Like, at all.

I make my way down to the dock and sit at the very end of it, dangling my bare feet over the edge. But let's say Cassie *is* the reason I'm still up. Obviously, this just means I'm a good friend. A friend who worries about the well-being of another friend. I mean, I know nothing about this Aaron kid. But I do know for a fact the carnival shuts down at eleven. So, really, she should've been home by now.

Unless she went back to his place.

My shoulders stiffen. His brother said they were staying in a rental on the north end, right on the water. The reminder makes me frown. I hope he doesn't convince her to take a late-night dip. The waters up there are choppier. It's where we usually go to surf. Swear to God, if fuckin' Aaron allows Cassie to get sucked into the sea by a freak midnight riptide . . .

I'm suddenly craving a cigarette. I only smoke if I'm drinking, and then maybe one or two max, but right now I could use some help easing the jittery sensations inside me. My smokes are in the house, though, so I debate going for a swim instead. I allow the toes of one foot to skim the water, finding it much warmer than expected. I'm about to strip off my shirt and dive in when my phone lights up.

Cassie: *You up?*

I laugh softly. Swim plan instantly abandoned, I reach for the phone.

Me: *Is this a booty call or a debriefing?*
Cassie: *Debriefing. I need my wingman ASAP.*
Me: *I'm on the dock.*
Cassie: *Be there in two.*

The heaviness in my chest lifts as if someone flicked a switch. I try not to question it too hard. It's crucial to this friendship that I don't.

The tall grass at the base of the slope rustles, and I turn to see Cassie emerge from the shadows. Her hair is no longer arranged in a side braid but falling around her shoulders. With her white dress, bare feet, and loose copper waves, she has an almost ethereal quality about her. Practically floating down the dock toward me.

She plops beside me, legs over the edge, and releases a moan of unhappiness. "Hi."

I grin. "That bad?"

"No. Not bad at all. We stayed out past midnight, so obviously there were lots of checks in the plus column." Yet she's visibly distressed.

"Okay, let's hear 'em. Give me the play by play."

"He's super funny. He's smart. He didn't monopolize the conversation. Asked me lots of questions, but it didn't feel like an interrogation. It was just, you know, a good conversation. Flowed easily."

"All pluses so far."

"He held my hand and didn't ask beforehand if he could. I figured you'd view the confident hand grab as a plus."

I snicker. "Oh, absolutely. What else?"

"He's scared of heights, but still rode the Ferris wheel after I said how much I love seeing the town from above. That was another plus."

"Agreed."

"The carnival grounds close at eleven, so we left and got slushies afterward. We sat in the parking lot and talked, and . . ." She pauses, and I notice a blush rising on her cheeks. "We were definitely feeling each other."

"This is all good so far," I point out, ignoring the weird clench in my chest. "How did he manage to fuck this up? What were the minuses?"

"Just one minus." She turns to me with a look of defeat. "The kissing. Oh my God, Tate."

"Aw, shit. Our boy Aaron can't bring it home? What was the issue? Saliva? Because that might not be his fault. My friend Chase dated a guy once who had something called hypersalivation and—"

"It wasn't the saliva," she interjects. "It was the tongue."

"Too much of it?"

"Too much is an understatement. And it was right from the get-go. I'm talking even *before* our mouths actually touched. He came at me tongue first, eyes closed. Want me to demonstrate?"

"No, I think I get—"

Cassie ignores my objection and demonstrates anyway. "It was like this." She squeezes her eyes shut, sticks her tongue straight out, and comes barreling toward my face.

It's so unsettling I instinctively rear back.

"Holy shit. He didn't."

"He did. It was terrible."

I try to control the laughter bubbling in my throat, but it's difficult. "Okay," I say carefully. "That sounds . . . unpleasant. But once the lips made contact, did it get better?"

"It did not," she groans. "It was just too much. He was trying so hard to be passionate, I guess, but it wasn't working in the slightest. When it finally ended I felt like I'd run a marathon. Or worse. Like . . . like I'd just changed a duvet cover."

"Did you ask him to slow down at any point?"

"No."

I roll my eyes. "Why the hell not?"

"I don't know." She offers a self-conscious shrug, her fingers toying with the hem of her dress. "I'm not that person."

"You're not the person who asks a dude not to shove his tongue halfway down your throat and pretend you're sword-fighting during a make-out session?"

"I'm not the person who tells someone they're a bad kisser," she corrects.

"Requesting to go slower isn't telling him he's a bad kisser," I argue. "You're just vocalizing your needs."

"Vocalizing my needs? What are you, a self-help guru?"

"Apparently you need one," I say in accusation, flashing a smile so she knows I'm half kidding.

"Why, because I'm too polite to tell a guy he's doing it all wrong?"

"Would you rather be polite, or would you rather enjoy a kiss? And anyway, you don't go about it that way, like *he's* doing something wrong. You make it about *you*. You pull away and say something like . . ." I ponder. "*I like it slow*. And make sure to sound all breathy, even apologetic, as if it's a *you* problem. Know what I mean?"

Wariness flickers through her expression.

"Or you could pull back and whisper something like, *I like being teased*. Then flutter your eyelashes and give him that hot-girl look and order him to tease you for a bit."

Now she looks fascinated. "Okay, you're not bad at this."

"I know," I say smugly.

"But it's easier said than done. It's easy to imagine myself saying and doing all those things *after* the fact. In the moment, though, I know I'll freeze. People are so vulnerable when they're kissing. It's like this super precarious state of being. When he's kissing me, his self-esteem hangs in the balance. One negative word from me, and it's an embarrassment he'll carry with him forever." She heaves a sigh. "Plus I don't like conflict."

"One, you're giving yourself way too much importance in this dude's life if you believe your criticism will haunt him forever. Either that, or *you* hang on to embarrassing shit a lot longer than most people, which is a whole other conversation altogether. And two, I'm pretty sure nearly everyone is conflict averse. Conflict fucking sucks." I cock my head. "Do you want to practice on me?"

"Practice what?" She wrinkles her forehead.

"Being assertive." I angle myself so I'm facing her. She's blushing again, a deep, noticeable red. "C'mon, I think this'll be good for you. I'll come at you tongue first and let's see how you handle it."

Cassie spits out an unequivocal, "No!"

"Nah, this is an excellent idea. It'll be an exercise in self-assertion and conflict mitigation." I roll my neck around my shoulders, stretching it out. When Cassie sighs at me, I lift a brow. "What? I need to be limber for this. Ready?"

"No."

"Great. Here I come!"

I shoot forward with my eyes closed and tongue spearing the air.

Cassie shrieks and pushes my chest, nearly knocking me off the dock. She doubles over in laughter, which makes me chuckle as I regain my balance. Her spirits are lifting, so that's good, at least.

"Oh my God. Are you sure you're twenty-three and not an overgrown child?"

"I've been informed by my mother that all men are overgrown children until the age of thirty." I snort. "Or in my dad's case, still a child in his midforties."

"So that's where you get it from."

"My dashing good looks? Yes."

"I meant your antics."

"Antics? I'm trying to help you here, ginger. You need to learn to speak up. Vocalize your needs. Don't tell me you're not sitting here wishing you handled tonight differently." I meet her suddenly troubled eyes. "You regret not saying something, don't you?"

"Yes," she confesses. "I wish I said something."

"Good. Then I'm serious—practice on me. Let's try again."

She eyes me suspiciously. "Are you going to launch yourself at me with your tongue again?"

"Nah." I wink. "But get ready for the worst kiss of your life."

CHAPTER 13

TATE

A few hours ago, I was ordering myself to sustain a platonic friendship at all costs. I guess that plan went by the wayside because, and I could be wrong, I don't think kissing falls under the *platonic* category.

In my defense, *this* can't be classified as kissing. At least not enjoyable or acceptable kissing. When our mouths collide, it's pure disaster. Nothing like the hot kiss we shared at the Hartley house, when the feel of Cassie's soft, warm lips got me so hard I had trouble walking afterward. This kiss is overbearing and sloppy. We're both having trouble breathing and not in a sexy way. My tongue is like an action star, kicking and punching around in her mouth as if we're dueling for dominance. It's actually exhausting.

Her outraged squeal vibrates against my lips. "Ahhh, stop! This is awful!" She shoves me.

I laugh, wiping the excess saliva off my chin. "Nope. We both know you'd never actually say that to him. Try again. Redirect the negative into a positive request. Make it a *you* issue, remember?"

She's instantly shamefaced. "Right. I forgot." Her lips press together in humor. "Sorry I pushed you."

"All good." I draw a deep breath to stock up on oxygen, then dive in for round two.

This time, when my tongue pillages its way through her parted lips, I feel a firm touch on the center of my chest. Then she awkwardly eases her mouth away and orders, "Slow!"

I narrow my eyes.

She softens her tone. "I mean, I like it slower." Then, as if struck by inspiration, a naughty smile tugs on her lips. "I love being teased. Slow kissing is *such* a turn-on for me . . ."

Oh man. Those words do something to *me*. My sweatpants suddenly feel too tight.

"Excellent ad-libbing," I tell her, my voice coming out a bit husky.

She brightens. "Thank you. What now?"

"Okay." I clear my throat. "I think we practice an even more proactive approach—this one deals with the aggressive entry. When he comes at you tongue first, this is what you do. You touch his cheek to stop him, stare at him, and give him a compliment."

"About what?"

"Anything. His eyes. His dimples. Anything on his face. Just slow it down before he even gets the chance to Hulk-smash his mouth against yours. Now *you're* in the position to get the kiss going, and that means you pick the pace."

"Genius."

"I know. Ready?"

Her throat dips as she swallows. When she licks her lips in preparation, I almost groan out loud. Lip-licking is my goddamn kryptonite. I can't see a woman do that, especially this one, and *not* want to rip her clothes off.

Platonic, I remind myself. *You're just helping her out.*

With a gulp of my own, I adopt my ridiculous pose—eyelids shut, mouth gaping open like a trout's—and move my head toward hers.

A pro at following orders, Cassie intercepts the trajectory of my tongue by touching my cheek. My pulse kicks up a notch from the feel of her soft fingertips stroking the stubble on my jaw.

Her eyes slowly meet mine. Those bottomless brown depths glimmer with desire. Our faces are inches apart, her sweet breath tickling my chin.

"You have the sexiest lips," she whispers, brushing the pad of her thumb over my bottom lip. "I'm obsessed with them."

Our gazes remain locked. This late at night, the breeze traveling along the water tends to be cooler, but I'm burning up. My dick is hard and my skin is on fire. Her touch feels like heaven along my flesh, and I instinctively sag into it, forgetting I'm supposed to be playacting. That I'm simply helping her shore up her boundaries so they're nice and firm the next time she sees that Aaron kid. The next time she makes out with someone else.

I abruptly straighten out. "That was smooth. Nice job."

Her answering smile is so relaxed and careless I have to wonder if I imagined what just happened. If I was the only one to feel the surge of raw need that traveled between us.

"When are you seeing him again?" I ask lightly.

"Saturday night. I would've invited him to be my date for that charity gala on Friday, but I'm already going with Joy and my grandmother. This year's charity is Habitat for Humanity, Grandma's pet cause, so she's giving me five grand to spend on the auctions. Can you believe that? *Five* grand."

"Oh shit," I say, feeling my face go pale. "I forgot that was this weekend. I'm in the auction."

She grins at me. "Of course you are."

"Not by choice," I growl. "It's a job requirement. My boss at the club forces all the sailing guys to volunteer. I fucking hate it."

"Uh-huh. I'm sure it's *such* a chore to stand on a stage while women literally throw money at your feet for a chance to date you."

An idea strikes. I look over hopefully. "Will you bid on me?"

"I'd rather not," she replies in amusement.

"Please? I can't go on a date with another cougar, Cass. I just can't."

She snickers. "How many years have you done it?"

"This will be my third. Last year I went on a sunset cruise with a fifty-something-year-old broad who offered me my own boat and a weekly allowance if I came over every Sunday when her husband was playing golf."

"You turned down a sugar mama? Oh, Tate."

I glower at her. "I'm not for sale."

"You're literally putting yourself up for sale in an auction!"

"And I'm *trying* to rig it by asking my friend to bid on me." I give her my best puppy-dog eyes. "Come on, you just said your grandmother is giving you money to bid."

"Yeah, and I wanted to bid on the Charleston Sanctuary package for me and Joy," Cassie whines. "It's literally the best spa in the country."

"What's more important? The spa or my dignity?"

"The spa."

I flip up my middle finger. "Asshole. Come on, do me a solid. I think last year I only went for a couple grand."

Her mouth falls open. "You're asking me to spend two thousand dollars on you? On *this*?" She vaguely waves a hand at my body.

"Like you don't want to be all up in this business."

"For two grand I don't."

"You think I could twist Lydia's arm into bidding on me?"

"Doubtful. She's too classy to participate in what's basically the equivalent of *Magic Mike* for rich people."

"Hey, is your dad going to be there too this weekend? Both my folks are coming."

Cassie shakes her head. "I don't think so. The country club is a Tanner family thing. The Souls are much more laid-back."

"He does seem like a super laid-back dude," I remark, remembering Clayton Soul's relaxed demeanor and quick laughter. "You two are close?"

"Sometimes."

I chuckle. "What does that mean?"

"I don't know. I just don't see or talk to him as often as I'd like." She gazes up at the dark sky, and her hair falls down her back in waves. "It sucks, because we were practically inseparable when I was a kid. I was much closer to him than my mother."

"How'd that happen anyway? Your parents, I mean. Your mom's a clone and your dad's a local—how'd they get together in the first place?" I lean back on my elbows and make myself comfortable. Despite the fact it's nearly 1 A.M., it doesn't seem like Cassie's in any hurry to head inside. Neither am I. The stars are out and the water's calm. And I like talking to her. A lot.

She brings her legs up and sits cross-legged, arranging her dress so it covers her thighs. "They met when Mom was a junior in college. Before my grandparents decided to live in the Bay year-round, they'd split their time between here and Boston, but summers were always spent in the Bay, no exceptions. Mom was visiting and they met at a party, I think. Somehow they fell in love, despite being so different in every conceivable way." She shrugs. "Opposites really do attract, I guess. And she had to have loved him, right? Because she came to live here full-time after college, which would've been a major sacrifice for her."

"You sound like you're trying to convince yourself of that."

"Maybe I am. I mean, I know what my dad saw in her. She's gorgeous, obviously. And she's very charming when she wants to be. Funny, sociable. When she puts on her act, she's the most lovable person you'll ever meet. She'll be coming to town mid-August, so I'm sure you'll experience the act for yourself."

I wrinkle my brow. "What makes you think it's an act?"

"Because I've seen the person behind the mask. She's manipulative. Entitled. Hypercritical. She gets a kick out of putting you down, then plays the victim when you call her out on it. And don't get me started on the total lack of empathy. There isn't an empathetic bone in her body. She's the most self-centered person I've ever known."

"Man, that's rough. Has she always been like that?"

"I think so. For as long as I can remember, anyway. And although my grandmother would never say a bad word about her own children, I can tell she's disappointed with Mom's behavior. Especially when it comes to all the passive-aggressive bullshit, the scathing criticism. She wasn't too awful to me when I was little, but she was constantly snapping at Dad. I remember thinking he had the patience of a saint. It wasn't until after the divorce, once she and I were alone all the time, that she turned most of her vitriol toward me. Suddenly she always had something to bitch about, some element of my appearance to disparage, some immoral behavior to call out." Cassie offers a weak laugh. "Lucky me."

I study her face, my heart squeezing at the thought of a young Cassie having to endure her mother's vile bullshit. But her expression remains detached, accepting even, as if any past—or present—trauma is no big deal.

"You always do that," I tell her.

"Do what?" Her teeth dig into her lower lip. Finally revealing a trace of emotion.

"Downplay all the shit that hurts you."

"Because I'm an optimist." She tucks a section of reddish hair behind her ear, her eyes shining in the moonlight. "No situation is entirely bad. There's always a silver lining. Always. You just have to look for it."

"Really? So there's a silver lining in having your mother treat you like crap?" I say dubiously. "Or your parents getting divorced?"

"If it weren't for the divorce, I wouldn't have my little sisters," Cassie points out. "And I'm quite happy that my sisters exist."

"You can be happy they exist and still wish the divorce hadn't happened."

"True. But honestly, it was probably for the best. Nothing Dad did could ever make her happy. He's definitely better off without her." Cassie pushes more hair out of her eyes. It's getting breezier out, causing those long, wavy strands to fly into her face. "Let me guess—your parents are happily married?"

"Yeah, it's disgusting."

We both laugh.

"They've always been great role models," I admit, albeit grudgingly. "That's why I hate disappointing them. I swear, I'm the only kid who would willingly ground himself or demand extra chores after getting in trouble. This one time in high school, I stayed out all night with the twins. My parents were up till dawn, wearing holes in the carpet from fear I was dead in an alley somewhere. The next morning, I walked in, hungover as fuck, sat on the sofa in front of them, and was like, *I think you should ground me for two weeks and put me on permanent dog-poop duty.*"

Cassie peals out a laugh. "You are such a loser."

"First of all—I got laid that night. Losers don't get laid. Second—don't tell me you wouldn't have done the exact same thing, Ms. I Avoid Conflict."

"Fair. But," she adds smugly, "I never got in trouble. Ever."

"I don't know if that's something to brag about."

She starts to answer, then breaks off in a wide yawn. "Oh

man. I'm tired." She blinks a few times. "That just hit me out of nowhere." She yawns again. "I think it's time for bed."

When she unfolds her legs and gets to her feet, I can't stop a pang of disappointment. I'm working two different jobs tomorrow and yet I want nothing more than to stay up all night talking.

As friends, of course.

But she's already pulling me to my feet. "Come on, walk me up the path so I don't trip on a rock or something and crack my head open."

I offer my arm, then yank it away before she can take it. Her jaw drops, and I cock a brow. "On one condition—you bid on me this weekend."

"Nope."

"You're really going to throw me to the wolves like that? The cougar wolves?"

"Oh my God, drama queen. All right," she relents. "How about this? I'll bid—only if I see the cougars making their move."

"Thank you. You're the best."

Cassie grabs my arm and links hers through it. "No promises," she warns.

CHAPTER 14

CASSIE

"That dress is so hot." Joy's approving gaze travels over my knee-length pale green minidress. "Honestly, I should become a stylist. I'm so good at this."

"I like how not once in that series of compliments did you mention me. The *dress* is nice and *you're* a great stylist."

"I assumed the Cassie part of the equation was a given. You always look hot." She links her arm through mine as we glide toward the next table.

We're part of the crowd by the far wall of the Manor's grand ballroom, browsing the tables that make up the silent auction, while canned piano music blares out of the PA system. Much to my chagrin, I haven't found the Charleston Sanctuary package yet. They fucking better not have decided to skip the event this year. I love that place, and they're always booked solid. It's impossible to get an appointment. One time I even demeaned myself by name-dropping my grandmother and still couldn't get a slot.

"Ooh, how about this?" Joy suggests, picking up the sheet of crisp ivory-colored cardstock. "Six golf lessons with . . . drum roll, please . . . *Lorenzo*!" She dons an Italian accent when saying his name.

Lorenzo has been working as a golf coach at the club for about a hundred years. If you told me he was a ghost trapped between worlds and forced to roam the Manor for all of eternity, I'd have no trouble believing it. There are honest-to-God pictures of my mother holding me as an infant at the club, with Lorenzo lurking in the background sporting the same long ponytail and leathery skin as he has now. The man doesn't age. He also has no concept of personal space, always leaning in way too close when he's talking to you. As teenagers, Joy and I used to hide whenever we saw him strolling our way.

I blanch at the listing. "I'd rather eat my own hair. No joke."

She howls before clapping a hand over her mouth to stifle the outburst, which has drawn the disapproving stares of the older country-club set milling around us. Damn, and we're not even drunk yet. These folks are going to despise us by the end of the night.

I approach the adjacent table, where my grandmother is bent over, using a black felt-tip pen to scribble an amount on a small white card. She's bidding on a jumbo gift basket donated by the Soapery, one of the local artisan shops in town.

"Oh my God. No. Mrs. Tanner." Joy peeks at Grandma's bid. "You just bid *two grand* on a basket of soap. Soap!" She shakes her head in disbelief.

"It's very good soap," Grandma says primly, then slides the card into the slot of the cardboard box on the table. "Have you found anything to bid on?" The question is directed at me.

"I haven't seen the spa package yet. That's the only thing I want." I set my jaw in determination. "And I'll murder anyone who outbids me. I swear, I fantasize about their hot stone massage on a daily basis."

"Don't blow all your cash on it," Joy reminds me, dark eyes twinkling impishly. "Gotta make sure you have enough left over to bid on your friend Tate in the bachelor auction."

Grandma looks amused. "You're bidding on Mr. Bartlett?"

"Maybe," I say grudgingly. "He asked me to rescue him if the cougar crowd gets overzealous."

"I like that boy." Grandma chuckles softly.

So do I.

It's becoming a real problem, in fact. Particularly after what happened between us the other night. Joy maintains it wasn't a big deal. Even Peyton sort of dismissed its importance when I told her about it. But they're both dead wrong.

When you return home after real-kissing one guy and proceed to pretend-kiss another one, that's a problem.

And when the guy you're pretend-kissing is the one you wish you were real-kissing, except you can't because he's not into you like that . . . this is also a problem.

Before I can dwell on my thorny predicament, my phone beeps with a text from, ironically, the person who *is* into me.

Aaron: *How's it going at the charity thing?*
Me: *My grandmother just bid 2K on soap.*
Aaron: *Bold move.*
Me: *Right?*
Aaron: *Are we still on for dinner tomorrow night?*
Me: *Yup. Looking forward to it.*

I tuck the phone back into my silver clutch while assuring myself I *am* looking forward to seeing Aaron again. And, hey, maybe in the days since the carnival he's been honing his kissing skills. Practicing on a pillow or something. A girl can hope, right? Because the memory of his forceful tongue repeatedly plunging into my mouth like it was mining for tonsil treasure almost makes me gag. It's a shame, because he's such a cool guy otherwise. He's been texting me every day since we met. Memes, random thoughts. He's hilarious.

But . . .

I don't know if Aaron is the one.

Don't get me wrong, I certainly haven't been saving my virginity for my one true love. I'm not sitting at home waiting for Prince Charming to sweep me off my feet. But at the very least, I'd like to be wildly attracted to the man. I want to be unable to contain myself when he's around. I want to want him so badly that I can't wait to rip his clothes off. I want *that* level of chemistry.

Still, one date isn't enough to assess the full scope of chemistry. At least that's what Peyton always insists. According to my best friend, a date introduces you to the potential, the spark. And if the spark is there, however small it may be, you need to give it a chance, kindle it to discover how hot the fire can burn. The spark was there with Aaron, I can't deny that, so I suppose it's time to see if it develops into an inferno.

"Here's the spa package!" I exclaim, spotting it at the next table.

I practically bulldoze my grandmother over to grab a bid card and a green golf pencil from the basket. I wish I could see what other people have already bid, but the format of this auction is asinine. It's a silent, *secret* auction. The bids go into the box, someone flips through them to find the highest number, and that's the winner.

"This isn't rocket science," Joy says, grinning at my indecision.

"The next available appointment at this spa is next July. July, Joy! They're booking a *year* in advance. This is my one shot. My one opportunity."

"You have issues."

While she taps her foot with impatience, I mentally calculate what I think the package is worth, then double it. Then I cross out that amount and triple it instead.

"Pray for me," I declare. I slip the card into the box.

"I need new friends," Joy tells Grandma.

"Laaaadies and gentleeeemen," a male voice booms from the stage at the front of the room. "If we could have your attention over here!"

The noisy ballroom quiets, but only slightly. Most of the formal-wear-clad crowd continues whatever they were doing and ignores our hosts. The gala has two emcees this year—a former running back for the Panthers whose name I didn't catch, and a news anchor from the local network whose name I also didn't catch. Joy and I have just been calling them Big and Blonde, because he's big and she's blonde.

"The silent auction is now closed," Big announces. "Our wonderful staff will start tallying the bids, and winners will be announced after the bachelor auction. Until then—eat, drink, and be merry!"

Blond teeters up beside him on dangerously high heels to shout into the microphone. "Let's get our gala on!" As her shrill voice reverberates through the cavernous ballroom, I don't miss the way Grandma winces.

"Are you all right?" I ask, touching her arm.

"A bit tired," she admits. "And, if I'm being frank, I don't think my eardrums will survive listening to that woman for another hour."

"Do you want to leave?"

After a beat, she nods. "I think so, yes. Are you all right taking a car service home?"

"Yeah, that's no problem. But are you sure? It's only eight o'clock."

Grandma gives that prim smile of hers, the one that always holds a trace of mischief. "I made my appearance, dear. Nobody will notice if I slip away."

"I'll walk you out, then." I glance at Joy. "Meet you back at the table."

"'Night, Mrs. Tanner," Joy says, leaning down to kiss my grandmother's cheek.

"Good night, dear."

After I've seen Grandma off, I return to the ballroom, weaving my way through tables. The centerpieces this year are massive—fancy crystal monstrosities with tall feathers and sprigs of baby's breath. I think they're supposed to look like swans. Or horses. It's really a toss-up. The riser extending out from the stage is meant to serve as the runway for the bachelor auction, and as I pass it I smother a laugh. Poor Tate. I haven't spotted him yet tonight, so I assume he's cowering in a corner somewhere.

Or he's chatting with Joy, which is what I find when I reach the table Grandma sponsored.

He's wearing a dark gray suit, the wool jacket stretching deliciously across his broad shoulders. He has a white dress shirt underneath, no tie, top two buttons undone. With his handsome face clean-shaven and his golden hair styled, he looks like one of those preppy boys he likes to call *clones*.

"Someone busted out the hair products," I tease.

"Damn right." Those blue eyes sweep over my dress. "That's a great color on you."

"Thanks," Joy says. "I picked it out."

I snort. "Yes. Joy deserves all credit. You ready for your big moment?" I ask Tate.

He nods briskly. "I've covered all my bases. Lined up a plan A *and* a plan B."

I narrow my eyes at him. "Which one am I?"

"A, definitely. I mean, no man wants to win a date with his mother."

That makes me laugh. "Your mom's here?"

"Her and Dad are sitting over there." He points to a table to the right of the stage. "She promised she'd save the day if you bailed on me. Hey, you know what, come meet them."

"What?" I shift in discomfort, the heels of my pointy nude pumps sinking into the burgundy carpet. "Ah, that's not necessary."

"No, come. They'd love to meet you. I was telling them about you earlier."

He was?

I notice Joy giving me a look that says *he's talking you up to his parents?*

When I respond with a panicky look that says *help,* she throws me into the deep end as usual. "I'll stay here," she chirps, snagging a flute of champagne from one of the waiters. She takes a sip, smiling impishly around the edge of her glass. "Go meet his parents, Cass."

Traitor.

"What, is this weird?" Tate asks as he loosely holds my arm to escort me through the crowd.

"No," I lie. "Why would it be weird?"

"Joy's acting like meeting my parents is a big deal or something." He offers a flippant shrug. "It's just my folks. They're nothing special."

He's wrong. The moment I meet the Bartletts, I become a bit starry-eyed. I'm not the only one either. The couple holds court in the middle of a large group, clearly the center of attention. Tate's dad, tall, blond, and gregarious, is regaling everyone with a tale that's making them yowl with laughter. A gray-haired man wipes tears of mirth from his eyes, declaring, "Jesus Christ, Gavin, that's the craziest thing I've ever heard."

When they notice Tate approaching, the Bartletts break away

from their friends, greeting us with broad smiles. Tate had described his parents as being *disgustingly in love,* and I pick up on it instantly. They emit a distinctive aura that surrounds them, and everyone around them, in a loving cocoon of tenderness.

And they're always touching each other in some way. Even while Tate's dad holds out a hand toward me, one arm remains wrapped around his wife's shoulder. "Gavin," he introduces himself. "Nice to meet you."

When Tate's mom shakes my hand, her other one remains nestled in the crook of Gavin's arm. "Gemma," she says. She's a petite, curvy woman with dirty-blond hair and warm brown eyes, appearing much younger than her age. A white sheath dress fits her body like a glove.

"I'm Cassie." I return the handshake before glancing over at Tate. "Aw, man. They even have the same initials. Gavin and Gemma. I love it." I grin in delight. "You guys totally missed an opportunity to go all Kardashian and give Tate a G name."

"We were definitely considering Gate," Gavin replies earnestly, "but Tate had a better ring to it."

I snort out a laugh. "Hear that, Gate? You dodged a bullet."

"Tate says you're his auction backup?" Gemma prompts, smiling at me.

"I don't know . . . I *thought* I was. Now it sounds like it's going to be a bidding war between you and I . . . ." I tip my chin in mock challenge.

Gemma feigns a glare. "Oh, it's on."

"Ladies, please. Don't fight over me." Tate grimaces. "Like, seriously, don't. I can't have my mother involved in any competition where I'm the prize."

Gavin booms with laughter. "Good point, kid." He claps Tate on the shoulder before focusing his attention on me. "Cassie, how are you enjoying the summer?"

"It's been nice. I've just been taking it easy."

"Tate says you grew up in the Bay?"

"I did. My dad and stepmom still live here, with my two half sisters, but I'm in Boston now. I go to college there."

"Did you tell her my news?" Gavin asks his son.

Tate is flabbergasted. "Of course not. Why would I do that?"

"Maybe because it's the most exciting thing that's ever happened to anybody?" his father shoots back.

Tate wasn't kidding about his dad being an overgrown child. And Tate is the spitting image of his father. The two of them are so similar in both looks and personality that I have to smile watching them interact.

"What's the news?" I ask curiously.

Gavin's entire face lights up, pride in his eyes. "Guess who's being featured in the newspaper."

Tate glances at me. "The *Avalon Bee* is doing a write-up on Dad," he explains. His voice lowers to a stage whisper. "He thinks this makes him special, but they run a profile on a local businessman every month. He's literally one of dozens."

"Front page?" challenges Gavin.

"Well, no," Tate relents. "But the only reason you're being featured on the front page is because you gave Harvey a deal on that speedboat. You basically bribed the guy."

"Me? You think *I'm* capable of bribing a journalist?"

"Yes," Tate and Gemma answer in unison.

I laugh, then dutifully *ooh* and *aah* as Gavin offers more details about the article. We chat for a few more minutes, until Big and Blonde return to the stage and ask everyone to take their seats. The bachelor auction is about to commence.

"Kill me now," Tate moans.

"You're going to do great," his mother assures him. "Everyone will bid on you, sweetie."

"Mom, no. You don't understand the assignment. We *don't* want everyone to bid on me. Just Cassie."

Gavin waggles his eyebrows at me. "Look at you, young lady. You seem to have captivated our son."

"Oh, we're just friends," I'm quick to protest.

"I'm just teasing," he says with a boisterous laugh.

I laugh awkwardly in response. "Oh. Anyway, it was nice meeting you guys. I should go join my friend, though."

"Wonderful to meet you, Cassie," Gemma says warmly.

"They're so normal," I hiss at Tate as he escorts me back to my table.

"I know. I told you."

Ten minutes later, the bachelor auction is in full swing. From the shiny podium at the head of the stage, Big clutches a stack of cue cards and introduces the first bachelor.

"Everyone, let's give a warm welcome to Morty!"

A tuxedo-clad man with glasses and a red bow tie takes the stage. He's pushing sixty, with an infectious smile he flashes to the entire room. He waves to the crowd and starts strutting.

"Oh, he's adorable," Joy exclaims.

"Morty is sixty-two years young, an accountant with a head for numbers and a love of pickles. And not just *eating* pickles! Creating them! In his spare time, Morty pickles anything he can get his hands on. Beets, peppers, tomatoes, peaches, squash, rhubarb—Farrah, did you know you can pickle rhubarb? I didn't!"

Right. Blonde's name is Farrah.

"Sounds yummy!" she chirps into her microphone.

"So how about it, folks? Who fancies a date with Morty? Bid high and maybe he'll pickle something for you! I'm told his entire garage features rows and rows of jars, all full of pickled delights . . ."

"I changed my mind," Joy whispers. "I think he might be a serial killer."

"The jars, right?"

"Oh yeah."

"We'll start the bidding at fifty dollars."

Three hands shoot up. "Fifty!"

"A hundred."

"A hundred and fifty!"

Before we know it, Morty the Pickler goes for six hundred dollars.

"That's about five hundred and fifty more dollars than I thought he'd go for," Joy whispers to me, and we nearly keel over in laughter. The champagne at this event has been free-flowing, and although I'm only on my first glass, I'm already feeling a buzz.

The next bachelor is a silver fox who causes a murmur to ripple through the crowd when he emerges from behind the black velvet curtains.

"Hot damn. Hello, Daddy," Joy coos.

"Oh gross. Don't say that."

"Come on, don't tell me you wouldn't hit that."

I study him. He's wearing a white linen shirt, fine-pressed gray trousers, and deck shoes. Sporting a deep summer tan. He's tall, handsome, and when it's revealed that he runs a hedge fund, the ladies are clamoring to bid.

Farrah the Blonde barely gets out his job title before a woman shouts, "Five hundred!"

"Six!"

"Seven!"

"Eight fifty!"

Joy looks over. "Can I borrow some of Grandma's money?"

I elbow her. "Absolutely not. You literally just got back together with Isaiah."

"Oh right. Fuck. I forgot."

After Silver Fox is taken for fifteen hundred smackeroos, several more bachelors grace the stage. The owner of the Good Boy brewery. A dog trainer. Two waiters from the club restaurant, then one of the golf instructors. Luckily, not Lorenzo.

When Tate's friend Danny is up, the winning bid for the attractive ginger is a staggering $2,300. Doesn't bode well for Tate if that's the going price for hot sailing instructors.

Danny's smile seems forced as he walks off the stage to greet his date. The pair isn't required to go out tonight, but it's customary to say hello to the person who "wins" you. Instantly, the woman's fingers curl around Danny's biceps and she peers up at him eagerly. Now I see why Tate was so worried. There are a lot of hungry women in this ballroom tonight.

"Our next bachelor is Tate!" Farrah announces.

"Here we go," I say.

Tate appears on the stage, hands loosely resting on his belt loops. His long stride eats up the runway, fair hair gleaming in the spotlight aimed at him.

"Tate is an avid sailor, splitting his workdays between the yacht club and Bartlett Marine, our number-one boat retailer in Avalon Bay."

"Yeahhhhh!" cheers a loud voice I recognize as Gavin Bartlett's.

"He loves being out on the water, any way he can. When he's not on a boat, you'll find him on a surfboard."

Tate reaches the end of the runway and stops to strike a cheesy pose. He seeks out my face in the crowd and winks before turning back.

"This golden boy is a romantic at heart. He enjoys long walks on the beach and stargazing with that special someone."

It's physically impossible for my eyes to roll any harder. I wonder if he wrote this himself.

Farrah sighs dreamily as Tate returns to stand beside her at the podium. "Oh, honey bear, I'll stargaze with you any day."

"Farrah," Big hisses into his mic to snap her out of it.

She blinks. "Right. We'll start the bidding at—"

"Five hundred," someone shouts instantly.

Joy snatches the flute out of my hand before I can drink. "Focus. It's your time to shine."

I swipe the flute back. "I'm waiting it out. Can't seem too eager." I grin over a gulp of champagne. "Plus, I want to make him sweat."

"Evil bitch."

"Six hundred!"

"Eight!"

"Nine fifty!"

From the stage, Tate's eyes implore me. His outward smile does nothing to conceal his agony. I tip my glass at him and take another dainty sip.

"One thousand dollars!"

"Eleven hundred!"

"Cassie," Joy warns.

"I've got a strategy," I insist. "Let them tire themselves out. That's what I do with my sisters when they're on a sugar high."

"Twelve hundred!" bids a nasally voice.

"Fifteen hundred." This voice is throaty.

Uh-oh. I turn to scope out the competition and raise an eyebrow. All right. Interesting. The current high bidder is a gorgeous brunette who doesn't seem as thirsty as the others. She's clearly in her late forties, though. So now I'm torn. Tate ordered me to not let any MILFs win. But maybe this is the kind of MILF he would like? She's a stunner and isn't giving off any predatory vibes.

"Going once—"

But I did make him a promise.

"Going twice—"

"Cassie," Joy hisses.

Shit.

Caught off guard, I end up blurting the first number that pops into my head because I wasn't paying attention.

"Three thousand!"

My friend gapes at me. "Dude. It was at fifteen. You just doubled it."

"Three thousand," Big crows. "Highest bid of the night! Someone sure wants to go stargazing!"

Farrah takes over. "Going once . . . going twice . . ."

The hot brunette on the other side of the room remains silent.

"Sold for three thousand dollars to the redhead in the green dress!"

On the stage, Tate beams at me.

I smother a sigh. Whatever. At least it's for a good cause.

CHAPTER 15

CASSIE

"Does this mean I get to order you around now?" I ask later. "Like for the rest of the summer?"

Tate snorts at the question. We walk down to the dock of the Jackson house, where the water laps quietly against the wooden pylons and the drone of insects buzzes in the air. It's eleven thirty and the night is calm and still. I'm in my minidress but abandoned the heels up on the lawn. He's taken off his suit jacket and rolled up his shirt sleeves.

"For the rest of the summer? Dream on."

"I just dropped three grand on you. Show me some respect, you ungrateful brat."

"Three grand of your grandmother's money."

"Which I stand to inherit one day. Well, along with my cousins, but still," I grumble under my breath. "So that's it? I don't get anything out of this deal? At the very least you should be my pool boy on the weekends or something. You know, wear a tiny Speedo and serve me drinks poolside."

"You donated money to a good cause. Isn't that enough?"

"No!"

He rolls his eyes. "Fine. I'll tell you what. I'll let you order me around for the rest of tonight."

"But I'll be going to bed in, like, an hour," I complain.

"Then you have one hour to call the shots."

I plant my hands on my hips. "Fine. Go get us some drinks." *Ugh.* Except, ordering someone around isn't in my nature, so I quickly add, "Please?"

He throws his head back and laughs. "You're terrible at this. But you're in luck—I'm already on top of the drink situation. Got a surprise for you."

That piques my interest.

"Get comfortable. I'll be right back."

I sink onto one of the loungers facing the water, twisting around to adjust the backrest. The weather is perfect tonight. Feels like room temperature outside, and I stretch my legs out in front of me and close my eyes, just savoring the night. My eyelids pop open at the sound of Tate's footsteps on the wood slats of the dock. He reappears holding two bottles of champagne.

I gasp. I recognize the gold label. These were the expensive bottles of bubbly they were serving at the Manor tonight.

"Did you steal those from the club?" I demand.

"Oh, I did."

"Oh God, you're a thief."

"Trust me, they owe me for all those safety classes they keep roping me in to doing without paying me overtime."

"I can't drink stolen contraband."

"You can and you will."

He sets the bottles on the small table between our loungers, then pulls two skinny glasses from his pocket, which he must have grabbed from Gil Jackson's kitchen. Picking up a bottle, he peels off the gold foil packaging around the lip.

Just as he's about to pop the cork, I balk, screeching loudly. "Don't aim it at the water!"

"I could aim it at your face," he offers.

I give him the finger. "Point it at the grass over there. But not the water. What if the cork lands in the bay and a fish eats it and chokes to death? Or a turtle? Oh my God, what if there's a Keanu Reeves turtle living under your dock and he thinks we're feeding him and then he *dies*—"

"The babbling never ends with you, does it, ginger?"

"Don't call me ginger, Gate."

He jabs the air with his finger. "No. Absolutely not. That is *not* becoming a thing."

"What's the matter, Gate?" I ask sweetly. "Did someone give you a nickname you don't enjoy?"

"Call me that again and I'll murder a turtle right in front of you."

"You wouldn't dare." I grin at him. "Oh! Speaking of turtles. My dad messaged earlier, and guess what—my stepmother agreed to the turtle. They're planning to give it to the girls after their birthday party in a couple weeks. The twins are going to die of excitement."

"Isn't your birthday coming up soon too?"

He remembered that?

My heart skips a beat, but I pretend to be unaffected. "Also in a couple weeks," I confirm. "My sisters and I share a birthday."

"Damn. Let me guess—somehow you've managed to find a silver lining for that too?"

"Yup." I nod at his hands. "You gonna open that bottle, Gate?"

"*Gate* is not becoming a thing," he growls, before turning in a safe direction to pop the cork. A moment later, he pours the bubbly liquid into our flutes, hands me one, and settles in the chair beside me.

As we sip our champagne, I try to ignore the pounding of my heart. The dampness of my palms. This feels like a date, even though I know it's not.

To hammer it home to my silly, smitten brain that such thoughts are counterintuitive, I force myself to say, "I'm going out with Aaron again tomorrow."

"Ah, right." Tate chuckles quietly. "Tongue battles part two."

"God, I hope not."

"We practiced for this. If it happens again, you're saying something," he warns.

"I will," I promise.

"And let's just hope kissing isn't the only activity he's bad at."

I straighten up in alarm. "Oh no. Oh *no*. I was planning to let him go to second base. Nobody can be bad at second base, can they?"

Tate drinks some more champagne, mulling it over. "He could be an aggressive tit squeezer."

I blanch. "If he is, I'll have no choice but to say something, because that'll earn him an involuntary scream of pain. The girls are sensitive."

Tate's eyes briefly flick my way. "Are they?" he drawls.

"Yes. Very." My throat is suddenly dry.

His must be too, because he chugs the rest of his glass and then pours himself another one.

"Easy, partner," I caution.

"Don't worry. Look how tiny these glasses are. It'll take a lot of refills to get me even close to drunk."

He has a point. So I hold out my own tiny glass, and he tops it off with that playful smile I'm beginning to crave on a daily basis. While we lie there on the dock, my gaze drifts up to the sky, sweeping over the twinkling carpet of lights.

"It's incredible how clear the sky is out here," I remark. "In Boston, the sky is different. All the pollution in the air, I guess. You hardly ever see any stars."

"I love it. Especially when you're on the open ocean. No land anywhere around you, this huge sky above you. That could freak anyone out, looking around and seeing nothing but water. But the stars, right? They're always there. They're fixed. You can't get lost when you can see the stars. Can't lose yourself."

"Holy shit," I accuse. "You're actually into stargazing? I assumed that bio they read at the auction was bogus." I snicker. *"He's a romantic at heart and enjoys long walks on the beach."*

"Nah, that part was BS. Whoever wrote the intro decided to improvise." He shrugs. "I listed four interests on the questionnaire they emailed, and all of them started with an S. Maybe they didn't like that."

"Four S's . . ." I start to list them. "Sailing. Surfing. Stargazing. Wait—what was the fourth?"

"They didn't read it."

I eye him curiously. "Why? What was it?"

"Sex." He winks.

My face almost bursts into flames, which isn't a favorable thing because I was already burning up from the alcohol. I don't even want to know what color my cheeks are right now.

Between the two of us, we've officially polished off an entire bottle of champagne. He's ingested more, but my tolerance is shit and the champagne loosens my tongue.

"Yeah . . . I don't have much experience with that," I confess.

Tate is already removing the foil from the second bottle. He stops for a second and meets my eyes. "You're a virgin."

"Man, you drop it like a statement of fact," I say dryly. "Not even a question, huh? What, is it written on my forehead or something?"

"Nah. Just an educated guess."

I stick out my glass for another top-up. "Well, the answer to the non-question is yes, I'm a virgin. I've done other things, though."

"Is that right?" Eyes dancing, he cocks his head at me.

"Don't you dare tell me to spill the tea."

"C'mon, let's hear it, ginger. Whatcha done?" When I remain quiet, he chugs nearly half his fresh glass. "All right, then. I'm going to start guessing. Okay. So. I know you've made out."

I roll my eyes. "Yes."

"Handjobs," he guesses.

"Yes."

"Blowjobs?"

"Yes." I turn toward him. "And I even swallowed."

Tate, who was mid-sip, spit outs his drink at my proud response. Laughing, he pours himself more champagne. "You wild thing," he says in amusement.

"Anyway. That's it. Sexy times by Cassie Soul. HJs and BJs. The end."

"Nuh-uh," Tate argues. "That's what *he* got out of it. What about you? Did he go down on you?"

"This is not proper friend talk."

"Sure it is. I talk about sex with my friends all the time."

"Your *girl* friends?"

"Sure. You should hear some of Steph's stories. And she's bi, so it's, like, twice the dirty. Sometimes she talks about pussy, other times it's dick. Exciting times."

I laugh. "Sounds like it."

He eyes me over the rim of his glass. "You ever had an orgasm?"

Oh my God.

"Yes," I grumble. "Both solo and with a partner, before you ask."

"I don't think I've ever seen anyone's cheeks turn that shade of red before."

"I told you, this isn't appropriate subject matter."

"Why, is it turning you on?"

Yes!

"No," I lie.

He just grins. "So why haven't you had sex? Waiting for Mr. Right?"

"No." I sigh. "I'd settle for someone I'm madly attracted to, but I rarely come across that. I swear, my friends walk out their front doors and, bam, they're hooking up with someone they can't keep their hands off of. Meanwhile, I'm a total disaster when it comes to meeting men. I babble—have you noticed I babble? And if I do manage to overcome my nerves and actually interact with someone I'm attracted to, they end up not being attracted to me. And then the ones I *don't* want are all over me."

"That's how it usually goes."

"I was dating someone last year," I admit. "Lasted about six months, and there was chemistry, for sure. But something just didn't fully click. Didn't feel right. I wasn't entirely comfortable with him, I guess. And I couldn't pull the trigger."

"If you couldn't pull the trigger with a guy you were dating for six months, how do you expect to do it in one summer? July's almost over," Tate reminds me. "Doesn't leave you with much time to execute your fling plan."

"I mean, in my defense, I tried pulling the trigger three weeks ago." A case of the giggles suddenly hits me. "You realize you were literally the first guy I spoke to this summer? What are the odds? I *never* meet guys I'm attracted to, and I meet one the first night I go out." I double over laughing. "And you friend-zoned me."

"Doing okay over there, Soul?"

"I'm great," I croak between wheezy laughs. "This is hilarious. I've been in town almost a month and look what I've accomplished. First I go on a date with a dude who learned to kiss in a barnyard. And now I'm lying here stargazing with a hot guy and neither of us is naked because he's not into it."

"I never said I wasn't into it," he protests.

"Let's not rehash this," I say, reaching over to pat his knee. "Don't worry, I'm not mad or anything. Just stating how absurd this whole situation is."

Clearly flustered, Tate goes to pour another glass. Only a few drops trickle out of the bottle.

"Shit." He sounds amazed. "We just killed two bottles of champagne, Cassie. In an hour. We're fucking barbarians."

"I think that's our cue to say good night, then." My knees are wobbly as I rise from the chair. I scoop up the empty bottles. "Come on, Gate. Walk me home so I don't trip in the dark and break my neck."

"Gate ain't happening, ginger."

"Oh, it *so* is."

Tate rests his palm on my lower back to guide me, keeping me steady as we walk. I'm certain I feel his fingertips move in a light caress. But it's probably an accident, a result of the fact that we're stumbling up the path, both a little drunk. Still, there's something very intimate about the feel of his hand at my back.

I want it on other parts on me.

He wasn't wrong. I *am* turned on. Painfully so. I'm practically squeezing my thighs together, desperate to go inside, as we stop and say goodbye on the stretch of manicured grass between our two houses. I want nothing more than to lock myself in my room, slide my fingers in my panties, and bring myself to orgasm thinking about him.

Inside, I make sure all the lights are off because Grandma is forgetful sometimes. Then I enable the alarm and sprint upstairs as quietly as I can. The throbbing between my legs has become unbearable. I'm already unzipping my dress while I hurry down the hall. I enter my room and throw my phone on the bed, hands tugging my bodice down. I let my dress drop to the floor about half a second before remembering I haven't shut the curtains yet.

Tate is at his window.

My heart jumps to my throat. I'm wearing nothing but skimpy panties and a strapless bra. And he notices. Of course he notices. His eyes rake over my body, admiring, lingering, then moving up to my face. I expect him to reach for his phone and text a smart-ass remark.

Instead, he starts unbuttoning his shirt.

My breath hitches.

It's impossible to look away. I've seen his bare chest before, but the act of undressing . . . it's almost more intimate than nudity itself. I can scarcely breathe. Slowly, he parts the front of the white dress shirt and eases it off his shoulders. His gaze never leaves mine as he tosses the shirt away.

I step toward the window, but I don't draw the curtains. Not even a gun to my head could compel me to close these curtains right now. I swallow, trying to bring moisture to my throat. It remains bone-dry.

Tate unzips his pants.

I moan out loud, and even though he's twenty feet away, I swear I see the corners of his mouth quirk up.

He pushes his gray trousers down his legs. Kicks them away. My gaze involuntarily lowers to his groin. There's no mistaking the long ridge of arousal straining against his white boxer briefs. The material is stretched taut over his erection, leaving very little to the imagination. I'm mesmerized.

This is dangerous territory. We're on the edge of a cliff here. He just stripped down to his underwear and now it's my move. I can shut the drapes and pretend this never happened.

Or . . .

I hear a buzzing from the bed. I look over, expecting an in-coming text. But it's a call. Gulping, I grab the phone with a shaky hand. I swipe to answer it.

"I'm not *not* into it." His raspy voice tickles my ear.

"W-what?" My mouth is so dry I can barely get that one word out.

"You said I friend-zoned you because I'm not into you. That's not true." He huffs out a breath. "I know it sounded like a bunch of excuses, but I meant it when I said it's easier to keep things platonic. But that's not to say I wasn't attracted to you. I was. I still am."

"Really?"

"Yeah." There's a beat. "You have no idea what you do to me."

"Show me."

The request slips out before I can stop it.

Forget the cliff. It's long gone. I've sailed over the edge and am basically free falling. My heart beats so hard and so fast that my ribs are sore. Every muscle in my body is tense, knees quaking as I move closer to the window.

Tate's got the phone to his ear. He's watching me. But he still hasn't responded.

And then his low voice slides into my ear.

"Are you calling the shots?"

This time there's no mistaking the naughty curve of his lips. And I realize this is the out we both require. A way to distance ourselves from the mistake we're probably about to make. He said I could order him around just for tonight. So why not. Let's treat it like a game. A fun little game without any consequences.

"Yeah." My voice is soft. "I'm calling the shots." I take a breath. "Show me how much you want me."

As I watch, he taps his phone and then sets it on the window ledge. He's put me on speaker. Three seconds later, he's naked. Naked and gorgeous and gloriously turned on. Long and hard, and bigger than I expected.

My mouth turns to sawdust again, and I gulp rapidly. Tate drifts a hand down his bare chest. Slow, leisurely. He wraps it around the thick shaft and gives a slow stroke. I bite back another moan.

"I'm drunk," I tell him.

"Me too."

I can't take my eyes off his hand. Those long fingers curled around his erection. "We're friends."

"We are," he agrees.

"Friends shouldn't do this."

"Probably not." He pauses. "See this?" Another long, deliberate stroke. "This is how hard you make me. Lately I've started jerking off before I know I'm going to see you, just to curb the temptation."

The filthy picture he paints makes my nipples tingle. "Are you serious?"

"Mmm-hmm. And I'm going to get myself off the moment you close those curtains."

My hand trembles so wildly I nearly drop the phone. "Who says I'm going to close them?"

From across the way, I glimpse the faint movement of his tongue, swiping across his bottom lip to moisten the corner of his mouth.

"You have no idea how good you look right now," he says roughly.

Clutching the phone to my ear, I bring my other hand behind my back, searching for the clasp of my bra. It's an easy one to undo single-handed. I flick it open and the bra flutters to the floor.

The moment my breasts are exposed, Tate makes a tortured sound. Husky and deep.

"How about now? How do I look?"

Oh my God, who is this woman? What are these words leaving my mouth? Whose throaty voice is that? I'm on display for him, and yet I'm not at all self-conscious.

"You look goddamn edible."

A smile flits over my lips, but dips into a slight frown when I realize his hand has gone still. "You're not touching yourself anymore."

"I'm waiting for your orders," is the gravelly response. "Tell me what you want."

I realize then, despite the bravado I just exhibited, I'm completely out of my depth here. I don't know how to direct an encounter like this. I don't know what to ask for. How to ask it. All I know is that my clit is throbbing and my nipples have never been harder.

"I want you to help me," I order. "I want you to take control and help me . . ." I trail off.

A strangled groan fills my ear. "Help you what? Help you come?"

"Yes."

"All right. Then I want you to slide your hand inside those panties for me. I want you to rub that hot pussy until you're coming for me. Can you do that for me?"

A wave of lust nearly knocks me off my feet. Sweet Lord.

"I don't know if I can," I confess. "Standing up, I mean." I'm certain my face is redder than it's ever been.

"Move closer." His voice is hypnotic. It's a lure and I'm drawn in like a fish, gliding beneath the surface toward it.

"Put me on speaker," he says when I'm a foot from the window. "Leave your phone on the windowsill."

My pulse is thudding, a rapid, rhythmic beat thrumming in my blood. He's touching himself again. A lazy stroke here and there. No rush at all. I admire the defined ridges of his abdomen, the sexy V of his oblique muscles. He's incredible. I wish he were here in my bedroom with me, that his warm, tanned flesh were pressed up against me.

I put him on speakerphone, grateful for the fact that my grandmother isn't a light sleeper.

"Good girl," he encourages when I set the phone down. "Now take your left hand and hold onto the ledge. Hold yourself steady."

I follow his instructions.

"I want to see your other hand inside your panties."

I slip the fingers of my right hand under my waistband, and the moment they collide with my clit, I almost keel over. "Fuck," I choke out, grateful to be holding on to something.

He chuckles. "Feel good?"

"Uh-huh."

We continue to watch each other. He's stroking a little faster now. I rub a little faster.

His gaze is fixed on me. I don't know if he's focused on my breasts or the motions of my hand, but either way his breathing is quickening. I can hear it over the speakerphone.

I'm starting to make breathy sounds too. I grind the heel of my palm over my core, rocking against it. Pinpricks of pleasure dance along my skin. My nipples are tight. Breasts tender.

I exhale slowly. "I wish you were here with me."

"Me too."

And yet neither of us take that thought to its logical conclusion. I don't ask him to come over. He doesn't offer. Instead, we continue to pleasure ourselves. Our eyes remain locked. My entire body is a live wire, desperately waiting for a spark to set it off.

"Do you wish my dick was inside you right now?"

A soft moan slips out. "I don't know," I answer truthfully. "I've never had a dick inside me before."

That summons a low groan from him. "Christ. Why is that the hottest thing I've ever heard?"

When I see his fist tighten around his erection, I rock faster against my hand. The tension is agonizing. I apply more pressure on the swollen nub that's hurting for release, and a shudder runs through me.

"I'm close." I barely hear my own voice over the persistent hammering of my heart.

"Yeah? Let me see it."

I bite my lip. My body feels heavy and weak, as if my limbs are about to give out on me. I grip the ledge, digging my fingernails into the white painted wood. I sag forward and lean my forehead against the window. My erratic breaths fog up the glass. A whimper escapes my lips as the pleasure mounts, gathering in my core. God. This is the most erotic experience of my life.

"Cass. *Yes*. You're gonna make me come."

Those husky words provide the spark. My body detonates. The orgasm surfaces in a flash of light, a surge of heat. A rush of bliss that sweeps me away, coursing through me in sweet, pulsing waves. When Tate grunts, my eyelids flutter open. I watch him climax, listening to the quiet noises he makes while he loses himself to release. Finally, his hand slows. His chest rises and falls with each shallow breath he sucks in.

"Holy hell," he curses, biting his lip as he meets my eyes.

Holy hell, indeed.

CHAPTER 16

CASSIE

The need to belong is deeply ingrained in us. I think it's because there's no worse feeling in the world than being on the outside looking in. Watching a group of friends laughing together in school and wishing you were in on the joke. Seeing your coworkers gathered around at the water cooler and longing to be part of the conversation. Or, in my case, desperately wanting to belong in my own family. From the moment Dad married Nia, I felt pushed aside. And then, when the twins were born two years later, I was more than pushed aside—I was pushed *out*. At least that's what it feels like. Nia never warmed up to me, and I'm constantly walking on eggshells with Dad, which in turn makes me all the more desperate for their approval.

That's probably why, when Dad calls thirty minutes before I'm supposed to meet Aaron for dinner and asks if I can babysit, I answer yes without hesitation.

"I thought Nia's friend's daughter was the best babysitter on the block," I joke, unable to stop from dropping a passive-aggressive jab under the guise of teasing. On past visits I offered to babysit numerous times so Dad and Nia could go on their monthly date nights, but they've always dismissed the offer, opting instead for some teenager on their street.

Dad chuckles. "Kendra's great. But she's no match for their big sister. Anyway, she sprained her ankle this afternoon, so she had to cancel. We hate to bug you on Saturday night, though. You didn't already have plans?"

"Well, I did. But I'm fine rescheduling. Unless . . . any chance I can invite a friend over? We had plans for dinner and a movie. Maybe I can talk him into coming by and watching Disney movies instead."

"Is this the friend from the fish store?"

"No, somebody else."

"Ms. Popularity over here! Sure, that won't be a problem. Go ahead and invite your friend. And thanks, Cass. I owe you one. We really didn't want to cancel date night—there's a CCR tribute band playing in the park tonight. I'm stoked."

"No worries. I've hardly seen the girls this month, so it'll be nice to spend some time with them."

After we hang up, I text Aaron.

Me: *I am SO sorry to do this, but there's been a last-minute change of plans. My dad's in a bind and needs me to babysit my sisters. Any chance you want to come by and keep me company? Their bedtime is nine, so we'll still have alone time. AND . . . there's a Disney movie in it for you . . .*

Aaron: *Make it Frozen 2 and you've got yourself a deal.*

Me: *I'm afraid you'll have to negotiate with two six-year-old girls on that. They run the show.*

Aaron: *Challenge accepted.*

Me: *I'll text you the address.*

An hour later, Nia opens the front door to let me into my childhood home, her reluctant expression telling me how little she's enjoying this change of plans.

"Thank you for babysitting, Cassandra." Her smile is a bit stiff. "I'm sure you have better things to do on a Saturday night."

"It's fine. I've barely seen the girls this summer."

It's not meant as an accusation, but I see a flicker of guilt in her eyes.

Before she can say anything, I change the subject. "Anything I need to know for tonight? Any new allergies since the last time I was here? Or still just coconut for Roxy?"

"Just the coconut." Nia leads me into the kitchen. "They already had their dinner, and they just finished their bath. Clayton is dressing them." When the faint sound of girlish shrieks rings out from upstairs, she gazes at the ceiling with amusement. "Or at least he should be. Your father always turns the simplest task into a game."

I grin. "He's always been like that."

She stops at the counter. "We went grocery shopping today, so there are plenty of snacks and drinks. But don't let them drink any soda. Not even a drop."

"I won't," I promise.

"Let me go upstairs and speed them up."

As Nia ducks out of the kitchen, I take off my jean jacket and drape it over the back of a breakfast stool. Setting my purse on the counter, I reach inside it for my phone and find a message from Tate.

Tate: *I've prayed to the kissing gods on your behalf. Good fortune be with you.*

I've been waiting for him to text all day. I hadn't wanted to do it first, and the longer today dragged on without a word from him, the more I worried just how badly last night had screwed things up between us. I'd passed out like a light after our mutual pleasure session, then woke up this morning wondering what the hell I'd done. A line had undeniably been crossed, but I didn't know how to address it. I figured when he got in touch and brought it up, I could blame it on all the champagne.

But this? This is the message I get?

We're just going to pretend it never happened? That I don't know what his face looks like when he ejaculates?

A warm flush spreads across my skin at the filthy memory. I'm never going to be able to erase that image from my mind. His teeth biting into his lip. Hand clenched around his cock. The husky noise he made. Watching Tate Bartlett shudder in orgasm was the hottest thing I've ever witnessed in my life.

But okay. I guess we're not going to talk about it.

Me: *LOL thanks. Might be hard to get some kissing in, though. I got roped into babysitting, so Aaron's going to keep me company.*
Tate: *Lame.*
Me: *I know. Maybe we'll go out afterward if the folks don't get back too late.*
Tate: *All right. Have fun.*

Sighing, I lay the phone down. Hell, maybe it's better we don't talk about it. Just forget it ever happened.

Only, as with most impossible tasks, forgetting last night is . . . well . . . impossible.

"Bedtime is nine," Nia is saying ten minutes later, as she and Dad slip into their shoes in the front hall. "They can watch one movie. Only one."

I watch as she secures the ankle strap of one gold sandal. She looks beautiful tonight. Her hair is loose, tight black curls framing her face and making her appear softer; usually it's pulled back in a low bun, giving her a more severe look. Her makeup is light, just the sweep of gold eyeshadow and a touch of mascara. She's clad in a flowy blue dress with a unique pattern on it, paired with those strappy gold sandals.

"You look gorgeous," I tell her, the compliment popping out before I can stop it. Experience has taught me that Nia is terrible at receiving compliments. Or at least ones that come from me. She typically dismisses them with a stiff wave of her hand.

Tonight, she surprises me. "Thank you." She smooths the front of her dress. "My mother sent me this dress last year, but this is my first opportunity to wear it."

"Care package from Haiti, huh? That's cool."

Nia smiles. "It's always a wonderful surprise. Makes me very homesick."

I'm pretty sure this is the first time she's shared something this personal with me. Holy shit. Are we bonding?

Dad ruins the moment by peering past my shoulder into the living room, where my sisters are on the couch babbling to each other in French.

"*Au revoir, mes petites chéries,*" he calls out.

"*Au revoir,* Daddy!"

"Don't give your sister too much trouble," he warns.

"We won't," Roxy promises.

Dad kisses my cheek and ducks out the door. Nia lingers, her expression taking on a glint of panic.

"No soda," she reminds me. "If they want a snack, there are rice cakes on the top shelf of the cabinet. Monique loves them, especially if you spread some peanut butter on them. Oh, and be sure to keep a close eye on her. She likes to climb the furniture."

"We'll be fine," I assure her. "I'll call you if I need anything. Go out and enjoy the concert."

"Thank you, Cassandra." Everyone else calls me Cassie or

Cass, but in the eight years I've known her, Nia's never called me anything but Cassandra.

I close the door behind them, lock it, and proceed to dance into the living room like a game show contestant who just got chosen to go onstage. "All right, the adults are gone!" I shout. "Let's party!"

The twins burst into giggles. I flop down on the couch between them and throw an arm around each girl.

"So, I should warn you," I say, "I invited a friend to hang out with us tonight."

Roxy squeals. "What's her name? How do you know her?"

"Well, firstly, it's a him—"

"Ewwwww," Mo says, making a face.

"What's his name? How do you know him?" Roxy demands.

"His name is Aaron. You'll like him. He's really funny. I told him he can watch a movie with us."

"I don't want a movie. I want a story," Monique whines. "I want Kit 'n McKenna!"

"We can do both," I tell her. "Movie now, and a story at bedtime."

At the reminder of their favorite bedtime story, I suddenly realize I haven't heard from Robb in a few days. I gave him the story line for our *Kit 'n McKenna* book last week, but he still hasn't sent back any concepts for the artwork. Since the printer I found takes about seven days to print the book, Robb and I need to finalize the illustrations by the end of next week if I want it to be ready in time for the girls' party.

As Roxy continues to interrogate me about Aaron, a message from him pops up, informing me he'll be here in forty minutes or so. When I told him we wouldn't be eating together, he ended up driving to Charleston with his brother for dinner, and they're on their way back now.

Me: *The girls are feeling very nosy today, so expect some grilling when you get here.*

Aaron: *Ha! I'm not worried. All kids love me.*

He's not lying. An hour later, we're watching *Moana,* and the twins are laughing their butts off while Aaron stands in front of the TV and belts out the entire number that The Rock sings in the movie. He knows every word, and when I demand an explanation afterward, he offers a sheepish smile and says, "My older sister has a four-year-old daughter. We watch a lot of movies together."

Halfway through the film, the girls declare they're bored and would rather play a game, so Mo brings out a ridiculous card game that Roxy tries valiantly to explain. It involves monsters and severed body parts and requires us to fight each other in weird card battles. I don't understand what the hell is going on, but Aaron picks it up fast, and the next thing I know he and Roxy are competing in a fierce monster battle rife with dark glares and very bad trash talk.

"Oh, you're going down," he warns my sister.

"Nuh-uh. You are."

"No, you are."

"No, YOU ARE!" Roxy sticks her tongue out at him.

Aaron sticks his tongue out right back at her.

I stare at him. "I'm dating a six-year-old."

"Dating, huh?" His eyes sparkle.

Smiling, I arch a brow. "I mean, yeah, isn't this a date?"

"Ewwww!" Monique cries.

"Cassie has a boyfriend!" Roxy yells.

I roll my eyes. "You guys are SO immature," I say haughtily, and Aaron snickers.

Eventually, I check the time and notice it's almost eight thirty, so I encourage everyone to wrap up the game. Roxy wins, but I think Aaron lets her, which is another check in his plus column. Not batting an eye about our change of date venue is another one. He really is a decent guy.

"You okay staying down here while I put them to bed?" I ask him.

He's already reaching for the TV remote. "I'm good," he assures me. "Preseason game is on. Gotta see how the Bills are looking so far."

I keep forgetting he's from New York. *Not that far from Boston,* a little voice in my head points out.

I suppose that's super convenient. If we keep dating, that is. Right now, though, while I'm having fun with him, it still feels very platonic. Our initial spark doesn't seem to be catching fire. I don't feel a sense of eagerness to kiss him, but I'm not sure if the lack of heat and passion is because of what happened last time we kissed, or if it's simply just not there with us.

I know I'm capable of feeling it. I felt it last night. I'm sure some of *that* had to do with the alcohol we'd consumed, but most of it had to do with Tate.

Upstairs, I tuck the girls in and switch on the little lamp atop the night table between their beds. When I turn off the main light, the lamp casts a yellow glow over the room and projects glowing mermaids on the walls. It's the coolest thing. I wish I'd had one of those growing up.

I drag a white-painted rocking chair closer to their beds. It's a remnant from when they were babies, and I suddenly have a memory of Nia sitting in this chair, rocking my tiny infant sisters to sleep.

"Okay," I say cheerfully. "Are we ready to find out what happens when McKenna's older brother finds Kit hiding in the garage?"

* * *

"Thanks for waiting." I come downstairs about thirty minutes later. Aaron's made himself comfortable in the living room. Feet up on the coffee table, leaning back against the couch cushions with one arm propped behind his head.

He looks kind of sexy in that position . . .

This is promising.

When his head turns toward the doorway and his eyes smolder at the sight of me, I feel a fluttering between my legs.

Promising, indeed.

"The girls asleep?" he asks.

I settle beside him on the couch. "Roxy's out like a light, but Mo will take a bit longer. She was drifting off when I left, though."

"They're cool kids. Half sisters, right?"

"Yeah. Their mom is Dad's second wife. Nia."

"And you don't have any other siblings?"

"Nope. I was an only child until I was fifteen, and then the twins came along."

We talk about families for a while, but I have to admit I'm not paying too much attention to what we're saying. Aaron's arm is around me now, and his fingertips are brushing my bare shoulder. Stroking lightly. It feels nice. I'm pleasantly surprised to find heat gathering in my belly. My heart beating faster. Okay, I can work with this.

"Cassie."

I look over to see him peering at me through heavy-lidded eyes.

"Yeah?" I swallow.

"I really want to kiss you."

I swallow again. "Good. So kiss me."

For all of Tate's advice about how to ward off the "aggressive entry," it happens so fast I barely have a chance to blink, let alone touch his face and compliment him. The speed with which his lips latch onto mine and his tongue is thrusting inside is almost remarkable. He's perfected the art of persistent passion with zero buildup. In fact, I've never met anyone who's *this* skilled at kissing *this* bad. Once again, I'm caught in the same predicament, a helpless participant in a kiss that makes my head spin, and not in a good way.

Tell him to slow down.

I hear Tate's voice in my head.

But I feel too awkward asking him to change gears. Not when he's moaning as if he's thoroughly enjoying this. His fingers are threaded through my hair. One hand strokes my thigh over my yoga pants. Fortunately, I'm granted a reprieve when he comes up for air. I suck in as much oxygen as my lungs will allow, while Aaron mumbles, "You're so fucking pretty," and abruptly starts "kissing" me again. At this point, I don't think it qualifies as actual kissing, so much as face banging.

Say something.

I say nothing.

Yup, I chicken out. I let him keep doing what he thinks of as sexy kissing for another solid minute. Until, to my sheer relief, a little voice interrupts us.

"Cassie?" Monique whines from the stairs.

Aaron and I break apart. "Hold that thought," I tell him, when inside I'm like, *please, forget that thought.*

I step into the hall and find Mo wobbling down the stairs in her PJs, wide awake.

"Hey, squirt." I frown. "Why aren't you in bed?"

"I can't sleep."

"Aww. Well, that's not good. How can we fix that?"

"Can you tell me another story?"

I glance at the clock hanging on the wall at the entrance to the kitchen. It's five past ten. An hour past her bedtime. And Nia and my dad should be home in the next hour or so. I bite my cheek. I can't have Monique up and about when they get back or Nia will never leave me alone with the girls again.

"All right." I let out a sigh. "Go up to bed and we'll do another story. Just give me a sec to say goodbye to Aaron."

"I'll wait here." With a stubborn jut of her chin, she plants her butt on the bottom step.

"Okay. But don't move."

When I reenter the living room, Aaron is already up, phone in hand. He swipes his keys off the coffee table.

"You heard that?" I say wryly.

"Yeah."

"I'm sorry. I need to go back upstairs and put her to sleep, and I feel bad making you sit and wait again." Monique's insomnia also happens to be the escape hatch I'd been praying for, but I keep that thought to myself.

"It's no problem," he says easily. "Why don't we meet again during the week? I heard there's a really good mini golf course on the south end of the boardwalk."

"Sure. Sounds good."

I walk him to the door, where he leans in to kiss me goodbye. Luckily, just a kiss on the cheek, his tongue remaining firmly in his own mouth.

"Good night, sexy," he says huskily, and I can't lie—it does nothing for me.

I close the door after him and lock it. Then I stand there for a moment, exhaling a long, tired breath when I hear his car driving away. I don't think this Aaron thing is going to work. A friendship, maybe, but I honestly can't envision anything more than that. Which means—

A resounding crash jolts me from my thoughts.

It sounded like it came from the kitchen.

A wave of fear slams into me, propelling me forward. "Monique?" I shout, running through the house.

I fly into the kitchen and my heart stops when I spot her small body sprawled by the tall cabinet where we keep the snacks. The bottom shelf has broken off, the splintered plank now lying on the floor. It's clear she tried to climb it, and it didn't hold her weight. Random items are strewn around her feet—bags of chips, a can of peanuts, an array of baking supplies. On the top shelf, another tin of nuts teeters on the edge before crashing down and missing Monique's head by mere inches. She screeches in surprise.

I dive onto the floor and help her into a sitting position. "Oh my God. Sweetheart. Are you okay? Where are you hurt?"

I snap into emergency mode and search her for injuries, the frigid chill of panic icing my veins when I notice the cut on her jaw. It's not bleeding, just a few red dots, but whatever hit her did break the skin and leave a small indentation.

Tears stream down Monique's face. "The thing fell on my face. That one." She points.

I follow her finger to a peanut can that's rolling toward the fridge. Okay. Thank God. It's a plastic container. Not glass. Although either way Nia is going to kill me.

"It broke my face," Mo sobs. "I just wanted the rice cakes."

"Come here, baby." I pick her up. She wraps her arms and legs around me and clings tight. Her wails begin to quiet, transforming into hiccups.

"Let's get you a Band-Aid."

"I don't want a Band-Aid," she cries, then hiccups again.

"Tough. I'm going to put you down now, okay?" I set her on the chair at the kitchen table. "Don't you move a muscle, you hear me? Not one muscle, Mo."

I duck into the hall bathroom, where I know Dad keeps a

mini first aid kit under the sink. I grab it and hoof it back to the kitchen, where this time Mo listened and didn't move from her chair.

Sinking to my knees in front of her, I tear open an antiseptic wipe. "This is going to sting just a little," I warn her. "Ready?"

She nods weakly.

When I swipe it over the tiny cut, her face scrunches up. "I don't like that!"

"I know, but it's over. See? It's over. All done." I check the wipe, gratified to find no blood on it. She might have a wee bruise, but that's it.

Once the Band-Aid is on, I scoop her up again and search her face. "Are you okay? Does it still hurt?"

She shakes her head. "No."

"Good. Come on, let's get you back to bed."

We reach the stairs as the front door opens.

Shit.

I hear Nia and Dad's voices. So does Mo, because she exclaims, "Mama! Daddy! I broke my face! Come see!"

I swallow a groan. "Monique," I chide.

It's too late. The adults are galloping in. Nia pries Monique from my arms, while Dad barks, "What happened? Is everything okay?"

"It's fine," I reassure them. "I promise. There's a broken shelf in the kitchen, but Mo is fine."

Eyes now completely dry, Mo shows off her Band-Aid. "Look! Maybe I'll have a scar."

"A scar?" Nia swivels on me in reproach. "What happened?" Her voice is sharp.

"I was walking Aaron to the door. Mo couldn't sleep and was alone in the kitchen—when she was *supposed* to be waiting for me in the hall." I frown at my sister.

"I'm sorry," she says meekly.

"She tried to climb the cabinet to get a snack—"

Nia's eyes blaze. "I told you not to let her climb anything, Cassandra."

"I know." Guilt jams in my throat. "I swear I only left her alone for thirty seconds. Aaron was just leaving."

"It's okay, sweetheart," Dad says gently.

"No, it's not." Nia's voice rises as she blasts Monique with a reprimand. "You're not supposed to be climbing the furniture!" Dad touches Nia's arm, but she pushes him away. "No. I'm taking Monique to bed. Say good night to your father and sister."

"Good night, Daddy. Good night, Cassie." Monique's face is forlorn as peers at me over her mother's shoulder. She knows she got me in trouble. *I'm sorry,* she mouths.

I flash a smile of assurance. *Love you,* I mouth back.

They disappear at the top of the stairs.

Dad observes my expression and sighs. "Don't worry. She'll be fine. Kids are resilient."

"I know," I moan. "It's just . . . Nia already doesn't like me."

His features soften. "What are you talking about? That's not true."

"You know it is."

"It's not," he insists. "She thinks you're wonderful. We both do."

Sure. If he says so.

His false assurances still echo in my head as I drive home ten minutes later. It's eleven o'clock and I'm exhausted. I was supposed to go on a fun date tonight, which somehow turned into my trying to prove to my stepmother that I can be a good big sister. Instead, I only validated her already low opinion of me. And I couldn't even be assertive with Aaron. Too afraid to hurt his feelings by asking him to slow things down.

God. I feel like shit. My self-esteem is in the toilet, and for the life of me I can't conjure up a silver lining for tonight. I simply want to go home and climb into bed and sleep the rest of this disastrous weekend away.

When I pull into the driveway of Grandma's house, I'm startled to find another car parked there.

A silver Mercedes.

Oh no.

No.

Please, don't let it be her.

Please.

My stomach churns as I shut off the engine. My mother's go-to rental car choice is a Mercedes. She hates driving Grandma's Range Rover when she's in town. Claims it's too clunky.

Only, Mom isn't due to arrive for another two weeks. She's scheduled to come on my birthday weekend, and there's no way she would show up in Avalon Bay early. Not willingly. Ever since the divorce, this town has become a source of deep hostility for her.

In the front hall, my worst fears are confirmed when I spy several Louis Vuitton cases stacked against the wall. She always leaves her bags down here. Waiting for poor Adelaide to cart them up the stairs as if it's our housekeeper's job to play bellhop.

I kick off my tennis shoes and swallow a sigh when I notice the light on in the kitchen. I reluctantly make my way toward it. Steeling myself. Because apparently only bad things happen in kitchens tonight.

I enter to see Mom at the kitchen table, sipping a glass of white wine.

Yup. Only bad things.

"Hey!" I exclaim, slapping on a cheerful smile. It's difficult, though. My spirits are already dismally low. And if there's one thing I know about my mother, it's that she has the power to drag me down even lower. "What are you doing here? You weren't due for two more weeks."

"I decided to come early," she replies. "Mother mentioned on the phone the other day that you two haven't even started going through the house to decide what she'll be shipping to the city next month. Clearly my presence is needed here more than in Boston, which, frankly, has been sweltering this summer. It will be nice to spend a month by the ocean." She takes another sip, then sets down the wineglass and rises from her chair. "Is that a problem?"

"No, of course not!" My voice sounds high, squeaky.

"Wonderful. Then come here and give your mother a hug."

I walk over and obediently step into her embrace.

"Ah, it's so good to see you," Mom says, planting a kiss on the top of my head. The reception is more genuine than I expect, her hug infused with more warmth than I'm accustomed to. "I missed you, sweetie."

"Oh. I missed you too." My guard drops a couple of feet. I seem to have caught her in a good mood tonight.

She squeezes me tighter. "I'm hoping we get a chance to spend a lot of time together this month."

Her brown eyes shine with what seems like sincerity as she releases me. Then they fix on my yoga pants and tight white tank, flicking briefly to the black bra straps peeking out of my top.

A frown twists her lips. "Is that what you wore out tonight?"

And so it begins.

CHAPTER 17

TATE

I don't know . . . I've never had a dick inside me before . . .

I thought I was cured of spontaneous boner syndrome once I turned fourteen. Turns out, my dick still has a mind of his own. Only, this time, I'm not in front of the class delivering a presentation on the founding fathers when I pitch a tent. I'm at the bar, standing up to greet Evan, whose gaze doesn't miss what's happening down below.

"Do you have a boner?" he demands.

"Say it louder for the people in the back," I grumble.

Luckily, I revert to a state of non-arousal the moment I'm presented with a distraction. Before Evan arrived, I was sitting alone with far too much time on my hands to ruminate over what happened with Cassie. Since the night of the charity gala, I've been playing it off like it's no big deal. Friends always masturbate in front of windows together. Like, come on, bro. It's just a cool thing platonic people do. But it's not working. She's not dumb and neither am I. A line had definitely been crossed. And every time I hear her breathy voice in my head, whispering those words—*I've never had a dick inside me before*—I get harder than granite.

"Seriously. Is that for me?" Evan sounds amused.

"You wish." I push the beer I ordered for him across the booth. "Here."

"Thanks."

It's Sunday night and I dragged Evan out for drinks because both Danny and Luke bailed on me after work. Pleading exhaustion after a long day on the water with a group of disastrous, albeit enthusiastic, would-be sailors. Me, I desperately need the diversion, so I pried Evan out of Gen's bed. At least that's what I assume he was doing when I called.

Evan raises the pint glass to his lips. "And you're still not answering the question. Clue me in already. I want to solve the case. The case of the mysterious boner."

"I have a sex problem," I confess.

His amusement grows. "Oh, I can't wait to hear this. Hold that thought." He waves at one of the waitresses, whose hips sway deliberately as she saunters over to us.

Her name is Nicole, and I'm pretty sure Evan hooked up with her during Genevieve's year in Charleston when she went radio silent on him. Dude attempted to cure his broken heart by sleeping his way through the Bay, hitting on any cute chick that crossed his path. Fortunately, like me, he's on good terms with most of his hookups.

"Hi, boys," Nicole chirps. She eyes me. "You look . . . flushed."

Evan snickers. "Could I grab an order of chicken wings? Hottest sauce you've got." He winks at her. "Please and thank you."

"Coming right up."

Once she's gone, Evan takes another swig of his beer. "Okay, what's the problem?"

"I think maybe I have a virgin fetish I didn't know about."

He almost chokes on his beer. "I'm sorry, what?" He coughs a few times.

"You know that chick Cassie who was at your place a couple weeks ago? Her grandmother used to own the Beacon?"

"Yes . . ." He shakes his head, sighing. "You stupid bastard. You took her virginity?"

"No, no. I mean, she did sort of proposition me. Asked if I was interested in a summer fling. But I said no."

Evan lifts a brow. "Since when do you turn down propositions like that?"

"Mac talked some sense into me," I admit. "And when I took a step back to really think about it, I realized it wouldn't be a smart idea. Cassie didn't strike me as the type who could keep things strictly physical. I don't want to hurt her."

"Worried she'll fall in love with you, huh?"

"Kind of, yeah. Do you remember what happened in high school with Lindsey Gerlach?"

"I'm pretty sure our entire graduating class remembers," he says dryly. "What did her friends spray-paint on your locker again? *Stupid asshole?*"

"*Selfish prick,*" I correct.

"Eh. I've been called worse."

I reach for my glass. "Anyway, I didn't want Cassie catching feelings. And now we're becoming good friends, and honestly, I kind of learned my lesson the last time I hooked up with a friend."

Alana and I haven't even spoken since she ended it. Granted, it hasn't made for any awkward group gatherings, but that's probably because I barely attended any parties this July. I've been too busy with work. Still, the idea of screwing up my friendship with Cassie bums me out. I don't want to lose her. I would miss talking to her.

"But—" I add.

He chuckles. "There's always a *but.*"

"The other night, we kind of had a moment . . ."

"Of course you did. What'd you do? Make out?"

"Nah, it was a phone sex thing." I omit the details, especially the window element of the scenario. He doesn't need to know all that. "But yeah . . . it came up a couple of times that night, the virginity thing, and now I can't stop thinking about it."

"About what? Popping her cherry?"

"Yes," I groan, then slug back nearly half my beer. It's so hard to articulate. I mean, I've watched porn. I'm sure some of that porn featured virgins, but the actual genre—virgin porn—isn't my thing. I prefer experienced women. I like women who know their way around a man's body.

And yet the idea of being the first guy inside of Cassie gets me going something fierce. I wonder if there's an anthropological reason behind it. Some recessive caveman instinct in us, a primal urge backed by science. Except this urge never existed in me before.

Another possibility occurs to me. Maybe it's not the fact she's a virgin that's making me crave her on such a deep level. Maybe it's because she's beautiful and funny and so damn easy to be around.

Maybe I just . . . like her.

Shit.

"I know it's not a good idea, though. It's a lot of pressure. I don't need that kind of pressure, right?"

"Christ, no. You never want to be a woman's first. You're literally going to be someone she remembers for the rest of her life. But what's your legacy gonna be? Best-case scenario, she's got you up on a pedestal because you rocked her world. Likely scenario? She'll be nervous, which'll make *you* nervous, and then you'll fuck it up and ruin the experience for her because you're both so uncomfortable. Either that, or you come too fast because she'll be so tight—" He breaks off abruptly. "Speaking of fast."

Our waitress is back, holding a platter of wings. "Do I even want to know?" Nicole asks politely.

Evan blinks. "Nope."

I offer an innocent smile. "Nothing to see here."

"Why do I get the feeling you're up to no good?" Her narrowed eyes shift between us.

"Who, us? We're choir boys," Evan says. "You know that."

"Yeah, sure." Snorting, she plants his chicken wings in front of him and wanders off.

Evan wastes no time pulling the plate closer and snatching up a sauce-drenched wing.

"So, now that we've discovered you have a deflowering kink," he says between bites. "What are you going to do about it?"

"Nothing," I say glumly.

"Nothing?" he echoes. "Well, that's no fun." He wipes his chin with a napkin, then slides out of the booth. "Be right back. Gotta hit the head."

He's only gone a minute before Nicole returns to check on our booth. She eyes Evan's empty side. "Where's Hartley? He abandon you?"

"Nah, he'll be right back."

"Pity. I'm almost done with my shift." One eyebrow flicks up. "I would've kept you company."

Well. This is interesting. Nicole and I haven't interacted much, but I've seen her around the Bay, and I can't deny I've always enjoyed the view. Tall. Curvy. Pouty lips and shoulder-length dark hair.

"Guess we need a raincheck," I say lightly.

"Yeah? How about Friday?"

"You asking me out, Nic?"

"Something like that. I've seen you around for years." She purses those full, red lips. "Maybe it's time we got to know each other better."

A faint smile tugs on my lips. Yeah. There's no mistaking her intentions. She's not asking me on a date—she's looking to hook up. And the more I think on it, the more I realize it's exactly what I need to clear my head. I haven't gotten laid since I met Cassie.

If I don't find an outlet soon, all that pent-up sexual energy will explode and push me right into Cassie's bed.

So, why not? Indulging in a no-strings hookup is a surefire way to stop myself from corrupting Cassie and blowing up our friendship. I can't keep jerking off before seeing her. That's not a viable long-term solution. Eventually my dick is going to require a lot more than my tired hand.

"I work until seven on Friday," I tell the smirking brunette. "Why don't you come by for a drink around eight? I'm staying at the Jackson place. Housesitting for the summer."

"Really? I pass that house on my dad's boat all the time. I've always wanted to see the inside."

"Is that a yes?"

"It's a yes." She licks her lips. "Sounds like fun."

"Great. See you then."

Evan returns as Nicole's sashaying off and doesn't miss the coy smile she tosses me over her shoulder. "Man, you move fast." He slides back into the booth. "Nic is good people, though."

"Yeah, she's cool." I steal a chicken wing off his plate. "She's coming by on Friday."

"I get it." He nods. "You need the distraction."

He does get it. "Yup."

Despite the plans I made with Nicole, I still have Cassie on the brain when I get home a couple hours later. I park my Jeep in the driveway and enter the house to conduct my usual security check. Everything looks good. Me, though, I'm still on edge. Restless. So after a quick shower, I head downstairs and grab the pack of smokes I stashed in the kitchen, along with a cheap plastic lighter.

I step onto the back deck, where I fish out a cigarette and pop it between my lips. It's nine thirty, and although the sun set not too long ago, the moon is high and shining bright, casting streaks of silver over the calm water of the bay. I flick my gaze toward Cassie's house. The patio light is on, but I don't see anybody out there. I approach the railing that overlooks the dock below and light my smoke. I inhale deeply. Let the nicotine lodge in my lungs until they feel like they're going to explode, and only then do I exhale, watching the thick cloud of smoke float away and dissipate.

I love this town, I truly do. But sometimes it's so damn oppressive. Especially when I look out at the water, when my gaze rests on that strip of land that curves at the very edge of the bay. Because I know beyond it is the open ocean, and every cell in my body cries out for me to go to it. I want to be navigating the ocean using the stars. I want to see new places, meet new people, experience things I know I'll never experience in Avalon Bay. Small towns are familiar. They're a comforting pair of arms that bring you close and keep you safe.

But those same arms hold you back. Keep you locked in place.

I'm feeling too introspective tonight. I should've stayed out with Evan, talked him into another round of beers, a game or two of pool.

I take another drag. Exhale again as I listen to the sounds of the night. Insects humming. Trees rustling. I hear a car drive by. A burst of laughter from the dock several houses down, where it sounds like they're hosting a small gathering. Then, another car engine, this one from the vicinity of the Tanner house. I hear a door shut. A flash of movement crosses my peripheral vision, and I realize the patio wasn't empty, after all. There's a woman on the deck, drinking a glass of wine. It doesn't appear to be Cassie's grandmother. Lydia Tanner has dark hair. This woman has red hair, several shades darker than Cassie's.

I furrow my brow. Is that her mother? I thought Cassie had said her mom wasn't arriving until mid-August.

The back door creaks open and another figure steps outside. The foliage shields her from view, but I recognize Cassie's voice.

"Hey, Mom. I just got back from dinner with Joy. Just wanted to say good night."

Okay, so it is her mother. I wonder when she got in. I've been at the yacht club all weekend, so I haven't paid much attention to the comings and goings next door. That, and I've been diligently avoiding Cassie since window sex.

"That's the outfit you wore to dinner?" her mother inquires.

"Yes. What's wrong with it?" Cassie's tone sounds strange to my ears. Forced, as if she's trying to remain neutral but can't quite master it. "We went to Joe's Beach Bar. Dress code is casual there."

"I thought we talked about the crop tops, Cass."

I crush my cigarette in the ashtray on the railing. Feels wrong eavesdropping. I don't mean to, but it's also hard not to, especially at night when there're no boats on the water. No shrieking children. No birds or seagulls squawking. Only the soft whine of mosquitoes, the occasional cricket, and the very clear voices of Cassie and her mother, who isn't letting up.

"It's really not a flattering look for you, sweetheart."

My body tenses up. Oh, screw that. Cassie looks good in everything. And as I recall, she was wearing a crop top the first time we kissed. I vividly remember the way it hugged her tits.

And now I also remember what she told me about her mother. The way she described the woman. Highly critical. Self-centered. Zero empathy.

Checks out so far.

"I don't know . . . I kind of like them." Cassie's flippant now, but the mere fact that she's defending her fashion choices makes me frown. She doesn't have to justify herself to anyone.

"I just think it's something you should leave to girls like Joy, or

Peyton. Girls with abs, you know?" Her mom gives an airy laugh, as if they're sharing some lighthearted joke. "You need to have a very flat, toned stomach to pull off that kind of top."

My eyebrows soar.

Fuck you. That's what Cassie ought to be saying. I get it, respect your elders, obey your parents and all that. But come on.

"Eh, abs are overrated." I have no clue how Cassie is managing to retain her composure. Somehow her voice remains calm and unruffled, when I suspect that inside she's anything but.

"Sweetie. You know I want you to always look and feel your best. And it's not only about showing the midriff. With your breast size? You need to choose your wardrobe carefully. I understand at your age you want to look sexy, but on your body type, most sexy outfits tend to have the opposite effect. There's looking sexy, and then there's looking like a bimbo."

Cassie remains silent.

"Large breasts are a curse and a blessing. Trust me, I know." Her mom laughs again, as if she hasn't just bullied her daughter to the point of silence. "I think right now you're seeing the curse aspect of it."

Finally, Cassie lets out an awkward laugh. "Well, I mean, it's not like I can get rid of these things, so . . ."

"*I* did it. There's no reason you can't either. We can talk to Dr. Bowers about doing a reduction."

"I don't want a reduction. I've already told you this."

"You said you were scared of the anesthesia, but—"

"It's not only that. I just don't want it."

"Cass—"

"I'm not doing a reduction," Cassie repeats. For the first time since she stepped outside, her tone brooks no argument.

There's a beat. Then her mother, totally unbothered, says, "You look tired. We probably shouldn't be talking about this when you're clearly exhausted. Let's discuss it another time. Why don't you head up to bed?"

"You're right. I *am* exhausted. Bed sounds like a wonderful idea."

"Good night, sweetheart. Love you."

"Love you, too."

After *that* conversation, it's hard to believe there's love on either end. Particularly Cassie's mother. What kind of parent talks like that to their kid? Hypercritical, Cassie said? Try downright cruel.

I'm startled by the torrent of anger that floods my gut. I remain on the deck and pull out another smoke, my fingers shaking when I flick the lighter. I lean into the flame, sucking hard on the cigarette. That dark, angry sensation inside me only heightens, forming a knot of tension between my shoulder blades.

A light turns on. A yellow glow radiating from the second floor of the Tanner house. I tip my head toward it. I don't have a direct view of Cassie's window from down here, but I catch a blur of motion and then a fleeting glimpse of her face. She's scrubbing two fists over her eyes.

Goddamn it. She's crying.

My jaw tightens to the point of pain. I force myself to relax it and take another deep drag.

No.

Fuck that.

I snuff out my cigarette and head next door.

CHAPTER 18

CASSIE

When the window rattles the first time, I assume it's the wind, though I was just outside and it wasn't windy at all. Nonetheless, that's the most logical assumption to reach when you hear your window shaking in its frame. But then it happens again. And again. And I realize I'm not hearing rattling. It's tapping.

God. I do not have the energy for this, whatever *this* is, right now.

Sniffling, I swipe at my wet eyes on my way to the window. I know I'm too old to be crying over my mother's veiled insults, and yet here I am. I think she just caught me off guard tonight.

I jump when a hand appears on the glass. Heart racing, I quickly lift the window open and see Tate's face.

"What the hell are you doing?" I whisper-shout.

He's literally clinging to the lattice like a monkey. And either I'm imagining it, or the delicate crisscross frame is beginning to bend under his weight. Everything about this situation seems extremely unstable.

Tate groans softly. "Can I come in or are you going to let me fall to my death? Because I'm pretty sure this thing is going to give out any second."

"Have you ever heard of a door? More specifically, a front

door? We've got one of those downstairs, and it has this little gizmo on it called a doorbell that you ring and then someone answers and—"

"This is not the time for your babbling, ginger. I'm about to plummet to my death."

Good point.

Sighing, I help him up, and a moment later he tumbles onto my floor. When he's standing, he runs both hands through his tousled blond hair to push it away from his face. He smooths out his T-shirt, which is rumpled from his climb, then fixes the waistband of his gray sweatpants. I notice he's barefoot and hope he didn't scratch his feet going up that lattice.

"To answer your question," he says, visibly frazzled, "I didn't use the front door because I was afraid I'd have to meet your mother, and I'm not her biggest fan right now."

I freeze. "Why do you say that?"

"I was outside having a smoke when you got home and—"

"You *smoke*?" I demand. "How come I didn't know—" I stop myself, because that is not the thing to focus on right now. "You heard us?"

He nods.

Oh God.

My eyes start to sting again. And now I feel like throwing up too, because the hottest guy in the world heard my mother disparage my body, insinuate I'm a slut, and encourage me to get a breast reduction.

I blink rapidly. Mortified.

Tate doesn't miss the way I hastily rub underneath my eyes with the pad of my thumb.

"No," he begs. "Please don't cry again."

Again?

He saw me crying?

I might actually be sick. I take a few breaths, attempting to keep the nausea at bay. My knees go weak, so I sink onto the edge of my bed, but because I'm wearing my bimbo crop top, it creates an inevitable roll in my stomach. Normally I wouldn't care about that—everyone gets it when they sit down—but after my mother's callous assessment of my figure, I'm now feeling extra self-conscious.

I shoot back up. "Look," I start, then trail off. I don't even know what to say. I draw another deep breath and opt for honesty. "I feel like throwing up knowing you heard all that."

His jaw ticks, as if he's clenching and unclenching his teeth. "You realize none of it's true, right? It was all bullshit. I almost stormed over there and gave her a piece of my mind. Does she always talk to you like that?"

"Pretty much. But she tries to disguise it as helpful advice, so most of her criticism falls under the *I just want you to look your best* umbrella." I shrug. "She's called me a lot of things over the years, but a bimbo? That's new. It's also extremely outdated, but I suppose *bimbo* is her generation's *slut*? And I guess I prefer *bimbo* to *slut*. It's more fun to say. Bim-bo."

"Stop it, Cass. It's not a joke."

I crack a half smile. "It is kind of funny."

Tate isn't amused. "Have you told her you don't like it when she says that shit?"

"I used to," I admit. "When I was younger. But it doesn't register. People like her only hear what they want to hear. Like I told you before, I eventually just gave up on . . ."

"Saying how you feel," he finishes, then shakes his head in disapproval. "You should never stop telling people how they make you feel."

"Doesn't make a difference, Tate. She'll never accept she did anything wrong, and she'll never apologize. That's not who my mother is." I smile sadly.

"You don't do it for an apology. You do it for yourself. Because when you don't release those dark emotions, you end up bottling them up. You let them consume you from the inside out until you're running upstairs in tears believing you're unworthy or unattractive or whatever other false ideas she planted in your mind—when in reality, you're the most beautiful woman I've ever fucking met."

My smile falters. "Okay, you're laying it on thick to make me feel better. I appreciate it, but—"

"You are. Christ. Just look at you."

He gestures toward me, his earnest gaze taking in the outfit I'd chosen for my boardwalk dinner with Joy. A wrap skirt, a burnt orange color, that swishes around my knees. The tight black top that shows off my abs-free but still decent (or so I thought) midriff. I left the house believing I looked nice, but now all I hear is my mother's voice in my head talking about girls with perfect abs and how big boobs will only ever look trashy. Never sexy.

"You're goddamn perfect, Cassie."

"Now you're just bullshitting." I start to turn away.

"I'm not." He grabs my hand, tugging me closer. "You didn't know I was listening earlier, right? Well, I could've gone inside and you would've been none the wiser. I didn't have to scale a tower tonight and stumble in through your window just to tell you how hot you look. Why would I do that, or say that, if I didn't mean it?"

Another good point. But . . . I still think he's bullshitting.

He notes my skepticism and chuckles. "Do you really not see what you do to me?"

Despite myself, my gaze lowers to his groin. And yeah, there does appear to be some . . . swelling . . . happening beneath his sweatpants.

The evidence of his arousal, however, only triggers a gust of frustration.

"What the hell!" I burst out.

Confusion creases his forehead. "What?"

"What do you mean, *what*? You're the king of mixed signals, Tate! Do you realize that?" I back away from him, aggravation rising inside me. "You can't do this shit, okay? It fucking confuses me. And it's fucking inconsiderate. And now look at how fucking much I'm swearing because that's how *fucking* frustrated I am with you!"

He takes a step forward. "Cass—"

"No." I whip up my hand to stop him from coming any closer. "You're confusing. And insensitive! First you kiss me—and then you tell me you want to be platonic. Fine. So now we're friends and suddenly you're my wingman, and I feel like, okay, things are moving in a platonic direction—and then you jerk off in front of me! Seriously, Tate. What am I supposed to think here?"

"I know." He releases an equally frustrated groan. He drags both hands though his hair, messing it up even more. "I'm sorry."

"Yes, you should be! I don't get it. If you're attracted to me like you insist you are, then why wouldn't you just agree to be my summer fling when I asked instead of feeding me a bunch of excuses and platitudes?"

His expression grows tortured. "I honestly thought it was the best idea at the time. I was worried I might hurt you if we got involved. That you might want something more. And I don't have a great track record with relationships. I'm sort of just the hookup guy."

"And I wanted a *hookup*! I literally approached the hookup guy for a hookup!" I realize I'm practically shouting at him and force myself to lower my voice.

"I know, but you said so yourself, you don't have a lot of experience in this department. You've never even had sex before. I felt like I'd be taking advantage of your inexperience."

I'm so horrifically embarrassed that my entire face is on fire. I wish I had a cold glass of water to hurl at my cheeks. "My virginity freaks you out *this* much?"

He hesitates. "I'm not freaked out, not really. It's . . . the pressure, you know? Being your first puts a lot of pressure on me to make it good for you. To make it the best you've ever fucking had. Well, I suppose you wouldn't know if it was the best, since you've never done it before, but you know what I mean."

Kill me.

Kill me now.

This time, I all but collapse on the edge of the bed. I don't even care what my stomach does. I bury my face in my hands and moan. "Please leave, Tate. I've had enough humiliation for one night."

"Cassie." I feel the mattress dip under the weight of him. "Come on, look at me."

"No," I mumble into my palms.

"Look at me."

"No."

"Don't you want to know the silver lining here?"

"There is none. We finally found a situation without a hint of lining, silver or otherwise. It's all black. Just big, black thunderclouds."

I twitch when I feel his thumb on the side of my jaw. He gently pries my face out of my hands and cups my chin, forcing me to look at him.

"Let me tell you the silver lining," he says. Gruff and sincere.

"Can't wait to hear it," I grumble. And although he's trying to impose eye contact on me, I keep my gaze downcast. Focusing it on his thumbnail.

"The silver lining is, if I hadn't heard your mother calling you a bimbo and—hey, you're right, it *is* fun to say. Bimbo."

I laugh faintly and accidentally meet his eyes, which are twinkling.

"If she hadn't said that shit, I wouldn't be sitting here right now telling you how beautiful you are."

Despite myself, my pulse speeds up. Because hearing those words spoken in his deep, earnest voice does something to me. Hits me in a different way. Aaron had called me beautiful the other night, but it hadn't elicited this kind of response. Hadn't made my heart flutter or my hands shake so wildly that I have to place them on my knees to keep them still.

"And if I hadn't heard all that shit, I wouldn't be saying: Cassie Soul, I would like to fling you."

My jaw drops. "What? Oh no. No way. I don't need a pity hookup." I peel his fingers off my chin.

He captures my hand and brings it to his groin.

I give a sharp intake of breath at the feel of an unmistakable erection beneath my palm.

"There is zero pity involved here," he says. "Not even a shred of it. Seriously. Feel how hard you make me. I want you so bad it hurts."

"What about my virgin status?" I challenge.

He visibly gulps. "I mean, I won't lie. That part is kind of scary. The pressure—"

"Stop," I order with a choked laugh. "There's no pressure. I promise."

Tate seems unconvinced.

"I mean it. I don't expect rose petals and declarations of love. And I certainly don't expect a commitment. All I want out of this is to have fun. And to gain some experience," I admit, suddenly feeling a bit shy. "I'm heading back to school after Labor Day weekend. I know this won't lead to a relationship, and I'm fine with that. I'm also not naïve enough to think that the first time—or even the first couple of times—is going to be a perfect, magical moment of sexual delights. But." I shrug. "Based on our previous encounters, I suspect we're going to have fun." I eye him. Daring him to contradict that. He doesn't. "So, really, where's the pressure?"

It's only after I conclude my speech that it occurs to me my hand is still on his dick.

Classy.

Noticing where my gaze went, Tate flashes those playful dimples. "Well. This is awkward."

"I don't know about *awkward.*" Before I can stop myself, I move my palm in a featherlight caress.

"Stop that. That was only intended to show you how on board I am." With a firm look, he pries my hand away from his crotch. "But I didn't come here for me. I came here for you."

My pulse quickens. "For me," I echo.

"Mmm-hmm." His blue eyes grow serious. "But if we do this, we take it slow. That means . . ." He raises a brow. "No sex. At least not tonight."

"Ugh," I say in mock disgust. "Then why are you even *here*? Jeez."

He lets out a laugh. "Slow," he repeats. "Deal?"

"Slow," I agree, nodding my assurance. I give him an expectant look. "So then what happens tonight?"

"Tonight . . . I want to make you feel good." He licks his lips, and I instinctively lick mine too. "I want to make you feel beautiful."

Our heads move closer, as if drawn together by a magnetic field. Then he kisses me. It's soft and gentle and almost too much of a tease. I make an anguished noise and deepen the kiss, clutching the back of his neck to keep him close. When our tongues meet with a teasing stroke, it's his turn to make noise, a hoarse groan that comes from deep in his chest and vibrates against my lips. *This* is what a passionate kiss is supposed to be like, I realize. You don't need your tongues to do all the heavy lifting. You don't need loud groans and grabby hands. Chemistry. That's all you need.

Despite his muttered objection, my hand seeks out his erection again. "You know what makes me feel beautiful?" I tell him. "*This*. Knowing I did this to you. Knowing you're so turned on you can't even think straight."

"Mission accomplished," he says wryly, then groans when my fingers dip beneath the waistband of his sweatpants.

He's not wearing underwear, and I find him hard and ready for me. I stroke him for a moment, enjoying the way his lips part, the way he breathes a little faster. Then I drop to my knees in front of him. I run my fingers along the heavy length of him. He's rock hard.

"I want you to tell me how good I make you feel."

His eyes are molten. Pure lust. "You mean you can't literally feel it?" He thrusts into my hand.

My thumb finds a streak of moisture at his tip and glides over it before my fingers curl around him again. When I stroke him, firmer this time, his expression burns hotter, a flash of pleasure bordering on pain. He wants me so bad it hurts, he said. I don't think he was kidding.

He continues gazing down at me as if I'm the most beautiful creature he's ever seen. It does wonders for my ego. Melts away that horrible lump of inadequacy that was jammed in my throat before.

When I bring my lips to his tip and place a soft kiss on it, his entire body jerks. "Tease," he growls.

Smiling, I plant another kiss on him, then swirl my tongue around the crown of his cock. Teasing again. His exhalations get heavier. Eyelids are heavy too. I peer up at him, loving the sight of his features stretched taut with need. How he looks like he's having trouble performing even the most basic task, like breathing.

My gaze locked with his, I take him fully into my mouth.

"Jesus," he swears, and I get a thrill knowing I'm responsible for the desperate groan that flies out of his mouth.

It's such a sexy sound that I proceed to do everything in my power to hear it again, to keep drawing those groans from his lips. I suck him deep, using my hand and tongue to drive him wild.

"Feels so good," he mumbles. Yet at the same time, he's suddenly trying to ease away from my hungry mouth. "I didn't come here for this."

I release him. "Well, this is what you're getting, so are we really going to complain about a blowjob, Gate?"

Tate shudders out a laugh. "I told you, that is not becoming a thing—" He halts when I take him in my mouth again. "Holy *hell*." A tortured moan escapes his throat. "I love this, I really do. I, ah—" Another moan. "I never want you to stop, but—ah, hell, that's good." He thrusts deeper. "But I want us to come together."

My nipples tighten at the lewd suggestion.

"Like, I'm right here. And you're right here. And I need you on me." He's basically fucking my mouth now, his hips moving in a restless, impatient rhythm as his long fingers tangle in my hair. "I need to touch you and see your face and hear that noise you make when you're getting close."

"What noise?" I lift my mouth off him, breathing hard.

"I can't describe it. It's just hot. Please," he begs.

I give him what he wants. Hell, what we *both* want. Because as fun as it is to tease him, my entire body is screaming for release. I climb onto the bed and we fall back on the mattress, his mouth instantly finding mine in a ravenous kiss. His hand fumbles to get under my skirt, where he pushes aside the crotch of my panties. I'm wet and ready, and he uses that wetness to stroke my clit, to drag a finger up and down my slit.

"Put your hand on me again," he whispers.

"Wait, I have an idea," I say.

He grunts in complaint when I roll over, but I'm not going far. Just reaching for the hand lotion I'd left out on the nightstand earlier. I squirt some on my palm and roll back toward him. That first smooth, wet glide of my fist along his shaft makes his eyes glaze over.

"Ah. Keep doing that."

I grin. "Good?"

"So good. Don't stop." His hips start rocking as he thrusts into my hand.

He props himself on his elbow and lifts my shirt, hurriedly undoing the front clasp. Then his mouth latches around one beaded nipple, while his fingers return between my thighs, rubbing, teasing, stroking my clit to bring me closer and closer to the edge.

When he pushes one finger inside me, his startled curse heats the air between us. "This is the tightest pussy I've ever fucking felt." He's practically moaning the words.

My breathing becomes labored as I strain against his skilled touch. "I'm getting close. Are you?"

"I was close before you even took off my pants." He raises his mouth from my breast to grin at me. "Just say when."

"Kiss me," I plead.

He does, and the moment our tongues meet, the orgasm breaks through the surface. My inner muscles clamp around his finger, and Tate groans and spills into my hand. We're both panting, hips moving as we lose ourselves in our respective bliss.

When my eyelids finally open, Tate is watching me. Pleased. "You made that noise." He sighs happily. "It's my favorite noise."

Our foreheads rest together, slightly damp with sweat.

"That was really good," I mumble with a satisfied sigh of my own. I try to nestle closer and realize my range of motion is constricted because my top is tangled around my collarbone. With a giggle, I attempt to free myself. "I'm stuck."

"Damn, ginger. You needed it so bad you forgot to take your clothes off?" Chuckling, he leans in to brush his lips over mine. "You're such a bimbo."

This time a whole slew of giggles shudders through me. "Shut up, Gate."

CHAPTER 19

CASSIE

I want my mother to go back to Boston. No, even better—let her go south. I want her to drive all the way down to Florida, find her way to Cape Canaveral, board a rocket ship, get launched into outer space, and make a new life for herself on a distant planet somewhere.

Ugh. All right. Maybe I'm being overdramatic.

Actually, no. You know what? I'm being a perfectly reasonable amount of dramatic.

Since she got here, Mom has been utterly insufferable. And maybe if she were behaving poorly toward only me, I'd have an easier time letting it slide off my shoulders. But she's been bitchier than usual to my grandmother, and that makes me see red. It's inexcusable and Grandma doesn't deserve it. Besides that, it's quite repulsive watching a woman in her forties act like a spoiled brat, which is what Mom is doing when I enter the kitchen for breakfast.

"Mother!" she snaps. "You *have* to give a speech. I'm not letting this go."

"It's no longer our establishment, Victoria. The new owner is the one who should deliver the speech."

"The new owner is a *child*," Mom retorts, lifting her nose up. "And she made the offer. She asked you to do it."

"And I declined."

"Mother."

"Victoria." Grandma's looking increasingly annoyed. "I already declined the offer. The subject is closed."

"This makes our family look bad." Mom, as usual, refuses to drop it. "The Tanners built the Beacon, and a Tanner should be the one to speak at the reopening. Say a proper goodbye. If we say nothing, it looks like we're just handing it over."

"We sold it, dear." Grandma gives her a pointed look. "Primarily because neither you nor your siblings wanted to take on the responsibility of renovating it. So, please, let the new owner reap the rewards of her efforts and enjoy her moment in the sun. I had nothing to do with this reopening and I wouldn't feel comfortable taking any credit for it."

I hide a smile. *Go, Grandma.*

"Good morning, dear." Grandma catches sight of me in the doorway. "Adelaide stopped by the bakery in town this morning and picked up some fresh croissants and pastries."

"Oh, nice." I feel my mother's eyes on me as I go to the counter to assess the goodies our housekeeper brought.

"Just take one," Mom warns. "We have a dress fitting today and you don't want to be bloated for it."

I resist the urge to roll my eyes. "I'll try my best not to eat this entire platter."

Grandma chuckles.

"You slept in," my mother says.

I don't miss her frown of reproach. Awesome. Now my sleeping habits are an issue. I genuinely can't do anything right in her eyes. Well, unless we're in public together. Then suddenly I'm the most wonderful, accomplished, thoughtful daughter in the world. That's the image Mom needs to project. That we're best friends. That my achievements, few as they are at this current time in my life, are all a credit to *her*.

"I had a late night." I duck my head and hope they don't notice my blush, aka the curse of the red hair.

Tate snuck into my bedroom again last night. We hooked up again, and it was better than the first time.

And the second time.

And the third, fourth, fifth . . .

I've seen him every night this week.

Last night, though, was one for the books. He went down on me for almost an hour, his mouth voracious, one hand squeezing and kneading my breasts while the other pushed two fingers inside me. I was biting my lip to stop from being too loud. Tate is very good at what he does.

Truthfully, his breadth of experience is overwhelming sometimes. He's so comfortable, not just with his own body, but mine. There's no hesitation when he touches me, only the confident hands of a man who knows what he's doing.

The one thing he refuses to do, however, is freaking *have sex with me*.

What? Who's bitter?

Okay, fine. I'm not actually bitter. I'm impatient. Tate keeps reminding me we're taking it slow, but part of me wonders if he's still too scared to be my first. Not just because of the supposed pressure, but for what it may mean for us. Peyton concurred with that suspicion when we texted about it earlier. She said men are terrified women will immediately expect promise rings and *I love you*s once they lose it to a guy. I told Tate I wasn't expecting a relationship out of this, but I have a feeling he doesn't trust that.

"Yes. It did sound like a late night for you." Grandma's voice interrupts my thoughts. "I heard you talking long past midnight. You had a friend over?" she prompts, looking like she's fighting a smile.

Shit. I thought we were being quiet, but evidently not.

"No, I didn't have anyone over," I lie. And there's no way Grandma could've seen him last night, since Tate still insists on climbing through the window when he comes over, claiming he doesn't want to bump into my family. I think he just enjoys the sneaky element to it. The excitement. What I'm learning about Tate, the more time I spend with him, is how much he loves leaning into his playful nature.

"I was just watching a movie," I add. "I didn't realize I had the volume on so loud. I'm sorry if it woke you."

Her eyes sparkle. I know she knows I'm lying. "My mistake. Well, then you really ought to lower that volume, dear."

Mom, of course, believes my lies. "Of course she didn't have anyone over, Mother. So late at night?"

In Mom's mind, there's no way her daughter could possibly have a guy over. Which is ironic since supposedly I look like a bimbo, soooo, apropos to *her* logic, there should be a line outside my bedroom door.

I grab a plate and a croissant, then reach for the butter. I expect a comment from Mom about going easy on the butter, but it doesn't come. She's busy checking her phone now.

I join them at the table, my own phone coming to life the moment I sit down. I peer at it, anticipation dancing through me when I notice the email subject line.

"Ahh! The printer sent me the digital proof!" I tell Grandma.

Mom looks up and asks, "What proof?" at which point I remember I hadn't told her about my foray into the world of children's book authorship. Wasn't planning on it, either.

But it's too late now.

"Oh, it's no big deal," I say, downplaying the project. "I put together a little illustrated book for Roxanne and Monique. You know, for their birthday." I shrug. "It's cute. I wrote the story, and asked Robb to do the illustrations—"

Shit.

What the hell is wrong with me? I'm two for two now with boneheaded slipups.

"Robb?" Mom is visibly displeased. "Robb Sheffield?"

"Yeah." I tear a piece off my croissant and shove it into my mouth. Maybe if I'm chewing she'll stop questioning me.

"I didn't realize you two kept in touch."

"Oh. Yes. Here and there."

"Here and there," she echoes.

"Uh-huh." I chew extra slowly. "We exchange the occasional message on social media, just to say what's up."

Her lips flatten as she picks up her coffee cup. "You know how I feel about that, Cassie."

Well, too frickin' bad. You can't give me a stepbrother for five years and then expect me to never speak to him again just because you got another divorce.

I don't say that out loud.

Honestly, though, I genuinely liked the man Mom remarried. Stuart Sheffield. Filthy rich, of course. I mean, with a name like that, of course he's wealthy. Stu was more serious than my dad, stricter as well, but he was kind. Sucks that he fell for my mother's Ms. Congeniality act, but I don't blame him for that. She's very skilled at charming people. And seeing as how the world revolves around her, the moment she decided Stu and Robb didn't exist, I was expected to follow suit.

"It's not a big deal," I repeat. "Not like Robb and I are vacationing together in the Hamptons. I just asked him to do a few drawings for me."

"And what's this, you're writing a children's book now?" She sounds irritated. "That's what my big, fancy college tuition check is going toward?"

"It's just a birthday present. The twins love the bedtime stories I make up for them. Dad suggested I put one in a book."

"Of course he did."

I grit my teeth, then force myself to release the tension in my jaw.

It tightens right back up when Mom coolly inquires, "And what is your father's nurse planning for the birthday celebrations?"

"Victoria," my grandmother snaps.

"What?" She flicks up an eyebrow.

"I thought I instilled better manners in you than that."

"Seriously, Mother? You're siding with Clayton's trophy wife?"

I swallow a laugh, because Nia is the furthest thing from a trophy wife. Nia doesn't care about image, about money, about clothes, about status. She's everything that my mother isn't.

"There's a party for the twins during the day," I say, ignoring the jab about Nia. "All their friends will be there. And afterward we're having dinner, just the five of us." Then, since I anticipate a bitchy comment about being left out of her own daughter's momentous twenty-first birthday, I add, "You and I are still going to Charleston that weekend, right? Spending all of Sunday there? I'm so excited for that."

Making it about her has the desired effect. She smiles warmly. "I'm looking forward to it too." She rises from her chair. "Anyway. We have the fitting in an hour, and I'd like to get there a bit early. Will you be ready to leave after you eat?"

"Yup."

"Okay, great. I need to make a phone call before we go." She saunters out of the kitchen.

I don't know why, but I have a feeling she's off to call my

former stepfather to gripe about the fact that their kids are still in contact.

And speaking of that . . . I quickly click on the email and open the attachment.

"Let me see too," Grandma urges, so I drag my chair closer to hers and together we *ooh* and *aah* over the final product. "Oh, Cassie, you did a tremendous job."

"It was a team effort." I'm not being humble—it really had been. I wrote the story. Robb did the drawings. And Peyton, who works for a graphic design firm in Boston, put together the layout that I sent to the printer.

I pinch the screen to zoom in on an illustration. Robb's creative interpretation of Kit the dragon is remarkable. Somehow, he found the perfect balance between scary and cutesy. He brought Kit to life.

"He is so talented," I marvel. "They look like real characters, don't they?"

"They are real characters. You created them, dear."

"I know, but now I can *see* them. This is so cool." I feel myself beaming.

"There's that smile." Grandma leans over and tucks a strand of hair behind my ear. "Cassandra . . ." Her voice softens. "I know your mother is . . . difficult. To say the least. I hope you don't hold some of the things she says too close to your heart. And I want you to know that I'm proud of you. I'm proud of the woman you're becoming and I think you are absolutely wonderful."

I blink back tears. I didn't know it, but that's exactly what I needed to hear this morning.

CHAPTER 20

TATE

"That was incredible!" Riley exclaims. The teenager's face is flushed with excitement as he helps me tie off the line. We just got back from a double-handed sail on the practice dinghy. It was windier than anticipated today, so we caught some major speed. Also ended up in the bay more times than I would've liked, but you've got to be prepared for that in competitive racing. That's why I love it so much. Always guaranteed a wild ride.

"I can't believe how fast we were going," the kid gushes.

"That was awesome," I agree, hopping onto the pier.

"When can we take the Optimist out?"

I snicker. "Yeah, hold your horses, kid. Not until you have a few more lessons under your belt." The boat we used today is far easier to handle. She's stable and basically unsinkable, whereas the Optimist dinghy capsizes easily.

"It's hard to right the Optimist," I remind him.

Riley's quick to protest. "I can handle it."

I study him for a moment. He looks back hopefully, shoving his blond shoulder-length surfer-boy hair behind his ear.

I shake my head. "No. You can't. Not yet. But soon."

"I'm telling Evan," he threatens with an evil grin. "I'll turn on the waterworks and cry about how sad I am that my Big Brother's best friend is depriving me of my dream of racing on an Optimist."

I respond with a loud snort. The kid's got balls, I'll give him that. Riley is the product of the soul-searching journey of reformation Evan decided to embark on a while ago. In other words, Evan needed to prove to Genevieve he was willing to stop being a boozing, brawling jackass and grow the fuck up. One way he did that was by enrolling in the local Big Brother program. He totally lucked out with Riley, who's a great kid.

"All right," I tell him. "Next lesson, we'll practice positioning at different angles, teach you some racing tactics. There're a couple different strategies you can use when rounding marks. And the next race you enter, don't partner with Evan. He's lousy."

Riley hoots. "No shit."

"If you're doing a double-handed race and need a partner, hit me up. I mean it—drop the zero and get with the hero." I wink at him.

I don't offer myself up like that to just anyone, but I like Riley. I like his enthusiasm. A lot of these kids who take dinghy lessons just want to go fast on the water. They don't want to think too deeply about the ins and outs of sailing. But Riley's different. He's thirsty for knowledge.

I clap him on the back. My favorite part of this job is working with the kids. The teens. Adults are fun too, but their eyes don't light up the same way.

"I'll see you next week."

"Cool. Later, Tate."

He dashes off, and I head back in the direction from which we came to double-check the boat is securely moored, as the wind's still blowing hard. Sometimes it sucks working on other people's boats; I'm always scared I'll fuck something up and be on the hook for it.

In the yacht club's employee quarters, I strip out of my damp uniform and change into my street clothes. A few minutes later, I cross the parking lot toward my Jeep, checking my phone while I walk. I find a couple messages from the twins. And one from Cassie.

> Cassie: *You, me, a bed covered in rose petals, and my virginity on a silver platter?*

I bust out laughing. I swear, this chick . . . Since the night we agreed to the fling, she's been persistently trying to get me to bang her.

> Me: *No.*

She instantly replies.

> Cassie: *You're mean.*
> Me: *Just taking it slow. Window time later?*
> Cassie: *Can't. You took too long to reply to my message, so I made plans with Joy. We're going to see a band at the Rip Tide. It'll probably be past your bedtime when I'm back.*
> Me: *Text me anyway. Maybe I'll still be up.*
> Cassie: *Only if you take the V-card.*
> Me: *Anyone ever tell you you've got a one-track mind, ginger?*
> Cassie: *Anyone ever tell you you're a tease?*
> Me: *Who's teasing? I'm pretty sure I made you come twice last night.*
> Cassie: *I was faking it, Gate.*

I grin at the phone and toss it on the passenger seat, then start the car. I can't believe I'm the one depriving someone of sex. Me, of all people. But despite Cassie's insistence that we don't need to make a big deal out of it, I feel like I should do something for her first time. Something special. Maybe not rose petals, but certainly not a quick bang while her family is right down the hall. That just feels wrong. It's all I would've been able to offer her this week, though. I've had early mornings, a packed sailing schedule, and late shifts at the dealership. Which means I'm always exhausted by the time I scale her wall and tumble through her window for an hour or so of mutual orgasms. Exhaustion is not conducive to good sex, and since I'm determined to make sure her first time is beyond good, I've been trying to stall her until the weekend.

Unbeknownst to Cassie, I took Saturday off. I'm planning to take her out on the water for the day. Anchor at my favorite cove. Spend the night . . .

My heart beats faster, and my palms suddenly feel slick around the steering wheel. Jeez. You'd think *I* was the virgin here.

At the Jackson house, I start prepping dinner. I throw a couple baked potatoes in the oven, then pop outside to turn on the barbecue. I'm doing shrimp skewers on the grill tonight. It's too bad Cassie's out with Joy. Would've been nice to cook dinner for her.

I falter, wondering where *that* thought came from. Cook dinner for her? I'm pretty sure I've never made dinner for a woman other than my mother. I force myself not to overthink it, though.

While the barbecue's heating up, I head to the dock to ensure the boats are secure because it's still so windy out. Then I walk back up to the house, reaching it just as Cassie's mother appears around the side of their house. She's clad in a long summer dress with sunglasses atop her head.

"Hi." I lift my hand in a wave. Honestly, I'm surprised it's taken this long for our paths to cross. It's been days since she arrived in town, but it seems she spends most of her time inside the house. Or shopping in Charleston, according to Cassie.

She startles at the sight of me. Eyes widening.

"Sorry, I didn't mean to scare you," I call out. "I'm Tate. I'm housesitting for the Jacksons. And I'm friends with your daughter."

Cassie's mom still hasn't spoken. Just keeps staring at me. I note the resemblance between her and Cassie, in their wide-set brown eyes and red hair, but while Cassie has a rounder face, her mother's is narrower, giving off a different vibe. Colder. Or maybe that's her personality.

She shakes herself out of her surprise and offers a smile far warmer than I expect. "Oh hello. I'm sorry. I was in my head. I'm Victoria." She stretches out an arm. "You can call me Tori."

I stride forward to shake her hand. "Nice to meet you."

"How long are you housesitting for?" Tori asks, her appreciative gaze still fixed on me.

Yeah. She's totally checking me out. Which is awkward as fuck, considering I'm hooking up with her daughter. "Gil and Shirley return Labor Day weekend, so I still have another month here."

"Lucky you."

"Yeah, it's not a bad gig," I admit. "It's my fourth summer doing it. I look forward to it every year now."

The Jacksons don't pay me much while I'm here—I'm responsible for my own food, gas, all the usual expenses—but I don't do it for the money. It's worth it to get out of my parents' house for a couple months. Living at home at the age of twenty-three cramps my style sometimes, but at the moment it's convenient, allowing me to save more money. Save up enough and eventually I can finance a boat that I'll probably call home.

"Anyway, I've got dinner going, so I need to check on it. Have a good evening, Mrs. Tanner."

"Tori," she corrects.

"Tori," I repeat clumsily.

She smiles. "It was nice to meet you, Tate. Don't be a stranger."

Inside, I find a missed call from Gil Jackson. Frowning, I quickly do the math, then realize it's not a cause for concern. With the time difference, he's sixteen hours ahead of me, making it 9 A.M. in Auckland.

I check on the baked potatoes, then return Gil's call.

"Hey, Gil," I say after he picks up. "Sorry I missed your call. I was outside chatting with the neighbor."

"Oh, how is Lydia?"

"She's good. But I was talking to her daughter. Tori?"

"You mean Victoria Tanner?" he asks in amusement.

"She said to call her Tori."

His laughter, a deep baritone, sounds in my ear. "Oh boy. I think someone has a crush on you," Gil jokes.

"No," I groan. "Don't even kid about that. Anyway, what's up? Everything okay?"

"Everything's great here. I wanted to check in and see how things are going on your end, discuss a couple matters. We haven't touched base in a few days."

"All good here too," I assure him. "I was just down at the dock securing the boats. The wind was really gusting on the bay today, and it's supposed to storm tonight."

"Thank you. Have you taken the Lightning out yet?"

My dick actually twitches. "What? Oh. No. I haven't even touched her."

"Are you crazy? Take her out for a ride!"

"Are you sure?" I gulp. "I mean, she's super expensive." Alarmingly expensive. The idea of anything happening to her makes me nauseous.

"Tate. Son. You can handle a boat better than anyone I know. Take her out. Enjoy yourself. I promise you, it's a thrill like nothing you've ever experienced."

I don't doubt it.

"In fact," he says, "your sailing expertise is the other reason I called."

I crinkle my forehead. "How's that?"

"Shirley and I just closed on a house down here."

"You did? Congratulations." My brain is scrambling to connect those two dots. What my sailing ability has to do with them purchasing a house in New Zealand. "Are you leaving the Bay?"

"No, no, but we will be splitting our time going forward. Half the year in Auckland, the other half in Avalon Bay. Shirley loves it down here, and the house we found is breathtaking. It's on a bluff overlooking the ocean. Just magnificent. We want to do some sailing while we're here. Cross the Tasman to Australia, explore the Gold Coast, see the Great Barrier Reef. Which means I need someone to bring the *Surely Perfect* over."

I'm startled. My gaze immediately travels beyond the French doors to the sailboat at the dock before I remember she's not the boat in question. The *Surely Perfect* is at the yacht club. And he wants someone to sail her?

"Bring her over?" I echo. "You mean to New Zealand?"

"Yes. Gotta hire someone to sail her. Shirley and I were discussing it last night, and she says, why not Tate, he has his captain's license. And I thought about it and realized, yes, why not? That boy could handle a solo voyage in his sleep."

I feel winded. I flop onto a kitchen stool, shrimp skewers forgotten on the counter. "I don't know about *in my sleep*," I say slowly. "But . . . yeah, I could probably manage it. How long would a journey like that take?" I'm playing it cool, but this would be a massive undertaking.

"It's a long way, no doubt. You'd be leaving from the Port of Miami, and according to the folks I consulted, if you're averaging eight to ten knots and the weather permits, you could do it in two months—I would help you chart out a course that makes the most sense for you. The wife and I are returning to the Bay next month and we'll be here through the holidays. Planning to return to Auckland in January," Gil continues, "which means we'd need her down here by New Year's. So, realistically, you could set sail in September if you wanted. Take three months. Four, even. It's entirely up to you."

I shake my head, dazed. "Are you serious right now?" I demand.

He laughs. "Quite serious. And, of course, you'll be paid accordingly." He proceeds to name a sum that makes my head spin. It's enough to put a down payment on a sailboat of my own. Not a Hallberg-Rassy, but definitely something higher end.

"You'll also have a credit card for expenses, so if you need to restock any supplies when you make port, it'll all be covered. Your only concern will be getting our girl from point A to point B."

"Can I think about it?" Obviously, I want nothing more than to shout out *yes!* But I can't just drop my entire life and sail to New Zealand. I have a job, responsibilities. Especially to my family. I hate letting Dad down. And I literally just agreed to run the dealership alone so my parents can take September off.

"Take your time," Gil says. "You can let me know the weekend we get back. If it's a no, that still leaves us plenty of time to hire somebody else. There's a company we can use that hooks you up with a captain. But we'd prefer to see you do it. I know you've always wanted to do a major crossing, and, selfishly, I'd rather pay someone I like and trust than a complete stranger."

"Wow. Thank you, Gil. I mean it. I really appreciate the opportunity."

"Of course, son. And don't forget to take the Lightning out for a spin." He chuckles. "You'll thank me for it later."

CHAPTER 21

CASSIE

Aaron: *Hey stranger.*

I stare at the screen, my stomach dropping. I'm parked in front of the post office and was about to get out of the Rover when his message came in. Aaron's been trying to get together all week. I keep turning him down, claiming to be busy with my mother. Which isn't exactly a lie; since she got in, she's monopolized all my time. Still, I can't deny it's been a relief to have a legitimate excuse to avoid hanging out with him. The moment Tate and I started hooking up, I all but forgot about Aaron. That makes me kind of a jerk, I know that. It's just so difficult to tell him I'm no longer interested.

But I also can't keep putting him off. He's going back to New York next week. I don't want him spending his last week sitting around waiting for me.

Unsure how best to phrase it, I text Peyton instead.

Me: *I need to tell Aaron I don't want to see him anymore, but I need to say it in a nice way. Suggestions?*

She must be right by her phone because her response is instantaneous. Or rather, her respon*ses*. As usual, six messages pop up in quick succession.

Peyton: *All right, this is what I always say:*
Peyton: *Hey! I've had so much fun hanging out with you, but I kind of see this as more of a friendship thing.*
Peyton: *I'm not really feeling a romantic spark.*
Peyton: *You're so awesome, and I know you're going to find someone you totally click with.*
Peyton: *I just don't think it's me.*
Me: *Wow. Not bad. Thanks!*

I do a bit of tweaking, copy and paste, then take a deep breath and hit send. Instantly, I get that weak feeling in my stomach and my heart starts pounding. The idea of an impending confrontation makes me queasy, but at the same time I experience a pang of pride. I may not be able to tell Aaron he's a terrible kisser, or tell my mother how much I hate her sometimes, but at least I was able to accomplish this one teeny, tiny thing. There's the silver lining, I guess.

I try to focus on that feeling of pride, but the nervous energy doesn't abate. It continues to wreak havoc on my gut as I approach the pickup counter at the post office.

"Hi," I greet the elderly clerk. "I need to pick up a package for Cassie Soul? I got a notice on my door saying they dropped it off here because nobody was home to sign." I hand him the notice.

"Let me go check." The gray-haired man shuffles into the back room.

While I wait, my phone buzzes in my hand. Aaron's name appears on the lock screen. The nausea returns. All I can see from the notification preview is: *Thanks for being honest. I really—*

Then it cuts off.

Oh God. *I really* what? Optimism eludes me as my brain fills in the blanks with all the worst-case scenarios.

I really hate you.

I really think you're a bitch.

I really hate that you wasted my time.

I click the notification.

Aaron: *Thanks for being honest. I really appreciate it. So many people just ghost these days. Thanks for being so cool.*

Relief flitters through me. Wow. Okay. That went way better than expected.

Me: *Thanks for understanding. You're really cool too.*

Aaron: *Enjoy the rest of your summer, Cassie.*

Me: *You too.*

Just like that, I handled the confrontation with such ease I almost want to call Tate and brag. Then I realize how weird that would be, considering I haven't brought up Aaron since Tate and I got together. And I don't want him to think I'm still seeing other guys.

"Here you are!" The postal clerk returns with a thin cardboard box. "Sign here, please."

My entire body vibrates with excitement as I get back into the car, where I tear open the package. I reach inside. The next thing I know, I'm holding the physical manifestation of *Kit 'n McKenna*. It's a hardcover, the front image featuring the titular characters, and it looks and feels incredible. Even more astonishing is the byline at the top.

WRITTEN BY CASSANDRA SOUL

At the bottom is a second listing:

ILLUSTRATED BY ROBB SHEFFIELD

Squealing out loud, I quickly snap a picture and text it to my former stepbrother.

Me: *LOOK!!!!*
Robb: *Holy shit!*
Me: *I had a second copy printed and shipped to the penthouse. You should receive it end of day tomorrow.*
Robb: *This is so cool. Thanks for including me. Imagine this takes off??*
Me: *What do you mean? We're not actually selling it lol*
Robb: *Why the hell not?*
Me: *It's just a present for my sisters.*
Robb: *Umm . . . Okay, we need to get on a call to discuss it. This could be a missed opportunity, Cass.*
Robb: *I'm away this weekend, heading to the Montauk house, but how about Monday? You free to chat?*
Me: *Sure. Sounds good.*

My head is spinning like a carousel now. I didn't plan on selling this book at all. Dad made that throwaway comment about self-publishing or submitting it to a publisher, but I'd brushed it off. Becoming a children's book author was never at the top of my career choice list. But now I've got a hardback copy of *Kit 'n McKenna* in my hands, and it looks *real*. Sharp, professional. This printer did an exceptional job. The pages are glossy, and the interior illustrations are gorgeous. As I flip through and read lines from the story, I find myself grinning like a silly schoolgirl. This is good. It's really, really good.

So why not? Why not try to make something happen? Turn this project into something other children can enjoy, not just my sisters. I suppose next weekend's birthday unveiling will be the real test. If Roxy and Mo love the book, that bodes well for the prospective success of this venture.

My phone buzzes again while I'm reading.

Joy: *Is that you sitting in the Range Rover giggling to yourself like an escaped mental patient?*

I look up and spot her by the smoothie shop. She gives a nonchalant wave.

Rolling my eyes, I hop out of the Rover and dart over to my friend. "Check this out!" I shove the hardcover into her hand.

"Ooooh!" Her eyes light up. "This is amazing!"

"Do you think the girls will like it?" I ask anxiously.

"Are you kidding? They're going to love it. I think a lot of kids would love it, actually." She flips through it, then stops on one page in particular. She giggles and twists it around to show me the visual of McKenna trying to jam her secret dragon into a too-small cupboard. In the next panel, the doors bust open and Kit bursts out in a flurry of purple scales. "This is great. I would read this to my little cousins."

"Robb wants to talk about publishing it properly—"

"Do it!" Joy says immediately.

I bite my lip as tiny ripples of excitement dance in my stomach. "I'll have to think about it."

"What's there to think about?"

"A lot. I'm about to start senior year of college. I don't have time to think about publishing children's books on the side." I shrug. "Anyway, what are you up to now? Want to grab lunch?"

"This is lunch." She holds up her gross-looking green juice. "But

230 • ELLE KENNEDY

I'll come and watch you eat." She waggles her eyebrows. "Sounds hot."

I snicker. "That's something Tate would say." I tuck the book under my arm and nod at the smoothie place. "I'll just grab a smoothie too. Treat me? I left my purse in the car."

"Jeez. So demanding."

We go in, and a moment later we're at the end of the counter, waiting for my order to be prepared.

"Did you see Tate when you got back last night?" she asks.

"Yes," I answer, thinking about the brief encounter. Joy and I left the Rip Tide around midnight, and despite needing to wake up early, Tate still snuck in through my window . . . to kiss me good night. Yup, just a kiss. I swear, he's the biggest tease I've ever met.

"I can't believe you still haven't been fully naked together," Joy says, marveling over what I told her last night at the show.

"It's weird, right? It's like he thinks if we have all our clothes off, his penis will accidently fall into my vagina."

She hoots. "Maybe he's a virgin too."

"Definitely not. Honestly, I think he's scared to deflower me. He's moving at a snail's pace. It's maddening."

"Then let's give him a nudge."

"What kind of nudge?"

"Um. Seduce the guy, Cass."

"How?"

"What do you mean, how?" She looks amused by my total lack of seduction proficiency. "There are *so* many options."

"Name one," I challenge. "Because it sounds like you don't actually know—"

"Sneak into his house and be naked in his bed when he comes back from work." Joy offers a self-satisfied smile. "There. That's one suggestion."

"I can't sneak into the house," I protest. I step up to the counter to take my banana-strawberry smoothie, courtesy of the teenage employee who just placed it on the counter. "There's an alarm."

"Really, that's what you're focused on?" she says as we step back onto the sidewalk. "You can find ways around it. Text him and say, *hey, where's your spare key? I need to pop over to your place to borrow some sugar.*" She tilts her head. "That's a neighbor thing, right? They always need sugar."

I snort. "Okay, I'll play. So I text him, tell him I need something from his house. And then?"

"You get naked. You lie on his bed. Instead of flowers, you cover yourself in a sea of condoms—"

"Oh my God." I start to laugh. "No."

"Fine, no condom décor. But I stand by the rest. Trust me, if he walks into his bedroom and finds you lying there naked? He won't be resisting you anymore."

I mull over the idea. Honestly, it does sound kind of hot. Exciting. And it'll be hot and exciting even if we don't end up having sex.

"I don't know if I can be naked," I admit, lifting my straw to my lips. I take a long sip of fruity goodness. "But maybe lingerie?"

"*Yes!* Even better! We need something positively slutty! Okay. Go get your purse." Joy has snapped into dictator mode. "We're going shopping."

* * *

Later that night, Grandma and Mom embark on a rare outing together, heading to Charleston for dinner. I think it was Grandma's idea, her attempt at giving me a reprieve.

Mom's been on my case all week, roping me into numerous shopping excursions, painful lunches, and constant criticism.

232 • ELLE KENNEDY

Mostly directed at my fashion choices, but she's also been throwing in complaints about Dad, Nia, and my friendship with Robb, just to keep me on my toes. The main reason she's bent out of shape, though, is because I refused to go along with her dress suggestion for the Beacon's reopening. I vetoed the floor-length gold gown on sight, which, in hindsight, may have been a mistake seeing as how it led to several more shopping trips to find another dress.

With my family gone the house is completely empty, so there's no reason Tate can't come over here, but the idea of him finding me in his own bed is a lot more appealing. More of a sexy shock for him. He's done working at seven today. He had to stay late so his dad could train him in some payroll matters, but said he'd be home by seven thirty. I told him I'd cook him dinner.

What he doesn't know is that we're having dessert first.

Me: *Hey. What's the keypad code to get in through your back door? I need to steal some spices. Can you believe we ran out of both salt and red pepper?*

Tate: *If I tell you the code, you can never share it with anyone.*

Me: *Of course not. I was only planning to post it on Twitter, not any of my other social media accounts. Keep it exclusive, you know?*

Tate: *Perfect. 25591. I'm on my way home now. Grabbing a quick shower and then I'll head over to you.*

Excellent.

I'm all ready to go. I shaved my entire body, so it's smoother and softer than a baby's bottom. I chose the color white for the lacy bra and matching thong I picked up in town earlier. According to the saleswoman, the official shade of it is honest-to-God called *virginal white*. Once I heard that, I would've bought the lingerie set for the comedy appeal alone. Thankfully, I look great in white. When I stepped out of the dressing room, Joy and the saleswoman assured me no man would be able to keep his hands off me.

There's really only one man I care about tonight.

I give my reflection one last inspection in the hall mirror. I've straightened my hair and am wearing it loose. No makeup, save for some lip gloss and light mascara. Definitely no blush, because I'll be doing that naturally anyway. It's my cross to bear. I don't even keep blush in my makeup case.

Since I can't strut next door in my underwear, I throw a loose tank dress over my head and slip my feet into a pair of flip-flops. I walk the path at the side of our houses toward the Jacksons' back deck, where I punch in the code on the door, and the lock releases.

Tate's been keeping the place super clean. I like that. I head for the wide spiral staircase in the front hall that's painted a nautical blue and features white wainscoting. At the top of the stairs, I get an idea. I dart back to the hall and kick one flip-flop off, leaving it on the hardwood floor. I leave the other flip-flop on the first step. My dress halfway up the stairs. Grinning at the little trail I've created, I head for the guest room where Tate's been staying.

His bed is made and the duvet smells good, like fabric softener and Tate's unique, masculine scent, which always makes me think of the ocean. I'm not surprised everything is so neat and tidy. He told me he picked up the habit at Scouts' camp. Because of course he was a Boy Scout. Apparently his dad was his troop leader, which also doesn't surprise me. Gavin Bartlett is the epitome of *fun dad*.

Speaking of Gavin, Tate said his parents had invited me over for dinner. So far, I've been putting it off. Dinner with his parents would make it feel like we're seriously dating, and I'm trying to keep a proper distance there. I know this is just a fling. I'm returning to Boston at the end of the summer, and it's not like long-distance relationships ever work. Besides, I already told him I don't want a relationship, and Tate doesn't want one either. He's simply having fun. We both are.

My heart rate spikes when I finally hear the front door open. The alarm beeps a few times, then stops once Tate arms it.

His muffled voice says, "What the . . ." and I smother a grin. Someone's spotted my abandoned flip-flops and dress.

"Cassie?" he calls warily.

Footsteps approach the stairs.

"Up here!" I tell him.

"Oh, thank God." His voice gets louder. "I was worried I was going to find you murdered up there."

I choke out a laugh. "Why would a murderer take the time to arrange my clothing in a trail?"

I hear him approaching the bedroom door. "I don't know. To fuck with my head and—" Tate halts in the doorway. His Adam's apple bobs when he spots me. Eyes instantly blazing. "Holy hell." He shakes his head. "Wow."

"What?" I ask innocently.

"Don't *what* me. You look . . ." He swallows again. "So . . . fucking . . . good."

His hungry eyes devour my body, which I've posed pinup style just for him. One knee propped. Head resting on his pillows and back arched, a position that makes my boobs jut out enticingly. It's rare for me to put the girls on display like this, but I love the way he's looking at them right now.

A cheeky smile springs free. "Are you just going to stand there and stare, or are you going to take your clothes off?" I inquire.

Without a word, Tate reaches for the hem of his shirt.

"Good choice."

Chuckling, he pulls his shirt off, revealing that tanned, muscular chest. "What did I do to deserve this?" he asks, and I don't know if it's a rhetorical question.

"Do you like?" I toy with the tiny lace bow on my bra, flashing a coy smile.

"I love."

He undoes his pants, shoving the material down. Boxers disappear next. Now he's naked, his erection out and proud.

He takes a step forward.

"Still want to take it slow?" I taunt.

"Don't know if that's possible," he growls, and then he's on the bed, covering my body with his.

Our lips meet, and it gets hot and dirty real fast. Greedy kissing and impatient hands running over each other's bodies. Tate makes no effort to remove my lingerie. He lifts his head, breathing hard, then kisses my breast over my bra.

"This is so sexy," he groans. His fingertips slim over the lacy edge. "Solid choice with white."

I'm pleased he approves.

Slowly, his hand glides along my stomach toward the delicate straps of my thong. "Goddamn," he croaks. "I don't even want to take these off you. The bra too. I want to fuck you while you're wearing them." He strokes my clit over the panties, and a rush of pleasure skitters through me.

His erection is heavy against my thigh, an erotic reminder of what I'm about to experience. I can't wait. Swallowing through my dry throat, I reach for him, circling his shaft with my fingers and—

The doorbell rings.

We both jump in surprise. "Are you expecting someone?" I ask him.

"No, not that I—" He cuts off. His face, which only a second ago was flushed, suddenly pales.

Then his phone chimes.

"Shit," Tate curses. He practically dives off the bed and grabs the phone from his pants pocket. He lets out another expletive when he reads the text.

"What's going on?" I sit up. For some reason, I instinctively lower one arm to cover my breasts, which are nearly overflowing from my skimpy bra cups.

The doorbell rings again.

"Who is that?" I demand.

He raises his head from his phone, features pained. "My date."

CHAPTER 22

TATE

Before I can blink, Cassie is off the bed and sprinting to the door.

"Cass, wait."

"Are you fucking kidding me?" she shouts back without turning around.

I grab my discarded boxers and hurriedly pull them on. I reach the doorway just as she makes it to the top of the staircase. Christ, her ass looks phenomenal in those cheeky panties. Her tits are practically spilling out of that bra, more so now that she's breathing so hard. A moment ago, I was about to devour her. Now I'm chasing after her to keep her from leaving.

She picks up the dress that's lying on the stairs, slipping it over her head as she descends. I hurry after her.

The doorbell rings again, making me wince.

I totally forgot about Nicole. I'm an asshole, I know. But I made the date last Sunday while I was trying not to think about Cassie and then forgot to call it off because I've had a busy week.

"I cannot believe you have another woman coming over tonight!" Cassie's murderous gaze eviscerates me. "What was the plan, exactly? You were going to meet her first, and me right after? Or go back and forth between the houses like Hannah fucking

Montana pretending to be in two places at once? Did I spoil your little plot by coming over here instead?"

"No, not at all," I say, reaching the bottom of the staircase.

She puts on her flip-flops and marches to the front door.

"Cassie, come on, wait. Can I please explain?"

"No," she barks, then flings the door open to reveal the startled face of Nicole.

"Oh, I'm sorry," Nicole hedges in. "Am I interrupting . . . ?"

"Nope," Cassie replies as she storms past. "He's all yours," she calls over her shoulder.

In completely misery, I watch her go.

"Fuck!" I groan, scrubbing my hands over my face. I briefly close my eyes, sucking in a frustrated breath. Then my eyes open, only to be confronted with the cloud of displeasure darkening Nicole's face.

"Uh, yeah, it's pretty obvious I did interrupt something. What the hell, Tate?"

"I'm sorry." I exhale a heavy breath. "I forgot you were coming over."

"Are you fucking serious?"

"I'm sorry." Shame now pours off me by the bucketload. "I started seeing someone this week—"

"Clearly," Nicole interrupts, jaw tightening.

"She and I were just friends when I asked you out, but then it turned into something more and I forgot to cancel with you. I'm sorry. I'm such an asshole. Honestly, I need you to hit me right now. Just clock me in the jaw. Please." I groan again. "You know I don't do this. I never play around with women. Ever. I'm so, so sorry."

She must recognize my sincerity—and immense remorse—because her face softens. "Dude. Dial it down. It's not like we just got married and you cheated on me on our honeymoon."

I spit out a weak laugh. "No, but this is a dick move."

"It is. I won't deny that." She runs a hand through her dark hair. "Can't say I'm not disappointed, either. I was looking forward to this all week."

"I'm sorry," I repeat through a lump of guilt.

"You're lucky you have a rep for being a good guy. I know you don't pull this shit with women."

"I don't," I moan. "I don't think I've ever felt this bad in my life. I can't apologize enough."

Nicole fiddles with the sleeve of her tight top. "I'm really embarrassed," she admits.

"Please don't be. This is all on me."

"Well, obviously. But that doesn't change the fact that I just walked in on—you know what, it's fine. Let's just forget it."

I search her expression. "Are we good?"

"Yeah, we're good." Sighing, she steps closer and gives me a little pat on the shoulder. "But I think you owe her an apology too. And I should probably let you get to that."

I still feel like shit as I walk Nicole to her car. Once she drives off, I glance toward Cassie's front porch. I don't want to go and ring the doorbell because I'm not sure if her mom and grandmother are home. But I also don't want to climb up to her window for fear she'll push me to my death.

Dismissing both options, I go back inside to get my phone.

Me: *Meet me out back so we can talk? Please?*

Part of me expects radio silence, but Cassie responds.

Cassie: *Date #2 is over already? Does someone have a stamina problem?*

And people say you can't discern tone over text.

Me: *It's really not what you think. Please. Just come outside?*
Cassie: *Fine.*

She meets me on the dock. Arms crossed, eyes apoplectic. She's wearing her dress, and now that I know what's underneath it I want to kick myself harder for forgetting to cancel with Nicole, because there's no way I'm seeing a single thread of that lingerie again tonight. Even if we do make up, the moment has passed.

"I made the date with her on Sunday," I explain. "After you and I . . . you know. Window sex."

Cassie nods, mouth flattening. "I think that might make it worse."

"I was trying to avoid temptation. I thought maybe if I found a distraction, I'd be able to see you again without being tempted to blow up our friendship. So when Nicole asked me out, I said yes. And then I got home that night and overheard you and your mom, and, well, you know what that led to." I gnaw on the inside of my cheek. "I screwed up. You and I have been hooking up all week, and I've been swamped with work, and I honestly just forgot to let her know the date was off."

"That is *such* a dick move. Especially to her."

"Trust me, I know. I just spent the past ten minutes begging her forgiveness. And now I'm begging yours." I meet Cassie's eyes. I know she hears the heartfelt note in my voice. "I don't juggle women. I might sleep with a lot of them, but never at the same time. Ask anyone who knows me—I don't play games. That's not who I am. You *know* that's not who I am, Cassie. I'm a Boy Scout. I'm the one who asked to get grounded. My parents raised me to treat women with respect. That's why I was afraid I'd be taking advantage of your inexperience."

She bites her lip in hesitation. "If you didn't want to be exclusive, you could've just told me."

"That's not it at all." I frown. "It didn't even cross my mind to not be exclusive. I assumed we were."

"Really?"

"I told you, I don't date more than one person."

"*Are* we dating?"

"Flinging. Hooking up. Whatever you want to call it."

My body is tight with frustration, because I can't quite explain how any of this makes me feel. All I know is the sheer panic, the helplessness that was squeezing my throat when Cassie stormed out and I thought I might never see her again.

"I like you," I say gruffly. "I have a great time with you. I'm wildly attracted to you. And I don't want to ever do anything that makes you look at me like that again. Like I was total slime."

She draws a breath. "When I thought you had another date . . . another girl lined up, or maybe even a whole roster of them . . . it upset me."

"I know. I'm sorry. I promise I'm not seeing anyone but you." I drag a hand through my hair, offering a rueful smile. "I had a whole thing planned for tomorrow. For you, I mean."

"You did?" Her forehead creases. "You never mentioned anything."

"I was planning on asking you tonight. You know how Gil told me I can use the Lightning? I thought . . ." I shift awkwardly. I don't think I've ever been so tongue-tied around a chick before. "I thought we could go out on the boat. Maybe anchor at Kearny's Cove. You wouldn't think it, but there's a roomy cabin below deck. It's cozy. We could do an overnight . . . ?"

The implication hangs in the air.

Cassie visibly swallows. We both know what will happen if we spend the night alone together in one bed.

"That sounds nice," she finally says, a soft smile tugging on her lips. "I'm in."

I almost sag over in relief. "Perfect. So it's a date."

"Just one date, Tate. Your *only* date of the evening." The humor dancing in her eyes tells me we're good again.

"My only date. Scout's honor."

* * *

"You ready?" I ask the following day, jumping on board the Lightning. I hold my hand out to Cassie. It's late afternoon and we're supposed to be leaving for our overnight, but she remains standing on the dock. Her gaze is focused on the gray and black life vests I set down on the copilot's seat.

"Do we need to wear those the whole time?" she asks warily.

"Only when she's moving. And it's only a precaution."

"Okay, now I'm kind of scared. Just how fast do you plan to go?"

"Fast." I'm practically shaking with excitement. "Gil says she can do 125, 130 miles per hour." I shudder happily. "I'm gonna come in my pants, ginger."

"Should I be jealous? Of the boat, I mean?"

"Probably."

That gets me a laugh. "Fine. Let's go."

I grip her hand to help her in. While she dons her life vest, I stash the cooler below deck, but grab two bottles of water out of it to throw into the cupholders. Once we're seated, I gently steer us away from the dock. Don't want to go all speed demon right from the jump. A bit farther out, I give her more juice. The boat comes to life. Anticipation coils in my gut as I ease the stick forward. When the Lightning's bow rises, Cassie jumps in alarm.

"It's fine," I assure her, and the bow settles. Oh man. This is nuts. Only cruising speed, and she's still going faster than any speedboat I've ever been on.

"Why are we going out so far?" Cassie looks worried the more miles I put between us and land.

"This is a no-wake zone. We need to go just past there, beyond the speed restrictions." I slice forward, cutting around the bend in the bay. Once we're far enough, I slow to a crawl, then idle for a minute. The Lightning gently bobs on the waves. I do a quick assessment. Wind is light, providing no resistance at all. Waves are decent, not too choppy.

I turn to Cassie with a grin. "All right. I'm gonna give it all I've got. All she's got. You ready?"

Cassie takes a breath. "Okay. Do it before I change my mind."

I accelerate and the Lightning takes off.

Cassie yelps, holding on for dear life. And we're not even going that fast yet. Maybe eighty, ninety miles per hour. It's incredible how much the Lightning still has left in her. Adrenaline surges through my blood as I speed up. The wind rushes past our faces, slicking my hair back. Cassie's ponytail hovers in the air like the tail of a kite, sticking straight out. Yet the Lightning is stable. So stable you'd never guess how fast we were going.

Like a little kid, I let out a loud whoop, and turn to see Cassie grinning at me. Then she throws her hands up and whoops too, and we surrender to the speed, the exhilaration. We're about a hundred miles an hour now, but I want more. Just a little bit more. I adjust the trim, play with the throttle, and then we're flying. One hundred and twenty miles an hour, and I'm on another plane of existence. We barely feel the chop. We're fucking soaring, so fast it feels like slow motion. It's unbelievable.

I let her fly for several more miles before slowing. My heartbeat takes a while to regulate. I look over and Cassie's still smiling. Her face is red, cheeks slightly windburned. The hull rocks as I bring us to a not-so-ass-puckering speed.

"That was incredible," I say, still breathing hard.

"You look like you just had an orgasm."

"I feel like I did. I've never piloted anything like her." She's a dream to handle. Tight turns, responsive.

"You should buy one."

I bark out a laugh. "Um, no. This is a million-dollar speedboat. And Gil got it used."

"Holy shit."

"Exactly. I'm saving up for a sailboat, anyway. That comes first. Powerboats are playthings for later in life."

"You're a plaything for later in life," she cracks.

"Nice."

As we cruise toward Kearny's Cove, she fixes her ponytail, which got messed up during the wild ride. I slow us almost to a crawl and grab my water bottle. I gulp down a much-needed swig, then offer it to Cassie, who shakes her head. She's busy examining the cockpit, running a hand over the sleek vinyl upholstery.

She glances around the deck. "How is there a cabin down there? Doesn't seem like there'd be any room on this thing."

"First of all, don't call my girlfriend a thing."

She snorts.

"And the cabin is shockingly spacious. Seriously, you're going to love it."

"Am I now?"

A heated look passes between us. My heart's beating fast again. This time it has nothing to do with the Lightning and everything to do with Cassie Soul. I'm dying to get inside her. I've been thinking about it all goddamn day.

We arrive at Kearny's Cove, a gorgeous private spot that's sheltered by a rock wall so the wind barely touches this part of the bay. There's a beach, albeit a tiny one. A narrow strip of sand, situated between the rock face and the reeds.

"This is such a pretty spot! Is this where we're having dinner?" Cassie asks.

"Yup."

She eyes me. "How many other women have you brought here?"

"None," I answer truthfully.

"Really?"

"Really."

"Why not?"

I shrug. "I guess I've never met anyone I liked enough to bring on a romantic overnight."

"Oooooh, Gate's trying to be romantic, huh?"

"Not anymore," I grumble.

"You didn't do this kind of stuff with Alana?"

"Nope. We only ever hung out at her house. Never even went out to dinner."

I anchor us and grab the cooler from below. Then I kick off my deck shoes and hop into the water. It splashes around my knees, soaking the bottom of my shorts. I deposit the cooler on the beach, then return to help Cassie off the boat.

Dinner consists of grilled chicken, Greek salad, fruit for dessert, and a bottle of champagne that makes Cassie snicker when I pull it out. "Stole that from the club again?"

"Sure did."

I pour her a glass. We're on the blanket I laid out on the sand, lazily eating our dinner while the sun begins its descent toward the horizon light.

"Okay, this is romantic," she relents, admiring the colors streaking across the sky. Brilliant pinks, reds, and oranges. The sunset is almost as pretty as she is.

After dinner, we stick our trash in the cooler and talk over champagne about nothing in particular. Cassie's birthday is next weekend. I offer to take her to dinner, but she has plans both days; dad on Saturday, mom on Sunday. She seems more enthused about the former, but I get the sense she and her stepmother have an awkward relationship, which puts a damper on most family occasions.

Cassie confirms that by adding, "Honestly, I don't think Nia likes me very much. I'm just a reminder of my mother. Aka, her husband's nasty ex-wife."

"Where did you say she was from again? The Dominican?"

"Haiti."

"Oh cool. Does that mean she speaks French? Wait, or is it Creole?"

"French, but according to Nia there's a perceivable difference between Haitian French and French French. She says it's in the intonation. Not that I would ever hear the difference. She's really nice," Cassie admits. "Dad found himself a good one."

Eventually, darkness falls over us, so we wade back to the boat. We kick off our shoes and go below deck where Cassie's eyes widen.

"See," I say smugly. "It's huge."

The cabin is more than just roomy—it offers plenty of amenities for an overnight in the cove. Built-in closets for storage, a pull-out refrigerator, a portable head. The center table converts into a bed, which I'd already set up before we left the dock.

"It even has air conditioning?" She gapes.

"Yup. Told you, this gal ain't cheap."

Cassie flops cross-legged in the center of the bed. "Do you think you'll accept Gil Jackson's offer? To sail to New Zealand?"

I'd mentioned it over dinner but didn't linger too long on the subject. It's been gnawing at the back of my brain since Gil's phone call. "I don't know. I'm still thinking about it."

"That's nuts that he has all these boats. His own fleet. Or is it an armada? What do you call a bunch of boats?" She wrinkles her nose. "A bushel?"

"Yes, baby, a bushel of boats. You nailed it."

"I sense sarcasm."

"You sense right."

Her indignant expression dissolves into a smile. "I will forgive that because you called me *baby* and that kind of turned me on."

"Oh, did it?"

Just like that, we're eye-fucking each other. And suddenly my entire body clenches in anticipation at the knowledge that it won't be long before we're real fucking.

"Come here." Her voice is throaty.

I join her on the bed. Try to sit at first, but she promptly pushes me onto my back. I land with a thump, smiling up at her. She looks so good right now. Eyes shining. Cheeks red. Windblown hair—copper, not ginger, although I won't give her the satisfaction of letting her know she's right about that. In her seated position, her shorts have ridden up her thighs. I reach out, unable to stop myself from stroking her smooth flesh.

She bites her lip. "Are you starting something here, Gate?"

"I don't know . . . you want me to?"

Rather than answer, she bends down to kiss me.

I kiss her back, sliding my fingers through her hair, giving a gentle tug to pull her closer. She's on top of me now, those delectable tits crushed against my chest, nipples puckered tight. I reach between us and give her left nipple a teasing pinch, knowing how sensitive her breasts are. As if on cue, she lets out a moan, and I smile. I love every single sound she makes when we're fooling around. None more than that soft, breathy whimper right before she's about to come. But we're not there yet, not even close to hearing that particular whimper. And I'm not bothered. It's not always about the destination. Sometimes it's all about the journey.

Rolling us over, I start off slow, kissing her neck and enjoying the way she shivers. Her hands idly run up and down between my shoulder blades, stroke the back of my head, tangle in my hair. It's fucking glorious. I grip the bottom of her tank top and drag it upward, my lips following the trail of exposed skin until they reach her collarbone and collide with the fabric of her top. I tug on it.

"Off," I order.

Laughing, she rises off the bed to pull the shirt off, along with her bikini top.

I touch her shorts then give the side of her ass a little smack. "Up," I growl.

"I love your monosyllabic caveman talk."

"Damn right you do."

She lifts her ass and I yank on her shorts and underwear, tossing them away. It suddenly occurs to me this is the first time I've seen her fully naked. I can't even believe that. I prop up on one elbow to admire her, my hand gliding over her perfect, naked flesh. Aside from her chest, she's kind of small everywhere else. I skim her rib cage, feeling the protrusions beneath my fingertips. The sharp jut of her hip bone.

She's watching me as I touch her. "You're teasing."

"No. Just enjoying." My fingers dance over one knee before sliding toward the juncture of her thighs. Licking my lips, I drag my knuckles over her slit.

Her breath catches. "That feels so good."

"I've barely gotten started." Grinning, I take off my shirt, but keep my shorts on. I don't need that temptation yet. Then I grip her ankles and start dragging her to the foot of the bed. There isn't a lot of space up there, so I kneel on the ground in front of her, bring her ass to the end of the mattress, and lower my face between her legs.

We both moan when my tongue makes contact. This is my favorite thing in the world. I don't think Cassie believed me when I told her that, but it's the truth. Nothing gets me harder than going down on a woman. Making her moan and squirm. Her gasps for air. Her thighs squeezing around my head, desperate to keep me right where she needs me. It's the pinnacle of sexual excitement. So fucking good.

As my erection strains against my zipper, I work her with my tongue, my fingers, until finally I hear it—my favorite noise. I groan happily, and know she feels that low, husky response on her clit. Her hips start moving. She grinds herself against my face, taking all the pleasure I have to offer, and it's not until she goes completely still that I abandon my post and kiss my way up her body.

She welcomes my kiss and I love that. Doesn't care that her taste is still on my tongue. She practically eats my face off, her nails digging into my shoulders as one hand fumbles for my zipper.

"Why are these still on?" she demands. "This vexes me."

"Oh, it vexes you?"

"Yes, it vexes me. I've very vexed."

I let her roll me onto my back. She's clawing at my shorts, wrenching them down my hips. My dick springs out, hard and eager.

Cassie gives an amused look. "Somebody's excited."

"Damn right I am." I suck a breath in when she takes me in her hand and starts to lower her head. Oh Christ. "No," I say, pulling her off me.

She looks offended. "What do you mean *no*?"

"No blowjobs."

"Ever?"

"No, not ever. Just now. I want to be able to last more than three strokes."

Her eyes twinkle. "You should have jerked off before we left. I read some guys do that to take the edge off."

"I did jerk off before we left," I growl, and she bursts out laughing.

"And you're still that close to ruining this experience for me? Jeez."

I know she's joking, yet I can't fight a self-conscious pang. "Damn, Cass. Don't say that. Now I'm going to have that in the back of my mind the whole time."

"No, don't." She launches herself at me again, our naked bodies colliding. Cupping my face, she looks into my eyes. "There's nothing to ruin. Even if we don't have sex right now, this is still one of the best days of my life. Honestly."

"Mine too," I confess. My first ride on a Fountain Lightning and I had Cassie by my side? Whatever happens between us in the future, I'll never forget that moment. And I'll never forget *this*. I squeeze one full, perfect breast. Sweep my thumb over her beaded nipple. When I bring my hand between her legs I find her wet and ready for me.

Yeah. I won't forget anything about tonight.

She's trying to reach for me again, and once again I intercept her fingers. "Hold that thought," I say and bend over the bed for the overnight bag. I unzip the side pocket for the condoms I stashed there.

Once I'm suited up, I ease my body on top of hers. Lightly touch her hip and lower my lips to kiss her nipple. Then I raise my head and meet her eyes. "You good?"

"I'm great," she says and guides me between her legs.

I only make it about an inch before we're both sweating. The sensation of her clamped so tightly around me short-circuits my brain. I forget how to fuck. Like, I actually do. I just lie there, my tip lodged inside, and it isn't until she groans impatiently that I snap out of it.

"Ready?" I whisper.

"Mmm-hmm."

I push myself inside her, past the resistance, kissing her to swallow the soft yelp of pain. "You okay?" I murmur against her lips.

"Uh-huh. Just give me one second."

I go still again, surrounded by her snug, warm heat. It's the greatest feeling in the world. Ever so slowly, she starts to move. Canting her hips. Digging her nails into my shoulder. It's torture. And I don't know if she's doing it on purpose, but her pussy is rippling around me, squeezing tight, releasing, then squeezing me in again. I clench my ass cheeks because I'm scared if I move I'm going to start pounding into her.

She squeezes me again, and my hips snap forward, hard and deep, summoning a startled sound from Cassie. I choke out a curse. I'm not going to survive this.

"All right," I mumble. "Here's what's going to happen."

A smile dances across her lips. "Yes, please share."

"I'm rolling us over and you're going to ride me. You're going to set the pace, okay? I'm trying so damn hard to go slow right now, but my body isn't going to let me in this position."

A moment later she's astride me. I shove a pillow under my head and soak in the sight of her. Flushed cheeks. Lust-drenched eyes. She hesitates, looking a bit uncertain.

"Take what you need," I say softly. I gaze up at her, completely at her mercy. "Every part of me is yours."

Cassie smiles. Slowly, she begins to ride me. Her palms flatten on my chest. Her lips part. She leans forward and her hair falls over us like a curtain, tickling my pecs. She kisses me, then makes a breathy sound.

"Oh, I like that."

"What?" I ask thickly.

"Kissing you while you're inside me." Her breathing quickens. So does the tempo, sending a bolt of pleasure through my body.

My balls tingle. Ass clenches again. I realize my fingers are curled over her hip, digging into her flesh. I loosen them. Force myself to relax.

She stops again. Dismayed. "What if I can't finish this way?"

"Then I'll go down on you again." I sigh happily. "All night, preferably."

"You really wouldn't care?"

"I really wouldn't care. Why should I, as long as this feels good for you?"

"It does," she assures me, leaning in to kiss me again.

I tug her so that she's draped over my chest. Then I lift my hips in a teasing, upward thrust at the same time I slide my tongue in her mouth.

Her eyes pop open and she gasps.

"What is it?" I ask, freezing.

"Oh. This position," she says, her voice dreamy. "It's rubbing the right spot." She rotates her hips, moving her lower body over mine. "This is the one."

Suddenly she's grinding her clit against me while I'm buried inside her, and I know she's found her rhythm. Her spot. Then I hear it, the telltale whimper, and my body fails me. With her nipples scraping my pecs, her ass filling my hands, her body gripping me tight, I can't fight it any longer.

"Cass, I'm gonna come. I can't stop it."

She mumbles, "It's okay," and I go off like a rocket. The pleasure is just starting to abate when Cassie reaches the place she needs to be. Her orgasm elicits another rush of heat in my body, like the aftershocks following an earthquake, tiny ripples after the initial blast.

Once our breathing is back to normal, she settles at my side, her head resting on my shoulder.

"So?" I say hoarsely. "Did I ruin it for you?"

"Definitely," she whispers. "It was so bad."

"So bad."

She giggles, her soft breath tickling my flesh. Silence falls over us. As we lie there in the dark, a sensation of pure serenity washes over me.

"I'm sleepy," she murmurs.

"Then close your eyes." I close mine too. Listening to the wind whistling beyond the cabin. Feeling the rocking of the hull on the calm water. The warmth of Cassie's naked body against mine.

I can't think of a better way to fall asleep.

CHAPTER 23

CASSIE

August

Only thirty minutes in to the twins' birthday party, and I'm second-guessing my desire to have children. I thought *two* six-year-olds were loud. Fifteen of them? It's one endless shriek that doesn't let up. The kind of unceasing noise that worms its way into your soul.

Dad and Nia rented a bouncy castle that takes up nearly half the backyard and currently contains eight little girls who are jumping up and down screaming at the tops of their lungs. It sounds like they're getting murdered in there, but I think they're having fun? The remaining seven girls are seated around the crafts table, where one of the counselors from the twins' day camp helps everyone construct their own sparkly tiaras. Dad hired the teenager for the afternoon, and she's a big hit so far.

Speaking of Dad, this is the fourth time he's hurried inside to "get something." Took me a while, but I'm starting to think he's not actually getting something, because he keeps returning empty-handed. On to him, I sneak away from the party and follow him inside. Sure enough, he's leaning against the kitchen counter, scrolling through his phone.

"You're not getting anything," I accuse.

He looks up, eyes dancing behind his glasses. "Sure I am. I'm getting peace and quiet."

I wander toward the other side of the counter and admire the girls' birthday cake, courtesy of Nia's bakery buddy Chandra, who ratted out Dad the day we were turtle browsing. Chandra and her daughter Sava are here today, the former chatting outside with Nia, the latter one of the kids getting murdered in the bouncy castle.

"Do you think the twins suspect?" I ask him. "About the turtle."

"Not in the slightest," he replies. "Last night Roxy was complaining again about having to wait till next year for a pet."

"Is everything all set up? The tank? The water? The—what did that Joel kid call it? UV light?"

"UVB," Dad corrects. "And it's all done. Even decorated the little dude's new digs with this waterlogged cypress tree decoration. It has all these branches he can perch on. I gotta admit, he's cute."

"Uh-huh. And what does Nia think about your new roommate?"

"She's still not thrilled about it, but she's just glad it's not a dog. As far as pets go, this one is low maintenance if you ignore the fact that it lives for a thousand years."

I snort.

"I'm glad you're here," Dad adds. "And I know I've already said it a bunch of times today, but happy birthday."

He comes up to wrap his arms around me in a warm hug. It's rare to receive any physical affection from my father, and I lean into his touch. I might not see him as often as I'd like, but when I do, I'm happy to be around him. It's so much easier with him than Mom. With her it's a minefield; I never know when I'll set off the next verbal attack.

As if reading my mind, Dad releases me with a light, "How's it been with your mom in town? You two getting along?"

"You know, the usual." And then, also as per usual, I change the subject. "I wish I hadn't wrapped the *Kit 'n McKenna* book already. I'm dying to show you how it turned out." I hesitate, feeling myself blush. "And you'll be happy to know I spoke to Robb about trying to publish it."

Dad's eyes light up. "You did? Excellent."

"His boss at the design studio has some contacts in the agent world. Talent agents, literary, that kind of thing. He's going to give Robb a few names of people who might want to rep us." I shrug. "Who knows—maybe this is the career path I'll end up on." When Dad brightens again, I raise my hand in warning. "Don't get your hopes up. Publishers might hate the concept."

"They won't," he says confidently. "And I can't wait to see it. I don't know what the girls are going to love more—the turtle or your book."

"The turtle, Dad." I roll my eyes.

A couple hours later, after all the birthday cake has been devoured and all the horrible shrieking children are gone, the remaining five of us gather in the living room for the grand unveiling. We decided to wait until their friends were gone, because as Joel the Pothead Turtle Whisperer had warned, turtles are highly sensitive. We didn't want to give the poor thing a heart attack when he swam out of his cypress tree and found fifteen screaming girls in his face.

A thirty-gallon tank now resides against the back wall of the living room, hidden by the black tablecloth Dad temporarily draped over it.

"What's happening?" Roxy demands, perpetually mistrustful. "What is that?"

"Why don't you go and look?" Dad beams at her. Even Nia looks like she's fighting a smile.

Wearing identical expressions of suspicion, the twins approach the covered tank.

"Pull the tablecloth off," Dad encourages.

Surprisingly, Roxy hesitates, and so it's Mo who ends up tugging on the cloth to reveal the turtle tank beneath.

Even more surprising, the girls stay deathly silent. Not a shriek to be heard.

"Girls?" Dad prompts.

They turn toward their parents, wide-eyed.

"Is . . . is it for us?" Monique whispers.

"He sure is." Nia's smile breaks free. It's hard not to smile when the girls are trembling with quiet excitement.

"Come," Dad says, urging them closer. "Come see him."

I step forward too. I also want to see the little dude. I peer at the tank and search the artificial rocks, branches, and little log that serves as a basking spot. That's where I find him. Dad's right—he's kind of cute. Small, maybe four inches max, with a mottled black shell and distinct stripes on his head.

"What's his name?" Roxy whispers.

"He doesn't have one yet," Dad says.

Not entirely true. I think this one was LL Cool J. But I don't blame Dad for wanting to rename him.

"I was thinking, though . . . maybe we can let your mama name him?" Dad tips his head as he awaits an answer.

Nia looks startled. "Me?"

He winks at his wife. "You. We all know Mama had her doubts about him, but she fell in love with him the moment she met him. So I think she should name him."

"Name him, Mama," Mo pleads.

Nia eyes the turtle for several long beats. Then she says, "Pierre."

I swallow a laugh. "Excellent choice."

"Pierre," Roxy echoes solemnly, pressing her nose to the tank.

"I will love him forever," Mo breathes. She's got both hands on the glass and is staring at him in adoration.

"Can I hold him?" Roxy begs.

"No, me first!"

Dad shakes his head. "We're going to go easy on the holding thing. At least for a little while. Pierre's experiencing a real culture shock right now."

"And," Nia adds, donning a stern look, "we need to have a serious talk about how to take care of Pierre, and what your responsibilities will be. *Oui*?"

"*Oui*," the twins promise.

"We'll do that tomorrow. Tonight, we still have a birthday dinner to eat," Dad says cheerfully. "And your sister has a present for you too . . ." he trails off enticingly.

My sisters spin toward me. "What is it?" Roxy demands.

I give her an innocent smile. "I don't know . . ." I walk into the hall to grab the wrapped present I left on the credenza, then return to offer it to Roxanne. "Why don't you two sit on the couch and open it?"

Unlike the awed silence Pierre received, my gift garners actual shrieks.

"It's Kit!" Mo shouts, trying to grab the hardcover out of her sister's hands. "Let me look!"

"We're looking together!" Roxy flips to the first page and stares at the drawing. "This is a real storybook!"

"It is," I confirm.

She scrunches up her forehead. "But it's *your* story."

"It is my story," I agree. "And I wrote it down and put it in a book for you. And . . ." I join them on the couch, settling in between them. "Look." I flip back to the intro page. "Can you read that for me?"

The twins are going into the first grade in September, but they've been at an advanced reading level for a while now. They squint at the page, eyes widening when they recognize their names.

"*To Roxanne . . . and . . . Monique*," Roxy reads in stilted pauses. "*The best . . . sisters . . . in the word.* I mean, *world*." She gazes at me, mouth gaping open. Then she screeches with joy. "I'm in the book!" she shouts. "Momo, you're in the book too!"

"We're in the book!" Mo jumps up and starts bouncing on the cushions.

"Monique," Nia chides, instantly plucking her off the couch and setting her on the floor. "We don't climb on the furniture, remember?"

Guilt pricks into me as I'm reminded of the last time she scaled the furniture. Under my watch, when a cabinet almost felt on her head and crushed my sister to death. At least Nia doesn't seem to be holding a grudge about it.

"Can you read it to us?" Roxy asks, hugging my arm.

"Please?" Mo launches herself at me, trying to climb into my lap.

"Why don't you girls do that now while your mama and I start fixing dinner?" Dad suggests. He's wearing a soft smile as he sweeps his gaze over the three of us.

He and Nia disappear into the kitchen, and I settle in to read my sisters a story.

* * *

Over dinner, Dad pours a glass of champagne and hands it to me. When I raise an eyebrow, he raises one back. "You're legal now," he says. "And I'm going to pretend this is your first glass of champagne."

"It is," I say innocently. "Never drank a single drop until this very moment."

That draws a genuine laugh from Nia.

Dad clinks his glass with mine. "Happy birthday, Cass."

"Happy birthday, Cassie," my sisters echo.

"Happy birthday, Cassandra," Nia adds in.

Dinner is tasty, as it always is when Nia cooks. Afterward, Dad hands me an envelope that serves as my birthday present. Inside is a gift card, which is pretty much what I expected. It's always a gift card.

"Figured this way you could go and pick something out for yourself," Dad tells me. Which is what he says every year.

"It's perfect. Thank you." But it's hard to ignore the pang of unhappiness that tugs at my insides. I know it's far easier to please first-graders than your college-senior daughter, but sometimes it would be nice if Dad made an actual effort.

The girls beg me to spend the night, and although I hadn't been planning on it, I can't say no to those faces. I text Tate to let him know I won't be coming by later.

Tate: *No birthday sex??!!*
Me: *Sadly not. My sisters don't want me to leave.*
Tate: *I'll allow it, but I'm not happy.*

I know he's kidding, which is confirmed when he sends a follow-up.

Tate: *Have fun. See you tomorrow?*
Me: *For sure.*

Hell, now I'm almost regretting agreeing to spend the night here, because just seeing his name on my phone gets me going. Sexually. Because that's what my world has been reduced to. Sex.

And sex. And then more sex. I'm voracious about it now. I crave it all the damn time.

I freaking love sex.

Or maybe it's Tate.

Of course it's Tate. You're falling for him.

Wait, what? Where the hell did that come from? I chide my mind for even suggesting such blasphemy. I can't, under any circumstances, allow myself to fall in love with the guy. I'm leaving in three weeks. He's staying behind. Not only that, but we agreed to a fling. We even discussed the terms. Therefore, I'm not allowed to engage my heart in this. Only my body.

Luckily, my body is very much in love with Tate's.

"Let me help you with those," I say when I spot Nia carrying in plates from the dining room.

"*Non, non.* It's fine."

"You cooked dinner for me," I protest. "The least I can do is help with the cleanup."

Nia once again dismisses me. "Go spend time with the girls. Their bedtime is soon."

I press my lips together, fighting a wave of irritation. Despite my best effort, the words biting at my tongue cannot be reined in.

"Why don't you like me?"

Her expression turns to shock. "What?"

"Why don't you like me?" I repeat.

"Cassandra . . ." She places the dirty dishes in the sink and slowly steps toward me. She rubs the bridge of her nose. Uneasy. "I—"

"Cass!" Dad calls from the living room. "Come check this out!"

"Pierre is swimming!" yells Roxy.

Relief sweeps through me. I'm immensely grateful for the interruption, because voicing the question made me realize I don't want to know the answer.

Why do we do that, anyway? Ask questions with glaringly obvious answers. Painful answers. I guess human beings really are gluttons for punishment. It's like Peyton, whenever she gets ghosted by a guy. She always wants to know the reason. Wants to know why. And I always counter with, *Why does it matter? Either way he's not interested in you*. But still she persists, *Yes, but I want to know WHY.*

Nia doesn't like me. That much is clear.

So, really, the *why* doesn't matter.

*   *   *

Tate: *Make sure not to throw out the newspaper today.*

The message comes in as I'm pulling into Grandma's driveway the next morning. Okay. Intriguing.

I hop out of the Rover and head into the house to have a look. Grandma wakes up ungodly early in the mornings, and if she'd already gone out to grab the newspaper, she would've tossed the *Avalon Bee* on the hall table and only brought her paper of choice—*The Wall Street Journal*—into the kitchen with her.

Sure enough, in the hall I find the abandoned Saturday edition of the *Bee*. Curious, I unfold it, then burst out laughing. Oh my God. This is incredible.

"Cassie?" comes my mother's voice.

Still giggling over the paper, I carry it into the kitchen, where Mom is drinking her coffee at the table.

She gives me a wry smile. "What's so funny?"

"This." I hold up the newspaper to show her the front page, which features a half-page photograph of the Bartlett family. Gavin, Gemma, and Tate (missed opportunity for *Gate*) pose in front of Bartlett Marine, with Gavin in the middle, his broad grin flying off the page. Tate's dad is definitely larger than life, and the headline reflects this:

MR. CONGENIALITY OF THE BAY

Mom leans forward to study the article, her eyes instantly narrowing. "What's this?"

"Tate's dad." Another giggle pops out. "The *Bee* did a profile on him. It was all he could talk about the first time I met him. He's so proud of it."

My phone buzzes in my other hand.

Tate: *He already has TWO framed copies. One for the dealership, one for his home office. He thinks he's a celebrity now. He just called me asking if he should schedule a press conference.*
Me: *Let the man have his moment in the sun, Gate!*

Laughing, I leave my phone on the counter and head for the fridge. At the table, Mom is scanning the article, still looking displeased. Well, of course. Someone other than her is getting attention. The nerve!

"Your grandmother tried to convince me the other day that you were dating that boy, but I didn't believe her." Raising one eyebrow, Mom pushes the newspaper away and picks up her coffee cup. "It appears I was wrong."

"Tate and I aren't dating." I stick my head in the fridge hoping the chill might cool down my suddenly warm cheeks.

"No? Because also according to your grandmother, the land-scaper says it looks like someone's been trampling the rose garden beneath the lattice at the side of the house. The one that leads right to your window."

Damn it. I poke my head out, my hand emerging with a container of yogurt. "It's not a big deal," I say, going to grab a bowl. "We're just hanging out."

Mom shakes her head in amusement. "It's not like I don't know exactly what that means, sweetie."

I shrug. "It's just a casual thing. We're parting ways at the end of the summer, so it's not going to lead to anything."

"I see. Well, I suppose so long as you're having fun."

"We are."

"And so long as you're taking precautions." Mom offers a pointed look.

My cheeks are scorching again. "We are."

"Then I guess I don't have anything to worry about," she finishes.

I'm confused as to why she was worried in the first place. Mom's never paid much attention to my love life, other than to criticize me for not having one.

She changes the subject, watching me as she sips her coffee. "How is your father?"

I brace myself. Waiting for the . . . *and his nurse?*

But it doesn't come.

"He's good. We had a nice time. The girls loved their gift."

"Speaking of gifts." Mom finishes her coffee and walks to the counter, and it's then that I notice the neatly wrapped gift near the knife block. A crisp lavender envelope sits atop it. "I decided I'd wait until today to give you this, since you were so busy yesterday."

Her tone lacks bite, but that had to be sarcasm, right? Some kind of resentful subtext, like, *You were so busy yesterday . . . because your father and his nurse kept you away from me all day long.*

Only, I see none of that on her face. Not an ounce of hostility.

"Yesterday was super busy," I agree.

I open the envelope first and pull out a card with a delicate purple flower pressed onto the front. Inside, the card is blank save for my mother's uber-concise handwritten message: *Happy birthday, Cassie. Love, Mom.* And there's a check for five thousand dollars.

"Some spending money for your senior year," she explains.

"Thanks." Gift card. Check. Both my parents enjoy taking the easy way out, apparently.

"Now here's your real present," she says, sliding the gift box toward me. Her tone is light, joking even, but it's belied by the anxiety in her eyes.

Okay. This is weird. Why does she look so anxious for me to open this?

I study the narrow box, which is around the size of a sheet of paper and not too thick. Clothing, I realize, when I lift the lid and glimpse fabric beneath the white tissue paper. I part the paper.

It's a crop top.

I steel myself. This must be some kind of attack, right?

"I had Joy pick it out," Mom says. A nervous look darts across her face.

Holy shit, this is not a joke. I repeat, this is not a joke.

It's a sincere gesture.

"Oh," I say in surprise.

I run my fingers over the ribbed material. I saw this top in one of the boutiques on the strip when Joy and I were shopping a few weeks ago. I'd picked it up, admiring it, asking Joy if emerald green was my color. I didn't end up buying it, only because I didn't feel like dropping two hundred dollars on a strip of fabric.

"I know I was out of line," Mom starts.

The shocks just keep coming.

"Last week when we spoke on the patio," she clarifies. "You'd just returned from dinner and I remarked on your outfit. I may have been a tad rude about it."

May have? A tad?

"Just a tad," I say lightly.

"I'm sorry. I was in a very bad mood that night, and I'm afraid I took it out on you." She laughs, and it sounds genuinely sheepish. "I don't think you're a bimbo. Obviously I don't think that. Like I said, I was in a bad mood. I apologize."

I can't get over the feeling that somehow, someway, this is an inexplicable ruse. A trick with an end game I don't know yet. It's difficult to trust my mother. You can't trust a person who's spent years making you feel unworthy.

Mom isn't done. "I spoke with your grandmother about it when we were in Charleston, and she pointed out that when I was your age, I was also insecure about my looks. And those insecurities aren't helped by someone sharing their negative opinion about your wardrobe choices. Also, if you do choose to have a breast reduction—"

I brace myself again.

"—I will happily accompany you to the consultation. But if you choose not to, that is also okay." She reaches out and touches the soft material of the crop top. "Either way, I'm sure you're going to look wonderful in this. Why don't you wear it today? Pair it with that long skirt we bought last week, the khaki one with the gold flowers? That might be a nice outfit for our day in Charleston." Mom pauses. "That's still the plan, right? Birthday Sunday in the city?"

"For sure. I just need to shower and change and then I'm ready to go." I clutch the top a little tighter, surprised by the lump of emotion that forms in my throat. "Thank you for this. I love it."

For once, I'm not lying.

CHAPTER 24

CASSIE

A few days after my birthday, Mom takes me and Tate out to dinner on the boardwalk. That in itself is a shocking development, but she continues to surprise me once we're seated at the Italian place and she generously hands over the leather-bound wine menu to Tate.

"Why don't you pick the wine, Tate?" It's a big honor coming from Mom, and I can tell he's fighting his amusement over the ceremonial tone with which she makes the offer.

I'm equally surprised Tate agreed to this dinner at all, considering he hasn't been my mother's biggest fan since the night she bimbo-shamed me. But Mom's been badgering me about it for the past couple days. I suspect a part of her still doesn't believe Tate and I are seeing each other and she wants visual proof.

I don't entirely blame her. I mean, let's not kid ourselves—Tate is probably the best-looking guy I've ever been in the same room as, and I've been surrounded by cute college boys for the last three years, so that says a lot. He surpasses them in looks. The perfect golden boy with his perfect face and perfect body. Even Mom can't stop checking him out. It's both creepy and validating, two things I didn't think could coexist in my mind. But I like knowing I'm not just some foolish girl blinded by a crush. That he's actually as hot as I think he is.

"I'm not a big wine drinker," Tate tells her. "You'd be doing yourself a disservice if you put me on wine-picking duty for the night." He hands the menu back. "But if you're interested in beer, then I'm your man."

Mom proceeds to do another shocking thing. "You know what? Let's have beer tonight."

My jaw drops. "You're going to drink beer? Here?" This is one of the nicest restaurants in the Bay. Normally she wouldn't be caught dead drinking anything other than the most expensive wine in the restaurant's cellar.

There's something different about her. Even her outfit gives off a different vibe. She's clad in an expensive sleeveless dress, a sky blue that complements her red hair, which she's uncharacteristically wearing down. She doesn't seem so uptight tonight. She'd even complimented my dress when Tate and I met her outside the restaurant.

And don't get me started on *that* perplexing exchange. Mom had greeted Tate with a warm smile and said, "Nice to see you again, Tate," and he'd responded with, "Nice to see you again too, Tori."

Tori.

My eyebrows almost jumped off my face as I turned to Mom to clarify. I don't think I've ever heard anyone call my mother Tori. Dad called her Vic sometimes, but mostly Victoria. Even Grandma always uses her entire name.

"All my friends call me that," Mom had responded, rolling her eyes at me. "Where have you been, Cass?"

To be fair, I always kept a safe distance whenever she had a friend over to the penthouse. It was much easier than putting on the whole mother/daughter act, the one she's so skilled at. When new friends, acquaintances, or strangers are around, she pretends we're the bestest of friends. We're Lorelai and Rory from *Gilmore*

Girls, giggling together in our pajamas and casually chatting about our crushes.

Which has never happened, nor will it ever.

But I guess we're pretending again tonight. Me and Tori. Best buds. Luckily, I know Tate can see through it.

When the waiter arrives, Tate orders an obscure-sounding beer, which he explains is locally brewed. Mom tells the server to make it two, but I beg off when he looks toward me. Instead, I order a Diet Coke. I need to keep a clear head. I don't know why the three of us are here and it still feels like a trap.

"This is nice," Mom remarks, only deepening my suspicions. What is she up to? "So, Tate. Cassie said you're a sailor?"

"Not professionally, but yes, I love to sail. Used to compete in high school." While he talks, he plays with the edge of his napkin, and I watch the way his long fingers move.

Heat tickles my core when I remember the feel of those fingers moving over *me.* Stroking my body. Biting into my ass, my hips, as I rode him.

Oh no. *Don't blush,* I tell myself.

He catches my eye and grins. Damn it. I'm blushing.

"I don't compete as much I'd like to anymore," he continues, while reaching for my hand.

He links our fingers together and I try not to smile. Holding hands during dinner? He's making a statement, and I notice Mom gazing on in approval. Now *that's* a rare look on her.

"Too busy these days with work," he says.

"You work at the Manor?" she prompts.

"Part-time, weekends mostly. The rest of the time I'm at the family business."

"And what would that be?"

"Bartlett Marine. Dad and I run it. It's a dealership, but we handle rentals and charters too."

I just listen to the conversation. Mom can be very charismatic when she wants to be. Disarming. I used to have friends from high school come over and look at me like I was crazy for even insinuating that my mother could be a raging narcissistic bitch. They all thought she was fabulous. I can't entirely gauge Tate's opinion of her. He was a bit reserved when we first sat down, but he seems to be warming up to her.

"Cassie showed me the newspaper article about your father," Mom says, smiling. "Sounds like you hail from a family of celebrities."

"Man, do not tell my dad that," Tate replies with a groan. "He's already walking around the dealership thinking he's hot stuff because they ran a profile on him. Like, dude, it's the *Avalon Bee,* not *GQ.*"

As Mom laughs, I come to poor Gavin's defense. "Have *you* ever been featured on the front page of a newspaper? Any newspaper, for that matter?"

"Uh, yeah," he shoots back. "I'm in the picture on the front page of the *Bee,* in case you forgot."

"For an article about your *dad.* Jeez. Get your own achievements." I give him a taunting smile. "You can't complain about his excitement until you've experienced your own fifteen minutes of fame. You'd probably be even worse, too. Accepting fake Oscars in front of the mirror every morning."

"Cassie," Mom chides, but her eyes twinkle with humor.

"What?" I protest. "Look at him. He looks like the guy who delivers fake speeches in the mirror. Don't deny it."

He snickers. "I would never."

Mom's gaze shifts toward him, assessing. Lingers a little too long, but when she turns back to me, her expression still contains humor. "He does seem like the type," she agrees.

I can't believe my mother and I sided on something. And even crazier, that I'm genuinely enjoying myself. At dinner. With my mother present. People in hell must be wearing parkas right about now.

Whether or not she's putting on an act remains undecided. But I'm still relaxed, my guard down. I end up ordering a cocktail. And now that I'm twenty-one, I can do that without stressing that someone is going to ask for my ID.

Dinner is excellent, which is to be expected from the most expensive restaurant in town. This place gets the freshest lobster and the best cuts of meat in the Bay. As we eat, Tate tells us funny stories about working at the yacht club. Seems like during every lesson, something ridiculous happens.

"Couples are the worst," he insists. "Any time we take out a sailboat that's bigger than thirty feet, at least one half of the couple demands to act out the king of the world scene from *Titanic*. Then I have to stand there taking pictures, like, a thousand of them, because the first nine hundred and ninety-nine are apparently never good enough for the 'gram."

"Oh dear," Mom says, giggling into her beer. She just shocked me by ordering a second one. "You poor thing."

I suppose I can overlook the way she's blatantly flirting with my sort-of boyfriend if it means she's not frowning at my outfit or talking about breast reductions. Over dessert, she even shares some stories about her own days at the country club.

"There was this golf instructor—Lorenzo." She sighs dreamily. "I had the biggest crush on him. Almost fainted with excitement when he asked me on a date. I think I was twenty-one, maybe? It was right before I met your father, Cass."

I almost spit out my drink. "Mom! You dated Lorenzo? The immortal Italian vampire?"

Tate snickers into his beer.

"I don't even know what that means," she says.

"It means he's worked at the Manor for five hundred years because he never ages." I suddenly feel the color draining from my face. "Oh my God, he could have been my father." I glare at her, aghast. "You almost got me sired by *Lorenzo*."

"No chance," she replies, lips pressed tight together as if she's fighting an onslaught of giggles. "Let's just say Lorenzo had some . . . performance issues."

I gasp.

Tate groans. "No. Why did you have to tell me that? Now I'll never be able to look him in the eye again."

When the bill arrives, he tries to reach for it, but Mom firmly divests him of that notion. "It's on me. I'm just glad you were able to join us. I wanted to meet the boy who's been sneaking into my daughter's window this summer."

He winks at me before answering her. "No comment."

"I'm glad you two are spending time together. It's so nice to see you with a boyfriend," Mom says to me, and I don't think she's mocking me.

What planet is this? Are we in another dimension? Either that, or I've snagged a guy so hot and perfect that even Mom can't find fault in him.

"Thank you. This was great," Tate tells her. "We should do it again while you're in town."

"Of course." She takes the black AmEx the waiter returns to her, quickly signing the check. "And you'll be accompanying Cassie to the Beacon's grand reopening in a few weeks?"

He glances at me. "We haven't really talked about it. I was planning on going, though." He flashes an awkward smile. A little bashful. "Wanna go together?"

I feel my cheeks reddening. "Sure."

"Excellent." Mom pushes her chair back and stands. "I assume your parents will be there too? According to my mother, the Cabot girl invited nearly half the town."

"I'm not sure," he replies, helping me out of my seat. "I don't know if there's an official guest list. I'll ask Mackenzie."

Mom waves a hand. "Your parents are welcome to come as our guests. The Beacon was in the Tanner family for decades." She winks. "We still have a bit of clout left."

We reach the door, Tate once again thanking her for dinner before we part ways. He and I have plans to go to the Hartleys' house, and Mom sashays off toward the Mercedes parked across the street.

Uneasiness swims inside me as I watch her drive away.

"You okay?" Tate asks, interlacing his fingers with mine.

"Yeah. I'm just . . . baffled."

"Baffled."

"Yes. Like, what the hell was that?" I gesture toward her disappearing taillights.

"I don't know. I thought it went pretty well. I was expecting a lot worse, but it ended up being kind of fun."

"Exactly. That's the baffling part. My mother is never this nice. Something's going on here. First she apologizes to me and buys me a crop top, and now this? This pleasant, condemnation-free dinner without a whiff of tension or a shred of criticism? No. I don't trust it."

He grins at me. "Aren't you the silver-lining girl?"

"This doesn't qualify as a silver-lining situation. This has never happened before. I told you, she's not this nice. Especially to me."

"You're saying there hasn't been a single genuine moment between you two in your entire life?" He sounds dubious.

I stubbornly shake my head. "There's always an ulterior motive with her. An agenda. The last time she buddied up to me this hard, she was going through her divorce with Stu and it turned out she wanted me to sign a written statement from her lawyer claiming Stu emotionally abused her throughout their marriage and she therefore deserved to have their prenup dissolved. Then when I refused, she told me Stu had never even liked me."

"Damn. Seriously?"

"Seriously. My stepbrother assured me that wasn't true. But still. That's why this—" I vaguely motion toward the street and the restaurant. "I don't get it."

He goes quiet for a moment. "Have you considered the possibility it's genuine this time?"

"Fool me once . . ."

"I get that. And I'm not saying you should blindly trust it. But . . ." He hesitates. "Maybe she's realized that having a combative relationship with her daughter isn't ideal."

"And when did she have this epiphany?"

He shrugs. "Who knows. Could be because you guys are selling your grandmother's house, the family business. It's the end of something, and endings make people nostalgic. Even narcissists. Sometimes it causes them to look inward and take stock of themselves. Triggers self-awareness they may have been lacking before."

"Maybe." I'm still not convinced.

"Look, we never truly know our parents. They lived entire lives before we ever came along, you know? All those experiences shaped them, made them who they are, and sometimes people become set in their ways and their personality defects, and it takes something major to jar them into making a change. Who knows what triggered your mother, but maybe she's ready for that change."

We start walking down the sidewalk, which is crammed with tourists even on a Wednesday night. It's so busy we had to park nearly a mile away.

"I think you should give her a shot," he says. "Be open to the possibility this olive branch is sincere."

I bite my lip. The problem with Tate is, he doesn't understand toxic parents. His family is perfect. As a couple, Gavin and Gemma are madly in love. As parents, they've always been there for him. He's the only guy I know who can proudly say that his mom is his best friend. And his dad too! If anyone has a *Gilmore Girls* relationship, it's Tate. He's Rory, and *both* his parents are frickin' Lorelai.

I envy him. Truly. I'd love having that sort of relationship with my parents. Hell, even just one of them. But I don't.

Tonight was nice, though. I can't deny that. My guard was nonexistent, and Mom didn't strike. I'm unscathed. Happy, even.

"I had a lot of fun tonight," I confess, albeit reluctantly.

"Then you should give her a chance. It's never too late to repair a relationship with somebody. To try and build the kind of relationship you want with them."

"You really believe that?"

"I do." His hand tightens around mine. It's comforting at first, but then he rubs the inside of my palm with his thumb, and the tone instantly shifts.

"You did a sexy thing," I accuse.

He nods in agreement. "I did a sexy thing."

We reach the parking lot, where he does another sexy thing by moistening his lips with his tongue.

"So." He licks at the corner of his mouth. "I know you lost your virginity less than two weeks ago, and, well, I don't want to throw everything at you all at once, but . . . how do you feel about car sex?"

"Yes," I say instantly and tug his hand toward the Jeep.

CHAPTER 25

CASSIE

On Friday morning, I stop by the Hartley house on my way to town to drop off a stack of photographs for Mackenzie. Since we're selling the house soon, I've been helping Grandma sift through the attic this week, digging through old boxes and decades' worth of treasures. I found a box of photographs of the Beacon Hotel throughout the years, and after we scanned them so Grandma could have a digital record, she suggested choosing a few of the originals to give to Mackenzie. When I called Mac about it, she'd been over the moon. She plans to frame and hang them at the hotel, along with an original map of Avalon Bay she somehow got her hands on. The map itself is so old the paper is virtually disintegrating and they need to keep it behind protective glass, away from any moisture.

While I'm at the house, Mac and Genevieve, who has the day off, drag me to the back deck so we can go over our plans for Beach Games, which commence tomorrow. It's a two-day affair that's bound to get ugly if the deadly determination on my teammates' faces is any indication.

"According to this," Mac says, reading from her phone, "the only events that require all four team members on the field of play at the same time are sandcastles, volleyball, and the water balloon toss. The others are either two-man only, or two-man heats."

"This is confusing," I inform her. "And so is that scoring system on the second page of the pdf. Who the hell organized this, a ten-year-old?"

Gen snickers. "Beach Games is spearheaded by Debra Dooley. She's the president of the Avalon Bay Tourism Board."

"*Debra Dooley* sounds like a cartoon character," Mac retorts.

"Trust me, that's not far off. Deb has the energy levels of thirty preschoolers. Just wait." Gen checks her own phone. "I'm down for the windsurfing and the swim. But I'd rather die than give Evan the satisfaction of watching me fall off the tightrope."

"Oh, I'll do that one," I volunteer. "I know you wouldn't think it because of these things—" I gesture to my boobs—"but somehow they aid my balance instead of toppling me over."

Mac snickers. "I can do the tightrope. But I'm not doing the tug-of-war. Rope burn sucks."

We look over the rest of the events, tentatively assigning players to each one. "I'll text Zale the assignments and see if he wants to make any changes," Mac says when we're done. I've yet to meet this Zale, Mac's new activities director, but from the way she describes him, he sounds like a blast.

"Tate and Danny will take any water sports easily," Gen says, still looking at the list. "But if good fortune is upon us, Evan will be the one windsurfing. He's a disaster, so there's no way Hartley and Sons will score."

"Speaking of Tate," Mac says, turning to eye me. "Coop said you two are dating."

"You needed Cooper to tell you that?" Gen demands before I can answer. She snorts loudly. "You mean the fact that they couldn't keep their hands off each other when they were here the other night and then left early with those guilty expressions— that didn't tip you off?"

I can't help but laugh. "She's got a point there."

Mac rolls her eyes. "Well, obviously I suspected at that point. But this is my first chance to be alone with Cassie. I wanted confirmation." She lifts one delicate eyebrow. "It's true, then?"

"We're not dating, per se. It's more of a fling."

"Flings never stay flings," Gen informs me. "They either turn into relationships, or someone gets their heart broken."

I shrug. "I'm not too worried. We live in different states, so it will have to end regardless. We're just having fun. And don't worry, my heart's still intact."

Because I refuse to engage it. I had one slip, one minor setback the other day at my dad's house, when my heart insinuated itself into what was supposed to be a summer of passion. *You're falling for him.* Okay, well, I heard you out, heart. And I've decided to ignore you.

Since then, I've been making a conscious effort to not get emotionally attached. And to temper my expectations. Luckily, I'm very proficient at not expecting too much out of people.

Whatever's happening between Tate and I, it's better if phrases like *falling for him* don't enter the equation.

Mac sets down her phone. "Want to stick around for a while? Take the dog for a walk on the beach?"

"I would," I say regretfully, "but I have to go. I'm meeting my mother at a salon in town. We're getting manicures."

"Must be nice to have a mom to do that kind of stuff with," Genevieve says, her voice surprisingly wistful.

"You're not close with your mother?"

"Well, she just died this past spring—"

"Oh gosh, I'm so sorry."

"It's all good." Gen shrugs. "Even when she was alive, Mom and I weren't close."

"Oh, this manicure doesn't mean we're close. Trust me. We've always had a very strained relationship. But she's been making an effort since she got to town, so I've decided to meet her halfway."

Because the silver lining to this, the best-case scenario, is that we manage to repair the relationship and have something better going forward. Worst case? She goes back to being a raging narcissist, which I've dealt with my whole life anyway, so there'd be nothing new there.

I bid the girls goodbye and drive into town. The salon is situated on a street parallel to Main Street, making it easier to find parking. It's a quiet location, sandwiched between a massage therapy clinic and a chiropractor's office.

Mom is already there when I walk in, seated at one of the manicure stations. "Cass!" she calls, waving me over.

"Hey," I greet her, while taking in the familiar surroundings. "I totally forgot about this place. Grandma used to bring me here when I was younger, remember? I'd always come home with neon pink nails."

"And then you'd shriek bloody murder when your father and I tried removing the nail polish once it started chipping."

"Because God forbid your six-year-old go outside with chipped nails," I say dryly.

That gets me a genuine laugh.

"Would you like to pick your color?" my manicurist asks while I settle at the table next to Mom.

"Oh, no color," I answer. "Just French tip."

"No color?" Mom frowns. "That won't look good for the grand opening."

It's the only critical remark she's made in a while, so I let it slide.

"I'll need to get another manicure before then, anyway. I have Beach Games this weekend," I remind her. "I'll be digging in sand and playing volleyball, so there's no point doing anything too fancy today."

She relaxes. "That's right. I forgot. You're competing for the Beacon."

"Yes. Really looking forward to it, too. It's going to be a blast."

"Maybe I can convince your grandmother to come watch some of the events," Mom suggests. "Or at least to attend the winners' ceremony."

"I honestly can't envision us placing, let alone winning." There's some stiff competition this year. The dudes from Jessup's Garage. The local fire station. Tate and the yacht club guys. The Hartleys. We'll be lucky if we win one event.

We settle in to be pampered as our nails are washed, buffed, and painted. My manicurist is a quiet teenager with long black hair, while Mom's is a super chatty woman in her thirties. She's visibly pregnant, informing us she's eight months along with her fifth child.

"Lord, you have four already? I could barely handle one," Mom jokes, nodding toward me. I make a face at her. "And now five? You deserve a medal of valor."

The woman laughs. "It sure is challenging at times. My boys are both under the age of six, and my girls are entering their tweens and becoming real handfuls, I tell ya."

Once our color is done, we're ushered to the drying area where we're ordered to sit for twenty minutes.

"Five kids?" I whisper when we're alone. "That sounds like a nightmare."

"Five is too many," Mom agrees.

A question bites at my tongue. It's one I'd never have dreamed of asking in the past, but we've been getting along so well lately, and my curiosity gets the better of me.

"Did you and Dad ever want more children?"

She looks startled. "Well. I suppose so. Your father did, certainly. He wanted at least three." A flare of bitterness darkens her expression. "And he got his three, so . . ."

"What about you?" I swiftly steer the subject away from Dad, partly because I've been enjoying our noncombative interactions, but mostly because we're stuck with our hands in these heaters which means I'm effectively trapped here with no escape.

"I didn't, no," she finally admits. "I was happy with just one child. You know I don't enjoy chaos. And growing up with three older siblings was very chaotic, especially having two older brothers who played sports. Your uncles were always tormenting me and Jacqueline. So, yes, I was content with one child." She hesitates again, for much longer this time. "With that said, I can't deny I was elated when I got pregnant for a second time."

I can't stop my loud gasp. "You were pregnant again after me?"

Mom's eyes flick across the room. The manicurists are chattering away with other clients, oblivious to our conversation.

"Yes." Her voice becomes very soft, as if she doesn't want to be overheard. Or maybe the subject is too emotional for her. Mom's not a fan of feelings. "I got pregnant when you were ten."

"How come I never knew this?"

"Your father and I didn't want to tell you yet. We were already having problems in the marriage, and then I lost the baby at nine weeks." She sighs. "They advise you not to announce the news to the world too early. Wait until the end of the first trimester to see if it sticks. And it didn't stick."

My heart squeezes. There isn't an ounce of emotion in her voice, but her eyes tell a different story. I don't think I've ever seen my mother appear this vulnerable.

"I'm sorry. I wish I'd known."

"No, I'm glad you didn't. You would have gotten your hopes up for a sibling and then been devastated when it didn't happen."

"You could have told me after the fact," I point out. "Once I was older."

"There was no point. The baby was gone, and then your father and I got divorced." Something in her tone changes, a sliver of regret slicing through it. "Although it may have contributed to why I fought for full custody of you."

She voices the confession then pulls her hand from the dryer and casually examines her nails, as if she hadn't just dropped a major truth bomb.

"What do you mean?" I push.

"Maybe it wasn't fair to your father, but after losing the baby, I clung to you a little tighter than I should have." She pauses. "Perhaps that wasn't the right thing to do, but . . . well, you can't change the past, can you?"

She quickly adopts a cavalier expression, unruffled by the fact that she just shattered my entire world view. Or at the very least, altered my view of *her*. I'd always believed she insisted on full custody to be spiteful, to get back at Dad, but this potential new motive provides another glimpse into my mother. A softer side I didn't know existed.

I reach over and touch her arm. "I'm really sorry, Mom. That must have been tough to go through. A divorce and a miscarriage around the same time."

"It's fine, sweetheart." She jerks away from my touch. Not in a rude way, but it's clear I made her uncomfortable. Physical comfort— any comfort, really—isn't something we typically offer each other. Maybe I was overreaching by going for that consolatory pat.

The main lesson I've taken from this conversation, though, is that Tate was right.

We never truly know our parents.

CHAPTER 26

CASSIE

I never gave much thought to pep talks. In school, I didn't play sports or belong to a team. But I'm fairly certain a pep talk is supposed to pump your teammates up, not make them fear you. The Hartley twins never got that memo.

"Let's hear it again," yells Evan. "Louder this time! What are we gonna do?"

"Murder," the two non-Hartley team members recite. Thoroughly unenthused.

"And who are we gonna murder?" shouts Cooper.

"Your girlfriends."

"Hey, assholes," Genevieve calls. "We're right here, you know."

Evan turns with an expression of the utmost innocence. "Baby, hey. Didn't see you there."

She just snorts.

Mac, meanwhile, seeks out the authorities. "Hey, Deb," she says, waving a hand. "Any chance we can switch sandcastle stations? Our neighbors are obnoxious."

"Tattletale," Cooper taunts.

Debra Dooley waves back. "No, siree! We're about to start!" Our Beach Games host looks exactly like her name sounds. Short, plump, with a helmet of brown hair and bangs slashing a straight line across her forehead. She's wearing khaki shorts, a white polo, and a pink adventure hat that would make my dad drool.

Looks like we're stuck next to Hartley and Sons. To our other side, huddled about six feet away, are the women from the Soapery, the store on the boardwalk that Grandma loves so much. Their team consists of the owner, Felice, her manager, and two employees. To be honest, I'm more worried about them than the Hartleys. They hand-carve all their soaps. A sandcastle should be easy for them.

Deb Dooley and her team of volunteers from the tourism office wrote up a practical event schedule for our two-day competition. The more labor-intensive events are taking place in the morning when it isn't too hot. Once the sun starts scorching us around noon, we'll be switching to water events. The teams arrived at nine, and I've been told we're done by one thirty. We also get an hour for lunch.

"All right," Gen says while the tourism people discuss some last-minute details among themselves. She lowers her voice. "Are we still doing a fish?"

"We *must*," insists Zale, who became my all-time favorite person within three seconds of meeting him. "We agreed to be ambitious."

"I know, but it'll be tough," Gen argues. "Especially the scales. How are we going to make them look all detailed?"

"Oh, my sweet talentless flower," Zale chirps, "leave the artistic endeavors to the designers. You and Cassie are the muscle. The pail bearers. Mac and I will handle our fish friend."

Gen rolls her eyes. "Did you just call me *talentless*?"

"'Fraid so." He flashes his bright white teeth, which he informed me he had professionally whitened just for this occasion. In the twenty or so minutes I've known Zale, I've become privy to his beauty routine, his family history, and the reasons he broke up with his last three boyfriends, two of whom were named Brian. With his tall, lanky frame, dazzling smile, and wild Afro held back by a navy bandana, Zale is larger than life. His exuberance is downright contagious.

A crowd has already gathered at the boardwalk. Deb and her army of volunteers roped off the sandcastle-building area from the public, and I smile when I catch sight of my dad and sisters. The girls insisted on showing up for the "opening ceremonies" to cheer me on.

"Go, Cassie!" Roxy shouts when Dad hoists her onto his shoulders.

I look over and wave, then scan the beach for Tate's team. I didn't see where Deb placed them. On the other side of Hartley and Sons are the mechanics. Beyond them is the team from the bakery—Nia's friend Chandra catches my eye and waves. I finally spot Tate's team about fifty feet away. They're huddled together, talking strategy. Last night I kept bugging Tate to tell me what they planned on building, to which he declared he would drown himself before sharing trade secrets with the enemy. And I thought I was overdramatic.

"Ladies and gentlemen, the twentieth annual Avalon Beach Games are about to commence!"

Damn, where did Deb get a microphone? And did she say *twentieth*?

"Twenty years they've been doing this shit?" Zale says. He's not from the Bay, only moved here this summer after Mackenzie's headhunter poached him from a golf resort in California. "Damn. You southern peeps have too much time on your hands."

Gen snickers.

"My name is Debra Dooley, and I'll be your host for this year's competition." Deb is bouncing around with excitement. "I'm the president of Avalon Bay's Tourism Board, and that means I love this town! I love it hard, folks!"

I smother a grin.

"The Bay is home not only to some very extraordinary people, but to the greatest, most unique businesses on the eastern seaboard! And we have a group of brave and beautiful participants for this summer's Games, including a team from the newly renovated Beacon Hotel, which is reopening at the end of the month."

"Whooo!" Genevieve shouts, jumping up and down. Since she's in tiny shorts and a black string bikini, her antics draw the eyes of nearly every male on the beach. My eyes aren't idle, either. She has great boobs. Perfectly proportioned.

"I know what you're doing," her fiancé warns from beside us.

"What?" she says innocently.

"You want to distract all the dudes into thinking about your tits instead of their sandcastles. Well, it ain't gonna work, Fred," he declares, using that completely random nickname he has for her that they both refuse to explain.

"Too late," his teammate Spencer says. "All I'm thinking about is her rack now."

Evan glowers at him. "That's the mother of my future children, asshole."

"The mother of your future children has a great rack."

"Our first event requires all four team members," Deb says into her mic. "The rules are simple—just build something! Anything! It could be a castle, it could be a flower, it could a self-portrait! You're allowed to use your hands and any of the tools provided. Shovels, pails, spatulas. Go nuts, everyone! You can also take advantage of any natural objects you find on the beach. Driftwood, shells, seaweed, and rocks are all fair game. What isn't allowed is anything man-made. If we see any food coloring or cement—"

"Who the fuck brought their own cement?" I hear Cooper mutter, and our respective teams shudder with laughter.

"—you will be disqualified." Deb claps her hands. "All right, everybody, get those sculpting hands ready! You have ninety minutes to wow the judges with the most impressive sand structure ever made. May I remind you that last year's winners, the beautiful ladies from the Soapery—"

I knew it. They're definitely our biggest competitors in this event.

"—constructed a five-foot sand interpretation of Cinderella's castle. That will be a tough one to top, ladies, but I believe in you."

"Someone's playing favorites," Mackenzie grumbles.

"For real. Dooley better not be one of the judges," Cooper growls.

"I think we found the competitive couple on the beach," I whisper to Gen, who giggles.

"Ready, set, sculpt!"

Anyone who thinks building something out of sand is easy is dead wrong. It's hard. And my only task so far is carting plastic pails from the ocean to our build site. It's nine o'clock and the sun's rays aren't even that strong, yet Genevieve and I are sweating profusely as we toil to replenish our team's water supply. After each trip, though, each sharp order from Mac and Zale to pat this, tamp this down, build this up, I'm starting to see a method to their madness. Gradually, our fish comes alive. It's about six feet long and three feet wide, its curved tail slashing a semicircle in the sand, scales intricately carved by Zale's spatula.

By the time our ninety minutes are up, I'm genuinely impressed by Team Beacon's creation.

"Not half bad," Gen says, admiring our handiwork.

"Not half bad?" Zale echoes. "It's exquisite."

"I wouldn't go that far—"

"Yes. You would. And you should." His tone brooks no argument, and Gen wisely shuts up.

I check out the Hartley team's creation, my eyebrows soaring when I notice it's not half bad either. They constructed a lion, complete with a wavy mane, thick paws, and an open mouth brandishing a set of lethal-looking teeth.

"Dammit," Mackenzie mutters, sidling up to Genevieve. They're surreptitiously studying their boyfriends' work. "It's pretty good."

"Ours is better," I assure them.

Zale agrees. "There's no structural integrity in that lion's mouth. One gust of wind and those teeth are falling off." He grins. "And my weather app has just informed me we should be expecting a lil' bit of wind."

Turns out he's a prophet. By the time the judges are nearing our section of the beach, the wind has picked up. They approach the Hartley lion just as half its face crumbles off.

"Son of a bitch," Cooper curses.

Mackenzie looks over with a sweet smile. "Better luck next time, sweetie."

This couple is vicious.

The three volunteer judges scribble something on their clipboards, then walk over to inspect our fish. I hear a couple *oohs,* which bodes well. Zale links his arm through mine, whispering, "We got this in the bag."

But there's no contest, not when the Soapery created a sprawling sand replica of Santorini, Greece. Even if I hadn't been told what it was, I could have easily guessed. Santorini's trademark staggered, dome-shaped buildings crop out of the sand, topped by colored shells the ladies scavenged from the beach. They've somehow managed to create blue accents. White walkways made of crushed shells. It's goddamn breathtaking.

The *oohs* and *ahhs* get louder. The judges furiously scribble and take pictures. Nobody is at all surprised when Felice and her team are declared the winners.

Team Soapery now leads the scoreboard with three points. The bakers, no surprise, come in second with their four-foot-tall sand cake, earning Team Bakery two points. And to my delight, our fish places third, which grants us one point.

"We're in this," Mackenzie exclaims, pumping her fist.

"Unlike *some* people," Genevieve says loudly.

I love my teammates.

* * *

The next few hours are some of the most fun I've ever had. Due to the windy conditions, the windsurfing race ends up being the most competitive. It's split into two heats, which means two scoring opportunities. Tate and Danny compete for the club; Mac and Gen for the Beacon. And Gen, who practically grew up on the water, causes an upset when she beats Danny. He crosses the finish line a mere second later, stunned to find himself in second. Zale and I cheer like maniacs from the shore, because Gen's win just earned our team three points. Mac, sadly, doesn't even place. Tate takes that heat easily, with Team Mechanics finishing second, and another upset occurs when Team Bakery steals third place from Team Firefighters.

I'm frankly shocked by all the upsets. There are eight teams in total, the participants ranging in age and skill level, but some of the competitors come out of left field. Like when the tiny waitress from Sharkey's Sports Bar defeats a gigantic mechanic in the footrace to take third. Or when one of the firefighters, who's two hundred and twenty pounds with tree trunks for legs, nimbly dances across the tightrope as if he were raised in the circus, winning first place.

After his windsurfing win, Tate strides down the sand, shaking water droplets from his golden hair. He smiles as he passes me.

"Nice win," I say grudgingly.

"Thanks, ginger." He winks before rejoining his team.

"Why does he call you *ginger*?" Zale asks blankly. "Your hair is clearly copper."

Gasping, I throw my arms around my teammate's neck. "THANK YOU!"

To cool off after the last water event, Debra Dooley announces it's time for tug-of-war.

Zale and I are representing Team Beacon. He's lean but muscular, and, as I told Mackenzie during our strategy session, I'm freakishly strong.

"All right, Cass, you ready for this?" Gen encourages. "Let's see you use that boob power!"

I roll my eyes at her. Normally I might bristle at the big-boobs joke, but that one was actually kind of funny. "I'll do my best," I promise.

Since Deb's scoring system makes very little sense to me, I struggle to understand as she explains how the tug-of-war event will work. It seems to be a bracket setup, four teams narrowed to two, narrowed to one winner. But you also get one point for every round you win along the way. And then the usual first-, second-, and third-place scores. Whatever. Just pull the rope, right?

Zale and I face off against the Soapery ladies: Felice and her manager, Nora. I feel like a sadist at the notion of destroying two fifty-year-old women, but they surprise us with their fortitude.

"Dig in!" Zale shouts. He's our anchor in the back. I'm in the front. "Dig your heels in, Cassie! We got this."

I hold on to the rope for dear life, while our teammates scream their encouragement from the sidelines. Inch by inch, we manage to drag our opponents closer to the red line. Sweat drips down my forehead. I see Felice's forearms straining. A red vein in Nora's forehead pulsating. They're losing steam. Giving up. Zale and I give a final tug and Team Soapery is out.

"One point for Team Beacon," Deb declares after blowing her whistle. "You guys are moving on to the next round."

Of the other three matchups, I'm not shocked that the teams with the biggest dudes make it through. The Hartley twins, the firefighters, and the yacht club guys.

We're facing the firefighters next, and I'm not optimistic.

"We can take them," Zale assures me.

We're huddled together several feet from the battle area. Deb's given each team a couple minutes to talk strategy, but the firefighters don't bother utilizing their allotted time. They're already in position, rope in hand. Cocky assholes.

Rightfully so, however. "Zale. There's no way. That big dude is, like, two hundred pounds."

He disagrees, his voice low and confident. "You saw what they did against the mechanics, right? They placed the short guy in the front, big one anchoring. Now look what they're doing."

I discreetly peek over. Interesting. The big dude is up front now.

"See?" Zale says knowingly. "Bad strategy. They think because you're in the front, he'll be able to single-handedly wrench you over the line."

"So I should go to the back this time?"

"No. Let's not talk crazy now. You need me to anchor. But you, my special goddess warrior, won't let him move you. You're not gonna budge, because we're gonna what?"

"Dig our heels in," I answer dutifully.

"Exactly. Dig those heels in. You're a stone, Cassie. Immovable. You're a statue. You're Stonehenge."

Now that's a pep talk.

"Now rub sand on your hands to dry them off," he orders. "A dry rope is a winning rope."

As we're getting in position, I notice Tate grinning at me. "Come on, ginger," he calls. "Let's see what you got."

Deb blows the whistle and the round begins. Somehow, against all odds, Zale's strategy works. We're statues. We don't move. Don't budge. I don't think the firefighters know what hit them, and they expend all their energy attempting to dislodge our heels, which are dug in so deep we're part of the sand now. Our opponents are dripping with sweat, but we're Stonehenge. We're immovable. Standing our ground.

"Now," Zale orders, and we make our move, yanking hard. The shorter guy can't control the rope and the two men go flying forward, landing face first in the sand.

"Another point for the Beacon!"

"Holy shit," I exclaim, dazed. "We're in the top two!"

Zale screams and lifts me off my feet to spin me around.

The Hartleys face off against Tate and his partner next, the latter team beating the twins after a competitive battle involving many an expletive. Then Tate's sauntering up to me with a shit-eating grin.

"Ohhhh, look what the cat dragged in," he taunts.

"You're the one who dragged yourself over to me, dumbass," I point out. I kneel down to stick my hands in the sand. They're sweaty, and I need them dry. As Zale says, *a dry rope is a winning rope.* That's not a real phrase, but hey, it got us to the finals.

Where, I suspect, our luck is about to run out. Tate's six-one and has those strong sailing hands. His partner Luke is six-five and also happens to have strong sailing hands. The two of them have dominated their matchups. But Zale and I did manage to beat the firefighters, so maybe there's a shred of hope for us.

"Don't look so worried," Tate tells me. "It'll be okay. I'll help you up after your face hits the sand."

"That's so romantic," I say. I look at Zale. "Isn't he so romantic?"

"You guys dating?" Zale asks, his gaze shifting between us.

I answer, "Sort of," at the same time Tate responds, "Just a little."

We look at each other and grin.

Then I drag my fingers across my throat and warn, "You're going down."

"Oh, I *am* going down. On you later tonight."

Zale lets out a howl.

"Is that supposed to be a threat?" I demand. "Because it sounds fun."

Tate winks. "More like a promise."

Then the whistle blows and we get our asses handed to us. The round lasts about four seconds, and I do indeed get sand in my face after I collapse. I'm pretty sure Luke was capable of taking us down all on his own.

Like the gentleman he is, Tate keeps his promise and helps me to my feet. "You okay?"

"I'm good. Nice win."

Although we lost, our efforts in the tug-of-war event awarded Team Beacon with four points. Mackenzie does some quick math and looks concerned when she realizes the Hartleys are closing in on the lead we accrued thanks to our windsurfing upset.

"It's fine," Gen reassures her. "We're still ahead by a lot."

Except suddenly we're not. Team Hartley embarks on a winning streak that makes Mac and Gen see red. They crush it in beach volleyball. Then Evan and Alex dominate their swimming heats, each coming in first. By the time one thirty rolls around, Team Hartley has added nine points to their total score.

Everyone's tired and ready to go, but we're stuck there for Deb Dooley's final speech.

"All right, everybody! How much fun did we have today? I think this was peak fun for me! And I'm looking forward to seeing all of you again tomorrow, bright and early! We'll be starting the obstacle course at eight forty-five sharp—the rest of tomorrow's events are listed on the schedule we emailed to you this week. We'll be wrapping up around one thirty P.M., with the winners' ceremony starting at two. Today's standings are being posted outside the tourism center as we speak, so make sure to take a peek before you head home for the day!"

The moment she finishes speaking, it's as if everyone on the beach has transformed from adult to child. A mob of us hurries across the street toward the tourism center, a little blue building that stands at the entrance to the boardwalk. Near the door, an easel holds a huge chalkboard with the scoreboard written on it. Genevieve practically hurls herself at it. She studies it, then threads her way through the other teams back toward us.

"We're in third place overall," she says flatly.

"That's great!" I counter. "Why do you look so pissed?"

"Hartley and Sons are in second place."

"Damn it," growls Mackenzie.

First place is currently held by the firefighters, with the yacht club in fourth. When I see Tate wandering my way, I stick out my tongue at him like an immature ass. "We're beating you."

He slaps his chest as if struck by a bullet. "Oh no. My ego can't handle it. I might need a blowjob to make me feel better."

I snicker, and he slings an arm around me and leans down

to plant a kiss on my lips. My heart skips a beat, because I still can't get used to the reality that Tate Bartlett just goes around kissing me.

"That was fun," he says.

"It really was. Did you compete last year?"

He nods. "We came in second overall. Third the year before."

"Look at you, collecting trophies left and right."

"Baby, don't even talk to me about trophies. My dad's kept every single trophy I've ever won in my life, since I was, like, five years old. They're collecting dust all over the house."

"What trophies were you winning at age five?" I challenge.

"You kidding me? I was five when I won my first dinghy race. Damn trophy was taller than I was." He grins. "Pretty sure Dad has a framed photo of it at the house. Tiny me struggling to hold up a monster trophy."

"I need to see that picture. Get on that."

"I'll see if my dad still has it prominently displayed in his office," Tate promises with a laugh.

"Hey," Evan interrupts, elbowing Tate in the arm. "Bonfire at our place later." He winks at me. "Gotta celebrate our lead."

I look at Gen, who's standing next to Evan. "Fraternizing with the enemy, are we?" I say, raising a brow.

"I mean, we live together."

"Fair. I'll allow it. Do you want to go?" I ask Tate.

"Like, a date?" He feigns uncertainty. "I don't know. That's a big commitment."

"Fine. I'll go alone."

"Nah, I'll go with you. I'm stopping in to see my folks for dinner, but I can come grab you after."

He removes his arm from my shoulder but doesn't release me completely—his hand instantly seeks out mine. As Tate laces our fingers together, I don't miss the amused gleam in Evan's eyes.

"So this is a thing now, eh?" Evan says.

Once again, Tate and I answer at the same time.

"Sort of."

"Just a little."

CHAPTER 27

TATE

Before I even turn the knob on the front door, I hear the explosion of noise behind it. The kids always know when someone's home. Especially when it's their papa. Sure enough, the moment I step inside, two tornadoes slam into me.

"Hey, guys." I drop to my knees to show them some love. "Aww, I missed you so much."

Fudge, our chocolate lab, has both paws around my neck. He's a hugger. Polly, our shepherd, waits her turn like the proper lady she is. She always plays it coy. Sits there looking pretty until I can't resist.

"Oh, you pretty girl, c'mere," I tell her, and soon she's trying to climb into my lap because these two always forget how big they are. Ninety-pound lapdogs. We used to have a third, a border collie named Jack, but he died this past winter. I miss the old guy.

As I rub behind her ears, Polly's tongue flops out happily. She collapses on the hardwood and offers me her belly. Fudge does the same, and suddenly I've got eight paws sticking straight up in the air and two bellies demanding to be rubbed.

Which is how my mom finds me. "Am I interrupting?" she asks dryly.

At the sound of her voice, the dogs jump to their feet, instantly bored of their prodigal papa's return. Their toenails click on the floor as they dash off to who knows where. I'm but a speck in their proverbial dust.

"Damn. And I thought they missed me," I remark, watching their disappearing tails.

"Speaking of missing. Hey, kiddo." Mom laughs and flings her arms around me. "I hate this housesitting gig of yours."

"No, you don't. You love the alone time with Dad."

"Well, duh. But I still miss my son."

"We text every day."

"Still miss you. Are you hungry? Dinner's almost ready."

"Famished. Where's Dad?"

"Upstairs in his office. He forgot to fill out some paperwork at work earlier, so he's taking care of a few things before dinner."

"Cool. I'm gonna go up and say hi to him. I need something from his office."

In the upstairs hall, I find Dad's door ajar. I approach and give it a light knock. "Dad?"

"Yeah, come in, kid." He greets me with a big smile. "How goes it? How was Beach Games?"

"Intense. We're currently in fourth place."

"Who's in first?"

"Frickin' dudes from the fire station. They always dominate." I walk toward the glass cabinet that spans one wall of the office.

It's pretty much a shrine to our family, containing all the accomplishments we've amassed over the years. Dad's baseball trophies and photos from his time in St. Louis. His and Mom's wedding pictures. All my childhood trophies and first-place ribbons. And there, sandwiched between Mom's framed college diploma and a copy of the deed to Bartlett Marine, is the photograph I was telling Cassie about. Me, posing after the first sailing race I ever entered, holding the first trophy I ever won. Or rather,

trying to hold it. My teeth-gritting expression reveals I'm struggling not to let the thing flatten me.

"Do you mind if I take this out so I can snap a picture of it?"
I point to the photo.

"Go for it." He chuckles. "Taking a walk down memory lane?"

"No, I was just telling Cassie about this earlier. Thought she'd
get a kick out of seeing it." I open the cabinet and carefully remove the frame, then place it on the edge of Dad's desk and fuck
with my phone camera until I'm not seeing any glare.

"Man, I was a cute kid," I remark.

Dad snorts. "And so humble too."

I take a pic of the pic, then return it to the cabinet. As I'm
shutting the door, my gaze snags on another framed photo, this
one featuring a younger version of my father hanging off the mast
of a shiny white yacht. He's grinning from ear to ear, loving life.

"Was this your Hawaii-to-Australia sail?" I ask, glancing over
my shoulder. "The one that took you a month?"

"Thirty-two days," he confirms. "Man, what an adventure. I
almost died in Hurricane Erma."

"Sounds fun." My smile falters when I suddenly think about
Gil Jackson's offer. It's constantly been on my mind, nagging at
me, but I haven't made any decisions yet. It would be a huge commitment, leaving the Bay. And sure, I can do it in sixty days, but
who knows if or when I'd get an opportunity like that again. If I
accept the gig, I want to maximize my time on the *Surely Perfect*.
That means four months. Four months and the adventure of a
lifetime.

"Uh-oh, you've gone serious on me." Dad spins around in his
chair, propping his hands behind his head. "What's going on,
kid?"

"Gil asked me to deliver the *Surely Perfect* to him in New
Zealand."

His eyebrows shoot up. "Really?"

"I know, right?" I lean against the bookshelf. Hesitant, because I value my father's opinion. But I also know he won't want me taking so much time off. "They bought a house in Auckland and plan to live there half the year. They'd need her there by New Year's Day. They'd pay me, obviously."

Dad is startled now. "You're considering this?"

"Of course I am. Why? You think I shouldn't?"

His casual pose changes, arms dropping, hands clasping together in his lap. His expression grows serious as he considers the question. "What's the starting point? California?"

"Florida. It'll take a couple days to sail from Charleston to the port in Miami. I'd stock up there. Prep the boat. And then I'd set sail to Auckland."

A frown mars his lips. "This is a transatlantic crossing, Tate. No. It's too much for you."

"I'd take it easy. Gil said he'll help me chart a manageable route."

"Easy? Manageable?" Dad shakes his head in disbelief. "We're talking about crossing the North Atlantic, the South Atlantic. Indian Ocean. Then you've got the gulfs, the Tasman Sea."

"It's a lot," I agree.

"It's too much," he repeats. "And he needs her there by the first of January? That puts you in hurricane season."

"The tail end of it," I argue. "It adds some risk, yes, but the tough sailing starts later in the journey. By November the season will have passed. Any developing hurricanes are likely to be west, right?"

"That's not the only concern, kid. The trades will be difficult. You'd be looking at fifteen, twenty knots. Not to mention squalls. I did an Atlantic crossing before you born, nothing too intensive, just to the Canaries. And even that was tough." He sounds unhappy.

"You gotta pay attention to what's happening north when you tackle a voyage like this. Those long trailing cold fronts from the North Atlantic can fuck with the trade winds."

"I'd adjust for all that."

"A friend of mine did an Atlantic crossing in winter once. Said it was the worst sailing of his life." Dad's eyes flicker with concern now. "Waters could get rough."

"I can handle it."

He rubs the bridge of his nose. "Look. I mean, part of me thinks, yeah, you can. I've never seen anyone handle a boat the way you do. But it's a big undertaking for your first solo, you know?"

"I know," I say, nodding.

"If it's something you're seriously considering, maybe wait until spring, then? And start off a little less ambitious, maybe only a week or two? Chart a course from here to, I don't know, the Virgin Islands. Yeah, BVI would be good. You could take the Beneteau 49 if she's not booked for a charter—"

She's not a Hallberg-Rassy, I almost blurt out, but bite my tongue.

"—and give yourself a small taste of the solo journey. Know what I mean?"

"Yeah, I guess." We can both hear my lack of enthusiasm for his alternate proposal.

"If you accepted Gil's offer, you'd be gone, what, two, three months?"

"About that. Longer if I take the scenic route," I joke.

Dad doesn't crack a smile. "That's a long time to be away from home. I need you at Bartlett Marine, kid. I can't handle it by myself."

I want to point out that he handled it by himself for years before I started taking on more responsibility. But it's clear what he thinks of this plan.

Sensing my unhappiness, he sighs. "I built this business for our family. For you, so that one day you would take it over. I thought that's what we were working toward these past few years. Teaching you how to run it."

"We are. But if I'm ever going to do a major solo voyage, shouldn't I do it now? Before I have even more responsibility?"

Dad is silent for several long beats. "I truly don't think you're ready for it," he finally says. "And I need you here, at the dealership. But if you want to go . . ."

I swallow my disappointment. "No," I say. "It's fine." He's probably right, anyway. It's a crazy idea. Dangerous. "I'll tell Gil to hire a more experienced captain."

"I think that's a smart idea. And if you did want to plan something for the spring, I'd be happy to sit down with you and—"

"Dinner's ready!" Mom's faint voice calls from below.

"Shit," Dad says with a pained look. "I still need to send this email. Tell your mother I'll be right down?"

"Sure thing."

Downstairs, I help Mom set the table, hoping she doesn't notice I'm feeling subdued. But she's a mom, so of course she notices.

"Everything okay?" she asks. "What were you talking to your father about?"

"All good. We were just going over some sailing stuff. And I needed to take a picture of Dad's trophy shrine to show something to Cassie. I'm meeting her after this."

Mom smiles and hands me a stack of silverware from the utensil drawer. "Which picture?"

"The one of me after my first dinghy race."

"Oh boy, I remember that day," she says with a laugh. "Standing there at the marina, worrying my five-year-old son was going to drown. Gavin assured me you could handle it, and what do you know—he was right. You won. Your dad was practically bursting with pride." She's quiet for a beat, then says, "You're spending a lot of time with Cassie."

I lay down the silverware on the table. "Yeah. I guess."

"Is it serious?"

I lift my head to see her fighting a smile. "Not really. It's going to end when she goes back to school in September."

"Do you want it to end?"

That gives me pause. "To be honest, I hadn't considered the alternative."

"But you like her."

I do like her. I like her a lot. In fact, I'm getting impatient for dinner to start, because the sooner it starts, the sooner it ends and I can go pick Cassie up for the bonfire. I saw her all day and I'm already dying to see her again.

"Yes. I like her."

"Then why does it have to end?" Mom asks.

For the life of me, I can't think of a good answer to that.

* * *

Later, at the bonfire, I'm still thinking about my mother's question.

Why does it have to end?

I mean . . . does it? Cassie and I agreed to a summer fling, but sometimes flings . . . evolve. My biggest fear was that I'd end up hurting her because of my need to keep things purely physical, but that need seems to have . . . evolved. We go out on the boat. We have dinner when I get home from work. Hell, I've gone for dinner with her and her *mother*. Somehow, without noticing it, I allowed all this to happen. And I don't even care. I *like* it.

Fuck.

Whatever we have going on these days, it's a lot more than physical.

I gaze across the fire where Cassie's sitting with Genevieve and Heidi. She and Heidi are laughing about something, which is a bit shocking because Heidi isn't the chatty, giggly type. She's the type who eats her own young. That's why she and Alana are such good friends. Stone hearts, those two.

Speaking of Alana, when I go to the coolers to grab another beer, my former flame sidles up to me. She looks gorgeous as always, and yet I'm startled to discover I'm not attracted to her anymore. She's gone back to being the Alana I first met in junior high, just another one of the awesome girls in my platonic friend group, someone it wouldn't even occur to me to sleep with.

"Hey," she says.

"Hey." I twist open a fresh beer.

"You've been avoiding me."

I glance over. "Not at all."

"Oh really? So it just happens that we used to see each other all the time and now I haven't seen you since . . ." Alana thinks it over. "Damn, since the last time we were here together."

"Shit, really? That was more than a month ago."

"Exactly."

"I promise, I'm not avoiding you," I assure her. "I've been slammed at work this entire summer. I haven't really hung out with anyone other than Cassie."

"Ah," she says knowingly. "The other redhead."

"Purely coincidental," I reply with a grin, although I do find it funny.

"So you're not avoiding me."

"No."

Those sharp eyes continue to study me. "I don't think you're lying."

"I'm not. I've been at the dealership, the yacht club, chilling with Cassie. This weekend is Beach Games. Lots going on. I've gone out with Evan for a couple drinks, but that's about it. And I'm housesitting for the Jacksons, so I've been away from the regular 'hood."

"Oh yes, you're lapping it up in the land of clone luxury."

"Pretty much. How've you been?"

"I'm good. Got a job as an au pair."

"You hate kids," I remind her, grinning.

"These ones aren't too bad. And the pay is great. I swear those clones like to throw their cash around like their entire life is one long strip club visit."

I think about how much Gil offered me to sail the *Surely Perfect* and I have to agree. "You dating anybody?" I raise a brow.

"I am not . . . unlike some people." Alana laughs. "It's weird seeing you with a girlfriend."

"She's not my girlfriend."

"Uh-huh, that's what they all say." With that, Alana saunters off.

Beer in hand, I wander to the fire and grab a chair, dragging it next to Evan's. Heidi's gone, and Gen and Cassie are now near the deck in an intense huddle with Mackenzie and their Beach Games teammate Zale. When Cooper passes their huddle, Mac lifts her head and all but hisses at him like a feral cat. He holds his hands up in surrender and keeps walking, rolling his eyes when he approaches us.

"I just got accused of espionage for walking by their team," Coop says cheerfully.

I snicker. My eyes remain on Cassie, who's laughing at something Gen said.

"Gen really likes your girl," Evan remarks, following my gaze. "And Gen hates most people."

"It's hard not to like Cassie," I admit.

Cooper's brows jerk up. Then he chuckles. "Interesting."

"What?"

"Nothing."

"You sound like my mother. She was just grilling me about Cass."

"I mean, you're acting very boyfriendly," Evan pipes up, sounding amused. "So if that's not the path you want to take," he warns, "you should probably course correct right about now."

I take a swig of beer. "Boyfriendly how?"

"Every time I turn around you're holding her hand."

"So?"

"You never held Alana's hand," Cooper points out.

"Alana would bite a dude's dick off before she let him hold her hand."

"Did you even try?" challenges Evan.

I pause. "No."

"Why not?" His smug smirk tells me he already knows the answer to that.

And he's right. I never felt that sort of tenderness toward Alana. We both kept an emotional distance because we knew it was never going anywhere.

But there's no distance with Cassie. She's always within my reach. She melts into me when I come to her. She doesn't keep me at arm's length. Doesn't play games. I'm happy when I'm with her. And as I think about all the ways she and I just fit, that question once again surfaces in the forefront of my mind.

Why does it have to end?

CHAPTER 28

CASSIE

"This is it. What we've trained our entire lives for. And by entire lives I mean the last two days. And by trained I mean we randomly decided who would compete in what event. I mean, I didn't train—did you?" Zale glances around the huddle.

"I swam some laps in my pool," I tell them. "Does that count?"

"Now that's dedication to the team," Mackenzie teases.

"The Beacon is forever indebted to you," Genevieve says solemnly.

I snicker. I had a lot of fun with my teammates this weekend, and I'm sad to see it end. Alas, only one event remains in the twentieth-annual Avalon Beach Games: the water balloon toss.

It's been a frustrating day thus far for Team Beacon. We didn't place in either of the obstacle course heats this morning. Team Yacht Club won both, which had Tate strutting around like a self-righteous peacock. We also lost out on third place in the bucket relay to those damn firefighters. We made up for it by placing third in the three-legged race, thanks to Mackenzie and Zale. Unfortunately, "the stupid twins because they have the same stupid size legs," as Mackenzie had poetically framed it, won that race to give Team Hartley three points.

As it stands now for Mac and Gen's side bet, their boyfriends are beating us by one measly point. In the scope of the actual competition, I think our teams are vying for third place overall. But since my teammates are more concerned with their side hustle, they proceed to torture my brain with a bunch of math that makes no sense.

"All right," Mac is saying. "They're up by one, so that means we need to place third in order to tie—"

"What's the tiebreaker?" Zale interjects.

"No idea. We didn't anticipate a tie. We'll have to come up with something. But if we place second, that becomes moot, because then we get two points and we win. First place, we get three points and we win. *But*—we only win if *they* don't place."

"Wait, what if they place third and we place first?" Gen points out. She squints as she does some mental math. "Then they get one point, which puts them up by two. But we get three points, which puts us up by one. We win."

"Right. But . . . damn it, if we win and they come in second, we tie again. So—"

"Stop," I wail, covering my ears. "I can't listen to this anymore."

"For real," Zale moans, his face scrunched in sheer pain. "This is too complicated. You sound like my brothers droning on about their dumbass fantasy football standings, trying to figure out if they made the playoffs."

"All right, everyone!" Debra Dooley yells into her microphone. I swear, she brought that thing from home. None of the other volunteers have mics. "We're about to start!"

A few yards away, Evan calls out to his fiancée. "Hey, Fred, what size should I order your French maid costume in?"

"In your dreams," Gen shoots back.

"Every night," he promises.

Mackenzie's gaze travels to Cooper, and she cocks her head at him. "Well? I'm waiting. Where's *your* smartass comment?"

Cooper smirks. "I don't heckle the downtrodden."

"Heckle this," she retorts, flipping him the bird.

I smother a laugh. It's funny seeing each of them interact. Gen and Evan are chemistry personified, every word exchanged practically oozing sex. Cooper and Mac are more adversarial, yet when they look at each other, their connection is unmistakable.

I look over at Tate, remembering the way he held my hand last night at the bonfire. His fingers laced through mine feels so natural, and I wonder how on earth I'm going to say goodbye to him in two weeks. My flight to Boston leaves three days after the Beacon's reopening, and a part of me is already thinking, well, I *do* get a week off for midterms in October. And I *do* get Thanksgiving off. And Christmas. New Year's.

Maybe we can make something work. Not a relationship or anything; I'm still doing my best to keep my heart disengaged. But who says we can't keep sleeping together? Hooking up when we have the opportunity? We're not sick of each other yet, so doesn't it make sense to keep the fling going until we are? That is, if Tate's even interested in extending the fling.

For some reason, though, I get the feeling he is.

"We'll do a random draw to determine the order for the toss," Deb says, and a volunteer rushes over with a baseball cap containing slips of paper with our team names. "Up first will be . . . the handsome sailors from the Manor!"

The rest of the names are pulled from the hat, and we're gratified to hear we'll be going last. Gives us an opportunity to watch the other teams and learn from their mistakes.

As Tate and his team come forward, Deb quickly goes over the rules again. The water balloon toss requires all four members to stand in a line, starting at about two feet apart. The balloon is thrown down the line from one person to the next, and after each completed leg, the team members must take a step back. The distance between each person gets bigger and bigger, and the team that makes it the farthest distance without popping their balloon wins those coveted three points.

"Ready?" Deb shouts. "Annnd toss!"

This is it. Do or die.

Team Yacht Club makes it to a distance of fifteen feet separating each member before the balloon hits Luke in the face and explodes, soaking him. Tate shoots me a wry look as they return to the sidelines, as if to say, *you win some, you lose some.* He takes everything in stride. I love that about him.

"Fifteen feet is the distance to beat!" announces Deb.

The bakers and mechanics are up next, finishing with an impressive twenty-two feet for the former and a dismal twelve for the latter. The firefighters finish with twenty feet. The Sharkey's staff with nine.

Then it's Team Soapery, working together like a well-oiled machine. Each time Deb shouts, "Annnd step!" the four ladies take a step to widen the distance. Deb shouts, "Annnd toss!" and the balloon exchanges hands.

Three minutes in, and they're already twenty feet apart.

"Whoa," Zale marvels.

"It's the underhand throw," Mac whispers to our team. "We need to go underhand."

Team Soapery makes it a spectacular twenty-nine feet before Felice catches the balloon wrong and it bursts in her outstretched hands. Still, the ladies know they kicked ass, grinning from ear to ear as they head for the sidelines. They've got a good seven feet on the best team, the bakers.

"Hartley and Sons, you're up!"

Cooper smirks at his girlfriend as he saunters by. "You're saying all we have to do is beat twenty feet and we're guaranteed to place? Oh no! So hard!"

312 • ELLE KENNEDY

Mackenzie and Genevieve simultaneously throw up their middle fingers, sparking a burst of laughter from the gathering crowd. When I glance toward the onlookers, I'm alarmed to spot my dad's face. He's with Nia and the twins, and they all smile and wave when they notice me looking. Shit. I didn't know they were coming back today. Mom and Grandma are supposed to show up too. For the winners' ceremony.

Panic flares inside me, while I strain to remember the last time Mom and Dad were in the same vicinity.

The saving grace here is that Mom and Grandma haven't arrived yet. That means I have time to warn Dad off before they get here. But first, we need to murder this water balloon event.

On the field of play, the Team Hartley line moves with swift precision. They nail their five-foot throws. Ten. Fifteen.

At nineteen feet, the biggest upset of today's Beach Games occurs.

Spencer, their day laborer, tosses the balloon to Evan. His hand slips on the release, just slightly, but it's enough to alter the trajectory. The balloon veers toward Evan's right, forcing him to take an abrupt step, and his body isn't quite in position as he attempts the catch.

Splat.

The water explodes in Evan's hand.

"Man down!" Deb crows into the mic, and the firefighters cheer loudly, maintaining their current third-place score of twenty feet.

"Oh baby, why are you all wet?" Genevieve coos when Evan stomps back. She pretends to be confused. "What happened? I wasn't looking. Did it pop?"

"Use that little-girl voice again"—he narrows his eyes—"and it better be tonight. In bed."

Mac winks at Cooper as he passes. "I'm pretty sure that wasn't twenty feet . . ."

He snorts. "You haven't placed yet, princess. And right now we're still beating you by one point."

Finally, it's our turn. I can't even believe how nerve-wracking this is. How is this low-stakes, small-town beach competition making me sweat this much?

"We got this," Zale says.

"We got this," Gen echoes.

"Annnd toss!" Deb yells once we're in position.

Team Beacon makes fast work of it. Five feet. Ten. Fifteen. Those are the easy ones. Now come the scary little one-footers between fifteen and twenty. If we hit twenty, though, we only tie with the Hartleys, and we can't have that. We want the win. Which means we need to beat not only the firefighters but also the bakers in order to move to second place.

At eighteen feet, my palms are so clammy I have to bend down and wipe them off in the sand.

At nineteen feet, I can't feel my legs anymore.

The pressure is monumental. We're tossing for twenty now. If we make it, we've tied the firefighters.

We make it.

"Annnd step!"

We take another step. If we succeed in this next sequence, we've knocked the firefighters out.

"Annnd toss!"

Zale tosses. I make the first catch.

I look at Genevieve. "Ready?"

She wipes her hands on the front of her denim shorts. "Ready."

Very methodically, I throw underhanded in a perfect straight line. The balloon floats like a weightless feather into her waiting palms. She catches it, and a collective breath of relief travels through the crowd.

Gen turns to face Mac, features creased with deep concentration. She tosses.

Mackenzie makes the catch.

"Twenty-one feet!" Deb declares.

"Holy shit!" Zale screams. "We did it! We did it!" He starts jumping around, thrusting up both arms and punching the air.

I choke out a laugh. "We're not done!" I remind him. "We're still playing."

"Oh, right."

"We have an actual shot at second place here," Gen marvels.

And we do it. We make it to twenty-three feet before my balloon explodes at Gen's feet. Doesn't matter, though. We successfully edged out the bakers to finish second place in this final event.

We've beaten the Hartleys at Beach Games.

By *one* point.

That was really fucking close.

"What size thong do you need?" a smirking Gen asks the twins once our team celebration dies down. Her gaze shifts to Evan's groin. "I don't know if they make it in extra small, sweetie."

"Extra large, you mean." Growling, he lifts Gen off her feet as if he's going to toss her, but instead brings her close. She wraps her legs around him and they start making out.

Rolling my eyes, I wander over to my dad, who now stands alone on the boardwalk. "Nice job!" he exclaims, giving me a quick side hug.

"Thanks. Where are the girls?" I ask, glancing around.

"They got bored of watching you throw balloons, so Nia took them to get ice cream."

I nod. "Hey, so I should probably warn you—Mom and Grandma are going to be here any minute. They're coming for the winners' ceremony."

"Really? Your mother?" He lifts a brow.

I smile ruefully. "I know, right? But . . . I haven't said anything to you about this, mostly because I didn't trust it at first, but Mom really has been making an effort since she got to town."

"Has she?" I can't quite discern his tone.

"She has. It's been fun, actually."

Dad is taken aback by that. I don't blame him. I've never used the word *fun* in relation to my mother.

"Oh. Well. That's great, Cass. I'm glad to hear you're enjoying yourself and that she's putting in the effort."

This time, I easily pick up on the skepticism lining his voice.

"Like I said, I didn't entirely trust it. But she's been good lately. Attentive. Funny. Forthcoming . . ." I hesitate for a beat. This probably isn't the most appropriate time to take the conversation deeper, but I also suspect we likely won't get another opportunity to discuss my mother, and so the words just slip out. "She told me about the miscarriage."

Dad lurches as if I struck him. "She did?"

"Yes." My palms are sweaty again. Dad and I rarely discuss anything this sensitive, so I'm unsure how to navigate it. "I'm glad she did. It made me understand her better, you know? Why she fought you so hard for custody. I thought she was trying to keep you away from me, but I guess she was trying to keep me close after her loss. So . . . yeah. I'm grateful that she told me."

"Yes. Well." His expression shutters, but not before I glimpse a flash of anger.

"Cassie!"

I turn in time to see my sisters racing toward me. Nia trails after them, wearing brown sandals and a loose-fitting sleeveless dress.

"Wanna know what Pierre did today?" Roxy exclaims. "He farted!"

The girls proceed to double over in high-pitched laughter, while their mother grimaces.

"It was very unpleasant," Nia says stiffly.

I glance at Dad. "You didn't warn them about the whole stink-pot thing?"

"*Clayton?*" growls his wife.

"Thanks, Cass. Thanks a lot."

I snicker. "Hey, you knew going into this purchase that if they handled him too roughly he'd unleash a fart attack."

"Fart attack!" Mo squeals, and the girls start skipping around shouting those two words over and over again. A resigned Nia offers an apologetic smile to all the people who turn to stare at us.

"Attention, Avalon Bay!"

A voice suddenly blasts out of the boardwalk's PA system. Deb, of course. I've heard Debra Dooley scream into microphones so many times these past two days that I could now pick her voice out of a lineup.

"The winners of the twentieth-annual Avalon Beach Games are about to be announced. Please make your way over to the Tourism Center."

"Did you win?" Mo asks me, wide-eyed.

"I don't think so. But if my teammate's math is right, we may have come in third. I'll see you guys later, okay? Gotta find my team."

"We're heading out now," Dad says, which tells me he took my warning seriously. "But I'll call you later. Good job today."

"Thanks, Dad."

There's a large crowd gathered at the tourism hut when I arrive. I search the sea of faces until I spot Zale's familiar Afro. "Cass!" he shouts. "Over here!"

I join my team, and we wait impatiently while Deb delivers another one of her speeches about how much she loves this town. She stands atop a low stage that barely holds two people, let alone a team of four. The winning teams select one member to go up and accept their trophy.

The firefighters win first place, while the yacht club takes second. And for the Beacon's long-awaited return to the world of Beach Games, our team comes in third.

We break out in cheers as Gen hops on to the small stage to accept our third-place trophy from a beaming Deb Dooley. It's about ten inches tall with a copper finish and gold accents around the beach ball figurine at the top. The brown wooden base just has a generic THIRD PLACE engraved on it.

Gen flashes the Hartleys a smile as she saunters past them holding our trophy. "Aww, they don't give these out for fourth?" Gen asks sweetly. "Look how cute it is."

"A third-place trophy, Genevieve?" Cooper shoots back. "Grow the fuck up. If you don't win, you lose."

Mac offers a brisk nod of agreement. "He's not wrong."

"You two psychos are made for each other," Evan mutters.

"Hey, Cassie," Mac says, turning to smile at me. "Thanks so much for being on our team—this was such a blast. Will you come back next year?"

"Really? Even though I don't work at the hotel?"

"What do you mean? The Beacon was in the Tanner family for fifty years. You'll always have a place here."

I'm so touched, my eyes start to sting. I didn't expect to form genuine connections this summer, but I'm so glad I did. Stupid Grandma was right. It is nice being part of a group.

Speaking of Grandma, I suddenly spot her in the crowd, a frown staining my lips when I notice she's alone. I excuse myself and make my way toward her. She greets me with a smile, but it's clearly strained.

"Hey," I say, leading her toward a less busy section of the boardwalk. "Where's Mom?"

"Well . . ." Grandma presses her lips together.

"What's wrong?"

"Nothing's wrong. But . . . perhaps a little hiccup. We just ran into your father and his family in the parking lot." Grandma pauses. "Your mother stopped to speak to Clayton."

Shit.

"Damn it," I mutter. Then I force a smile so Grandma doesn't worry. "Are you cool waiting here for a minute? I want to go and make sure nobody's been killed."

I race off in the direction of the little gravel lot behind the tourism center. This situation needs handling ASAP. Last thing I need is for Evil Mom to make a reappearance when we still have a week left in the Bay. Which means I need to defuse any bombs that might blow the rest of my summer to smithereens.

I catch sight of them immediately, gratified that it's just the two of them. Nia and the girls must be in the car already. Silver lining, I guess.

Hurrying toward them, I manage to catch the tail end of Dad's incensed accusation.

"Using the miscarriage to turn our kid against me? Trying to make yourself look like some sort of martyr? That's low, Vic, even for you. You fought for custody because you're a selfish—" He stops abruptly. "Cassie, hey. Hi, sweetheart."

Mom whirls around. Her brown eyes blaze with anger. Not directed at me, though. She's still wholly focused on my father.

"Guys," I beg. "Please. I don't want you two to fight."

"Neither do I, Cassandra. But I'm not the one fighting, am I, Clayton?" Mom says coldly.

Dad frowns. "Victoria . . ." I don't know if it's a warning or an appeal.

"No, I think this conversation is over. Why don't you go now? Your nurse and her children are waiting in the car."

"*My* children," he growls.

I reach for Mom's arm. "Come on," I urge. "Tate's taking us to lunch. He and Grandma are waiting."

Her thunderous expression doesn't change, but she also doesn't object when I start leading her away. I glance over my shoulder at Dad, whose face is bright red, his movements jerky as he repositions his glasses on the bridge of his nose.

"I'll see you this weekend," I tell him. "We're still doing dinner, right?"

"Yes, of course. See you then, sweetheart."

And then Dad stalks off and Mom is still fuming, and I feel like I just fought off a pack of rabid dogs. *This* is why confrontations should be avoided at all costs. They never lead to anything but misery.

CHAPTER 29

TATE

"That was so brutal today," Cassie moans against my shoulder, her breath tickling my skin. We're lying together on the dock. Sharing one lounge chair, which means we're practically on top of each other. Not that I'm complaining. I welcome any opportunity to have her delectable body pressed up against me.

"You're still thinking about it?" I say gently.

"How can I not? I don't even want to know what would've happened if I hadn't been able to drag Mom away. They looked like they were going to murder each other."

"That's rough."

"I mean, it's par for the course with them."

It's difficult for me to relate to that. My parents rarely fight. They bicker, sure. They've gone through a rough patch or two, but I've never seen them treat each other with anything close to the level of vitriol that Cassie describes with her parents. Their confrontation really affected her today, and the lunch that followed wasn't much of a palate cleanser. Tori was plainly in a bad mood, and I was glad when the check finally arrived.

I spent the rest of the day trying to distract Cassie from her parents' argument. We passed the afternoon swimming, barbecuing, and hanging out on the dock. At sunset we took the Lightning out for a ride again, which in turn got me so hot I couldn't even wait to find a bed when we returned to the house. We had sex on the dock, which, I won't deny, is a bit risky. But Tori and Lydia had gone out for dinner, and we tried to be quiet, mindful of the other houses along the water. Not sure if we succeeded. I can be loud when I come.

Now, we're still in our bathing suits, cozied up on the lounger, while the night breeze floats along the bay and I absentmindedly stroke her soft hair.

Cassie snuggles closer, and a sense of pure contentment washes over me. Even now, a solid hour postcoital, I'm still recovering from the sex. I swear it only gets better with this woman. I forget myself when I'm inside her. The entire world disappears and it's just me and her. Her warmth. Her pussy. Her smile. It's perfection. And the more I think about it, the more I don't want this to end. I'm already thinking about the holidays, the possibility of flying to Boston to see her.

Or, even better, accepting Gil Jackson's offer and asking Cassie to join me on the *Surely Perfect*. For a weekend. A week, a month. As long as she wanted. A horde of images suddenly swarms my mind. Cassie and I on the open water. Her hair blowing in the wind as she helps me sail. Having sex on the deck. Falling asleep in the cabin. Cooking together in the galley—

Jesus. What the hell is my brain doing right now?

None of that is ever going to happen, least of which because I already decided not to go. I promised Dad I wouldn't.

"Are you going to talk to your dad about the argument?" I ask, my gaze focusing on the darkening sky.

"God no."

"Why not?"

"Because clearly it's a sore subject for him."

"As it should be. She had a miscarriage. She fought for sole custody of you instead of agreeing to joint custody like he wanted." I lightly stroke Cassie's arm. "Don't you want to know more about that? His perspective about the miscarriage and everything that followed it?" Now I find myself frowning. "Don't you want to talk to him about *real* shit?"

"We do," she protests. "Sometimes. Sporadically." She sighs. "All right, fine. We don't talk about anything deep. I hold a lot of it back, but—"

"But there's a silver lining?" I guess with a dry chuckle. "Okay, let's hear it."

"I have him in my life," she says simply.

I furrow my brow. "And he'd go away if you shared your feelings?"

"He might. I . . ." Her voice cracks. "I don't want to be a burden on him. He already has his hands full, raising two little kids. He doesn't need his grown-ass daughter whining about her feelings and demanding to know why he never fought for custody. Telling him how much it hurts that he gave her childhood bedroom away, how awful it is to feel like I've been replaced. How fucking jealous I am of his new family."

I take a breath, tightening my arm around her. "Man. I didn't realize you felt any of that."

"Yeah. I do." Her hand trembles against my abdomen. "Right after the twins were born, when Dad suddenly had even less time for me, I used to listen to this one song all the time. It was called 'Jealous,' and I'd lie in my bedroom in Boston and listen to it on repeat because it just encapsulated everything I felt. How jealous I was that Dad had this new life I was no longer a part of."

Damn. I remember the lyrics to that song, and they're heartbreaking. Soul crushing. The idea of Cassie feeling that way brings a hot clench of emotion to my chest.

"And don't get me wrong—I treasure my sisters, I do. And I

like Nia. But I can't tell you how many times I used to lie there crying about it. Sometimes, I'd fantasize that Dad would randomly show up in Boston and come get me. He'd push past my mother and announce he was bringing me home because he was miserable without me. Like in the song." Cassie lets out a shaky breath, a flimsy laugh. "It's stupid, I know. But I was fifteen. Angst was my middle name."

My vision goes a little blurry, and I'm startled to realize there's moisture clinging to my eyelashes. I blink rapidly, but that proves to be a mistake. One tear slips out and plops onto the cheek Cassie has pressed on my shoulder.

"Oh my God, Tate. Are you crying?"

Someone goddamn kill me.

I swallow hard. My throat is so tight it hurts.

"You are," she says in amazement, rising on her elbow to peer at me. "I'm sorry. I didn't mean to bum you out."

I lift my fist to my face and scrub it over my eyes. "Sorry. It's just so fucking sad, Cassie." I hold her closer and she's so soft and warm, and suddenly I'm hit with the vision of a ten-year-old Cassie being forced to leave Avalon Bay and her father behind, whisked away to live with her shitty mother.

My eyes feel like they're burning again, and I gulp down the lump obstructing my throat.

Christ.

"This is the sweetest thing ever," she whispers, burying her face in my neck. "Nobody has ever cried on my behalf before."

Hell, *I've* never cried on anyone's behalf before. But this is Cassie. She's the kindest soul I've ever met. The funniest, sexiest, most compelling woman I've ever been with, and I feel—

I take a sharp inhale as understanding strikes me.

I feel it.

The elusive *it*.

Whatever the hell it is that makes my parents look at each other the way they do. The feeling I'd been waiting for but could never find with any of the girls who've crossed my path over the years.

I feel it now.

The irony of this doesn't escape me. I almost didn't get involved with her because I was worried *she'd* catch feelings. Meanwhile, my feelings for *her* hit me out of nowhere and knocked me on my damn ass.

But what does that mean for us? She lives in Boston, and I can't leave the Bay for the time being. Long-distance relationships are hard to maintain, but maybe we could manage it. She graduates this year anyway. Maybe she'd consider moving back here. This was where she was born. Where her father lives. And it's evident she loves him deeply.

"You have to talk to him," I say. "To your dad. Hell, and your mother too. She should know how much her words have hurt you. Don't you want parents you can be honest with, instead of sweeping everything important under the rug? Just be honest, Cass. With both of them."

"Sort of like how you're honest with your father about how badly you want to sail to New Zealand?"

"I mean, it's not like I *didn't* tell him about it. I did. I just can't go."

"Sure you can. Your contract ends soon. You have all of autumn and winter off."

"I already promised Dad I'd work full-time at Bartlett Marine."

"The dealership will be waiting for you when you get back," Cassie says softly. She sits up, watching me, her eyes shining with encouragement. "It's only a few months. Bartlett Marine isn't going to implode if you're gone for three months."

I chew on the inside of my cheek. "I know. I just . . . I don't want to let him down."

That earns me a gentle smile. "See?"

"See what?"

"We both do it. Hold back our own feelings because we don't want to disappoint our parents or make any waves."

She's right.

She's right about everything.

If I go, Bartlett Marine will still be there when I get back. If I don't go, I'm letting the opportunity of a lifetime slip away. I might never get another chance to sail a goddamn Hallberg-Rassy halfway across the goddamn world. I'm twenty-three years old, for fuck's sake. I have the rest of my life to stay in one place and work a nine-to-five job. Three months will pass in the blink of an eye. My father will survive it.

"You know what? You're right. I think I need to practice what I preach. I'll make you a deal," I announce, a smile tickling my lips. "How about this? You talk to your dad and tell him everything you just told me. Talk to your mom and tell her how she's hurt you. And I'll talk to my dad and tell him I'm going to New Zealand. Deal?"

Cassie purses her lips, thinking it over. "Only if it's after the Beacon's reopening."

"You're stalling," I tease.

"No, just being practical. Any conversation with my mother creates the potential for sheer and utter catastrophe, and I still have to live with her for the next week."

"Fair. Then we'll schedule our respective conversations for the day after the reopening." I lift a brow. "Deal?"

She shakes my hand. "Deal."

My chest feels surprisingly light at the notion of telling my father I'm going to accept Gil's offer. Or maybe that feeling of ease has more to do with the other confession I plan to make.

Because after I tell Dad about the trip, I'm going to tell Cassie I'm in love with her.

CHAPTER 30

CASSIE

Last time I was in this ballroom, it was a year after the hurricane and my grandparents were giving me a walk-through of the damage. By then, the sea had done its worst, leaving behind a gaping space that could've doubled as the setting of a ghost ship in a horror movie. Everything needed to be ripped out. The drywall, the flooring. Gutted right to the studs.

Now, after all of Mackenzie's hard work, the ballroom has been completely restored. The old wallpaper and gilded wall ornaments are gone, replaced by cream paint and white panels with intricate detailing. Brand-new hardwood flooring gleams beneath our feet. The most impressive change, however, is the ceiling. It still soars impossibly high, only now there are skylights, glass panels that open up the room and provide a dazzling view of the inky sky streaked with a dusting of stars.

On the stage, a ten-piece jazz band performs an up-tempo number that makes me feel like I've stepped into another time. Everything about this ballroom feels both modern and vintage at the same time, and I watch Grandma's face as she takes it all in.

"Incredible," she says under her breath, and I see the relief in Mackenzie's green eyes.

"You did an amazing job," I tell Mac.

"It was a team effort." She links her arm with Cooper, who looks gorgeous in his tux. With his tattoos covered and his face clean-shaven, he resembles a preppy boy from Garnet College. I would never tell him that, though. I feel like it would ruin his entire night.

Mac introduces my grandmother to Cooper. As Grandma shakes his hand, she's still gazing around the room, marveling over it. Her attention lands on the chandelier. "Is that the same—"

"No, it's a replica," Mac cuts in. Her smile is hopeful. "It looks the same, though, right? I asked the designer to copy it from a photograph."

"It's breathtaking," Grandma assures her. "All of it."

The two of them wander off, Mac pointing out other updates to the ballroom. Meanwhile, I notice several familiar faces entering through the arched doorway. It's only eight o'clock, so people are still trickling in. The hotel itself isn't open for business until tomorrow morning, when guests from near and far will be checking in at the newly christened Beacon Hotel. Mackenzie says they're booked to capacity, and Genevieve has been stressing about it all week, grumbling about how she'd been promised a soft opening. I guess Mac's original plan was to only book half capacity for opening weekend, just to "dip her toe in," but Cooper talked her out of it, convincing her to make a big splash instead.

"Cass!" My cousin Liv breaks away from the crowd and hurries over to hug me.

"Hey! You look incredible."

Liv is eighteen and about to start her freshman year at Yale. She's Uncle Will's daughter, and the only cousin close to my age. The others are all thirteen or under, with Aunt Jacqueline's late-in-life baby Mariah being the youngest at five. My aunt had her at forty-four.

"Hi, squirt," I greet the little girl who waddles up beside Liv. Mariah looks adorable in a white tutu dress and shiny silver barrettes. She reminds me of my sisters, which makes me wish they were here tonight. But Dad and Co. weren't invited, and even if they had been, I'm sure Nia would rather be caught dead than interact with my mother. Not that I blame her.

I greet my aunt and uncles, who flew in last night from Massachusetts and Connecticut.

"It's a family reunion!" Uncle Max gives me a kiss on the cheek and then ruffles Mariah's hair. "Where's Victoria?" he asks me.

"I don't know. She arrived with us but then disappeared. I think she went to the ladies' room." I scan the ballroom, which isn't super crowded yet. Still, there's a fair number of people milling around, in an array of beautiful gowns and tailored suits and tuxedos. "Oh, there she is."

Mom saunters over. I can't deny she looks stunning in her form-fitting black gown, red-soled Louboutins, and elegant updo. She's forty-five and honestly looks ten years younger. Genetically, that bodes well for me.

I'm quite pleased with my own dress too. It's emerald green, with a halter-style bodice that covers my boobs nicely and a pleated skirt that swirls around my ankles. Picked for me courtesy of Joy, who's looking gorgeous herself in a white minidress and impossibly high stilettos. Isaiah is her plus-one, but from the way they've been bickering since they got here, I have a feeling this latest reconciliation won't stick.

Mom's gaze sweeps around the room, resting on the lively band, before she turns back and grudgingly admits, "This is lovely."

"Isn't it?" Aunt Jacqueline says. "Almost makes me wish we held on to this place."

Mom is quick with a reprimand. "Don't you say that, Jacqueline. We had to sell."

330 • ELLE KENNEDY

Uncle Will chimes in agreement. "It was time to say goodbye. Remember Mom and Dad with this place? It was their entire life. They didn't have any time for themselves."

"The world revolved around the Beacon," Uncle Max concurs.

"I know," my aunt says sullenly. "I guess I'm just sad to see it go."

Mackenzie returns to give us a private tour. Just the family, and everyone is suitably impressed by what she's done with the hotel. The tour ends on the top floor, where Mac strides down the carpeted hallway looking like a supermodel in her black satin gown and silver heels. She leads us to a pair of double doors at the very end of the hall.

"The presidential suite," she says. Eyes twinkling, she steps aside to show us the plaque on the wall.

THE TANNER SUITE.

Grandma looks like she might cry. "Oh, Mackenzie, dear. You didn't have to do that."

"No, I did." Mac's expression becomes serious, her voice thick with emotion. "If it wasn't for you, the Beacon wouldn't have stood on this boardwalk for fifty years. It's your legacy, Lydia."

The suite is as posh as you would expect. Even has a grand piano. Afterward, we return to the ballroom, and I'm surprised to witness some genuine nostalgia swimming in Mom's eyes.

"Aww, you're sad to see it go too," I accuse, my smile telling her I'm teasing. "After all the grumbling about how you didn't want it . . ."

"Oh stop," she says, patting me good-naturedly. She looks around the ballroom that's slowly filling up. The band is now playing a jazzy rendition of a Taylor Swift song, which is sort of cool. "Where is your boyfriend tonight?"

"Um . . ." I pull my phone out of my clutch and check the screen. Tate was supposed to let me know when he was coming inside. Last time we texted, he was in the parking lot waiting for his parents. "Oh, perfect. His parents just got here. They're walking in now."

A server appears brandishing an array of champagne flutes, and Mom plucks two of them off the tray. With a broad smile, she hands me one.

I eye her in amusement.

"What?" she says. "We're celebrating. Let's make a toast." She raises the delicate flute. "To our family."

"To our family." We tap our glasses. I don't know why her spirits are suddenly so high, but hey, I'll take it.

We weave our way through the ballroom, stopping to say hello to several people Mom knows. Then I turn my head and see Tate entering.

My throat instantly turns into an arid wasteland. I thought Tate in a suit was nice. Tate in a tux? It's a sight to behold. Although of course, Tate in nothing at all would be my ultimate preference. Any time we're naked together, I forget my own name. And it's not just the sex that turns my mind to mush. It's everything. His laughter. The way his blue eyes become so animated when he talks about something he's passionate about. How he's far more sensitive than he lets on. He tries to hide that under the guise of surfer-boy man-whore, but he's not fooling me. Not anymore.

I'm still floored by what happened last week. Tate shedding real tears when I spoke of my fragile relationship with my father. I plan on sticking to my end of the deal—I'm going to talk to both my parents about our relationships. But I think I'm adding Tate to that list, because it's getting harder and harder to deny my feelings for him.

I tried not to get attached and I failed.

My heart is officially engaged.

It was supposed to be a summer fling, but I don't want it to end. I don't think he wants it to end either. I wish he'd be the one to bring it up, to suggest we continue seeing other, but so far he hasn't. A part of me wonders if he's waiting for me to take the lead. I was the one who wanted the fling. I insisted I didn't want a relationship to come of it. And Tate's the kind of guy who isn't going to push the issue. If I want more, I need to ask for it. Vocalize my needs and all that fun stuff.

I take another sip, then touch Mom's arm. "Tate's here. Let's say hi."

"Of course." She sips her own champagne as she follows me toward the tuxedo-clad golden god who stole my virginity and my heart.

"Who invited *you*?" I mock glare when we reach him.

"I know, right?" Tate's appreciative gaze eats me up. "You look incredible."

"You clean up nice too." I smile and rise on my tiptoes to kiss his cheek.

His parents are standing nearby, talking to Cooper's uncle Levi, but Gemma breaks away when she notices me.

"Cassie. You look beautiful." Gemma gives me a warm hug.

"Thank you. So do you." She's wearing a yellow dress, her fair hair arranged in an updo with wavy strands framing her face. A small diamond pendant is nestled in her cleavage.

I greet Tate's dad, who's less boisterous than usual as he leans in to kiss my cheek. Maybe he's toning himself down because this is such a classy event, but when he speaks, his demeanor feels more polite than lively. "Cassie. Good to see you."

"Good to see you too. This is my mom, Victoria. Mom, this is Gemma, and this is—"

"Gavin," Mom finishes, greeting him with a tight smile. She barely acknowledges Tate's mother, offering a brisk nod in lieu of hello. "It's been a long time."

"It has." Gavin looks ill at ease, fidgeting with his bowtie. "Nice to see you again, Tori."

I blink in surprise. "Oh, you two know each other?"

"Oh yes, we're well acquainted." Mom takes another sip of champagne.

I wait for her to continue, perhaps even, you know, *explain*.

But she doesn't, and neither does Gavin.

Tate appears as befuddled as I am. We exchange a mystified look, as if to say, *what are we missing?*

Grandma chooses that moment to approach, and I try to transmit to her with my eyes that maybe now is not the time. Something's brewing here. Like the way I know whenever a storm is coming. I can smell it, feel it in the air.

"How long has it been, Gavin?" Mom asks, studying him over the top of her glass. She sips again. "Eleven years?"

"About that," he says, not quite meeting her eyes.

I notice Tate's mom shooting him a questioning look. Okay. At least Tate and I aren't the only ones who are out of the loop. And whatever this loop is, it's beginning to trigger all my internal alarms.

Grandma reaches us, her expression one of concern. "Is everything all right?" she murmurs to me.

"I have no idea," I murmur back. Then I slather on a bright smile and make a last-ditch attempt to ward off the impending storm. "Hey, Mom, I think Aunt Jacqueline is waving us over—"

"The last time I saw you . . ." she muses to Gavin, effectively ignoring me. "It was the month of August, I remember that much. And I believe we met . . . here, actually. At this bar." She absently waves her arm toward the ballroom doors. "Before it was that café out there. It was the lobby bar, remember?"

Tate's dad doesn't answer. Either I'm imagining it, or his forehead has taken on a sheen of sweat.

"Refresh my memory? I can't recall exactly when we last saw

each other . . ." With a smile that's more a baring of teeth than anything resembling amity, Mom locks eyes with Gavin Bartlett. "Oh, silly me! I remember now. It was the night you ordered me to abort our baby."

CHAPTER 31

CASSIE

What in actual tarnation . . .

I stare at my mother. I'm not the only one.

Everyone has been stunned to silence.

Well, not everyone. All around us, other people are still enjoying themselves. They're laughing and chatting. They're nibbling on hors d'œuvres and drinking their champagne. Even the band is still playing. I long to be one of those blissfully oblivious people. I miss my old life, the one from five seconds ago before I heard my mother utter those inexplicable words in that ice-cold yet oddly smug tone.

Her shocking admission hangs like a cloud in the air, lingering, refusing to dissipate.

I'm the first one to find my voice, though it comes out hoarse and unstable.

"Mom." I shake my head a few times, unable to formulate any more words.

"What?" She is completely unbothered, cheerful even, as she drains the rest of her glass before signaling a passing server for another.

Is she fucking drunk?

I look at Gavin and Gemma. Tate's dad is paler than the crisp linen napkins being handed out with the hors d'œuvres. Gemma, on the other hand, is flushed, her cheeks stained a deep, dark red. Whether from anger or humiliation, I don't know.

Mom's amused gaze flicks my way. "Weren't you the one who was so curious about my past the other day?" she reminds me. A mocking note colors her tone. "And now, not a single question?" She *tsks*. "Really, Cass?"

"Victoria." Grandma's sharp voice slices the air.

"Oh, Mother, don't look at me like that. You knew about it."

My gaze flies to Grandma, flashing a hundred different questions at her. She says nothing to remedy my bewilderment. Does nothing to assuage my distress. Her shuttered expression is vexing and it's all I can do not to growl at her.

"Okay, what is *happening* right now?" I finally shout, and this time we draw some attention. Several startled gazes. Curious eyes.

Mom takes another sip.

Gavin, who hasn't uttered a single word yet, doesn't meet my gaze. His jaw is stiff, a muscle twitching.

"Gavin?" The distrustful voice belongs to Tate's mother. And it succeeds in getting a reaction from him. His blue eyes shift, locking on to his wife. I see nothing of note in his expression, but Gemma must, because her cheeks turn redder. Lips tightening.

"Her?" she demands in disbelief. "That's who it was?"

Tate stares at his parents, his face darkening. "Seriously, what the hell is going on? What baby is she talking about?"

My stomach begins to churn. An eddy of disgust and shame. I'm looking at my mother and I realize she's enjoying this. She stands there smirking, unruffled, sipping her drink. She doesn't care to expound on this tale. She's not purposely delaying the pay-off to keep everyone on the edge of their seats. That wasn't her intention. All she wanted, I realize, as she aims her satisfied smirk at a visibly sweating Gavin Bartlett—was *that*. She wanted to make Tate's father squirm. Wanted to put him in this position of having to explain himself to his family.

Without addressing his son's question, Gavin touches Gemma's arm. "Why don't we go speak privately, darlin'?"

My mother doesn't like that one bit. Whatever her original plan, I see the moment she mentally adjusts it.

With a harsh laugh, she says, "What's the matter, Gavin? You don't want to take a trip down memory lane among friends? Why on earth not?" She pretends to think it over. She's the star of this sick movie and she's relishing every second. "Is it because you don't want your son and your wife and the good people of Avalon Bay to know the kind of man you really are?"

Anger twists and cuts at my insides. "Stop it," I snap. "That's enough, Mom. Time to go."

I plan on getting this whole story, damn right I do, but not now. Not here, in a ballroom full of people. I notice Mackenzie starting to make her way toward us, Cooper at her heels. But they stop when I give a slight shake of my head.

"No, we can't have that, can we?" Mom doesn't heed my warning. She's laughing again. Cold and punishing. "You're Mr. Congeniality of the Bay. Mr. Perfect who can do no wrong. Perfect Gavin who can have an affair, screw another woman behind his wife's back, knock that woman up, and still smile to all those people who walk into his place of business and talk about how much he *loves* his boats and *let me tell you about the time I sailed to Hawaii!* Right, Gavin?" Scorn drips like tar from her every word. "Well, I'm sorry, you don't get that luxury anymore. You don't get to pretend anymore."

"Victoria." It's Grandma again. She touches Mom's elbow. "This is neither the time nor the place."

"Why not?" Mom flashes a mocking look. "This is the last time I'll ever be in this fucking town, so why *not* now?"

I flinch at the expletive. Mom is usually a lot classier than this. There's nothing classy about her now. The contemptuous smile. Those gleaming eyes, aimed at Tate's parents. It's insidious. Everything about this is fucking insidious.

And Tate. God, I can't even look at Tate. I see him in my periphery and I'm diligently trying not to let our eyes meet. I don't want to know his expression. Nobody wants to see what their sort-of boyfriend's face looks like after you both find out your parents had an affair. Allegedly. I'm still not certain what the whole story is here, but it's evident they were involved in some way.

"Mr. Perfect has nothing to say?" Mom seems almost disappointed that Tate's dad isn't taking her bait.

The man hasn't even acknowledged her since she dropped her bomb. And that's a problem. Narcissists can't handle being ignored. That's usually when they go for the jugular. And Mom is no exception.

"Perfect Gavin Bartlett, who has his cake and eats it too. Who flashes a huge smile to the world and then sits down and offers to pay for the abortion."

Someone needs to stop this. But nobody is. Grandma has gone deathly silent. Tate is motionless. Gavin just stands there taking it. And I'm too stunned, my heart pounding too fast. Too loud. I can barely hear my own thoughts, let alone string some together and verbalize them. I feel nauseous, bile burning like acid in my throat.

The person who finally puts an end to our collective torture is Tate's mom.

It's a testament to her southern upbringing, the way Gemma Bartlett wipes her palms on the front of her dress before taking a breath and stepping closer to my grandmother.

"Avalon Bay will be sad to see you go, Lydia. I've enjoyed running into you around town and chatting with you, and I do wish we'd gotten to know each other better over the years. I hope Boston treats you well." With a soft smile, Gemma clasps Grandma's hand, then releases it. "Now, I'm afraid I must take my leave. I'm feeling a wee bit under the weather."

Without sparing a glance at my mother, Gemma drops the proverbial mic like a fucking rock star and walks away.

It's chaos after that. Not the kind of chaos where people are screaming and running and making a scene. A quiet chaos, where everyone disappears in the blink of an eye. Tate's father goes after Gemma. A stricken Tate follows Gavin. My mother drains her glass and hands it to a waiter, then calmly saunters toward the arched doorway.

I stare at her retreating back, the casual sway of her hips in that black cocktail gown. I remain frozen for a moment. Before the rage propels me into action.

Heart rate dangerously high, I hurry after my mother. She's walking at a fast clip, and I don't catch up to her until she's gliding through the lobby doors to step outside.

"Are you *kidding* me?" I grab her arm before she can approach the valet. "No way. You're not going anywhere."

"Don't speak to me in that tone." Mom flings my hand off.

"Me? You're unhappy with the way *I'm* speaking to *you*? How about the way you spoke to everyone in there? *What the hell was that?*"

My voice is shaking wildly. A leaf in a hurricane. My palms feel numb, pulse racing. And through my blood surges the kind of rage that produces tears. That makes you sob like a helpless child because the ferocity of the fury is too strong for even an adult to handle.

As my throat tightens to the point of pain, I snatch Mom's hand and drag her away from the valet station.

"Cassie! Let me go."

"No," I snap.

"Cassie," she says sharply as she stumbles on her heels.

I slow down to allow her to regain her balance, but I don't stop moving until we're well out of earshot of the Beacon.

"You had an affair with Gavin Bartlett?" I demand.

She looks amused by the question.

"Don't smile at me like that." I clench my teeth. "Are you getting pleasure out of this?"

"A little bit, yes." She chuckles. "I don't think I've ever seen you so angry. You can relax. It was a long time ago."

I gape at her. "You want me to relax? You cheated on Dad."

"We were already separated." She pauses. Mulling. Then she amends that. "Talking about separation, anyway."

"But you weren't separated." I drag a tired hand over my eyes, willing myself not to cry. "When did this happen? The year before the divorce?"

"Yes. I was trading in your grandfather's boat and dealt with Gavin at the dealership. And, well . . ." She shrugs. "You've met the man. He's charming. Not to mention gorgeous."

My head is spinning. I don't want to know the details, and yet I do. "Who initiated it?" I ask warily.

"He did."

For some reason that surprises me. I pictured Mom as the instigator, strutting into the dealership in a tight dress, set on ruining a man's life.

"And it took a lot of persuasion on his end. I'd never cheated on your father in all the years we were married. If we hadn't already been having problems, I'm sure I would have remained faithful."

I feel sick again. "How long did it go on for?"

"Four months. Then I got pregnant." The humor and indifference finally abandon her, replaced by bitterness. Dark and acute. It fills her eyes, burning hot. "The thrill of an affair fades awfully fast when real life creeps in. He asked—no, he demanded—that I get rid of the baby. Said he couldn't do that to his family." She shakes her head angrily. "It was perfectly acceptable for him to be sleeping around on his wife, hurting her every single day by betraying the vows he took. Getting his rocks off in hotel rooms on his lunch break and then going home acting as if he was the perfect husband and father. So long as *he* was having a good time, then I was useful to him. And then, when his perfect little bubble burst, I became an inconvenience." Mom laughs without a shred of humor. "Victoria Tanner is nobody's inconvenience."

"So, what, you were going to keep his baby out of spite?" Oh my God. I want to throw up.

"No, I was keeping it because it was *mine*." She sounds offended I'd even voice that question, yet doesn't realize her answer is equally disturbing. As always, she talks about people, including an unborn child, like they're possessions. Tools for her to use whichever way she wants.

My eyes well up again. I feel the tears on my lashes and when I blink, a streak of moisture slides down my cheeks.

"Cassie. Stop it. You're acting like a child."

"I'm acting like a child?" I start to laugh. I'm so fucking astounded. I'm astonished that I'm related to this woman. "I shouldn't cry when I find out my mother cheated on my father? Got pregnant by another man. Decided to keep that baby. Did you really have a miscarriage?"

"Yes," she says stiffly.

"And Dad knew."

"He did, yes."

342 • ELLE KENNEDY

"He knew it wasn't his?" I challenge.

"Would've been hard for him not to guess when we hadn't been intimate in months by that point."

"And Grandma knew too?" I ask, remembering the way Mom snapped at her in the ballroom. "That you had an affair?"

"She only found out after the divorce. She and I weren't seeing eye to eye on something, and it came out during an argument."

Of course it did, because apparently my mother doesn't behave like a normal human being. She saves up all her ammunition and shoots it at you when it suits her. When she wants to hurt you, or needs some sort of validation.

Grandma's ears must have been burning because she appears then. Her gait is slower than usual, exhaustion lining her eyes. But her features sharpen when she reaches us, her shoulders straightening as if fortifying her for a fight.

"Not now, Mother," Mom snaps. "I really don't need your input at the moment."

"You're right, Victoria. You don't need my input. You don't need anyone's input, do you? Because you're always right." Grandma focuses on me, all but dismissing her own daughter. "Are you okay, dear?"

"Not really," I admit. "I just hope Tate and his parents are all right—"

Mom practically growls at me. "There is absolutely no reason for you to worry about Gavin and his family. He made his own bed. You don't get to cheat on your wife and lie about it for years, go on with your life as if nothing ever happened. He doesn't get that, and you shouldn't feel sorry for that man."

"I don't feel sorry for him," I say sadly. "I feel sorry for *you*."

She rears back. "Excuse me?"

"You heard me. You've been a selfish, manipulative jerk my entire life. Nothing is ever good enough for you. The way I look, the way I act, the guys I date—" I stop in horror. "Wait, is this why you've been so nice to me lately? Because I was going out with Tate? You knew he was Gavin's son."

"Of course I knew. I figured it out the moment I saw him outside the Jackson place. He's the spitting image of his father."

"So you were just pretending to be nice to me—"

"Stop being so dramatic, Cassie!" she interrupts, blowing out an exasperated breath. "Nobody was pretending. I'm your mother. I enjoy spending time with you."

"I don't think I believe that." I swallow my bitterness. "But now I get it." Shaking my head, disappointment embedded deep inside me, I meet her eyes and ask, "Was this some big plan to get Gavin in public and humiliate his family?"

"No," she scoffs. "I'm not a psychopath. But as I've always told you, if an opportunity presents itself, you take it. Tonight, an opportunity presented itself."

"Really," I say dubiously. "You didn't plan it. And you had no ulterior motives for constantly inviting Tate to join us for dinner."

"Of course not. I enjoy Tate's company too. It's completely incidental that it also gave me insight into what his family's been up to in the years since his father's indiscretion."

Incidental, my ass.

"And, I will admit, it annoyed me. Hearing about Gavin's life. How everyone in town still adores him. Getting articles written about him in the paper, photographed with his oblivious wife and perfect son. Maybe I was a bit out of line in there," she nods toward the hotel behind us, "but this town needed to know what kind of man he is."

I stare at her and see someone I don't recognize. Someone I don't want to know. I see a bitter, miserable woman who hates herself so much she lashes out at everyone around her. A woman who couldn't stand seeing the man she had an affair with living a seemingly happy life and thus felt the need to humiliate him and his wife. In public. In front of their son.

I see a woman I don't want in my life anymore, and I feel a profound sense of loss.

And no matter what she says, I no longer believe the story she fed me about fighting for sole custody because she was feeling *vulnerable* and longed to keep her daughter close after the miscarriage. She did it to hurt my father, plain and simple. I was a possession to her, something she could use against him and keep from him to make him suffer.

"You're sick," I tell her. "You have an actual sickness, Mom. And I'm done."

"Cassie—"

"No. Stop. Don't tell me I'm being dramatic. Don't blast me for not taking your side or whatever else you want to bitch about. You just humiliated my boyfriend and his family at a public event that was supposed to honor *our* family—" I cut myself off, because she's not worth it. Not worth the energy I'm expending by even saying any of these futile words. This entire time we've been out here, she hasn't once apologized for her actions. In her mind, she did nothing wrong tonight.

I jerk when I feel Grandma's hand on my arm. "I think it's time to go."

"I think so too," I say, nodding.

My grandmother glances at Mom. "And I think it's better if you stay in a hotel tonight, Victoria." With a look of irony, Grandma gestures to the Beacon. "There's one right there, dear. Perhaps Ms. Cabot will comp you a room."

"Mother. Seriously."

"Yes, seriously. I'm done listening to you tonight. You destroy everything you touch. You always have. I tried to instill the right values in you, to teach you the importance of being compassionate, humble. It appears I failed." Grandma shakes her head sadly. "I'll have Adelaide's husband deliver your bags tomorrow morning to wherever you choose to stay. But for tonight, and for the rest of the visit, Cassie and I would like to be alone. Isn't that right, Cassie?"

"Yes. It is."

Arms linked tightly together, Grandma and I walk away.

CHAPTER 32

CASSIE

Me: *You okay?*
Me: *Tonight was brutal.*
Me: *I don't even know what to say.*

I stop texting after the trifecta, because no matter how upset I am, I refuse to become a person who texts in one-liners.

My heart jumps when I see Tate typing back. I've been dying to talk to him since I got home, but he had his own shit to deal with. His own parental confrontations. I would've killed to be a fly on the wall when Tate spoke to his parents, especially his dad. I need to know Gavin's side of the sordid story, because I don't trust a damn word my mother says.

As I wait for Tate's message to appear, I stare up at the ceiling, wishing he were here with me. It's eleven o'clock and I doubt I'll be getting so much as a wink of sleep. My brain keeps running over every word that was uttered tonight. Every horrible, horrible word. I could use the distraction. But Tate is home with his parents, and I assume he'll be spending the night there.

Tate: *Yeah, that was rough. How are you doing?*

He was typing for so long, I expected more. But I guess it's better than nothing.

Me: *I don't even know. Is your mom okay?*
Tate: *Not really. She hasn't said much since we got home. Just been quiet. We're about to take the dogs for a walk.*
Me: *This late?*
Tate: *She doesn't feel like going to bed yet.*

There's a beat. Then another message.

Tate: *Dad's crashing on a friend's couch.*

Fuck. Guilt lodges in my throat like a wad of gum. I know that I, personally, didn't do this to his family, but I feel responsible, complicit in my mother's actions.

Gavin cheated too . . .

Right. I have to acknowledge that too. Not all the blame can be placed on my mother; Tate's father was equally responsible. And I doubt I'll ever know the real story about who initiated the affair, because cheaters tend to twist the truth to portray themselves in the best possible light. I'm not sure I envision Gavin as the seductive rogue who wooed my mother into his bed. But I can't entirely picture her seducing him either. Mom might be charming, but she's never been a flirt or a, well, bimbo.

I suspect as with most situations the truth is somewhere in the middle.

Either way, tonight left hurricane-scale damage on both our families. Grandma and I sat together in the kitchen for more than an hour after we got home. She was candid with me, admitting how disappointed she'd always been in her youngest daughter. Mom hadn't experienced any traumatic events in her childhood that made her this way—she was just spoiled. She was the baby, the youngest of four. Grandma didn't explicitly blame Grandpa Wally—she would never speak an ill word about him—but after our talk tonight, I get the sense he was the one who did most of the spoiling.

But spoiling your kid isn't a reason for someone to become as callous and entitled as my mother, not reason alone anyway. Some people are just born assholes, I guess.

Grandma said we'd talk about it more tomorrow, but really, what is left to say? I want nothing to do with my mother. For the time being, and possibly longer. The way she was smirking over her champagne tonight as she destroyed another woman's marriage was despicable. One of the cruelest things I've ever witnessed.

Tate: *I wish I was in bed with you right now.*
Me: *Me too. Will I see you tomorrow?*
Tate: *Yeah. Gil and Shirley return on Sunday so I gotta head back and clean the house from top to bottom.*

I can't believe the summer's over. I leave for Boston on Monday. And my relationship with Tate still hangs in the balance, unresolved. Except, now I realize there might never be a resolution. Whether we keep seeing each other or not, our families are now intrinsically intertwined. Forever.

But we're not our parents, I remind myself. We're not. I would never judge Tate for his father's actions, and I know he wouldn't judge me for what my mother's done. I'm hoping this doesn't change us. If it does, I can't be certain my heart will survive.

Tate: *I'll call you in the morning. Night, Cass.*
Me: *Night.*

I set the phone on the nightstand and crawl under the covers, but sleep eludes me. It simply won't come. My thoughts are running and running around in my head in an unceasing loop.

Mom got pregnant by Tate's dad.

And my father knew it wasn't his baby, which raises so many more questions. Did Dad know it was Gavin Bartlett's or think it was some anonymous man? And does it matter? Either way, Dad knew she was having an affair. He knew what kind of shitty person she was. And he still let me go live with her. He let me be alone with her from the age of ten to eighteen. Eight years of her attention solely focused on me. Her verbal punching bag. How could he do that?

I'm suddenly hit by a gust of anger. Sleep is all but forgotten. It all spills out, all the things I want to say to him, all the questions plaguing my mind, and it pushes me out of bed, because you know what? I'm done. I'm done bottling it up. Done not voicing my feelings. Vocalizing my needs, as Tate likes to say. I'm fucking done.

I don't bother changing, just head downstairs in my plaid shorts and gray T-shirt. As quietly as I can, I walk to the front hall and stick my feet in a pair of Grandma's gardening Crocs. Then I grab her keys and go out to the car.

It's 12:10 when I pull into the driveway of my childhood home. I stare at it through the Rover's windshield, my throat closing up. I love this house. I grew up here. My dad was here. And although I know the affair wasn't the sole reason for the divorce—they were already discussing separation by then—my mother was still the cause. The way she treated people, the way she treated him, that's what ended their marriage. But it didn't have to end my relationship with him. He didn't have to passively stand by and let her take me.

He could have fought for me.

I fling open the car door and jump out, heart pounding as I march toward the porch and then—

And then nothing. I halt, suddenly furious again. At *myself.* Because what the hell am I doing? There are two sleeping six-year-olds in there. It's midnight. If I storm in and start making demands on my dad right now, I'm no better than my mother causing a scene at the Beacon Hotel's grand reopening. Making it all about herself.

Swallowing the lump in my throat, I slowly turn and walk back to the Rover. I'll come back in the morning. It's what I should have done in the first place.

When I reach the car, I hear a soft voice say my name.

"Cassandra?"

It's Nia.

My stomach drops. Fucking hell. No. Not her. I can't do this right now. I just can't.

But she's already striding toward me, wearing white slippers and a red robe, the sash tied haphazardly around her midsection. Her tight curls are loose around her face, and there's no mistaking the concern that fills her dark eyes when she notices my tear-streaked face.

"Are you all right?" Nia frets, and for some reason the question unleashes a fresh onslaught of tears.

"*No,*" I moan and then I throw myself into her arms.

They weren't outstretched, weren't inviting me in, but the moment I'm there she wraps them around me, hugging me without hesitation. I shudder in her arms, crying uncontrollably. Gasping for air and feeling like my entire world has just crumbled around me, like I'm ten years old again and my parents are getting divorced and Daddy is telling me I can't live with him anymore but *don't worry I'll see you all the time, Cass.*

"He lied," I choke out, as the tears continue to fall. "He didn't see me all the time."

"What?" Nia says in confusion.

"He let her have me. After the divorce. He promised nothing would change and everything changed." If I had the ability to think coherent thoughts right now, I know I would be mortified. But I'm too distraught, sobbing in her arms as we stand there in the driveway. As Nia, the stepmother who doesn't even like me, provides me with the comfort that neither of my parents have been capable of giving me my entire life.

"I had to live with that woman, and he knows what it was like living with her. But he got rid of her, he got to leave. I didn't have that luxury, did I? I had to keep living with her, keep listening to all the ways I wasn't fucking good enough. And meanwhile he gets to stay here in *my* house," I spit out. It's a half growl, half sob. "With his new kids and their mother. Their perfect fucking mother."

I bury my face against her bosom and shake from my tears. She holds me tighter and runs her hand over my back, strokes my hair, and that only makes it worse because it's what a mother is supposed to do. And that makes me cry harder.

Somehow, I manage to lift my head even though it feels like it weighs a thousand pounds.

"I wish you were my mom," I tell her, my voice barely above a whisper.

And then it finally happens—the mortification kicks in, in the form of a panic attack that knocks me off my feet. It all bubbles over and I can't breathe. I've never had a panic attack before, the kind where you're hyperventilating. Suddenly I'm on the ground, the gravel biting into my bare knees. I gulp for air, crying and panting and avoiding Nia's worried eyes because I can't believe I just said that to her.

She's kneeling beside me now. "Breathe," she orders. "Breathe, Cassandra. Look at me."

I look at her.

"Do what I'm doing. Take a very deep breath. Inhale. Ready?"

I inhale.

"Good. Now exhale."

I exhale.

For the next couple of minutes, she helps me remember how to breathe. In and out, in and out, until my heartbeat has regulated and my hands are no longer numb.

"I'm so sorry," I croak. I glance toward the house, realizing the porch light is on. I catch a glimpse of movement in the living room window. Was that my father? "Did I wake up the whole house?"

"*Non, non,* you didn't."

"How did you know I was outside?"

"The doorbell camera sends an alert to my phone. It woke me up, but your father was still asleep."

"I'm sorry. I didn't mean to barge in. Something just happened tonight, and . . ." I trail off.

"Is everything all right? Your grandmother?"

"It's fine. She's fine." I inhale again. "We were at the grand reopening of our family hotel, and . . ." I shake my head, a bitter laugh sliding out. "Well, long story short, my mother decided to announce to the entire ballroom that she had an affair with my boyfriend's father when I was ten."

Nia's eyes widen. "Oh."

"According to her, Dad knew about the affair." I study my stepmother's face. "Did he tell you about it?"

After a beat, she nods. "He told me, yes. But I don't believe he knew who the other man was."

"I don't think he knew. Tate's mom didn't know about my mom." God. This is such a twisted mess. "It was so embarrassing, you have no idea. I was looking at Mom and she was this total stranger to me. Getting enjoyment out of it. My whole life, I've just wanted a mom. And tonight I realized that's never going to happen. Not with her." I give Nia a sad smile. "I'm sorry. I know I'm not your kid. You don't need to be sitting out here in the middle of the night comforting me."

Nia's tone becomes stern. "I may not have birthed you, Cassandra, but I certainly view you as a daughter."

"Bullshit." Then I wince. "Sorry, I didn't mean to swear."

She laughs quietly. "Don't worry, every day the word *merde* gets spoken in this house more times than I can count. And it's not bullshit. I admit, I've kept my distance over the years. Not because I didn't consider you a part of the family or didn't love you." She hesitates. "Your mother is . . . difficult."

"No, really?"

We both laugh.

"I figured that's what it was," I admit. "That you kept your distance because of her. But I'm not her. And I'm not *like* her. At all."

"You're not," Nia confirms. "But there is much you don't know, *chérie*. When your father and I became lovers—"

I choke on another laugh. "Please don't say it like that."

"What should I say then?"

"Say . . . *got together.*"

Her eyes sparkle. "When your father and I got together, your mother was very unhappy. She didn't have nice things to say to me, or about me, at the beginning. There were many warnings, including what would happen if I tried to take her daughter from her or speak badly of her when you were around. There was a meeting with the judge—"

Shock slams into me.

"She was threatening to take away your father's visitation."

Nia sighs. "You were twelve when Clayton and I got together, and she told the judge she didn't want her ex-husband's bimbo—I had to look up that word in the dictionary—she didn't want me brainwashing her daughter into hating her. There was a mediation session, and for the first year I wasn't even allowed to be alone with you."

I gasp. What in the actual fuck? "I had no idea."

"I know. We didn't tell you. And keeping a distance became a habit for me, I suppose. But I've been watching you grow up all these years, and I think you are a wonderful young woman. So creative, with your stories, and your humor. I'm very proud of you."

"Then why don't you want me around my sisters?" The wounded question slips out before I can stop it.

She looks alarmed. "Why do you say that?"

"You've always been so protective of them when I'm around. Like you don't trust me to be around them. Last month, after Monique fell, you looked so furious and—"

"I was very furious," Nia interrupts. "With Monique!" She's flustered now. "That girl knows better than to climb on furniture! I told you before we left that night how much it was upsetting me."

She did tell me. But, I suddenly realize, when you think someone doesn't like you, everything they say becomes warped. Every look becomes distorted. Her eyes might transmit aggravation with Monique's disobedience, but my eyes see condemnation. Her tone might convey concern, but I hear accusation. I made it all about myself, and I'm ashamed when I realize that's something my mother would do.

"I thought you didn't want me around. Dad too."

"Your father? Never. Your father loves you, Cassandra. You're all he ever talks about."

A lump forms in my throat. "Really?"

"There isn't a day that goes by in this house where your name isn't spoken," Nia says. "He loves you very much."

"He never tells me that."

"Do you ever tell him how *you* feel?"

"No, but is it just my responsibility?"

"No," she agrees. "And this is why we will go inside now, so you can speak to him."

"You said he was asleep."

"When I got up, yes. But he's awake now." She nods toward the kitchen window. "I signaled for him to give us a minute when he came outside."

"He came outside?"

"Yes. When you were . . . being sad."

Being sad. Understatement of the year.

"I suspect he's preparing the tea you like. And I would like you to say to him all the things you just said to me. Why don't we go inside and do that?"

I hesitate.

She brushes driveway gravel off her knees and gets to her feet. "Cassandra?" She extends her hand.

I take it and let her help me up. But the doubts are returning, the old insecurities whipping up and making me bite my lip. "If you like me, why do you always call me Cassandra?"

"That's your name, *oui*?"

"*Oui*—I mean, yes. But . . . everyone else calls me Cassie or Cass and you never do. I thought it meant something. Like maybe you were being intentionally formal because you didn't like me."

Her lips curve with humor. "Not at all. I just think it's a beautiful name. Cas-san-dra. I enjoy the way it rolls off my tongue."

I swallow my laughter. Of course she does.

The human brain is so ridiculous sometimes. It creates these elaborate intentions for people, attributes motives, when at the end of the day, she just likes how my name rolls off her tongue.

CHAPTER 33

TATE

I walk into the kitchen the next morning to find my father at the table, drinking his coffee and reading the Saturday edition of the *Avalon Bee* while Mom scrambles eggs at the stove. I do an honest-to-God double take. I have to blink several times to convince myself I'm not imagining this charade of domestic bliss.

Dad crashed at his friend Kurt's house last night and now he's in our kitchen. He must have woken up and come straight home, and instead of slamming the door in his face, Mom allowed him in and is goddamn serving him breakfast.

I stand in the doorway, staring. They don't notice me, too caught up in their mundane activities. Mom's sticking two slices of bread in the toaster. Dad's reading the paper, no care in the world after blowing our family apart.

"What the hell is he doing here?"

They both look over in shock.

When my eyes lock with Dad's, his fill with shame. Good. He fucking better be ashamed. Since the second Cassie's mother dropped that bomb, the events of last night have been running on a loop in my head. When Mom and I got home, she refused to even discuss what happened. I've never been so frustrated in my life, but hey, I thought, it's not just my life that got completely upended. This is her marriage. So I kept my mouth shut despite all the questions burning at my tongue. I didn't push her. We walked the dogs and then she bid me good night and went up to bed.

Now she's cooking breakfast for my cheating father as if nothing happened?

"Tate," Dad starts. Cautious. "Sit down. We should probably talk about last night."

"First of all, *probably*?" I'm equal doses dumbfounded and enraged. "And second, why are you here? Why are you sitting there drinking coffee? You should be upstairs packing a fucking bag."

He recoils.

Even as I spit out the words, a bolt of hot agony rips a hole in my chest. Packing a bag. Christ, the idea of my father leaving, my parents divorcing . . . I scrape a hand through my hair, wanting to tear it out by the roots.

My father had an affair. He slept with another woman. And not just any other woman—Cassie's mother. I'm still reeling from that. I'm sure Cassie is equally horrified. I'll talk to her about it later when I see her, but, fuck, I don't even know what there is to say. Yes, this mess was caused by our parents, not us. But everything about this situation just feels fucking wrong. As wrong as Mom carrying two plates of eggs and toast to the table as if our world is unchanged. The dogs trail after her, Fudge settling at her feet and staring longingly at their plates as if he hasn't had a bite of food in forty-five years. Polly keeps a respectable distance because she has better manners.

I gape at my parents. "Why is he here?" I ask Mom. Without letting her respond, I turn to glower at him. "You couldn't even give her twenty-four hours?"

Disdain drips from my tone and he flinches. His eyes widen and I realize I've never spoken to him this way before. But I've also never been this furious.

"You couldn't even give her a full day to absorb that bomb-shell? Try to deal with—"

"We dealt with it eleven years ago." That comes from Mom. Calm and resigned.

I swivel my head toward her. "What do you mean?"

"I mean, we dealt with it eleven years ago. Granted, I didn't know it was Victoria Tanner." She gives a rueful look at Dad. "I know, I know, I was insistent about you not telling me who it was. But—"

"You knew he had an affair?" I interject.

But I don't need to see her nod to know the truth. Of course she knew. I'd been so caught up in my own shock over Victoria Tanner's bombshell that I'd overlooked *Mom's* reaction to it. When I think back to last night, I realize she hadn't acted as shocked and horrified as she should have.

"I did, yes," she says.

I turn back to Dad. This time, he won't meet my gaze. Of course not. That was the one thing Victoria—sorry, *Tori*—had gotten right last night. Mr. Perfect always needs to look good to the world.

Another rush of anger burns a fiery path up my spine. All these years, he's been acting like the model of virtue. Preaching about how family is so important, it always come first. *Never forget that, Tate.* And Gavin Bartlett does everything for his family.

Where was his family when he was banging somebody else?

Dad sees it all in my eyes, every thought I'm thinking, and it deepens the cloud of shame that darkens his face, sags his shoulders. He deserves to feel like shit after what he's done.

What's more shocking is that Mom knew all along. I think back to eleven years ago. I would have been twelve, turning thirteen. It was right when we moved to Avalon Bay. The memories surface. The arguments around the house, always behind closed doors. They made sure I wouldn't overhear them, but I knew something was up. When I asked Mom about it, she just said they were going through a rough patch and not to worry. So I didn't worry, because my entire life my parents never gave me any reasons to.

Turns out, they were arguing about the fact that he can't keep his dick in his pants.

"Tate, sit down. Please," Dad begs.

"No." I stalk over to the counter and pour myself a cup of coffee. I gulp down the scalding liquid, wishing I could just fucking disappear.

"The affair happened when we moved here from Georgia," Mom says quietly, seeking out my gaze. The total lack of anger or betrayal on her face only pisses me off more, though. "Your dad just opened a new business. I couldn't find a job. We were arguing—"

"And that gives him a free pass to cheat?"

"Of course not," she says. "I'm just providing the context—"

"It's okay, darlin'," Dad interjects, his voice gentle. "This is for me to fix." With a ragged breath, he finally meets my eyes. "I fucked up, kid. Eleven years ago, I committed a very selfish act—"

"Several selfish acts," I remind him coldly. "Because it sure doesn't sound like it was a one-time thing."

"No, it wasn't. It lasted for four months. And I hated myself for it every single day."

I snort. "If you expect me to have any sympathy—"

"I don't. I don't expect sympathy. I know what I did. Your mother knows what I did. And yes, it took me four months to come clean to her."

I narrow my eyes. "You told her yourself?" For some reason I imagined Mom breaking into his phone or stumbling across a hotel receipt in his pocket.

"Yes, I did," he says, and there's a sliver of pride in his tone that triggers a fresh rush of anger.

"Sure, Dad, pat yourself on the back there."

"Tate." He looks hurt.

"So you came clean, big deal. It doesn't change the fact that you slept with somebody else."

"We were struggling with the new business. We were low on money. My ego was in the gutter."

"All I'm hearing is more excuses."

"No, you're hearing the truth. And like your mother said, it's context. People aren't black-and-white creatures. Sure, we know what right and wrong ought to be. But sometimes the line between those is a bit gray. Life clouds your judgment and you cross lines you never thought you'd cross. People do stupid things. *I* did a stupid thing, and for eleven years I've woken up every single day with the intention of showing your mother that I recognize the pain and suffering I caused her, and that I consider each day she continues to stay with me the greatest gift of my life."

At the table, I notice Mom's eyes welling up with tears.

I don't know how I feel about this. To me, cheating is unforgivable. I don't know how she forgave him. But she must have, because I haven't picked up on any bitterness or resentment in our home since then. No closed-door arguments. No hostility. As far as I know, they're open with each other. They seem as in love today as they have been my entire life.

"I don't expect you to understand." Dad shrugs. "And I'm not asking for your forgiveness."

I laugh harshly. "Gee, thanks."

"The person I hurt already forgave me," he says simply.

I scoff at him. "You don't think you hurt me?"

"Has your life been different this past decade?" he asks. "Have we loved you less? Have I treated you worse?"

"No, but . . ." I'm mad again, because . . . yes, he's been a good father. No, it didn't affect me then. But it's affecting me *now,* goddamn it. A growl escapes my throat. "You fucked my girlfriend's mom."

Dad flinches.

Mom goes pale.

"So, please, don't sit there and act like that's cool. I don't care if Mom didn't want to know the name of your mistress. You should've said something the moment I started dating Cassie—"

"I didn't even know she was Victoria's daughter. I had no idea!"

That gives me pause. When I think on it, I realize he might be telling the truth. I told them Cassie was a neighbor, but I didn't specifically say which house. I don't think I even mentioned her last name . . . I shake myself out of it. Fuck that. I'm not getting hung up on minor details.

"You've spent my whole life harping about family," I mutter. *"Family is the most important thing, Tate.* Team family! And then you almost blow up our family. And she was right about how hard you try to present yourself as this good guy. Some selfless, perfect saint. But you were selfish when you cheated, and you're selfish when you go on about the dealership and how you built it for me—"

"Tate—" he tries to interject, looking alarmed.

"Because it's not about me. It's about *your* selfish needs. You want me at the dealership so you have someone to look at boat pictures with. You want to have someone there so you can take Mom on vacation. It's not about me." I slam my cup down. Liquid sloshes over the rim and splashes the cedar island.

Mom stands up. "Tate," she says sharply. "I understand that this is a big shock for you, but we're still your parents. You can't speak to your father like that."

I just stare at her. Then I snort and stalk out the back door.

I don't know where the hell I'm going. I'm barefoot, clad in plaid pajama pants and an old yacht club T-shirt. I just round the side of the house and walk down the street. This street on which I've lived since I was twelve. The town I fell in love with the moment we got here. My first day of school, I met the twins, Wyatt, Chase. I met Steph and Heidi and Genevieve, and immediately had this big friend group. I was swept away, so caught up in this new awesome life of mine that I wasn't paying attention to my parents' lives. I was vaguely aware of "the rough patch" and then it passed, and I never even stopped to consider what it meant.

And now I'm stalking down the street on bare feet, trying to figure out why I'm so angry, and that's when it hits me.

I'm mad because he's fallen off the pedestal. Not that I intentionally placed him on one, but I had always looked up to my dad. I admired him. I never wanted to let him down. He was the strongest, kindest person I knew. He could do no wrong, and now here I am, discovering that at the end of the day, he's perfectly capable of being a selfish prick.

I mean, I should've known. Everyone's capable of that. But I guess you never really expect it of your parents.

I end up at the small park at the end of our street. It's only seven o'clock on a Saturday morning, so the park is empty. I spot a mother pushing a stroller along the path about a hundred yards away, and that's about it.

I find a bench and sit down, burying my face in my hands. I regret snapping at my mother. My father, not so much.

They worked through it. I get it. They had eleven years to do that. I had eleven fucking minutes.

I smother a sigh when I hear his footsteps. I know it's him and not Mom because I know my mother, and she would want us to mend our relationship first. Which just makes me angrier.

"She always puts you first," I accuse.

"I know." His voice shakes.

I look over. His eyes are wet, rimmed with red.

"Always," he repeats as he sits down beside me. "Because that's your mom. She's the best person I know, and I don't deserve her. I don't know where she found the strength to forgive me. Trust me, I thank the Lord every day that she did. I never take that gift for granted."

"I can't believe you cheated on her."

"Me too," he admits. "Never thought I was capable of hurting someone like that. I'm not proud of it. I carry that shame with me every day."

We stare for a moment at the swings that begin swaying in the sudden breeze. As if invisible children are making them move. It invokes images of me in this park, hanging out with my friends. I was so happy to move to Avalon Bay. I didn't realize that move was the precipitating factor in almost losing my family.

"Did you really demand she get an abortion?" Bile coats my throat.

"I didn't demand it. I just said we should." Dad looks as sick as I feel. "I was planning on breaking it off with Victoria that night at the Beacon. The guilt had been eating me alive and I came clean to your mother the day before. Begged her to give me another chance. So I went to meet Tori to tell her it was over, and that's when she told me about the baby. I said I'd support her either way, but that I loved your mother and would never leave her. And, yeah, I told her I thought it would be best, for both of us, if she didn't keep the baby. I was selfish. I didn't want a child with her." He blows out a breath. "But you're wrong, kid. After the affair almost cost me everything I hold dear, I made a vow to never be selfish again. These past eleven years haven't been an act. I devoted my life to your mom and to you."

"I didn't ask you to do that."

"Of course not, but you're my kid, my blood. I *was* trying to leave you a legacy. I know you don't believe me, though, so if it means canceling a vacation or writing you out of my will, then so be it." He shrugs. "Nobody's perfect. Least of all me. We're all just human. Good, bad, and everything in between. Luckily, I found a woman who shares my belief that one mistake doesn't have to define a person. I'm not perfect," he repeats, then pauses for a moment. "With that said, I think you should accept Gil's offer."

The sudden change of subject makes my head spin. "What?"

"Take that voyage, Tate. I shouldn't have talked you out of it."

I stare at my feet. "You didn't. I'm going. I was planning on telling you today, actually."

He laughs under his breath. "Of course you're going." Another chuckle, before he goes serious again. "Tate. The reason I didn't want you to go isn't because I need you at work. To be honest, that sounded better than saying I'm fucking terrified."

I lift my head. "What do you mean?"

"It's a dangerous crossing. I don't know if your mother and I would survive if anything happened to you. But we've never sheltered you. We've let you make your own mistakes, and you're pretty good at recognizing them. And we need to let you take your own risks too, so if your heart is telling you to go, and I know it is, because—" He laughs again. "—my heart did the same damn thing when I was your age. You should go."

I nod slowly. "I will."

"And I know I said I didn't need your forgiveness, but I'm going to ask for it anyway."

Dragging my hand through my hair, I glance over with a rueful smile. "If Mom can get past it, then so can I. Just give me a little time."

"You got it, kid." He claps me on the shoulder. "Why don't we head back to the house before your mom sends Fudge and Polly on a rescue mission. I don't like making her worry."

And she must have been *really* worried, because her entire body sags with relief when we trudge into the house five minutes later. She was standing vigil at the front door, the dogs sitting at her feet, like some weird oil painting. I flash her a smile of assurance, and then Fudge rips a dog fart and we all snicker.

"Everything okay with my boys?" Mom prompts, studying our faces.

I shrug. "Getting there."

A faint smile touches her lips.

"Hope you don't mind if I skip breakfast," I tell her. "I'm just gonna go upstairs and change, then head back to the Jackson house. Gotta start cleaning."

"No problem, sweetie."

Up in my room, I shuck my pajama pants and grab a pair of faded jeans from my dresser. I shove them up my hips, then grab my keys and phone off the nightstand.

There's a knock, and I look up to see Mom lightly rapping her knuckles against my half-open door. "Hey. Got a second for me before you leave?"

"Always. What do you need?"

She walks in and sits at the edge of my bed. After a beat, I sit beside her. And then she begins to talk.

CHAPTER 34

CASSIE

"Hey."

My head lifts at Tate's approach. "Hey."

It's nine in the morning and he's back from his parents' house. I was up in my bedroom when I heard his Jeep pull in, and a moment later his text popped up, asking me to meet him down on the Jacksons' dock.

He looks tired as he lowers his body next to me, dangling those long legs over the edge of the dock.

"Did you get any sleep last night?" I ask.

"What do you think?" he says wryly. "You?"

"What do you think?" I mimic. I let out a sigh. "My mom's gone."

He's startled. "Gone how?"

"Oh, I mean she left. Caught a flight to Boston last night. Grandma told her not to come home, to stay at a hotel. I guess her pride wouldn't allow her to do that. She sent Grandma a message this morning asking to have her bags shipped to Boston."

"Did you two talk at all?"

"Oh, we did." The memory of the confrontation outside the Beacon is going to stay with me for a very long time. Hell, the events of that one night alone will take ten years' worth of therapy to unpack.

"She had her excuses. Claimed she didn't plan on ambushing them at the party."

Tate snorts. "Bullshit."

"That's what I said. It doesn't matter, though. What's done is done."

He studies my face. "So where did you leave it, you and her?"

"It's over," I say flatly. My heart clenches, a ripple of pain moving through me. "The relationship is irrevocably broken."

"Cass . . ."

"It is. And now I feel . . . free. No longer feel trapped by it. I always told myself I *had* to be in this relationship. I *had* to take the abuse because, well, it's my mother. That's what people always say, right? *It's your mother.* They can't fathom cutting a parent out of their lives."

I lean closer to him, resting my head on his shoulder. After a beat, he puts his arm around me. His fingertips stroke my bare shoulder. A part of me feared he would show up this morning and announce he wanted nothing to do with me after my mother's nauseating actions. But he's here and he has his arm around me, and I'm weak with relief.

"I don't need to be in that relationship, Tate. Maybe one day, if she has that moment of self-reflection you were talking about. But that's not happening anytime soon. And in the meantime, I need to live my own life. Without her in it."

"And you're okay with that?"

"I am. I mean, it hurts. But having her in my life hurts more."

"I guess that's the silver lining?" He runs his palm over my shoulder again, a comforting gesture.

"Oh. No. The silver lining would be that if I hadn't had a complete breakdown after confronting my mom, then I wouldn't have gone over to my *dad's*—where I had another complete breakdown. I was very busy." I can't help but laugh. "But enough about me. How did it go with *your* parents?"

"It went." His answering laugh is dry. "But you can't just leave me hanging like that. What happened at your dad's?"

I peek up at Tate with a self-deprecating grin. "Well, I went to confront him and ended up curled in a fetal position of tears on their front lawn. Nia came outside and we had a moment. A good one, actually. Then I went inside and talked to my dad. I did what you told me. Shared my feelings. Vocalized my needs and all that crap."

Tate snickers.

"I told him I want a relationship that involves more than light-hearted banter and turtle shopping. That I want to be able to come to him when I need him and not worry he'll push me away. It went well. I feel very grown up now." I tip my head, smiling again. "You've changed me."

Those chiseled features soften. "How did I do that?"

"You taught me how to stand up for myself. How to be honest with the people around me. I used to be a real chickenshit. But you make me feel strong and—"

He kisses me.

It comes out of nowhere. Dare I say, reminiscent of the old Aaron days, but at least Tate's tongue is still in his mouth. He presses his lips to mine in a soft caress before pulling back.

I run my fingertips over the stubble rising on his jaw. "You okay?"

"Just kiss me again," he says, and our mouths collide. Now his tongue slides through my parted lips, bordering on desperate. His fingers are in my hair and he's groaning against my lips. There's an urgency there, a thick thread of emotion wrapping around the two of us, and I realize both our hearts are engaged.

I pull back and the words just slip out.

"I love you."

His eyelids pop open. "What?"

"I know I said a lot of things before. That I didn't want a relationship. This would end in September. There was no pressure. I know I said all those things. But something's changed. I don't know how, but it just has, and now I'm in love with you." I gulp, staring at my hands. They're trembling. "You told me to talk about my feelings. Those are my feelings. I love you."

"I love you too."

My gaze flies to his. "You do?"

"I do. I've known for a while. Just didn't have the balls to tell you."

"Wait, so I'm suddenly dropping feelings bombs and you're holding them in? Is that what you're saying? We've switched places?"

"Something like that." With an indecipherable look, Tate strokes my cheek. Then he brings my face toward him, and his lips touch mine in an infinitely gentle kiss.

But this kiss . . .

It doesn't feel right.

A drop of moisture splashes the tip of my nose and I look up in confusion. Tate's blinking rapidly. He drags the side of his thumb over his eye.

"What's going on?" I ask uneasily.

"I don't want it to end either," he confesses, emotion creasing his features.

Joy flickers through me. "Okay, good—"

"—but it has to," he finishes, his voice a scant whisper.

My heart sinks like a stone to the pit of my stomach. "W-why?" I stammer.

"You asked how it went with my parents." He lets out a breath.

"They worked through the affair. Mom forgave him a long time ago. All these years of being disgustingly in love, it wasn't fake. They are in love. They love each other a lot, in fact."

"That's good, no?"

"It's great. And I understand my dad's reasons for what he did. That's not to say I condone his actions. He was wrong. He did a shitty thing and he hurt her. But she forgave him. Their marriage is rock solid."

"This is all good, Tate . . ."

"Dad and I had a moment alone and talked about our own stuff, too. Worked through some shit. I'm going to sail to New Zealand."

I nod, the dots suddenly connecting in my head. "I see. And you think it has to end with us because you're leaving for three months—"

"No, that's not it."

I rub the bridge of my nose. I'm so confused. "I don't get what's happening right now."

"I spoke to my mother alone too."

"Okay . . ." None of this is making sense yet.

"She forgave him," Tate reiterates, his voice breaking slightly, "but that doesn't mean she needs to be reminded of it every single day."

A sick sensation crawls into my stomach and wraps around my intestines. "And I'm a reminder of it," I whisper.

He nods. Agony flashing in his eyes.

"We talked for a while. Mom never wanted to know who he had the affair with, but she knows now. She knows it's your mother. She admitted it'll be hard to see you if you and I were together, if we were a couple."

I feel the tears coming. I briefly close my eyes, hoping to ward off the onslaught. I can't even blame Gemma for this. That's the worst part. I *understand*. Of course she doesn't want this reminder. Every time her son brings his girlfriend home, she has to be reminded that her husband cheated on her? With the girlfriend's mother?

"I can't do that to my mom," Tate says hoarsely. "I love you, Cass. I do. But I wouldn't be able to live with myself knowing I was hurting my own mother. I can't do that to her."

His jaw is working. Throat squeezing as he swallows repeatedly. He looks so upset.

I reach for his hand, lacing our fingers together. "It's okay. I understand."

"I'm so sorry." Sheer misery hangs from every word.

"You can't bring home the girl whose mother almost destroyed their marriage. It's going to be a dark cloud over our entire relationship going forward, especially if your mother can't get past it. There's no silver lining." My bottom lip starts quivering. I bite hard on it. I don't want to cry. "So I guess this is goodbye."

"Guess so." His voice cracks again, and so does a piece of my heart.

"I had a good summer," I tell him.

"Best summer of my life."

I smile. His eyes are looking a little misty again. Mine are rapidly following suit. I can barely see him now, my vision is so blurry. We're both weepy, and I know if I sit here any longer, I'll break.

"I'm glad I met you, ginger."

"Glad I met you too, Gate."

I leave him there on the dock. I don't know how my legs manage to carry me all the way into the house. But somehow I make it. Even in my bedroom I continue to fight the tears, because what if he's in *his* room now and we pass our windows at the same time, so I step into the bathroom and sit on the edge of the tub. And only then do I cry.

CHAPTER 35

CASSIE

November

"We did it!" Tate's flushed face fills my laptop screen. He rakes a hand through his wind-kissed golden hair, beaming from ear to ear. Relief jolts through me. I've been in a constant state of worry since he set sail, and every time I see him, safe and sound, I want to weep with joy. "I mean, it was touch and go a couple times. Definitely almost pissed myself during that squall last month—"

I shiver. That was a bad one. I saw the video he shot of the deck after the squall and it still haunts my dreams.

"—and I'm never going to stop apologizing for subjecting you to my a cappella version of 'Poker Face' the night I killed that bottle of Jack."

I giggle.

"—but the voyage has officially come to an end. Sort of. I'm going to stick around here till my girlfriend's parents steal her back from me." He lovingly sweeps those blue eyes over the *Surely Perfect*'s topsail. "Spend the next month sailing around Australia. See what the fuss is all about. So, stay tuned, folks. Journey's not over yet. Talk soon. Cheers."

The video ends.

I start to cry.

It's a weekly routine now. Every Monday, when Tate posts his travel vlog, I sit on my bed, open the laptop, and subject myself to thirty or forty minutes of Tate recapping his week. I'm not sure what editing software he's using, but his videos are excellent. Photo overlays, date cards to show when certain footage is from. Some footage is fixed, when Tate sets the camera somewhere and just lets it film. My heart always soars when I watch those capable hands hoisting a sail, tying a rope. But my favorite part of his videos is *this*—when it's just him, sitting on the deck, or at the table in the galley, talking to me. Well, to everyone. But I like to think he's talking to me.

Peyton says I'm torturing myself. Joy has threatened to fly in from Manhattan and stage an intervention. They think I need to move on. I'm sure they're right. There's nothing helpful about this, nothing to be gained from staring at Tate's handsome face week after week for three months straight. All it did was make me miss him more.

This semester has dragged. I can't concentrate on school. Can't be bothered to see friends or attend any parties. I haven't gone full recluse yet—I still shower. Still wash my hair and eat food. I clean my dorm room and text people. I even respond to emails from my new literary agent Danna Hargrove, who sold the Kit 'n Mc-Kenna series for us in a five-book deal. It was a modest advance, but Danna's excited for the potential. She thinks the series will take off. She's already talking about TV adaptations and merch.

I, as always, am tempering my expectations. But I'm hopeful. Robb's on board as illustrator, and the first book, the one I gave to my sisters, releases next fall. The deadline for the second book is in the new year, so luckily I don't need to force myself to be creative right now.

I'm not feeling creative. Not feeling anything, really, least of all happiness. But now it's Thanksgiving, and my spirits are slightly elevated. I'm looking forward to seeing my family. Since the night I showed up at Dad's house and cried in Nia's arms, things have been really good. Dad's been making an effort to check in about how I'm feeling, and Nia and I even started texting.

With my mother, it's the opposite. I haven't spoken to her since that night. I have no interest. She's texted several times, calls frequently, and though I can't bring myself to block her, I don't take her calls. According to Grandma, it's driving my mother crazy. I'm discovering that narcissists don't like the no-contact method. Every now and then I worry she'll show up on campus and try to wrest a reconciliation out of my stubborn hands, but so far, she's kept her distance. Who knows how long that will last.

I shut my laptop, leaving it on the bed as I head downstairs to rejoin my family. Nia's prepping dinner, while Dad pretends to watch football in the den when everyone knows he can't name even one player on any of the teams playing today. In the living room, my sisters are sitting in front of Pierre's tank, showing him the drawings they made of him.

I walk over to them and peer at the glass. Pierre's chilling on his cypress tree. I give him a wave. "Hey, little dude." I look at Mo. "Any fart attacks lately?"

"*No,*" she complains, and Roxy heaves a disappointed sigh.

Snickering, I wander into the kitchen where I find Nia at the counter glaring at her cutting board.

"Um. Everything okay?" I eye the pile of diced onions she's amassed, trying to figure out what the problem is.

"I ran out of onions," she grumbles.

"You, Nia Soul, ran out of an ingredient? Didn't you just give me a whole braggy speech when I was here at midterms? The one about your fancy sixth sense that allows you to always purchase the *exact* amount of potatoes required?"

"Yes. *Potatoes*." She's gritting her teeth. "These are onions." Nia curses under her breath, a mixture of English and French expletives that make me grin. "*Merde*. I don't have time to go look for a store that's open right now. I have too much to do—"

"I'll go," I offer. "I'm pretty sure Franny's Market is open till four today. They're always open on holidays."

Relief loosens her shoulders. "Are you sure you don't mind?"

"Yeah, it's no problem at all." I grab Dad's keys off the counter. "I'll go now. How many do you need?"

"Two. So get four."

I snicker. "Four it is."

"Thanks, Cassandra."

I leave the house and get into Dad's truck. It's so strange not to be driving Grandma's Rover. Or staying at her house. But Grandma doesn't live in the Bay anymore. She's in Boston now, residing in the same building as Aunt Jacqueline and Uncle Charlie and loving her quality time with the grandkids. Our house in Avalon Bay belongs to another family now. Some venture capitalist, his much younger wife, and their three children. Grandma says they seemed like a nice family. I hope they enjoy the house. It holds a lot of good memories for me.

At the market, I bypass the carts and march toward the produce aisles. I pick out four large onions, managing to stack two in each hand, then turn around—and slam right into Tate's mother.

"Gemma," I squeak. "Hi."

"Cassie." She's equally startled. "Hello."

Then silence falls.

Oh boy. This is awkward.

I stand there, trying to figure out what to say. I haven't seen her since that awful night at the Beacon. Do I bring it up? Ask how she's doing? Apologize on behalf of my mother?

Now we're both fidgeting with whatever's in our hands. In my case, unfortunately, it's onions. And then I *forget* that it's onions, and stupidly raise one hand to rub the bridge of my nose. My fingers, now covered in the onion curse, trigger a reflexive rush of tears. Shit.

Gemma takes one look at my face and bursts into tears too.

"Oh, no, no," I assure her, trying to wipe my eyes with my elbow. "I'm not crying. It's the onions."

"Well, *I'm* crying," she blubbers. "And it's not because of onions."

"Oh."

Our gazes lock.

Sniffling, she rubs her eyes with her sleeve, then gives me a sad smile. "Do you have a minute to talk? I know it's Thanksgiving, but . . ."

"Sure. Let me just pay for these. I'll meet you outside."

A few minutes later, we reconvene in the small parking lot. The market is the only store open in the plaza, but the café at the end of the row has an outdoor patio. I gesture toward it.

"Let's sit," I suggest.

She nods. We walk to the patio, where I flip over two of the chairs and set them on the ground.

We sit across from each other. I watch her, sorrow tightening my belly. "How are you doing?" I finally ask. "We haven't spoken since the night . . . you know, the night."

"The night," she echoes wryly.

"Just so you know—I had no idea what my mother was going to do. She took me by surprise, same as she did everyone else."

Gemma's eyes widen. "Oh. No. I never for a moment thought you were involved."

"Ah, okay. Good."

Another silence falls.

"I've been watching all of Tate's videos," I say. "That was some voyage, huh?"

"Took ten years off my life." She shudders. "He could have died in that squall. Lord! And then when his GPS broke!" She's now swallowing repeatedly, appearing nauseous. "Never have kids, Cassie. You're constantly living in fear they might die."

"Nah, when the GPS broke, that's when I was the *least* concerned about him."

"Really? Because I was picturing my boy lost in the middle of the Indian Ocean."

I shake my head. "Tate will never get lost, not as long as the stars are still in the sky."

My heart suddenly swells with emotion. I miss him so much. I think about him all the time. Sometimes I dream that I'm on the *Surely Perfect* with him. We're lying on a blanket on the gleaming teak deck and gazing up at the stars. He points out all the different constellations and tells me where the fuck we are.

Gemma must see the raw pain in my eyes because hers fill with tears again. "Can you ever forgive me?" she blurts out.

I blink in surprise. "What?"

Rather than clarify, she seems to change the subject. Her face takes on a faraway look. "His videos, Cassie . . . he's happy, yes. He's always happy when he's sailing. But I know my son. He's not at peace. His eyes are troubled."

I never saw any indication of that, but she's his mother. She knows him better. She's probably catalogued every last expression on Tate's face. Every flicker of emotion.

"We've spoken three times," she tells me. "Once a month. He calls from the satellite phone. It's expensive, so he keeps the calls short. But I hear it in his voice. He's sad."

A sob rises in my throat. I hastily swallow it down. *I'm sad too,* I want to say. But I don't. Because I understand the reason we broke up—she's sitting right in front of me. And I don't blame her for it, not one bit.

"I asked him to break up with you," Gemma confesses. "I told him I couldn't stand to have you around."

"I know. I get it. Honestly, I do."

"I was wrong."

I frown at her. "What?"

"I was wrong," she repeats with a firm shake of the head. "Gavin cheated on me, but I took him back. That's all that matters."

"But my mother . . ." I furrow my brow.

"I don't care about your mother. The affair was never about your mother. It was about my husband. It was about his own insecurities, his perceived inadequacies. And he's worked so hard on himself over the years. I'm proud of him. And I'm ashamed of myself for putting my own needs ahead of my child's."

"Gemma, come on. You're being too hard on yourself."

"No." She shakes her head. "Tate comes first. Always. Forever."

I gulp down another lump of emotion at the proof that they exist—good mothers. The proof is in Nia, and how fiercely she loves her girls. In Gemma, and how fiercely she loves her son. I might not have that, but it makes me happy to know others do.

"He loves you. You're the first girl he's ever felt that way about. I've watched him over the years." She sighs. "I know my boy. He was always a player—that's what we say these days, right? A player?"

Mmm. Not quite. I believe the term is *fuckboy*. But I keep that to myself. Besides, that's not what Tate is. It's not who he is. He's the best man I've ever known. Wise beyond his years. More sensitive than he lets on.

And, fine, he's great in bed.

"Then this summer, he met you and fell in love, and his own mother took that away from him. I'm ashamed."

"Gemma. Stop."

"So, please, can you ever forgive me?"

"There's nothing to forgive."

I reach over and take her hand. She clasps it with both of hers. "I miss him," I confess.

"I know. So do I." She smiles. "I put together a care package for him last night. I need to send it to Auckland before he sets sail for his Australian adventure. Do you know how much it costs to ship something to New Zealand? Gavin almost choked on his tongue."

I laugh. "Well, I mean, it's literally at the bottom of the world. It's bound to be expensive." Then I bite my lip, as something nags at the back of my mind. It starts as a tiny seed, then grows into a full-fledged idea that has me squeezing Gemma's hand. "But if you need a delivery person . . ."

CHAPTER 36

TATE

December

I exit the tiny grocery store three miles from the marina, muttering a string of curses under my breath. The kid that loaded these bags overfilled this one. And it's a paper bag. A delicate fucking creature. As I feel the bottom about to give out, I execute a swift maneuver, readjusting my grip at the same time I heave the danger bag on top of the meat bag. I swear, if this thing bursts and all my carefully hand-picked fruit rolls away? And then my apples go rolling on the dirt and I have to chase after them like an asshole—

"Tate."

I stop. Frowning.

Weird. I swear I heard Cassie's voice saying my name. I snap myself out of such insanity and keep walking.

"Tate! I know you heard me! Are you running away from me?"

Now it's Cassie's *outraged* voice.

Wait, is this actually real?

I spin around. Unfortunately forgetting the delicate paper-bag pyramid in my hands. I manage to hold on for dear life, but the fruit bag is in great peril, and Cassie runs over to grab it out of my hands.

"You okay there?" she teases.

All I can do is stand and gawk.

"Tate?"

Finally, I find my voice. "What are you doing here?"

"Oh, I asked the guy at the marina where you were, and he said you came here to buy groceries, so my cab driver brought me—"

"No, I mean *here*. In New Zealand. You realize you're in New Zealand, right?"

"No! Really? I thought I was on a beach in Miami!"

A smile springs to my lips. Goddamn. I missed her. And I can't stop staring at her. Her red hair is twisted in a loose knot on top of her head. She's wearing jean shorts and a blue T-shirt. White sneakers. Her eyes are shining and her cheeks are flushed, but the latter might be because of the sun beating down on us. It's hot as hell here in the winter. Or rather, their summer.

"I'm still trying to figure out if you're real." I blink. Blink again. But she's still standing in front of me.

Cassie smiles. "I'm real."

"And you're in Auckland."

"I'm in Auckland."

"Because . . . ?"

"Oh. Right." She brightens. "I'm dropping off a care package from your mother. It's kind of bulky, so I left it at the office in the marina. We can grab it when we get there."

I stare at her again. "Now you're just talking gibberish."

Cassie starts to laugh. "No, I really did bring a care package from Gemma. I ran into her last week when I was home for Thanksgiving."

I narrow my eyes. "I spoke to her the day after Thanksgiving. She didn't mention seeing you."

"I asked her not to. I wanted this to be a surprise. But I had to write a couple final papers before I could get away."

"Cass."

"Yes?"

"I am not complaining that you're here. Not one bit. But what is happening right now? Why did you come?"

"I came because . . ." She bites her lip, suddenly bashful. "Because I missed you."

My pulse quickens. "I missed you too," I say hoarsely.

More than she'll ever know. These last few months have been the most challenging of my entire life. Me against the elements. Singled-handedly sailing some of the toughest waters I've ever navigated. I'm not gonna lie—I was scared. Terrified I wouldn't even reach my destination. But I persevered, and one of the reasons I did was Cassie. Whenever I thought, *fuck, I might actually not make it,* I heard her voice in my head, making some smartass remark. You can do it, Gate.

Now she's right here, and while I don't have a proper explanation yet, I can't help myself. I set the grocery bags on the ground and pull her into my arms. She squeaks in surprise, but I just tighten my grip and let out a ragged breath. "Just let me hold you for a minute."

And she melts into me. I bury my face in her hair, inhaling the sweet scent of her shampoo. The soft strands tickle my chin. Her arms wrap around my waist.

"I really fucking missed you." My voice is still so hoarse. Thick with gravel. I force myself to release her, searching her enigmatic expression. "What exactly did my mom say to you?"

"She said she wants her son to be happy."

My chest clenches. The notion of hurting Mom is still so soul crushing. But these past three months without Cassie have also been pretty fucking awful.

"And she asked me to forgive her," Cassie says. She meets my eyes. "I think that means she's okay if I'm your girlfriend."

Heart racing, I put on a cocky grin. "Girlfriend, eh? That's rather presumptuous of you. Who says I want you as my girlfriend?"

"Sweetie. I think you kind of ceded the upper hand when you smelled my hair and told me how much you missed me."

She has a point. My smile widens so big I feel like it'll crack my face in half. The sun is almost blinding, but I don't slide my aviators on because I want her to see my eyes. To see the sincerity in them when I say, "I love you."

Happiness warms her gaze. "I love you too."

"Are you really here?" I ask.

"I'm really here. And you have me for three weeks. I need to go home for Christmas," she says regretfully.

Three weeks. Damned if my dick doesn't twitch hearing that. It's been three months since I've seen her. Kissed her. Touched her.

"Three weeks, you say?" I cock a brow.

"I have to warn you, though . . . I might need to put in some work on my next children's book while I'm here."

My jaw drops. "No."

"Oh yeah. Five-book deal, baby. The first book in the Kit 'n McKenna series debuts next fall. They love it so much they want to rush it out."

"You're a fucking rock star."

I tug her into my arms again and then my lips are devouring hers. Hot. Desperate. Because three months' worth of pent-up lust is now bubbling inside me.

"I want you naked so bad right now," I growl.

Cassie grins. "Then let's go get naked."

I lead her toward the dusty black Jeep parked a few yards away. Yup, I traveled to the ends of the earth and they give me another Jeep. I wanted something cooler, like a Humvee. But this was all the rental place had.

We load the bags in the back and hop in. Cassie is beaming. Her lips are curved in a smile. Cheeks flushed with excitement. Everything about her sends joy rippling through me.

"Wait, let me get my sunglasses." She twists toward the back seat to rummage in her purse. And I can't help copping a feel of one delectable tit.

"Save it for the boat," she teases. When she turns back, shades in hand, she suddenly makes a happy noise. "Look at the silver lining."

I glance over, grinning. "All right, let's hear it."

"No, I mean, *look* at it." A brilliant smile fills her face as she points to the sky.

I follow her gaze and realize she's right. Backlit by the sun, today's clouds have very distinct edges.

"I've never actually seen clouds with silver linings before," Cassie marvels. "It's beautiful."

I lean over and place a kiss on the corner of her jaw. "Beautiful," I agree, and I'm not looking at the clouds.

EPILOGUE

CASSIE

March

"I'm worried about Pierre."

One might expect to hear that from my sisters.

Or my father.

Or maybe even Tate, who's developed a close relationship with my little sisters' turtle over these past few months. Dad is constantly texting pictures of Pierre to my boyfriend.

But no, the worry-laced remark comes from none other than Nia, who walks up and slides into the booth next to Dad. The three of us are still finishing up our coffee and dessert; across the restaurant, Tate and the girls are crowded around one of those toy machines where you have to maneuver a claw hand to try and capture one of the plushies in the glass box. Roxy demanded he win them the stuffed turtle, and I'm discovering that Tate is incapable of walking away from a challenge.

"Why?" Dad asks his wife, his forehead creasing. "What's wrong? What did Joel say?" Nia had just stepped out to answer a call from their turtle sitter, and has returned looking quite distraught.

"I asked him how Pierre is and he kept saying LL Cool J is

fine." She sounds flustered. "I told you we should have asked Chandra instead. That boy's brain is jumbled from the ganja."

"*Jumbled from the ganja,*" I howl into my coffee. "I love it. Title of my next book."

Dad snickers. "Nice," he tells me, before putting a reassuring arm around Nia. "Don't worry. Joel's not in some stoned stupor—well, he probably is, but not about this. LL Cool J was Pierre's former name."

"Oh. I see." She relaxes.

"And trust me," I add, "nobody will take better care of that turtle than Joel. He's the turtle whisperer."

Although they may need to spray the house down with air freshener when they get back to the Bay tomorrow, because I guarantee Joel smoked pot in there while he was housesitting.

Dad, Nia, and the girls flew to Boston over March break to visit me. Technically, I live in Hastings, the small town an hour from the city that houses the Briar University campus, but I drove into Boston to spend the weekend with my family. And Tate, who heard about the visit and insisted on tagging along.

He and I have seen each other twice since our Australia adventure. A weekend at the end of January, and another one during my February break, but Tate bemoans it's not enough. He's right. I miss him every second we're not together, and I'm counting the days till graduation. I've already booked my flight to Avalon Bay. I'm going to stay with my family, but lately Tate's been dropping hints that we should find a place together for the fall.

"Cassie! Look!"

I grin when I glimpse my sisters racing toward the booth. Both their hands are clasped around the stuffed turtle, which they're holding up in a victory pose. Behind them, Tate struts over with a smug look.

"And you doubted me," he accuses. He glances at my sisters. "Remember how she doubted me?"

Roxy nods sternly. "She did. I remember."

"I remember too," Mo says.

I roll my eyes at all of them. "Of course I doubted. That machine is rigged. Nobody ever wins."

"Oh really?" Tate points at the turtle. "Does that look rigged? I don't think so, ginger."

"Don't think so, ginger," Roxy echoes, while Nia and Dad laugh into their coffees.

I glare at Tate. "You're a bad influence on them."

"Nah."

"Nah," Mo mimics.

I sigh and take the last bite of my lemon cake.

Tate sits beside me, slinging one sculpted arm around my shoulders. "I think you're just jealous, babe. Want me to win something for you? There's a lobster in there that's almost the same shade of red as your face."

"You're *so* funny." I glower at him, but he just winks. Besides, we both know I'm not actually mad. If anything, I'm so happy he's here with me right now.

We're happy.

Like, disgustingly happy.

The last thing I expected from my summer fling was to get a boyfriend out of the deal. All I wanted was passion. Fun. Maybe a little bit of romance.

But I got so much more than what I bargained for. I found true love with the greatest, funniest, sweetest man I've ever met in my life. A man who taught me how to express my feelings, even when they suck. And thanks to him, I got my dad back. I was finally able to free myself from my mother's clutches and end a relationship that was hurting me. I made a genuine connection with my stepmother. Hell, I even got to see Australia—from the deck of a yacht piloted by the hottest captain on the planet.

"It's cold!" Mo complains, burrowing closer to our dad. A group had just entered the restaurant, and since our table is near the door, a gust of cold March wind cools the air.

"Seriously," Dad grumbles. "Isn't it supposed to be spring? I don't know how you survive living up here in the Arctic."

I grin at him. "The northeast is not the Arctic. And I don't mind the weather. Especially in winter. The snow is so pretty."

"Winter sucks," Roxy informs me.

"Totally sucks," Tate agrees, before planting a kiss on my cheek. "Summer's my favorite season."

I meet his playful blue eyes. "Yeah? Why's that?"

"You know. All those cute summer girls rolling into town . . ."

"*All* of them?" I accuse.

"Well, just one." He finds my hand under the table. "And this summer is going to be even better than the last."

I lace our fingers together. "I can't wait."

ACKNOWLEDGMENTS

Every time I return to the world of Avalon Bay, there's a smile on my face from the words *Chapter One* all the way until *The End*. This little beach town is so much fun to immerse myself in, and I'm so grateful that I get to spend my days losing myself in fictional worlds. Even more, I'm grateful to the people who allow me to do that:

My editor, Eileen Rothschild, who let me lean into my silly side with this book and write about Keanu Reeves turtles and whatever other random things came to mind.

The Griffin all-stars: Lisa Bonvissuto, Alyssa Gammello, and Alexis Neuville, for their support and cheerleading for this series, and Jonathan Bush, for another amazing cover.

My agent, Kimberly Brower, for finding such a good home for this series.

Assistants Natasha and Nicole, who keep me on task when I'd rather be binge-watching TV shows.

Ann-Marie and Lori at Get Red PR for helping spread the word about the Avalon Bay series.

And as always: every reader, reviewer, blogger, Instagrammer, Tweeter, BookTokker, and supporter of my books. Your continued love and enthusiasm is what makes this job worthwhile!

ABOUT THE AUTHOR

Amanda Nicole White

A *New York Times, USA Today,* and *Wall Street Journal* bestselling author, ELLE KENNEDY grew up in the suburbs of Toronto, Ontario, and is the author of more than forty romantic suspense and contemporary romance novels, including the international bestselling Off-Campus series and Briar U series.

BAD GIRL
REPUTATION

ALSO BY ELLE KENNEDY

Good Girl Complex

BAD GIRL REPUTATION

An Avalon Bay Novel

Elle Kennedy

ST. MARTIN'S
GRIFFIN
NEW YORK

First published in the United States by St. Martin's Griffin, an imprint of St. Martin's Publishing Group

www.stmartins.com

Designed by Steven Seighman

Library of Congress Cataloging-in-Publication Data

Names: Kennedy, Elle, author.
Title: Bad girl reputation : an Avalon Bay novel / Elle Kennedy.
Description: First edition. | New York : St. Martin's Griffin, 2022.
Identifiers: LCCN 2022013550 | ISBN 9781250796752 (trade
    paperback) | ISBN 9781250796769 (ebook)
Subjects: LCGFT: Novels.
Classification: LCC PS3611.E55857 B33 2022 | DDC 813/.6—
    dc23/eng/20220323
LC record available at https://lccn.loc.gov/2022013550

Our books may be purchased in bulk for promotional, educational, or business use. Please contact your local bookseller or the Macmillan Corporate and Premium Sales Department at 1-800-221-7945, extension 5442, or by email at MacmillanSpecialMarkets@macmillan.com.

First Edition: 2022

10 9 8 7 6 5 4

BAD GIRL
REPUTATION

CHAPTER 1

GENEVIEVE

Everyone even vaguely related to me is in this house. Dressed in black and huddled together in awkward conversation around cheese plates and casserole dishes. My baby pictures on the wall. In fits and starts, someone clinks a fork against a bottle of Guinness or a glass of Jameson to raise a toast and tell an inappropriate story about how Mom once rode a Jet Ski topless through the Independence Day boat parade. While my dad looks uncomfortable and stares out the window, I sit with my brothers and pretend we're familiar with these old stories about our mother, the fun-loving, life-by-the-balls-grabbing Laurie Christine West . . . when in reality we never knew her at all.

"So we were hot-boxing it to Florida in the back of an old ice-cream truck," starts Cary, one of my mother's cousins. "And somewhere south of Savannah, we hear this noise, like a rustling around, coming from the back . . ."

I cling to a bottle of water, fearing what I'll do without something in my hands. I picked a hell of a time to get sober. Everyone I've run into is trying to shove a drink in my hand because they don't know what else to say to the poor motherless girl.

I've considered it. Sliding up to my old bedroom with a bottle of anything and knocking it back until this day ends. Except I'm still regretting the last time I slipped.

But it would certainly make this entire ordeal slightly more tolerable.

Great-aunt Milly is doing circles around the house like a goldfish in a bowl. Every pass, she stops at the sofa to pat my arm and weakly squeeze my wrist and tell me I look just like my mother.

Great.

"Someone's gotta stop her," my younger brother Billy whispers beside me. "She's going to collapse. Those skinny little ankles."

She's sweet, but she's starting to creep me out. If she calls me by my mom's name, I might lose my shit.

"I tell Louis to turn down the radio," Cousin Cary continues, getting excited about his story. "Because I'm trying to figure out exactly where the noise is coming from. Thought we might be dragging something."

Mom had been sick for months before she was diagnosed with pancreatic cancer. According to Dad, she'd dealt with a constant pain in her back and abdomen that she'd ignored as the aches of getting older—and then a month later she was dead. But to me, this all started only a week ago. A call in the middle of the afternoon from my brother Jay urging me to come home, followed by another from my dad saying Mom wasn't going to be around much longer.

They'd all kept me in the dark. Because she hadn't wanted me to know.

How messed up is that?

"I'm talking about, for miles, this knocking around in there. Now, we're all pretty baked, okay? You gotta understand. Ran into this old-timer hippie freak back in Myrtle Beach who hooked us up with some kush—"

Someone coughs, grumbles under their breath.

"Let's not bore them with the details," Cousin Eddie says. Knowing glances and conspiratorial smirks travel among the cousins.

"Anyway." Cary starts up again, hushing them. "So we hear this, whatever it is. Tony's driving, and your mom," he says, gesturing his glass at us kids, "is standing in front of the freezer with a bong over her head like she's about to beat a raccoon to death or something."

My mind is far, far away from this ridiculous anecdote, jumbled and twisted with thoughts of my mother. She spent weeks lying in bed, preparing to die. Her last wish was for her only daughter to find out she was sick at the last possible moment. Even my brothers were forbidden from being at her bedside in the slow, agonizing slip into her final days. Mom preferring, as always, to suffer in silence while keeping her children at a distance. On the surface it might seem she did it for the benefit of her kids, but I suspect it was for her own sake—she wanted to avoid all those emotional, intimate moments that her impending death would no doubt trigger, the same way she avoided those moments in life.

In the end, she was relieved to have an excuse not to act like our mother.

"None of us want to open the freezer, and someone's shouting at Tony to pull over, but he's freaking out because he sees a cop a few cars behind us and, oh yeah, it occurs to us we're carrying contraband across state lines, so . . ."

And I can forgive her. Until her last breath, she was herself. Never pretending to be anything else. Since we were kids, she'd made it clear she wasn't particularly interested in us, so we never expected much. My dad and brothers, though—they should have told me about her illness. How do you keep something like that from your child, your sister? Even if I was living a hundred miles away. They should have told me, damn it. There might have been things I wanted to say to her. If I'd had the time to think about it more.

"Finally, Laurie tells me, you're gonna flip open the lid and we're gonna throw open the side door and Tony is gonna slow down enough to kick whatever it is out onto the shoulder of the road."

Chuckles break out from the crowd.

"So we count to three, I close my eyes, and I throw open the lid, expecting fur and claws to leap for my face. Instead, we see some dude in there asleep. He wandered in who knows when. Somewhere back in Myrtle Beach, maybe. Just curled up and took a nap."

This isn't how I pictured coming back to Avalon Bay. The house I grew up in crowded with mourners. Flower arrangements and sympathy cards on every table. We left the funeral hours ago, but I guess these things follow you. For days. Weeks. Never knowing when it's acceptable to say, *okay, enough, go back to your lives and let me go back to mine.* How do you even throw out a three-foot flower heart?

As Cary's story winds down, my dad taps me on the shoulder and nods toward the hallway, pulling me aside. He's wearing a suit for maybe the third time in his life, and I can't get used to it. It's just another thing that's out of sorts. Coming home to a place I don't quite recognize, as if waking up in an alternate reality where everything is familiar but not. Just a little off-center. I guess I've changed too.

"Wanted to grab you for a minute," he says as we duck away from the somber festivities. He can't keep his hands off his tie or from tugging at the collar of his shirt. Loosening it, then seemingly talking himself into straightening and tightening it again, like he feels guilty about it. "Look, I know there isn't a great time to bring this up, so I just got to ask."

"What's going on?"

"Well, I wanted to see if you might be planning to stick around for a while."

Shit.

"I don't know, Dad. I hadn't given it much thought." I didn't expect to get cornered so soon. Figured I'd have time, maybe a couple days, to see how things went and decide then. I left Avalon Bay a year ago for a reason and would have preferred to stay gone if not for the circumstances. I have a life back in Charleston. A job, an apartment. Amazon deliveries piling up at my door.

"See, I was hoping you could help with the business. Your mom managed all the office stuff, and things have kind of gone to hell on that since . . ." He stops himself. None of us know how to talk about it—her. It feels wrong no matter from which angle we try to approach it. So we trail off into silence and nod at each other to say, *yeah, I don't know either, but I understand.* "I thought, if you weren't in too much of a rush, you wouldn't mind jumping in there and making sense of it all."

I expected he might be depressed for a while and need some time to himself to cope, to get his head around it all. Maybe run off and go fishing or something. But this is . . . a lot to ask.

"What about Kellan, or Shane? Either one of them have got to know more about running that place than I do. Doesn't seem like they'd want me striding in there jumping the line."

My two oldest brothers have been working for Dad for years. In addition to a small hardware store, he also owns a stone business that caters to landscapers and people embarking on home renovations. Since I was a kid, my mom managed the inside stuff—orders, invoices, payroll—so Dad could worry about the dirty work outside.

"Kellan's the best foreman I've got, and with all these hurricane rebuilds we're doing down on the south coast, I can't afford to take him off the jobsites. And Shane spent the last year driving around on an expired license because the boy never opens his damn mail. I'd be bankrupt in a month if I let him anywhere near the books."

He's not wrong. I mean, I love my brothers, but the one time our parents had Shane babysit us, he let Jay and Billy climb onto the roof with a box of cherry bombs. The fire department showed up after the three boys started launching bombs with a slingshot at the neighbor's teenage sons in their pool. Growing up with two younger brothers and three older ones was entertaining, to say the least.

Still, I'm not getting roped into being a permanent replacement for Mom.

I bite my lip. "How long are you thinking?"

"A month, maybe two?"

Fuck.

I think it over for a moment, then sigh. "On one condition," I tell him. "You have to start looking to hire a new office manager in the next few weeks. I'll stick around until you find the right fit, but this isn't going to become a long-term arrangement. Deal?"

Dad wraps an arm around my shoulder and kisses the side of my head. "Thanks, kiddo. You're really helping me out of a jam."

I can't ever say no to him, even when I know I'm getting hosed. Ronan West might come off as a hard-ass, but he's always been a good father. Gave us enough freedom to get in trouble but was always there to bail us out. Even when he was pissed at us, we knew he cared.

"Grab your brothers, will ya? We gotta talk about a couple things."

He sends me off with foreboding and a pat on the back. Past experience has taught me that family meetings are never a positive affair. Family meetings mean more upheaval. Which is terrifying, because wasn't getting me to uproot my life to temporarily move back home already the big ask? I'm running through things in my head like breaking my lease or getting a subletter, quitting my job or pleading for a sabbatical, and my dad's still got more on the docket?

"Hey, shithead." Jay, who's sitting on the arm of the sofa in the living room, kicks my shin as I walk up. "Grab me another beer."

"Get it yourself, butt sniffer."

He's already ditched his jacket and tie, his white dress shirt unbuttoned at the top and sleeves rolled up. The others aren't much better, all of them in various states of giving up on the whole suit thing since getting back from the cemetery.

"Did you see Miss Grace? From middle school?" Billy, who's still not old enough to drink, tries to offer me a flask, but I wave it off. Jay snatches it instead. "She showed up a minute ago with Corey Doucette carrying her stupid little purse dog."

"Moustache Doucette?" I grin at the memory. In freshman year, Corey grew this creepy serial killer strip of hair on his lip and just refused to shave the nasty thing until it escalated to the threat of suspension if he didn't get rid of it. He was scaring the teachers. "Miss Grace has got to be, what, seventy?"

"I think she was seventy when I had her class in eighth grade," Shane says, shivering to himself.

"So they're, like, screwing?" Craig's face contorts in horror. His was the last class she taught before retiring. My youngest brother is now a high school graduate. "That's so messed up."

"Come on," I tell them. "Dad wants to talk to us in the den."

Once assembled, Dad starts in again on his tie and shirt collar until Jay hands him the flask and he takes a relieved swig. "So I'm just gonna come out with it: I'm putting the house up for sale."

"What the hell?" Kellan, the eldest, speaks for all of us when his outburst stunts Dad's announcement. "Where did this come from?"

"It's just me and Craig here now," Dad says, "and with him

going off to college in a couple months, it doesn't make much sense to hang on to this big, empty place. Time to downsize."

"Dad, come on," Billy interjects. "Where's Shane gonna sleep when he forgets where he lives again?"

"One time," Shane growls, punching him in the arm.

"Yeah, fuck you, one time." Billy gives him a shove. "What about when you slept on the beach because you couldn't find your car parked not even fifty yards away?"

"Will y'all knock it off? You're acting like a bunch of damn idiots. There are people still out there mourning your mother."

That shuts everyone up real quick. For just a minute or two, we'd forgotten. That's what keeps happening. We forget, and then the truck slams into us again and we're snapped back to the present, to this strange reality that doesn't feel right.

"Like I said, it's too much house for one person. My mind's made up." Dad's tone is firm. "But before I can put it on the market, we've got to fix it up a little. Put a spit shine on it."

Seems like everything's changing too fast, and I can't keep up. I barely had time to get my head around Mom being sick before we were putting her in the ground, and now I've got to pick up and move my whole life back home, only to find out home won't exist much longer either. I've got whiplash, but I'm standing still, watching everything swirl around me.

"There's no sense clearing out until Craig gets settled at school in the fall," Dad says, "so it'll be a little while yet. But there it is. Thought y'all should know sooner rather than later."

With that, he ducks out of the den. Damage done. He leaves us there with the fallout of his announcement, all of us shell-shocked and staggering.

"Shit," Shane says like he just remembered he left his keys on the beach at high tide. "You know how much porn and old weed is hidden in this house?"

"Right." Affecting a serious face, Billy smacks his hands together. "So after Dad falls asleep, we start ripping out floorboards."

As the boys argue about who gets dibs on any lost contraband they might dig up, I'm still trying to catch my breath. I guess I've never been good with change. I'm still fumbling to navigate my own transformation since leaving town.

Swallowing a sigh, I abandon my brothers and step into the hall—where my gaze snags on probably the only thing about this place that hasn't changed one bit.

My ex-boyfriend Evan Hartley.

CHAPTER 2

GENEVIEVE

The guy's got some nerve walking in here looking like that. Those haunting, dark eyes that still lurk in the deepest parts of my memory. Brown, nearly black hair I still feel between my fingers. He's as heart-stabbingly gorgeous as the pictures that still flicker behind my eyes. It's been a year since I last saw him, yet my response to him is the same. He walks into a room, and my body notices him before I do. It's a disturbance of static in the air that dances across my skin.

It's obnoxious, is what it is. And that my body has the audacity to react to him, *now*, at my mother's funeral, is even more disturbing.

Evan stands with his twin brother Cooper, scanning the room until he notices me. The guys are identical except for occasional variances in their haircuts, but most people tell them apart by their tattoos. Cooper's got two full sleeves, while most of Evan's ink is on his back. Me, I know it from his eyes. Whether they're gleaming with mischief or flickering with joy, need, frustration . . . I always know when it's Evan's eyes on me.

Our gazes meet. He nods. I nod back, my pulse quickening. Literally three seconds later, Evan and I convene down the hall where there are no witnesses.

It's strange how familiar we are with some people, no matter how much time has passed. Memories of the two of us wash over me like a balmy breeze. Walking through this house with him like we're back in high school. Sneaking in and out at all hours. Stumbling with hands against the wall to stay upright. Laughing in hysterical whispers to not wake up the whole house.

"Hey," he says, holding out his arms in a hesitant offer, which I accept because it feels more awkward not to.

He always did give good hugs.

I force myself not to linger in his arms, not to inhale his scent. His body is warm and muscular and as familiar to me as my own. I know every inch of that tall, delicious frame.

I take a hasty step backward.

"Yeah, so, I heard. Obviously. Wanted to pay my respects." Evan is bashful, almost coy, with his hands in his pockets and his head bowed to look at me under thick lashes. I can't imagine the pep talk it took to get him here.

"Thanks."

"And, well, yeah." From one pocket, he pulls out a blue Blow Pop. "I got you this."

I haven't cried once since finding out Mom was sick. Yet accepting this stupid token from Evan makes my throat tighten and my eyes sting.

I'm suddenly transported back to the first time a Blow Pop ever exchanged hands between us. Another funeral. Another dead parent. It was after Evan's dad, Walt, died in a car accident. Drunk driving, because that's the kind of reckless, self-destructive man Walt Hartley had been. Fortunately, nobody else was hurt, but Walt's life ended on the dark road that night when he'd lost control and smashed into a tree.

I was twelve at the time and had no clue what to bring to a wake. My parents brought flowers, but Evan was a kid like me.

What was he going to do with flowers? All I knew was that my best friend and the boy I'd always had a huge crush on was hurting badly, and all I had to my name was one measly dollar. The fanciest thing I could afford at the general store was a lollipop.

Evan had cried when I clasped the Blow Pop in his shaking hand and quietly sat beside him on the back deck of his house. He'd whispered, "Thanks, Gen," and then we sat there in silence for more than an hour, staring at the waves lapping at the shore.

"Shut up," I mutter to myself, clenching the lollipop in my palm. "You're so dumb." Despite my words, we both know I'm deeply affected.

Evan cracks a knowing smile and smooths one hand over his tie, straightening it. He cleans up nice, but not too nice. Something about a suit on this guy still feels dangerous.

"You're lucky I found you first," I tell him once I can speak again. "Not sure my brothers would be as friendly."

With an unconcerned smirk, he shrugs. "Kellan hits like a girl."

Typical. "I'll make sure to tell him you said so."

Some wandering cousins glimpse us around the corner and look as though they might find a reason to come talk to me, so I grab Evan by the lapel and shove him toward the laundry room. I press myself up against the doorframe, then check to make sure the coast is clear.

"I can't get hijacked into another conversation about how much I remind people of my mom," I groan. "Like, dude, the last time you saw me, I still wasn't eating solid food."

Evan adjusts his tie again. "They think they're helping."

"Well, they're not."

Everyone wants to tell me what a great lady Mom was and how important family was to her. It's almost creepy, hearing people talk about a woman who bears no resemblance to the person I knew.

"How you holding up?" he asks roughly. "Like, really?"

I shrug in return. Because that's the question, isn't it? I've been asked it a dozen different ways over the past couple days, and I still don't have a proper answer. Or at least, not the one people want to hear.

"I'm not sure I feel anything. I don't know. Maybe I'm still in shock or something. You always expect these things to happen in a split second, or over months and months. This, though? It was like just the wrong amount of warning. I came home, and a week later she was dead."

"I get that," he says. "Barely time to get your bearings before it's over."

"I haven't known which way is up for days." I bite my lip. "I'm starting to wonder if there's something wrong with me?"

He fixes me with a disbelieving scowl. "It's death, Fred. There's nothing wrong with you."

I snort a laugh at his nickname for me. Been so long since I've heard it, I'd almost forgotten what it sounded like. There was a time when I answered to it more than my own name.

"Seriously, though. I keep waiting for the grief to hit, but it doesn't come."

"It's hard to find a lot of emotion for a person who didn't have a lot for you. Even if it's your mom." He pauses. "Maybe especially moms."

"True."

Evan gets it. He always has. One of the things we have in common is an unorthodox relationship with our mothers. In that there isn't much relationship to speak of. While his mom is an impermanent idea in his life—absent except for the few times a year she breezes into town to sleep off a bender or ask for money— mine was absent in spirit if not in body. Mine was so cold and detached, even in my earliest memories, that she hardly seemed to exist at all. I grew up jealous of the flower beds she tended in the front yard.

"I'm almost relieved she's gone." A lump rises in my throat. "No, more than almost. That's terrible to say, I know that. But it's like . . . now I can stop trying, you know? Trying and then feeling like crap when it doesn't change."

My whole life I made efforts to connect with her. To figure out why my mother didn't seem to like me much. I'd never gotten an answer. Maybe now I can stop asking.

"It's not terrible," Evan says. "Some people make shit parents. It's not our fault they don't know how to love us."

Except for Craig—Mom certainly knew how to love him. After five failed attempts, she'd finally gotten the recipe right with him. Her one perfect son she could pour a lifetime of mothering into. I love my little brother, but he and I might as well have been raised by two different people. He's the only one of us walking around here with red, swollen eyes.

"Can I tell you something?" Evan says with a grin that makes me suspicious. "But you have to promise not to hit me."

"Yeah, I can't do that."

He laughs to himself and licks his lips. An involuntary habit that always drove me crazy, because I know what that mouth is capable of.

"I missed you," he confesses. "Am I an asshole if I'm sort of glad someone died?"

I punch him in the shoulder, to which he feigns injury. He doesn't mean it. Not really. But in a weird way I appreciate the sentiment, if only because it gives me permission to smile for a second or two. To breathe.

I toy with the thin silver bracelet circling my wrist. Not quite meeting his eyes. "I missed you too. A little."

"A little?" He's mocking me.

"Just a little."

"Mmm-mmm. So you thought about me, what, once, twice a day when you were gone?"

"More like once or twice *total*."

He chuckles.

Truthfully, after I left the Bay I spent months doing my best to push away the thoughts of him when they insisted their way forward. Refusing the images that came when I closed my eyes at night or went on a date. Eventually it got easier. I'd almost managed to forget him. Almost.

And now here he is, and it's like not a second has passed. We still have this bubble of energy building between us. It's evident in the way he angles his body toward mine, the way my hand lingers on his arm longer than necessary. How it hurts not to touch him.

"Don't do that," I order when I notice his expression. I'm caught in his eyes. Snagged, like catching my shirt on a door handle, only it's a memory tripping up my brain.

"Do what?"

"You know what."

Evan's lips lift at the corner. Just a twitch. Because he knows the way he looks at me.

"You look good, Gen." He's doing it again. The dare in his eyes, the implications in his gaze. "Time away agreed with you."

The little shit. It isn't fair. I hate him, even as my fingers make contact with his chest and slide down the front of his shirt.

No, what I hate is how easily he can have me.

"We shouldn't do this," I murmur.

We're tucked away but still visible to anyone should they get the urge to glance in our direction. Evan's hand skims the hem of my dress. He pushes up under the fabric and softly drags his fingertips along the curve of my ass.

"No," he breathes against my ear. "We shouldn't."

So, of course, we do.

We slip into the bathroom next to the laundry room, locking the door behind us. My breath lodges in my throat when he lifts me up on the vanity.

"This is a terrible idea," I tell him as he grips my waist and I brace myself against the sink.

"I know." And then he covers my mouth with his.

The kiss is urgent and hungry. Lord, I missed this. I missed his kisses and the greedy thrust of his tongue, how wild and unbridled he is. Our mouths devour each other, almost too roughly, and still I can't have enough of him.

The anticipation and frantic need is too much. I fumble with the buttons of his shirt, pulling it open to drag my nails down his chest until the pain makes him pin my arms behind my back. It's hot and raw. Maybe a little angry. All the unfinished business working itself out. I close my eyes and hold on for the ride, losing myself in the kiss, the taste of him. He kisses me harder, deeper, until I'm mindless with need.

I can't stand it anymore.

I force my arms free to unbuckle his belt. Evan watches me. Watches my eyes. My lips.

"I've missed this," he whispers.

So have I, but I can't bring myself to say it out loud.

I gasp when his hand travels between my thighs. My own hand is trembling as I slip it inside his boxers and—

"Everything okay in there?" A voice. Then a knock. My entire extended family is on the other side of the door.

I freeze.

"Fine," Evan calls back, his fingertips a scant inch from where I was just aching for him.

Now, I'm sliding off the vanity, pushing his hand off me, withdrawing mine from his boxers. Before my flats even connect with the tiled floor, I already hate myself. Barely in the same room with him for ten minutes, and I lose all self-control.

I almost had sex with Evan Hartley at my mother's funeral reception, for fuck's sake. If we hadn't been interrupted, I have no doubt I would've let him take me right then and there. That's a new low, even for me.

Damn it.

I'd spent the last year training myself to at least approximate a normal functioning adult. To not surrender to every destructive instinct the second it pops into my head, to exercise some damn restraint. And then Evan Hartley licks his lips and I'm open for business.

Really, Gen?

As I'm fixing my hair in the mirror, I see him watching me with a question on his tongue.

Finally he voices it. "You okay?"

"I can't believe we almost did that," I mumble, shame lining my throat. Then, I find my composure and steel up my defenses. I lift my head. "Just so we're clear, this isn't going to be a thing."

"The hell does that mean?" His affronted gaze meets mine in the reflection.

"It means I have to be in town for a bit for my dad, but while I'm here, we're not going to be seeing each other."

"Seriously?" When he reads my resolved expression, his sours. "What the hell, Gen? You stick your tongue down my throat and then tell me to get lost? That's pretty shitty."

Turning to face him, I shrug with feigned indifference. He wants me to fight him because he knows there's a lot of emotion here, and the more he drags it out of me, the better his chances. But I'm not going there again, not this time. This was a lapse in judgment. Temporary insanity. I'm better now. Head on straight. Got it all out of my system.

"You know we can't stay away from each other," he tells me, growing more frustrated at my decision. "We spent our whole relationship trying. Doesn't work."

He's not wrong. Until the day I finally left town, we were on and off since freshman year of high school. A constant push-and-pull of loving and fighting. Sometimes I'm the moth, other times the flame.

What I eventually figured out, though, is that the only way to win is not to play.

Unlocking the door, I pause to offer a brief look over my shoulder. "There's a first time for everything."

CHAPTER 3

EVAN

This is what I get for trying to be a nice guy. She needed to forget for a little while—that's cool. I'll never, ever complain about kissing Genevieve. But she could've at least played nice afterward. *Let's get together later and have a drink, catch up.* Blowing me off altogether is harsh even for her.

Gen has always had sharp edges. Hell, it's one of the things that draws me to her. But she's never looked at me with such dead disinterest. Like I was nobody to her.

Brutal.

As we leave the West house and walk toward Cooper's truck, he gives me a look of suspicion. Beyond appearances, we're entirely different people. If we weren't brothers, we probably wouldn't even be friends. But we are brothers—even worse, twins—which means we can read each other's minds with one measly look.

"You're kidding me," he says, sighing with what has become a near-permanent state of judgment plastered on his face. For months now, he's been on my case about every little thing.

"Leave it." Honestly, I'm not in the mood to hear it.

He pulls away from the curb among the long line of cars parked on the street for the reception. "Unbelievable. You hooked up with her." He slides a side-eye at me, which I ignore. "Jesus

Christ. You were gone for ten minutes. What, you were like, I'm so sorry for your loss, here, have my penis?"

"Fuck off, Coop." When he phrases it like that, it does sound kind of bad.

Kind of?

Fine. Alright. Maybe nearly having sex at her mother's funeral reception wasn't the brightest of ideas, but . . . but I missed her, damn it. Seeing Gen again, after more than a year apart, was like a punch to the gut. My need to touch her, kiss her, had bordered on desperation.

Maybe that makes me a weak bastard, but there you have it.

"I think you've done enough of that for the both of us."

I grit my teeth and force my gaze out the window. The thing about Cooper—when our dad died and then our mom basically abandoned us as kids, he somehow got it in his head that I wanted him to become both. A constantly nagging, grumpy bastard who's always disappointed in me. For a little while, things got better after he settled down with his girlfriend Mackenzie, who managed to yank the stick out of his ass. But now it seems like finally being in his first stable relationship has got him back to thinking he's qualified to pass judgment on my life.

"It wasn't like that," I tell him. Because I can feel him fuming at me. "Some people cry when they're grieving. Gen's not a crier."

He half shakes his head, twisting his hands on the steering wheel while his jaw works on grinding down his molars, like I can't hear what he's thinking.

"Don't give yourself an aneurysm, bro. Just spit it out."

"She's barely been in town a week and already you're in it up to your neck. I told you it was a bad idea going over there."

I would never give Cooper the satisfaction, but he's right.

Genevieve shows up and I lose my damn mind. It's always been that way with us. We're two mostly harmless chemicals that when mixed become an explosive combination, leveling a city block with salt water.

"You act like we robbed a liquor store. Relax. All we did was kiss."

Cooper's disapproval pours off him. "Today it's just a kiss. Tomorrow is another story."

And? It's not as if we're hurting anybody. I frown at him. "Dude, what does it matter to you?"

He and Genevieve used to be cool. Even friends. I get that maybe he holds a grudge about how she left town, but it's not like she did it to him. Anyway, it's been a year. If I'm not still making a thing of it, why should he?

At a stoplight, he turns to meet my eyes. "Look, you're my brother and I love you, but you're an ass when she's around. These last few months you've really gotten your shit together. Don't throw all that away on a chick who's never going to stop being a mess."

Something about it—I don't know, the contempt in his voice, the condescension—sticks right in my craw. Cooper can be a real self-righteous prick when he wants to be.

"It's not like I'm dating her again, okay? Don't be so dramatic."

We pull up to our house, the two-story, low-country cottage-style on the beach that's been in our family for three generations. The place was all but falling apart before we started making renovations over the past several months. It's taken most of our savings and more of our time, but it's coming along.

"Yeah, you keep telling yourself that." Cooper shuts off the engine with an exasperated breath. "Same old pattern: takes off whenever she wants, suddenly pops back in, and you're ready to bake cookies together. Sound like any other woman you know?" With that, he hops out of the truck and slams the door shut.

Well, that was uncalled for.

Of the two of us, Cooper has held the hardest grudge against our mother, to the point he's resented me for not needing to hate her as much as he does. In her latest episode, though, I backed him up. Told her she wasn't welcome to hang around anymore, not after what she did to him. Shelley Hartley had finally crossed one line too many.

But I guess taking Cooper's side wasn't enough to get him to ease up on me. Everyone's full of low blows today.

At dinner later, Cooper still hasn't let the Genevieve thing go. Not in his nature.

It's damn irritating. I'm trying to eat my damned spaghetti, and this asshole is still laying into me while he tells Mackenzie, who's been living with us for the past few months, about how I basically screwed my ex on top of the still-warm casket of her dead mother.

"Evan says he'll just be a minute, then leaves me by myself in that house to give our condolences to her dad and five brothers, who pretty much think it's Evan's fault she ran out of town a year ago," Cooper grumbles, stabbing a meatball with his fork. "They're asking where he is; meanwhile, he's got Mr. West's baby girl bent over the bathtub or whatever."

"We just kissed," I say in exasperation.

"Coop, come on," Mac says, wincing away from her fork, which is coiled with pasta and hanging mid-air. "I'm trying to eat."

"Yeah, have some tact, jackass," I chide.

When they're not looking, I slip a piece of meatball to Daisy, the golden retriever puppy at my feet. Cooper and Mac rescued her off the jetty last year and she's nearly doubled in size since then. At first I wasn't thrilled with the idea of taking care of this creature Cooper's new girlfriend had dumped on us, but then she spent a night curled up at the end of my bed having puppy dreams, and I broke like a cheap toy. Dog's had me wrapped around her paw ever since. She's the only girl I can trust not to take off on me. Luckily, Coop and Mac worked out, so we didn't have to fight a custody battle.

It's funny how life works out sometimes. Last year, Cooper and I hatched an admittedly mean-spirited plot to sabotage Mac's relationship with her boyfriend at the time. In our defense, the guy was a douchebag. Then Cooper had to spoil all the fun and catch feelings for the rich college girl. I couldn't stand her at first, but it turned out I'd read Mackenzie Cabot all wrong. I was at least man enough to admit I'd misjudged her. Cooper, on the other hand, can't keep his thoughts to himself so far as Gen's concerned. Typical.

"So what's the real story with you two?" Mac asks, curiosity flickering in her dark-green eyes.

The real story? How do I even begin to answer that? Genevieve and I have history. Lots of it. Some of it great. Some, not so good. Things have always been complicated with us.

"We got together freshman year of high school," I tell Mac. "She was basically my best friend. Always good for a laugh and down for anything."

My mind is suddenly flooded with images of us messing around on dirt bikes at two in the morning with a fifth of tequila between us. Surfing the swells as a hurricane moved in, then riding out the storm in the back of her brother's Jeep. Gen and I constantly dared each other's limits of adventure, getting into a few scrapes with death or mutilation that we had no right escaping unscathed. There was no adult in the relationship, so there was never a point when someone said stop. We were always chasing the rush.

And Gen was a rush. Fearless and undaunted. Unapologetically herself, and to hell what anyone had to say about it. She made me crazy; more than once I broke my hand wrestling some asshole cornering her in a bar. Yeah, maybe I was possessive, but no more than she was. She'd drag a chick out by her hair for looking at me the wrong way. Most of it had something to do with the off-and-on part—getting jealous, fighting, and turning around to make the other one jealous. It was a little messed up, but it was our language. I was hers and she was mine. We were addicted to make-up sex.

The quiet moments were just as addictive. Lying on a beach blanket at our favorite spot in the Bay, her head in the crook of my neck, my arm slung around her as we looked up at the stars. Whispering our darkest secrets to each other and knowing there'd never be any judgment on the other end. Hell, aside from Cooper, she's the only one to ever see me cry.

"There was a lot of breaking up and making up," I admit. "But that was our thing. And then last year, she was suddenly gone. One day she just picked up and left town. Didn't say a word to anyone."

My heart squeezes painfully at the memory. I thought it was a joke at first. That Gen had taken off with her girlfriends and wanted me to freak out and drive to Florida or something to track her down, then fight a little and bang it out. Until the girls promised me they hadn't heard a peep from her.

"I found out later she'd settled down in Charleston and started a new life. Just like that." I swallow the bitterness that clogs my throat.

Mac contemplates me for a moment. We've grown fairly close since she started living here, so I know when she's trying to formulate a nice way to tell me I'm a disaster. Not like it's anything I don't know.

"Go ahead, princess. Say what's on your mind."

She puts her fork down and pushes her plate away. "Sounds like a toxic situation for both of you. Maybe Gen was right to end it for good. It might be better you two stay away from each other."

At that, Cooper slides me a glare because there is almost nothing he loves more than an I-told-you-so.

"I said the same thing to Cooper about you," I remind her. "And now look at you guys."

"For fuck's sake." Cooper throws his utensils on his plate, and his chair squeaks against the wooden floor. "You can't compare the two. Not even close. Genevieve is a mess. The best thing she ever did for you was stop taking your calls. Let it go, dude. She's not here for you."

"Yeah, you must be loving this," I say, wiping my mouth with my napkin before tossing it on the table. "Because this is payback, right?"

He sighs, rubbing his eyes like I'm some dog refusing to be house-trained. Condescending prick. "I'm trying to look out for you because you're too dick-blinded to see where this will end. Where you two always end up."

"You know," I say, getting up from the table. "Maybe you should stop projecting all your hang-ups onto me. Genevieve isn't Shelley. Stop trying to punish me because you're mad your mommy left you."

I regret the words even as they leave my mouth, but I don't turn back as Daisy follows me to the kitchen door and we head for the beach. Truth is, no one knows better than me all the messed-up shit Gen and I have been through. How inescapable we are. But that's just it. Now that she's back, I can't ignore her.

This thing between us, this pull—it won't let me.

CHAPTER 4

GENEVIEVE

I regret this already. My first day in the office at Dad's stone business is worse than I imagined. For weeks, maybe months, the guys walked in here to leave invoices in a haphazard pile on the desk in front of an empty chair. Mail was tossed in a tray without so much as looking at who it was from. There's still a mug of sludge that used to be coffee sitting on top of the filing cabinet. Opened sugar packets the ants have long since scavenged are sitting in the trash can.

And Shane isn't helping. While I sit at the computer trying to discern Mom's file-naming system to track down some kind of record of paid and outstanding accounts, my second-oldest brother is down a TikTok hole on his phone.

"Hey, fuckhead," I say, snapping my fingers. "There are like six invoices here with your name on them. Are these paid or still pending?"

He doesn't bother raising his head from his screen. "How should I know?"

"Because they're your jobsites."

"That's not my department."

Shane doesn't see me shake my hands in the air as I'm imagining throttling him. Asshole.

"There are three emails here from Jerry about a patio for his restaurant. You need to get on the phone with him and set up an appointment to do a walk-through and give him an estimate."

"I've got shit to do," he says, barely muttering the words as his attention stays focused on the tiny glowing box in his hands. It's like he's five years old.

I launch a paper clip at him with a rubber band. Nails him right in the middle of his forehead.

"Shit, Gen. What the hell?"

That got his attention.

"This." I push the invoices across the desk and write down Jerry's phone number. "Since you've already got your phone out, make the call."

Utterly disgusted with my tone, he sneers at me. "You realize you're basically Dad's secretary."

Shane is sincerely testing my love for him and desire to let him live. I have four other brothers. Not like I'll really miss one.

"You don't get to boss me around," he gripes.

"Dad made me office manager until he finds someone else." I get up from the desk to put the papers in his hand and shove him out of the office. "So as far as you're concerned, I am your god now. Get used to it." Then I slam the door on him.

I knew this would happen. Growing up in a house with six kids, all of us were always jockeying for position. We all have an autonomy complex, everyone trying to exert their independence while getting shit on from the upper rungs of the age ladder. It's worse now that I'm the twenty-two-year-old middle kid telling the big brothers what's what. Still, Dad was right—this place is a wreck. If I don't get it all sorted in a hurry, he'll be broke in no time.

Later, after work, I meet up with my brother Billy for a drink at Ronda's, a local dive for the retired swingers crowd that spends their days driving up and down Avalon Bay in golf carts and trading keys in a fishbowl over a game of poker. The rising May temperatures in the Bay means the return of wall-to-wall tourists and rich pricks clogging the boardwalk, so the rest of us have to find more creative places to hang out.

As Billy smiles at the leathery-faced bartender for a beer—nobody in this town cards the locals—I order a coffee. It's unseasonably sweltering outside, even at sunset, and my clothes are sticking to my skin like papier-mâché, but I can always drink a cup of hot, unleaded caffeine. It's how you know you're from the South.

"Saw you and Jay bringing in some boxes last night," Billy says. "That the last of it?"

"Yeah, I'm leaving most of my stuff in storage back in Charleston. Doesn't make much sense to haul my furniture down here just to move it all back up in a few months."

"You're still set on going back?"

I nod. "I'll have to find a different place, though."

My landlord was a total jerk about breaking my lease a couple months early, so I'll still be paying him while I'm here living in my childhood bedroom. Leaving my job didn't go much better. My boss at the real estate agency all but laughed at me when I mentioned taking a leave of absence. I hope Dad's planning on paying me well. He might be a grieving widower, but I don't work for free.

"So guess who walked into the hardware store the other day?" Billy says with a look that tells me to brace myself. "Deputy Dogshit came in hassling me about the sidewalk sign. Something about town ordinances and blocking pedestrian traffic."

My nails bite into the weathered bar top. Even after a year, the mention of Deputy Rusty Randall still coaxes a special kind of anger.

"That sign's been there for, what," Billy says, "twenty years at least."

As long as I can remember, definitely. It's a staple of the side-walk, our wooden A-frame sign with the cartoon handyman announcing, *YES, WE'RE OPEN!* and waving a pipe wrench. The other side features a chalkboard with the week's sale or new products. When I was little and loved following Dad to work, he used to yell at me from inside that I better not be drawing on the sign. I'd hastily erase my artwork and begin transferring it to the concrete, doing my best to force traffic around my masterpieces and just about biting the ankles off tourists who stomped their Sperrys through my sidewalk gallery.

"The guy wouldn't leave until I brought the sign inside," Billy grumbles. "He stood there for fifteen minutes while I pretended to help some customers and haggled with him about his bullshit ordinance. I was about to call Dad to talk some sense into him, but he went for his cuffs like he was about to arrest me, so I said, screw it. I waited a few minutes after he left and then put it back out."

"Asshole," I mutter into my coffee. "You know he gets off on it."

"I'm surprised he didn't tail you into town. Half expected him to be sitting outside the house in the middle of the night."

I wouldn't have put it past him. About a year ago, Deputy Randall became my cautionary tale. That night was my rock bottom, the moment I realized I couldn't go on living like I was. Drinking too much, partying every night, letting my demons get the best of me. I had to do something about it—get my life back—before it was too late. So I made a plan, and a couple months later, I packed up everything I needed and set off for Charleston. Billy was the only person I told about that night with Rusty. Even though he's two years younger than me, he's always been my closest confidant.

"I still think about her," I tell my brother. The guilt churning in my gut at the thought of Kayla and her children is still potent after all this time. I'd heard a while back she'd left Rusty and taken the kids. "I feel like I should find her. Apologize."

Though the idea of facing her, and how she might react, is enough to send me into an anxiety spiral. It's become a new feeling for me since that night. There was a time when nothing scared me. The stuff that left other people biting their nails rolled right off my shoulders. Now, I look back on my wilder days and cringe. Some of those days were not so long ago.

"Do what you want," Billy says, taking a deep swig of his beer as if to wash the lingering topic out of his mouth. "But you have nothing to apologize for. The guy's a jackass and a creep. He's lucky we didn't find him down a dark dirt road somewhere."

I'd sworn Billy to secrecy; otherwise, he definitely would've run and told Dad or our brothers what had happened. I'm glad he kept it quiet. No sense in all of them winding up in prison for beating the pulp out of a cop. Then Randall would win.

"I'm going to run into him eventually," I say, more to myself.

"Well, if you've got to skip town in a hurry, I still have about eighty bucks stashed in my old bed frame at Dad's house." Billy grins at me, which does go a long way to unwinding the knot in my chest. He's good like that.

As we're closing out the tab, I get a text from my best friend Heidi.

Heidi: *Bonfire on the beach tonight.*
Me: *Where?*
Heidi: *The usual.*

Meaning Evan and Cooper's house. The place is loaded with emotional landmines.

Me: *I don't know if that's a good idea.*
Heidi: *Come on. A couple drinks then you can bail.*

Heidi: *Don't make me come get you.*
Heidi: *See you there.*
Me: *Fine. Bitch.*

I stifle a sigh, as my tired brain tries to work through yet another pitfall to consider. Settling back into town, I was excited to reconnect with old friends and spend more time with others, but trying to dodge Evan makes that more complicated. I can't very well draw a line down the center of town. And no part of me wants the summer to devolve into tests of loyalty and calling dibs on our tight web of friends, ties crossing and overlapping. It isn't fair to either of us. Because as much as I know nothing good comes from letting Evan back in, I have no intentions to hurt him. This is my punishment, not his.

CHAPTER 5

EVAN

All the freaks come out at night. Under a full moon, we're the hidden images of ourselves, revealed in silver light. It's the Bay turned wild with inhibition and mischief, everybody hot and bothered and aching for a good time. Any excuse for a party.

On the beach, dozens of our friends, and more than a few random tagalongs, surround a bonfire. Our house is set back just beyond the dunes and grassy tree-dotted lawn, its outline evident only in the orange porch lights. It's a good time, kicking back with a few beers, smoking a bowl. A couple people with guitars haggle over song requests while a nearby group plays strip glow frisbee. Whatever it takes to get laid these days, I guess.

"So this clone is wasted, right," Jordy, an old high school friend of ours, says to those of us gathered around the fire, sitting on a driftwood log while he rolls a joint. Dude could do this shit with his eyes closed and it'd still be the tightest, neatest roll you've ever seen. "And the guy stumbles into our table. Like knocks right into us. He keeps calling me Parker."

We laugh, because it's such a clone name. Those collar-wearing pansy-ass Richie Riches who go to Garnet College are nothing if not predictable. Can't hold their liquor and making it everyone else's problem.

"For like twenty minutes he's talking to us, holding on to the table to keep from splattering on the floor. No idea what the hell he's babbling about. Then suddenly he's like, *hey, come on, bros, after-party at my house.*"

"No," Mackenzie says, eyes flashing wide and dread in her voice. "You did not." She's keeping Cooper in a better mood tonight, sitting in his lap with her tits shoved up in his face. Got him well occupied, which is a relief. I was getting sick of his tantrums.

Jordy shrugs. "I mean, he insisted. So the four us, right, are pretty much having to carry this guy out of the bar. Then he hands me his keys and says, *you drive, it's the blue one.* I press the button on the fob, and this Maserati SUV flashes its lights at me. Like no way, right? That's a hundred-thousand-dollar car. I'm pretty sure I stepped in piss at some point in that dirty bar bathroom, but sure, guy."

"Just tell me he still has his kidneys," I say with a grin.

"Yeah, yeah. We didn't chop him or the car for parts." Jordy waves his hand, then lights the joint. "Anyway. So the guy goes, *Car, take me home.* And the thing is like, *okay, Christopher, here's your route home.* At that point I'm thinking, well, shit. So I rev that baby up and start driving. About a half hour later we get to his stupid-huge mansion down the coast. I'm talking iron gate and topiaries and shit. So we make it there alive and the dude's like, *hey, want to see something cool?*"

Always the famous last words. Like the time our buddy Wyatt tried the knife trick from *Aliens* and had to get thirty-seven stiches and have a tendon reattached. Come to think of it, that was one of the last times Genevieve and I hung out. Which, until all the blood, was a pretty good time. Can't say for sure how we ended up on the sixty-five-foot Hatteras sportfishing boat out in the middle of the bay, only that we had a nightmare of a time getting it to the dock and somehow still managed to come ashore about ten miles from where we were aiming. Navigating gets a hell of a lot harder in the dark after a few Fireballs.

I can't believe I'd almost forgotten about that night. But I guess I've done a lot of forgetting over the last year. Or tried to, at least. For a while, I expected Gen would show up as if nothing had happened. Like she overslept for six months. Then seven, eight months—a year gone, and I'd finally trained myself to stop thinking about her every time this thing or that reminded me of another time when. So of course, just when I've almost got her out of my system, she's back. A fresh, unfiltered shot straight into my bloodstream when I was damn near clean. Now all I taste are her lips. I feel her nails down my back every night while I'm lying in bed. I wake up hearing her voice. It's infuriating.

"This crazy bastard thinks he's Hawkeye or some shit," Jordy says, passing the joint around the circle. "Running around with a bow, shooting flaming arrows all over his backyard. I'm like, *nah, white boy, I've seen this movie.* The guys and I are gonna bail but, oh, right, we drove this dude's car and we're stuck out here behind an iron gate."

I can't help glancing toward the house. I keep expecting Gen to come walking out of the shadows. I feel Mackenzie giving me the eye and realize she's caught me looking. Or rather, caught me *hoping.* Because I know Heidi or one of the girls will have invited Gen, and if she doesn't come, it's because she'd rather hide out at her dad's place than chance seeing me again. The notion seriously grates.

"We have to make a run for it because this dude is out of his mind, and we're climbing through these damn hedges and getting all cut up. I've got Danny on my shoulder to heave him up over the fence. Juan is trying to get an Uber but the reception sucks, so the app isn't loading. We're hauling ass, hearing all kinds of commotion behind us, while I'm thinking, one of these rich folks are going to think that house is burning down and call the cops on us. Sure enough, about ten minutes later, we're heading back toward the main road and a car comes up real slow behind us."

I hear a voice and look over my shoulder. It's Gen, standing a few yards away with Heidi and some of the girls. She's wearing a long-sleeve shirt falling off one shoulder and barely revealing a tiny pair of shorts hugging her ass like they're painted on. Long black hair cascades down her back. Kill me.

Gen's got this way about her. Confident and cool but with this edge of absolute batshit terror, like at any moment she could blow a kiss and drag a knife through your parachute, then push you out of a plane. There's nothing sexier than the way her blue eyes smile when she's got mayhem on her mind.

"Then the car stops. Man, my chest is pounding. A guy sticks his head out the window and shouts at us: *Get in, assholes. Drunk Lannister is on the loose and it's the Battle of the Blackwater out there.*"

The group erupts in laughter. The fire flashes as someone coughs up a mouthful of beer. I note Gen is pointedly not looking in this direction.

Jordy gets the joint back and takes a hit. "Turns out Luke went home with some clone chick down the street and was outside when they saw this dude shooting off these arrows, which caught at least two boats on fire at their docks. Neighbors were running out of their houses firing back flares. Like, sheer madness."

Cooper catches me watching Gen. Without a word, I hear him scolding me. Then he shakes his head, which may as well be a dare. He might be settled down, but I still intend to have a good time. And I know Gen. Maybe she was on some cold turkey kick before, but now that she's back, there's no point in either of us pretending we know how to stay away from each other. It's chemistry.

Wandering away from the bonfire, I approach her. I'm half

hard already, thinking about the last time I saw her. Legs wrapped around me. Teeth digging into my shoulder. My skin still bears the marks she left behind. Just the sight of her has me wanting to take her to bed and make up for time lost.

She feels me coming before I open my mouth, casting her gaze over her shoulder. There's the briefest flicker of recognition—the shared spark of lust and longing—before her expression turns impassive.

"What are you drinking?" I say as what I figure is an easy way in.

"I'm not."

It's awkward right from the off. All the familiarity of our conversation back at her house—gone. To the point that even Heidi and Steph wince with embarrassment.

"What do you want?" I ask, ignoring her attitude. If that'd ever worked on me, we wouldn't have kept getting back together. "I'll run up to the house and make you something."

"I'm good, thanks." Gen stares off at the waves climbing up the sand.

I stifle a sigh. "Can we talk? Take a walk with me."

She pulls her hair over her shoulder in a move I recognize right away. It's her fuck-off flip. The I've-already-stopped-hearing-you hair toss. Like we're strangers.

"Yeah, no," she says, voice flat and all but unrecognizable. "I'm not even sticking around. Just stopped by to say hey."

But not to me.

"So it's like that?" I try to curb the bite in my tone and fail. "You come back here and pretend you don't know me?"

"Okay," Heidi interjects with a bored roll of her eyes. "Thanks for stopping by, but this is a penis-free zone tonight. Run along, Evan."

"Fuck off, Heidi." She's always been a shit-stirrer.

"Yep, happy to." At that, she and Steph drag Gen closer to the bonfire and leave me standing there like an idiot.

Cool. Whatever. I don't need this aggravation. Genevieve wants to play games, fine. I grab a beer from the cooler and notice a group of girls stroll up to the party looking like they stumbled out of Daddy's Bentley. They're all dressed in the same sort of little ruffle tops and short skirts—straight off the clone assembly line. Definitely Garnet students, and my money's on sorority sisters. Gen's complete opposites in every way. They stand around looking lost and confused for a minute, until one of them homes in on me.

She tries her best to look chill while slipping in the sand to stride over. With too much lip gloss, she smiles at me. "Can I get a drink?"

I happily pop the cap off a beer for her and grab a few more for her friends. The best part about rich girls coming to slum it out here with the townies is they're easily amused. Tell them a few embellished stories about near-death exploits and running from the cops, and they eat that shit up. It scratches their sticking-it-to-the-parents itch, allowing them to live dangerously from a safe, vicarious distance, and gives them something to tell their friends about. Normally, feeling like I'm an attraction at a zoo would piss me off, but tonight I'm not the one with the sour face.

As the chicks let their hands linger on my arms while they laugh at my jokes and peel up my shirt after I tell them I have tattoos, Gen is staring daggers from her spot near the fire. Hitting me with a glare that says, *really, them?* And I don't give her the satisfaction of a response, because if she wants to pretend I'm dead to her, then I'm cold all over.

"I've got one too," the bravest of the girls informs me. She's cute, in a cookie-cutter clone sort of way. Nice rack, at least. "Got it on spring break last year in Mexico. Want to see?"

Before I can answer, she pulls her skirt up to flash the inside of her thigh at me. Her tat is a jellyfish, looking like it's gliding up into her lacy panties. I don't know how that's supposed to be sexy. But Gen watches me look, and that's kind of hot.

"Did it hurt?" I ask her, meeting Gen's eyes over the girl's shoulder.

"A little. But I like the pain."

"Yeah, I get that." It's almost too easy. This chick is practically begging me to take her back to the house. "It's pain that teaches us what pleasure is. Or how would we even know the difference?"

Eventually, her friends give up trying to share me and wander off to find their own one-night stands, and it doesn't take long before she kisses me and I'm copping a handful of her ass. It's a familiar routine, one I've indulged in plenty of times this past year. Forgetting myself in a hungry tongue and eager body meant forgetting about Gen for a while, not having to remember the cold truth that she'd left me without a word.

But right now, she's the only thing on my mind. When I come up for air, I spot Gen biting her lip at me like she'd slit my throat if there weren't so many witnesses. Ha. Too damn bad. She started it.

"Motherfucker!"

I blink, and suddenly there's some polo-wearing douchebag crowding my sightline. His face is red with anger, making him look like a pissed-off lobster. He calls the girl Ashlyn, who scrambles away from me with a guilty look about a second before the dude sucker punches me. It isn't a great shot and barely naps my head sideways.

"Well, that was rude," I remark, readjusting my jaw. I've taken so many hits in my life, I barely feel it anymore.

"You stay the hell away from her!" He's all hopped up on his macho bullshit, and he's got his buddies behind him.

I look over at Ashlyn, but she's not at my side anymore. She's huddled with her friends five yards away, refusing to meet my eyes. The smug gleam on her face as she watches Mr. Polo tells me I was more than frivolous entertainment for her tonight. I was payback.

"Easy, there," I tell the guy. A few heads turn, then several more as the party becomes aware of the confrontation. "Your sister and I were just getting acquainted."

"That's my girlfriend, asshole."

"You're sleeping with your sister? That's fucked up, dude."

His second punch is stronger. The taste of blood fills my mouth as I lick at the gash in my lip. I spit a wad of red mucous in the sand.

"Come on, pretty boy," I taunt, smiling with red, wet teeth. My arms tingle with expectant energy. "You can do better than that. She even showed me her tattoo."

He comes at me again, but this time I dodge the shot and send him to the ground with blood pouring out of his nose. We wrestle, sand sticking to the blood streaking down our shirts. We exchange blows, rolling around until some of his buddies and mine finally jump in to tear us apart. My friends tell the clones to get lost. They're outnumbered, after all. Still, as pretty boy and his group are retreating, I can't help feeling interrupted, my muscles not nearly tired and the adrenaline still running hot.

"Come again any time," I shout after them.

Then I turn around to a wave of salt water splashing me in the face.

When I wipe my eyes, Gen's standing there with an empty red cup. I smirk at her. "Thanks, I was thirsty."

"You're an idiot."

"He hit me first." My lip stings and my hand is sore, but I'm otherwise unscathed. I reach for her, but she steps away.

"You haven't changed a bit." At that, she tosses the cup at my feet and leaves with Heidi and Steph, her look of dismissive disgust landing harder than any blow I endured from the party crasher.

I haven't changed a bit? Why *should* I change? I'm the same person she's always known. Only difference is she disappeared for a year and came back with a superiority complex. Pretending to be someone she's not. Because I felt it, the other day at her house. The real Genevieve. This new chick is an act, and not a very good one. I don't know who she thinks she's impressing, but I'm not about to feel bad about being honest. At least one of us is.

"What was that?" Cooper follows me up to the house as I reach the back deck.

"I don't want to hear it," I say, pulling open the sliding glass door to the kitchen.

"Hey." He grabs my shoulder. "Everyone was having a good time until you had to start some shit."

"I didn't start anything." This is so typical. Some random dude messes with me, and Cooper makes it my fault. "He decided to throw down with me."

"Yeah. It's always the other guy. But somehow they always pick you. Why is that?"

"Just lucky, I guess." I try to walk away again but Cooper gets in my path and shoves my chest.

"You need to get your shit together. We're not kids anymore. Picking fights because you've got some chip on your shoulder has gotten real old, Evan."

"Just once, it'd be nice if you took my side."

"Then stop being on the wrong side."

Fuck this. I push him aside and go upstairs to take a shower. Cooper has always refused to see my side of anything. He's too busy being a judgmental prick. Must be all warm and cozy in his Good Twin delusion, but I'm sick of it.

Waiting for the water to heat up, I stare at my reflection in the mirror and experience a jolt of shock. My lip's a bit swollen, but not too bad. No, it's the ravaged look in my eyes that startles me. It matches the broken, battered feeling I've been struggling to ignore since my best friend skipped town on me, but I hope like hell I wasn't wearing that expression back there with Gen. She knows she stuck a knife in me when she bailed, but I'll be damned if she sees the damage it wrought.

CHAPTER 6

GENEVIEVE

It's dark outside by the time I shut off the computer in the office Friday night. I hadn't intended to work so late—everyone else had long since gone home—but I was in a spreadsheet trance and just kept going until Heidi texted to remind me that I'd agreed to meet up later with the girls. It's taken me the better part of two weeks, but I've finally managed to get a handle on the invoice tracking system. By next week, I should be caught up on all the outstanding accounts just in time to make payroll. I had to give myself a Google crash course on the software, but thankfully Mom had it set up to automate most of the process. Last thing I need is a bunch of angry employees when their paychecks are screwed up. While part of me is worried that doing too good a job might make me indispensable, I'm hoping that efficiency will help motivate Dad to allow someone else to take over soon.

As I'm locking up the building, a familiar pickup truck pulls into the parking lot. My shoulders tense when Cooper steps out and approaches me with the determination of a man with something on his mind.

"Hey, Coop."

He's identical to his brother, with dark hair and daunting brown eyes. Tall and fit, both arms covered in tattoos. And yet, strangely, I've never been attracted to Cooper. Evan caught my eye, and even in the dark I could tell them apart, as if there was some distinct aura about each of them.

"We need to talk," he tells me with an angry edge to his voice.

"Okay." His abrupt tone puts me off, raising my defenses. I grew up the middle child with five brothers. Absolutely no one gets to come in hot at me. So I plaster on a placating smile. "What's the problem?"

"Stay the hell away from Evan." At least he's direct.

I knew it was a bad idea showing up at the bonfire the other night. Every instinct said going anywhere near Evan wouldn't end well, but I'd convinced myself if I kept my distance, didn't engage, it wouldn't be so bad. Clearly it was too close.

"Maybe you should be having this conversation with him, Coop."

"I'm having it with you," he bites back, and for a second I'm unnerved. I've never gotten over the uncanny feeling of arguing with Evan's face but Cooper's words. I've known them since we were kids, but when you're as close as Evan and I were, it's hard to reconcile these feelings of intimacy that belong to a completely different yet similar person. "He was doing fine until you came back. Now you're not even here a few weeks and he's beating the tar out of some college prick because you've got his head all fucked up again."

"That's not fair. We've barely even spoken."

"And look at the damage it's done."

"I'm not Evan's keeper," I remind him, uncomfortable with the animosity wafting off him. "Whatever your brother's up to, I'm not responsible for his behavior."

"No, you're just the reason for it." Cooper is all but unrecognizable. He used to be the nice one. The reasonable one. Well, as reasonable as a Hartley twin can be. Cornering me in a parking lot isn't like him.

"Where's this coming from? I thought we were cool. We used to be friends." The three of us had been a trio of trouble once upon a time.

"Fuck off," he says, scoffing. It startles me. He might as well have spit in my face. "You tore my brother's heart out and took off without even a goodbye. What kind of cold-ass person does that? You have any idea what that did to him? No, Gen. We're not friends. You lost that privilege. Nobody hurts Evan."

I don't know what to say to that. I stand there, mouth dry and mind blank, watching this person I've known practically my whole life look at me like I'm scum. Guilt burns at my throat, because I know he's partially right. What I did *was* cold. No warning, no goodbye. I may as well have taken a match to my history with Evan and set it on fire. But it hadn't occurred to me Cooper would give a shit that I'd left his brother. If anything, I figured he'd be relieved.

Apparently I was wrong.

"I mean it, Gen. Leave him alone." With a last glare of contempt, he gets in his truck and drives away.

Later, at Joe's Beachfront Bar, I'm still distracted by the encounter with Cooper. Amid the crappy music and scents of perfume and body spray wrestling in the salt air blowing in from the open patio, I keep rehashing the interaction. It was unsettling, the way he sought me out to basically say stay away or else. If I didn't know Cooper, I'd have good reason to feel intimidated. As it is, though, I do know him. And his brother. So the more I spin the conversation over in my head, the more pissed off I get that he had the nerve to come and, what, tell me off? As if Evan weren't a grown man with more than a few malfunctions of his very own that have nothing to do with me. Coop wants to play the protector? Fine, whatever. But despite my lingering guilt over my abrupt departure, learning that Evan's still going around causing trouble only strengthens my conviction that leaving had been the right thing to do. Evan's had plenty of time to straighten himself out. If he hasn't, that's on him.

"Hey." Heidi, who's seated across from me at the high-top table, snaps her fingers in my face, waking me from my bitter stewing. Of all the girls in our group, I'm closest with Heidi, who's probably the most like me. With her platinum bob and razor-sharp tongue, Heidi's a total badass, a.k.a. my kind of girl. She also knows me far too well.

"You alive in there?" she adds, eyeing me with suspicion.

I answer with a half-hearted smile, ordering myself to be more present. Although we texted often when I was gone, I haven't hung out with my friends in ages.

"Sorry," I say sheepishly. I stab at the ice in my virgin cocktail with a straw. Nights like this, I could use a real drink.

"You sure you don't want something stronger?" Alana asks, temptingly holding out her glass of tequila with just the lightest mist of lime and simple syrup.

"Leave her alone." Steph, ever the defender of the weak, throws herself between me and peer pressure. "You know if she has a drink the convent won't take her back."

Okay, so she isn't all that nice.

"Yes, Sister Genevieve," Heidi says with a sarcastic smirk, speaking slowly like I'm an exchange student or something. An attempt at a crack on how long I've been away. "It must be overwhelming with all these lights and loud music. Do you remember music?"

"I moved to Charleston," I tell her, throwing up my middle finger. "Not Amish country."

"Right." Alana takes another sip of her drink, and the salty-sweet smell really does make me thirsty. "The notorious dry city of Charleston."

"Yeah, no, that's funny," I say to their teasing. "You're hilarious."

They don't get it. Not really. And I don't blame them. These girls have been my best friends since we were kids, so to them there's never been anything wrong with me. But there was. An uncontrollable destructive streak that drove my every decision when I was drinking. I wasn't making good decisions. Couldn't find the middle ground between moderation and obliteration. Other than a regrettable lapse last month on a trip to Florida where I woke up in a stranger's bed, I've kept pretty well to sobriety. Not without effort, though.

"Then here's to Gen." Heidi raises her glass. "Who may have forgotten how to have a good time, but we'll take her back anyway."

Heidi's always been good for a backhanded compliment. It's her love language. If she's not insulting you at least a little, you might as well be dead to her. I appreciate that about her, because there's never any confusion about where she stands. It's an honest way to live.

But she throws me for a loop by softening her tone again. "Welcome home, Gen. I really did miss you." Then, as if realizing she'd actually—gasp—revealed a sliver of emotion, she scowls at me, adding, "Don't ever leave us again, bitch."

I hide a smile. "I'll try not to."

"Welcome home," Steph and Alana echo, raising their glasses.

"So fill me in," I say, because I'd love to talk about literally anything else. Between the funeral and moving back home, all anyone does is ask me how I'm doing. I'm sick of myself. "What else is going on?"

"Alana's banging Tate," Steph spits out with too much enthusiasm, as if the declaration has been nervously pacing in the wings all night, waiting for its entrance. While Heidi and Alana are notoriously tight-lipped, Steph's a huge gossip and has been since we were kids. She gets off on the drama, so long as it doesn't involve her.

"Jesus, Steph." Alana throws a cardboard coaster at her. "Say it a little louder."

"What? It's true." Steph sips her drink with an unrepentant sparkle in her eyes.

"How'd that happen?" I ask curiously. Our friend Tate gets around, to put it mildly. Even among the more promiscuous in our wider circle of friends, he's notorious. He's not usually the type Alana goes for. She's . . . well, particular, is a way of putting it.

Alana shrugs in response. "Darndest thing. I was stumbling around in the dark one night and, whaddya know, I tripped and fell on his dick."

Interesting. Tis the season for summer hookups. Good for her, I guess.

Heidi rolls her eyes, unamused with Alana's evasiveness. "More like hooking up since last fall."

I raise an eyebrow. Since last fall? I'd never known either of them to be interested in long term. "So is this a thing, or . . . ?"

She gives another noncommittal head tilt that fails to convince. "An irregular occurrence of one-night stands. Of the extremely sporadic sort."

"Then there's Wyatt," Steph adds like she's sitting on a secret, all dumb smiles and arched eyebrows.

"Wyatt?" I echo in surprise. This revelation is even more baffling than the Tate one. "What about Ren?"

"You know how they've been doing the on-again/off-again dance for like three years? Dumping each other every other week? Well, it finally backfired," Heidi reveals with a smirk. "She dumped him over something stupid, and he moved on."

Wow. I definitely didn't see that coming. Lauren and Wyatt were similar to me and Evan in that way, constantly breaking up and making up, but I never expected them to end it for good.

"And you moved in on him?" I demand, turning to Alana. "Ren's our friend—isn't that against girl code?"

"I didn't move in on him." Alana huffs at the suggestion. "We're not hooking up, no matter what this one thinks—" She glares at Steph. "For some ludicrous reason, he's decided he has a thing for me." She flips her copper-colored hair over one shoulder, looking annoyed. "I'm trying to shut it down, okay?"

Taking pity on her, I swiftly change the subject. "Catch me up on Cooper and the new girl," I tell Heidi. It wasn't so long ago Heidi was doing the "will they, won't they" dance with Coop. In their case, however, the friends with benefits arrangement blew up in her face. "What's her deal?"

"Mackenzie," she replies, without the hint of irritation that had at one point tinged her occasional texts to complain about Cooper and his new rich girlfriend. "Garnet dropout. Basically walked out on her parents and let them cut her off."

"It was a whole thing," Steph agrees. "Oh, and she bought the old boardwalk hotel. The Beacon. She's been restoring it to reopen soon."

Damn. She *is* loaded. Must be nice. Me, I'd settle for having any kind of direction about what I'm doing with my life. Filling out spreadsheets and chasing down my brothers for invoices isn't exactly my lifelong dream. And as much as I appreciate everything my dad's built to support us, the family business feels more like a trap than an opportunity. It isn't me. Though hell if I know what is.

"She's actually kind of cool," Heidi says, albeit grudgingly. "I wasn't a fan at first. But they're good together, and Coop's usually in a better mood since she's been around, so that's something."

Could've fooled me. Whatever this girl's effect on him, it isn't foolproof.

"What's that look?" Alana asks.

"He sort of accosted me when I was leaving work."

"He what?" Heidi's evident alarm snaps her upright.

It sounds stupid to say out loud. Cooper's got a reputation for being a bit of a hellion, but he's easily the tamer of the Hartley twins. Scolding me in a parking lot still feels wildly out of character for him. Then again, where his brother's concerned, he's always had a short fuse. Evan has that effect on people.

"Yeah, I don't know," I tell them. "He all but threatened me to stay away from Evan. Said he doesn't consider me a friend anymore after the way I hurt his brother."

"Harsh," Steph says with sympathy.

"I guess he has a point about that part." I pretend to be unbothered, shrugging. "But he also blamed me for Evan being out of control, which isn't exactly fair. Evan's a grown man. He's responsible for his own actions."

Alana looks away like she's got something to say.

I narrow my eyes. "What is it?"

"No, nothing." She shakes her head, but there's clearly more she's reluctant to elaborate on. When the three of us press her with silence, she finally relents. "It's just, I mean Evan went and got the shit kicked out of him to make you jealous. Seems like the kind of thing Cooper would notice and disapprove of."

"So you're taking his side, then? It's all my fault?"

"No. All I'm saying is, the way Cooper thinks, he's going to look at that and you showing up as a bad omen of things to come. Let's be honest, he's always been terrible at keeping Evan in line. He probably thinks if he can scare you off, it'll make everything easier."

"That's a crappy thing to do," Steph says.

"Hey, I'm just guessing." Alana finishes her drink and drops her glass on the table. "Another round?"

Everyone nods, and she and Steph leave for a pit stop at the restroom before putting in an order for round two.

After draining the last of her drink, Heidi eyes me warily and makes an uneasy entreaty. "So, listen. This is awkward, but, um, you know Jay and I are sort of dating."

My eyes widen. "Jay as in my brother Jay?"

"Yeah."

"Um. No. I did not."

"Yeah, well, it's new-ish. Honestly, he'd been chasing me for a date since the fall, but I wasn't sure it was a good idea. He finally broke me down a couple months ago. I wanted to make sure you're cool with it. I don't want things to be weird with us."

What's weird is seeing Heidi squirm. Hardly anything penetrates her don't-mess-with-me exterior or puts her on the defensive. She'd spook a bull shark. So it's cute, I guess, that she wants to ask my permission to date my older brother.

"You want my blessing, is that it?" I tease, sucking air from the bottom of my glass of mostly ice melt while I make her wait. "Yeah, it's fine. This town is so small it was only a matter of time before one of you ended up with a West brother. I'm just surprised it's Jay."

Jay's the sweetest of my brothers. Well, after Craig, anyway, but Craig doesn't count because he literally just graduated high school. Jay is twenty-four and doesn't have a mean bone in his softie body. He's almost the complete opposite of Heidi, who's all sharp edges.

"Trust me, I'm equally surprised," she says dryly, running a hand through her blonde bob. "I swear, I've never gone out with anyone so damn nice. Like, what's his problem?"

I burst out laughing. "Right?"

"The other night we were on our way to the drive-in and he pulled over to help a little old lady cross the street. Who the fuck does that?"

"Please don't tell me you screwed my brother at the drive-in."

"Okay, I won't tell you."

"Oh God. I walked right into that one, huh?"

"Uh, hi there, Genevieve," a male voice interrupts.

Heidi and I turn as a cheerfully nervous guy arrives at our table, dressed in a short-sleeved button-down shirt and khaki pants. He's cute, in a Boy Scout sort of way, with brown hair and freckles. If it weren't for a vague feeling I recognize him, I'd say he was a tourist who got lost and stumbled away from the boardwalk.

"I'm Harrison Gates," he says. "We went to high school together."

"Oh, sure, right." The name barely nudges my memory, but now that he's placed his face for me, he does seem familiar. "How's it going?"

"Good." He directs a smile at Heidi as well, but his gaze remains focused on me. "I don't mean to bother you. I just wanted to offer my condolences about your mom."

"Thank you," I tell him sincerely. Whatever my mixed feelings about her death, the nice part about coming home to a small town is that people do generally give a damn. Even people who would have sooner run me over with their car a few years ago have come up to say a few kind words. It's what you do. "I appreciate that."

"Yeah." His smile grows larger and somewhat less anxious as his posture relaxes. "And, you know, I wanted to say welcome back."

Heidi gives me a look that appears to be a warning to bail, but I don't understand her alarm. Harrison seems nice enough.

"So what are you up to these days?" I ask, because it seems rude not to talk to the guy for a minute, at least.

"Well, I just joined the Avalon Bay Sheriff's Department, if you can believe it. Still sounds weird to say it out loud."

"Really? Huh. You seem too nice to be a cop."

He laughs. "I hear that a lot, actually."

Even before the incident last year, I'd had plenty of unfortunate run-ins with the local police. When we were kids, it seemed they had nothing better to do than to follow us around town harassing us. It was a sport for them. The school bullies but with guns and badges. That asshole Rusty Randall being the biggest bully of them all.

"Watch out with this one, Rookie. She's more trouble than she's worth."

As if he heard me cursing him in my head, a uniformed Deputy Randall saunters up and slaps a hand on Harrison's shoulder.

My entire body instantly goes ice-cold.

Heidi snaps a comeback at him that I don't really hear above the deafening fury screaming through my skull. My teeth dig into the inside of my cheek to keep me from spouting off at the mouth.

"If you don't mind," Randall says to Harrison, "I need a moment of her time."

He's gained weight since I last saw him. Lost a lot more hair. Where he used to hide his true self behind a friendly smile and a wave, now his face is contorted in a permanent scowl of resentment and malice.

"You know what, we're a little busy here," Heidi says, cocking her head at him in a way that begs a fight. "But if you'd like to make an appointment, maybe we'll get back to you."

"Was that your car I saw parked across the street?" he asks me in a mocking tone. "Maybe I ought to run the tag for unpaid tickets." Even Harrison seems uncomfortable at Randall's threat, eyeing me with confusion. "What do you say, Genevieve?"

"It's fine," I interject before this gets out of hand. Heidi's looking like she's about to flip a table. And poor Harrison. He really has no idea what he's stepped in. "Let's talk, Deputy Randall."

What more can he really do to me, after all?

CHAPTER 7

GENEVIEVE

I'd always had a bad feeling about Rusty Randall. When I used to babysit his four kids back in high school, he would say things—little offhanded comments that made me uncomfortable. But I never said anything back, preferring the money and figuring I only ever had to see him for a few minutes coming and going, so it wasn't a big deal. Until that night last year.

Some friends and I had gone out to a bar on the outskirts of town. We knew it was a cop hangout, but after a couple hours of pre-partying, Alana had gotten in her head it would be a hoot. In hindsight, it was not one of her better ideas. We were knocking back tequila shots and rum runners when Randall slid up to our table. He was buying our drinks, which was fine. Then he started getting handsy. Which wasn't.

Now, outside Joe's, Deputy Randall leans against the cruiser parked at the curb. I don't know what it is about cops resting their hands on their equipment belts, fingers always flirting with their weapons, that incites an instinctual rage in me. My nails dig into the flesh of my palms as I brace myself for what comes next. I'm careful to stay in the light of a streetlamp where people from the bar's entrance are still visible.

"So here's how it is," Randall says, talking down his nose at me. "You're not welcome back here. Long as you're in town, you stay the hell away from me and my family."

Not his family anymore, the way I heard it. But I bite back the snarky remark, along with the rush of scorn that rises in my throat. He has no right to speak to me in that tone of disgust, not after the way *he* behaved last year.

We were admittedly wasted that night back then, the girls and me, while Rusty kept trying to talk me into going out to his car with him and fooling around in the parking lot. I was gentle, at first. Laughing it off and making my way around the room to avoid him. Clinging to the girls because there was safety in numbers. Until he cornered me against the jukebox, tried to slather his mouth on mine, and jammed his hand up my shirt. I shoved him away and told him, loud enough for the whole bar to hear, to fuck off. Thankfully, he'd left, albeit cranky and dissatisfied.

That could have been the end of it. I could have gone back to my friends and let it go. Certainly wasn't the first time I'd been hit on by an overaggressive older man. But something about the encounter had stung me right to the bone. I was pissed. Fuming. Absolutely irate. Long after he'd gone, I sat there stewing over the encounter and all the ways I should have stuck my foot in his groin and rammed the heel of my palm into his throat. I kept throwing down shots. Eventually Steph and Alana left, and it was just me and my friend Trina, who's probably the only person in our old circle of friends who had me beat for wild instincts. She wasn't ready to let what Randall did go and said neither should I. What he did was wrong, and it was my responsibility to not let him get away with it.

In front of me now, Randall stands up straight, bearing down on me. I back up onto the sidewalk, glancing around for my best exit. Frankly, I have no idea what this man is capable of, so I assume everything.

"Look," I say. "I own that I acted crazy by showing up at your house the way I did. But that doesn't change the fact that you felt me up in a bar after I spent the whole night trying to get away from you. Far as I'm concerned, it's you who needs a reminder to keep his distance. I'm not the one looking for a confrontation."

"You better keep your head down, girl," he warns, growling at me with a wet, phlegmy voice full of impotent anger. He's getting off on the power trip. "None of that partying bullshit. I catch you with drugs, you're gonna find yourself in the back of this car. So much as sniff trouble around you, you're going to jail. Hear me?"

He's aching for a reason, the slightest provocation to nail me. Too bad for him, I left that Genevieve behind a long time ago. From the corner of my eye, I spot Heidi and the girls standing at the entrance to the bar, waiting for me.

"We done here?" I ask, keeping my chin up. I'd walk into traffic before giving Randall the satisfaction of knowing his threats affect me. "Good."

I walk off. When the girls ask, I just tell them to watch their backs. Wherever we are this summer, whatever we do, it's a sure thing he'll be watching. Biding his time.

I'm not about to play his game.

Later, at home, I lie in bed still rigid with anger. There's tension tugging at the muscles in my neck. A throbbing pressure pushing against my eyeballs. I can't be still. So that's how, at nearly midnight, I find myself sitting on the floor at my closet, surrounded by boxes, yearbooks, and photo albums, taking a walk down memory lane. An ill-advised walk, because the first picture in the first album I open? One of me and Evan. We're eighteen, maybe nineteen, standing on the beach at sunset. Evan has both arms wrapped around me from behind, one hand holding a bottle of beer. I'm in a red bikini, resting my head against his broad, shirtless chest. We're both smiling happily.

I bite my lip, trying hard to fend off the memories attempting to bat their way into my brain. But they barrel through my mental defenses. I remember that day on the beach. We watched the sunset with our friends, then took off alone, walking in the warm sand toward Evan's house where we locked ourselves in his bedroom and didn't come out till the next afternoon.

Another picture, this one at some party at Steph's house, and this time we're sixteen years old. I know it's sixteen because those awful blonde highlights in my hair had been a birthday present from Heidi. I look ridiculous. But you wouldn't know it from the way Evan is staring at me. I don't know who took the photo, but they managed to capture in his expression what I can only describe as adoration. I look equally smitten.

I find myself smiling at our young, besotted selves. It wasn't long after that party that he told me he loved me for the first time. We were hanging out in my backyard floating on our backs in the pool, engaged in a pretty serious conversation about how much we wished our mothers gave a shit about us, when he suddenly cut me off mid-sentence and said, "Hey, Genevieve? I love you."

And I'd been so startled to hear him utter my full name and not *Fred*, the dumb nickname whose origins I don't even remember, that I sank like a stone. I didn't even register the second part of that statement until I came up to the surface, eyes stinging, coughing up water.

His indignant expression had greeted me. "Seriously? I tell you I love you and you try to drown yourself? What the hell?"

Which made me laugh so hard I peed myself a little and then stupidly *confessed* to peeing a little, at which point he swam to the ladder and heaved his wet body out of the pool. He'd thrown his hands up in exasperation and growled, "Forget I said anything!"

Laughter tickles my throat. I'm half a second away from texting him to ask if he remembers that day when I realize I'm supposed to be keeping my distance.

My phone buzzes beside me.

A glance at it triggers an anguished groan. How does he do it? How does he always know when I'm thinking about him?

Evan: *I'm sorry about the other night.*
Evan: *I was an idiot.*

I sit there staring at the texts until I realize all the tension I'd been feeling over my run-in with Randall, all the anger and shame, has dissipated. My shoulders are limp, the ten-ton boulder on my chest finally removed. Even my headache has subsided. I hate that he can still do that too.

Me: *Yes you were.*
Evan: *I think I've still got sand in my eye, if that makes you feel better.*
Me: *A little.*

There's a long delay, nearly a full minute before I see him typing again. The little gray bubbles appear, then disappear, then reappear.

Evan: *Missed you.*

Already I feel the tug, those old ties pulling me back to a place I swore I wouldn't go again. Backsliding would be so easy. Making a promise to myself and actually keeping it this time is much harder.

It isn't his fault—Evan didn't make me this way. For once, though, I'm choosing me.

Me: *Missed you too. But that doesn't change anything. I meant what I said.*

Then I shut off my phone before he can respond.

Although it brings an unbearable ache to my chest, I force myself to look through the rest of the albums and piles of loose photos. Our entire relationship plays out in scenes preserved in single perfect moments.

You tore my brother's heart out and took off without even a good-bye. What kind of cold-ass person does that? You have any idea what that did to him?

Cooper's words, his accusations, buzz around in my head, making my heart squeeze painfully. He's right—I didn't say goodbye to Evan. But that's because I couldn't. If I had, I know he would have succeeded in convincing me to stay. I've never been able to say no to Evan. So I left without alerting him. Without looking back.

It's past one a.m. when I finally shove the photos in their boxes and slide them to the back of the closet under clothes and old shoes.

Only dead things pine for the past. Sad things. I might be sad, but I'm not dead. And I intend to live while I still can.

CHAPTER 8

EVAN

Cooper and Mac are already sitting down in the kitchen with Uncle Levi when I walk through the door on Sunday night. The plans for Mac's hotel are spread out on the table. She has her laptop open, hunched over the keyboard while gnawing on a pen. Daisy is the only one to acknowledge me, running up to climb my leg as I kick off my shoes.

"Hey, pretty girl," I coo at the excited puppy.

"You're late," Cooper informs me.

"I stopped to pick up dinner." I drop the bags of Chinese takeout on the counter. My brother doesn't even turn his head from the blueprints. "No, don't sweat it. My pleasure."

"Thank you," Mac says over her shoulder. "No egg in the fried rice, right?"

"Yes, I remembered." For fuck's sake, it's like I'm the damn help around here.

"Leave that," Levi says. "Come here. We need to talk about next week."

Levi is our dad's brother. He took us in after Dad died in a drunk driving accident when we were little and raised us when our mom couldn't be bothered to care. Our uncle's the only real family Cooper and I have left, and although it was difficult to bond with him growing up—he's the gruff, quiet type whose idea of spending quality time together is sitting silently in the same room—the three of us have gotten closer lately.

He's been running his own construction business for years. And after the recent hurricanes that ravaged Avalon Bay, he's been flush with more renovation and demolition work than he can handle. Since Levi made Cooper and I partners in the business not too long ago, we've got a hell of a lot more on our plates too.

Our biggest and most pressing gig is The Beacon, the old landmark hotel on the boardwalk that Mac bought several months ago. The hotel had been gutted from the storm and sat abandoned for a couple years until Mac impulsively decided to fix it up. Her family is disgustingly wealthy, but she'd purchased The Beacon with her own money—I only recently found out that she'd made millions running her own websites that post cheesy relationship stuff.

"Got a call from Ronan West," Levi is saying. "He needs some renovations on his house before he puts it up for sale. So that means we need to split one of you to run a crew out there."

"Let one of the guys do it," Cooper says, copping an attitude at the mention of Gen's dad. Because Coop's a damn child. "I don't want things slipping at the hotel because we leave someone else in charge over there."

We're in the final stages of the renovation at Mac's hotel, which is supposed to have a soft opening a few months from now in September. The idea being: She'll bring in a select guest list to feel the place out and build up a reputation for the spa through the winter season, then hold the grand opening in the spring.

"Ronan's a friend," Levi counters. "I can't send some knucklehead to him. I want to know he's taken care of right."

"I'll do it," I offer.

"Of course." Cooper says with an exasperated sigh. "I don't think that's a good idea."

"No one asked you." Starved, I edge away from the table to grab one of the boxes of lo mein and dig in.

"We've got a good handle on the hotel." Mac eyes my lo mein, then gets her box of fried rice and hops up on the counter to eat. "Shouldn't be a problem."

Cooper shoots her a look for contradicting him, but she just shrugs. Maybe the best part of having Mac around is that she loves to wind my brother up. Which usually means taking my side in an argument.

"You're a glutton for punishment." Cooper shakes his head at me.

Maybe I am, but he doesn't understand Gen like I do. Sure, we've had our toxic moments, the fights, the reckless nights. But there were great times as well. Together, we're fusion. Perfect energy. Right now she thinks there's some righteous atonement in keeping our distance, but that's only because she's let herself forget what it's like when we're at our best.

I simply have to remind her. But to do that, I need to get close to her.

"Hey." Levi demands my attention. "You sure you can keep it professional? I don't want you acting like a fool over there while you're on the job. We might be Hartley and Sons now, but that's still my name on the business card."

"Don't worry," I promise through a mouthful of noodles. "I got this."

Cooper sighs.

On Monday afternoon, Levi and I pull up to the West house. Ronan had dropped off a key at Levi's this morning so we could let ourselves in to have a look around. The purpose of today's visit is to walk the property and come up with a task list of anything that needs replacing, fixing, painting. Ronan's left it up to Levi to give him his opinion and a price quote for what he thinks it will take to get the best offer when it goes on the market. After twenty-some years and six kids, the rambling two-story house has definitely seen better days.

It is a little odd being back here under the circumstances. Even weirder to be walking through the front door after all those times Gen and I got caught sneaking in or out through her window. And don't get me started on all the pool parties we threw when Gen's parents were away.

My uncle and I conduct a sweep of the interior first, scribbling on our clipboards as we point out various issues that jump out at us. We scope out the exterior next, looking at the siding that needs replacing and deciding the wobbly wooden fence around the back-yard probably warrants a PVC upgrade. Looks better and is easier to maintain. After some more clipboard notes, we let ourselves through the gate to check out the pool and—holy sweet Jesus.

I come up short at the sight of Gen tanning on one of the lounge chairs.

Topless.

Kill me.

"I thought they stopped making pornos like this in the nine-ties," I drawl, getting an irritated grumble in response from Levi.

Totally unbothered, Gen rolls onto her side, looking like a swimsuit model with her long legs and oiled skin glowing under the sun. Those astounding, perky breasts are pointing right at me. Not as though I'd forgotten what they look like, but the sight of her in just tiny bikini bottoms and sunglasses gets me reminiscing about old times.

"You don't knock anymore?" Gen says, then reaches for a glass of water.

"Did I ever?" My gaze keeps flitting back to her perfect rack.

It's taking all my wits to remember my uncle is standing next to me.

"Your, uh, dad asked us over to give him a quote for the renovation," Levi answers, staring uncomfortably at the ground. "He didn't say anyone would be here."

I stifle a laugh. "Come on, Gen, put those things away. You're gonna give the poor man a stroke."

"Aw, Levi's not interested in anything I've got, anyway." She sits up, reaching for her bikini top. "How's Tim doing?" she asks Levi.

He grunts out a, "Yeah, good," while still diligently averting his eyes. My uncle doesn't talk much about his long-time partner, who works from home as an editor for academic journals. Levi prefers to keep their personal life private. It wasn't always easy for him being a gay man in this town, and I think he finds it simpler to let most people believe what they want. Even among his friends that know, they don't ask about it. As a couple, he and Tim don't tend to go out much on account of the latter being sort of a recluse. They like things quiet, those two. It suits them, I suppose.

"What are you doing home?" I ask Gen. I heard her dad had her working at the stone yard.

"We're open on Sundays," she says, covering her chest with her forearm as she untangles the strings of her top. "So we get Mondays off. You guys need anything from me?"

Levi finds his voice while dutifully looking at his clipboard. "Is Ronan going to want any landscaping back here?"

Gen shrugs. "No idea."

Relieved, he takes the excuse to go inside and call Ronan, leaving me alone with Gen.

After a moment of noticeable reluctance, she shifts in her chair. "Tie me up?" Holding her top to her chest, she turns her back to me.

"Or . . . we could leave it off."

"Evan."

"You're no fun." I sit at the edge of her lounger and reach for her bikini strings. I've had worse jobs.

"Does this happen to you a lot? Catching cougars and rich college girls in various states of undress?" Her tone is dry.

"This is exactly how every one of these projects start," I say solemnly, tying the thin strings of her bikini. "First time I've had a hard-on in front of my uncle, though, so that's a whole new level of family trauma."

"You could have warned me," she accuses, turning to face me once she's adjusted herself. "Dropping in without notice was sneaky on your part."

"I didn't know you'd be here," I remind her. "I was planning to help myself to some underwear and be on my way."

Gen just sighs.

"You know, this whole topless scheme of yours—"

"Scheme? I didn't know you were coming," she protests.

I ignore that. "Reminds me of that field trip senior year," I finish, not even pretending I'm not watching the little beads of condensation that fall off her water glass and travel down her chest as she takes a sip.

"What field trip?"

"Don't play dumb. You know exactly what I'm talking about." That trip was pretty damn unforgettable.

Her lips curve slightly before flattening in a tight line. "How about we don't go there?" she says with another sigh.

"Go where?" I blink innocently. "The aquarium?"

"Evan."

"It was raining that day. You were mad at me because you said I was flirting with Jessica in math class, so you showed up the next day for the field trip in a white tank top with no bra to throw yourself at Andy What's-his-face. So we get off the bus in the rain, and then everyone's catching an eyeful of your twins."

There's a long beat, during which I can see her resolve crumbling.

"You stole me a T-shirt from the gift shop," she says grudgingly.

I hide a smile of satisfaction. So easy to get her to join me on this trip down memory lane. "Because I would have had to break Andy Fuck Face's nose for staring at your tits the whole trip."

Again, she pauses. Then, "Maybe I thought it was hot when you got jealous."

My smile breaks free. "Speaking of jealous . . ."

Her expression goes cloudy. "What?"

"I saw the murder in your eyes at the bonfire the other night." When she doesn't take the bait, I toss out another lure. "You know, when I was talking to that college chick."

"Talking?" she echoes darkly. A familiar hint of murder glints in her eyes before her lips quickly curl in annoyance—directed at herself.

I know Genevieve, and right now she's kicking herself for showing weakness. So, as expected, she deflects.

"You're referring to the girl whose boyfriend beat you up?" Gen flashes a saccharine smile. "The one who only pretended she wanted to get with you to make her man jealous?"

"One, you're not allowed to look that gleeful at the idea of someone beating me up. Two, I didn't get beat up—that dude's crew had to carry him away, in case you didn't notice. And three, if I'd wanted to get with her, I would've gotten with her."

"Uh-huh. Because from where I was standing, it looked like you tried to shoot your shot and she left with her boyfriend."

"Tried? I wasn't trying." I tip my head in challenge. "Genevieve. Baby. We both know I have no trouble convincing women to take their clothes off."

"And he's modest too."

I wink at her. "Modesty is for guys who don't get laid."

I'm gratified to see her swallow. Christ. I want to fuck her. It's been so long. *Too* long. Doesn't matter how many girls I hooked up with in Gen's absence. No one compares to her. No one gets me as hot, makes me as crazy.

"Well, since seduction comes so easy for you, why don't you skedaddle and go find someone who wants to be seduced?" With a bitchy flick of her eyebrows, Gen picks up her water and takes another sip.

I snort. "Stop pretending like you don't want to rip my clothes off and fuck me in that pool."

"I don't." Her tone is confident, but I don't miss the flare of heat in her eyes.

"No?" I say, licking my suddenly dry lips.

"No," she repeats, but her confidence is slipping.

"Really? Not even a teeny, tiny part of you is tempted?"

Her throat dips as she gulps again. I see her hand trembling slightly as she puts down her glass.

I lean closer, breathing deeply. The salty, sweet scent of tanning oil is rich in the humid air. I want to rip her top off with my teeth and wrap her hair between my fingers. She tries to act like she's so above it all, but I can see her pulse thrumming on the side of her neck, and I know she feels the same insatiable need.

"Meet me later," I say without forethought but then commit to the idea. "Our spot. Tonight."

She's impassive behind those silver reflective sunglasses. But when she bites her lip and hesitates to answer, I know she's considering it. She wants to say yes. It'd be so easy. Because we've never had to try to be together, it's just natural. Our tides always flowing in the same direction.

Then she pulls away. She stands and wraps a towel around her waist. The impenetrable wall goes up and I'm locked on the other side.

"Sorry," she says with a dismissive shrug. "I can't. I have a date."

CHAPTER 9

GENEVIEVE

Three hours after my encounter with Evan, I'm still kicking myself. In a moment of triumphant stupidity, my mouth ran away from me, and now I've got to materialize a date for tonight out of thin air. After the lie popped out of my foolhardy mouth, Evan was naturally pissed, though he was doing his best to act like it was no big deal. Sometimes he forgets I know him too well. All his tics and tells. So, while pretending he wasn't fuming inside, he'd quizzed me on the where and when, which compounded one lie with another, and then another. I managed to dodge on the question of who by insisting Evan wouldn't know the guy, but I wouldn't put it past him to check up on me, so therein lies the rub.

By eight o'clock tonight, I need to come up with a man to take me out.

Since I'm not about to hop on Tinder for a fake date to dissuade my ex, I throw up the SOS in our group chat, then end up at Steph and Alana's place to get the brain trust together on this one. Heidi's at work, which is probably a good thing because her advice in the chat thread was utterly useless. *Tell stupid lies, win stupid prizes*, she'd texted in her typical no-nonsense way.

Ugh. I mean . . . she's not wrong.

"So you emotionally masturbated to teasing Evan with your boobs and then swerved him," Alana says to my explanation of events. We're sitting on their back porch while I try visualizing my sweet tea with vodka in it. "I mean, not to take his side, but I'd call that mixed signals."

"I don't think I'm telling it right. He walked in on me."

Steph regards me in amusement. "Yeah. But you kinda liked it."

"It's fine if you did," Alana tells me, reclining on the porch swing while she sways back and forth. "Everybody's got a kink."

"It's not a kink."

Although, now that she's named it, I suppose she isn't so far-off. Evan and I have always had this tension between us. Pushing and pulling. Making each other jealous and manipulating a response. It's all part of the bad habits I'm trying to break. Yet, in doing so, I'm repeating the steps. New tune, same old dance.

"It's the bad-boy dick magic," Alana says in her flat intonation, devoid of humor. "Makes us crazy. It isn't our fault the screwed-up ones are the best in bed."

I mean, she has a point. And when it comes to Evan Hartley, it's the most random stuff that gets me all messed up. The little things that trigger memories and invite involuntary responses. My body has been programmed to certain stimuli. It's instinct. Second nature. He licks his lips and I start imagining his face between my legs. Today, it was the way his hair smelled.

And it certainly didn't help that he taunted me about pool sex and then asked me to meet him at our spot later.

I only came up with the date excuse because I was so close to accepting his invitation. Because what would be the harm in a little consensual sex between friends, right? No harm at all . . . until a little sex leads to a lot of sex, and then we're spending every waking minute together, starting trouble and picking fights because every bit of adventure and conflict wrings a few more drops of adrenaline out of each other.

"I can't help myself around him. He's an addiction. I try to stay aloof, but then he smiles and flirts and coaxes me into flirting back," I find myself confessing. "But if I don't break the habit, I'll never get a fresh start."

"So we break the cycle," Alana decides. "We just have to find someone who is everything that Evan isn't. Shock the system, so to speak."

"Well, that pretty much eliminates everyone we know." Scratching off the list of names that are either his friends or people I can't stand, there are hardly any people left in this town who aren't related to me. Trolling college bars for a random Garnet dweeb isn't my idea of a good time either.

"What about that guy from the other night?" Steph asks. "The one who approached you and Heidi."

"Who, Harrison?" She can't be serious.

"No, that's good." Alana sits up. Her face lights as the scheme assembles behind her eyes. She's the queen of schemes, this one. "That's really good."

Steph nods. "The way Heidi told it, it sounded like the guy had a crush on you."

"But he's . . ." It even tastes bad on my tongue. "A *cop*. And he wears khakis. Tourists wear khakis."

"Exactly," Alana says, nodding her head as she sees all the pieces come together. She lands her determined gaze on me. "The Anti-Evan. He's perfect."

"It's one date," Steph reminds me. "Gets Evan off your back, and there are worse ways to spend a night than getting a free meal out of a guy who has zero chance of trying to get laid."

There is that. And she's right; Harrison was plenty nice. As far as dates go, this one comes with bare minimum expectations and is super low risk. The worst part, I guess, will be running out of things to talk about and realizing right away that we have absolutely nothing in common. But we'll just part awkwardly at the end of the night and never have to see each other again. Simple. And if Evan shows up, he takes one look at Harrison, decides to feel sorry for me, and walks away laughing. I can handle that if it keeps Evan at bay.

"Alright," I agree. "Operation Boy Scout is a go."

Since I don't know anyone who would have a cop's number in their phone, and there is no chance that I call a police station just to, like, chat, it takes some creative social media sleuthing to slide into Harrison's DMs. His Instagram is adorably if not pathetically bland. But I remind myself, this makes him a completely harmless suitor and reinforces the message that I am reforming. No more bad boys.

> Me: *It was nice seeing you the other night.*
> Me: *Sorry we got interrupted. Dinner tonight?*

It's a bold opening, but I'm a woman on a mission. And a deadline. Thankfully, Harrison responds within a few minutes.

> Harrison: *This is a surprise. Yeah, that'd be great.*
> Harrison: *Should I pick you up around 7?*
> Me: *Sure. But leave the cruiser at home.*
> Harrison: *Copy. See you then.*

There. That wasn't so hard.

What I've come to realize over the last year of my makeover is that change is a choice we make every day, a thousand times a day. We choose to do this one thing better. Then the next. And the next. And the one after that. So maybe duping a nice guy into a fake date in order to let my ex down gently isn't exactly putting me up for sainthood—but baby steps. The point is, the old me wouldn't have been caught dead in the same room as Harrison. And who knows, maybe we walk away from this as friends.

CHAPTER 10

EVAN

She does this shit on purpose. She likes to know she still has the power to mess with my head, dangling the possibilities in front of my face just to yank the carrot away at the last moment. What I'm more concerned about is the guy. This fucking guy who thought it'd be a good idea to run up on Genevieve right under my nose. Dude better have his affairs in order.

Needless to say, I'm buzzing when I get back to my house after work. But I don't make it three steps through the door before Cooper pounces on me.

"Hey," he calls from the living room, where he and Mac are sitting on the couch watching TV, "did you get in touch with Steve about the pipe fittings?"

"What?" I kick off my shoes and throw my keys at the side table with too much force. "No, I was out at Gen's house with Levi."

"And after that you were supposed to stop by the office to call Steve about the order for the hotel. We need those fittings tomorrow so we can replace the plumbing on the second floor."

"So you do it." I stalk into the kitchen and grab a beer from the fridge. Daisy rushes up to wag her tail at my feet, more hyper than usual.

"I think she wants to go out," Mac says. "Mind taking her for a walk?"

"You stuck to the couch or something?"

"Whoa." Cooper jumps to his feet, apparently still capable of using his legs. "What's with the attitude?"

"I just walked in the damn door and you two can't wait ten seconds before jumping down my throat." I flick the bottle cap into the trash and snap my fingers at Daisy, which sends her whimpering back to Mac. "Meanwhile, you both have done what today, exactly? Instead of bitching about stuff not getting done, why not get off your asses and do it yourself?"

Having exactly no interest in this conversation, I head outside to the garage.

What gets me is Gen doesn't date. The thought of her putting on a pretty dress and doing her makeup to sit nicely at dinner is laughable. She'd sooner gnaw off her own arm than make small talk over appetizers. So what is this, some elaborate attempt to convince me she's changed? Bullshit. Gen's the type of girl who steals a motorcycle from outside a biker bar just to take a joyride. She does not, under any circumstances, let a guy pull her chair out.

Maybe she does now.

The nagging voice in my head pokes a hole in my conviction. What if pretty dresses and sit-down dinners are her thing now? Is it so far-fetched? Maybe the girl I knew last year isn't the same one who—

I banish the thought. Because, no. Just no. I know Genevieve West like the back of my hand. I know what excites her. I know what makes her smile, and I know what brings tears to her eyes. I know her every mood, and I know the deepest fucking parts of her soul. Maybe she's got herself fooled, but not me.

As my head turns itself over, I strip off my shirt, toss it aside, and start hitting the heavy bag hanging from the ceiling in the corner of the garage. Dust explodes off the surface with every strike of my fists. Great billowing plumes of fine gray powder. The first few hits shock my nerves, slap the noise from my mind. The sharp, shooting pain radiates through my hands, then my arms, elbows, and shoulders, until the pain dulls and I barely feel it anymore. But I still feel her. Everywhere. All the time and growing more insistent.

She *left* me. Me, who'd slept all night in a chair by her hospital bed that time she got a concussion after falling off a tree during a climbing race with two of her brothers. Me, who'd let her cry in my arms every time her mom missed an important event in Gen's life.

She just left without telling me.

No. Worse—without asking me to come with her.

"You're not going to have any skin left if you don't tape those up." Cooper sneaks up on me. He positions himself behind the bag to hold it in place while I mostly ignore him to concentrate on my aim. Small clusters of blood have already appeared on the synthetic leather. I don't care.

When I don't respond, he presses on.

"Come on. What's going on? Something happen?"

"If you're going to talk, you can leave." I punch through the bag. Past it. Driving my fists harder with every swing. The distraction dissipates with every repetition, and as my nerves become desensitized to the impact, my brain finds the effects wearing off too.

"So it's about Gen." There's a sigh of equal parts disapproval and disappointment, as if I came home with a D on my report card. It's exhausting having a brother who thinks he's my dad. "When are you going to let that go? She ghosted you, dude. What more is there to say?"

"Remember how much you appreciated my input on Mac last year?" I remind him. Because I learned my lesson. When I was all up in his business about crossing over to the dark side to catch feelings for a rich chick, he told me no small number of times to get bent. And he was right. "Well, same."

"I'm just trying to look out for you," he says, like somehow I've missed the point. Then, sensing I'm quickly losing my tolerance for him, Cooper changes tacks. "Come on, let's get out of here. Go out. Take your mind off everything."

"Pass." What I figured out a long time ago is there's nothing that bleaches thoughts of Genevieve out of my head. She's woven into the fabric. I can't rip her out without tearing myself apart.

I catch Cooper's eyes for a second between hits to the bag. There's unhappiness in them. But it isn't up to me to make him feel better, and I don't take responsibility for trying. "You can go now, Coop."

With a clenched jaw, he stalks out of the garage.

Not long after he's gone, I give up on the bag. My knuckles are bloody; bits of flesh hang off in kernels. It's gross as fuck.

When my phone buzzes in my pocket, I entertain a moment of dim-witted anticipation expecting it to be Gen, then curse to myself when I see it's my mother.

Shelley: *Hey baby. Just checking in to see how you're doing.*

Yep, my mother is not in my contacts list under *MOM*, but Shelley. Which speaks volumes.

She's been messaging me in an attempt to resurrect our relationship after Cooper briefly had her arrested for stealing several grand from him a few months back. He's had it with her shit for a long time, but that was the last insult for him. The final betrayal.

I haven't told Cooper about the texts yet, because as far as he's concerned, she's dead to him. Admitting I've been in contact would have him downright furious.

Not that I'm so forgiving either. Not anymore, at least. For years, I was willing to give her the benefit of the doubt, even when I knew she couldn't be trusted. That every visit was simply a precursor to another broken promise and another exit without a goodbye. I just don't know how to ignore her.

Sighing, I shoot a quick text back.

Me: *All good here. You?*
Shelley: *I'm in Charleston. Was hoping maybe you'd come visit?*

I stare at the screen for a long moment. For weeks, she has been insisting she's reformed. New leaf and all that. Her last message said she wants a chance at reconciliation, but the amount of chances this woman has gotten from us is comical at this point. There were times Cooper and I needed a mother when we were kids. Now, we get along just fine without one. Hell, we get along *better*. Life's much less stressful without a person that blows into town every few months or years to spin some bullshit about a big opportunity and getting her life together, and all she needs is a place to stay and a few bucks, yada yada. Until we wake up one morning and she's gone again. The coffee can above the fridge empty. Cooper's room ransacked. Or whatever new low Shelley decides to sink to.

When I don't respond right away, another message pops up.

Shelley: *Please? We could start off easy. Coffee? A walk? Whatever you want.*

My hesitation earns me another message.

Shelley: *I miss my sons, Evan. Please.*

I grit my teeth. Thing is, I didn't pack for a guilt trip. She can't play the mom card after years of negligence.

Her next message names a time and place. Because she knows I'm the soft one when it comes to her, and I always have been. She wouldn't dare come at Cooper like this. Which is all the more conniving and unfair.

Still, even understanding all this, a part of me wants to believe her, to give her a chance to prove she can be a decent person. If to no one else, then to us.

Me: *I'll think about it and get back to you.*

But reconciliation is a stretch goal. Coop is intent on taking this grudge to the grave. I'm sure he'd be happier if he never had to think about her again. For me, well, if I'm honest with myself, I guess I'm still raw about the whole thing. Last time she was here, she put on a good act, her best performance yet. She had me most of the way to believing she'd stick around and give it a try. Be a real mom. As much as she could be to two grown men who barely know her.

Needless to say, it blew up in my face with Coop getting in another *I told you so.*

And since I'm not in the mood for a repeat when I sit down for dinner later, I keep the news of Shelley being in Charleston to myself. She's the least of my concerns, anyway. The thoughts of Gen on her date scream much, much louder in my head.

While Mac is passing me the mashed potatoes, I'm imagining Gen laughing over salads and appetizers with some asshole. Cooper's talking shop, but I'm picturing this dude sizing up how to get Gen back to his place tonight. He's thinking about what she looks like naked, and will some steak and lobster buy him a blowjob on a first date?

My jaw's so tight I can barely eat.

Then, as we're clearing the table, a bug crawls in my ear asking, *what if Gen actually likes this bastard?* What if she's falling for his bullshit, eating his game with a spoon? Maybe she wore some sexy outfit with the intentions of leaving it on his bedroom floor. Maybe later tonight, she'll be dragging her nails down his back.

I nearly put my fist through the wall, curling both hands over the countertop as I help Mac load the dishwasher.

And what happens if Gen and this guy get together for real? It's one thing if she dated someone in Charleston, because I wouldn't have to see it. But she's home now. If she finds a new guy, I'll be forced to watch them walk around, rubbing it in my face while I'm at work, fixing up her dad's house? Walking in on them in the kitchen suddenly trying to act chill with that flush on her face that says she just had his fingers inside her? Oh, hell no. I'd end up taking a hammer to his hand.

"We're going for a walk on the beach with Daisy," Mac says, neatly folding the dishcloth and placing it next to the sink. "Wanna come?"

"Nah. I'm good."

I'm not good. I'm not good in the slightest.

The moment Cooper and Mac exit onto the back deck, I grab my keys and head to the front door.

In no time at all, I'm riding into town on my motorcycle to see for myself. Damned if I'm going to be made the cuck.

CHAPTER 11

GENEVIEVE

"I think I screwed up," I whisper to Harrison as the waiter in a white dress shirt and black vest lays the linen napkin in my lap. There are already three sets of glasses on the table and we haven't even ordered anything yet. When the waiter offered us still or sparkling water, I asked for the free kind. "I had no idea this place was so fancy."

Or expensive. It only opened recently, and I noticed it as I passed by the other day. When I was concocting this diversion for Evan earlier, it just popped into my head. Now, I'm wearing my best summer dress, even put on makeup and did my hair, and yet I still feel underdressed.

For his part, Harrison does a decent job of passing as one of the yacht club guys that wash into Avalon Bay for the season. Button-down shirt and those damn khakis with a belt that matches his shoes. It works for him, though.

"I don't mind." Harrison pushes some glasses out of the way to make room for his menu. "I don't eat out much. It's nice to have an excuse."

"Okay, but I'll obviously split the check."

With a Disney Channel smile, Harrison shakes his head. "I can't let you do that."

"No, seriously. I wouldn't have suggested this place if I'd known. Please."

He sets the menu aside and meets my eyes with stern conviction. It ages him ten years. "If you keep trying to shove money in my pocket, I'm bound to get offended." Then he winks at me, those boyish freckles blossoming on his cheeks, and I realize he's putting me on.

"That's your cop face, isn't it?"

"I've been working on it in the mirror," he confirms, leaning in with his voice hushed. "How am I doing?"

"I'd say you've got it down pat."

Harrison sips his water as though he's just remembered that first dates are supposed to make us nervous. "There was a little old lady the other day I pulled over for running a stop sign. I made the mistake of asking if she'd not seen the sign, which I guess she took to mean I thought her vision was the trouble, and so this woman gets on the phone to the sheriff telling him some high school kid's stolen a cruiser and a uniform and is out terrorizing the community."

I burst out laughing.

"Anyway. I've been told I better figure my way to looking more the part," he finishes.

The waiter returns to take our drink order, and would we care for a bottle of wine? I wave off the wine list when Harrison offers it to me. My experience is generally limited to the five major food groups: whiskey, vodka, tequila, rum, and gin.

"Hang on, I got this," Harrison says, getting excited as he scans the list. "I watched a wine documentary on Netflix once."

A smile springs free. "Nerd."

He shrugs, but with a satisfied smirk that says he's quite proud of himself. "We'll have two glasses of the 2016 pinot grigio, please. Thank you."

The waiter nods his approval. I consider speaking up to refuse, but what's the harm in one glass of wine? It's not like I'm pounding shots or downing cocktails. I won't even get a buzz on a stingy pour. Besides, I don't want to dive headlong into the details of my reputation recovery before we've even ordered food. Not a great conversation starter. I think of it like an accessory to complete my ensemble of mature adult Gen.

"I think that went well," I tell him.

"I was nervous there for a minute, but I think I pulled it out in the end," he agrees with a laugh.

Honestly, as far as fake first dates go, this one's off to a better start than I had any right to expect. We ended up meeting at the restaurant instead of him picking me up, and part of me worried he might walk up holding flowers or something. As he'd kissed my cheek in greeting, he admitted he'd considered bringing a bouquet but realized I wasn't the type, and it'd probably embarrass both of us. He was right, and the fact that he figured that out put him in an entirely new perspective. Now, the vibe is chill and we're getting along. None of those uncomfortable silences and darting glances to avoid eye contact, while we both struggle to devise an exit strategy. Dare I say, I'm having a good time. Strange as that is.

The old me wouldn't have been caught dead in this place. Which I suppose is the point. I'm stepping out of the long shadow my past has cast over my life. Harrison is certainly living up to his part of this plot. A bit shy and reserved in comparison, but sweet and funny in a nineties family sitcom sort of way. And although I can't muster up any sexual attraction to him, perhaps that's a good thing. Evan and I were all but defined by our rabid sexual chemistry. It ruled us.

But if I'm going to be serious about this good girl turn, maybe I need a good boy to match.

"Anyway," he says once we've ordered our meals, after going off on a tangent about why he can't eat mussels anymore. "I feel like I'm being rude, doing all the talking. I tend to ramble sometimes."

"No, you're fine," I assure him. I'd much rather not have the conversation focus on me. "Tell me, what's the weirdest call you've gone out on?"

Harrison ponders, staring into his glass of wine while spinning it in little circles on the table by the base. "Well, there was this one. Second week on the job. I've still got a babysitter, this guy Mitchum, who, if you picture a disgruntled math teacher with a gun, is pretty much spot-on. From the second we meet, his personality is he wants me dead."

I snort out a too-loud laugh that disturbs the tables nearby and has me hiding behind my napkin.

"I'm serious," Harrison insists. "I don't know what it was, but I walked into the boss's office before my first shift, and Mitchum was standing there looking at me like I'd knocked up his daughter."

I can't imagine anyone being put off by Harrison's first impression. Then again, I've never been too fond of the cops in this town, so maybe that's all the explanation there needs to be.

"We get called out to this house in Belfield," he continues. "Dispatch says a couple of neighbors are having some kind of dispute. So we arrive on scene to find two older fellas jawing at each other in the front yard. Mitchum and I separate them to get their stories and figure out real quick they both started hitting the bottle early that day. They were arguing over a mower or a mailbox, depending on which one of them tells it. Nothing especially interesting, but they've both got rifles they're waving around, and somebody let a few shots off."

I'm trying to anticipate where this story is headed when Harrison shakes his head at me, as if to say, don't even try.

"Mitchum asks the one guy, *why don't you put the gun away?* He tells us he only got his gun because his neighbor got his own. And the other neighbor says he only got his gun after the other guy put the gator on his roof."

"What?" I bark out another disturbing noise that disrupts the entire restaurant, though now I'm too preoccupied to feel contrite. "Like a real alligator?"

"This fella's been trying to shoot the thing down, if you can believe that. Pumping rounds into his own roof, the walls, wherever. We can't be sure they're even all accounted for—thank goodness we never got any reports of stray bullets."

"How'd he get it up there in the first place?" I demand.

"Turns out the guy works for the phone company. He's out driving to a job when he finds this gator in the middle of the road. On his lunch break he decides to drive the cherry picker home and drop that poor animal up there, though I can't for the life of me imagine the mechanics of that situation. Turns out they'd had a run-in that morning which precipitated the retaliation."

"I almost have to admire the guy," I admit. "I've never had a grudge that warranted a biblical plague. I guess I need to find a better class of nemesis."

"But get this. Mitchum, sweet guy that he is, tells me I have to climb up there and get the gator down."

"No way."

"Now remember, it's my first shift on the street, and if this guy goes back to the station and says I can't hack it, I could be banished behind a desk for good. So I don't have much of a choice. Still, I ask, *shouldn't we get animal control out there instead?* And he tells me, *sorry, kid, the dog catchers only work on the ground.*"

"Wow." I'm honestly stunned. Not that I didn't know cops were bastards, but that's some cold shit right there. Talk about friendly fire. "What'd you do?"

"The short version," he says with the haunted stare of a man who's seen things, "involves a ladder, a ribeye, some rope, and about four hours to get that thing down."

"Damn, Harrison, you're my hero. Here's to protecting and serving," I say, clinking my wineglass with his.

We make it halfway through our entrées before he tires of dominating the conversation and once again tries to turn it on me. This time, the topic being my mother.

"I'm sorry again," he says. "This must still be a difficult time. With moving back and all."

His consolatory tone reminds me that I'm still putting on an act, playing a part I've written of the person I should be: the grieving daughter, still mourning her dear mother. Wallpapering a better story over our absent relationship, because it sounds good.

Which is something I've never had to do with Evan.

Fuck. Despite my best efforts, thoughts of him creep in through the seams. He's the only person who understands my darkest thoughts, who doesn't judge or try to dissect me. He understands that the empty place where everyone else holds their mothers in their hearts doesn't make me a bad person. For all our failings, Evan never needed me to be anyone but myself.

"Ooh, that looks good."

Speak of the fucking devil.

Completely blindsiding us, Evan suddenly drops a chair at our table and sits down between Harrison and me.

He grabs a scallop off my plate and pops it in his mouth. His daring gaze flicks to me with a self-satisfied grin. "Hey."

Unbelievable.

My jaw doesn't know whether to drop or tighten, so it alternates between the two disparate movements, I'm sure making me appear unhinged. "You're out of your mind," I growl.

"Brought you something." He places a green Blow Pop on

the table, then appraises me with almost lewd interest. "You look nice."

"Nope. Not doing this. Go home, Evan."

"What?" he says with mock innocence. He licks lemon-butter sauce from his fingers. "You've made your point. I came to spring you from this stuck-up nightmare."

He stands out among the other diners, wearing a black T-shirt and black jeans, hair wind-tossed, and all of him smelling like motorcycle exhaust.

"Come on." Harrison, to his credit, takes the interruption in stride. A bit confused as he questions me with his eyes, but maintaining a polite smile. "We're having a nice time. Let the lady finish her dinner in peace. I'm sure whatever you two have to talk about can wait until later."

"Oh, shit." Laughing, Evan cocks his head at me. "This guy's serious? Where'd you find him? I mean, damn, Gen, you're basically dating our seventh-grade science teacher."

That wipes the friendly smile from Harrison's face.

"Evan, stop it." I grab his arm. "You're not funny."

"Alright, I've asked you nicely," Harrison says. He stands up and I'm reminded of all the times cops chased me and Evan out of convenience store parking lots and abandoned buildings. "Now I'm telling you. Leave."

"It's fine," I warn Harrison. "I've got it."

Still holding Evan's arm, I tighten my grip. There's no way I'm letting him start a brawl in the middle of this restaurant and get his ass thrown in jail for breaking a cop's nose.

"Please, Evan," I say flatly. "Just go."

He ignores the request. "Remember when this place was a clothing store?" Evan leans in closer, brushing his fingers over my hand on his arm, which I snatch away from his touch. "Did you tell him about the time we did it in the dressing room while the church ladies were just outside the door trying on their Sunday hats?"

"Screw you." My voice shakes with anger, cold and brittle, the words barely passing through my lips as my throat constricts. I'd slap him if I didn't know for certain it would only encourage his sabotage. The more emotion Evan can pull from me, the more proof he has to continue his pursuit.

Pushing back from the table to stand, I catch a brief glimpse of Harrison's sympathetic gaze before I turn away and leave.

I hit the railing that separates the boardwalk from the beach below like a car slamming into an embankment. I might have kept on walking into the ocean, blind with rage, if it hadn't stopped me. I want to throw something. Launch a brick through a storefront window to hear it shatter. Take a baseball bat to a china shop. Anything to get this restless static out of my arms, the thick, stone-hard ball of fury throbbing in my chest.

When I hear footsteps behind me, my fist tightens. A hand touches my arm and I'm mid-swing when I turn to see Harrison with his hands up, braced for impact.

"Oh gosh, I'm sorry." I drop my hands. "I thought you were Evan."

Harrison laughs nervously and flashes a relieved smile. "No worries. This is what all those de-escalation courses are for at the academy."

It's sweet, his commitment to deflecting everything with a joke and a heaping, sugary spoonful of optimism. I don't have that stuff in me.

"Really, though. I'm sorry for everything back there. That was so embarrassing. I'd make some excuse for him, but Evan's kind of a jerk on his best days." I lean over the railing, resting my arms on the splintered wood. "And here all you did was say hi in a bar to be nice. Bet you didn't expect all this drama, huh? Got more than you bargained for."

"Nah, I knew there was a chance I'd have a pissed-off Hartley on my ass if I went out with you."

I lift a brow. "Oh really?"

"We went to the same high school," he reminds me, his voice wry but gentle. "Everyone had a front-row seat to the Genevieve and Evan show."

Embarrassment heats my cheeks, and I avert my eyes. Somehow, knowing Harrison witnessed our high school antics is even more humiliating than having Evan crash this date.

"Hey. Don't look away like that. Everyone has baggage." He comes to lean against the railing beside me. "We've all got a past. Things we'd rather people not judge us for. How can anyone grow if we only let them be who they were yesterday, right?"

I glance over in surprise. "That's an unusual outlook for a cop."

"Yeah, I get that a lot."

We stand there for a while, just listening to the waves and watching the way the lights of the boardwalk float on the water. I'm about to pack it in, pick up my dignity off the ground and head home, when Harrison makes another suggestion.

"You want to take a walk?" As though he's spent this whole time mustering the courage, he offers his hand. "I don't think I'm ready to go home. Besides, we didn't make it to dessert. I bet the ice-cream place might still be open."

My first instinct is to say no. Just go home and nurse my anger. Then I remember what Alana said. If I'm going to walk a different path, I have to start making different choices. And I suppose that starts with giving Harrison a chance to change my mind.

"That sounds nice," I say.

We stroll down the boardwalk toward Two Scoops, where he

buys us a couple of ice-cream cones. We keep walking, passing families and other couples. Teenagers running around, making out in the shadows. It's a balmy night with a warm breeze of salt air that offers the slightest relief from the heat. Harrison holds my hand, and while I let him, it feels wrong. Unnatural. Nothing like the feeling of anticipation and longing that comes with touching that person you can't wait to kiss, the one who sets your nerves racing, gets your fingertips excited.

Eventually, we end up in front of the old hotel. Last time I saw this place, it was gaping open, walls collapsed, with furniture and debris pouring out. The Beacon had been all but eviscerated in the hurricane. Now, it's like it never happened. Practically brand new, with its sparkling white façade and green trim, shiny new windows, and a roof without any holes in it.

Now that Cooper's girlfriend owns this place, I'll probably never be allowed to step foot inside.

"It's remarkable what they've managed to do with the place," Harrison says, admiring the renovation. "I heard it's supposed to open in the fall."

"I loved this place when I was a kid. For my sixteenth birthday, my dad brought me and my friends in for a spa day. Got our nails done, facials and stuff." I grin at the memory. "They gave us robes and slippers, water with cucumbers in it. All that fancy stuff. It probably sounds stupid, but I remember thinking this was the most beautiful place. All the dark wood and brass, the paintings on the walls, the antique furniture. It was how I imagined palaces must look on the inside. But, you know, kids are stupid, so . . ." I shrug.

"No, it's not stupid," Harrison assures me. "We had my grandparents' anniversary dinner here years back. They served all this really pretty-looking food—real rich-people stuff, because my family wanted to give them a special party—and my grandad got so mad, kept yelling at the waiter to just bring him some meatloaf. I swear," Harrison laughs, "he left that party like it was the worst night of his life. Meanwhile, the family spent a small fortune to cater the thing."

We trade a few more stories, and eventually he escorts me back to my car parked outside the restaurant. While much of my irritation with the ordeal from earlier has dissipated, nothing makes this part of the night any less awkward.

"Thank you," I say. "For dinner, but really for being so nice. You didn't have to be."

"Believe it or not, I had a great time." His earnest expression tells me he actually means that.

"How are you even like this?" I demand, befuddled by him. "So positive and upbeat all the time. I've never met anyone like you."

Harrison shrugs. "Seems like a lot of work being any other way." Like the true gentleman he is, he opens my door for me. Then, with a tentative gesture, he offers me a hug. It's a relief, honestly, not to do the whole dance around a kiss. "I'd like to call you, if that's okay."

I don't get a chance to contemplate the possibility of a second date.

"Step away from the car," a voice shouts.

Frowning, I turn around in time to spot Deputy Randall crossing the street. He's got a mean way about him. A look that intends to do harm.

"Put the keys on the ground," he commands.

For fuck's sake. I shield my eyes as he approaches with a flashlight shining in my face. "It's my car. I'm not stealing it."

"I can't allow you to drive impaired," Randall says, resting a hand on his utility belt.

"Impaired?" I look at Harrison, seeking confirmation I'm not hallucinating this. Because Randall cannot be serious. "What are you talking about?"

"Rusty," Harrison says timidly, "I think you've made a mistake here."

"I clearly observed the young lady standing in an unsteady manner and leaning on the door for support."

"Bullshit," I spit at him. "I barely touched a glass of wine over an hour ago. This is harassment."

"I gotta say, Rusty, I've been with her all night." Harrison is soft-spoken and polite, presenting a nonthreatening contradiction to Randall's nonsense assertions. "She's telling the truth."

"Told you before, kid," Randall says with an almost gleefully cruel sneer. "This ain't one you want to waste your time on. If she's awake, she's either drugged out or drunk, making a sloppy embarrassment of herself all over town." He huffs out a sarcastic laugh. "If drunk and disorderlies were frequent flyer miles, she could book a trip around the world. Ain't that right, Genevieve?"

"Fuck you. Asshole." I know I'll regret the words even as they're coming out of my mouth, but I don't bother clamping my lips shut. It feels good to let it out, ineffectual as it is. A brief fantasy of snagging his pepper spray flickers through my mind.

The faintest twitch of a smirk tugs at the corner of Randall's mouth. Then, forehead creased, he orders me to come stand behind the car and take a field sobriety test.

My jaw snaps open in shock.

"You can't be serious," protests Harrison, who's clearly starting to understand what an utter dickweed Randall is.

"No." I cross my arms and consider just driving away. Daring Randall to stop me. Those old instincts of mayhem and defiance roar back with a vengeance. "This is ludicrous. We both know I'm not drunk."

"If you fail to comply with a lawful order, you will be under arrest," he informs me. Randall is practically drooling at the prospect of putting me in handcuffs.

I turn to Harrison, who, though plainly alarmed, admits with a shrug there's nothing he can do about it. Seriously? What the hell's the point of dating a cop if he can't get you out of a trumped-up traffic stop with a disgruntled egomaniac?

What truly pisses me off, however, what really tears the nails from the bed, is knowing Randall gets off on this. He loves applying his authority to humiliate me. Busting a nut with his power trip.

Not wanting to make a scene, I stalk toward the rear bumper and appraise Randall with a cool look. "What would you like me to do? *Officer.*"

A smile stretches across his face. "You can start by reciting the alphabet. Backwards."

If he thinks this weakens me, he's sorely mistaken.

That which doesn't kill me makes my anger stronger.

CHAPTER 12

EVAN

For some reason, I saw that encounter going better in my head. I thought it'd be charming, in our kind of demented way. At the very least, make her laugh. Because as much as she'd given me a hard time back in the day, she always ate that stuff up, getting me jealous and riled until I snapped and stormed in to throw her over my shoulder. Then we'd fuck it out and be cool again.

This time, not so much.

I rake both hands through my hair and stare out at the dark water beyond the long pier. After Gen stormed out of the restaurant and her dipshit date gave me some unconvincing advice to leave her alone, I walked out here to get some air, get my head on straight. But so far, all I've succeeded in doing is wallowing over how much I miss Gen.

With a tired exhalation, I shove my hands in my pockets and leave the pier. Coming up the steps to the boardwalk, where my bike is parked along the curb, I'm not quite sure what I'm looking at until I hear Gen's voice across the street telling a cop with his flashlight pointed at her to suck her dick.

My eyebrows soar in confusion, then knit in displeasure. The cop's got her on the street behind a car, with her arms spread, touching her finger to her nose. Meanwhile, her dweeb date is there doing nothing while she begrudgingly walks a straight line and recites the alphabet, muttering obscenities along the way. Even from a distance I can feel the humiliation in Gen's expression. The way her eyes stare into the distance.

I'm halfway to running over there before I stop myself. Damn it. The last thing I need right now is to go to jail for bouncing a cop's face off the pavement. I wouldn't make it out of a cell alive. Besides, Cooper's already up my ass about fighting—getting locked up would give him a lifetime *I told you so* account that I'm not about to pay into. So I stand there, hugging the railing, fists clenched.

I recognize Rusty Randall, though I don't know him well. Just that he's got a reputation as a creep with a not-so-secret drinking problem of his own. To her credit, however, Gen takes it like a champ, never the type to let anyone see her rattled.

Still, it turns my stomach to watch this degrading episode. Dozens of people stare at her as they pass. She was stone-cold sober when I saw her an hour ago. And by how easily she's navigating the test, I'd say it's clear she didn't pop into a bar to pound a bunch of shots after she left the restaurant. Which means Randall is only being a dick because he can.

Finally, after a brief conversation, she's allowed to get in her car. I'm gratified to note she barely glances at her polo-clad date as she leaves.

I quickly get on my bike to follow her, making sure to keep my distance. I just want to make sure she gets home okay. After a while, though, I realize we aren't headed to her house. We leave the lights of town behind, headed north along the coast where the population thins out and the stars appear overhead. Soon we're winding down a two-lane road through the black wooded landscape where the moon over the bay appears in brief glimpses through the trees.

Eventually, she pulls onto the dirt shoulder near a narrow

footpath you can only find if you know it's there, even in daylight. She gets out of her car, grabs a blanket from the trunk, and proceeds through the trees. I wait a few minutes before following her. At the end of the path, where the trees give way to the sandy beach, I find her sitting on a driftwood log.

Her head lifts when she hears me approach. "You suck at tailing people," she says.

I take that as an invitation to sit. "I stopped trying to be sly about it after I realized where you were headed."

"I didn't come here to meet you." With the blanket wrapped around her shoulders, she buries her toes in the cool sand. "This is just where I come to think. Or it was."

That she chose this place hits me right in the chest. Because it's our spot. Always has been. It was our emergency rendezvous after running from the cops, the make-out spot when we were grounded and sneaking out of the house. Our secret hideout. Not even Cooper knows I come here.

"I saw what happened back there," I tell her. She's not much more than a black outline against the night. It's so dark out here, moonlight gets swallowed before it hits the ground. The stars, though, are really something. "What was that all about?"

"Nothing. Just some asshole giving me a hard time."

"That was Randall, right? Didn't you used to babysit for him?" He wasn't a super nice guy or anything, but I remember once or twice he let her slide on this or that in high school when other cops had it in for us pretty bad. It was sort of a transactional understanding.

"Yeah, well, things change." Her voice is tight and sour.

She doesn't elaborate just yet, and I don't push. Thing I learned a long time ago: Gen will talk when she wants to. She's a locked box—nothing gets in or out unless she wants it to. A person could spend a lifetime trying to pick her open.

So I wait, silent, listening. Until minutes pass and she lets out a sigh.

"Not long before I left town, I blew up Randall's family."

I slant my head. "How'd you manage that?"

In a voice heavy with fatigue, she explains how he assaulted her in a bar after he failed to coax her to do him in the parking lot. My fists clench so hard my knuckles crack. I want to hit something. Tear it to shreds. But I don't dare move because I want to hear everything she has to say.

"When I got home after we closed down the bar, that's all I could think about. Vengeance. I was raging," Gen continues. "The Randall house was only a few blocks away, so I got it in my head to walk my ass over there at three in the morning. Next thing I know, I'm banging on the door with my hair sweaty and makeup melting off my face. His wife Kayla answered the door all bleary-eyed and confused. I forced my way past her to start shouting in the middle of her living room until Rusty came downstairs."

I don't miss the deep crease of shame that digs into her forehead. I have to stop myself from reaching out and taking her hand.

"I told her how her sleazeball husband tried to coerce me into sex then assaulted me in a bar. How everyone in town but her knew he was sleeping around behind her back. He denied it all, of course. Said I'd come on to him. The jilted, jealous girl." Gen laughs humorlessly. "I was a screaming lunatic who probably looked like I'd just washed in with the tide. Meanwhile, her four kids were peering out from the hallway, terrified. Kayla had no reason to believe me, so she told me to get the hell out of her house."

I wish I'd known, wish I'd been there for her. I could have stopped this entire ordeal dead in its tracks. Kept her from leaving. Now, I'm not sure what's worse. Wondering this whole time what made her leave, or understanding now that if I'd just been there, we wouldn't have lost the last year of our lives together.

"The next morning, I woke up with a monster hangover and a perfect memory of what I'd done. Every terrible moment of my total meltdown. It would've been less mortifying to set his cruiser on fire. At least then I'd still have had my self-respect. I couldn't bear the shame and regret. Not for that skeezy douchebag, but for storming into that poor woman's house and traumatizing her kids. Kayla didn't deserve that. She was a kind woman who'd always been nice to me. Her only fault was being married to an asshole and not knowing any better."

"I'd have killed him," I tell her, now seriously regretting I didn't take my shot when he had her on the boardwalk. "Beat him within an inch of his life and dragged him out to sea behind a boat."

The urge to hop on my bike and find Randall is almost irresistible. In seconds, a montage of brutal fantasies spin through my head. Knocking every tooth out of his skull. Snapping his fingers like matchsticks. Putting his nut sack under the rear tire of my motorcycle. And that's all for starters. Because absolutely no one lays a goddamn hand on my Genevieve.

I hate what he's done to her. Not just that night, or this latest power trip, but the way she's resigned herself to defeat, the exhaustion in her voice. It rips me up inside and I can't stand it. Because there's nothing I can do. Short of kicking his ass and spending the next twenty years in prison, I don't know how to fix it.

"I wish you'd told me," I say quietly.

"I—" She stops for a beat. "I didn't tell anyone," she finishes.

Yet I have a suspicion she'd been about to say something else.

"It's a big part of the reason why I left," she admits. "Not only him, but his wife and those kids. I couldn't stomach walking around town knowing people would hear about what happened, how I made a first-rate ass of myself and ruined that family."

"Oh, screw that." I shake my head emphatically. "To hell with him. You did his wife a favor. And better those kids find out sooner than later that their dad's a bastard. Trust me, the prick had it coming." I've got no sympathy for him, and neither should she.

A half-hearted *yeah* is all she mutters in response. And all I want is to make this better for her. Take away the garbage that's clogging up her head. Help her breathe again. Then it occurs to me, I haven't been much help tonight. Her evening had gone to hell before Randall even got there, and that's on me.

"I'm sorry," I say roughly. "For crashing your date. I wasn't thinking clearly."

"You don't say."

"I'm not sure I ever am when it comes to you. Truth is, my head hasn't been right for about a year now."

"I can't be responsible for your happiness, Evan. I can barely account for myself."

"That's not what I'm saying. When you left, my whole life changed. It would be like if Cooper suddenly disappeared. A huge piece of me broke off and was just gone." I scrub a hand over my face. "So much of me was wrapped up in us. And then you came back, and it's got me all twisted up inside. Because you're here, but you're not really back. Not like it was. I don't know how to fit everything into place the way it was before, so I'm just walking around all out of sorts."

Agony lodges in my throat. For as long as I can remember, I've been a goner for this girl. Turning myself inside out to keep her attention. Always terrified that one day she'd realize I was a loser who wasn't worth her time, figure out she's always had the option to do better. Last year, I thought she'd reached that conclusion, but it turns out I was the idiot thinking her leaving had anything to do with my dumb ass.

"I'm not trying to hurt you," she says softly.

Silence falls over us. Not strained or uncomfortable, because it's never that way with me and Gen, even when we want to murder each other.

"I remember the first time I knew I wanted to kiss you," I finally say, not quite sure where the sentiment even came from. But the memory is clearer than day. It was the summer before eighth grade. I'd been making a fool of myself for weeks trying to impress her, make her laugh. I didn't know yet that's how crushes start. When the balance tips from friendship to attraction. "A few weeks before we started eighth grade. We were all out there diving off the old pier."

She gives a quiet laugh. "God, that thing was a death trap."

It really was, that decrepit wooden pier half sunken into the waves and falling apart. Victim of a hurricane years prior, infested with rusty nails and splinters. At some point, high school kids had hauled a metal ladder out to the part of the pier that was still standing and tied it to a pylon with bungee cords. It was a sort of rite of passage to swim out through the crashing waves, climb the rickety thing, and leap off the top railing. Then all you had to do was not let the waves throw you back against the pylons covered in barnacles that would tear the flesh off your bones.

"There was that ninth-grader—Jared or Jackson or somebody. He'd been flirting with you all afternoon, doing flips off the pier like he was so damn cool. And being all obnoxious about it too. Like, *hey, look at me, I'm such a badass.* So you dared him to jump to one of the pylons from the pier. It was maybe a ten-foot leap to a one-foot target, and right below were all sorts of torn-up, jagged pieces sticking up out of the water. With the waves just absolutely thrashing below us." I grin. "Suddenly he wasn't so loud anymore. Starts making excuses and shit. And while everyone's ragging on him for chickening out, you take a running start and go flying through the air. I was looking at Cooper for the split second like, oh fuck, we're gonna have to jump in after you and drag you back to shore when you break your neck or get impaled on something. But then you nailed it. Perfect landing. Coolest thing I'd ever seen."

She laughs to herself, remembering. "I got stung by a jellyfish after I jumped down. But I had to be chill about it, you know. Didn't want to look like a dumbass for jumping out there in the first place."

"Yeah, probably a good idea. You would've had ten pervert boys whipping their tiny dicks out to pee on your leg." We both shudder in disgust at that dodged bullet.

"You didn't kiss me that day, though," she points out. "Why not?"

"Because you're fucking scary."

"Oh." She laughs, elbowing my arm good-naturedly.

"I mean, I know we'd been friends for years by then, but when you figure out you have a crush on someone, it's like you're starting from scratch. I didn't know how to approach you."

"You figured it out."

She shifts beside me, and I sense the change in the air between us. Something happens. Without her saying a word, I feel her decide to not be mad at me anymore.

"Didn't have a choice," I admit. "I was going to claw out of my skin if I didn't find out what your lips felt like."

"Maybe you should have." The blanket drops from around her shoulders. She turns to look at me. "Eaten yourself alive. Spared us both the trouble."

"Believe me, there's no version of this"—I gesture between us—"where we don't get together, Fred. One way or another. I can tell you that for certain."

"And to hell with the collateral damage."

"Yes." Without hesitation.

"While it all burns around us."

"I like it that way." Because nothing else matters when she's mine. Nothing. She's everything and all of it.

"There's something wrong with us," she murmurs, closing the space between us until I feel her arm brush mine and her hair sweep across my shoulder in the breeze. "It shouldn't feel like this."

"How should it feel?" I haven't the slightest idea what that means, but I wouldn't change the way I feel about her for anything.

"I don't know. But not this intense."

I can't resist the urge any longer. I reach out to tentatively brush her hair behind her ear, then thread my fingers through the long, soft strands at the back of her neck when she tilts her head into my touch.

"Do you want me to leave?" I ask hoarsely.

"I want you to kiss me."

"You know what'll happen if I do, Gen."

Heat flares in her eyes, those vivid blue depths that never fail to draw me in. "Yeah? What'll happen?" she asks, the slight curve of her lips telling me she already knows the answer but wants to hear me say it.

"I'll kiss you." I drag my thumb along the nape of her neck. "And then . . . then you'll ask me to fuck you."

Her breath hitches. "And then what?" Her voice is shaky.

"You know what." I gulp through the sudden onslaught of pure, carnal lust. "I can never say no to you."

"I know the feeling," she says, and then her lips touch mine and from there I'm no longer in control. We become this autonomous thing with a mind of its own. Like blacking out. She bites my lip with a soft moan, grabbing a fistful of my T-shirt. I'm rock hard and ready to be inside her, but I don't want this to end.

"Let me taste you," I whisper against her mouth.

Lying back on the log, the blanket beneath her, she parts her legs for me, granting me the access I desperately crave. Not even trying to be polite about it, I pull down her lacy panties, shove them in my pocket, and throw her leg over my shoulder.

"I've missed this," I say with a happy groan.

God, and I have. I missed the way she pulls my hair when I suck her clit, arching her back to grind against my face as I drag my tongue over her delicate flesh. I missed her soft sighs of pleasure. Her fingers tangled in my hair.

I push her knees up to her chest, spreading her open, as she trembles against my mouth. She's quiet, all but holding her breath. At least until I work two fingers inside her. Then she moans uncontrollably, and it's almost unfair how fast she comes. I want to make it last for her, but I'm also greedy to make her shake for me.

I don't even expect her to fuck me. I'd be happy to go down on her every day and twice on Sunday just to go home and yank it to the memory. But afterward Gen throws the blanket on the sand and starts unzipping my jeans. She takes my cock in her hand and strokes me, slow and firm. We don't speak. As if we're both afraid words will shatter the darkness, the seclusion that makes this all possible. Out here, alone and in secret, is it even real? We can be anyone, do anything. If no one knows, it never happened.

She sits me on the blanket, both of us still clothed. She knows I've got a condom in my pocket because I almost always do, so she takes it, rips it open and slides it on me before sliding herself down on my dick. So wet and tight. Her hips rock back and forth, taking me deep, summoning a ragged breath from my lungs. I drag down the zipper of her dress and unhook her bra to grab two handfuls of her breasts. Squeezing. Sucking her nipples while she rides me. Burying my face in her warm skin.

It's fucking perfection.

Small noises start to escape her lips. Sighs that become louder, more desperate. Then she loses all control of her voice, moaning against my ear.

"Harder," she begs me. "Please, Evan. Harder."

I grab her ass, holding her above me while I thrust into her. She bites my shoulder. I don't know why that always does it, but seconds later I come, hard, shaking as I hold her tight to my chest. Every time with Gen is the best sex I've ever had. Raw and unfiltered, the most honest we know how to be.

If only that feeling could last forever.

CHAPTER 13

GENEVIEVE

I forget to be afraid of myself, of what I become inside Evan's orbit. It's so much work, worrying, constantly guarding my own worst instincts, thinking and then unthinking every decision. I forget to hate myself and instead let my dress fall to the sand. I walk naked out into the waves while Evan pulls his shirt off, watching me from the shore. I remember how it feels to have his eyes on me. Knowing me, searing me into his mind. I remember the power in it, the excitement in what I do to him by just standing here.

Up to my waist in the water, I turn around to watch him wade in after me—and remember he has the same power. I'm transfixed by the lines of his muscles and broad shoulders. The way he grabs a handful of water and runs it through his hair. A shudder runs through me at the magnificent sight.

"Yeah, so, it's been fun," he says glibly. "But I gotta run."

"Oh yeah? Somewhere to be?"

"Yeah, I got a date, actually. In fact, I'm already running late. Gonna have to stop at the store for more condoms."

"Right, sure," I say, dragging my hands through the water to keep myself steady against the tide. "Anyone I know?"

"Doubt it. She's a meter maid."

"Hot." I bite back a laugh. "Just your type. I know how wild you go for civic authority."

"You know, it's the polyester, if I'm honest. Tacky uniforms get my dick hard."

"So if I told you I became a UPS girl in Charleston—"

"I'd destroy that."

"Promises, promises."

Grabbing my waist, he lifts me and I wrap my legs around his hips. I hang on to him with my hands clasped behind his neck as he keeps us firm against the push and pull of the waves.

Evan squeezes my ass in both hands. "Please, Gen, dare me to bend you over. I'm begging you."

To that I smack a handful of salt water at him. "Animal."

He shakes the water from his face, flipping his hair out of his eyes. "Woof."

We're good like this. That's the thing. It'd be easy to walk away if he were a bastard who treated me badly and was only nice when he wanted to get laid. But it's not like that at all. He's my best friend. Or was.

"So, go on," Evan says gruffly. "Tell me about Charleston. What kind of trouble were you getting into?"

"You're going to be disappointed." This past year was decidedly drab, but that's what it was meant to be. A complete social detox. "There's not much to tell, really. I got a job working for a real estate office. Secretary slash assistant slash miscellaneous. If you can believe that."

"That must have been a hell of a job interview." A wave comes at us sideways and tosses us toward shore. Evan sets me on my feet but keeps those strong hands on my hips.

"Why's that?"

His eyes sparkle in the moonlight. "Well, I assume under relevant experience, you listed the Goldenrod Estates."

The mention of that place brings to mind all sorts of mischief. A few years ago, Goldenrod Estates was a housing development still under construction just south of Avalon Bay. Another gated community for people with more money than taste, all those gaudy McMansions sitting on top of each other. But when the hurricane came through and tore down half the town, construction halted as every company rushed to snap up all the restoration and repair work they could get. The places were abandoned for months, leaving kids like us to roam free through the empty, open homes.

"That was a good summer," I admit. One of our fonder memories.

"The empty pool party."

"Oh, shit. Yes. Like fifty people crammed in a huge concrete hole."

"Then Billy comes running up and says the cops are coming."

The night in question flashes through my mind. I remember my brother's frantic entrance, how we'd shut off the music and turned out the flashlights. All of us holding our breath, crouched down in the dark.

"And your dumb ass decides to be the hero," I say, more in amusement than accusation. "Climbs out of the pool and runs across the street."

"You didn't have to follow me."

"Well, yeah." I sway with the current, letting my toes drag in the sand as the force of the tide pushes and pulls. "But I wasn't letting you go to jail alone."

The memories keep surfacing. Evan and I got up on the roof of a house across the street, watching the red and blue lights grow brighter against the walls of the unfinished houses as cars drew closer. Half a dozen cruisers, at least. Then, hoping to distract the cops from our friends, we began waving our flashlights, shouting at the officers to get their attention. We leapt off the roof, pounding pavement and darting through houses as we ran from the cops, eventually losing them in the woods.

God, we were invincible together. Untouchable. With Evan, I was never bored a minute in my life. Both of us were constantly feeding the high, looking for the next shot of adrenaline as we pressed the limits of our own capacity for trouble.

"There a guy?" he asks suddenly. "Back in Charleston?"

"What if there was?" But there wasn't, not really. Just a series of unimpressive dates and short-lived relationships that mostly passed the time. It's tough when you're comparing every guy you meet to the one you ran away from.

"No reason," he says, shrugging.

"Just want to talk to him, right? Just a chat."

Evan smirks. "Something like that."

I can't help that his jealousy excites me. It's stupid and petty, I know, but in our bizarre way, it's how we show we care.

"What about you? Any girls?"

"A few."

I frown at his vague tone. Feeling the claws trying to come out, I force myself to retract them. Force myself not to picture Evan with another woman. His mouth on someone who isn't me. His hands exploring curves that aren't mine.

But I fail. The images swarm my brain and a low growl escapes my throat.

Evan laughs mockingly. "Just want to talk to them, right?" he mimics. "Just a chat?"

"No. I want to burn their houses down for touching you."

"Damn, Fred, why do you always go right to arson?"

I snicker. "What can I say? I run hot."

"Damn right." His hands glide up my stomach to cup my bare breasts. He squeezes, winking at me.

I shiver when his fingertips dance over my nipples, which pucker tightly. Evan notices the response, and a faint smile tugs at his lips. He's so good-looking it's almost unfair. My gaze sweeps from his chiseled features to the defined muscles of his bare chest. His sculpted arms. Flat abdomen. Those big, callused hands that had just pinned me down while his hungry mouth feasted between my legs.

"You're killing me, Gen." Evan growls the words at whatever he sees playing out on my face. His fingers bite into my flesh. "Don't do that unless you mean it."

"Do what?"

"You know what." Holding onto my waist, he walks us backward toward shore. "You're having fuck-me daydreams. I'm pretty much there, if you want to go again."

"I didn't say that."

He presses himself against me, letting me feel him hard against my leg. "You're a tease, you know that?"

"I do." We reach dry sand. Standing there, we stare at each other, until a tiny smile tickles my lips. "You like it."

Then I kiss his neck. His shoulder. Down his chest until I'm on my knees with his erection in my grip, stroking him. Evan runs both hands into his hair and drops his head back, breathing heavy.

When I don't do anything, he peers down at me, his dark eyes burning with need. "Are you just going to sit there, or are you going to suck it?"

"Haven't decided yet." I lick my lips, and he lets out a tortured groan.

"Tease," he says again, trying to thrust forward.

I tighten my grip in warning, but that just makes his eyes gleam brighter.

"More," he begs.

"More what?" I use my index finger to draw teeny circles around the tip of his cock, prolonging his torture.

"More everything," Evan chokes out.

His hips snap forward again, seeking contact, relief. Laughing at his desperation, I slide my tongue up his shaft and then take him in my mouth.

He moans loud enough to wake the dead.

There are things about Evan I've missed more than others. Getting wasted, blacking out, waking up in a random closet of some random warehouse wearing clothes that weren't my own—I could live without some of those memories. But how he makes me feel when we're alone? How he gives himself over to me, trusts me completely—I love this version of us. The good us.

I relish in the soft groans that vibrate in his chest and the tension tightening his muscles. The way his hands drop to his hips, then to my hair, as he resists the urge to thrust hard and fast, because one time I gently bit him in warning and now he lives in fear of me—just a little. It's our game. I'm on my knees but he's the one at my mercy. I make him feel only what I give him. The pleasure and anticipation. Slowing to prolong the experience, rushing to pull him to the edge of frustration. Until finally, he breaks.

"Gen, *please*."

So I let him come, pumping him until he reaches his release. Then, totally spent, he slinks to the ground and tugs me to lie with him on the blanket.

We're quiet for a while. Surrounded by the comforting darkness, surrounded by only the sound of the breeze rustling the palm trees and the waves rushing up the sand.

"Did I tell you my mom texted me?" Evan says suddenly.

It's not at all where I expect his mind to go, and I hesitate to entertain the subject. Not because it bothers me in any particular way, but I know it tends to upset him.

"She wants me to meet her in Charleston. Make amends or whatever."

"Does Cooper know?"

"Nope." Evan stretches to clasp his hands behind his head, prone under the stars. His beautiful profile is strained when I turn to peek at him. "Last time she was in town, she stole his life savings."

"Oh jeez. That's rough."

"He got most of it back, but . . . yup. Needless to say, he's not rolling out the welcome mat for her anytime soon."

"Do you want to see her?" I ask carefully.

Shelley is a sore spot for Evan and his brother, and always has been. Whereas I was relieved to finally be freed from the standoff of my failed relationship with my mom, I've spent years watching Evan get his hopes up that one day his mother will come to her senses and love him, then have them utterly devastated. I don't share his faith.

"I don't want to be made a fool of again," he confesses. He sounds bleak, exhausted. "I know how I look. Cooper thinks I'm an idiot, that I don't get it. I do, though. I understand what he does, but I can't help that I don't want to miss the one time she might mean it. Maybe that sounds stupid."

"It doesn't," I assure him. Naïve, maybe. Wishful, yes. Both qualities I've never put much stock in. But not stupid.

"It'd be different if it weren't just Coop and me, I think. If our dad was still around." He glances at me with a sad smile. "I mean if he wasn't an asshole. And if we had a bunch of brothers and sisters."

"My mom had too many damn kids," I interject. "Trust me, that didn't make her a better person. I guess having my brothers around helped me to not feel so lonely in that house, but nothing fixes it when you know your mom doesn't give a damn about you."

It's strange how saying those words out loud—saying my mother didn't give a damn about me—brings comfort rather than heartache. I told myself a long time ago I didn't need her love or approval or attention. That I wouldn't waste my breath on someone who couldn't be bothered. And I kept telling myself that until I believed it, entirely and without hesitation. Now that she's dead, I don't miss the wasted years or regret all the times I saved myself the grief of trying. The best gift we give ourselves is respecting our needs first. Because no one else will.

"You wouldn't want a big family?" Evan asks. "Your own, someday?"

I pause in thought, considering all the times one of my brothers walked into the bathroom to take a dump while I was in the shower. The times I came home to one of them in my bed with a girl because another one locked them out of their own room. And then on the flipside: my older brothers all piling in the car to teach me to drive because my dad by then couldn't take the stress of it. Teaching me to play pool and shoot darts. How to drink and throw a punch. They're a bunch of stinking, disgusting brutes. But they're my brutes.

"Yeah, I guess I do." Although I don't particularly want to think about *making* that big family—when I imagine what the six of us must have done to my mother's vag, I blame her a little less for her casual animosity toward us. "Not anytime soon, though."

"I do," he says. "Want a big family, I mean. I'd even be the stay-at-home dad. Do the diapers and make lunches and all that."

"Right." I snort out a laugh at the image of Evan standing in the front yard with two arms full of tiny naked children while the house burns behind him. "Find yourself a sugar momma whose uterus isn't entirely shriveled to sawdust yet."

He shrugs. "What the hell else am I doing, you know? Let's be honest, I tripped and fell into the business with Levi. I didn't really do much to earn that, except mostly show up on time to work. Cooper's got the plans and ambition. Getting his furniture business going and whatnot. So why not be the guy who stays home with the kids?"

"I really wouldn't have figured you for the type." Evan's never been interested in what's expected of him—in all the ways society tells us to get a job, get married, have kids, and die with a mortgage we can't afford and generational credit card debt. "Guess I thought you always had a plan to hop on your bike one day and set out on the open road or whatever cliché shit."

"That's a vacation, not a life. I love the small-town beach life. Where everyone knows everyone. It's a good place to raise a family."

Yet there's uncertainty lingering in his voice. "But?"

"But what the hell do I know about being a father, right? Given my role models, I'd probably permanently scar my kids too."

I sit up to meet Evan's eyes. In his flippant dismissals I hear his pain, the years of trauma buried under bravado. Beating himself up for what's been done to him because there's no one else around to take the blame.

"You'd be a good dad," I say softly.

Another shrug. "Eh. Maybe I wouldn't entirely ruin them."

"You'd have to be more than just the fun dad, though," I remind him as he tugs me back down. I rest my head on his chest and drape my leg over his hip. "Learn discipline. Can't have your kids ending up like us."

"The horror." He kisses the top of my head.

Even after we've closed our eyes, we still mutter about this or that late into the night, until our words become further apart and eventually we drift to sleep. Naked under the stars.

CHAPTER 14

GENEVIEVE

The sun creeps in slowly at first, then all at once, an explosion of light prying my eyelids open. I wake up with sand in my butt, and I can't even blame a hangover. Because it's him. It's always him.

Still naked on the ground from the night before, I haul myself up to fish for my clothes. I find my phone half buried and my underwear hanging out of the pocket of Evan's jeans. There are a dozen missed calls and texts from my dad and Shane asking where the hell I am. I'm more than an hour late for work, and judging by their increasingly worried messages, they're about ready to send out a search party and start calling hospitals.

Evan is still asleep on the blanket. I've got hell waiting for me at the shop, but still I can't tear my gaze away from him. The long lines of his body, tan and strong. Memories of last night skitter across my limbs like a flurry of tiny sparks. I'd do it all again, pick up right where we left off and to hell with responsibilities and obligations.

And that's the problem.

He rolls over, exposing his back, and I realize for the first time what was too dark to see last night. On his lower back, just above his right hip and tucked in among his other tattoos, there's an illustration of a small beach cove with two distinctive palm trees bent from hurricanes and crisscrossing each other. Identical to the ones behind me. It's our spot. Our one perfect place on earth.

Which only makes this harder.

Evan stirs as I'm wrapping my hair in a bun and digging my keys out of the sand. "Hey," he mumbles, adorably drowsy.

"I'm late," I tell him.

He jerks upright with a concerned expression. "What's wrong?"

It's only when I rub my eyes that I realize my vision's blurry with tears. I inhale deeply, exhaling a feeble sputter of air that makes me feel a bit wobbly. "This was a mistake."

"Wait. Hold on." He grabs his pants and shakes them out to start getting dressed, a hurried panic evident in his movements. "What's happened?"

"I told you we couldn't do this." I ease backwards, blinking away the moisture in my eyes. All I want to do is run. Get away from him as fast as I can, because every second I linger in his presence weakens my resolve.

"Gen, hey. Stop." He grabs my hands to still me. "Talk to me for a second."

"We can't keep doing this." I implore him to understand what I already know is beyond his reasoning. "We're no good for each other."

"But where's this coming from? Last night—"

"I have people who are counting on me." Desperation clogs my throat. "My dad, my brothers. We're all working on keeping the business afloat. I can't blow them off to hide out with you all night." I gulp down a massive lump of sadness. "As long as we're around each other, I can't trust myself."

"What's the big deal?" He turns his back in frustration, tugging at his hair. "We had a good time and no one got hurt."

"We're both late for work because we stayed up all night fucking like teenagers whose parents are out of town. When are we going to grow up, Evan?"

He rounds on me, dark eyes blazing with frustration. "What is so wrong about wanting to be with you? Why do you want to punish us for this?" he demands, gesturing between us. "Why are you punishing yourself for caring about me?"

"I've just decided to start caring about myself more. That means being responsible for the first time in my life. I can't do that when every time I see you I forget anything else exists. That's why I didn't say goodbye to you before I left. Because I knew—" I stop before the rest of that sentiment can escape.

"You knew what?"

I hesitate, remembering the pain I'd seen on his face last night when he'd confessed how much my leaving had affected him. *A huge piece of me broke off and was just gone.* I'd hurt him badly, a hell of a lot more than I'd realized. And hurting Evan makes me sick to my stomach. I don't like doing it, and I don't want to do it now, but . . . I'm not sure I have a choice.

"You said last night that you wish I'd told you about the showdown with Randall," I finally say.

"Yeah . . ." His tone is wary.

"Well, I tried. I didn't sleep a wink that night. I stayed up all night thinking about what I'd done, stewing in my humiliation. It wasn't a total rock-bottom moment, but it was definitely a wake-up call. It was obvious the partying had become a problem and was starting to cloud my judgment. There's no way I ever would've showed up on Kayla Randall's doorstep in the middle of the night if I'd been sober."

I shake my head in disgust. At myself, not him. Although,

I certainly hadn't been impressed with him either, the morning after my unhinged visit to the Randall house.

"I knew you were out with the guys that night and would probably sleep in, so I waited around all morning for you to call or text," I tell him. "And when you didn't, I finally drove over to your place so I could tell you what happened with the Randalls."

A frown touches his lips. "I don't remember you coming over."

"Because you were still passed out," I say flatly. "It was one in the afternoon, and I walked into your house to find you snoring on the couch, empty bottles and full ashtrays all over the coffee table. There was spilled beer on the floor, all sticky under my shoes, and someone must've dropped a joint on the armchair at some point, because there'd been a hole burned into it." I sigh softly, shaking my head again. "I didn't bother waking you. I just turned around and went home. And started packing."

Now he looks startled. "You left town because I was hungover after a night with the boys?" There's a defensive edge to his voice.

"No. Not entirely." I try not to groan. "It was just another wake-up call, okay? I realized I'd never be able to change my ways if we were together. But I knew that if I told you I wanted to leave, you would convince me to stay." There's a bitter taste in my mouth, but I know it's not Evan's fault. It's mine. "I can't say no to you. We both know that."

"And I can't say no to you," he says simply. He exhales a ragged breath. "You should've just talked to me, Gen. Hell, I would've gone with you. You know that."

"Yes. I knew that too. But you're a bad influence on me." At his wounded look, I add, "It's a two-way street. I was an equally bad influence on you. I was worried that if we left the Bay together, we'd just bring those bad habits to wherever we ended up. And I was done with those habits. I'm done with them now."

Gathering my shoes, I steel myself for what comes next. After all this time away, it hasn't gotten any easier. "You ought to think about getting your shit together too. We aren't kids anymore, Evan. If you don't make a change, you're going to wake up one day and realize you've become the thing you hate most."

"I'm not my parents," he grits out between clenched teeth.

"Everything's a choice."

I hesitate for a beat. Then I step forward and kiss him on the cheek. When his gaze softens, I step out of his reach before he can change my mind. Because I *do* care about him. I care about him way too fucking much.

But I can't take responsibility for his life when I'm barely capable of running mine.

After stopping by the house to change clothes, I finally make it into work, where my dad's waiting for me in the office. I know it's bad when he's sitting in Mom's chair. Well, my chair now. Dad hardly ever comes into the office and absolutely never sits down, preferring to be out at the jobsites and meeting with clients. The man hasn't stopped moving since the day he first went to work for his dad when he was eleven.

"Let's talk," he says, nodding at a chair in front of the desk. "Where've you been?"

"I'm sorry I'm late. I was out and overslept. Won't happen again."

"Uh-huh." He sips his coffee, chair tipped back against the wall. "You know, I was sitting here waiting for you, and I got to thinking. And it occurred to me I never really disciplined you as a kid."

Talk about an understatement. Although Dad was never the overly strict type, I probably got it the easiest, being the only daughter in a house full of boys. It's one of the reasons we got along so well.

"And maybe I need to take some responsibility for how that turned out," he says slowly. Pensive. "All the partying and getting in trouble . . . I didn't do you any favors letting you carry on like that."

"I'm pretty sure I would have done what I wanted either way," I admit.

He answers with a knowing grin.

"At least this way I didn't grow up hating you."

"Yeah, well, teenagers are supposed to hate their parents at least a little, at some point or another."

Maybe that's true, but I prefer it this way, knowing the alternative. "I am trying to do better," I tell him, hoping he can see the sincerity on my face. "This was a slip, but I promise I won't make it a habit. I want you to know you can count on me. I understand how important it is to chip in around here right now."

He sits forward. "We can both do better, kiddo. Truth is, you've been great around here. Got the place running smooth. Customers love you. Everybody's always going on about what a charming young woman you turned out to be."

I grin. "I clean up nice when I want to."

"So." Dad gets up and comes around the desk. "I'll get out of your hair. Consider this your first official reprimand, kiddo." He pats me on the head and strolls out.

Oddly, I think I kind of enjoyed that, talking with my father like adults. I appreciate that he respected me enough to tell me I messed up without beating me over the head about one mistake. And I'm thrilled that he thinks I'm doing well here. When I agreed to run the office, I was terrified I'd screw it up, drive the whole thing into the ground, and leave Dad bankrupt and broken. Instead, it turns out I might actually be *good* at this stuff.

For once, I'm not a total disaster.

CHAPTER 15

EVAN

I used to enjoy being alone on a jobsite, hanging drywall or pouring in a driveway. Give me a list and eight hours, and I'd have that shit knocked out no problem. I always work faster by myself, especially when I don't have to listen to some asshole's radio or him telling me about his sick pet fish or whatever. Today is different. I've been at the West house all morning installing new kitchen cabinets, but it's taking me twice as long as it should. These cabinet doors don't want to level out. I keep dropping stuff. At one point, I damn near ran a drill over my finger.

It's been days of unanswered texts since Gen ran off from our spot. My calls are going straight to voicemail. It's maddening. She just drops all those truth bombs and accusations in my lap and then ghosts me? She barely gave me a chance to respond.

Then again, what the hell could I even say? Apparently, I hadn't been that off-base when I blamed myself for running her out of town. Randall set the ball in motion, but I kicked the damn thing in the net. Goal! Gen's gone!

I was a wake-up call for her. Christ. My hungover, passed-out self drove the girl I love more than anything else in this world right out of my life.

Damned if that doesn't rip apart my insides.

I fight the pain tightening my throat, my hand once again squeezing the drill a little too hard. Fuck. I'm going to get myself killed on this job if I don't start focusing.

But no, I refuse to take *all* the blame. Since when did I become the root of all her problems? Seems like a convenient excuse to avoid dealing with her own baggage. I might have been a delinquent for most of my life, but at least I'm not trying to lay that blame on everyone else.

"Hey, man." Gen's youngest brother Craig strolls into the kitchen wearing a T-shirt and a pair of basketball shorts. He gives me a nod as he grabs a soda from the fridge. "Thirsty?"

I'd love a beer, but I accept the soda anyway. "Thanks." I might as well take a break, seeing as how I've entirely lost track of what I was doing anyway.

"How's it going in here?" he asks after scanning the dust-covered disaster that is the half-demolished kitchen. He takes a seat at the kitchen table that now sits under a drop cloth and my toolboxes.

"Slow," I reply honestly. "But I'll get it done." *Or Levi will have my ass.* "You ready to get the hell out of here?"

Craig shrugs, sipping his soda. "I guess. It's weird thinking this won't be our house the next time I come home from college."

He falls quiet, examining the writing on the side of his can. He was always a quiet kid. Four years younger than Gen and a total mama's boy, which, despite making her resentful, also made Gen especially protective of him.

I lean against the counter. "What are you up to this summer? Any big plans?"

He evades the question, staring down at the table for a beat. Then his attention wanders the room, his shoulders hunched like a kid in the back of the classroom who doesn't want to get called on. "You'll think it's dumb," he finally answers.

"What is it?" I say. "Spit it out."

Reluctant, he sighs. "Jay and I signed up to do the Big Brothers program. Mentoring kids and whatever. So, yeah."

Why am I not surprised? Those two were always the Boy Scouts of the family. While Gen and her two oldest brothers were out raising hell and being a bad influence on Billy, Jay and Craig were doing their homework and cleaning their rooms. I guess when you have six kids, some of them are bound to turn out straight-edge.

"That's cool," I tell him. "You like it so far?"

He nods shyly. "It feels good, like, when my Little Brother looks forward to hanging out. He doesn't have a lot of friends, so when we get to go do stuff, it's a big deal for him."

Craig's the right type for that sort of thing. A little dorky and soft, but a nice kid. And, most importantly, smart and responsible. Leave me with a kid for ten minutes and they would probably catch fire somehow. Which gets me thinking again about Gen and our conversation on the beach about family and children. I guess she isn't wrong that if I ever had a family, I'd have to at least learn how not to kill my kid. I don't have a clue how my parents kept Cooper and me from drowning in the bathtub. Those two could barely stand up straight after ten a.m.

"She's not coming back as long as you're still here," Craig says.

I frown. "Huh?"

"My sister. She left early this morning so she wouldn't run into you, and she won't come home until she knows you're gone." He pauses knowingly. "If you were thinking of waiting for her."

Damn. Somehow, it's even colder coming from this kid. "She told you that?"

He shrugs. "You guys fighting?"

"I'm not." I wish I could make her understand she can have me however she wants. Whatever she needs from me, I'll do it.

"You know, I always kind of looked up to you when I was a kid."

Craig's words catch me off guard. "Oh yeah?"

"Not so much anymore."

Ouch. The kid's full of bullets today. "This unfiltered honesty thing gets a lot less cute when you're old enough to get your ass kicked," I remind him.

He has the decency to blush. "Sorry."

"So what's changed, huh?"

He considers the question for several seconds. Then, with a look of pity that would knock other men out cold, he says, "The bad boy thing gets old."

Well, shit.

It's not every day I get dressed down by a Boy Scout.

Later that night, I hit up one of the usual haunts for a few drinks with Tate, Wyatt, and the guys. After a couple rounds of beers, we drift over to the pool tables and indulge in our favorite pastime: hustling tourists. Eventually they catch on to us, so we start playing for fun. We split into teams, me and Tate versus Wyatt and Jordy. The cash we'd just squeezed out of the tourists sits in a neat pile at the corner of the table. Winners take all.

From the next table, a cute blonde in a pink sundress watches me, while her boyfriend, I presume, is completely oblivious as he stalks around the table sinking shots. I might have been able to work up some enthusiasm about the scenario if Genevieve West didn't have my head in a vise. But since she came back to the Bay, I've had zero interest in hookups with other women. Just one.

"Coop coming?" Tate asks me, shoving the pool cue in my hand for my turn.

I line up my shot and scuff the felt. "Doubt it."

"The wifey doesn't let him out anymore," Wyatt cracks as he easily follows up my scratch by nailing a bank shot.

He's not entirely wrong. Though it isn't necessarily Mackenzie keeping Cooper from drinks with the boys these days, so much as the two of them mind-melding into a single entity that prefers its own company to that of others. They're happy and stupid in their gooey love bubble. For a while, it was a relief when Mac managed to mellow Cooper out, but now their bubble is absorbing the whole house, and it's not so fun anymore.

Or hell, maybe I'm just jealous. Maybe I'm resentful that Coop throws his perfect relationship in my face but does everything in his power to keep me miserable. There was no good reason he and Mac should have gotten together, much less stayed together. But they ignored all of us and made it work. Why can't I have that?

"You're up." Tate smacks me with the cue again.

"Nah, I'm tapping out." I glance toward our table. "Yo, Donovan, take my place."

"Aww, come on." Wyatt taunts me from across the table. "Let me embarrass your ass fair and square."

I reach for my beer and find it empty. "I'm gonna hit the head and then grab the next round."

"Well, you heard the man," Wyatt says, slapping our buddy Donovan on the back. "It's your turn to shoot."

I pay a quick visit to the restroom, drying my hands with a paper towel that I drop in the trash can by the door. I step into the corridor at the same time someone exits the ladies' room. None other than Lauren, Wyatt's ex.

"Evan. Hey," the brunette says.

"Ah, hey." I dutifully lean in for the hug she offers. She and Wyatt might be broken up, but Ren's been part of our crew for years. I can't very well shun her, and I doubt Wyatt would want me to. "How've you been, Ren?"

"Pretty good. Been spending a lot of time in Charleston with my sister." She lifts a slender arm to drag her hand through her glossy hair, drawing my attention to the full sleeve of tats on her skin. Most of the art is courtesy of Wyatt, who did a lot of my own recent ink. "How about you?" she asks.

"Nothing new to report," I say lightly.

"I heard Gen's back in town. We're supposed to grab lunch sometime next week."

"Yeah. She sure is back."

A dimple appears at the left side of Ren's mouth. Her eyes twinkle with amusement. "I'm guessing she didn't come running right back into your arms?"

I smile faintly. "Good guess."

Pensive for a beat, Ren moistens her bottom lip with the tip of her tongue. "We should grab lunch one of these days too. Or better yet, a drink."

My eyebrows shoot up. "You asking me out, Ren? Because you know I can't say yes to that." I might be a total asshole, but Wyatt's one of my best friends. I'd never date his ex.

"I don't want to hook up with you," she answers with a throaty laugh. "Just figured it could be a mutually beneficial arrangement if we went out a couple times." Ren grins. "Our respective exes don't handle jealousy too well."

"No, they don't," I agree. "Still can't do that to Wyatt, though, even if it ain't real."

"Fair enough." She gives my arm a warm squeeze. "See you around, Ev. Say hi to the boys for me."

I watch her saunter away, hips swaying. Women with asses like that are dangerous.

At the bar, I ask the bartender to pour me a shot of bourbon for myself, then line up another round of shots and beer for the guys. The place isn't too crowded tonight. Just the usual faces.

Sports highlights flash on the TVs overhead while '90s rock plays on the sound system. I knock back my bourbon just as I see Billy West grab a seat at the other end of the bar.

I hesitate. I'm not sure he's any more amicable to my situation than Craig was, but I've exhausted all other reasonable means of fixing this thing with Gen. If anyone knows what is going on inside her head, it'll be Billy.

Setting the empty shot glass on the bar, I walk over and grab the stool beside him. "We need to talk," I tell him. "The hell's up with your sister?"

Billy spares me a brief sideways glance. "What'd you do now?"

"Nothing. That's the point."

"So why are you asking me?"

I narrow my eyes. The little shit's two years younger than me, and I still remember all the pranks Gen and I used to pull on him, so I don't much appreciate the attitude he's slinging my way.

"Because she won't answer her damn phone."

"That sounds like a you problem."

Cocky little fucker. "Listen, I know she talks to you. So just tell me what I have to do to get her back, and I'll leave you alone."

Billy slams down his beer bottle and huffs out a sarcastic laugh as he turns to look me dead on. "Why would I want her to take you back? For the last year, I've watched you get drunk like it's your job, hook up with a nonstop parade of college chicks, fight every rich prick you can get your hands on, and do nothing meaningful with your life."

"Are you serious? I co-own a damn business now. Just like your old man. I work for a living. How's that nothing?"

"Right, a business you didn't build. It just got handed to you, same way my dad's business got handed to us. But I don't go around congratulating myself for it."

"Man, fuck you. Not all of us had Mommy and Daddy at

home cooking pancakes every morning. Maybe don't talk about shit you don't understand." I feel remorse the second I mention his mother, but it's too late to take it back. Anyway, I stand by my point. If Gen's brother wants to pass judgment on me, he can save it. I'm not interested in his judgment.

"Gen's finally trying to get her life together," he mutters, slapping some cash on the bar. "And you're doing everything you can to keep her down in the mud with you. That's not how you treat someone you care about."

I have to remind myself that beating the hell out of Gen's little brother is not the way to get in her good graces.

"I do care about her," I say roughly.

"Then here's my advice," he retorts, standing over me. "You want my sister to let you back into her life? Worry about getting your own life together first."

CHAPTER 16

EVAN

Two days later, I wake up at the crack of dawn after another restless night. Rather than laze in bed like a bum, I'm up with the sun to take Daisy out for a walk on the beach, then give her a bath in the driveway to get her looking all shiny and clean. After getting dressed in my nicest outfit that falls between funeral attire and dirtbag, I clip a leash on Daisy and head back to the kitchen for another cup of coffee.

When I find Cooper and Mac eating breakfast on the deck, I pop my head out of the sliding glass door. "Hey. Just so you know, I'm taking Daisy out for a few hours."

"Where?" Cooper grunts with a mouthful of waffles.

"Sit down," Mac tells me. "We made plenty. Have you eaten yet?"

"Nah, I'm good. I picked up a shift volunteering at the seniors' home. The lady on the phone said old folks love dogs, so I'm bringing Daisy."

"Is that like a euphemism for something?" she asks, laughing as she turns to Cooper for the punchline.

My brother looks as bewildered as his girlfriend sounds. "If it is, I don't know what it's code for."

"Alright, gotta run. Oh, by the way," I tell Cooper, "I'm taking your truck." Then I slap the door shut before he can respond.

I can only imagine the conversation they're having in my wake. *Has Evan gone nuts? Obviously he's not volunteering anywhere, right?*

Well, joke's on them, because I certainly fucking am. My last conversation with Gen, followed by my chat with Billy the other night, got me thinking about what "getting my life together" actually looks like. Truth be told, I hadn't thought my life was so scattered to begin with. It's not as if I'm a total deadbeat. I've got a job—my own business, partly. I have a house and a motorcycle. An old Jeep I spend more time fixing up than driving.

Plenty of people I grew up with around here aspired to a lot less. And a lot of people would have put money on me ending up a lot worse. Still, if all that isn't enough for Gen, fine. I can do better. She thinks I can't change? Watch me.

Starting today, I'm hella upstanding. Easing up on the drinking. No more fights. I'm officially on a mission of self-improvement, a complete Good Boy retrofit. Which, according to Google, includes volunteer work.

So bring on the seniors.

At the nursing home, Daisy is psyched at all the new, weird smells. Her little tail excitedly smacks the linoleum floor as she tugs on her leash, anxious to explore, while I check in at the front desk and introduce myself.

A volunteer coordinator named Elaine meets me in the lobby, offering a broad smile in greeting. "Evan! Nice to meet you in person! We always appreciate visitors." She shakes my hand before sinking to one knee to greet Daisy. "And we love having pretty girls around!"

I watch as the middle-aged woman fawns over Daisy, scratching behind her ears and dodging that tongue that just last night got into the garbage again.

This dog doesn't even understand how easy she's got it.

"Yeah, well, we like to give back," I say, then regret how skeezy it sounds coming from me.

Elaine takes us on a tour of the two-story facility. Honestly, it's less creepy than I imagined. I had pictured something at a cross between hospital and asylum, but this place isn't spooky at all. No one is wandering around dead-eyed in a nightshirt muttering to themselves. It simply looks like a condo building with hospital handrails on the walls.

"We underwent a major renovation a few years ago. We have a full-service restaurant that serves three meals every day, plus a café and coffee shop where our residents can grab a snack and sit with friends. Of course, for our less mobile residents, we deliver meals to their rooms."

Elaine proceeds to tell me about activities they organize as we pass one of the community rooms, where the old folks are sitting around easels, painting. Apparently, this is where most of my volunteer hours will be spent.

"Do you have any special skills or talents?" she asks. "Play an instrument, maybe?"

"Uh, no, nothing like that, I'm afraid." I did spend a few months in middle school thinking I might take up the guitar, but that shit's complicated. "I can build stuff, mostly. Just about anything."

"Crafts, then," she says with a placating smile that I choose to ignore. "And of course, our residents enjoy when four-legged friends come by. So we can set up a schedule for that as well."

Down one of the residential halls, Elaine pokes her head in an open door with a quiet knock. "Arlene, may we come in? You have a special visitor."

Arlene, a tiny pixie of a white-haired woman, sits in a recliner watching her television. She waves us in with a frail hand that looks like it might snap off if she moves too quickly. But she's smiling the second her cloudy eyes land on Daisy.

"Arlene, this is Evan and Daisy. They'll be volunteering here," Elaine says. "Arlene is one of our favorite residents. She's going to outlast all of us, isn't that right?"

Then, like shoving a kid into the deep end of the pool to make him figure out how to swim, Elaine abandons Daisy and me to the whims of Arlene and the Weather Channel.

"You better bring the car into the garage, Jerry," Arlene says to me, while petting Daisy, who has hopped up in her lap now. "TV says it's going to rain."

I don't respond at first, confused. But as she keeps chatting up a storm, it quickly becomes evident she thinks I'm someone named Jerry. Her husband, I take it.

I'm clueless about nursing home etiquette, so I'm not sure if I'm allowed to sit on the edge of the old lady's bed. But there's only one chair in the room, and Arlene is sitting in it. So I remain standing, awkwardly sliding my hands in my back pockets.

"Is your brother still up north?" she asks after the weather guy remarks on a line of severe thunderstorms moving up the New England coast. "You should make sure he replaced those gutters like you told him to, Jerry. He doesn't want more leaks like last season."

I nod briefly. "Yeah, I'll tell him."

She goes on like that for more than an hour, and I don't know what to do other than play along. I mean, how are you supposed to respond to someone who probably has dementia? Is it like waking a sleepwalker? Do you wake a sleepwalker? Hell if I know. It seems the kind of thing they should put in a brochure or something. In fact, I'm starting to think Elaine is a terrible volunteer coordinator and that this gig absolutely should come with some training.

"Jerry," Arlene says during a commercial. She's made me change the channel five times in the past five minutes because she never seems to remember what she's been watching, "I think I'd like a bath. Will you help me to the tub?"

"Uhh . . ."

Nope. I'm noping out. I draw the line at stripping little old ladies. Plus, Daisy's starting to get a bit restless, jumping down from Arlene's lap and sniffing around the room.

"Why don't I find someone to come help?" I suggest.

"Oh no, that's not necessary, Jerry. You're all the help I need." Smiling brightly, Arlene starts to stand, then drops back down in her chair, unsteady.

"Here," I say, helping her to her feet. The moment she's upright, she tightly holds on to my arm. "How about we hit that call button and—"

"Arlene, sweetie, where you trying to go?" A big guy in white scrubs walks into the room and pries Arlene out of my arms.

I glance at the newcomer. "She was having trouble getting up, so—"

"Jerry is going to give me a bath," Arlene says happily, walking with the orderly's assistance over to her bed.

"You had a bath this morning," he reminds her as he helps her take off her slippers and get in bed. "How about a nap before lunch, then?"

While he handles her, I get Daisy back on her leash, then follow the orderly out of the room when he gives me the nod.

"She thought I was her husband," I tell him, by way of an explanation.

The orderly grins and shakes his head. "Nah, brother. That old lady's mind is sharp as a tack. She's just trying to get a little frisky with the new guy. She pulls this stunt on all the handsome ones." Guffawing, he gives me a slap on the shoulder. "And she's not the only one. My advice: Trust no one."

Nursing homes are fucked up.

When Elaine finally returns after abandoning me to the wilds, she shows little sympathy for my ordeal. *Comes with the territory* seems to be her attitude; the staff has apparently resigned themselves to the lawlessness. The inmates are running the asylum.

Elaine eventually brings me to a Korean War helicopter pilot named Lloyd. His room is decorated in about a dozen old photographs of him in his helmet and jumpsuit. When we enter, he's in bed grumbling at the newspaper, which he reads with a magnifying glass on an arm attached to the bedside table.

"Lloyd," she says, "this young man would like to spend some time with you, if that's alright."

"Doesn't anyone edit these damn papers anymore? There are two spelling errors on this page alone. When did the newspaper start looking like some lazy kid's homework?" He lifts his gaze only long enough to spot Daisy standing at my side. "Get that thing out of here," he snaps. "I'm allergic."

"You're not allergic to dogs, Lloyd," Elaine tells him with a cadence that suggests this isn't the first argument they've had. "And Daisy is very sweet. I'm sure you two will have a lovely time."

Lloyd huffs and returns to inspecting his newspaper while Elaine leaves me with another pat on the back. It's like some weird handshake, everyone who works here warning me now that I've entered, I can never leave.

"He's harmless," she murmurs from the doorway. "Talk to him about Jessie. He loves to talk about the bird."

"The bird" is a little yellow thing I hadn't noticed in a cage by the window. Elaine ducks into the hallway, leaving me trapped in a tiny room with a crotchety old man who glares at me.

I notice another photo on his wall, and move closer to inspect it. "You met Buddy Holly?"

"What?" Lloyd squints toward the photograph of him and the musician outside a venue, posing beside a bus parked in an alley. "Yes, I knew Charles. Back when music meant something."

"You were friends?"

Daisy, apparently afraid of him, lies on the floor at the foot of the bed.

"I was a roadie. Hauled his gear, that sort of thing." With another huff, Lloyd loudly folds his paper and sets it aside. "Was getting on a train in New York after I got back from Korea when I saw this skinny kid who could barely lift his guitar and all these bags and cases. I offered him a hand."

Lloyd seems to warm up a bit, albeit reluctantly. He talks about traveling the country with Holly, Elvis Presley, and Johnny Cash. Running from the cops and unruly fans. Catching flat tires and getting robbed in the middle of nowhere, at a time before calling AAA from the side of the road was a thing. Lugging guitar amps ten miles on foot to the nearest gas station. Turns out Lloyd's got plenty to say, if I just shut up and let him talk. And in all honesty, I'm enjoying listening to his crazy anecdotes. This guy's *lived*.

Things are going well—he hasn't once asked me to bathe him or called me Sheila—until he asks me to feed his bird and put fresh water in the cage. When I open it up, the bird flies out, which doesn't seem to concern Lloyd at first.

But we both realize too late there's a puppy in the room, and she's been bored silly all afternoon.

Like a slow-motion crash, the parakeet flits over to the dresser. Daisy's ears perk up. She lifts her head, a low growl building in the back of her throat. Alarmed, the bird takes flight. Daisy pounces, snatching the tiny creature out of the air as it explodes in a burst of yellow feathers and disappears.

Goodbye Jessie.

CHAPTER 17

EVAN

Me: *Hey. Just checking in to make sure you're alive.*

Gen: *You've been asking me that question every other day for almost 2 weeks. Still alive. Just been busy with work.*

Me: *Same.*

Gen: *You realize usually when a guy "checks in" at 1 in the morning, it's considered a booty call?*

Me: *Blasphemy! I would never besmirch your purity like that.*

Gen: *Uh-huh.*

Me: *Tbh, I can't sleep.*

Gen: *Same.*

Me: *You good, other than being a busy insomniac?*

Gen: *All good here.*

Me: *Dinner one of these days?*

Me: *Just to catch up?*

It's been six hours since Gen stopped responding to my texts. As I help Mac set the breakfast table outside on the deck, I keep feeling a phantom vibration in my pocket, hoping it's her. But no. Now it's just been six hours, forty-two minutes.

"Grab the napkins, will you?" Mac says, handing me utensils to lay down.

My mind is elsewhere as I duck inside to grab some napkins. I'd thought things were getting better with Gen. We've been texting here and there for the past couple weeks, just random banter or quick hellos. Every time I mention getting together, however, she shuts down and stops responding. I can't get even a foot in the door. She won't go for coffee, won't eat lunch with me—nothing. She's the most infuriating person I've ever known. Worse, she likes it that way.

"So what's your plan for the day?" Cooper asks after we're seated to eat. "Got some orphans to pull out of a burning building, or what?"

Mac passes me the scrambled eggs. "Still doing the nursing home?"

Daisy pokes her head up from under the table to beg for a piece of sausage. When I start to hand her a piece, Mac points a knife at me.

"Don't you dare. That stuff will kill her."

While Mac is preoccupied with chastising me, Cooper slips a chuck to Daisy, and I stifle a grin.

"Anyway, no," I say in response to their badgering. "I'm not allowed back there since our crazed beast ate that dude's bird."

"Wait, what?" Mac's utensils clang on her plate as she drops them. "What the fuck?"

"Well, ate is probably an exaggeration," I relent. "I'm pretty sure most of the bird was intact when Daisy spit it up."

Coop barks out a hysterical laugh, to which Mac shoots him the scary eyes.

"This happened last week?" she shouts. "Why didn't you tell me?"

"I told Coop. Guess I forgot you weren't there." Cooper was falling on the floor cracking up when I told him about the incident with Lloyd. In fact, he'd suggested we keep it on the DL because Mac would flip out. Guess I forgot that part too.

"You didn't think to mention it?" Mac cuts a glare at my brother.

"She's a dog," he says lightly. "It's what they do."

"This isn't over, Hartley," she replies in a voice that says he's not getting his dick sucked anytime soon.

"Anyway, I've got a new gig," I continue just to save Coop from the weight of his impending punishment. "I signed up to be a Big Brother."

Yup, it's happening. I'm hopping on the Big Brothers band-wagon. I tried out a few other volunteer gigs after the nursing home didn't work out, the most recent one being a shift picking up trash on the beach. Which was going well until I was attacked by a homeless dude under the boardwalk. He chased me off by throwing bottles at my head. I swear, nobody had warned me civic responsibility was so treacherous. At any rate, I figured some disadvantaged kid has got to be less dangerous than hobos and handsy old ladies.

"Oh, Christ, no," Coop groans. "You realize you can't just take him to a bar for four hours, right?"

"Fuck off." Just for that, I steal the last pancake. "I'll be a great role model. Teach him all the things adults don't want to tell kids."

"Child endangerment is a crime, Evan." Mac smirks at me. "If the cops find you stumbling out of the Pony Stable with a ten-year-old, you're going to end up in jail."

"As always, I appreciate your support, princess." Their lack of confidence is disappointing if not unexpected. "Anyway, he's fourteen. Plenty old enough to learn how the world works."

"God help that kid," Coop mutters.

I get it. They'd rather keep me in the screwup box than believe I'm evolving. I guess that's not entirely unwarranted, but an ounce or two of faith, a little benefit of the doubt, would be appreciated. They make it sound like I'm gonna kill the poor kid. But how hard can it be? Feed him, water him, turn him in at the end of the day. I mean, hell. I've rented a car before.

Is this really so different?

His name is Riley and he's a typical skinny Bay teenager with shaggy blond hair and a summer tan. I had pictured a little punk-ass like me, some dude with a smart mouth and more attitude than sense, ready to tell me to get bent. In reality, he's a bit shy. Looking at the ground as we wander the boardwalk, because I hadn't thought too much about what there is to do with him that doesn't involve any of the nonsense I was getting up to at his age.

It was weird, if I'm honest, going into the public library to meet him. Like checking out a library book, but a whole damn human. I walked out of there with a person it's my job not to lose or get maimed, and suddenly that seems like a big ask. They didn't even hand me a first aid kit.

"So what are you into, kid?"

"I dunno," he says with a shrug. "Stuff, I guess."

"Stuff like what?"

"Sailing, sometimes. Fishing. And, um, surfing. But I'm not very good. My board's kinda old, so."

He's killing me. He's got his head bowed and hands in his pockets, sweat starting to trickle from under his wispy mop of hair. It's a blistering June day and the boardwalk is swarmed with tourists, all hot and sticky. We're like hot dogs in a sidewalk cart, rolling around in each other's sweat.

"Hey, you hungry?" I ask, because it really is too boiling out here to spend all afternoon walking around.

"Sure, I guess."

Cooper was right—with a lack of any better ideas, I pull Riley into a bar. Well, not exactly a bar. Big Molly's is a kitschy kind of tourist trap, with random tchotchkes on the wall and live music on the weekends. The waitresses run around in skimpy outfits. Turns out, the kid notices. He perks right up when he gets an eyeful of the hostess in a crop top and tiny skirt.

"Hey you," she coos by way of a greeting. "Been awhile."

I flash a grin at her. "Got a table for two?"

Stella leans over the hostess stand, pushing her tits together. "Who's your friend?" She winks at him, which would have been more than enough to give me a boner at that age. It's unfair, torturing the kid like that. "He's cute."

"Riley, this is Stella."

"Hey, sweetie," she says when he can't quite work up a reply. "Come on, I'll get you seated."

"You ever been here before?" I ask him as we settle at a high-top table. A band onstage is playing some early nineties covers. At the bar counter, college guys and dads who escaped while their wives went shopping occupy the old wooden stools.

Riley shakes his head no. "My aunt hates these places."

"So what's the story there?" No one ends up in a program like this if their lives are going totally to plan. "If you want to talk about it, that is."

Another shrug. "I live with my mom's sister. She's an ER nurse, so she works a lot. My mom died when I was little. Cancer."

"Where's your dad?"

He stares at his menu without reading it, flicking the laminated edge with his fingernail. "Went to prison about six years ago. He was out on parole for a while, but then he took off. Got arrested again, I think. My aunt doesn't like to talk about him, so she doesn't really tell me stuff. She thinks it upsets me."

"Does it?"

"I dunno. Sometimes, I guess."

I'm starting to understand why they stuck him with me. "My dad died when I was younger too."

Riley meets my eyes.

"Drunk driving accident," I add. "My mom hasn't been around since then either."

"Did you have to go live somewhere else? Like, in foster care or with another relative?"

"My uncle took care of my brother and me," I explain, and it's not until this very moment that I consider what might have happened to me and Cooper if Levi hadn't been there. Funny how our lives teeter on these rails, riding the edge over a dark unknown. How easy it is to fall off. "Do you like your aunt? You two get along?"

A slight smile erases the gloom from his expression. "She's nice. But she can be kind of a lot sometimes. She worries about me." He sighs quietly. "She thinks I'm depressed."

"Are you?"

"I don't think so? I mean, I don't really have many friends. Don't like being around a lot of people. I'm just, I dunno, quiet."

I get that. Sometimes things happen to us when we're young, and we learn to stay inside ourselves. Especially when we don't know how to talk about what's going on in our heads. It doesn't always mean anything or indicate a bout of depression. Being a teenager is hard enough without real shit getting in the way.

"There's nothing wrong with that," I tell Riley.

"Hey, boys." Our waitress sets down a basket of hush puppies and dipping sauce, along with two tall glasses of water. "How we doing?" The brunette greets me with a wry smile and an arched brow that suggests I better prove I remember her.

Come on now. Give me a little credit here. "Hey, Rox. How's things?"

At that she smiles, satisfied. "Another summer."

"I hear ya."

She gives the kid a once-over. "This guy giving you a hard time, sweetie?"

"No," he says, grinning like he's never seen a pair of fake tits before. "I'm fine."

"Good. What'll you have?"

Riley grabs his menu again and rushes to scan it front and back, realizing he hadn't actually read it.

"What's fresh?" I ask Rox.

"Grouper's good. I'd get it Cajun style."

I glance at Riley. "You like grouper?" It occurs to me he might feel weird about what he should order when some dude he only met today is paying. I would.

"Sure," he says, looking almost relieved.

"Cool. We'll do that."

When she's done taking our order, Riley takes a second to admire her retreating backside before leaning in toward me. "You know her?"

"In a manner of speaking."

"Hey, Evan." Another waitress saunters by. Cass, a short, cute blonde in a tank top she took a pair of scissors to, waves as she passes our table.

"You know a lot of girls here," Riley remarks.

I swallow a laugh at how much he sounds like Mackenzie in that moment. Every time we walk into a place and a girl gives me a nod, Mac rolls her eyes. Like we didn't meet because she was out helping her roommate hunt me down for a one-night stand.

"It's a small town."

"So you've, like, slept with all of them?"

Well, that's more forward than I thought he was capable of. "To some extent or another, yeah, sure."

I realize then his eyes aren't wandering because he's avoiding eye contact with me. As I track his attention around the room, it's clear he's checking out all the teenage tourists, the bored girls perusing their phones while their families sit around tables scarfing down nachos and inhaling two-dollar margaritas. Suddenly, I'm just hoping this kid doesn't ask me to buy him condoms. Not that I wouldn't, but I don't need to get kicked out of another volunteer program because he goes home to tell his aunt I'm trying to get him laid.

"What about you?" I counter. "Got a girlfriend or anything?"

He shakes his head. "Girls think I'm weird. I don't know how to talk to them."

"You're not weird," I assure him. Yes, he's shy, but he doesn't give off any creep vibes. The kid just needs someone to build up his confidence. "Girls can be complicated. You just need to know the signs."

"Signs?"

"When a girl likes you. When she wants you to come talk to her."

"Like what?"

"Well, for one." I scan the room and locate a hot redhead in her early twenties. She's sitting with her girlfriends around a fishbowl of blue liquor with four straws. "When you catch each other's attention and she smiles at you—that means she thinks you're cute."

Riley follows my gaze, his eyes glazing over slightly.

It takes less than two seconds for the redhead to notice me. A mischievous smile curves her full lips. I offer a faint half smile in return.

"Then what?" Riley sounds almost eager now.

"You go introduce yourself. Get her number."

"But how?" he insists, mindlessly popping hush puppies in his mouth. "What do you say to them?"

Me, personally? Not much, really. But I can't tell him to buy her a drink or ask if she wants a ride on his motorcycle. Once I had a driver's license, all I had to do was ask a chick if her parents were home. But that's neither here nor there. Riley is the sensitive type, I'd guess. He needs a different approach.

"Okay," I tell him. "So, if she's alone—you never want to approach a girl standing with her family; dads are a surefire cockblock—but if she's alone, you go up and say hi."

"Hi? That's it? But what do I say after that?"

"Ask her . . ." I mull it over. I don't want the kid to sound like a tool. If I send him out there to get his heart broken, I'm not a very good Big Brother. "Okay, do this. You see a girl you like, she smiles at you. You say hi, introduce yourself, then say something like, what do you like to do at the beach. Then what's her favorite day. Her favorite time of day. And once you get those answers, you take out your phone and tell her you've set a reminder for that day and time to pick her up for a beach date."

Riley studies me with a skeptical grimace. "That seems kinda corny."

"Wow. Okay. Getting heckled by a fourteen-year-old."

He snorts a laugh.

"Look. Chicks like a guy with confidence. They want you to take charge of the situation. Show some game."

He shakes his head, stabbing his straw into his glass of water. "I don't think I can do that."

I ponder some more. How hard can it be to pick up a teenage girl these days? "Right, how 'bout this. You see a girl you like?"

Riley is hesitant, glancing around the restaurant. Beyond the bar, the place is stuffed with the lunch rush. Eventually, his gaze lands on a brunette sitting with her family; she looks to be the youngest of two older sisters. As the girls chat among themselves, the mom grabs her purse from the back of her chair and heads off toward the restrooms.

"Quick, before her mom comes back. You go over there and say to her sisters, 'Hey, I'm Riley, and I'm not very good at this but I'd really like to ask your sister out on a date, and I was hoping you could help me.'"

"I don't know," he says, watching them with trepidation. "What if they laugh at me? Or think I'm a weirdo?"

"They won't. Trust me, they'll think it's cute. Just smile, be natural. You're a good-looking guy, Riley. You've got that sweet-boy face that girls love. Have a little faith in yourself."

For a second or two, I think he's going to psych himself out. He remains glued to his chair. Then, with a deep breath, he gathers his confidence and stands from the table. He takes a couple steps forward before doubling back. "Wait. What do I do if she says yes?"

I smother a laugh. "Get her number and tell her you'll call her tonight."

With a nod, he's off.

Rox comes back with our food just as he's reaching their table, and together we watch him nervously approach the sisters. The girls look uncertain, guarded at first, but when Riley gets a few words out, their faces soften. They smile, amused, looking at their sister. Blushing, she says something in response, which eases the anxiety in Riley's expression. Then he tosses his hair out of his face and hands the girl his phone. They exchange a few more words before he struts back to us and throws his phone on the table like a goddamn hero.

"So?" I demand.

"We're going to play mini golf tomorrow."

I flip my palm up for a high five. "Hell yeah."

Rox's lips twitch wildly, as if she's fighting a rush of laughter. "Be careful with this one," Rox warns Riley, hooking her thumb in my direction. "He'll get you into all sorts of trouble." With a wink, she dashes off again.

I grin at Riley with a strange rush of pride filling my chest. "See, I told you, kid. You got game."

After lunch, we spend a couple hours at the arcade. Turns out I'm kind of a bastard, as far as the whole Big Brother thing goes.

"Some people," Riley says as we're leaving. "*Some people* might find your behavior in poor taste."

"Can't expect life to give you everything you want."

It started at air hockey. Five straight games during which I utterly humiliated him. In the fourth game, it looked like he might've turned it around, going on a pretty good run of scoring, but then he got a bit too pleased with himself and I took him to the cleaners.

"I'm just saying."

"Sounds like whining to me."

"I'm just saying, you wouldn't go to the kids' cancer ward and do victory laps around the room after beating them at Mario Kart."

Next, we played Skee-Ball. I don't know if it's his skinny little arms or lack of trapezius muscles, but I owned him at that too. If he had any cash, I'd have started putting money on those games.

"Who says I wouldn't? What do they have to do all day but hone their skills? I've got a job and responsibilities."

"That's messed up."

I was almost starting to feel bad for him. Even considered taking it easy on the kid. Until he started talking all kinds of smack and challenged me to a Jurassic Park shooting game. At that point, it was an educational imperative—I had to teach the kid some manners.

"You know you're supposed to set a good example for me, right?"

"These are important lessons. Eating shit is the first lesson of adulthood."

"You're terrible at this," he informs me, rolling his eyes.

"You're welcome."

We're making our way down the boardwalk to where I parked my Jeep when a familiar face appears in my line of sight. She's exiting the smoothie place five feet ahead of us and looks over her shoulder to meet my eyes, as if she felt me coming. It always strikes me how good her skin looks under a midday sun.

"You following me now?" Dark sunglasses hide her expression, but I know in the goading tone of her voice she isn't entirely disappointed to see me. Then her attention falls to Riley. "Oh dear. Is this man bothering you?"

"Why does everyone keep saying that to me?" I grumble. "Do I look like I drive a panel van?"

"I'm Riley," the teen says with a shy smile.

"Genevieve, but you can call me Gen." She nods in the direction we'd been heading, asking us to walk with her.

As we fall into step with my drop-dead gorgeous ex-girlfriend, it's as if a switch flips in Riley. His entire demeanor changes as he tips his head toward her. "What do you like to do at the beach, Gen?"

She questions me with a look before answering. "Well, I guess I like to tan and read a book."

"What's your favorite day?"

"Uh . . . Sunday, I suppose." Gen licks her lips, growing more skeptical as the interrogation continues.

"What's your favorite time of day?"

I'm here, watching this happen. Still, I can't believe what I'm seeing. Surreal.

"Sunrise. When it's still quiet." An amused Gen watches Riley pull out his phone and type in a quick note. "What are you writing?"

"There," he says smugly. "I just set a reminder to pick you up for a sunrise date on the beach this weekend."

"Wow." She turns with an arched eyebrow, peering at me above the rim of her sunglasses. "Can I assume this was your doing?"

"They grow up so fast."

Once again, I'm practically bursting with pride. I don't know if Riley is a quick study or if I'm an extraordinary mentor, but I think it's safe to say he's conquered his confidence problem. Although the superpower persuasion of Gen's spectacular rack might have had something to do with it. Kid's been staring so hard I'm worried I might have to take him home cross-eyed.

"I might look young," he tells her. "But I assure you I'm an old soul."

"Oh my God." Gen playfully mashes his face with her palm. "Where'd you find this kid, Evan?"

"I'm his Big Brother."

She scoffs at me, incredulous. "No, seriously. This is Mackenzie's little brother or something, right?"

"Really. I'm giving back to my community."

"Huh."

I'm not sure what to make of her response, but at least she's not telling me to get lost again.

When we come up on Mac's hotel, Gen pauses near the new white-and-green sign with the elegantly scrawled words *The Beacon Hotel*. Sipping her smoothie, she examines the building. There isn't much going on outside anymore, as far as the renovation goes. The façade is all patched up and painted. Most of the work left to do is on the inside. Decorating, installing the mirrors and fixtures, all that tedious stuff. Mac's been getting more anal by the minute about every microscopic detail.

"I've always loved this place," Gen says to no one in particular.

"Is it open yet?" Riley asks curiously.

I shake my head. "Soon. Couple months, I think."

"The woman who owned this place would come to the stone yard sometimes," Gen says, a faraway note in her voice. "She'd hire Dad to do seasonal landscaping. There was something so glamorous about her, even in a place like that. She'd be walking through stone dust and mulch looking like a million bucks. I used to tell my folks I was going to work here someday."

"Mac's hiring," I tell her.

Gen cocks her head at me. "What, seriously?"

"Yeah. Cooper's been giving her a hard time about needing to hurry up and pick some people, or she'll never open." Though I can't see her eyes, I feel the intensity of Gen's interest in the way she presses her lips together. "I could put in a good word, if you're interested."

She hesitates for a beat. Then she nods slowly. "Yeah. Yes. I'd actually really appreciate that. If it's not too much of a thing."

"No sweat." Hell, I'm just happy she's letting me do this for her, rather than making it a whole argument about fending for herself or me getting too involved in her life. "It's done." At that, though, it really is time I bring Riley back to the library. I was warned at least four times that tardiness is frowned upon. "Listen, we gotta go, but I'll talk to Mac and let you know how it goes. Cool?"

"Cool. Thanks again."

She says goodbye to Riley, and we shuffle through an awkward hug that still gets my blood rushing like I haven't touched a woman in months. Something about the smell of sunscreen and her flowery shampoo makes me all stupid, and I can't walk straight. The haze lingers as we walk off in different directions.

Riley and I make it five yards away before something stops me. A nagging sense of money left on the table. This was the longest conversation Gen and I have had in weeks, and I'm just letting her leave? What the hell is wrong with me?

"Give me a sec," I tell Riley. Then I dart off, jogging after Genevieve. "Hey. Fred. Wait up."

She stops, turning to face me. "What's up?"

I let out a hurried breath. "No bullshit, I took what you said seriously. I'm getting my act together."

A groove digs into her forehead. "Is that what this Big Brothers thing is all about?"

"Sort of. I'm reformed," I say earnestly. "And I can prove it to you."

"How's that?"

"I intend to court you."

Gen bites back a laugh, looking away. "Evan."

"I mean it. I'm going to court you. All gentlemanly and shit."

"Is this your latest creative attempt to get me naked?"

I haven't heard a no yet, so I take it as a good sign. "If we do this, sex is off the table. I'm going to prove to you I've changed. Woo you the old-fashioned way."

"Woo me," she echoes.

"Woo you," I confirm.

Twisting her lips as she studies me, Gen considers my offer. Every second she's silent, I know the idea is finding root in her brain. Because she wants me to give her an excuse, to make it okay to say yes. I know her. Better, I know *us*. There's no world in which she can stay away from me. No more than I can tolerate distance from her. Truth is, we've never had any resistance to each other, no chance of severing the immutable connection that always pulls us back together. And because I can't lie to her, she knows when I'm sincere.

"You should know," Gen says, "you wouldn't be my only suitor."

I narrow my eyes. "Baby cop?"

She chides me with a grimace. "Harrison asked me out on another date, and I said yes. You've got some competition."

We have very different concepts of competition, but sure, whatever. If she needs a guy to make me jealous, either as some form of punishment or just to keep things interesting, that's fine by me. It'll make winning all the more satisfying. Because this guy's already been knocked out. He just hasn't hit the ground yet.

I flash the cocky lopsided grin that I know drives her wild. "Bring it, baby."

CHAPTER 18

GENEVIEVE

I'm not sure how it happened. A couple months ago, I was certain coming back to the Bay was a temporary situation. Confident that things would eventually level off with Dad, the house, and the business—he'd find someone to replace me, and everyone would move on from Mom's death. Now, it seems every day I stick around, I'm digging my toes in deeper. Despite my best efforts, my instincts keep me rooted home, and my life in Charleston is slowly becoming blurred with distance.

I wake up to the faint aroma of coffee and the muffled sounds of Billy and Craig arguing over something downstairs. There's a shower running in the hall bathroom, and I hear Jay singing what sounds like a Katy Perry song.

I roll over in bed and strain to make out the words. Oh, that is definitely Katy Perry. I make a mental note to tease him mercilessly at breakfast. Jay crashed here last night after Kellan kicked him out of their apartment because he had a hot date. Who knows where Shane slept. That boy is a walking disaster.

I won't lie. It's good to be home.

On the nightstand, my phone buzzes with an incoming text.

Evan: *Morning, Fred.*

I'd like to say Evan is irrelevant to the roots that are taking hold and tethering me to this town. But since agreeing a few days ago to give him another chance, I've felt nothing but pure relief. My shoulders suddenly feel lighter and unburdened from the effort of avoiding him. I hadn't realized how much it'd hurt, staying away from him.

Me: *Morning.*
Evan: *Good luck.*

The phone rings before I can ponder the meaning of his text.

Wrinkling my forehead, I swipe the screen to answer the call. "Hello?"

"Genevieve? Hey. It's Mackenzie Cabot. Cooper's girlfriend."

My brain snaps to attention. "Oh. Hi. How's it going?"

"Evan told me you were interested in working at the hotel. He gave me some details about your experience, but I figured we should meet in person and have an official interview. How'd you like to come by and talk about the manager position? See if it's something you'd be up for."

Excitement quickens my pulse. "Yes, absolutely."

"Great. If you're not busy, I've got time today."

"Give me thirty minutes."

Once we're off the phone, I throw myself into the shower and forego blow-drying my hair to wrap it in a tight bun. Then I race around my room, digging out a nice outfit that isn't still wrinkled from unpacking and hunting through boxes and under the bed for shoes. I don't bother with much makeup other than some lipstick and mascara. I always do this to myself. Instead of asking for the reasonable time I need, I promise too much and then tie myself in knots to meet my own unreasonable deadline.

Somehow, I manage to get myself out of the house with enough time to make the short drive out to the Hartley house. My mind races over the meager details Mackenzie had provided over the phone, constantly getting stuck on the word "manager." Honestly, I hadn't considered what position I'd aim for when Evan said he'd mention me to Mackenzie. Something supervisory, sure. Operations, maybe. But managing an entire hotel—events, restaurants, catering, a spa—is more than I'm accustomed to.

Then again, I've never been afraid of taking a big leap. Looking down is defeatist. If I want to turn my life around, I might as well aim high right out the gate.

With two minutes to spare, I ring the doorbell.

The front door swings open to reveal a tall, stunning girl with shiny dark hair and big green eyes. I remember catching glimpses of her the night of the bonfire, when Evan threw down with that college guy, but we'd never been properly introduced.

"It's nice to officially meet you," Mackenzie says as she lets me in. She's wearing a striped T-shirt and khaki shorts. The overly casual outfit makes me feel overdressed in my navy linen pants and white button-down shirt with the sleeves rolled up to my elbows.

"Nice to meet you too," I tell her.

She brings me through the house to the back deck, where she has a table set with two glasses and a pitcher of water with lemon.

"The guys have done a lot of work on the place," I remark as we sit down. The short walk inside had revealed new floors and old peeling wallpaper removed. Out here, I note that the siding's been replaced and painted.

"They've been at it for months. Seems like every morning I wake up to a sander or a saw running, and then I go to work and it's the same thing," she says, with an exhausted smile. "I swear to God, when it's all over, I'm going to spend two weeks in an isolation chamber." She pours us a couple glasses of water before relaxing back in her chair. A warm breeze whips across the deck, blowing the wind chimes hanging from the roof.

"I know the feeling," I say wryly.

"Oh, right. The renovation at your dad's house. It must be so hectic over there."

"I'm working most of the day, so it isn't so bad. And when I am home, noise-canceling headphones are my best friend."

"I hope I didn't make you skip work for this," she says, and I wonder if she's thinking I blew off my current job to interview for this one.

"No," I assure her. "My dad gave me the morning off, so I don't start until noon."

With the small talk over, I'm aware that I need to make a good impression here. Evan might have gotten me in the door, but a woman doesn't go out of her way to restore a derelict old hotel just to hand the keys over to some random townie with no sense. She's about to get an uncut dose of Professional Genevieve.

"So," Mackenzie says, "tell me about yourself."

I hand her my résumé, which is admittedly lacking in hotel experience. "I've been working since I was eleven years old. Started out cleaning up and stocking at my dad's hardware store. Worked summer jobs as a hostess, waitress, bartender. Customer service at the stone yard. I even did a summer stint as a deckhand on a sailing yacht."

I tell her about Charleston, where I fudge my title a little. Assistant slash secretary slash adult in the room is basically the same thing as an office manager, right? Wrangling a bunch of real estate agents with massive egos and attention deficit disorders should certainly qualify.

"Now I'm the office manager at the stone yard. I process invoices and payroll, scheduling, ordering. There isn't anything that goes on in that place that I don't keep my finger on. And I see that clients are well cared for, of course."

"I understand you've taken on a lot of responsibility since your mother's passing," Mackenzie tells me, putting my résumé aside after reading it carefully. "I'm very sorry for your loss."

"Thank you."

It's still awkward when someone brings up my mom. Mostly because I've moved on. I've been over it almost since the moment it happened. Yet I get pulled right back in every time someone else pauses to process or acknowledge it. Sucked out of time and transported to the funeral all over again, back to those first days scrambling everyone on the phone.

"It's been a lot to learn, but I've gotten a good handle on things," I say. "I'm a quick study. And I think now is the right time to leave the stone yard and hand the reins off to someone else."

If given his way, my dad would keep me in the office forever. Despite our deal, I know the only way to force his hand is to give him a deadline. I can teach just about anyone else to run the yard for him; he just needs the proper motivation to pick someone.

"I can understand getting thrown into the deep end. Or in my case, jumping. I mean, what business do I have owning a hotel, right?" There's something disarming about her self-awareness, her self-deprecating grin. Mackenzie doesn't take herself too seriously, so it's easy to talk to her like a real person, not just another clone throwing their money around. "I just saw the place and fell in love, you know? It spoke to me. And once my heart was set, there was no talking myself out of it."

"I had the same reaction when I was a kid," I admit. "I don't know how to explain it . . ." I trail off pensively. I can still picture the old brass fixtures, and the palm trees casting shadows on the pool cabanas. "It's a special place. Some buildings, they have character, personality. I'm sure you've seen pictures, but I wish you could have known The Beacon before it closed. It was like a time capsule—entirely unique. I have great memories there."

"Yeah, that's something the previous owner said to me when

I convinced her to let me buy the property. Her only request was that I maintain the original intent as much as possible. The personality, as you put it. Basically, I promised not to go mangling a piece of history." Mackenzie grins. "Hopefully, I've kept that promise. I mean, we've certainly tried. Cooper's exhausted himself tracking down experts to make sure every detail is as close to authentic as possible."

"I'm honestly excited to get a look."

"For me, part of that authenticity is about finding people who know and truly understand what we're trying to recreate. People who care as much about that history as I do, you know? People make the hospitality, after all."

She goes quiet, lingering on what feels like an open question as she sips her water.

Finally, she says, "I do have some other interviews this week, but just so you know, you're comfortably among the top candidates."

"Seriously?" I don't mean to say that out loud and roll my eyes at myself. I offer a sheepish smile. "I mean, thank you. I'm grateful for the opportunity."

Somehow, I'm always surprised when anyone takes me seriously, especially as a matter of trust and responsibility. No matter how well I dress up or maintain good posture, it feels like they all see through me. Like they look at me and see only the screwup teenager running around drunk on the back of a motorcycle.

Nerves dampen my palms. If I get this job, there's no room for mistakes. No spending the night naked on the beach and showing up to work late. If history is any indication, I'm a piece of twine over an open flame. Just a matter of time before I snap. So to get this job—and *keep* this job—the training wheels have to come off this newly self-proclaimed good girl.

As I'm about to make my way out, a golden retriever comes

galloping onto the deck. She's got that gangly look that tells me she's still very young and not in complete control of her limbs. She nudges me with her nose and plops her head in my lap.

"Oh my goodness. Look at this cutie! What's her name?"

"Daisy."

I rub behind Daisy's ears and she makes a happy sound, her brown eyes glazing over. "She's very sweet."

"You want to hang out for a bit? It's about time for her walk. We can take her down to the beach."

I hesitate. Not because Mackenzie isn't perfectly nice, but because I think the interview was pretty great, and the longer I stick around, the more chance I have to screw that up. I'm better in small doses around people who don't know me well. If I'm going to get the job, I'd rather sign the paperwork before my boss figures out I'm a potential disaster.

"Don't worry," she says, apparently discerning my anxiety. "We're both off the clock. Consider this family time."

She winks, and I catch her meaning. A job isn't the only thing we have in common.

"Sure," I agree, and a few minutes later we've got our sunglasses on and are following Daisy as she runs up and down the beach digging for crabs and chasing the waves.

It isn't long before the subject of Evan rises to the surface.

"You two go way back, huh?" Mackenzie says. "It sounds like kind of a complicated history."

"No," I answer, laughing, "not that complicated. A couple teenagers running amok while the town burned in the background. Pretty simple, actually."

Smiling, she picks up a stick and tosses it for Daisy. "That doesn't sound awful, if I'm honest."

"Oh, it wasn't. Especially not when we were drunk, high, naked, or some combination of the three most of the time. It was incredible, even. Until the buzz wore off. Then I looked back at the destruction in my wake and decided I couldn't live with the consequences."

"And that's why you moved?"

"Essentially."

"Evan talked about you a lot while you were gone."

I know she doesn't mean anything by it, but it seems there's no end in sight to being reminded that Evan was one of those consequences. That to fix myself, I had to hurt him. Maybe my decision to leave town was rash—cowardly, in some respect—but looking back, I still think I made the right decision.

"I hit a nerve," Mackenzie says, pausing as we stroll the beach. "I'm sorry. I only meant to say he missed you."

"It's fine. I've made this bed."

"He said you're trying to work things out, though, right?"

Daisy brings her stick to me, pushing her nose into my hand until I accept the stick and fling it down the beach. Her tail furiously slashes through the air as she chases it down.

"He's wooing me," I say with a sigh.

Mackenzie breaks out in a grin. "Oh my God. Please tell me those were his words."

"They were. He's wooing. I'm being wooed." I can't help but laugh. "We never dated in the traditional way, so I guess he's trying to change that. And I figured, what the hell, let's give it a shot."

Ever since he asked me out on the boardwalk, I'd been waiting for the tug of regret, the jolt of dread over this impending date, but it hasn't come. When I moved back home, I convinced myself that I needed to stay away from Evan out of sheer self-preservation, but the more I think on it, the less it makes sense to rest my problems at Evan's feet. He didn't make me drink. He didn't make me blow off school or sneak into abandoned buildings. I did those things because I wanted to, and doing them with him let me pretend I wasn't responsible for myself.

Truth is, we're both different people now. And in all the ways we've changed and grown up, we've also grown closer somehow. He's made the effort. Only seems fair to give it a chance.

"So when's the big date?" Mackenzie asks. "Tonight?"

"Next weekend. And before you ask, I have no idea what he's planning." I groan. "I'm worried there might be a corsage and limo involved."

She hoots in delight. "Please, *please* take a picture for me if that's the case."

"Tonight I'm meeting Alana at the Rip Tide. If you want to come," I hedge. "Our friend Jordy's reggae band is performing."

"Ahh, I can't." She appears genuinely disappointed. "Coop and I are having dinner at his uncle's place."

"Next time, then. Say hi to Levi and Tim for me." I hesitate for a beat. "And thank you again for considering me for this position, Mackenzie."

"Mac," she corrects. "We're dating twins, Genevieve. I feel like that moves us into nickname territory."

"Deal. Mac." I smile. "And you can call me Gen."

"Hey, sorry, I'm late." Alana slides across from me at the table near the small stage of the Rip Tide. Her dark-red hair cascades over one shoulder, appearing a bit tousled.

"Swear to God, if you're late because you were hooking up with Tate—"

"I wasn't," she assures me. Then she rolls her eyes. "And even if I was, you're the last person who should judge. Your love life is a series of bad decisions."

"Ouch." I grin. "But true."

As we laugh, Alana flags down a server and orders a beer. Friday nights are half-price pitchers at the Rip Tide, a deal I would've taken full advantage of not so long ago. But I'm drinking a virgin mai tai, which is damn good if I'm being honest. Who knew the taste of virgin cocktails would start growing on me.

"What's the holdup?" she asks, nodding toward the empty stage. "Weren't they supposed to go on at nine?"

"Technical difficulties." About ten minutes ago, one of Jordy's bandmates came up to the mic to make a vague announcement. Naturally, I'd texted Jordy for more details, and he admitted their steel drum player showed up with a hangover and has been puking backstage since his arrival.

"Technical difficulties?" Alana says knowingly.

"Yeah, as in, Juan is technically having difficulties not projectile-vomiting all the Jägerbombs he inhaled last night."

She gives a loud snicker, before smoothing out her rumpled hair. "Sorry I look like a scrub. I came straight from the club. I was caddying today and it was so windy. I didn't have an elastic, so my hair was blowing all over the place."

I wrinkle my forehead. "I didn't know you were working at the country club again. What happened to the receptionist gig at the *Avalon Bee*?"

"I'm doing both." She rubs her temples, visibly tired. "I'm saving up for a new car because old Betsy's engine is finally threatening to give out for good. So I called my old boss at The Manor and she gave me a few shifts a week over there. I might be landing a better gig, though—some lady at the club approached me about possibly working as her au pair for the rest of the summer. I guess their current one just up and quit."

"An au pair? You realize that's just a fancy word for nanny, right? Also, you hate kids," I remind her, then snicker at the thought of Alana wrangling a bunch of screaming kids into a minivan. She'd kill them in two days, tops.

"Nah, I can tolerate kids. What I *can't* tolerate is caddying for one more pompous jackass. I swear, the group today had four of them and they all took turns offering to buy me expensive shit in exchange for sex." She snorts. "One said he'd settle for a handy in the bathroom, which was sweet of him."

"Gross." I take a sip of my drink. "Speaking of career changes, I had a job interview today with Mackenzie."

"Yeah? How'd that go?"

"Good, I think. She said she'll be in touch once she's done interviewing all the candidates."

After our server drops off Alana's beer, she clinks her bottle against my glass. "Cheers, babe. Glad you're home."

"Glad to be home."

"Did you end up reaching Heidi? Her phone kept going to voicemail when I called."

A sigh slips out. "She's hanging out with my brother tonight. I think they're watching a movie at his place with Kellan serving as third wheel."

"Kinky."

"Please don't ever say the word *kinky* when we're discussing two of my brothers. Thank you."

Alana snorts. "I can't believe she's still dating Jay. No offense, but Heidi eats guys like him for breakfast."

"I know, right? But hey, it seems to be working. I guess opposites really do attract."

We both wince when the screech of microphone feedback pierces through the low murmur of voices in the dive bar. Goodbye, eardrums. Turning to the stage, I see the keyboardist adjusting his mic, while Jordy settles on a stool with his guitar. The other band members take the stage, including a very pale Juan, who staggers toward his drum.

Alana cackles. "Ten bucks says he turns green and runs off the stage after three songs."

"I say he only lasts two."

"Deal."

We're both wrong. Halfway through the first song—a pretty good Bob Marley cover—poor Juan gags, slaps a hand over his mouth, and practically dives backstage. Laughter breaks out in the bar, along with several loud whistles and some applause.

"Looks like we got a bird down," Mase, the smooth-voiced lead singer, drawls into the mic. "But don't you worry, my little pelicans, we're gonna keep chirping without him."

Did I mention Jordy's band is called Three Little Birds? Without fail, every one of their sets involves an obscene amount of bird references and incredibly unfunny fowl puns.

"Hey, girlies," says a familiar voice, and then our friend Lauren sidles up to us. She leans down to smack a kiss on my cheek. "We still on for lunch next week?" she asks me.

"Absolutely. It's been ages since we had a proper catch-up." We've known Ren since grade school, but she's been joined at the hip with Wyatt these past few years. She's one of those chicks who disappears when she has a boyfriend and then comes slinking back whenever they're on a break. Or over for good, which seems to be the case this time.

Still, Ren's good people. She's hilarious and always has your back.

Which is why I'm slightly confused by Alana's reaction to our friend. After a lackluster hello, Alana busies herself by studying the label on her bottle, as if she's never actually read the ingredients in a Corona before and *must* know what they are. Right now.

It doesn't take long to figure out what's what, though.

"I hear you've been spending a lot of time with Wyatt," Ren

says to Alana. Her tone has gone frosty, but she's still got a smile pasted on.

"Well, yeah, we're friends," Alana answers. Her tone has dropped several degrees too.

Ren pauses thoughtfully. "Friends, huh."

"Yes, Ren. We're friends." Alana gives her a pointed look. "So, please, just chill, alright? It's not like we suddenly developed some random friendship after you guys broke up. I've known him since kindergarten."

The brunette nods a few times, briskly. "Uh-huh. I know you guys are friends. But the thing is, you were never the kind of friends who crashed at each other's places or lay on the beach stargazing at two in the fucking morning."

Uh-oh. What on earth has Alana gotten herself into?

I'm the one who's now fascinated with her beverage. My gaze drops to my glass as I pretend I'm seeing ice cubes for the very first time.

Alana quirks up a brow. "You spying on us now, Lauren?"

Ren's jaw tightens. "No. But I was with Danny yesterday, and he said he took a date to the boardwalk the other night and saw you and Wyatt on the beach. And then last week, Shari was driving past your house at like five in the morning and saw Wyatt's truck parked outside. So . . ." Ren trails off deliberately, waiting for Alana to fill in the blanks.

But Ren ought to know better. Alana is not and has never been one to explain herself. She simply stares at Ren as if to say, *are you done?*

On the stage, Mase is singing an original song about a young couple having sex on the beach at dawn while seagulls squawk overhead.

Despite my better sense, I get involved. "Come on, Ren, you

know it's not like that with them." Or is it? Truthfully, I have no idea what Alana's up to. She insists she's not hooking up with Wyatt, but who knows with that one.

"*Do* I know that?" Ren bites out, voicing my own doubts. "Alana sure as shit isn't denying it."

"Because she doesn't feel she needs to defend herself over an accusation so ridiculous," I respond with confidence I'm not sure I should have. "She and Wyatt aren't hooking up. They're friends. Friends go to the beach together. Sometimes they get drunk and crash at each other's houses. Big deal."

"Are you kidding me, Gen? You of all people should be backing me up right now." Ren gapes at me. "You used to cut a bitch for even looking at Evan. There was one time you didn't speak to Steph for days after she kissed him in a game of spin the bottle."

"Well, I was young and stupid back then," I say lightly.

"Oh, really?" she challenges. "So you're saying you wouldn't care if one of your friends was taking moonlit strolls on the beach with Evan?"

"Wouldn't bat an eyelash," I say, shrugging. "He might be my ex, but I don't own him. He's allowed to have friends, and it's perfectly cool if he's friends with my friends."

A smug gleam lights Ren's eyes. "Yeah? Then I guess you won't mind if I ask him to dance."

Ask him to what? But she's already gone, sauntering off toward—

Evan.

He'd just entered the dimly lit bar with Tate and their buddy Chase in tow.

As always, he senses my presence before our gazes even meet. His shoulders tense, chin shifting to the side before his head follows suit. And then those magnetic dark eyes lock onto mine and I can feel the change in the air. The electricity.

I'm helpless to stop the rush of heat that fills my body and tingles between my legs. Evan looks good enough to eat. Dark-green cargo pants encase his long legs. A white band shirt stretches across his broad chest. I squint in the darkness and realize it's one of Jordy's shirts, with the Three Little Birds name and trademark logo scrawled on the front. His hair's swept back from his chiseled face, emphasizing those gorgeous, masculine features. It's infuriating. Why does he have to be so hot?

Ren wasn't making idle threats. Her curvy frame sashays toward my ex-boyfriend, and she takes his hand and gives it a teasing tug. I can't hear what she's saying to him, but it earns her a lopsided smile and a nod of surrender, as Evan allows her to drag him to the dance floor.

"Bitch," I growl under my breath.

Alana barks out a laugh.

"Shut it," I order, pointing a finger at her. "You're the reason she's out there proving a point."

And Ren's definitely making a statement. As the sultry reggae beat thuds in the bar, she loops her arms around Evan's neck and starts moving to the beat.

I breathe through my nose and pretend I don't care that Evan's hands are resting on another woman's hips. In his defense, he seems to be trying to keep at least a foot of distance between their bodies. And he doesn't look very comfortable. But still. He could've said no.

Wearing identical looks of amusement, Tate and Chase wander over to our table. I notice Alana stiffen at Tate's approach. They greet each other with nods, as if they're complete strangers—when we all know they've been sleeping together for months now.

"What's going on there?" Tate nods his blond head toward the dance floor.

"Ren's pissed at me so she's retaliating by pissing off Gen,"

Alana explains, then takes a long swig of beer, draining the rest of the bottle.

"How does that make any sense?" Chase looks confused.

"It doesn't," I grind out through clenched teeth. My fists are clenched too, because Ren's hands are veering dangerously close to Evan's ass. Would I be breaking my good girl vows if I marched over there and dragged her away from him by the hair? Probably.

Evan seeks out my eyes over Ren's shoulder, frowning slightly when he discerns my expression. Yeah, he knows my feelings on this matter. I've never been good at hiding my jealousy.

"Gonna grab drinks," Tate says. He nudges Alana's arm, then gestures to her empty bottle. "Want a refill?"

"Nah. Thanks, though." To my surprise, Alana slides out of her chair. "Gen and I were about to take off. We're meeting Steph."

I don't call her out on the lies. Frankly, I wouldn't mind getting out of here too. Before I do something I'm going to regret. It's taking all my willpower not to rip Ren away from Evan and fuck him right there in front of everyone to stake my claim. And that's terrifying to me. He's not mine anymore. I have no claims on him, and these raw, visceral emotions he evokes in me are too overwhelming.

"Yeah." I stand up and touch Chase's arm. "Would you tell Jordy we had to duck out early, but that he totally crushed it tonight?"

"Sure thing," Chase says easily.

"Alana—" Tate starts, then stops abruptly. His blue eyes cloud over for a second before taking on a careless veil. "Enjoy the rest of your night."

"You too."

Alana and I practically sprint out of the bar. I feel Evan's gaze boring a hole into my back as we flee.

"Are you going to explain what that was all about?" I grumble as we step into the warm night breeze.

Alana just sighs. "I don't want him to think we're together, so every now and then I remind him by being a bitch."

I nod slowly. "Fine. And Wyatt? You going to tell me what the hell is happening there?"

Her expression darkens. "I told you before, there's nothing happening except that he thinks he has a crush on me."

"Maybe he does."

"He doesn't," she says flatly. "We've been friends forever, and he doesn't know what he's fucking talking about."

In other words, *back off.* So I do. I don't press her, and in return she doesn't press me about what's happening between me and Evan. Not that I would have been able to answer that question. My feelings for Evan Hartley have always been far too complicated to articulate.

Alana and I part ways. Ten minutes later, I'm pulling into my driveway at home when my phone buzzes. I fish it out of the cup holder and check the screen.

Evan: *Why'd you run off?*

Sighing, I tap out a quick response.

Me: *Alana wasn't in the mood for Tate.*

The urge to type a follow-up makes my fingers itch. I try to resist it and fail.

Me: *And I wasn't in the mood to watch you rubbing up all over Ren.*

Evan: *Ha! She was rubbing up all over me. I was an innocent bystander.*

Me: *I'm sure it was torture for you.*

Evan: *It was. Whenever there's a chick grinding up on me, my poor dick yells at me and demands to know why that chick isn't you.*

My cheeks feel warm all of a sudden. He's not the most poetic man out there, but he does have a way with words. And those words never fail to turn me on.

Me: *I thought you were reformed. "We're not having sex, yada yada."*
Evan: *I didn't say we were going to have sex. Just that my dick misses you.*
Me: *You still with Ren?*
Evan: *No, she wandered off the moment she realized she didn't have an audience anymore. Just chilling with the boys now.*

There's a short delay. Then:

Evan: *We still on for next weekend?*

This is my chance to back out. To say, "You know what, I changed my mind about the whole wooing thing. Let's just try to be friends."
What I say instead is:

Me: *Yes.*

CHAPTER 19

EVAN

Wyatt taps two fingers on the kitchen table. Cooper also checks after the turn. I'm sitting on a possible jack-high straight, but I've got a fairly good idea that Tate's got the king, and I'm not about to blow my stack to see the river. I check.

"Tate, it's your call, hurry up," Wyatt shouts.

"He checks," Coop says, huffing as he peeks at his cards again, like they've changed since he looked at them twenty seconds ago.

"Yeah, I bet your pair of threes says he checks."

"Then you should have raised," Coop tells Wyatt, getting irritated. "Let's see that king already." At that, Wyatt shakes his head with a knowing smile. Because Coop is a poor sport and it's sort of a running gag at this point.

When we were kids, he'd steal from the bank in Monopoly and throw a fit when he was losing. After numerous tantrums, we started egging him on for fun just to see the fireworks. Really, it's one of the few things that keeps poker interesting when I'm playing my brother. Play with anyone long enough and there ceases to be any mystery left. With twins, it's worse. I might as well be staring at his cards. We can't bluff each other.

"Tate, what the hell?" Wyatt yells. "I'm about to divvy up your chips."

"Coming," he calls from the garage, where we keep the drink coolers.

"I check," Chase says, skipping Tate.

"And dealer checks." Our old high school buddy Luke burns one card off the top of the deck and turns the next faceup on the table. "Queen of clubs. Possible straight, possible royal flush on the board."

"Oh, come on. That's not cool." Tate comes in with his arms full and sets several beers on the kitchen counter. "I was going to raise."

Coop and I smirk at each other across the table. He definitely has the king. We both fold out of turn.

"Yeah, screw you both," Tate says, watching his best hand of the night go belly up.

"Where'd you go? Milwaukee?" Wyatt reaches out an impatient hand for his beer. "Or did you have to brew them yourself?"

"Next time you can get your own damn drink."

It's boys' night at our house, a usual poker game we host every month or so. Enough time for the guys to replenish their wallets after the cash Coop and I took off them the game before. You'd think they'd catch on that the odds are stacked against them. Yet every month, here they are, swimming upstream and right into the bear's mouth.

The rest of the hand quickly plays out, with Tate taking a small pot as everyone either folds or calls. Hardly worth the excellent hand. I almost feel bad for the guy. Almost.

"You gonna have the boat ready for tomorrow?" Danny glances at Luke for an answer, while Tate deals the next hand. Danny's another friend from high school, a tall ginger who works with Tate at the yacht club as a sailing instructor.

"We put it on the water this morning." Luke sighs. "The thing's more duct tape than fiberglass at this point, but it'll float."

"Think you'll try to stay on the race route this time?" Coop glances at his cards, then tosses his chips in for the small blind.

The big blind falls to me this time. Peeping my cards, I luck out with a pair of nines. I can work with that.

"Let me ask you something," Danny says, popping the cap on another beer. "When the teenage girl on the Jet Ski had to tow your sad little dinghy back to the dock, did your balls physically recede back into your body, or just fall off altogether?"

Luke flicks a bottle cap that smacks him between the eyes. "Ask your mom. They were in her mouth last night."

"Dude." Danny deflates, his expression sad. "That's not cool. My dad's in the hospital. He has to have hernia surgery from railing your sister last night."

"Whoa." Luke flinches, staring horrified at Danny. "Too far, man. That's messed up."

"What, how is that different?"

They go on like that, occasionally remembering to call or raise as Tate lays down the flop then the turn. Meanwhile no one is noticing I'm running up on a full house. Easy money.

"I'm racing tomorrow," I say casually, raising the pot again.

"Wait, what?" Cooper arches an eyebrow at me. "In the regatta?"

I shrug while the guys call my bet to see the river. "Yeah. Riley mentioned it sounded like fun, so I put our names in."

"Riley?" Tate asks blankly.

"His Little Brother," Chase supplies.

"You guys have another brother?"

"No, nimrod." Chase shakes his head. "His Little Brother, like that charity thing."

"Where did you get a boat?" Tate demands, dealing out the river card. And there's my flush.

"Weird Pete had one at the yard," I tell him, watching everyone limp into the pot. "Some guy stopped paying rent a few months ago, so it's been sitting around."

"You do realize you don't know anything about sailing, right?" Coop's been paying attention, though, and he quietly folds.

"I watched a couple videos. Anyway, Riley can sail. How hard can it be?"

The regatta is an annual event in the bay. It's a short course, the entrants a fairly even mix of tourists and locals sailing two-man crews on little boats. Some of the guys have competed for years, but this will be my first time. While I warned him we might be lucky to finish at all, Riley seemed stoked on the idea when I brought it up. I figured I ought to start relating to what he's into if I'm going to take this Big Brother thing seriously.

"Welp," Danny says with a self-assured grin. "Good luck with that."

I win the pot with little trouble, the guys all looking at the table like they blacked out for the last ten minutes, uncertain how they let me run away with that one. Poker's as much a game of misdirection as anything else.

"I hope Arlene can come out for the race." It's Cooper's turn to deal. He tosses the cards at us while peering at me sideways. "I'm sure she'd hate to miss your big day."

"Eat me." My cards are trash. Best I can hope for is to pick up a flop pair.

Luke tucks his cards away like they tried to bite him. "Who's Arlene?" he asks.

My brother grins broadly. "Evan's got a stalker."

"Jealous," I answer.

Cooper continues, chuckling to himself. "Old lady from the nursing home got his number somehow and calls him at all hours. She's smitten."

"You should hit that." Tate chucks his empty beer bottle in the garbage can and is rewarded with a glare from Cooper when we hear it shatter. "Old broads put out."

"First, gross," I say, stunned as I find myself with three of a kind when Cooper deals the flop. "Second, I've taken a new vow of abstinence."

Wyatt snorts. "Come again?"

"Not anytime soon," Cooper answers, swallowing a laugh. Child.

"You got the clap or something?" Danny gets some bright idea to steal this pot and splashes it with an overaggressive raise that says he's working on a full house.

"No." I roll my eyes. "Call it a spiritual cleanse."

Tate coughs out a "horseshit" while folding.

"I say Evan doesn't make it one week." Danny throws a ten-dollar bill on the table. Dick.

"I'll take that action," Coop scoops up the bill, adding his own to it. "Anyone say five days?"

"I got five." Tate slaps down his money.

"Wait, does the stranger count?" Wyatt makes a jerking motion in the air with his left hand.

"You offering?" I wink at him.

He flips up his middle finger, then places his ten-dollar bet that I won't last forty-eight hours. My friends are supreme jackasses.

We keep playing. A few beers in now, everyone's playing with one eye closed, fast and loose with their chips. Which is fine by me, as I take nearly three hands in a row.

"So Mac went to pick up Steph for brunch the other day," Cooper says, contemplating his cards. "Said your car was outside in the same place it was parked the night before." He aims the accusation at Tate. "What's up with you and Alana?"

Tate shrugs while pretending to count his chips. "We hook up sometimes. It's not serious. Just great sex."

It's been "not serious, great sex" for a while now. Long enough that some people might start mistaking habit for addiction. And addiction for commitment. Which is to say, if Tate's not careful, he'll find himself settling down whether he realizes it or not. It's uncertain, at this point, whether he's given any thought to the idea beyond the special kind of denial that is friends with benefits. Cooper found himself in a similar trap last year, which damn near split our crew right down the middle when it looked like him and Heidi were headed for war. Thankfully, they called a cease-fire before more damage was done.

Then again, there's a lot to be said for great sex. Gen and I have great sex. Phenomenal, even. The kind of sex that makes a guy forget about promises and good behavior. But for the time being, good behavior is my creed. I made a commitment to Gen, and I want to show her I can be trusted to keep my dick in my pants. It'll be worth it. Eventually. Or so I hope, anyway.

"Of course it's not serious," Wyatt says to Tate. "Alana's just toying with you, bro. Like a lion playing with its dinner. She gets off on it." I don't miss the sharpness to his tone.

Neither does Tate. But rather than confront Wyatt about whatever bug crawled up his ass, Tate throws me under the bus instead. "If you wanna talk about chicks who get off on games, why don't you ask Evan over here about him dirty dancing with your ex last night?"

Asshole. I shoot Tate a glare before turning to reassure Wyatt. "It was only dancing, minus the dirty. Ren's just a friend, you know that."

Luckily, Wyatt nods, unfazed. "Yeah, she's been pulling out all the stops to get me back," he admits. "I'm not surprised to hear she's been flirting with my friends. She likes to make me jealous. Thinks it'll drive me so crazy that I'll get back with her."

Cooper lifts a brow. "But you won't?"

"Not this time," Wyatt replies. He sounds dead serious, and that gives me pause. Wyatt and Lauren's relationship had always followed a similar pattern to mine and Genevieve's. Is he really out for good? His grim expression tells me yes, yes he is.

For a moment I entertain the idea of doing the same— extracting myself from this push-and-pull routine with Gen. Saying goodbye to her, for real.

Just the thought sends a hot knife of agony directly into my heart. Even my pulse speeds up.

Yeah . . .

Not happening.

CHAPTER 20

GENEVIEVE

"Okay, I've got one," Harrison says as we walk past the crews rigging their boats. He's been at this since he picked me up this morning. "Why do they put barcodes on the side of Norwegian ships?"

"Why?"

"So when they return to port, they can be Scandinavian." He beams, so proud of his latest dad joke.

"You should be ashamed of yourself." I don't know where my life took a turn off the misspent youth, coming-of-age CW drama and wound up stranded inside a Hallmark movie, but this must be what blondes feel like every day.

This Sunday morning date is so wholesome it's almost surreal. Harrison brought me out to the marina to watch the regatta. It's a mild, clear, sunny day with a steady breeze—perfect sailing weather. I inhale the scents of ocean air and sugary confections from the carts set up along the boardwalk selling cotton candy and funnel cakes.

"No, wait," he says, laughing happily. "Here's a good one. So one night, there are two ships caught in a storm. A blue ship, and a red ship. Tossed in the wind and rain, the ships can't see each other. Then a rogue wave throws the vessels crashing into each other.

The ships are destroyed. But when the storm clears, what does the moonlight reveal?"

I suppose I'm a glutton for punishment, because as torturously unfunny as his jokes are, I like how excited he gets to tell them. "I don't know, what?"

"The crew was marooned."

Wow. "You talk to your mother with that mouth?"

He just laughs again. He's got those damn khakis on, paired with a tourist-dad button-down shirt. The kind of guy I'd have been making fun of while I sat with my friends smoking weed under the pier. Now here I am, one of the yuppie tools. It doesn't feel as dirty as I'd imagined.

"Have you ever entered this race?" he asks me.

I nod. "A few times, actually. Alana and I placed twice."

"That's awesome."

He insists we stop for lemon slushes, then carries them both because they're melting quick and overflowing a little, and he doesn't want any to drip on my dress. Just another reminder that he's far too nice for someone who once stole a girl's bike to jump it off a collapsed bridge and lost it down the river.

"I took a sailing lesson one time," he confesses as he leads me to a decent viewing position along the railing. "Wound up hanging overboard by my ankle."

"Were you hurt?" I ask, taking back my slush because I'm far less concerned than he is about getting sticky.

"No, just a little bruised." He smiles behind his sunglasses, in that cheerful secrets-of-the-universe way of his that makes me feel bitter and empty. Because people this happy and content must know something the rest of us don't. Either that, or they're faking it. "Lucky for me, there was a resourceful twelve-year-old girl on board who managed to pull me out of the water before I got to experience keelhauling."

It isn't his fault, though, that he makes me feel this way. Harrison is a catch. Well, except that he's a cop, and I'm a fortunate favor or two from being a convict. But the real issue? No matter how hard I try, I can't muster up a sexual attraction to him. Not even a warm, fuzzy, platonic spark. A fact I'm sure isn't lost on him, because for all his small-town charms, he isn't a dope. I've seen the wistfulness that turns to disappointment in his eyes, the slight falter in his smile, at the knowledge that while we get along and have a nice time together, we're not quite a love story. Nevertheless, until I have a reason otherwise, there's no harm in giving this a shot and letting him grow on me. Water and sunlight work wonders on plants, so why not us?

"Sailing's fun, but honestly, it's more work than it's worth," I grumble. "All that running around, pulling, and winding for a few bursts of speed. You spend the whole time making the thing go, you don't get to sit back and enjoy it."

"Sure, but it's romantic. A few ropes and sheets against the forces of nature. Harnessing the wind. Nothing between you and the sea but ingenuity and luck." His tone is animated. "Like the very first navigators who saw the new world as it appeared over the horizon."

"Did you get that out of a movie or something?" I tease.

Harrison offers a contrite grin. "History Channel."

A voice over a loudspeaker announces a ten-minute warning for boats to approach the starting line. On the water, masts tilt and sway, jockeying their way into position.

"Of course," I say, because as terrible as it is, I do appreciate his particular sense of humor. "I bet you stayed up all night watching an eight-part Ken Burns documentary on the history of nautical expedition."

"Actually, it was a program about how Christopher Columbus was an alien."

"Right." I nod, smothering a laugh. "A classic."

I'm finally starting to warm up to this date when I make the mistake of glancing over my shoulder. A familiar face meets my gaze as she leads her four kids away from the fried Oreo stand. Kayla Randall.

Shit. We're both frozen in trepidation. The eye contact lasted too long to blink away and pretend we didn't see each other. The moment has been acknowledged and is now begging for a resolution.

"What's wrong?" Harrison says in concern, noticing my apparent apprehension.

"Nothing." I hand him my lemon slush. "I see someone I need to talk to. Would you mind? I'll just be a minute."

"No problem."

Drawing a breath, I walk toward Kayla, who watches me while she makes a futile attempt to shove napkins in her kids' hands.

"Hi," I say. A wholly inadequate greeting under the circumstances. "Can we talk for a minute?"

Kayla appears rightfully uncomfortable. "I suppose we better." She shifts her feet. "But I've got the kids right now and—"

"I can watch them," comes Harrison's helpful voice. To Kayla's brood he asks, "You guys want to get a closer look at the boats?"

"Ya!" they shout in unison.

God bless this guy. I swear, I've never met anyone so agreeable.

Harrison leads the kids to the railing to watch the boats getting in position. As I'm left alone with Kayla, a familiar nervous sense of anticipation builds in my gut. It's like hanging my toes over the edge of the roof with a backyard full of chanting drunks standing around the swimming pool with their cameras on me. For some people, the fear makes their stomachs weak. But I find fear is a lens. It focuses me, if I aim it right.

"I'm glad you found me," Kayla says before I can arrange my thoughts. We stand in the shadow of a shop awning while she removes her sunglasses. "For a while, I was relieved when you left town."

"I understand. Please know—"

"I'm sorry," she interjects, stunning the words from my lips. "I've had a lot of time to think about that night, and I realize now I overreacted. That I was more angry at having to face the truth than I was with you—which was that Rusty was a bastard."

"Kayla." I want to tell her I was out of my mind for barging into someone's home, drunk and hysterical. That being right didn't make it right. She's kinda stealing my wind here.

"No, the problems were there for a long time. He was emotionally and verbally abusive. But it took you showing up to put that reality into perspective. To make me accept that it was not normal to live the way we were." Grief flickers in her eyes.

"I'm so sorry," I admit. It was an open secret that Randall was a creep and a bad cop, but I had no idea it was so bad at home. In a way, I feel worse now. I feel sorry for Kayla and the kids, and what was surely an ugly aftermath that I invited into their home. "I had no right to barge in like that. The way I behaved that night was . . . I'm so embarrassed."

"No, it's okay."

She squeezes my shoulder, reminding me that for a long time, we were sort of friends. I'd been their babysitter for years. I used to chat with Kayla on the couch after she'd get home from work. I would tell her things I couldn't share with my mom, about boys and school and teenage stuff. She was like an aunt or a big sister.

"I'm glad it was you," Kayla adds. "Things weren't good between me and Rusty for a long time, but my friends were so afraid of, I don't know, pissing him off or getting involved, they didn't want to tell me the truth. And the truth was, I needed to get out of there. I needed to get my kids out of that situation. Because of you, I finally did. And we're much happier for it. Honestly."

It's a relief to hear, although unexpected. I've spent the better part of the last year tied up in knots over the guilt and remorse for how I behaved. I'd uprooted my entire life to get away from the crippling embarrassment. And this whole time, I was hiding from my own shadow.

I can't help but think what might've been different now if I'd stayed. If I had the courage to get myself cleaned up without having to change zip codes. Did I need to remove temptation to get sober, or had I underestimated myself? Had I left to escape my worst instincts, or because I was afraid how everyone would react?

We both glance behind us at the sound of Kayla's kids laughing and squealing in delight. Harrison is probably enthralling them with a magic trick. Some more of his world-renowned comedy stylings.

"He's good with them," she remarks, putting her sunglasses back on.

Of course he is. Harrison has a natural ease with just about everyone, a sincere goodness that disarms people. Especially with kids, who see everything.

She tips her head curiously. "That your new boyfriend?"

"No. It's only been a couple dates."

Watching Harrison with the kids, I suddenly hear Evan's voice in my head. I flash back to the night at our spot, the two of us naked under the stars while he mused about kids and a family. The preposterous notion of Evan as a stay-at-home dad, his motorcycle rusting in the yard. Sure.

Yet as difficult as that image is to conjure, it's not entirely unattractive.

As Kayla and I part with a hug and no hard feelings, the mayor of Avalon Bay takes the mic on a small platform in front of the marina to announce the race participants. I half tune him out, at least until a familiar name greets my ears.

"—and Evan Hartley, sailing with Riley Dalton."

My head jerks up, and I nearly choke on the melted remnants of my lemon slush at the sound of Evan's name. I would think I'm hallucinating if not for Harrison raising an eyebrow at the same time.

Huh.

I wonder if Evan remembers he can't sail.

CHAPTER 21

EVAN

"Mistakes were made."

Riley laughs.

"That much is clear. It may have started when I steered us into another boat coming off the starting line. It may have been when we failed to make the first turn around the buoy. Who's to say, really?"

A hysterical noise escapes his throat, a cross between a snort and a howl. Riley hasn't stopped laughing since we rammed the dock. No, not rammed. We *nudged* the dock. Rammed would suggest a great rate of speed, which I don't think we achieved during the entire race.

Sopping wet, I wring out my T-shirt over the railing of the boardwalk while the trophy presentation kicks off at the other end of the marina.

"Dude," he chokes out between giggles. "We failed miserably."

"Not true," I protest. "There was a high point there when we managed to right the ship and not entirely capsize."

He's still laughing as we make our way to the crowd gathered around the platform, cheering for the winners and politely congratulating all those who placed. I'm just glad we're not getting stuck with a bill for salvaging the boat off the bottom of the bay.

As it turns out, I can't sail for shit. It's hard, actually. So many ropes and pulleys and winches, who the fuck knew. I thought you just put the sail up and steered, but apparently there's such a thing as oversteering, and steering left to go right for some stupid reason. Almost the second the starting gun went off, we were discombobulated. Came in dead last after tipping the boat and nearly going in the drink.

But Riley's still laughing, absolutely stoked on the whole ordeal. Mostly at my suffering, I think, but that's okay. The kid had a great time, which was the whole damn point to begin with.

"There's my guy." His aunt Liz, a petite woman with pretty brown eyes and long hair tied in a low ponytail, finds us among the spectators and gives him a hug. "You have fun?"

"It was a blast," Riley says. "For a minute there, I thought we were goners."

"Oh," she says, covering her alarm with a laugh. "Well, I'm glad you both survived."

"Don't worry. I'm a much better swimmer than I am a sailor. I wouldn't let your kid drown." I say this, of course, shirtless, with a full back of tattoos. Lady probably thinks I look more like Riley's drug dealer than his role model.

"Can I have some money for the hot dog stand?" Riley pleads. "I'm starving."

With an indulgent smile, Riley's aunt hands him a few bucks and sends him off.

"Trust me," I assure her, now concerned that putting a kid's life in mortal peril might reflect poorly on my participation in the program. "He wasn't in any danger. Just a minor mishap."

Liz waves off my concern. "I'm not worried. He hasn't had this much fun in a long time."

I think about the Riley I met that first afternoon—the shy, quiet teen who spent the first couple hours staring at his feet and mumbling to himself. Cut to today, where he's shouting commands at me and taking snarky jabs at my lack of nautical prowess. I don't know if it's what the program had in mind, but I'd call that improvement. For our relationship, at least.

"He's a cool kid. Who knows, maybe he can teach me how to sail and we can try again next year." I surprise myself when it occurs to me what I've just said. I hadn't given much thought to how long this arrangement would last. But now that I give it some consideration, I couldn't imagine Riley and I not being pals a year from now.

"You know, I think you mean that." Liz studies me, and I can't help wondering what she sees. "I do appreciate everything you've done for him. I know it's only been a couple weeks, but you're starting to mean a lot to Riley. You're good for him."

"Yeah, well . . ." I slide my sunglasses on and make another attempt at wringing out my wet shirt. "He's not a total asshole, so . . ."

She laughs at that, letting me off the hook. I've never been great at taking compliments. Being the consummate screwup doesn't often give a lot of reason for praise, so I guess you can say I haven't had much practice. And yet somehow, this kid turns out to be one of the few things I've gotten right. I've seen him several times a week for more than two weeks, and despite all odds, I haven't screwed him up yet.

"I need to get him home so I can head to work," Riley's aunt says. "But I'd like it if you came by for dinner one night. The three of us. Maybe next week?"

The fleeting notion of what would be in some alternate universe if Liz took a shine to me skips through my brain. Until I glance over her shoulder to spot black hair and long, tan legs, and the universe—*this* universe—reminds me there's only one woman for me on this plane.

Gen is strutting down the boardwalk in some girly white dress that gets my blood hot. Because she's trying. She's trying to impress this dweeb, to look the part by dulling herself to his milquetoast sensibilities. She's grinding down the sharp edges that make her everything that's fierce and dangerous and extraordinary, and I won't stand for it.

"Sure," I tell Liz, while my attention remains elsewhere. "Let's do that. Tell Riley bye for me? Just saw a friend I need to say hi to."

I jog through the crowd, dodging sweaty tourists and sunburnt children to catch up to Gen. Then, I slow down and manage to get in front of her and the guy, because now she'll have to notice me and say something, alleviating all guilt of crashing her date for a second time.

"Evan?"

I feign surprise as I turn around. "Oh, hey."

I can sense her rolling her eyes behind those reflective sunglasses. She smirks and shakes her head. "Oh, hey? You get you're terrible at this, right?"

Sometimes I forget I've never been able to put one over on her a day in my life. "Yeah, you know, I'd love to hang around, but I'm kinda busy, so . . ."

"Uh-huh."

With my shirt slung over my shoulder, I nod at Deputy Dolittle in his standard-issue Tommy Bahama. "Nice shirt."

"Stop," Gen warns, though she's still smiling. Because she knows, dude walks around dressed like that, he's asking for it. "What do you want?"

"Hey, there's no hard feelings, right?" I offer my hand to the deputy. "Truce?"

"Sure." He grips my hand with what must be all the force he can muster. I almost feel bad for the guy. Almost. "Bygones."

"Evan . . ." She cocks her head at me, impatient.

"You look nice."

"Don't do that."

I fight a grin. "I can't give you a compliment?"

"You know what I mean." She likes it. The amusement in her voice betrays her words.

"You do look nice." I'll always prefer the real Gen, the girl in a pair of cutoff shorts and a loose tank top over a bikini. Or nothing at all. But that doesn't mean I can't appreciate this little white slinky number that, in the right light, I can all but see through against her tan skin. "Big plans today?"

"We saw your race," the guy says. He could tell me his name a thousand times, and it still wouldn't stick. I could cover my eyes right now and have no idea what the guy looks like. He should have gone into the CIA or something; a dude this incapable of leaving an impression would do well, I imagine.

"It was, um, eventful." Gen tries and fails to pretend she isn't checking me out.

"These things are always so boring," I tell her. "Thought we'd add a little drama."

"Is that what that was? Drama?"

"Rather be last than boring."

Even behind those sunglasses, I feel her dragging her eyes down my bare chest. The way her teeth tug at the inside of her lip conjures all sorts of images in my head. I want to shove my fingers in her hair, put her up against the wall, and make this guy watch her melt against my lips. Whatever ideas she's got about playing the field or making me jealous, we both know he can't kiss her like I can. He'll never know her mouth, her body, the way I do.

"Why don't you join us for lunch?" the chaperone interjects.

Even Gen looks like she'd forgotten he was there. She startles, glancing over at him. "No, you don't have to do that."

"Lunch sounds great," I say cheerfully.

"Seriously?" This time her exasperation is directed at him. "Harrison. We had plans."

Surprisingly, he doesn't budge. "I insist."

Oh, buddy. I don't know what he thinks he's playing at, but there's no scenario where he puts Gen and me in a room together and it goes in his favor.

"Fine. I'm going to the restroom first." She points a finger at my chest. "Behave. And put a shirt on."

Gen leaves us standing outside a tacky gift shop. I'm content to keep my thoughts to myself, but it's Officer Chuckles who speaks up.

"She's a special woman," he starts.

That he talks about her like he knows her at all grates my nerves. "Yep."

"This sounds silly, but even back in high school I had a crush on her."

Back in high school we were making out in the yearbook darkroom while skipping third period.

"I know what this is," he announces, squaring up to me like he just found his balls. "You think you can intimidate me or scare me. Well, I promise it won't work."

"Dude, I don't know you." I remind myself he's a cop, and that I promised both Gen and Cooper I was done picking fights. Still, he's got to know I'm not the guy you test. "But if I were trying to scare you off, I wouldn't be shy or cute about it. I'd just do it."

"What I'm saying is, I like Genevieve. I intend to keep dating her. And nothing you do is going to change that. Keep crashing our dates, if you want. It won't make a difference."

I have to hand it to the guy. Even when putting himself between me and what's mine, he does it with a Boy Scout smile. Almost polite. Civil.

But it doesn't erase the fact that I'd step over his bleeding carcass to get to her. However long it takes for Gen to come back to me, I've already won this fight. He just hasn't figured it out yet.

"Then by all means," I say with a half smile. "Let the best man win."

CHAPTER 22

GENEVIEVE

These days, not much surprises me. For two months now, my life has become a predictable routine of the nine-to-five grind, with the occasional evening where I find a few hours to have a life. That isn't so much a complaint as an observation, because I asked for this. I went to great pains to tame my wilder tides.

But Evan, well, Evan Hartley still manages to surprise me. The weekend after the regatta, he picks me up for our date looking all primped and polished. He's wearing a clean white T-shirt and cargo pants without a single wrinkle in them. He even shaved—an especially rare treat. And where I expected one of his usual hair-brained schemes to get us into trouble on some ill-conceived adventure, we find ourselves sitting down to a late lunch at a modern vegan restaurant overlooking Avalon Beach.

"I have to ask," I say, enjoying the roasted eggplant pasta. "What made you decide on vegan? I can't remember the last time I've seen you eat a vegetable that wasn't wrapped in meat or cooked in animal fat."

As if to prove some point, Evan dabs the corner of his mouth with his napkin. "We're going against the grain, aren't we? I thought that was the whole point."

"I suppose." Not sure I meant we had to apply that philosophy to food, but okay.

"Clean living, Fred." Evan grins as he pops a bite of gnocchi in his mouth, then washes it down with a glass of water. He'd waved away the drink menu when we sat down. "Anyway, after our last dinner—"

"You mean my date you crashed."

"I thought I'd show you I can be civilized."

"You're not funny."

He ponders, then nods to himself. "Yes I am."

It was only a week ago when he barged his way into yet another date with Harrison at the marina, smirking and quite pleased with himself. I might muster up more annoyance if it wasn't so hard to be mad at him. With those eyes that dance with arrogance and mischief. The upturned corners of his lips that hint at secrets and whisper dares. He's impossible.

"You know this isn't what my life is now, right?" I gesture at the elegant table setting. "Dressing up in our parents' clothes, playing adult."

He snickers softly. "Not my parents."

"Or mine, but you know what I mean."

"You looked pretty comfortable in those clothes with him."

And we were having such a nice time.

I swallow a sigh. "Do you really want to talk about Harrison?"

Evan seems to consider this for a second, then dismisses the thought. "No."

"Good. Because I didn't agree to this date because I want you to be more like him. Try to remember that."

This, too, feels familiar—the somewhat adversarial rapport. Arguing for the sake of arguing because we like getting a rise out of each other. Never knowing when to quit. Wrapped up in sexual tension so that our fights become indistinguishable from flirting.

Why do I like it so much?

"Tell me this," he says roughly. "Who are you trying to be?"

Hell if I know. If I had that figured out, I wouldn't still be living at home, afraid to break it to my dad that he needs to move on without me in the family business. I wouldn't be dating one guy who I know is about as close to boyfriend material as anyone gets, while guarding myself from the million bad decisions sitting across the table.

"At the moment, shedding my bad girl reputation, I guess."

He nods slowly. He gets it.

And that's something I appreciate about Evan above all others—I never have to lie to him, or conceal something because I'm embarrassed about what he'd think of the truth. Whether I'm good, bad, or indifferent, he accepts me in all my iterations.

I offer a wry smile. "There're only so many times a girl can break into the waterpark after-hours to tube down the raging rapids before delinquency loses all meaning."

"I hear you. This is probably the longest I've gone without a hangover or a black eye since I was ten." He winks at me, which might as well be an invitation to throw my legs over his shoulders. Gets me every time.

"It's weird, though. Sometimes I'm out with the girls, and it's like I don't know what to do with my hands. If every instinct I have is what was getting me in trouble before, how am I supposed to know what the right ones are? What being good is supposed to look like, you know?"

"You're looking at a guy who Googled *model citizen*, okay? I've narrowed it down to this: Whatever sounds like a good idea, do the opposite."

"I'm serious," I say, flinging a sugar packet at him from the ramekin on the table. "What would you and I do on a normal date?"

"Normal?" He cocks his head at me, grinning.

"Normal for us."

"We wouldn't have left my bedroom," Evan says. Deadpan.

Well, yeah. "After that."

"Hit a bar. A party, maybe. End up in a stolen car doing laps at the old speedway until security chases us out. Getting drunk on top of the lighthouse while you suck me off."

My core clenches at the naughty suggestion. I pretend to be unaffected by hurling another sugar packet at his face. "You've given this some thought."

"Fred, this is all I think about."

He needs to stop doing that. Looking at me like he's starving, with his teeth nipping at his lower lip and those hooded eyes gleaming. It isn't fair, and I shouldn't have to put up with these conditions.

"Well, like you said, we're playing against type now, so . . ." I gulp my virgin cocktail, still expecting the burn of alcohol and left wanting. It seemed like a good idea at the time—trick my brain into believing it's getting what it wants—but the overly sweet concoction feels like sucking down a bottle of straight corn syrup. "What else you got?"

"Alright." He nods briskly, accepting the challenge. "You're on. For the rest of the night, we do the opposite of whatever our instincts tell us."

"You sure about this?" I lean in, elbows on the table. "I don't want to hear about you bailing on the idea . . ."

"I'm serious." He's got that look. A man possessed with a consuming notion. It reminds me of another thing that's always attracted me to Evan. He's shamelessly passionate. Even about the stupidest things. It's endearing. "Prepare yourself for an evening of well-mannered civility, Genevieve West."

I sputter out a laugh. "Hold on to your knickers."

"What do you think?" Evan crouches on the worn green turf beside the imitation Polynesian totem. He lays his putter on the ground, aiming the head of the club at the wooden crate labeled *dynamite*. "Take the left route around the pile of gold doubloons, yeah?"

Bending over beside him, I align my view with his. "I think that patch of old bubble gum stuck at the entrance of the mouse hole is going to give you trouble. The left fork over the ramp is a trickier shot, but once you're there, it's a cleaner descent to the hole."

"Let's go already." Behind us, a shaggy-headed kid grows testy. His friend sighs with loud impatience. "I'd like to get through this game while my clothes still fit."

Evan ignores him. Still evaluating his shot, picking leaves and bits of debris from around his golf ball. "I'm going left. I don't like the look of that turtle on the right." He gets to his feet, adjusts his stance. He takes a practice swing and then another.

"Come on!"

The club smacks the ball, launching it toward the high embankment, up and around the spilled pile of gold doubloons, where it sails straight into the rushing stream and down a waterfall. With a plop, it lands in the pool below, filled with colored golf balls like a hundred painted clams.

"After all that!" the friend heckles, while Shaggy Head guffaws loudly.

"Hey." I round on them, pointing my club. "Get fucked, shitheads."

"Whoa." The boys retreat a step with mocking expressions. "Ma'am, this is a family establishment."

I've got a mind to dangle them over the water feature, because these dudes have been getting on my nerves since the second hole, but Evan throws his arm around my shoulder to hold me back.

"Best behavior," he whispers at my ear. "Remember?"

Right. Nice young ladies don't drown little punk teenagers at the mini-golf course. "I'm cool."

"Get a handle on your chick, bro," Shaggy says.

His friend makes a taunting face. "She's crazy."

That snaps Evan's spine straight. Eyes glittering, he strides up, his fist tight around his club. He backs the kids up into the bushes as they stumble to escape him, expecting a beating.

Instead, Evan grabs a golf ball from the friend's hand and stalks back to me.

"Hey!" the kid complains.

"Consider it an asshole tax," Evan barks over his shoulder. He makes a grand show of sweeping his shoe over the ground to clear the tee for my turn. "My lady."

I fight a smile. "So chivalrous."

Then, knowing better, I hit my shot through the mouse hole, where it travels through an unseen underground passage and spits out from a canon, rather than the apparent turtle's mouth exit, and straight into the hole. Too easy.

Looking back at Evan, I see him twist his lips, cocking his head. "Cold-blooded, Fred."

At the next hole, we place a little wager on the game with the kids behind us after Evan decides to play nice and make friends. The matchup is closer than he'd like, in fact, but my hot hand keeps us up over the boys. In the end, Evan manages a clutch hole-in-one to push us over the top.

"That was decent of you." In the parking lot beside his motor-cycle, I crack open a bottle of water. The afternoon is waning into evening, but the sun is still furiously insistent. "Giving the boys their money back."

Leaning against his bike, Evan shrugs one shoulder. "Last thing I need is some irate mom hunting me down for hustling her kid, right?"

"If I didn't know better, I'd almost think you had a good time. Despite the lack of police chasing us."

He straightens, closing the small space between us. His prox-imity makes it difficult to remember why we aren't getting up to more tactile activities. I want to kiss him. Feel his hands on me. Straddle him over his bike until security chases us away.

"When are you going to accept that I'd be happy watching paint dry with you?" His voice is low, earnest.

"Challenge accepted."

We end up at one of those paint-your-own-pottery places. It also happens to be overrun with a little girl's birthday party. A dozen eight-year-olds run around while a haggard shop girl strug-gles to keep ceramic horses and knockoff Disney figures on the shelves before they topple into mounds of dust and sharp edges.

At the back of the store, Evan and I pick our table and decide on our canvases.

"I just remembered we've been here before," I inform him, pull-ing an owl off a shelf. A similar one sits in my bedroom at home.

Evan studies a giraffe. "Are you sure?"

"Yeah, we left homecoming early freshman year and wandered in because you were tripping balls and saw a dragon in the win-dow display, so you wouldn't let us go until you painted a purple dragon."

"Oh, shit," he says, backing away from the animals. "Yeah. I started freaking out because the dragon turned evil, and it was going to burn down the whole town."

I chuckle at the ridiculous memory. Turned out he'd pre-partied a little without me and consumed some pot brownies before the dance.

A sudden shriek rips through the room. The birthday girl in her crown and pink feather boa is red in the face and gesticulating wildly, her mother wide-eyed and horrified as the girl's friends cower in their seats. A tantrum poised to bubble over.

"I want the castle!" The girl fumes.

"You can have the castle, sweetie." The mom places a clearly substandard royal dwelling in front of her petulant offspring with the deliberate motions and sweaty brow of a bomb tech.

"Not that one!" The girl grabs for another child's far superior castle, which the other girl clutches, defiant. "It's my party! I want that one!"

"If I ever have a kid like that," I tell Evan, "I'm leaving it in the woods with a sleeping bag and some granola bars."

"Remind me not to leave you alone with our kids."

Casting a grin over his shoulder, Evan picks a seahorse off the shelf and strides over to the party. He gives the mom a reassuring nod then kneels in front of the angry birthday girl to ask if she'd do him the honor of an original artwork by painting the animal for him. Her bloodshot eyes and feral snarl return to a mostly human expression. She's even smiling.

Evan sits with her, talking and generally maintaining her attention, allowing the mother to take a deep breath and the other girls to go about their projects without fear of reprisal.

A half hour or so later, he rejoins me at our table, now the proud owner of the pink feather boa. Which is oddly fetching on him, for some reason.

"You're some kind of brat whisperer," I say as he takes a seat beside me.

"How do you think we've been friends for so long?"

For that I smear blue paint across his cheek. "Careful. I can do worse than throw pottery."

He flashes a crooked smile. "Don't I know it."

I'd have never thought him capable of wading into such treacherous territory and emerging unscathed. Triumphant, even. Paternal. It does something to me on a primal brain-chemistry level that I'm not entirely ready to unpack.

When this date started, I wasn't convinced we'd know how to be around each other if we weren't drunk, naked, or some variation approaching one or the other. Now, we've been at this a few hours, and I can't say I miss it. Well, I do, but not so much that I can't find enjoyment in the mundane activities of dating. Turns out there's something to be said for normal.

Leaving a while later with my new ceramic fish, we stroll the boardwalk, neither of us ready to go home but understanding the deadline fast approaching. Because once the sun sets, bad ideas come. We're creatures of habit, after all.

"You never told me," he says, reaching to hold my hand. Yet another surprise in this evening of firsts. Not that he's never held my hand before, but this feels different. It's not intentional or leading, but natural. Absent-minded. Like it's the only place our hands belong. "How'd your interview go with Mac?"

"You tell me. Did she say anything?"

"She thinks you're great. I'm more concerned how you feel. If you get the job, you two will be spending a lot of time together. That means Coop too. That means me."

The thought hasn't escaped me. Mac seems cool. It was only one meeting, but we got along well enough. Cooper, on the other hand, might be trickier. Last time we spoke, he was all but trying to run me out of town. Burrowing deeper into his inner circle is likely not going to improve that rift. But that's not what Evan's asking, not really. We both know that.

"If I get the job," I say with a poke to his chest, "that doesn't mean anything about you and me one way or another."

With that cocky grin, he doesn't break stride. "You keep telling yourself that."

Our path is interrupted by a group of old folks walking out of the ice-cream parlor. A couple ladies wave at Evan with disturbingly lewd intent. Meanwhile, a tall, gangly man whose sagging ears are racing his drooping jowls to his shoulders zeroes in on Evan.

"You," he says in a hoarse grumble. "I remember you."

Evan tugs my hand. "We better go."

"Lloyd, come on now." A man in a polo and name tag tries to coax the unruly seniors. "It's time to go."

"I'm not going anywhere." The man's cup of vanilla soft serve splatters to the ground. "That's the son of a bitch who killed my bird."

Um, *what?*

Evan doesn't give me even a second to digest that. As the elderly man launches himself at us, Evan yanks my arm and rockets us forward.

"Run!" he orders.

I'm struggling to keep my balance as Evan drags me behind him, hurtling down the boardwalk. I turn toward the wheezing exclamations at our backs to see Lloyd barreling after us. Unusually spry for a man his age, he's at a dead sprint, dodging food carts and tourists. He's got the devil in his eyes.

"This way," Evan says, pulling me to the left.

We cut down an alley between a couple of bars that leads behind the boardwalk carnival that is set up through much of the summer. We dart between a couple of midway games and through a back door, where we're promptly bombarded by a soundtrack of something I can only describe as trance music overlaid on nursery rhyme melodies with the disconcerting laughter of clowns. It's pitch-black, save for an occasional strobe light that reveals a maze of hanging painted mannequins.

"I always knew this is what I'd see before I died," I say in resignation.

Evan nods solemnly. "There are definitely dead kids walled up in here somewhere."

Catching my breath, I run a hand through my disheveled hair. "So. You killed a man's bird?"

"No, Cooper's Satan dog killed the bird. I strenuously object to any guilt by association."

"Uh-huh. And this happened how?"

Before he can answer, a shard of daylight enters the room from somewhere unseen. We both crouch, hugging the wall to avoid getting caught.

"Who's in here?" a voice shouts from the other side of the room. "We ain't open yet."

Evan puts his finger over his lips.

"You get out here, you hear me?" The angry man's demand is followed by a loud, startling crack of noise. Like a bat hitting a wall or something. "If I gotta hunt you down, I'm gonna turn your insides out."

"Oh my God," I whisper. "We have to get the hell out of here."

We feel around for the door we came through, but it's still dark and disorienting, the music and haunting laughter, and the strobe lights make the whole room appear to stutter. Practically crawling, we creep off in another direction until we find a small alcove. We stop there, listening to our pursuer's heavy footfalls.

Confined, hunted, not making a sound, Evan presses us into

the shadows of the tight corner. With his hands on my hips and his body warm against mine, I almost don't hear the nightmare soundtrack anymore. Just the sound of my own breathing in my ears. My mind trips over random thoughts and sensations. The scent of his shampoo and motorcycle exhaust. His skin. Memories of it on my tongue. His fingers.

"Don't do that," he rasps in my ear.

"What?"

"Remember."

It'd be so easy to grab handfuls of his hair and pull his lips to mine. Let him have me in this funhouse of horrors while we brace to be hacked up by Crazy Willy out there.

"We said we wouldn't," Evan reminds me, reading my mind because we've never needed words to speak to each other. "I'm trying to be a good boy, Fred."

I lick my dry lips. "Just out of curiosity, what would Bad Boy Evan do?" I ask, because apparently I'm into self-torture.

He licks his lips too. "You really want me to answer that?"

No.

Yes.

"Yes," I tell him.

Evan's palms lightly caress my hips, sending a shiver up my spine. "Bad Boy Evan would take his hand and slide it under your skirt."

To punctuate that, one big palm travels south to capture the hem of my pale-green skirt between his fingertips. He doesn't pull it up, though. Just plays with the filmy fabric, while a slight smile lifts the corners of his mouth.

"Yeah?" My voice is hoarse. "And why would he do that?"

"Because he'd want to find out how hot you were for him. How wet." He bunches the fabric between his fingers, giving a teasing tug. "And then, when he felt how bad you wanted it, he'd put his fingers inside you. Wouldn't even need to take your panties off, because Bad Girl Gen doesn't wear 'em."

I almost moan out loud.

"Then, after he made you come, he'd spin you around. Tell you to put your palms flat against the wall." Evan brings his lips close to my ear, eliciting another shiver, a flurry of them this time. "And he'd fuck you from behind until we both forgot our names."

Still smiling, he releases my skirt, which flutters down to my knees. That teasing hand glides back north, this time to cup my chin.

I stare up at him, unable to breathe. Crazy Willy's footsteps have dissipated. And the clown music has all but receded into the background of my brain. All I hear now is the pounding of my heart. My gaze is stuck on Evan's lips. The need to kiss him is powerful enough to make my knees wobble.

Feeling how unsteady I am, he lets out a husky laugh. "But we're not going to do any of that, are we?"

Despite my body screaming *please, please, please* at me, I exhale a slow breath and manage a nod. "No," I agree. "We're not going to do that."

Instead, we check that the coast is clear and then double back the way we came until we find the broken exit sign above the door. We emerge unscathed, but I can't say the same for my libido. My body is throbbing with need that borders on pain. Not putting my hands all over Evan is much, much harder than I thought it would be.

I honestly have no idea how long I'll be able to resist.

CHAPTER 23

EVAN

Come sunrise, I'm on Riley's porch with my phone to my ear. It's the fourth time in ten minutes it's gone to voicemail. I told the kid, *when I say early, I mean it.* So I jump down the steps and round the side of the tiny, pale-blue clapboard house to his bedroom window. I knock on the glass until the groggy teen pushes the blinds aside to rub his eyes at me.

I flash a grin. "Shake a leg, sunshine."

"Time is it?" His voice is muffled behind the window.

"Hurry-up time. Let's go."

When Riley had asked me to take him surfing, I'd warned him that we weren't going to mess around with crowded afternoon beaches. If he wanted to get on the water, he'd have to paddle out with the big boys. That means hitting the waves before breakfast.

I hop in Cooper's truck out front to wait for the kid. A few minutes later, I'm thinking about climbing through his window to drag him out when his aunt knocks on the passenger window.

"Morning," I greet her, turning off the radio. "I didn't wake you, did I? I'm supposed to take Riley surfing."

Wearing a zippered hoodie over a pair of scrubs, Liz glances at my surfboard in the bed of the truck. "Right, he mentioned it last night. You didn't wake me, though. I've got an early shift. He should be out in a minute." She holds up a large tray wrapped in tinfoil. "This is for you. Since we never had that dinner."

"Sorry about that." I slide across the bench seat to take the tray from her and lift up the foil. The homemade pie inside smells terrific. "I've been slammed at work."

"Hope you're not allergic to cherry."

I break off a piece of pie crust to pop in my mouth. Oh fuck, that is delicious. "What if I am?"

She grins. "Eat small bites."

"Ready!" Riley comes jogging out of the house with the screen door snapping shut behind him. He's lugging his board under his arm, with a backpack slung over his shoulder.

"Remember, you need to get some laundry done while I'm at work." Liz moves to let Riley jump in the truck as I slide back to the driver's side. "And taking some bleach to that bathtub wouldn't hurt."

"Yep, okay." He pokes his head out the window to give her a kiss on the cheek. "Call you later."

Smiling, Liz points a finger at me. "Don't drown my nephew."

I smile back. "I'll do my best."

Turns out Riley isn't half bad on a board. He's got good balance and a feel for the rhythm of the water but is just a little rough on technique. Unfortunately, the waves today aren't much worth the effort. We sit on our boards out beyond the breakers, bobbing on the swells. Even when the surfing isn't great, I'd still rather be out here than almost anywhere else.

"How'd you get better?" Riley asks as we watch the occasional intrepid rider attempt to paddle after a minor wave.

The sun at our back slowly climbs the sky, casting long orange streaks across the water. About a dozen other surfers float nearby, spread out, watching the undulating tide and hoping for something to crest.

"I just watched what the other guys did and tried to mimic them. But other than being on the water and getting tossed a lot, the thing that helped me the most was learning to control the board and my body."

"Like how?"

"Well, I swiped a piece of scrap metal pipe from a construction site and put a two-by-four over it. Sort of like a skateboard, you know? And I'd spend hours balancing on it. Learning how to shift my weight to move around. It really helped engage those muscles and train my body."

"So step one: theft. Got it."

I grin at him. "See, this is how you get me in trouble."

One zealous chick turns her board to shore and drives her arms through the water, paddling into position for what amounts to a gentle shove of a wave. Some assholes mockingly whistle after her.

"No worries," Riley says. "You won Liz over a long time ago. I think she's maybe got a little thing for you."

I'd been getting that vibe too. The guy at Big Brothers had even warned that sort of thing wasn't unheard of, but under no circumstances should I entertain the idea—if I was serious about helping my Little. Which isn't to say Liz doesn't have attractive qualities.

"Kind of got my hands full," I tell him.

He eyes me knowingly. "That girl from the boardwalk the other day?"

"Genevieve. We go way back."

Even saying her name gets my heart beating faster and fills me with anticipation. I think about her even a little, and I become impatient for the next time I can see her. I'd spent a year fighting a losing battle against this, driving myself crazy. Now she's here, never more than a few minutes away, and I still barely see her for some reason that I've yet to understand.

"Do you like the guys your aunt dates?" I ask Riley.

He shrugs. "Sometimes. Really, she doesn't get out much because she works all the time."

"What's her type?"

"I don't know." He shakes his head, laughing at me. "Boring dudes, I guess. When she's off work, she just wants to order takeout and watch movies. Relax, you know? I don't think she'd tolerate anyone with too much energy, even if she thinks it seems like a good idea at first. I just want her to have someone nice."

If I wasn't sure it'd set Gen off, I might try and point Liz and that Harrison guy at each other. In another life, maybe.

"I think we ought to do something nice for your aunt," I decide, forcing my brain to a change of topic. "Take her out to dinner or something." Regardless of the skewed Nightingale syndrome emerging here, she's a nice lady who does her best with limited resources. She should get some thanks for that.

"Yeah, she'd like that."

"She's good people." To most kids, moms are a given. They just assume their moms will love and take care of them. Nurture them. Band-Aids and school lunches and all that. Some of us know better. "Don't ever take her for granted."

"You hear from your mom lately?"

I've talked to him about Shelley before, but the question still hits me sideways. Thinking about her puts me in a constant state of whiplash. She sure isn't baking any cherry pies.

"She keeps texting, wanting to get together and reconnect. Make amends, or whatever. I told her I'd think about it, but every time she suggests a time and place to meet, I make up some excuse."

"What are you going to do? Do you want to see her?"

I shrug, scooping a handful of water to douse my hair. Even though it's not over our heads yet, the sun is already at baking temperature. "I don't know how many times I can let her make me the sucker before I haven't got any dignity left."

Riley drags his hands through the water, aimless. "I know it's not exactly the same situation with us. Mine got sick. She didn't leave. But I'd give anything to see her again, to talk to her."

His heart's in the right place, but I wish he hadn't said that. "Yeah, it's really not the same." Because missing his mother doesn't make him feel like an idiot.

He places both hands on his board and gives me a serious look. "I guess what I'm saying is, if your mom died tomorrow, would you regret not speaking to her one more time?"

Riley's words burrow into my brain like a worm eating through an apple. The question festers for hours, days. Until finally, a week later, I'm sitting in a diner in Charleston, placing bets against myself after fifteen minutes whether Shelley is going to stand me up. The pitying eyes of my server aren't giving me great odds as she refills my coffee mug.

"You want anything to eat?" asks the waitress, a middle-aged woman with overgrown roots and too many bracelets.

"No, thanks."

"The pie came in fresh this morning."

Enough with the damn pies. "Nope. I'm good."

Thirty minutes. This is why I didn't tell anyone, least of all Cooper. He would've told me this would happen. After he kicked my ass and took my keys to spare me one more humiliation.

I have no idea when I became the trusting one. The dupe.

I'm about to throw a few bucks on the table just as Shelley

drops into the booth and settles across the table from me. Blown in like a gust of wind.

"Oh, baby, I'm sorry." She pulls her purse off her shoulder and picks up a laminated menu to fan the heat-and-asphalt smell out of her dyed blonde hair. Her energy is hectic and frazzled, always in motion. "One of the girls was late coming back from lunch because she had to pick her kid up, and I couldn't leave on my break until she got back."

"You're late."

She stills. Presses her lips together with a contrite tilt of her head. "I'm sorry. But I'm here now."

Now. This impermanent state between wasn't and won't be.

"What'll you have?" The waitress is back, this time with an accusatory curtness to her tone. This woman's growing on me.

"Coffee, please," Shelley tells her.

The woman walks off with a grimace.

"I'm glad you called me back," Shelley tells me as she keeps fanning herself with the menu. I've never been able to put my finger on it before, but I just figured it out. Her frenetic nature gives me anxiety. Always has. The perpetual motion is so chaotic. Like bees in a glass box. "I've missed you."

I purse my lips for a second. Then I let out a tired breath.

"Yeah, you know what, before we go another ten rounds on this, let me say: You're a bad mom, Shelley. And it's pretty shady how you're pitting Cooper and I against each other." She opens her mouth to object. I stop her with a look. "No, that's exactly what you're doing. You came to me with all your pleas and apologies because you know Cooper won't hear it. You take advantage of the fact that I'm the soft one, but you don't care what that does to your sons. If he knew I was here—I don't know, he might change the locks on me. I'm not kidding."

"That isn't what I want." Any pretense of a sunny disposition fades from her face. "Brothers shouldn't fight."

"No, they shouldn't. And you shouldn't be putting me in this position. And you know what else? Would it have killed you to bake a pie every now and then?"

She blinks. "Huh?"

"I'm just saying," I mutter. "Other moms bake pies for their kids."

She's quiet for a while after the waitress brings her coffee. Staring at the table and folding her napkin into smaller and smaller shapes. She looks different, I can't help but acknowledge. Her eyes are clear. Skin is healthy. Getting sober is a hell of a drug.

Leaning forward on her elbows, she begins in a subdued voice. "I know I've been awful to you boys. Trust me, kid, I know what rock bottom is now. Getting thrown in jail by my own son was kind of an eye-opener."

"Stealing from your own son," I pointedly remind her. "Anyway, he dropped the charges, which was probably more than you deserved."

"I'm not arguing with you." She drops her head, watching her fingers pick at the peeling nail polish on her thumb. "Sitting in that cell knowing that my own kid had me locked up, though . . . Yeah, that was a wake-up call." Hesitant, she lifts her gaze to search mine, probably for some hint that her contrition is landing. "I'm trying here, baby. This is my new leaf. I got a job now. My own place."

"That tree's looking a little bare from where I'm sitting, Mom."

"You're right. We've been here before."

She smiles, all heartsick and hopeful. It's sad and pathetic, and

I hate seeing my own mother so beaten. I don't enjoy kicking her while she's down. But what else is there when she's been down so long, and she's got both hands around my ankle?

"I promise, Evan. I'm ready to be better. I got my shit together. No more of that old stuff. I just want to have a relationship with my sons before I die."

I hate that. It isn't fair, playing the death card on a couple orphans who've already buried one parent in the ground and another in our minds. Still, something strikes a chord with me. Maybe because the two of us have found ourselves on entirely different yet similar journeys of self-improvement. Maybe I'm a sap who will never stop wanting his mother to love him and act like she does. Either way, I can't help feeling she's sincere this time.

"Here's how it is," I say slowly. "I'm not saying no."

Her eyes, dark and daunting like mine, light with relief.

"I'm not saying yes, either. You're gonna have to do more than make promises if you want to be part of my life. That means keeping a steady job and your own place. Sticking around town for a solid year. No running off to Atlantic City or Baton Rouge or wherever else. And I think we should do a monthly dinner." I don't even know why I say that. It just spills out of me. Then I realize I don't hate the idea.

She nods, too eager. It makes me nervous. "I can do that."

"I don't want you coming to me for money. You don't drop by the house to sleep one off. Matter of fact, you don't come by at all. If Cooper sees you, I can't be sure he won't think of a reason to have you arrested again."

She reaches for my hand and squeezes. "You'll see, baby. I'm better now. I haven't even had a drink since you agreed to meet me."

"That's great, Mom. Let me tell you something, though, that

I've started to figure out myself: If the change is going to stick, you have to want it to. That means doing it for yourself, not only because you're trying to impress someone else. Change, or don't. Either way, you're the one who's got to live with the result."

CHAPTER 24

GENEVIEVE

There are few things I love about this town more than a bonfire on the beach. Cool sand and warm flames. The scent of burning pine and salt air. The coastal breeze that carries tiny orange embers into the waves. These things feel like home. And no one does it better than the twins. Summer nights at the Hartley house are a tradition in the Bay—like boardwalk carnivals and hustling Garnet freshmen.

The party is well underway when I arrive. Heidi and Jay are attached at the face. Alana's dancing in the flickering firelight with some roughneck deckhand, while Tate watches from the distance with his fist around a beer bottle like he's thinking about cracking it over the guy's head. Mackenzie, who's sitting beside the fire with Steph, waves when she spots me coming down from the house.

Just a few hours ago, she called to tell me I got the job. I'm officially the new general manager of The Beacon Hotel, which is a little terrifying but a lot exciting. I warned Mac that although I work hard and learn quickly, I don't pretend to know anything about running a hotel, and she reminded me that until a few months ago, she didn't know anything about owning one. Besides, I've never stopped to wonder if the landing might hurt before jumping off a pier or out of a plane. Why start now?

So while I'm not sure Cooper would appreciate seeing me here, I accepted Mac's invitation to the party. My new position doesn't start until the end of the summer, but still. You don't turn down the boss. Or maybe that's an excuse. Maybe the real reason I came tonight is because after I hung up the phone with Mac, there was only one person I couldn't wait to tell. Rather than linger too long on the implication of that instinct, I just got myself in the car and drove over here.

Evan finds me across the flames through the many shadowed faces. He nods for me to come meet him by the folding table and coolers, where they've practically got a whole liquor store stashed.

"Tell me something," he says when I approach. "You get perks, right? Maybe swing a presidential suite with some room service? You and me spend a weekend naked, eating chocolate-covered strawberries in a hot tub?"

"I see Mac already told you."

"Yep. Congratulations, Madam GM." With an elaborate hand motion, Evan presents me with a red Blow Pop.

This asshole is damn sweet sometimes. I hate that he doesn't have to try at all in order to turn my gut to giddy mush. That my nerves never dull to his dark, mischievous eyes and crooked smirk. He throws on any old T-shirt and a pair of jeans splattered with interior paint and plaster, and I get positively slutty.

"Now it feels real," I say with a laugh. "This makes all the fretting worth it."

My brother Billy wanders past us, throwing me the side-eye when he notices how close Evan and I are standing. I give a nod of assurance, making it clear it's all good here, and he keeps walking.

"Let me fix you a drink. I've been working on something special." Evan fills up a cup of ice from the cooler and starts assembling bottles of ingredients.

"I can't."

He waves off my hesitation. "It's non-alcoholic."

Words I never thought I'd hear come out of a Hartley's mouth. Especially this one.

I watch as he caps the shaker and begins vigorously mixing the drink. "Honestly, I was debating not even coming tonight," I confess.

A frown touches his lips. "Because of me?"

"No, because of this—" I gesture at the beer-filled coolers and table laden with booze. "On the drive over, I was trying to convince myself I could have a drink. Just one, you know, to take the edge off. But then, all these worst-case scenarios flashed through my head. One drink turns to two, and suddenly six drinks later, I wake up in a fire engine half submerged in the YMCA pool with the lights still flashing and a llama treading water." And only half of that scenario is hypothetical.

Amused, he pours the drink into the cup of ice. "Gen. You've got to cut yourself some slack. This kind of hypervigilance isn't sustainable. Trust me. If you don't let yourself have a little fun now and then, you're gonna end up burnt out or on a bender. Learn to embrace moderation."

"You get that off a T-shirt?" I ask in amusement.

"Here." He hands me the fruity concoction. "I'll be your chaperone tonight. If you reach for a real drink, I'll smack it out of your hand."

"Is that right?" He must think I'm new here.

"I'm sober tonight," Evan says without a hint of irony. "I plan to stay that way."

Ordinarily, I might laugh in his face. A sober Hartley at a party is like a fish out of water. But taking a good look at him, I note that his eyes are clear and focused. Not a whiff of booze on his breath. Hell, he's serious. If I didn't know him, I might start believing he was sincere about being reformed.

I guess there's only one way to find out.

"Okay," I say, accepting the drink. "But if I wake up on a stolen Jet Ski in the middle of the ocean, surrounded by Coast Guard cutters, you and me are gonna fight."

"Cheers to that." He hoists a bottle of water to clink with my plastic cup.

Turns out Evan can mix a decent virgin cocktail.

"Not for nothing," he says hesitantly. "You know this 'good girl' mission doesn't have to entirely change who you are, right?"

"What does that mean?" I'm somewhat taken aback. Not because Evan might be less than enthusiastic about this new lifestyle, but that there's some genuine distress in his voice I haven't heard before.

"I just think it'd be a shame if you let growing up dull your edges. I'm all for whatever makes you happy," he qualifies. "You don't need to be drinking for me to enjoy your company—you've always been fun no matter what. Lately, though, it seems like the real Gen is slipping away. Becoming a muted version of the incredible, terrifying, vibrant woman you used to be."

"You say that like I'm dying." I won't lie—it hurts a little to hear that from him. The disappointment, the chord of loss. It's like attending my own funeral.

His eyes drop, fingers running over the ridges of the bottle in his hand. "In a sense, maybe it feels that way. All I'm saying . . ." He lifts his attention again to me. A brief, wistful smile is quickly chased off by his typical irreverent grin. "Don't go getting soft on me, Fred."

I've always loved myself best in Evan's eyes. The adoring way he looks at me: part impressed, a little intimidated. But more so, the person he thinks I am. The way he tells it, I'm invincible. Thunder and lightning. Not much scares me, and even less when he's around.

I wash down the thought with another generous sip of my faux cocktail. "Wouldn't dream of it."

There's got to be a way to do both. Straighten out my more destructive tendencies without lobotomizing myself. Somewhere in the world are respectable, functioning adults who've staved off blandness.

Because Evan isn't alone in his concern. I've felt the slow slipping of self too, the image in the mirror becoming less familiar with time. Every morning waking as one person. The day spent tearing myself out and up, clawing through layers like breaking free of my own skin. And I hit my pillow each night as someone else entirely. At some point, I better settle on a persona before I'm not me at all, but another discarded husk on the floor.

"Tell you what," Evan says. "No more serious talk. I've missed the hell out of us. And you deserve to celebrate. So trust me to stop you from falling into old habits, but . . ." His voice roughens. "Not all habits are bad. For tonight, let's just say to hell with it and have a good time."

In other words, let's pretend it's the old days and we're still together. No more rules and boundaries. Feel the moment and let our instincts move us.

It's an attractive offer. And maybe he's caught me in just the right mood to accept.

"Temping . . ." I trail off.

"Oh, come on." He throws his arm over my shoulder and kisses the side of my head. "What's the worst that could happen?"

"Famous last words."

Evan shrugs, hauling me toward the music and dancing couples. "There are worse ways to go."

For a few hours, we are ether. Evan doesn't dance so much as stand there peeling my clothes off with his eyes. I lose my half-empty drink somewhere in the beat. I'm high on sensation. Fabric sticking to my body in the humidity. Sweat down my neck. His hands finding bare skin across my stomach, my shoulders. Lips pressed against my hair, my cheek, under my jaw until they meet my own. Kissing like everyone is watching. Grabbing fistfuls of his shirt and hiking my knee up his leg until I remember where we are.

It's the most fun I've had with my clothes on in a long time, and all we do is everything we've ever done. Laughing with our friends and kicking up sand. Nothing on fire but the burning logs in the pit, and the only flashing lights coming from the flames and cell phone cameras. Lumberjack Jimmy has trotted out his ax-throwing target, and everyone's placing bets as we take turns hurling sharp edges at the upright wooden board. At first glance the concept of mixing medieval weaponry and alcohol might appear like a recipe for a noisy ride to the emergency room, but so far, egos have taken the worst damage tonight.

"You should have a go," I urge Evan. Seeing as he's dead sober, no one's got him beat for aim.

With his arm around my waist as we watch another matchup, Evan strokes his thumb under the hem of my shirt. The seductive touch gets me dizzier than anything from a bottle. "What'll you give me if I win? And feel free to be as lewd as you'd like."

"My respect and admiration," I deadpan, to his utter dejection.

"Mmm-hmm, that's just as good as a blowjob."

When Jimmy asks who's going next, Evan steps up to the lane to take an ax in hand. Someone grabs Cooper to *get a load of this*, and the mass of interested spectators swells. They give him a wide berth, though. Because Evan Hartley with an ax is about as close to death as anyone gets with air in their lungs.

Until the sharp, shrill wail of a siren spooks the crowd. The music cuts out abruptly. Firelight reveals a cop trudging through the sand. He barks orders into a bullhorn, sending those of questionable parole status scattering into the darkness.

"Party's over," he announces. "You have three minutes to clear the premises or be subject to arrest."

For a split second, I hold out some faint hope it's Harrison having a laugh. But then the cop's face is revealed from the shadows.

Deputy Randall.

Of course.

Evan jerks his head at Cooper. Still gripping the ax, Evan struts up to Randall with his brother, shrugging off my weak attempt to stop him. I'm already feeling my pocket for my keys and wondering if Mac will understand when I have to miss a few days of work to skip town and drive Evan over the border.

As if sharing my prophetic vision, Mac comes up to take my arm as we follow our men to the confrontation.

"What's the deal?" Cooper asks, doing his best to control the deep streak of Hartley contempt for law enforcement from seeping into his voice.

"Everyone's got to go," Randall informs the entire crowd.

"This is private property," Evan shoots back with no such restraint. I know without a doubt that right now images of Randall cornering me in a bar and trying to feel me up are spinning in his mind as he holds the smooth wooden ax handle in his fist.

"Your property ends at the grass. This sand here is a public beach, boy."

Evan cocks his head, licking his lips. The madman thrill he gets from tasting his own blood.

"What's the problem?" Cooper takes a step forward to put a bit more of his body between Evan and Randall. "Don't try to tell me you got a noise complaint. All our neighbors are right here."

Without a flinch, Randall spits out a flat response. "You don't have a permit for this bonfire. It's against city code."

"Bullshit." Thin on patience, Evan raises his voice. "People have bonfires all the time. No one's ever needed any damn permit."

"This is harassment," Cooper says.

Looking bored, Randall reaches into his shirt pocket. "My badge number's on the card. Feel free to file a complaint." He flicks it at Cooper, who lets it fall to the sand. "Call it a night, or take a ride with me to the station."

Evan picks up the business card. "Don't want to be litter bugs, do we, deputy?"

With that, the party's over. Meandering toward the house, people begin to disperse. Evan and Cooper retreat, albeit reluctantly, to pack up the drinks. With a regretful shrug, Mac goes to break down the chairs and folding table. Meanwhile, I have no idea where I left my purse. I'm hunting for it, saying goodbye as friends pass me, when I nearly bump into Randall, who's blending into the night in his dark sheriff's uniform.

"That didn't take long." He sneers, arms crossed, that unearned sense of superiority bearing down on me.

"What?" I don't really want a response, so I try to dodge him, but Randall steps into my path.

"Harrison didn't stand a chance, eh? Barely got his foot in the door, and you're already stepping out on him."

"What is that supposed to mean?" He's got me zero to fed up in no time flat. I don't like what he's insinuating, and I'm not about to entertain his garbage on my home turf. We're not in public. Out here, all sorts of things can happen, and no one would say a word.

"Means you're not fooling anyone, sweetheart. Least of all me." Randall leans in, growling words coated in the sickly stench of gas station corn dogs and coffee. "You're still a lying little slut. Out to ruin another man's life."

"I'm sorry." Evan comes striding up beside me, the ax slung with one hand over his shoulder. "I didn't quite catch that." He tilts his ear to Randall. "You'll need to speak up. Say that again?"

"It's fine," I say, grabbing Evan's free wrist. If I was worried about becoming a fugitive before, I'm downright concerned now. "Walk me to my car?"

"Go on, boy." Randall moves his right hand to rest on his gun. The strap on the holster is unbuttoned. "Give me a reason."

Evan flashes a wild smile I've seen a hundred times. Right before he took a running leap off a cliff or unloaded a paintball gun at a police cruiser. It's a smile loaded with the serenity of madness saying, *watch this.*

"Yeah, you see . . ." Evan admires the ax, turning it in hand. "As a respected business owner and upstanding member of my community, I'd never run afoul of a lawman." He flicks his thumbnail across the blade.

It's then I realize this conversation has attracted an audience. A smaller contingent than the aborted party. In fact, with Cooper, Wyatt, Tate, and Billy, the remnants are made up almost exclusively of certified members from the Fuck Around and Find Out Society.

"But you come at me and mine sideways," Evan says, not a hint of humor in his grave tone. "You better come to dance."

For second or two, Randall appears to contemplate the offer. Then, sizing up the opposition, he thinks better of it. He barks a final order into the bullhorn. "Three minutes are up. Clear out."

He doesn't wait for compliance before trudging back through the sand and tall grass to the road and his waiting cruiser. I don't release my breath until I watch the taillights blink red and then disappear.

Following Evan up to the house, I'm still a bit winded by the whole ordeal. Somehow, he's still got the ax, which he tosses on the dresser when we enter his bedroom upstairs. I haven't been in here in a year, and it feels oddly like stepping into a museum of my own life. Memories on every wall.

"What's that look?" he says, pulling off his shirt and tossing it in the hamper. My throat goes dry as my attention is drawn to the lines of his chest, the defined muscles of his abs.

"It still smells the same."

"Hey, I did laundry yesterday."

I roll my eyes, taking a trip around the room. "Not like that. I mean it smells familiar."

"You okay?"

"For a minute there . . ." I'm distracted as I wander the bedroom. He's never been the sentimental type. There are no photographs tacked to the wall. No old concert tickets or souvenirs. Wasn't much into sports either, so none of those little gold men. "I thought you might find a use for that ax. You impressed me back there."

My gaze conducts a final sweep. His room is just a utilitarian composite of some basic furniture, TV, game system, and the contents of his pockets on any given day tossed on the nightstand. Except for one frill on top of his dresser: a decorative glass dish, like something an old lady would put potpourri in, filled with years' worth of Blow Pops.

This jerk is so damn sweet sometimes.

"Which part impressed you?" he asks.

I turn to find him leaning against his bedroom door. Legs crossed, hands shoved in his pockets. Jeans riding low on his hips. Everything about him demands to be consumed. And I'm locked in here with him.

"I admired your restraint." I don't know what to do with my hands now, so I rest them on the edge of his desk, hop up, and sit on them.

"I couldn't remember if we were still playing the opposite game. But I'll go hunt his ass down if we're not."

"No, you did good."

He raises an eyebrow. "How good?"

"Are you leaning against that door because you're afraid I'll leave?"

"Do you want to?"

When Evan looks at me from beneath those thick, dark lashes, all full of memories and hunger, I forget what I'm doing. All the rules and hesitations fly out the window.

"No," I admit.

He pushes off the door and stalks toward me, planting his hands on the desk on either side of me. Reflexively, I open my legs for him to stand between them. I fixate on his mouth. On the warmth radiating from his body and the way my limbs grow restless. When I think he's going to kiss me, he turns his face to brush his lips against my temple instead.

"I've missed you," he says, more a groan than words.

"I'm right here."

My pulse throbs in my neck, in my palms, the phantom echo of my thumping heart resonating across every nerve ending. I'm all but choking on the anticipation of something to happen and uncertain what it should be. Because I made myself a promise. Right now, though, I can't for the life of me think of a good reason to keep it.

With the lightest touch, Evan's hands slide up the outside of each leg, over my knees, thighs. "I've got it bad, Fred." His voice comes out hoarse. "The way I see it, you better send me to a cold shower before this thing gets serious."

I bite my lip to smother a smile. "Serious, huh?"

He grabs my hand and places it on his chest. "As a heart attack."

His skin under my palm is hot to the touch. In the quiet part of my mind, I know he's dangerous. But the rest of it, the loud, screaming voice between my ears, tells me to drag my hands down his chest. To undo the zipper on his jeans, reach into his boxer briefs, and wrap my fingers around his thick, throbbing erection.

Evan sucks in a breath when I stroke him. He looks down, watching me, his abdomen clenching. "Good choice."

Without warning, he draws my hand away and spins me around. I grip the edge of the desk to steady myself as he hastily tugs my shorts down to expose my bare ass. He squeezes my warm flesh with one hand, humming an appreciative sound. I hear a drawer open and shut, followed by the rip of a condom wrapper. His fingers slide between my legs, finding me wet, and then I feel him rub himself against my feverish skin as he leans over to whisper in my ear.

"I don't mind if you want to be loud."

A thrill shoots through me.

He leaves a kiss on my shoulder as he drags his erection along my aching core, before slowly pushing inside me. With one hand on my hip, and the other knotted in my hair to pull my head backward and arch my back, Evan fills me completely. My nails bite the worn desktop as I push back, taking him. The exquisite ache fogs my vision and quickens my pulse.

"Fuck, Gen." He grinds out the words. Lays another kiss at my temple.

I breathe out his name because I can't take the static anticipation a moment longer. I just want him already. I need him to put me out of my misery.

Evan glides his hand up my spine, under my shirt, to unhook my bra and let it slide down my arms. I grab his hand, guide it to my breast. Still, he stubbornly refuses to move.

"Why are you teasing me?" I demand.

"Because I never want this to end." His thumb brushes over my nipple in the most feather light of caresses.

I groan my desperation and buck against him, grinding on his dick.

Chuckling softly, he brings his other hand up and clasps both breasts now. "Better?"

"No," I mumble. "You're still not moving." And the feel of his entire length lodged inside me, completely motionless, is a new form of torment. No oxygen is reaching my lungs. My skin is on fire, and I'm close to self-combusting.

"Breathe." His voice is soft in my ear, his fingers playing with my nipples. "Take a breath, baby."

I manage a shaky inhale, and just as the air fills my lungs, Evan withdraws slowly. I'm mid-exhalation when he slides back in, sending a wave of sensation through my body.

My head drops back on his shoulder, experiencing every inch of him. Pleasure tingles in my nipples and tightens my core as he moves inside me, slow and deliberate. When I can't quell the need alone, I move his right hand between my legs.

"I'm close," I whisper.

"Already?"

"Feels too good." A ragged breath slips out. "Missed having you inside me."

That earns me a satisfied growl. He runs his finger over my clit. Gentle at first, then more insistent when I moan for him. It isn't long before I'm shaking, leaning against him for support as the orgasm sweeps through me.

"You're gorgeous when you come," he rasps against my neck.

As tiny flutters of pleasure continue to dance inside me, Evan bends me over the desk. He takes my hips with both hands and pumps into me with strong, forceful thrusts. Just the right intensity. Having me like it's his last night on Earth.

I twist my head to look at him, floored by the raw need darkening his eyes, the blissed-out haze. When our gazes lock, he stills, groaning through his climax. He runs his hands up my back, soothing my muscles, laying kisses across my sensitive flesh. I'm sated and spent, panting, when he steps away to throw out the condom.

"I'm gonna grab a Gatorade," he says, biting his lip as he stares at me. "Then we're doing that again."

CHAPTER 25

EVAN

"So there's something I need to tell you," Shelley says after our waiter seats us at a table overlooking the water. It was her choice to have dinner at this upscale restaurant, and as I pick up the menu and get a look at the prices, I'm already assuming I'll be the one footing the bill.

More than that, I'm now suspicious as hell, because any time my mother starts a sentence with "there's something I need to tell you," it's usually followed by the confession that she's skipping town again, or she's broke and needs cash. This is only the second time I've seen her since agreeing to give her another chance; last week we had lunch near the budget hotel where she works in housekeeping. She didn't hit me up for money during that meetup, but I shouldn't have presumed it'd be a lasting trend.

Catching my wary expression, she quickly waves a hand to dismiss my concerns. "No, no, it's nothing bad. I promise." But she doesn't elaborate. Her cheeks turn a little pink.

"What is it?" I push, only to be interrupted by our server, who returns to take our drink orders.

Shelley requests a sparkling water. I ask for a pale ale, which could end up being a risky move depending on Shelley's news. This past week, though, I've been testing myself to see if I can live that cheesy motto I gave Gen at the party last week: *Learn to embrace moderation*. I'd never push alcohol on Genevieve when she's hell-bent on sobriety, but, personally, I'd like to be able to have a beer or two at poker night without worrying about taking it too far.

"You know how I've always loved doing my hair and makeup and that kind of stuff?" Shelley shifts awkwardly in her chair, one hand fidgeting with her water glass. "Pretty good at it too."

"Yeah . . . ?" I don't know where she's going with this.

"So, well, I was talking to Raya . . . you know, that coworker I was telling you about last week?"

I nod. "Right. The chick with the psycho toddler who killed their goldfish."

Shelley sputters with laughter. "Evan! I told you, baby, that was an accident. Cassidy's only three. She didn't know fish can't breathe out of water."

"Sounds like something a psychopath would say."

My mom lets out a loud snort that causes the couple in the neighboring table to glare at us with deep frowns. The woman is wearing a string of pearls and a high-necked silk blouse, while the man's rocking a polka-dot ascot. I'm surprised they don't go all out and shush us. They look like shushers.

Shelley and I exchange an eye roll, a moment of shared humor that makes me falter for a beat. This is a whole new mother-son experience for us. I mean, having dinner on the waterfront, exchanging conspiratorial looks about the uptight patrons next to us. Laughing together. It's surreal.

Yet I don't entirely hate it.

"*Anyway*," Shelley says, picking up her glass. She takes a quick sip. "Not sure if I mentioned it before, but Raya has a second job. Works at a hair salon on the weekends. And yesterday, she tells me her salon's opening a second location and is gonna have a bunch of chairs available to rent."

"Chairs?"

"Yeah, that's how it works in the industry. The stylists rent the chair from the salon." She takes a breath. "I think I wanna do it."

I wrinkle my brow. "What? Become a hairdresser?"

Shelley nods earnestly.

"Okay. Don't you need some kind of degree for that? Or a certificate at the very least?"

Her cheeks turn even redder. If I'm reading her right, she looks embarrassed. "I, um, enrolled in cosmetology school. Fees for the first semester are due at the end of the week, and I start next Monday."

"Oh." I nod slowly, waiting for the rest.

I wait for: *But I'm a little short on funds, baby, so can you . . . ?*

Or: *I'm gonna have to quit this housekeeping gig to focus all my attention on school, which means I'll need a place to crash . . . ?*

I stare at her and wait . . . but it doesn't come.

"What?" Shelley's face turns anxious. "What is it, baby? You think it's a bad idea?"

"No. Not at all." I clear my throat and try to paste on an encouraging smile. "It sounds great. It's just . . ."

She gives a knowing look. "You thought I was gonna hit you up for cash."

"Uh. Well. Yes."

Regret flickers through her eyes. "I mean, you have every right to think the worst of me. But let me tell ya, when you're not blowing every paycheck on booze? The savings are out of this world."

I grin wryly. "I bet."

"I've got enough saved up for the first semester," she assures me. "And the classes are at night, so I don't have to quit my gig at the hotel. It's all good, baby. I promise." She picks up her menu. "What looks good? I'm thinking the mussels. My treat, by the way."

Luckily, her head is buried in the menu, so I'm able to wipe the shock from my face before she sees it. Forget surreal—this is downright miraculous. Who is this woman and what has she done with my mother?

I continue to battle my astonishment as we order our meals and proceed to enjoy a really nice dinner. I'm not naïve enough to dive right into the She's Changed camp, but I'm willing to dip in a toe or two. The conversation flows easily. There's no tension, no uncomfortable silences. The only time we come close to one is when she brings up Cooper, but I brush off the subject by saying, "Let's not go there," and we move on.

"You didn't tell me Genevieve is back home," Shelley says, her tone tentative as she watches me devour my surf and turf.

"Yeah," I answer between bites. "She came back for her mom's funeral and stuck around to help Ronan out at the stone yard."

"I was sorry to hear about her momma. I know they weren't close, and God knows Laurie wasn't the easiest woman to get along with, but it can't be easy for Genevieve."

"You know Gen. She's resilient."

Shelley smiles. "Oh, that girl's a fighter." She eyes me from across the table. "You gonna marry her?"

The question catches me so off-guard I choke on a scallop. Coughing wildly, I scramble for my water glass, while the jerk couple at the next table glower at me for the disruption.

"Gee," I croak after I've cleared the obstruction, glowering right back at them. "So sorry to disturb you with my near-death experience."

The woman huffs and honest-to-God clutches her pearls.

My mom is trying not to laugh. "Evan," she warns.

I gulp down some more water before picking up my fork again. "To answer your question," I say, lowering my voice, "I'm pretty sure Gen isn't interested in marrying me."

"Bullsh—nonsense," Shelley corrects herself, shooting a

glance at the judgey table, because God forbid we upset the Pearl Clutcher. "You two are meant to be together. I knew from the second you started dating that you'd get married someday and live happily ever after and all that."

"Uh-huh. I'm sure you knew from the *second* we started dating."

"It's true," she insists. "Ask your uncle. I told Levi my prediction, and he did that thing he does—you know, that half sigh, half grumble—because he knows my predictions always come true." She smiles smugly. "I called it with Levi and Tim, much as he hates to admit it. And I knew it with your brother too, when I met his new girlfriend. Mark my words, he's gonna marry her."

I don't doubt that Cooper and Mac are endgame. But that doesn't mean I'm ready to accept that my mom—who couldn't keep her own marriage together, not to mention all her subsequent relationships—is some kind of love clairvoyant.

"I don't think Gen's as confident as you are in our future," I say ruefully.

Hell, I can barely convince Gen to spend the night, let alone agree to date me again. Since the bonfire, she's been over at my place nearly every night. If I didn't know any better, I'd think she was using me for sex. But it's a lot more than that. She doesn't bail the moment we recover from our respective orgasms. She stays to cuddle. She takes Daisy for walks with me. She even dropped off dinner for me a couple times.

But whenever I push her to define what this is, she clams up. Tells me not to overthink it. So of course, all I do is think about it.

"Then give her confidence," Shelley says with a shrug. "You want her back, yeah?"

"Oh yeah," I sigh.

"Then keep working at it."

"Trust me, I'm trying." Now I groan. "But she made it clear she's not looking to be my girlfriend again and that all we're doing is fucking."

"Ahem!" comes an incensed cry. It's Husband Pearl Clutcher. "Is it too much to ask to enjoy our meals without being surrounded by filthy language?"

I open my mouth to retort, but my mother beats me to it.

Eyes gleaming with irritation, she addresses the other table by jabbing a finger toward the man. "Hey, mister, you wanna talk about filth? You've been checking out my rack since the moment I sat down. And you"—she directs that at the wife—"don't think I didn't see you slipping your phone number to that handsome young stud of a waiter when your hubby was in the john."

I snicker into my hand.

"Now, I'm trying to have a conversation with my son, so how 'bout you two Nosy Nellies focus on your own boring lives and mind your own damn business?"

That shuts them both up.

Shelley lifts a brow when she sees me grinning. "What? I might've turned a new leaf, but you can't expect me to always turn the other cheek. Even Jesus had his limits, baby."

I'm feeling oddly giddy as I cross the bridge and drive back to the Bay after dinner with Shelley. I can't lie—that wasn't awful. In fact, I . . . truly had a good time. Who would've thought?

The instinct to tell my brother about it is so strong that I end up veering off the road home, turning left instead of right. No, I can't risk seeing Cooper right now. He'll just ask why I'm in such a good mood, at which point I'll have to lie, and he'll see through the lie because of twin telepathy, and then we'll get in a fight.

So I drive to Gen's house instead. Parking on the curb out

front, I hop off my bike and fish my phone out of my pocket. I shoot off a quick text to Gen.

Me: *I'm standing outside your place like some lovesick stalker. Debating whether to throw rocks at your window or just knock on the front door.*

She responds almost instantly.

Her: *Use the door, you heathen. We're adults now, remember?*

I grin at the phone. True. But this is definitely a first, I reflect, as I tread up the front walk to the door, which swings open before I can ring the bell. I'm met by the sight of Genevieve's dad, who startles when he finds me standing there.

"Evan," he says gruffly, nodding in greeting. His gaze takes in my outfit. "You wearing khakis?"

"Uh. Yeah." I shove my hands in the pockets of said khakis. "I had a thing in the city."

He nods again. "Gen's upstairs. I was just heading out to meet your uncle for a beer, actually."

"Oh, nice. Tell him I said hey."

"Renos are looking great," Gen's dad adds, gesturing in the vague direction of inside. "The new kitchen cabinets turned out nice."

"Thanks." I feel a little burst of pride, because I installed those cabinets myself.

"Anyway." Ronan eyes me again. "Glad you and Gen are getting along again." He claps my shoulder before striding off toward the pickup truck in the driveway.

I let myself in, half expecting one of Gen's million brothers to intercept me, but the house is quiet as I head for the stairs. Last time I was here, the place was jam-packed with mourners and reverberating with hushed conversation. Tonight, all I hear are the creaks and groans of the old house, including the very loud protest of the second step from the top when I walk over it. Gen and I always made sure to skip over it whenever we snuck in after curfew, but tonight there's no need for stealth.

Gen's lying on her side reading a book when I enter her room. My gaze feasts on her sexy body and the curtain of black hair cascading over one shoulder. She looks up at my entrance.

"Are you wearing khakis?" she demands.

"Yup." I throw myself on the bed, causing her paperback to bounce on the mattress.

She grabs it before it falls over the edge. "Jerk."

Grinning, I clasp both hands behind my neck and get comfortable. Gen smiles in amusement as she watches me kick off my shoes and stretch out my legs. I'm too damn big for this bed, my feet hanging off the end.

"You're in a good mood," she remarks.

"I am," I agree.

"Are you going to elaborate?"

"Had dinner with Shelley tonight."

"You did?" Gen sounds surprised. "You didn't mention anything about it when we spoke this morning. Was it a last-minute thing?"

"Not really."

"So why didn't you tell me?" When I shrug, she pokes me in the rib. Hard. "Evan."

I glance over at her. She's sitting cross-legged beside me, her astute blue eyes studying my face. "I don't know. I guess I didn't say anything just in case she bailed."

Gen nods in understanding. "Ah. That's why you keep telling me about these meetings after the fact. You don't want to get your hopes up beforehand."

She gets it.

"Honestly?" I say quietly. "Every time I drive to Charleston to see her, I've given it fifty-fifty odds on whether she'll show." A lump forms in my throat. "So far she hasn't missed a date."

Gen moves closer to curl up beside me, resting her palm on my abdomen. The sweet scent of her hair wafts up to my nose. "I'm glad. And I hope to God she keeps it up. My mom's gone, but yours still has a chance to redeem herself."

I wrap my arm around her shoulder and plant a kiss atop her head. "I ran into your dad at the front door, by the way. He was happy to see me."

"Uh-huh."

"Face it, Fred. Your dad's always loved me."

"There's no accounting for taste."

"He said he's glad you and I are getting along again." I slide my hand down to lightly pinch her ass. "So, the way I see it, all that's left to do now is make it official."

"Or . . ."

She trails off enticingly and rolls over—directly on top of me. I'm semi-hard almost instantly, and her tiny smile tells me she notices.

"We can quit talking and take advantage of this empty house," she finishes, and then she's lifting my shirt up and kissing my chest, and my brain short-circuits.

A groan slips out when she undoes the button of my khakis.

"Gen," I protest, because I know she's trying to distract me with sex. And it's working.

She peers up at me with big, innocent eyes. "It's okay, baby. I don't mind if you want to be loud."

She's throwing my own words back at me, uttered the night of the bonfire before I spent hours making her gasp and moan and scream. I was relentless in my seduction that night. But now it's my turn to be weak and helpless, to fight for control as she leaves a trail of hot kisses along my stomach on her way down south.

When she takes my cock in her mouth, I give up on resisting. There's no better feeling in the world than having Gen swallow me up. She curls one delicate hand around my shaft and sucks me deep, while her other hand strokes my chest, her nails scraping along my sensitized flesh.

I give an upward thrust, pleasure gathering inside me, pulse quickening with each languid swipe of her tongue. And as I tangle my fingers in her hair and rock against her wet, eager mouth, I tell myself that we can talk after. Later. When my heart isn't hammering against my ribs, and my balls aren't drawn tight with need.

But we never get around to having that talk.

CHAPTER 26

EVAN

Weeks later, I lie in my bed while Gen is getting dressed. It's past noon, the two of us having slept in after staying up late with Mac and Cooper in a Mario Kart death match that damn near came to blows. Girls are such sore losers.

"I told you I should have gone home last night," she grumbles.

"You see how screwed up this is," I answer, watching as she shimmies a tiny pair of cutoff shorts up her long, tan legs. I'm still here with a semi and she's running off to *him*.

"And if you'd let me go home last night, we wouldn't be having this conversation." She ties her hair up in a ponytail and walks over to sift through the sheets for her phone.

"Stay."

Gen lifts her head to glare at me. "Stop it."

"I'm serious. Blow him off and let me go down on you instead."

"Isn't your Little Brother coming over for a barbecue today?"

"Yeah, in like an hour. Think of all the orgasms I can give you until then."

She finds her phone tucked under my back and snatches it.

I blink innocently. "How'd that get there?"

Gen rolls her eyes before straightening up and hunting for her shirt. "You knew this was the deal. Stop acting like I changed the rules."

The deal being that for the last several weeks, Gen and I have been going at it like it's the end of the world, while she's still dating Deputy Dumbfuck. Now she's jumping out of my bed and right into his car. How is this happening?

"Guess I thought there may have been some implied amendments to that deal after you begged me to spank you last night, but sure."

She pauses, after pulling her top on, to direct a frown my way. "And if you want to keep those spanking privileges, mind your mouth."

For no good reason, an unbidden image of her going down on the dweeb in his cruiser flashes behind my eyes. My dick goes soft as I shake the thought. This is why I don't ask. Very little could stop me from running up on him at the gas station and flicking a lit match his way.

And yet . . . "Are you sleeping with him?" I find myself blurting out.

Gen looks at me, tilting her head with sympathy as she comes to sit on the edge of the bed. She brushes her lips over mine in a fleeting caress. "No."

At least there's that.

"We haven't even kissed."

Relief floods my chest. "So then what are you getting out of it?"

With a frustrated sigh, she stands and grabs her keys from the nightstand. "Let's not, okay?"

"I'm serious." I sit up. "What are you getting out of it?"

She doesn't answer, and that's when I realize she doesn't have to. I already *know* the answer. We both do. There's only one reason she's continuing to date Harrison despite the fact they haven't so much as kissed—it's her way of keeping that final bit of distance between us. Keeping me at arm's length.

Now I'm the one sighing in frustration. "What's it going to take to make this official between us? I'm done messing around."

"Done, huh?"

"You know what I mean." I know this chick well enough to understand an ultimatum is the quickest way to drive her away. And that's the last thing I want to do.

We might've had a rocky start when she first moved back to the Bay, but the path is smooth now. It's as if all the bad parts of us, the fighting and jealousy and chasing highs—it's morphed into something else. Something softer. Don't get me wrong, the passion's still there. The soul-deep need to be together, to lay ourselves completely bare and raw, is stronger than ever. But there's something different about us now. About her. About me.

"I want us back together for real," I tell her. "What's the holdup?"

Gen leans against my dresser and stares at the floor. The summer's almost over, and still this question hangs between us. All this time I thought we were of the same mind, moving in the same direction—together. Now, every second she spends deciding what not to say, the fracture gets wider.

"You still don't trust me," I answer for her. My tone is grim.

"I do trust you."

"Not enough." Frustration jams in my throat. "What do I have to do to prove myself?"

"It's hard," she says, anguish drawing lines across her face. "I have a lifetime of instinct about you that says there's no way Evan Hartley gave himself a complete personality makeover in one summer. Yeah, you didn't chase Randall off with an ax and you're not getting wasted every night, but I guess I'm still hesitant to believe you've changed. Feels too easy."

"Has it occurred to you there's something more important to me in this room than drinking and fighting?"

"I know you want this to work." Most of the agitation leaves her voice. "But you're not the only one I have doubts about. Every day I question whether I can trust myself. How much I've really changed. Put the two of us back together, and maybe we realize this condition is temporary and we end up right back in our old roles."

I go to her, holding her. Because right here, the two of us, is the only thing that's ever made sense to me. And whatever she tells herself, I know she feels it too.

"Trust me, baby. Give us a chance to be good for each other. How am I ever going to convince you we can if you won't try?"

Her phone buzzes in her pocket. She gives me a contrite shrug as I release her to answer it.

"Trina," she says, wrinkling her forehead.

I haven't heard that name in a while. Trina went to high school with us, though she was more a friend of the girls in our crew than of Cooper or me. If I remember right, she moved not long after graduation. But her and Gen used to be tight. Two peas in a chaos pod.

"She's in town for the weekend," she reads aloud. "Wants to grab a drink." Gen swipes her finger across the screen to delete the text, then shoves the phone back in her pocket.

"You should go."

She lets out a sarcastic laugh. "Pass. Last time she came home for a visit, I got piss-drunk and stormed into Deputy Randall's house in the middle of the night to scream at his wife about what a creep she married."

"Oh."

"Yeah."

An idea springs to my mind. "Go anyway."

Her skeptical gaze says there'd better be more to that suggestion. And as I roll it over in my head, the plan starts to make more sense. Maybe the thing she needs to finally trust herself is the only thing she fears more than me. The thing that drove her out of town in the first place.

"Treat it as a test," I explain. "If you can behave yourself around the girl who once slipped acid to the girls' volleyball coach in the middle of a match, I'd say you conquered your demons."

Sure, it might be a little hairbrained, but I'm desperate here. One way or another, I need to get Gen on my side. The longer we stay trapped in relationship limbo, the more she gets used to the idea of us not being a couple. And the further away she slips.

"A test," she echoes dubiously.

I nod. "The final exam to your journey of reform. Show yourself you can spend an evening with Trina and not burn anything down."

Hesitation lingers on her gorgeous face, but at least she's not shooting down the idea outright. "I'll think on it," she finally says. Then, to my chagrin, she heads out my bedroom door. "Talk to you later. Harrison's waiting."

Riley shows up around one o'clock with a rack of marinated ribs and another homemade pie courtesy of Aunt Liz. God bless that woman. I lead him out to the back deck, my mouth watering as I inhale the aroma of meat and pastry. My two favorite things.

"How's your week been?" I ask him as we prep the barbecue.

He shrugs. "Meh."

"You looking forward to school starting in a few weeks?"

"What do you think?"

I grin. "You're right. Dumb question." I always hated it too, watching with dread as the calendar neared closer and closer to September.

"But," he says, brightening slightly, "Hailey's family is coming back and they'll be here till Labor Day."

"Hailey . . . That's the girl whose number you got at Big Molly's, right?" Riley went out with her a few times over the summer, but every time I asked for details, he'd clammed up.

Today, he's a bit more forthcoming. "Yeah. We've been texting since she went back home." He shoves his hands in the pockets of his board shorts, then removes them and starts fidgeting with a pair of metal tongs.

"What's going on? You're acting all bouncy."

"Bouncy?"

"Fidgety. Whatever. Are you nervous about seeing her, is that it?"

"Sorta?"

"But you guys have already gone out before," I remind him. "What's there to be nervous about?"

"We played mini golf and went to the movies a couple times. Oh, and ice cream on the boardwalk. So, like, four times. But we never—" He stops abruptly.

I narrow my eyes at him, but he avoids my gaze. He's antsy again, now pretending to check the temperature on the barbecue like some grilling expert, when we both know he's never grilled anything a day in his life.

"You never what?" Then it dawns on me. I stifle a curse. "Aw man, nope, don't tell me. I don't need to hear about how you're planning on having sex. Your aunt would murder—"

"Jeez!" he yelps. "We're not having sex, you idiot."

I'm swamped with relief, although a tad intrigued by the genuine shock on his face, as if he can't fathom the idea of sleeping with the chick. Riley's fourteen, the age I lost my virginity, but I suppose not everyone is an early bloomer like I was.

"I just wanna kiss her," he adds, the confession coming out as an embarrassed mumble.

"Oh. *Oh.* Okay." Kissing? I can handle a chat about kissing. There's no way Aunt Liz can be mad at me for that, right? "Well. Judging by your tomato face, I take it you've never done it before?"

He awkwardly jerks his head from side to side, a reluctant *no.*

"Dude, you don't need to be embarrassed. Lots of guys your age haven't kissed anyone." I lean against the railing of the deck, slanting my head. "So what do you want to know? How much tongue is too much tongue? Whether to grab her boobs when you do it?"

He squawks out a laugh, but some of the blush has left his face. Relaxing, he wanders over to stand beside me. The mouthwatering smell of the ribs cooking on the grill floats toward us.

"I'm just, like, not sure how to go for it. Like, do I say something beforehand?" He rubs his forehead with the back of his hand. "What if I lean in and she's not ready for it, and our heads smash together and I break her nose?"

I choke down a laugh, because I know he wouldn't appreciate being laughed at during such a sensitive topic. "I'm almost certain that won't happen. But yeah, you don't want to just go for it while she's mid-sentence or anything. There's a thing called consent. So, read the moment, you know? Wait for a lull in the conversation, gauge her expression and look for the signals."

"What signals?"

"Like, if she's licking her lips, it usually means she's thinking about kissing you. If she's staring at your mouth, also a good sign. Actually, that's the way in," I tell him, pushing away from the railing and heading for the cooler near the door. "Alright, listen up. This is what you gotta do."

He trails after me, accepting the soda I hand him. For myself I get a beer, twisting off the cap and tossing it in the plastic bucket on the deck. I return to the wooden railing and hop up to sit atop it.

"So at the end of the date," I continue, "or in the middle, or whenever you gather up the courage to do it, this is what you do—you stare at her lips. For like five seconds."

Riley sputters out a laugh. "That's so creepy!"

"It's really not. Stare at her lips until she gets all awkward and says, *why are you looking at me like that?* Or some variation of that question." When he opens his mouth to protest, I interject, "Trust me, she'll say it. And when she does, you say, *because I really want to kiss you right now—can I?* So now she's prepared, right? And based on her response, you go from there."

"What if her response is no?"

"Then you handle the rejection like a man, tell her you had a great summer with her, and wish her luck on her future endeavors."

I can't help but marvel at the sheer maturity I'm exuding. If only Gen were here to see it.

"But for what it's worth, a chick doesn't go out with someone four times if she's not interested," I assure him.

"Truth," Cooper's voice echoes from the sliding door. "For once, my brother's not talking out of his ass."

Riley's gaze snaps to the door. His jaw falling open, he glances at Cooper, then me, then Coop again, and finally me. "Holy shit, you didn't tell me you guys were identical," he accuses.

I roll my eyes. "I said we were twins. Figured you'd extrapolate from there."

Grinning, Coop extends a hand toward my Little Brother. "Hey, I'm Cooper. It's nice to finally meet you."

Riley's still blinking like an owl, astounded at our twinship. "Wow. It's scary how alike you look. If you weren't wearing different clothes, I don't think I'd be able to tell you apart."

"Not many people can," I say with a shrug.

"What about girls? Like, your girlfriends? Did they ever get you guys mixed up?" He's utterly fascinated.

"Sometimes," Coop answers as he grabs a beer for himself. He strides toward the barbecue, lifts the lid, and groans happily. "Oh man, those ribs look amazing." He turns back to Riley. "Serious girlfriends usually know the difference, though. My girl says she can tell us apart by our footsteps."

"I don't believe that for a second," I crack, sipping my beer. Yes, Mac can tell us apart, but from the sounds we make while we walk? I call bullshit.

Coop flashes a smug smile. "It's true."

Beyond his shoulder, I glimpse Mac through the open sliding doors. She just entered the kitchen and is removing items from the fridge. Then she starts preparing a sandwich at the counter, her back to us.

I slide off the railing. "I request permission to test that theory."

Cooper follows my gaze, smirks, and nods magnanimously. "Go for it."

Utilizing the stealth mode I'd perfected after years of sneaking in and out of houses and girls' bedrooms, I creep into the kitchen. Mac is focused on arranging cheese slices on her bread, singing softly to herself. Only when I'm close enough that she won't have much time to turn around, I walk normally and come up behind her.

Wrapping both hands around her waist, I nuzzle her neck and speak in my perfect, uncanny Cooper voice. "Hey, babe, your ass looks good enough to eat in those shorts."

An outraged cry fills the kitchen as she spins around and tries to knee me in the groin. "What the fuck, Evan! Why?"

Luckily, I capture her knee with both hands before it connects with the family jewels. Then I dart backward and raise my hands in surrender. From the deck, loud laughter greets my ears.

"Told you!" Cooper calls out.

"What is *wrong* with you!" Mac huffs.

"It was just an experiment," I protest, keeping my distance. "Question, though. How did you know it was me?"

"Your footsteps," she growls. "You walk like it's a game."

"What does that even mean?"

"Evan, please get out of my sight before I punch you in your stupid face."

I go back outside with a defeated sag to my shoulders. "She says I walk like it's a game," I inform my brother, who nods as if that makes any goddamn sense.

Riley, as usual, is in hysterics. Seems like all I do is make this kid bust out in laughter.

But maybe that's a good thing.

It ends up being a good day. Good food, good company, good everything. Even Cooper is in high spirits. He doesn't get on my case about Gen or whatever else disappoints him about me, not even once. He's, dare I say it, downright chipper. He and Mac face off against me and Riley in a game of beach volleyball, and when Liz comes to pick Riley up around four o'clock, he looks bummed to leave.

But in my life, "good" is a fleeting concept. Which is why I'm not surprised when later, while I'm on the beach with Mac and Cooper watching Daisy chase seagulls, I'm faced with a new dilemma.

Shelley's blowing up my phone about random stuff in between trying to set up another date. I usually don't spend much time on my phone, so answering the barrage of texts has Cooper eyeing me in suspicion. Normally I'd just turn it off and ignore the messages until later, but I've found Shelley gets impatient. If I don't answer, she goes into a panic spiral, thinking I've blown her off.

I'm worried she might impulsively drive out here, and I can't have that.

It's still weird, spending time with her like a normal mom-and-son duo. Talking about our days and pop culture. All the while delicately trying to avoid mention of Cooper to stave off the inevitable question of when he might join us at one of our meetups. I hate lying to my brother, but Cooper's a long way from ready to know about any of this.

Playing with Daisy, he shouts something at me about pizza for dinner. I nod absently, while Shelley is telling me there's a stray cat hanging around outside her work, and she's gotten it in her head she's going to take it home. Which makes me think she probably should have had to practice with a pet before having twins, but what the hell do I know?

A chewed-up, sandy tennis ball suddenly lands in my lap. Then a blur of golden fur is flying at my face. Daisy barrels into me to snatch the ball before running away again.

"Hey! What the hell?" I sputter.

Cooper stands over me, all puffed up and bothered. "You talking to Gen?"

Not this again. "No. Fuck off."

"You've been hunched over that thing ever since Riley left. Who is it?"

"Since when do you care?"

"Leave him alone," shouts Mac, who's still tossing the ball with Daisy at the tide line.

Cooper does the opposite—he yanks the phone from my hand. Instantly, I'm on my feet, wrestling him for it.

"Why are you such a drama queen?" I get one hand on the phone before he sweeps my leg and we end up rolling around in the sand.

"Grow up," Cooper grunts back. He digs his elbow into my

kidney, still reaching for the phone while we toss around. "What are you hiding?"

"Come on, quit it." Mac stands over us now with Daisy barking like she's waiting to get tagged in.

Fed up, I throw sand in his face and climb to my feet, brushing myself off. I shrug in response to Mac's looks of exasperation.

"He started it."

She rolls her eyes.

"You're up to something." Shaking sand out of his hair, Cooper stands up and snarls at me like he's ready for round two. "What is it?"

"Eat shit."

"Quit it, will you?" Mac, ever the peacemaker, utterly fails to get through to him. "You're both being ridiculous."

I don't particularly care that Coop's suspicious or annoyed. It's whatever. But he's got this perpetual sense of entitlement to know and have an opinion on everything I do—and I'm so over it. Over him acting out his hang-ups on me. My twin brother playing a poor approximation of a father I never asked for.

"Can we move on?" Mac says in frustration, glancing between the two of us. "Please?"

But it's too late now. I'm pissed, and the only thing that will make me feel better is rubbing it in his self-righteous face. "It's Shelley."

Cooper comes up short. His face is expressionless for a moment, as if he isn't sure he heard me right. Then he smirks, shaking his head. "Right."

I throw my phone at him.

He looks at the screen, then at me. All humor and disbelief has been replaced by cold, quiet rage. "Your brain fall out of your head?"

"She's getting better."

"Jesus Christ, Evan. You get how stupid you sound?"

Rather than answer, I glance at Mac. "This is why I didn't tell him."

When I turn back, Cooper's up in my face, all but standing on my toes. "That woman was ready to run off with our life savings and you just, what, go crawling back to Mommy the first chance you get?"

I set my jaw and back away from him. "I didn't ask you to like it. She's my mother. And I'm not kidding—she's making a real effort, man. She has a steady job, her own apartment. She enrolled in beauty school to get her hairdressing certificate. Hasn't had so much as a sip of booze in months."

"Months? You've been doing this behind my back for *months*? And you actually believe her crap?"

I swallow a tired sigh. "She's trying, Coop."

"You're pathetic." When he spits out the words, it's like he's had them sitting in his mouth for twenty years. "The time for getting over your mommy issues was when you stopped sleeping with a night-light."

"Dude, I'm not the one flying off the handle at the mention of her."

"Look at what you're doing." He advances on me, and I take another step back, only because I was just praising my self-restraint to Gen earlier. "One drunk, deadbeat woman walks out on you, so you go fall in love with another one. Man, you can't hang on to either one of them, and you never will."

My fist itches to put a dent in Cooper's face. He can say what he wants about our mother. He's earned his anger the honest way. But no one talks like that about Gen while I'm around.

"Because you're my blood, I'm going to pretend I didn't hear that," I tell him, my voice tight with restraint. "But if you feel like you got too many teeth in your mouth, go ahead and try that shit again."

"Hey, hey." Mac wedges herself between us and manages to walk Coop back a couple paces, though his glare still says he's thinking about my offer. "Both of you take it down a notch." She puts both hands on Cooper's chest until he drops his gaze to hers. A few breaths later, she's got his attention. "I know you don't want to hear this, but maybe give Evan the benefit of the doubt."

"We tried that last time." He flicks his gaze to me. "How'd that turn out?"

"Okay," she says quietly. "But this is now. If Evan says Shelley's making an effort, why not trust him? You could go have a look for yourself. If you'd be open to meeting her."

He tears away from Mac. "Oh, fuck off. Both of you. This ganging up stuff isn't cute most of the time, but about this?" Cooper levels Mac with a withering glare. "Mind your goddamn business."

At that, he storms off, marching back up to the house.

Unfortunately, this isn't the first time he's lost his cool over Shelley, and it's not likely to be the last. Mac has more experience with his tantrums than she should. Which is to say, she isn't fazed.

"I'll work on him," she promises me with a sad smile before going after him.

Well. No one walked away bloody. We might call that a success, under the circumstances.

I don't hold out much hope for Mac's mission, though. Cooper's been burned one too many times, so I can't say his reaction is entirely unwarranted. In our family history, Shelley's done more wrong than right, the worst of it practiced on Coop, as he was always the one trying to protect me from her latest betrayal. His self-imposed, older-by-three-minutes big brother complex insisted it was his job to shield me from the awful truth: that our mom was unreliable at best and downright malicious at worst.

So I get it. Because now it feels like I've betrayed him, thrown all the brothering back in his face to take her side. But the thing is, while he reached his tolerance for her a long time ago, I've still got some left. And I have to believe people can change. I *need* to believe it.

Otherwise, what the hell am I doing with my life?

CHAPTER 27

GENEVIEVE

Trina is a piece of work. We met in detention in the sixth grade and became fast friends. She enjoyed skipping class and smoking cigarettes in the baseball dugout as much as I did, so really, it was inevitable that we'd cross paths. And while I have more good memories of Trina than bad, I'm still nervous when I walk into the bar to meet her. Even when we were kids, she always had an infectious quality about her. Like she was having so much fun, you wanted in on whatever she was getting up to. Insatiable and alluring.

Evan's right, though. If I can survive Trina's temptations, I'll most definitely be cured.

"Damn it, Gen."

Winding through the crowded high-top tables, I turn at the familiar voice. Trina sits at a table against the wall, an empty highball and a bottle of beer in front of her. She hops to her feet and gives me a tight hug.

"I hoped you'd gotten hideous since the last time I saw you," she says, brushing my hair off my shoulder. "Would it have killed you to sprout some heinous zits for the occasion?"

"My bad," I laugh.

"Sit down, slag." She looks over my shoulder and waves for a waitress. "Catch me up. What the hell have you been up to?"

We didn't really talk after I left Avalon Bay. As I did with most of this town, I quit cold turkey. Other than some texts here and there, I'd kept my distance, even muting her on social media so I couldn't be tempted by her exploits.

"As it turns out, I start a new job soon. Cooper's girlfriend is reopening The Beacon Hotel. I'm the new manager."

"For real?" She's incredulous at first. Then, apparently realizing there isn't a punchline coming, she throws back a swig of her beer. "That means the next time I come to town, you're hooking me up with a room. I think me and my dear mother have exceeded our quota of quality time."

I grin. "Didn't you get in last night?"

"Exactly." Her eyes widen. "Shit, I'm sorry. I heard about your mom. You okay?"

It seems like ages ago now, though it's only been a few months. The reminders of Mom are fewer and further between. "Yeah," I say honestly. "I'm good. Thank you."

"I'd have been at the funeral if I'd known. But I only heard recently."

I don't think she means them to, but the words come out like an accusation. She'd have been there if I'd bothered to tell her, is the subtext. If I hadn't all but ghosted her a year ago. But that's probably my own guilt talking.

"It's fine, really. Was mostly a family thing. She didn't want a big fuss." Least of all from her kids.

Trina gets a menacing glint in her eye as she sips her drink. "You seeing much of Evan lately?"

I swallow a sigh. For just one night, can't something be about anything but him? My head's been on backwards since I came back to town. I'm my favorite self when I'm with him—and also my worst. Everything at both extremes wrapped up in this volatile cocktail we become.

"Sometimes, I guess. I don't know. It's complicated."

"You've been using that same line since we were fifteen."

And I don't feel much better equipped than I was then.

"So what's up?" With another mouthful of beer, she plasters on her usual irreverence when she reads the heaviness closing in. "You back for good now?"

"Looks that way." It's strange. I don't remember making the decision to stay. It just snuck up on me, the ties reattaching overnight while I slept. "Dad's selling the house, so I need to find a new place soon."

"I've given some thought to sticking around too."

I snort a laugh. "Why?"

Trina always hated this town. Or rather, the people. She loved her friends fiercely, the few she kept. Beyond that, she'd have lit a match and never looked back. Or so I thought.

We're briefly interrupted when the waitress finally makes it to our table. She looks young and flustered, a new hire struggling through the waning weeks of the summer crush. I order a club soda and ignore Trina's judgmental eyebrow.

"I don't know. . . . This place is a drag," she says. "But it's home, I guess." There's something in the way her gaze drifts to the soggy coaster, the way her fingernail picks at the corners, that suggests a deeper explanation.

"How are things?" I ask carefully. "LA not agreeing with you these days?"

"Eh, you know me. I've got a four-second attention span. I think maybe I've seen and done everything worth doing in that city."

Only from Trina would I believe that. "You still working at the dispensary?" The least surprising part of her West Coast move was getting a job doing stuff that, around here, still gets you thrown in jail.

"Sometimes. Also bartending a little. And this guy I know, he's a photographer, I help him out now and then, too."

"This guy . . ." I watch as she dodges eye contact. "Is that a thing?"

"Sometimes."

The conundrum of Trina is a bitter one. Few others I know manage to suck as much out of every minute of their lives as she does—eyes open and arms wide, try anything once, twice as much—and yet, at the same time, be so utterly unfulfilled. There's a hole in the bottom of her soul, where everything good leaks out and all the worst, thickest, blackest muck clings to the sides.

"He's an artist," she says by way of an explanation. "His work is important to him."

Which is the kind of thing people say when they're making excuses for why their needs aren't being met.

"Anyway, I didn't tell him I was coming here. Probably still hasn't noticed my stuff is gone."

A wave of sympathy swells in my chest. I felt like that for a long time. I kept grasping for anything at all to satisfy me, whether it was good for me or not. How could I know unless I found out for myself, though? It takes a lot of trial and error to realize all the good advice we ignored along the way.

When our drinks arrive, she drains the last of her previous beer and gets a start on the next. "Enough chat," she announces, running a hand through her hair. She's wearing it shorter these days, which gives her even more of a tough girl vibe. "I'm bored with myself."

"Okay. How shall we entertain ourselves?"

"If I remember right, you owe me a rematch. Rack 'em up, West."

I follow her to the pool table, where we split two games and call it a draw. From there, we barhop down the boardwalk, with Trina ingesting a quantity of shots and beers that would kill a man twice her size.

It's a relief, actually. A taste of the old life without the accompanying blackout. And it's incredible the things you notice when you're not wasted. Like the guy who hits on Trina at the second bar. She thinks he's twenty-five, but really, he's pushing forty with a spray tan, Botox, and a tan line from his missing wedding ring. Still, he's good for a couple drinks before she instigates him up to the karaoke mic for shits and giggles, as if he's her personal court jester. I'd feel bad for the dude if I wasn't sure there's a kid at home somewhere, whose college fund will be a little lighter after this midlife crisis.

"He was not forty," she insists too loudly when I inform her, as we trudge down the boardwalk in search of our next venue. "It was the lighting!"

"Babe, he had white chest hairs."

Trina shudders, a tremble of revulsion that vibrates through each limb. She makes a dry gagging noise while I howl with laughter.

"No," she moans.

"Yes," I confirm between giggles.

"Well, where were you? Tell a girl next time. Throw up some hand signals or something."

"What's sign language for pendulous, sagging testicles?"

Now we're both doubling over in hysterics.

The boardwalk at night is a drag strip of lights and music. Shops with neon signs and bright window displays. People pouring out of bars with the competing soundtracks mingling in the humid salt air. Patio restaurants bursting with tourists and souvenir cups. Every dozen steps or so, a young guy is barking about two-for-one drinks or free cover.

"Live music," one of them says, shoving his arm out to give Trina a pale green flyer for the music venue around the corner. "No cover before midnight."

"Are you in a band?" A flicker of interest brightens her eyes.

Trina has this way about her. Flirtatious in a vaguely threatening manner. It's hysterical when she's had a little to drink. When she's had a lot, it's not dissimilar to a lit firecracker that's stalled. You stand there. Waiting. Watching. Certain the moment you try to intervene, it'll explode and take your fingers and eyebrows with it.

"Uh, yeah," he says, hiding his fear behind an alert smile. Some guys like the hot, scary ones, and some have a sense of self-preservation. "I play bass."

He's cute, in a Disney Channel punk rock sort of way. The kid who grew up with parents that encouraged his creative endeavors and put out a plate of fresh-baked cookies while he did homework. I'll never understand the well-adjusted.

"Oh." Trina's carnivorous grin flattens to a grimace. "Well, no one's perfect."

We take the invitation, nonetheless, if only because it's the closest restroom that doesn't require a purchase in advance. Together, Trina and I stand in line down a dingy hallway covered in framed concert photographs and graffiti. It smells of cheap liquor, mildew, and perfume-scented sweat.

"You realize you've probably jinxed that poor guy, right?" I tell her.

"Please."

"Seriously. You just put ten years of bad mojo on him. What if he was supposed to become the next great American bassist? Now he's going to end up vacuuming baseboards at the Spit Shine car wash."

"The world needs bass players," she says. "But I can't be responsible for their misplaced notions of fuckability."

"Paul McCartney played bass."

"That's like saying Santa is fuckable. That's nasty, Gen."

Six women stumble out of the single-toilet restroom, sloppy and laughing. Trina and I take our turn. She splashes water on her face while I pee.

After we've both finished up and washed our hands, Trina pulls a small compact out of her purse. Under it is a little plastic baggie of white powder. She dips her finger in to gather some in her nail and snort it up her nose. Takes another up the other nostril, then spreads the excess on her teeth, sucking them dry.

"Want a bump?" She offers the compact to me.

"I'm good."

Cocaine was never my vice. I smoked plenty and drank like a sailor. Dropped acid every now and then. But I was never tempted by the harder stuff.

"Oh, come on." She tries shoving it at me. "I haven't said anything all night, but your sobriety is starting to become a buzzkill."

I shrug. "I think you've got enough buzz for both of us."

Big saucer eyes plead with me. "Just one little hit. Then I'll shut up."

"But then who's going to stop you from going home with some middle-aged car salesman?"

"You make a good point, West." Backing off, she snaps the compact shut and drops it in her purse.

To each their own. Trina gets no judgment from me. We all have our coping mechanisms, and I'm in no position to fault anyone for theirs. Just not my bag.

"So this straight-edge thing," she muses as we exit the restroom and scout a good table for the show. "You serious about that?"

We spot a two-seater high-top beside the stage and make a beeline to snag it.

I nod slowly. "Yeah, I think so."

I'm rather proud of myself, in fact. A whole night together, and I've yet to hop on a table or steal a pedicab. I'm still having a good time, not once missing a drink. That's progress.

Lifting a flask from her purse, Trina nods. "Cheers to that, then. May your liver bring you many years of health and prosperity."

Hell, if Trina can accept the new me, maybe there's hope yet. Maybe I really can make this change stick, and I'm not simply fooling myself.

Our party swells during the concert. A group of friends we went to high school with wander by our table and pull up a few stools. Some, like Colby and Debra, I hadn't seen in years. When the second act of the night turns out to be a '90s one-hit-wonder cover band, the entire place goes bonkers, everyone singing slurred, slightly wrong lyrics at the tops of our lungs. We're all breathless and hoarse by the time Trina and the rest of the group go outside to the smoking patio, while I babysit her purse at the bar and order a very big glass of ice water. I pull out my phone to find a missed text from Evan earlier in the night.

Evan: *You haven't asked for bail yet. Good sign?*

I have to admit, he was right. Meeting up with Trina turned out to be an affirming experience. Hardly the catastrophe I'd worked it up to be in my head. But I'm definitely not going to tell him that. Evan doesn't need any ego stroking from me.

Me: *We're on 95 with a one-eyed bounty hunter and his pet wolverine hot on our trail. Send snacks.*

When I feel a hand tap me on the shoulder, I'm impressed

Evan managed to track us down. But then I turn around and am met with the dark, pleated polyester of a sheriff's deputy uniform and the potbelly of Rusty Randall.

"Genevieve West." He grabs my wrist and roughly jerks it behind my back. "You're under arrest."

My jaw drops. "Seriously? For what?"

I'm pulled off my stool, struggling to find my feet. People around us retreat, some taking out their phones to record. Camera flashes blind me while my brain stutters to understand what's happening.

"Possession of a controlled substance." He wrenches my other arm behind my back, where metal cuffs bite into my skin. Deputy Randall grabs Trina's purse, picking through it, until he pulls out the compact and opens it to reveal the baggie of cocaine.

"That's not even my purse!" I shout, my head spinning with the instinct to run or fight or . . . something. I look desperately at the door to the smoking patio.

Wrapping his hand around my biceps, he leans close to my ear and whispers, "Should've left town while you had the chance."

CHAPTER 28

GENEVIEVE

Outside, I'm pushed up against the side of Randall's car, my face to the window, while he runs his fat, sweaty hands down my arms, ribs, and legs.

"You're just loving this," I say through gritted teeth. "Pervert."

He takes my phone, keys, and ID from my pockets and throws them on the roof of the car with Trina's purse. "Know what your problem is, Genevieve? You don't appreciate discretion."

"The hell does that mean?"

"It was only a matter of time before you screwed up again." His fingers comb through my hair as though I've got some needles and maybe a bowie knife stashed in there. "I told you, I've got eyes everywhere."

"Then your snitches are even dumber than you are."

He chuckles cruelly. "Yet you're the one in cuffs."

As he finishes patting me down, I'm trying to figure out how someone would have known about the coke. The person Trina bought it from in town? A lucky guess? Either option feels equally unlikely. But then, who knows the shady deals Randall's cut? The man is as corrupt as they come.

It occurs to me, then, that at any point in the night when Trina and I were separated—while one of us went to the bar for another round or to the restroom alone—she might have done a bump in front of any number of witnesses. It only takes one of them to have seen us together.

He grabs a plastic bag from the trunk of his cruiser and throws my stuff and Trina's purse inside. Then, with a sick grin, he opens the rear door and pushes my head down to shove me into the backseat.

"Sorry about the smell," he chirps. "Haven't had a chance to clean it out after the last guy threw up."

As long as I live, I'll remember his sadistic smile as he slams the door shut. And if it's the last thing I do, I'll get to wipe it off his smug face.

At the sheriff's office, I sit in a plastic chair against a wall down a narrow hallway with the drunk and disorderlies, prostitutes, and other pissed off victims of tonight's dragnet.

"Hey!" The frat boy with a bloody nose at the end of the row shouts at a passing deputy. "Hey! You get my dad on the phone. Hear me? My dad's gonna kick your ass."

"Man, shut up." A few chairs down, the townie with a black eye stares up at the ceiling. "No one cares about your stupid daddy."

"You're so dead. Every one of you idiots are so dead." The frat boy rattles around in his chair, and I realize they have him cuffed to it. "When my dad gets down here, you'll all be sorry."

"Dude," the townie says. "I'm already sorry now. If I have to keep listening to this pussy whine, someone just hand me a gun. I'll pistol-whip myself."

I'm tired, hungry, and I've had to pee since the moment Randall tossed me in the cruiser. My foot bounces with the anxiety of waiting. My mind runs a mile a minute, picturing Trina walking inside to find me and her purse gone, and wondering if she's figured out what's happened. I ponder the chances she'll have gotten in touch with my dad or one of my brothers, considering her phone is likely sitting in an evidence locker right now. Then I realize, if she *has* figured it out, she's not coming back for me. She's getting the hell out of the state before the cops pull her driver's license out of that purse and go looking for her too.

"You're doing fine." The woman in a sequin tank top and miniskirt has an almost Zen-like quality about her as she sits beside me, utterly relaxed. "Don't worry. It's not as scary as it looks on TV."

"When do we get to call someone? We get a phone call, right?"

Ironically, as many times as I've gotten myself in and out of trouble, I've never sat in this police station before. Given my previous lifestyle, I probably should have made a greater effort to understand the finer details of the criminal justice system.

In response, the woman tilts her head back and closes her eyes. "Get comfortable, sweetie. This could take a while."

"A while" is an understatement. It takes more than an hour just to get fingerprinted. Another hour for photographs. Another hour of waiting some more. It feels like every deputy in the station comes by to leer at me, each one with a look of amusement or smug satisfaction. I recognize some of them who'd wagged their fingers and sneered at me when I was in high school. They leave me with a visceral sense of the powerlessness of incarceration, and I'm only sitting in a well-lit hallway. Within these walls, they have all the power and we have none. We're guilty degenerates because they say so. Unworthy of respect or basic human decency. It's enough to radicalize even the softest suburbanite.

There's another hour of paperwork and more sitting around before we're finally placed in holding cells. Men and women separated. My wrists are sore and bruised when I take a seat on a bench beside a sleeping homeless woman. In the corner, a blonde tourist, probably about my age, cries silently into her hands, while her friend sits beside her looking bored. The metal toilet-sink combo on the far wall smells like every bar bathroom in the Bay flushes into it, curing me of any thoughts of having to go.

Sometime in the middle of the night, my name snaps me out of my meditation on the stains on the floor.

I glance toward the iron bars and almost burst into tears. It's Harrison. In uniform.

Because this night hasn't been mortifying enough.

Reluctantly, I go meet him at the front of the cell. "This is fitting, huh? Like a blind date game show reveal."

"I heard you were here and came as soon as I could." The poor guy appears genuine in his concern. "You alright? Anyone mistreating you?"

I don't know if he's asking about the people inside this cell or out. "I'm fine, given the circumstances." I smile wryly. "Don't suppose you want to accidentally drop a key and walk away."

"Okay," he says, his voice lowering to a stage whisper. "But you need to make it look convincing so I can tell them you over-powered me when I tried to stop you."

"Seriously, though. How does this work? I have money. If you can post my bail or whatever, I'll pay you back. They haven't even let me call someone yet."

He looks away with a sigh of frustration. "The sheriff's out of town at some family thing, so no one's in a big hurry to push papers."

Meaning any hope I had that Sheriff Nixon might realize I'm in here, and at least let my dad know, is right out the window. It wasn't a sure thing, but Hal Nixon and Dad play in a monthly poker game and have gotten chummy over the past couple years. I thought maybe, if I was extremely lucky, Nixon would let me plead my case that this whole thing is a misunderstanding blown sideways by a vindictive asshole.

"Can't post bail until they file the arrest," Harrison continues. "I don't know what the holdup is on phone calls. I'll see about that."

"I didn't do it." I look him square in the eye. "This is Randall again. You saw him. He's got a vendetta."

"We'll get this straightened out." Conflict and indecision contort his face.

Not that I'm feeling especially magnanimous, given my current situation, but I've had some time for deep contemplation lately, and I can appreciate that the fragile worldview of a rookie cop is perhaps a bit shaken when confronted with such blatant shitfuckery. These are his people, after all.

My tone softens. "It was sweet of you to check on me. Even if it was just to confirm I'm stuck here."

His tense posture relaxes. "I'm sorry. I feel like there's more I should do, but I really don't hold a lot of cards here."

"Tell you what," I say, sticking my hand through the bars to hold his. "When they give me the chair, I want you to be the one to throw the switch."

"Jesus." Harrison coughs out a disturbed laugh. "You're something else."

Which is a nice way of saying I'm better in small doses. "Yeah. I get that a lot."

"I'm going to see what I can find out. I'll try to make it back if I can. You want me to call anyone for you?"

I shake my head. As much as I want out of here, it'll be worse if Dad gets the call from Harrison instead of me. Besides, I've just gotten used to the smell in here.

"Go on, Deputy. Get out of here."

With a last regretful nod, he walks away.

Harrison never does find his way back. Instead, it's a sleepless night and an impatient morning before I'm allowed to make a phone call.

"Dad . . ." The embarrassment I feel when he answers, knowing what I have to say to him—I've had all night to agonize over it, and it's still worse than I anticipated. "Listen, I'm at the sheriff's office."

"Are you okay? What happened?" Dad's concern ripples over the line.

I hate this. Standing at a phone on the wall with a line behind me, I etch nervous patterns into the chipping paint with my thumbnail. My stomach churns queasily as I force myself to say the words.

"I was arrested."

He's quiet while I rush to explain. That the purse wasn't mine. That Randall's got it out for me. And the more I talk, the angrier I get. All of this started when I wouldn't accept the sexual advances of a married man with a badge. For so long, I felt guilty for wrecking that family with my drunken intrusion, but it hits me now that I didn't do that to him. *He* did. He set this entire year-long chain of events in motion because he's a sick, petty person. I should have kicked him in the scrotum when I had the chance.

"I swear, Dad. It wasn't mine. I'll take a drug test. Anything." My heart clenches tight against my rib cage. "I promise you. This isn't like before."

There's a long silence after I've stopped talking, during which I start to panic. What if he's had it with my shit, and this is one time too many? What if he leaves me in here to learn a lesson he should have taught me a long time ago? Gives up on his worthless, wayward daughter who was going to run out on him and the family business anyway.

"You sure you're okay?" he asks gruffly.

"Yeah, I'm okay."

"Alright, good. Hang tight, kiddo. I'm on my way."

It's only minutes before a deputy calls my name and opens the cell. As he escorts me from the holding area and through the bullpen of desks, I'm relieved that Randall isn't skulking around somewhere waiting for me. After our first run-in when I returned to the Bay, I understood that he had an ax to grind. When he showed up to hassle Harrison and I after our date, I prepared myself that he would become a perpetual annoyance. But this was a drastic escalation. And who knows what else is in store for me? This time, he throws me behind bars. Next time, maybe he isn't satisfied with conventional means of retribution. I'd hate to see what happens when he decides to be creative.

The deputy opens an office door and points me inside, where the sheriff is sitting in a polo shirt behind his desk. My father stands from his chair and gives me a tight nod.

"Good?" he says.

"Fine." As fine as I can be, anyway. When I notice the paper bag and cup of coffee sitting on the corner of the desk, I quirk a brow. "That for me?"

"Yeah, I brought you something," Dad says. "Figured you might be hungry."

I tear into the bag and practically inhale the two greasy sausage-and-egg sandwiches. I don't taste any of it when I wash it down with hot black coffee, but I feel better immediately. The exhausted haze has been chased away, my belly no longer fighting itself. Though now I really need to pee.

"Let me say," Sheriff Nixon speaks up, "I'm sorry about this whole mix-up."

That's a start.

"I had a look at the purse," he continues. "The ID, credit cards, and other personal items clearly all belong to a young lady named Katrina Chetnik."

I look to my father. "That's what I tried to tell him."

Dad nods, then narrows his eyes at the man behind the desk. "Sitting next to a purse at a crowded bar ain't a crime. Correct?"

"No, it isn't." To the sheriff's credit, he looks irritated with the whole scenario too. Annoyed to have been dragged down here on a Sunday to clear this mess up. "We'll make an effort to locate the owner."

Meaning Trina's problems are just beginning. But I can't say I care much about that. After spending a night in jail, I'm not about to run interference for her. She knew the risks. In hindsight, it was shitty of her to leave me sitting there with her coke in the first place.

There's a sharp knock on the door. A moment later, Rusty Randall enters. Apparently called in from home, he's dressed in a T-shirt and jeans, and I do take some small joy in the idea he was woken by an urgent call telling him the boss said *get your ass down here.*

Randall appraises me, then my father. Nothing about the scene appears to jostle him in the slightest. With his hands on his hips, he stands in the center of the room. "You needed to see me, sir?"

"Rusty, we'll be sending Ms. West home with our sincere apologies for her trouble. You can take care of the paperwork. I'll want to see a report on my desk by EOB."

"Fine," he says, voice tight.

"Anything you'd like to say?" the sheriff prompts, cocking his head.

Randall doesn't so much as blink in my direction. "I acted on probable cause for the arrest. My actions were entirely appropriate.

Of course, I respect your decision, and will handle that paperwork at once."

Coward.

But we both know he'd sooner wax his legs than apologize or admit he was wrong. Doesn't make much difference to me, though, because I couldn't care less what that man thinks.

"Ronan," Sheriff Nixon says, "go and get her home. And Ms. West . . ." He regards me for a moment. "I don't imagine I'll see you in here again."

I'm not sure how much I should read into his remark. Whether he means he'll see to it there aren't any further dirty arrests, or that he expects I've been scared straight. Either way, no, I don't believe we'll be seeing much more of each other. Not if I can help it.

"Not a chance," I agree.

Despite having my name cleared, the ride home only exacerbates my shame. I might have been wrongfully arrested, but my dad still had to call the sheriff first thing in the morning to get his only daughter out of jail. It was humiliating for me, so I suspect it was no picnic for him, either.

"I'm sorry," I say, cautiously studying his profile.

He doesn't respond, intensifying my guilt.

"I get that what I do reflects on you and the business. And even though the drugs weren't mine, and I wasn't using, I still placed myself in that situation. I knew Trina had the coke and I should have walked away. 'Cause let's be honest, a couple years ago, it wouldn't have been unheard of that the purse would have been mine."

"First of all," he says. "I'm not mad."

He watches the road as his jaw works, like he's trying to arrange his thoughts.

"Sure, you've made some mistakes. A couple years is a long time, though, and you're not that girl anymore." His voice softens. "I'd have gone down there no matter what you told me. You're my daughter, Genevieve." Dad glances at me. "But let's be clear. I had no doubt you were telling the truth. Don't think I haven't noticed the changes you've made. They matter."

Emotion clogs my throat. It suddenly occurs to me that I've spent so much time trying to convince myself I was for real, I missed when other people started to believe it. My dad. My friends. Evan.

I speak through the lump threatening to choke me. "I didn't want you to think this was me acting out or backsliding. That because of Mom or whatever . . ." The thought dies on my tongue. He doesn't acknowledge the mention of her, which I immediately regret. "But that's not the case at all. I'm trying so hard to be a better person, to take myself more seriously and have others do the same. I would never jeopardize that, especially now that I've got a new job starting soon."

Dad nods slowly. "Right. I don't know if I said this when you told me about the hotel, but . . . I'm proud of you, kiddo. This could end up being a big career for you."

"That's the plan." I give him a faint smile. "And no, you didn't say anything about being proud. If I recall correctly, you said 'congratulations' and then kind of grumbled about how Shane will make a terrible office manager."

He chuckles sheepishly. "I don't like change."

"Who does?" I shrug, adding, "Don't worry, we're not going to let Shane anywhere near that office. I already promised I'll help you interview candidates. We'll find an even better office manager than me."

"Doubt it," Dad says gruffly, and damned if that doesn't make my heart expand with pride. My throat closes up a little too.

"Hey, at least my replacement won't have a rap sheet," I say to lighten the mood.

"What's the deal with Rusty, anyway?" my father asks, glancing over suspiciously. "He have it out for you for some reason?"

Sighing, I tell him the truth. Most of it, anyway; there are still some things I won't repeat in front of my father. But he gets the gist. How Randall accosted me in the bar. How anger and too much to drink drove me into his living room to traumatize his family. The threats and run-ins since then.

"He blames me for destroying his family," I admit. "To some extent, I did too."

"That man did it to himself." Dad's features are cold and unforgiving. Randall's not going to want to bump into him in a dark alley anytime soon.

We ride in silence for a while. I don't interrupt what feels like his attempt to process all the information I just gave him. At which point I realize we're taking the long way home. My palms go damp. I guess this is the talk we've been putting off since I returned home.

"You're the most like your mother," he says suddenly. His eyes remain squarely on the road. "I know you two didn't get along. But I swear you're the spitting image of her when she was younger. She was a wild thing, back then."

I settle back in my seat, staring out the window at the little passing houses. Flickering, blurry images of my mother come to mind. They get fuzzier with every passing day, the details fading.

"Having a family changed her. I think I changed her first, if I'm honest. I've been wondering a lot lately, you know, if I broke her spirit—wanting to have a big family."

My gaze flies to his. "I don't understand."

"She was this energetic, lively woman when I met her. And

little by little, she dimmed. I don't even know how much she noticed until the light was all but gone."

"I always figured it was us." My voice cracks slightly. "I assumed she didn't like us, that maybe we didn't turn out the way she hoped."

Dad takes a deep breath, which he expels in a gust. "Your mom suffered a rough bout of postpartum depression after Kellan. Then we found out she was pregnant with Shane, and that seemed to help some. For a little while. Truth is, I don't know if she wanted so many kids because I did, or if she hoped the next one might snap her out of it. The next one would come along and fix her." He glances at me, full of remorse and sadness. "When she had Craig, something changed. The depression didn't come. Whatever hormones or chemicals are supposed to kick in that help women bond with the infant—well, it finally happened. And that only made her feel guiltier. She'd tried so damn hard to bond with the rest of you and was constantly fighting the depression, the dark thoughts, and then with Craig it was suddenly easy, and—"

He exhales a ragged breath, gaze still fixed on the road ahead. By the time he speaks again, I'm holding my breath. On pins and needles.

"Christ, Gen, you have no idea how much it ripped her apart, having that easy relationship with him when her relationships with the rest of you were so difficult. Her greatest fear was being a bad mom, and it crippled her. She couldn't get past the idea she was screwing you kids up. I don't know everything that went on in Laurie's head, but you've got to understand it wasn't her fault. Whatever it is, you know. The chemicals in her brain or whatever. She hated herself the most."

My eyes feel hot, stinging. I never thought about it that way. It wasn't something we talked about in our family. It felt like she hated us, so that was the truth we believed. Or I did, at least. Not once did it occur to me it was an illness, something she was incapable of controlling and even ashamed of. It must have felt so much easier for her to stop trying, to back away from the fear of breaking her kids. But, God, how much we all suffered for it.

Nothing changes our childhood, the years lost without a mother. The pain and torment of growing up believing that the act of being born, a decision we had no part in, was the reason she hated us. But Dad's pained confession, this new, sad piece of knowledge, changes a lot of how I feel about her now. How I look back on her.

And how I look at myself.

CHAPTER 29

EVAN

There's something in the air. I've got a crew at a storm-damaged house we're renovating for a flipper, and since lunch, the guys have been acting weird. I keep catching furtive glances and whispered conversations. People going silent when I walk into a room, yet feeling their eyes, everywhere, watching me. It's creepy is what it is. The scene before the pod people turn in unison and descend to assimilate their hapless target. Swear to God, if anything tries to probe me or vomit down my throat, I'm swinging a sledgehammer and aiming for nut sacks.

In the second-floor master bath, I catch my shift chief, Alex, hunched over a phone with the guy who's supposed to be installing the new tub.

"Grady, I'm pretty sure you billed us for something like thirty hours of overtime on that Poppy Hill job," I say loudly, and the tub guy startles and drops his phone into his pocket. "How do you figure Levi's gonna react when I tell him you're up here standing around on your phone with your dick in your hand?"

"I got you, boss. No problems. Gonna have all this . . ." Grady gestures at the tub, sink, and toilet left to install. "Gonna get it wrapped by today. Don't worry."

Amazing how agreeable people become when your name is on their paychecks.

To my shift chief, a young guy I vouched for to get this job, I give a nod to follow me down the hall. Alex and I step into one of the empty bedrooms, where I narrow my eyes. "What the hell is going on with everyone today?"

He hesitates to answer, taking off his baseball cap to scratch his head and then adjust and readjust it, hoping perhaps I might forget my question in the meantime. It sets my teeth on edge.

"What is it, for chrissake?" I demand.

"Yeah, um, so . . ." Oh, for the love of God. "Well, word is Genevieve got arrested. For like cocaine or something."

"What?" A cold tide rushes through my limbs. "When?"

"Last night. I mean, the rumor is she was caught moving a kilo of coke to an undercover agent on the boardwalk, but that's just talk. The way I heard it from my cousin who was working barback last night, some cop came in and found drugs in her purse, only she was telling him it wasn't her purse. Anyway, that girl Trina was looking for her a little while after that."

Damn it.

"We weren't sure you heard," Alex continues. "So the guys—"

"Yeah, fine." I wave him off. "Just get back to work. And tell them to put their damn phones away. Nobody's getting overtime for screwing around."

Trina.

Of course.

I should have seen this coming. I know as well as anyone the shit that girl gets up to. Anger burns my throat, most of it self-directed. What part of driving Gen toward her did I think would end any other way? Especially with Deputy Randall skulking around trying to pin something on Gen. If I'd given even a single thought to Genevieve's best interest instead of my own, I would've seen this coming.

Fuck.

No wonder she ran away from me. This turn of events was so predictable, Gen tried everything short of beating me back with a baseball bat to keep me away from her. And as it turns out, with all my efforts to prove she was overreacting and that nothing bad would come of us being together, I proved her right the first chance I got. I was so wrapped up in pleading my case, changing her mind, that I didn't give a single thought to the repercussions if it went badly.

What kind of asshole is so damn selfish?

This isn't a minor consequence either. Gen was cuffed. Probably perp walked out of the bar in front of half the town and a hundred tourists. Paraded through the police station and degraded by the same jerks who've been telling her she was no good her whole life. She must have been tearing out of her skin.

And I put her there.

I spent all this time trying to convince her that I'd be good for her and make her life better. What a goddamn joke.

It's hours before I can leave the jobsite to see Gen. Throughout the day I agonized over whether to call her, but eventually decided having this conversation over the phone was more insulting than waiting to do it in person. Or maybe I'm a coward who hoped the delay would help me figure out what to say to her.

As I'm pulling up to her house, I'm still at a loss.

Gen's little brother Craig answers the door. With a knowing look that says *good luck*, he nods upstairs.

"She's in her room."

I knock a couple times, then let myself in when there's no answer. Gen's asleep on her bed in pajamas and a bathrobe, hair still wet. The largest part of me wants to leave. Let her sleep. The longer I can put this off, the more time I have to come up with something sufficient to say. But then she opens her eyes to find me standing in the doorway.

"Sorry," she says drowsily, gathering herself to sit up against her headboard. "I didn't get much sleep in the clink."

"I can go. Come back later."

"No. Stay." She draws her knees up to make room for me. "I take it the whole town knows by now?"

She doesn't look so bad, all things considered. A bit groggy and pale from exhaustion, but otherwise unscathed. It doesn't help the lump of guilt stuck in my throat, though.

"You okay? He try anything with you?" Because throwing a Molotov cocktail through Randall's bedroom window might go a long way to improving my mood.

She shakes her head. "It was fine. Not much worse than the DMV, honestly."

"That's what you've got? A night in the slammer and you're doing '90s sitcom humor?"

A weak smile curves her lips. It breaks my fucking heart. "I'm thinking about touring the prison circuit with some new material."

"Have you heard from Trina?"

"Nope." Gen shrugs. "I wish her well. If she's smart, she's well into Mexico by now."

When I open my mouth to speak again, she cuts me off.

"Can we not talk about it? Later, fine. Right now, I don't want to think about it anymore. It's been a long day."

"Yeah, of course."

Taking my hand, she pulls me to sit beside her against the headboard. "Hey, I never said this, but the house looks great. You guys did a stellar job on the renovations. I'm almost sad it's over."

"I am gonna miss you wandering around the house in skimpy silk nighties, watching me work up a sweat."

Gen snorts. "You have an active imagination."

"Oh, were you not there for that? Must have been some other leggy brunette with nice tits."

Her elbow jabs my ribs. "I meant now that it's over, Dad's going to put the house on the market. This won't be my room for much longer. And the place is so nice now, it's a shame to leave."

"A lot of good memories in this room." Climbing in her window after everyone's gone to bed. Sneaking her out of it.

"Kellan and Shane tried smoking some old pot they found hidden under the floorboards in Shane's closet." This time when she laughs, it reaches her eyes. The sound is comforting and debilitating all at once. "They were throwing up for hours. Shane swore he was going blind."

I want to laugh with her and reminisce about all the stuff we got away with in this house. Every time we held our breath under the covers having sex while her entire family slept a few feet away. Constantly in fear for my life that one of her brothers would barge in and break my dick off if he found me on top of her.

But all I can think about is that if circumstances were different, she might've been facing serious jail time because of me.

Only now does it occur to me that some of those memories—running from cops or whoever we pissed off that night, stumbling in drunk at fifteen, getting high and blowing off class—aren't as cute as they seemed in high school.

"Dad wants me to look at houses with him. With Mom gone, he's feeling a little overwhelmed with the decisions."

The words barely reach my ears. A thought spiral drops like a heavy blanket on top of me, my mind weighted with all the ways I haven't conceived of yet that I'll ruin this girl. She was happy when she came back. Maybe not right away, thanks to the funeral and everything. But when I compare the person who showed up at that first bonfire to the person sitting next to me now? She looks burnt out. Dried up. A couple months around me and I've already sucked the life out of her.

And no matter what I do to think my way out of this, I come

back to one undeniable conclusion: I did this to her. And if given the chance, I'll do it again.

"Actually, a couple days ago I drove by a house on Mallard. That blue one with the palms. It's a newer home. I looked it up on—"

"Gen." I launch to my feet. "Look, you were right."

"Huh?"

Agitated now, I pace the room. How do I do this? I don't want to come off as an asshole, but maybe it's well too late for that.

"Evan?" Her voice ripples with worry.

"I should have listened to you."

Fuck, why didn't I listen? She gave me a dozen opportunities to respect her wishes and keep my distance. I ignored every one of her warnings and went straight off a cliff. Slowly, I turn to face her, all the guilt and regret bubbling up and spilling over. What did she ever do to deserve me?

"I'm sorry, Fred."

Alarm grows in her expression. "About what?"

"You were right. This can't work. You and me."

"Evan." A wary look of disbelief sucks the color from her face. "This is because of last night? You didn't put the coke in Trina's purse. You didn't sic Randall on me. None of that is your fault."

"But I talked you into going. That's on me." My voice rises of its own volition. It feels like I don't have control of my own mind. The frustration running away with me. The anger at myself that I let this happen. "I'm no good for you. I'm sorry it took me so long to figure that out." I swallow. It hurts to do so. "You need to stay the hell away from me."

"You don't mean that." Gen jumps off the bed. "I get that you feel responsible, but it was not your fault."

"Don't do that." I pull myself away when she reaches for my arm. "You've been making excuses for me my whole life."

She rolls her head in frustration, huffing out a breath. "That's not what I'm doing. I was only nervous about going out with Trina because I didn't think I could resist getting trashed around her. You had more faith in me, and you were right. I didn't drink at all last night. She offered me some of her coke, and I didn't take it. The rest of the night was my choice. I stuck around. I let her leave her purse with me. At any point I could have said no and gone home." Fight flashes across her face. "You've been taking bullets for me *my* whole life. But I'm all grown up now, Evan. I don't need a martyr."

I appreciate what she's trying to do, but I can't let her. This is how habits start. She forgives me this time, and the next. And the next. Until inch by inch, she backslides into all the self-destructive patterns she's worked so hard to break. She always was the best part of us.

I love her. I'd rather never see her again than be the reason she hates herself.

"You should stick it out with your cop," I tell her, my voice cracking slightly before hardening with resolve. "He's a decent guy, and he'll bend over backward to make you happy. Better influence than I'll ever be."

"Evan."

I watch the realization cement in her eyes. Watch as she grasps for some lever to pull to make this stop. Then I turn my back on her.

"Evan!"

I'm out the door and down the stairs. Practically running to my bike. I have to get out of here before I lose my nerve. I know she's looking at me from her bedroom window when I speed away from the curb. The ache begins before I've reached the end of the block. By the time I get home, I can't feel anything. Not sure I'm even awake.

It's dark when I take a seat on the back deck later. Clouds block the stars and make the sky feel small and too close. The cricket songs and katydids roar inside my skull. This is shell shock. I'm not fully present in the aftermath.

A cold beer lands in my lap. Beside me, Cooper pulls up a chair.

"You check on Genevieve?" he asks.

I twist open my beer and take a swig. I don't taste a thing. "Think I broke up with her," I mumble.

He stares at the side of my face. "You okay?"

"Sure."

Turns out I could've saved everyone all sorts of grief if I'd listened to both of them. Coop doesn't know his head from his asshole where Gen is concerned, but as much as I hate his second-guessing, he does know me.

"I'm sorry," he tells me.

"She's not a bad girl." People have always given her a hard time for the crime of trying to enjoy her life. Maybe it's because her lust for it sparked envy, longing. Most people are too afraid to truly experience their lives. They're passengers or passive observers to a world happening around them. But not Gen.

"I know," Coop says.

When she left a year ago, it never really ended. Nothing was said. She was gone, but we remained frozen in place. Even after it'd been months and everyone told me to take the hint, I couldn't let go of where we'd left off. It was only ever a matter of time before she came home and we picked up again. Except it didn't happen that way. She changed. And though I hadn't noticed, so did I. We tried to shove ourselves back together, fill in the same blank spaces, but we don't fit the same way we used to.

"You love her?"

My throat closes up to the point of suffocation. "More than anything in the world."

She's the one. The only one. But it's not enough.

Cooper lets out a breath. "I am sorry. Whatever my beef is with Gen, you're my brother. I don't like seeing you hurting."

He and I have been through a lot with each other this past year. Finding one reason or another to be at odds. It's exhausting, honestly. And lonely. Nights like this remind me that whatever else happens, it's just the two of us.

"We've got to do a better job of being brothers," I say quietly. "I know this thing with Mom gets you mad, but do we have to come to blows about it every time her name comes up? Man, I don't want to keep this stuff from you. I don't like lying about where I am or sneaking away to take phone calls so you can't hear me. I feel like I'm tiptoeing around my own house."

"Yeah, I get it." Coop takes another swig of his beer, then turns the bottle between his palms while the breeze kicks up and blows in salt air from the beach. "I've spent so long being mad at her, I guess I wanted you to be upset at her with me. Kinda lonely out in the cold."

"I'm not trying to leave you out in the cold. I knew you weren't ready to let her back in. That's cool. I told her not to expect anything. Hell, I warned her you'd tell the FBI she had Jimmy Hoffa buried in her backyard if she came around here."

He coughs out a stiff laugh. "Not a bad idea. You know, if needed."

"Anyway, I didn't ask you to see her because I know how bad she messed you up last time. I'd wanted you to give her a chance and she'd betrayed you. Both of us. Yeah, I was worried she'd make me a sucker again. Still am. I'm not sure that feeling goes away when it comes to Shelley. This is just something I need to do. For me."

"I was thinking." His attention is drawn to his lap, where he picks at the melting label from the sweaty bottle. "Maybe I'd be willing to consider meeting up with her."

"Seriously?"

"Oh, what the hell." Cooper downs the last of his beer. "As long as you and Mac are there. What's the worst that can happen?"

I wouldn't have put money on such a dramatic change of heart. I doubt it was anything I said; more likely Mac worked on him. But it's all the same to me either way. We don't have much of a family left. It got even smaller today. I'm just here trying to cobble together as much as I can out of the bits and pieces. If we can stop fighting about this one thing, it'll go a long way.

"I'll set it up."

"Telling you now, though," he warns. "If she comes looking for a kidney, I'm giving her one of yours."

CHAPTER 30

GENEVIEVE

I've been sitting on the floor in the same place I landed when Evan walked out. Staring at the patterns in the carpet, the scuffs on the wall, trying to understand what just happened. I crawl back into bed, turn the light out, and hug the blankets tight around my shoulders with the scene playing through my mind. His cold detachment. The way, even when our eyes met, he seemed to look through me. Untouchable.

Did he actually break up with me? Yesterday I would've said he wasn't capable of such a cruel and sudden turn.

My memory of the conversation we just had is fragmented, as though I wasn't entirely present for it. Now I'm sewing clips together and still can't fathom how I ended up alone in the dark with an ache tearing at my chest.

It was one thing when I left last year. He was still here. The way we think of home as permanent. Safe in a memory. Unmovable.

Then I came back, and I thought I could keep him there. Perfect and preserved. Always the boy with more daring than sense. If I didn't let myself take him seriously or see him as a whole complex person, I wouldn't have to answer the hard questions about what these feelings were and what to do with them. What happens when the party girl and the bad boy grow up.

Now he's stolen that possibility from me, made the hard choice for us both. Except I wasn't ready. Time ran out and I'm left sitting here alone.

Why'd he do this to me? Make me care about him all over again, test every boundary and knock down every wall, if only to walk away now?

It hurts, damn it.

More than I thought it could.

And my mind won't stop running over what-ifs and if onlys. What if I hadn't been so obstinate at the start? If I hadn't set up quite so many hurdles to a relationship? If only I'd been more open, would we have had this all figured out by now?

I don't know.

None of it helps me sleep. I'm still staring at the ceiling well after one in the morning. And that's when a noise outside startles me.

I'm not sure what it is at first. A passing car with the radio on? The neighbors? For the briefest moment, my pulse lurches with the thought it might be Evan climbing his way up.

Suddenly something smashes against my bedroom window.

Loud and piercing. I'm frozen in panic for a second before I turn on my bedside lamp and run to the window. There I see the foaming liquid sheeting down the windowpane and the brown shards of glass littering the sill. A beer bottle, from the looks of it.

"You fucking slut bitch!"

Below, Rusty Randall stands unsteady on my front lawn, his outline barely visible in the outer edge of the streetlamp's glow. He staggers, shouting almost incoherently except for every other word or so.

"Bitch ex-wife . . ." He growls something about *won't let me see my damn kids* and *my own damn house.*

On the bed, my phone lights up, and I make a mad dash for it.

Kayla: *I know it's late but I wanted to warn you. Rusty was here. He's drunk and angry. Stay away if you see him.*

Kayla's house is just down the street. A quick walk on his belligerence tour. One more stop on the midnight grievance stroll. Tonight, of all nights, I'm not interested in entertaining his rage.

Luckily, I don't have to.

"What the hell was that?" Craig barges into my room rubbing crust out of his eyes as he comes to stand beside me at the window. "Is that the one who arrested you?"

"You did this!" Randall shouts again. "You fucking bitch!"

Craig and I both turn our heads when we hear the stairs creak followed by the front door opening. The floodlights from the front porch pop on, lighting Randall on the front lawn. A second later, our dad walks out in shorts and a T-shirt with a pump-action shotgun in his hands.

"Oh, shit. Dad's pissed," Craig breathes.

He's not the only one. More footsteps follow, down the stairs and out the door. Then Billy, Shane, and Jay walk out to stand behind our father. Six-foot-five Jay has a baseball bat slung over his shoulder. I didn't even know he and Shane were here tonight. Kellan must've kicked them out again for a chick.

Randall drunkenly grumbles at Dad. I can't hear them well, but by the gesticulations, I catch the gist.

"I don't care about a badge," Dad says, raising his voice. "You get the hell off my property."

When Randall doesn't move quick enough, Dad pumps the shotgun to reiterate his demand.

That gets Randall backpedaling, growling along the way to his car. The Fuck Around and Find Out Society remains undefeated.

Craig and I make our way out to the porch in time to see his taillights pass.

"That guy's a real weirdo," Jay says, strutting in like he just chased off the British Army single-handedly with his Louisville Slugger.

"Should have put one in his ass," Shane laughs as Dad comes in and safely stows the shotgun.

"He's driving drunk," Craig pipes up. "We should tell the sheriff."

"I'll call him," Dad says before glancing at me. "You okay, kiddo?"

"Yeah, good." I flick on the living room lights, and we all congregate on the sofas.

"We were watching upstairs," Craig tells them, a big dumb grin on his face. "I thought for sure you were going to shoot that guy."

Dad leans against the back of his recliner, grimacing.

I fight a rush of guilt-tinged anger. "I'm so sorry, Dad. I had no idea he'd show up here. Kayla texted me after he was already out there to tell me he'd been by her place too. Guess she wouldn't let him in."

"Uh-huh." After a beat, he walks around to sit in the big leather chair. "I think I'm gonna stay up for a little while. Make sure that numbskull doesn't get any dumb ideas."

"What's that guy's deal?" Craig searches all of us for an answer. "I mean, something happened, right?"

Billy meets my gaze.

It was bad enough having that conversation with my father. No way I'm rehashing it for my youngest brother.

"You knuckleheads get on back to bed," Dad tells the boys.

"I can't sleep now." Shane all but bounces at the end of the sofa. "I'm hyped. I'll stay up too. Sit on the front porch with the shotgun in case he comes back."

Jay rolls his eyes, then gives me a sympathetic nod. "Let's go."

"Oh, come on." Craig huffs at being dismissed. "I never get to hear the good stuff. Gen?"

He searches me for support or permission, but I just shrug and say, "I'll tell you when you're older."

He flips up his middle finger. "Aw, you're no fun."

Jay yanks Craig by the arm and then wrangles the others, pushing Billy and Shane up the stairs, while cooing, "Bedtime, kiddos." Which gets him more middle fingers and a "fuck off" from Billy.

I remain with Dad, watching him cautiously. To his credit, he'd remained remarkably cordial out there, given that a deranged man was screaming obscenities at his daughter and hurling bottles against the house. While his clenched fists and white knuckles suggest he'd like to reach for the shotgun again, he gives up only a threatening throat clearing as he reaches for his phone.

"I'm going to have a talk with the sheriff." Dad rises from his recliner to kiss the top of my head. "Go to bed, kiddo. I'm taking care of it."

Sometimes, a girl just needs her dad. As far as they go, mine's pretty alright.

CHAPTER 31

EVAN

I dream about her. One of those half-awake meanderings of the mind after my eyes have blinked open a couple times to clench shut again against the spill of sunlight across my face. It's not so much a dream as a memory of something that never happened, indistinct and evaporating before I can consciously hold on to it. But we're together, and when my brain finally rocks me awake, I'm reminded there's no sleeping this one off. I let her go. And dreams are all I have left.

Rolling over, I grab my phone from the nightstand to check the time. The screen is full of texts from Gen. It takes me a minute to get up to speed, not understanding what I'm reading because I'm seeing it in reverse order. Only the most recent show up first, so I scroll up to read them properly.

Gen: *Randall showed up here last night.*
Gen: *Screaming on my front lawn.*
Gen: *Threw a beer bottle at my window.*

That one slaps any lingering grogginess from my head.

Gen: *Dad chased him off with a shotgun.*
Gen: *Please, we need to talk.*

I'm out of bed and throwing on the first shirt and pair of shorts I find.

Gen: *I wouldn't ask if it wasn't important.*
Gen: *Things have changed. Meet me at our spot as soon as you get this. You owe me that much.*

Already, I'm regretting how I went at her yesterday, especially considering everything she'd already been through. I could have done it better. Gently. Now she sounds like she's afraid I'd ignore her, and that's never what I wanted. Distance, yeah. Enough for both of us to get used to the idea of living our own lives. So she could get on with hers without interference from me. But thinking she'd have to beg for my help when she's in trouble? That's an awful feeling.

I'm out the door only minutes later, peeling out of the driveway on my motorcycle. When I arrive at the narrow path that cuts through the trees to the hidden beach, Gen is already there, wearing a pair of cutoffs and a loose red T-shirt. She's on a blanket just above the tide line, staring at the waves.

"Hey," I say, announcing myself as I approach. "You okay? What happened?"

She doesn't stand, but encourages me to sit. "I'm fine. Good thing we didn't have any loose pavers lying around or we might have had you out installing new windows."

"I'm serious." I search her face, but she seems okay. Just a little tired. "Your messages sounded—"

"Right." She ducks her head. "Sorry. Didn't mean to scare you."

"It's fine." When Gen won't look at me, I bow to meet her eyes. "I mean it, it's cool. You need me, I'm here. No problem."

After a breath, her shoulders relax. Her finger draws aimless patterns in the sand as she explains what exactly went on last night. Finding the ranting lunatic in her yard. Ronan West walking out to meet him like Dirty Harry.

"So then Dad called the sheriff and told him to get his ass down to the station. They brought me in at the crack of dawn to fill out a petition for a restraining order. We hung around for a while making a formal police report while Sheriff Nixon had Randall brought in. He was arrested for drunk driving, and they put him on leave." A glint of vindication lights her expression. "They have to do a whole internal investigation thing, but Dad says he's getting canned."

"Good." It's about time. I get why it didn't go that way in the first place, but at least something's finally being done about that guy. Hopefully, it brings Gen some peace of mind. "Do you see now that none of his problems were your fault?"

She slides me a sarcastic side-eye. "Yeah."

"Feel better?"

"If this keeps him away, sure. I'm honestly tired of thinking about him."

"He's gotten more of your time than he deserved."

"Exactly."

I'm glad she told me, and I'm relieved that she's alright. If I'd heard about it through the rumor mill, I would've been making a pass by Randall's house, and then there'd be nobody to talk some sense into me. Anyway, she deserves to catch a break. This thing's had a hold of her for more than a year.

As much as I want to, I don't know, console her, keep her company, the longer we sit here, the less I know what to say or how to act. I basically dumped her last night, so I can't imagine she wants me here any longer than necessary.

"Yeah, so I'll head out." I climb to my feet. "Leave you be."

She jumps up after me. "I'm not done. I didn't call you out here just to tell you about Randall."

My heart clenches. I'm not sure I can go another round about us today. Last night was brutal. Even now, I'm not sure how I managed to walk out of there without losing my nerve. If we have to rehash the whole argument, I can't be certain my resolve will hold. I've never been good at saying no to her.

"I stopped for coffee with Harrison on the way here."

Well, then. There it is.

I swallow the hysterical laughter that bubbles in my throat. Was I really just thinking she'd come here asking me back when I all but shoved her at another man yesterday? Idiot. Gen's got everything going for her. She doesn't need my dumb ass making things harder. But this is good, actually. It takes all the wishful thinking and foolish notions right off the table.

"He's a stand-up guy," I tell her.

"He is."

"Still a doofus." Alright, maybe I can't help myself. "But he's nice, polite. Probably sorts his laundry according to the care instructions, so you won't have to worry about him shrinking your clothes."

Gen smirks, biting her lip as she turns her head. "You are so weird sometimes."

"Your kids are going to be short, though. He's got kind of an odd-shaped head too. That might be hereditary. You should probably put them in karate or something. Get them into boxing. With a cranium like that, they're gonna need to know how to defend themselves."

Exasperated, she shakes her head. "Will you stop?" Still, she's beaming. "I told him I couldn't see him anymore."

Our gazes lock. "Why would you do that?"

"Because." Gen's smile is so infectious, I can't help but mimic her. "I told him I was in love with Evan Hartley."

I can feel my heartbeat in my face. Yet somehow I still manage to play it cool. "That's so strange, 'cause I know that guy."

"Uh-huh." There's a bizarre gleam in her eyes that's almost got me frightened. "Took me a little while, but as it turns out, I've been in love with him for a long time."

Part of me wants to throw her over my shoulder and toss caution to the wind, but we ended up here for a reason.

"What about Trina's coke? You spent the night in jail because of me," I remind her. "If Randall hadn't been the one who arrested you, or your dad wasn't friends with the sheriff, maybe the whole thing doesn't go away so easy."

"No, see." She holds one finger in the air. "I've decided I reject your premise."

She's so cute sometimes. "Really?"

"Indeed." She nods sharply. "I already told you, I'm glad I went out with Trina. You said I needed to see that I could go out and have a good time without losing control. And I did. I proved a lot to myself that night. Like I said before, nothing about how it ended was your fault."

When my expression reveals I'm less than convinced, she digs in.

"You and I could go back to single digits trying to take the blame for everything that ever happened to either of us. It's a zero-sum game. None of it is useful."

"It worries me that you're starting to make sense," I say, smothering a grin.

"I had to convince myself I'd really changed. To me, that night shows I have. And I did it with you in my life. You know what else? You've changed too. For most of the time I've known you, you've had this chip on your shoulder. Fighting the whole world on a thousand fronts, always ready to throw a punch before it threw one at you. I don't see that anymore. Like it or not, Evan, you've mellowed in your old age."

"Jesus . . ." I grab my chest. "Right for the heart, Fred."

She shrugs at me. "It's called growth. Get over it."

I don't know where this new energy is coming from, but I don't hate it. She's alive, happy. Glowing with that old fire and verve. Like she could turn sand to glass with a wink.

"We've grown as a couple," she continues. "But I'm hoping we can grow a little more."

This feels like being blindfolded, as if she's walking me around in the dark and I'm following her, a little terrified and expectant. She's up to something. Something both terrible and exciting. It's like that first time watching her take a running leap off the pier, but this time she's got me by the hand.

"I've been sitting here for a while. And I was thinking . . ." Gen steps closer and puts her hands against my chest. My muscles quiver beneath her palms. We both know what her touch does to me. "I think you should probably marry me."

My mouth goes dry. "That right?"

"Make a whole bunch of babies."

"An entire bunch?" I can't feel my fingers. The sounds of the ocean turn to a sharp ringing in my ears as my chest expands with a rush of pure, unfiltered joy.

"I'll run Mackenzie's hotel, and you can be the stay-at-home dad raising our seven kids."

Going quiet for a beat, Gen looks up at me through thick lashes. Then she holds out a red Blow Pop.

"If you want," she says impishly, though her expression conveys utter sincerity, "this is me asking."

I'm not even sure if I'm still standing. But I'm not a moron, either. "Yeah, I want."

Fingers tugging my shirt, she leans up to press her lips to mine. I'm still half stunned for a few seconds before my brain reboots and I wrap my arms around her, kissing her deeply. This amazing, absurd woman who has no idea what she's getting herself into.

"You're going to get sick of how much I love you," I tell her, brushing her hair off her shoulders. "Totally disgusted with it."

"I'll take that bet." She tips her head to smile at me, then tries to kiss me again.

"Listen." I hold her still. "Don't get me wrong, I love this plan. Whatever you had for breakfast, let's stick with that. But what about . . ." Hell, I don't know how to say it. "You know, your dad. And your brothers. I'm pretty sure they have a hole dug somewhere with my name on it."

"What about your brother?" she counters. "Who cares. They'll come around or they won't. You're what I want. The only thing I've ever asked for. I think I'm kind of entitled at this point."

"Well, I have a feeling Cooper will come around sooner than you think."

For the first time in my life, I can picture my future more than a few days out. A sense of family and security. Permanence. Me and Gen, married and blissfully happy. I'm catching glimpses of what waking up to someone feels like, knowing they aren't rushing to sneak out with their shoes in their hands.

"Seriously. We're doing this?" I ask roughly. "Because if you think you had to come up with some grand gesture to get me back, you could have just shown me your tits. I would've caved right away. No question." I chew on the inside of my cheek. "I don't want you to think we need to get married to prove this is real."

She flashes a cocky grin. "Trust me, I've known I've had you whipped since seventh grade."

"See." With my arms around her, I slide my hands into her back pockets to grab her ass. "You think that's an insult, but I don't mind a bit. My masculinity is entirely intact. I'd follow this ass anywhere."

This time when she tries to kiss me, I let her. She does me in when she bites my lip. By then, I've got no sense left. Instead, I wrap my arms under her thighs to lift her up around my hips as we kiss.

How did I ever think I could live without this? Her skin under my palms. Her taste on my tongue. The way my heart beats almost painfully fast when she weaves her fingers into my hair and pulls. *This woman.*

As Gen begins to breathe harder, sliding her tongue in my mouth to tangle with mine, I shove my hand up her shirt to grab a handful of her breast. She arches into my hand, grinding herself on me. I'm hard and pushing against the zipper of my shorts as she scrapes her teeth against the stubble on my chin and runs her tongue down my neck.

"Wait." She lowers her legs to stand. "Get in the backseat of my car."

I stare at her. "You know, if a cop comes by, this time we'll both end up spending a night in jail."

"Maybe. But I'll take my chances." She plants a sweet kiss on my cheek. "Gotta be a bad girl some of the time, right?"

Good enough for me. Because I'll take her any way I can.

Forever.

EPILOGUE

GENEVIEVE

I've got my head in the twins' linen closet looking for an outdoor tablecloth when I'm jolted by a pair of arms coming around me from behind. Evan's lips brush my neck. His hands travel up my ribs, under my shirt, to sneak their way past my bra and cup my breasts. I feel his erection pressing against my ass.

"I want you," he breathes.

"So you keep saying." This is the fourth time this afternoon he's cornered me somewhere around the house to make his intentions clear. "Dinner will be ready soon."

One hand slides down my stomach and into my shorts. "I want to eat now."

A hot shiver rolls through me. He isn't playing fair. Since we made the engagement official, we can't keep our hands off each other. Evan's new favorite game—which I've been less than sincere about deterring—is seeing how close he can get to outright seducing me in public before I call a time-out.

So far, pretty damn close.

"Have I mentioned I love you?" he whispers, his fingers slipping between my thighs. "Especially this part."

"Especially?" I yank his hand free and turn to face him, eyebrow raised.

"Equally. I meant equally. As I love all the . . ." His eyes drag over my body. "Parts of you."

"Just for that"—I reach under my shirt and unclasp my strapless bra, letting it drop to the floor—"I'm not wearing a bra to dinner."

"Whoops." Mac appears around the corner of the hallway. She pauses, then spins on her heel. "Carry on. Not even here."

With a devilish grin, Evan bends down and picks up my bra. He shoves it in his back pocket. "I'm keeping this."

Among the stranger things he's done, this is up there. "Why?"

"You'll find out."

Far too happy with himself, he saunters off.

Once I've found the tablecloth, I head back to the kitchen where Mac is placing trays of food on a larger serving tray to carry outside. I toss the cloth at Evan and order him to go set the table on the deck.

"So what's the score?" Mac asks me.

"Honestly, I've lost count." I spoon the potato salad into a big bowl then pull the roasted carrots out of the oven.

We're having an al fresco buffet-style dinner tonight. Several of our friends, along with Riley and his aunt, are already outside milling about. Steph keeps joking that it's our engagement dinner, but it's really not. More of a spur-of-the-moment suggestion on the part of Evan, whose impulsive tendencies haven't completely abated.

He bumps into me while pulling utensils out of a drawer. "I'm winning."

"I'm gonna say this again—" Cooper announces, coming to stand in the middle of the kitchen.

"Coop, stop." Mac rolls her eyes as she picks up a tray laden with various salads.

"No, I'd like to reiterate. If I find out anyone but me is having sex on my bed, I'm setting theirs on fire in the backyard."

"Dude." Evan laughs at him. "Seriously, what makes you think I'd want to blow a load in your room? I've heard what you get up to in there."

For that, he gets a swift smack to the arm from Mac.

"Just so you know," Cooper shoots back as Evan is picking a cucumber spear off the cutting board to pop in his mouth. "I've had sex with her on that counter. So enjoy."

"Jesus." Evan shudders. "I know you confuse me with a mirror, but we don't actually share a dick, man. Keep it to yourself."

Lately, most of the ribbing has come at our expense. Just a little good-natured teasing about our newly engaged bliss. That we're too young to get married and, before we know it, we'll both be bored with each other and drowning in baby diapers. Still, it doesn't faze us. Like Evan told Cooper when we announced it, we know we're forever. We've always known.

As Mac and Evan drift onto the back deck, I set my oven mitts on the counter and give Cooper a sidelong glance. He cocks a brow when he notices. "What?" he says defensively.

My answering smile is saccharine. "Still haven't gotten my apology for the day."

"Fuck's sake. Are you seriously going to hold me to that?"

"Sure am."

A few days ago, Cooper and I took a walk on the beach and had a long overdue chat. And it didn't even take any urging from Evan or Mackenzie. My future brother-in-law and I were mature enough to know we needed to squash the beef. So I apologized for being a bad influence on Evan in the past, while Cooper apologized for confronting me outside my place of business and telling me what a horrible person I was. He then offered me the privilege of his friendship again, to which I'd laughed and informed him if he wanted the privilege of *my* friendship, he would need to apologize to me every day until the wedding. Whenever that'll be. We're on Day Four now, and I'm having a blast.

"Fine." Cooper lets out an annoyed breath. "I'm sorry for telling you to fuck off and saying we weren't friends."

"Thanks, Coop." I walk over to ruffle his hair. "Appreciate it."

Mac returns to witness the exchange, laughing under her breath. "Cut him some slack, Gen. He promised to be nice from now on."

I think it over. "Fine. I release you from your apology obligations," I tell Cooper.

He rolls his eyes and heads outside to assist his brother.

"Need some help?" Alana appears at the open sliding door, uncharacteristically eager to help out. She practically grabs the potato salad bowl from my hand.

I stare at her. "Why are you being weird?"

Beside me, Mac peers past Alana's shoulder toward the deck. "She's avoiding Wyatt," Mac supplies. "He's glaring daggers at us right now."

I don't know whether to laugh or sigh. Whereas my love life finally straightened itself out, Alana's seems to be growing ever more complicated. "What did you do to him this time?" I ask her.

She scowls at me. "Nothing."

Mac lifts a brow.

"Fine." Alana huffs. "I'm getting my left wrist inked for my birthday next week. So I had a tattoo designed."

I'm confused. "And?"

"By someone other than Wyatt."

I gasp. "No!"

Even Mac, who's only lived in the Bay for a year or so, grasps the implications of that. Wyatt is the best artist in town. Going to anybody else for a tat is sacrilege.

"I'm allowed to use someone else," Alana argues. "Preferably someone who doesn't think they're in love with me."

"Guess you can't go to Tate either, then," Mac cracks, and she and I giggle.

Alana's mouth twists in another scowl. She swiftly sets down the potato salad. "You know what? I'm not helping anymore. I hate you both."

She stomps off, leaving us laughing in her wake. Through the sliding door, I see her march past Wyatt to join Steph and Heidi on the other side of the deck, where she tries to camouflage into the railing.

"Oh, the tangled webs we weave," Mac remarks, still chuckling.

We step outside and start arranging the serving dishes on the table. Another folding table has an array of drinks, and a few coolers of beer sit on the floor nearby. Cooper goes to check the meat he's grilling on the barbecue, while Evan wanders out with a stack of napkins and places them next to the pile of utensils.

"Where's Riley?" he asks, glancing around.

I nod toward the yard below, where Riley and Tate are on the sand engaged in an animated conversation about sailing. Riley's aunt Liz stands a few feet away, checking her phone.

"He told me he has a crush on a girl in his biology class," I whisper to Evan, nodding at his surrogate baby brother.

"Oh, Becky? Yeah, I know all about her."

"Becky? No, he said her name was Addison." My jaw drops. "Oh my God. He's turning into a little player."

Evan grins proudly. "Good. Let him play the field a bit. He's too young to settle down."

I sigh, about to offer a comeback, when a flash of movement catches my peripheral vision. I turn toward it and suck in a breath.

"What the hell," I hiss at Evan.

He's still all smiles. "Harrison!" he calls to the khaki-and-polo-clad deputy who approaches the deck from the side of the Hartley house. "Glad you could make it!"

He invited *Harrison*? And he's actually calling him by his proper name instead of some passive-aggressive taunt?

"Evan," I growl softly. "What have you done?"

"Chill, baby," he whispers back. "Just think of me as the love fairy. Spreading all the love around."

What in the actual fuck. I've barely registered the absurdity of the remark before Evan is gone, sauntering down the steps toward the new arrival. I find my footing and hurry after him, prepared to do damage control. Just how much of it will be required? Undetermined.

I reach them in time to witness Evan clap Harrison on the shoulder and say, "Been wanting to introduce you two for ages."

You two?

I blink in surprise as my crazy fiancé ushers Harrison over to Riley's aunt and starts making introductions. Harrison and Aunt Liz? That's just . . . genius, I realize. As my initial surprise wanes, it occurs to me that this might be the greatest matchmaking scheme in history. I'm almost disappointed I didn't think of it first.

"Liz is, like, the best nurse ever," Evan is raving. "At least that's what I hear in all my nursing circles."

I choke down a laugh and add to the pitch. "Harrison once carried a gator down from a roof with his bare hands," I inform Liz.

Evan's brows raise. "Seriously? Dude. I need to hear this story—"

"Another time," I chirp, latching a hand onto his arm. "We need to finish bringing the food out first. 'Scuse us."

With that, we leave a slightly dazed Harrison and an amused-looking Liz to their own devices.

"Damn, Mr. Love Fairy," I murmur as we return to the kitchen. "That was some good thinking. They're the perfect match."

Evan nods vigorously. "Right?"

I'm grabbing the last of the condiments from the fridge when the doorbell rings.

"I'll get it," he says before darting off.

I set down the ketchup and mustard bottles, then wipe my hands and go to see who's at the door.

Standing in the doorway is Shelley Hartley. I haven't seen Evan's mother in . . . I don't know how many years. She looks good, though. Like she's taking care of herself. Her hair is no longer dyed blonde, but her natural dark brown. Her skin looks healthy, and her jeans and tank top actually cover all the important bits.

Last time I asked Evan about her, he'd said he wasn't quite ready to spring her on me. Until now, it seems.

"I baked a pie." She holds up a tin wrapped in foil. Then her smile falters. "Okay, that's a lie. I bought it at the grocery store and rewrapped it. But it's a start, right?"

Evan is clearly trying not to laugh. "That's great, Mom." He gives her a kiss on the cheek and invites her in. "We appreciate it."

Cooper's standing in the living room as she enters. He offers to take the pie from her. While he doesn't entirely manage a smile or a kiss for his mother, he gives her a nod. "Thank you," he says brusquely. "That was thoughtful."

By the relief on her face, it's more than Shelley hoped for.

"Mom. You remember Genevieve." Evan coaxes me forward.

"Of course I do. And oh my goodness, you've gotten so gorgeous." She pulls me into a tight hug. "Evan told me about the engagement. I'm so happy for you two," she gushes, holding me out with her hands on my arms. She glances at her son with an oddly smug smile. "See, baby? Didn't I tell you? My love predictions always come true." She turns back to me. "I always liked you two together. Even when you were little. I said, he's going to marry that girl someday, if he knows what's good for him."

I get a tad choked up. "That's really sweet."

"Man, your kids," she exclaims, eyes huge. "Such beautiful kids you two are gonna have. I can't even."

Shelley is already planning playdates with her grandkids before we've even set a date for the wedding. Not that we're stalling, but with the grand opening at The Beacon coming up, scheduling is a nightmare.

Anyway, I think my dad is still in denial about the whole thing. A little upset that I asked Evan to marry me without talking to him first—and a lot scared that his only daughter isn't five years old anymore. Bad enough he's losing Craig to college next week. Billy and Jay insist he'll work his way through the grief process in time for the wedding. Well, that's if Evan survives the ritual hazing Shane and Kellan have promised to execute until he cracks or goes into hiding. But I have faith Evan can hold his own. One way or another, we're mashing these families together, and consequences be damned. Kicking and screaming if need be.

After the greetings, we all go outside and start loading up our plates. It's a super-casual affair. Harrison and Liz seem to have hit it off, so busy talking and smiling that they're ignoring their food. Heidi and a few others gather at the railing to eat standing. Riley scarfs down hot dogs and coleslaw on the deck steps.

Meanwhile, the twins sit at the table, with me and Mac at their sides and their mom sitting across from them. Evan squeezes my hand under the table. He'd been anxious the past couple days. Tense. I hadn't understood why, but now, seeing the contentment in his eyes, I realize this is a big moment for him. Having Shelley and her boys at the same table has been a long time coming. Despite the different roads we've taken to get here—and because of them—we've all found our second chances.

A cool breeze wafts over the deck and flutters our napkins. The season's changing in the Bay, summer's almost over. My arms break out in goosebumps, and a tiny shiver travels down my spine. It's then I realize my shirt feels a bit drafty. I glance up to see Evan's smug grin and remember I'm not wearing a bra. At my first dinner with his mother. And my nipples are hard.

Evan draws a tick mark in the air.

I walked right into this one. "So it's going to be like that, huh?" I grumble under my breath.

He pulls my hand up to kiss my knuckles. "Always."

ACKNOWLEDGMENTS

Some stories are harder to write than others, and some are an absolute joy to put down on the page. This book falls into the latter category—I loved every second of writing *Bad Girl Reputation* and breathing life into Genevieve and Evan. Their story is one of redemption, forgiveness, second chances, and the difficulties that come with shedding your past and trying to be a better, healthier version of yourself. I'm so thankful for everyone who helped me shape the Avalon Bay world and bring this book into your hands:

My editor Eileen Rothschild and the SMP all-stars: Lisa Bonvissuto, Christa Desir, Beatrice Jason, Alyssa Gammello, and Jonathan Bush for another incredible cover.

Kimberly Brower, agent extraordinaire and fellow *Felicity* fanatic.

Ann-Marie and Lori at Get Red PR for helping spread the word about this book and the Avalon Bay series.

Every single reader, reviewer, blogger, Instagrammer, Tweeter, Booktokker, and supporter of my books. I couldn't do this job without you, and I'm forever grateful to you.

And to all the former bad girls out there, know that second chances and new beginnings are always within your reach.

ABOUT THE AUTHOR

Amanda Nicole White

A *New York Times, USA Today,* and *Wall Street Journal* bestselling author, ELLE KENNEDY grew up in the suburbs of Toronto, Ontario, and is the author of more than forty romantic suspense and contemporary romance novels, including the international bestselling Off-Campus and Briar U series.

GOOD GIRL
COMPLEX

GOOD GIRL COMPLEX

Elle Kennedy

ST. MARTIN'S
GRIFFIN
NEW YORK

First published in the United States by St. Martin's Griffin, an imprint of St. Martin's Publishing Group

GOOD GIRL COMPLEX. Copyright © 2022 by Elle Kennedy. All rights reserved. Printed in the United States of America. For information, address St. Martin's Publishing Group, 120 Broadway, New York, NY 10271.

www.stmartins.com

Excerpt from *Bad Girl Reputation* copyright © 2022 by Elle Kennedy.

Library of Congress Cataloging-in-Publication Data

Names: Kennedy, Elle, author.
Title: Good girl complex / Elle Kennedy.
Description: First edition. | New York : St. Martin's Griffin, 2022. |
Identifiers: LCCN 2021039188 | ISBN 9781250796738 (trade
    paperback) | ISBN 9781250796745 (ebook)
Subjects: LCSH: College students—Juvenile fiction. | Rich people—
    Juvenile fiction. | Self-confidence—Juvenile fiction. | Young adult
    fiction. | South Carolina—Juvenile fiction. | CYAC: Love—Fiction. |
    Universities and colleges—Fiction. | Self-confidence—Fiction. |
    South Carolina—Fiction.
Classification: LCC PZ7.1.K5025 Go 2022 | DDC 813.6 [Fic]—dc23
LC record available at https://lccn.loc.gov/2021039188

Our books may be purchased in bulk for promotional, educational, or business use. Please contact your local bookseller or the Macmillan Corporate and Premium Sales Department at 1-800-221-7945, extension 5442, or by email at MacmillanSpecialMarkets@macmillan.com.

First Edition: 2022

20 19 18 17 16 15 14 13 12

CHAPTER ONE

COOPER

I'm up to my eyeballs in Jägerbombs. Yesterday, I was married to the blender, pumping out piña coladas and strawberry daiquiris like sweatshop labor. Tonight, it's vodka Red Bulls and Fireballs. And don't forget the rosé. These dipshits and their rosé. They're all slammed against the bar, wall-to-wall pastel linen shirts and three-hundred-dollar haircuts, shouting drink orders at me. It's too hot for this shit.

In Avalon Bay, the seasons are marked by an endless cycle of exodus and invasion. The way the tides turn in a storm: Summer ends and the churn begins. Sunburned tourists pack up their mini-vans and sugar-slathered kids and head inland, back to suburbs and cubicles. Replaced by the surge of spray-tanned college brats—the clone armies returning to Garnet College. These are the trust-fund babies whose coastal palaces block out the ocean views for the rest of us scraping by on the change that falls from their pockets.

"Hey, bro, six shots of tequila!" some clone barks, slapping a credit card down on the sticky wet wood of the bar top like I should be impressed. Really, he's just another typical Garnet fuckhead who walked straight out of a Sperry catalog.

"Remind me why we do this," I say to Steph as I rack up a line of Jack and Cokes for her at the waitress stand.

She reaches into her bra and lifts each breast so they sit higher and fuller in her black *Joe's Beachfront Bar* tank top. "The tips, Coop."

Right. Nothing spends faster than somebody else's money. Rich kids spitting bills in a game of one-upmanship, all courtesy of Daddy's credit card.

Weekends on the boardwalk are like Mardi Gras. Tonight is the last Friday before the fall semester at Garnet begins, and that means three days of raging straight to Monday morning, the bars bursting at the seams. We're practically printing money. Not that I plan to do this forever. I moonlight here on the weekends to save up some extra dough so I can stop working for other people and start being my own boss. Once I've got enough saved, my ass is out from behind this bar for good.

"Watch out for yourself," I warn Steph as she places the drinks on her tray. "Holler if you need me to grab the bat."

It wouldn't be the first time I roughed someone up who couldn't take no for an answer.

Nights like this, there's a different energy. Humidity so thick you can slather the salty air on like sunscreen. Bodies on bodies, zero inhibitions, and tequila-infused testosterone full of bad intentions.

Fortunately, Steph's a tough girl. "I can manage." With a wink she takes the drinks, plasters a smile on her face, and spins around, long black ponytail swinging.

I don't know how she tolerates it, these dudes pawing all over her. Don't get me wrong, I get my fair share of female attention. Some get pretty bold, too friendly. But with chicks, you throw them a grin and a shot, they giggle to their friends and leave you alone. Not these guys, though. The crew team douchebags and Greek Row fuckboys. Steph is constantly getting grabbed and groped and having all manner of vulgarities slithered into her ear over the screech of the blaring music. To her credit, she hardly ever punches any of them.

It's a constant grind. Catering to the seasonal parasites, this invasive species that uses us locals up, sucks us dry, and leaves their garbage behind.

And yet, this town would hardly exist without them.

"Yo! Let me get those shots!" the clone barks again.

I nod, as if to say *Coming right up*, when what I really mean is *This is me ignoring you on purpose*. Instead, a whistle at the other end of the bar catches my attention.

Locals get served first. Without exception. Followed by regulars who tip well, people who are polite, hot women, little old ladies, and then the rest of these overfed jackasses. At the end of the bar, I put down a shot of bourbon for Heidi and pour another for myself. We toss 'em back and I give her a refill.

"What are you doing in here?" I ask, because no self-respecting local is on the boardwalk tonight. Too many clones kill the vibe.

"Dropping off Steph's keys. Had to run by her place." Heidi was the prettiest girl in the first grade, and not much has changed since. Even in ratty cutoff shorts and a plain blue crop top, she's undeniably the hottest woman in this bar. "You closing tonight?"

"Yeah, won't be outta here till three, probably."

"Wanna come by after?" Heidi pushes up on her toes to lean across the bar.

"Nah, I'm pulling a double tomorrow. Gotta get some sleep."

She pouts. Playfully at first, then more flippant when she realizes I'm not interested in hooking up tonight. We might've indulged in a string of hookups earlier this summer, but making that a regular thing with one of my best friends starts to resemble a relationship, and that's not where I'm trying to go. I keep hoping she'll realize that and stop asking.

"Hey. Hey!" The impatient towheaded dude at the other end of the bar tries flagging me. "I swear to God, man, I will toss you a hundred-dollar bill for a fucking shot."

"You better get back to work," Heidi says with a sarcastic smile, blowing me a kiss.

I take my sweet time walking over to him. He's straight off the clone conveyor belt: standard-issue preppy Ken doll with a side part and the best smile dental insurance can buy. Beside him are a couple of factory-made sidekicks whose idea of manual labor is probably having to wipe their own asses.

"Let's see it," I dare him.

The clone slaps down a Benjamin. So proud of himself. I pour a single shot of whiskey because I don't remember what he asked for and slide it to him. He releases the bill to take the glass. I snatch it up and pocket it.

"I ordered six shots," he says, smug.

"Put down another five hundred and I'll pour 'em."

I expect him to whine, throw a fit. Instead he laughs, shaking his finger at me. To him, this is some of that charming local color they come slumming it down here to find. Rich kids love getting rolled.

To my absolute amazement, this knucklehead flicks out five more bills from a wad of cash and lays them on the bar. "The best you got," he says.

The best this bar keeps in stock is some Johnnie Walker Blue and a tequila I can't pronounce. Neither is more than five hundred dollars retail for a bottle. So I act impressed and get up on a stool to pull the dusty bottle of tequila from the top shelf because, okay, I did remember what he asked for, and pour them their overpriced shots.

At that, Richie Rich is satisfied and wanders off to a table.

My fellow bartender Lenny gives me the side-eye. I know I shouldn't encourage this behavior. It only reinforces the idea that we're for sale, that they own this town. But screw it, I'm not about to be slinging drinks till I'm dead. I've got bigger plans.

"What time do you get off?" a female voice purrs from my left side.

I turn slowly, waiting for the punch line. Traditionally, that question is followed by one of two options:

"Because I want you to get *me* off."

Or, "Because I can't wait to get *you* off."

The follow-up is an easy way to determine whether you're ending up with a woman who's selfish in the sack or one who loves doling out BJs.

Neither is a particularly original pickup line, but nobody said the clones who swarm the Bay every year were original.

"Well?" the blonde presses, and I realize there's no cheesy line in store for me.

"Bar closes at two," I answer easily.

"Hang out with us after you get off," she urges. She and her friend both have shiny hair, perfect bodies, and skin glowing from a day spent in the sun. They're cute, but I'm not in the mood for what they're offering.

"Sorry. Can't," I answer. "But you should keep an eye out for someone who looks exactly like me. My twin brother is around here somewhere." I wave a hand toward the throng of bodies packing the place like sardines in a tin. "I'm sure he'd love to entertain you."

I say it mostly because I know it'll annoy Evan. Though on the other hand, maybe he'll thank me. He might despise the clones, but he doesn't seem to mind the rich princesses when they're naked. I swear the dude's trying to sleep his way through this town. He claims he's "bored." I let him believe that I believe him.

"Omigod, there's two of you?" Almost immediately, both girls become starry-eyed.

I grab a glass and shovel some ice cubes into it. "Yup. His name's Evan," I add helpfully. "If you find him, tell him Cooper sent you."

When they finally wander off, fruity cocktails in hand, I breathe a sigh of relief.

Bartending is such a crap gig.

I push a whiskey on the rocks toward the skinny dude who ordered it, take the cash he hands me. I run a hand through my hair and draw a breath before going to the next customer. For most of the night, the drunken masses manage to keep their shit together. Daryl, the doorman, kicks out anyone he suspects might projectile vomit, while Lenny and I smack away any idiots who get it into their heads to reach behind the bar.

I keep an eye on Steph and the other female servers as they work the crowd. Steph's got a table full of Garnet dudes salivating over her. She's smiling, but I know that look. When she tries to walk away, one of them grabs her around the waist.

My eyes narrow. It's the same guy I took for six bills.

I'm damn near over the bar when her eyes find mine. As if she knows what's about to happen, she shakes her head. Then she slyly disentwines herself from the handsy prick and comes back to the waitress stand.

"Want me to toss 'em?" I ask her.

"Nah. I can handle them."

"I know. But you don't have to. I pulled six hundred from those dumbasses. I'll split it with you. Let me get rid of them."

"It's all good. Just get me three Coronas and two Jäg—"

"Do not even say it." My whole body winces at the word. If I never have to smell that vile black shit ever again, it'll be too soon. "I gotta get some nose plugs."

"It's like you've got shellshock," she laughs, watching me suffer through these pours.

"I should be getting hazard pay." I finish up and push the drinks to her. "Seriously, though, if those guys can't keep their hands to themselves, I'm coming over there."

"I'm fine. But, man, I wish they'd just leave. I don't know who's worse tonight—Mr. Grabby Hands, or that senior on the patio who's crying about his daddy reneging on his promise to buy him a yacht for graduation."

I snicker.

Steph waltzes off with a sigh and a full tray of drinks.

For the better part of an hour, I don't look up. The room is so dense the faces blur into a smudge of flesh, and all I do is pour and slide credit cards until I'm in a trance, barely aware of my actions.

The next time I check on Steph, it's to see Richie Rich trying to persuade her to dance with him. She's like a boxer, bobbing and weaving to get away from the dude. I can't make out her exact words, but it's easy to guess—*I'm working, please let me get back to work, I can't dance with you, I'm working.*

She's trying to remain courteous, but her blazing eyes tell me she's fed up.

"Len," I call, nodding toward the unfolding scene. "Gimme a sec."

He nods back. We take care of our own.

I stride over, knowing I pose a menacing picture. I'm six two, haven't shaved in days, and my hair could use a trim. Hopefully I look menacing enough to deter these bros from doing something stupid.

"Everything okay here?" I inquire when I reach the group. My tone says I know it's not and he'd better stop or I'm going to toss him out on his ass.

"Fuck off, carnie," one of them cracks.

The insult rolls right off me. I'm used to it.

I raise a brow. "I'm not leaving unless my colleague tells me to go." I look pointedly at Richie Rich's hand, which is latched onto Steph's arm. "She didn't sign up to get groped by rich boys."

The guy has the sense to remove his hand. Steph uses the opportunity to clamber to my side.

"See? All good." He sneers at me. "No distressed damsels requiring rescue."

"Make sure to keep it that way." I punctuate the warning with a sneer of my own. "And keep your hands to yourself."

Steph and I are about to head off when a glass breaks.

No matter how loud a room, how full to the brim with sound-dampening bodies, a glass shatters on the floor and, in the immediate seconds after, you can hear a hummingbird's wings flutter two counties away.

Every head turns. One of Richie Rich's buddies, who'd dropped the glass, is blinking innocently when I meet his gaze.

"Oops," he says.

Laughter and applause crush the momentary silence. Then conversation bubbles up again, and the collective attention of the bar returns to its previously intoxicated amusements.

"Fuck's sake," Steph mutters under her breath. "Go back to the bar, Coop. I got this."

She marches off with an annoyed frown, while the douche crew dismisses us from their holy presence and proceeds to chat loudly and laugh amongst themselves.

"All good?" Lenny asks when I return.

"Not sure."

I glance back toward the group, frowning when I notice their leader is no longer with them. Where the hell did he go?

"No," I say slowly. "I don't think it's good. Give me another sec."

Once again, I leave Lenny to man the battle stations alone while I duck out from behind the bar to find Steph. I head toward the back, figuring she went for a broom to sweep up the glass.

That's when I hear, "Get *off* me!"

I throw myself around the corner, my jaw tightening when I spot Richie Rich's pastel polo. He has Steph cornered at the end of the short, narrow hall where the supply closet is located. When she tries to dip around him, he steps in her way, grabbing her wrist. His other hand slides downward and attempts to cup her ass.

Nah, screw this.

I charge forward and yank him by his collar. A second later, I lay his ass flat out on the sticky floor.

"Get out," I growl.

"Cooper." Steph grabs me, even as gratitude shines in her eyes. I know she appreciates the save.

I shake her off, because enough is enough. "Get up and leave," I tell the startled punk.

He's yelling out angry curses as he climbs to his feet.

Because the restrooms are right around the corner about ten feet away, it doesn't take long for his shouts of outrage to draw an audience. A group of screeching sorority sisters hurry over, followed by other curious bystanders.

Suddenly more voices fill the corridor.

"Pres! Bro, you alright?"

Two of his friends break through the crowd. They puff up their chests beside him, flanking their champion because if they get chased out of here in front of all these people, it's going to be a long year of drinking alone at home.

"The hell's your problem, man?" the groper spits out, glaring daggers at me.

"No problem anymore," I reply, crossing my arms. "Just taking out the trash."

"You smell that, Preston?" his buddy says to Richie Rich with a goading grin. "Something sure stinks in here."

"Was that a dumpster outside or your trailer?" the other mocks.

"Please, take two steps closer and say that again," I encourage them because, whatever, I'm bored and these dudes' faces are begging to get smashed.

I assess my chances. It's three on one, and they aren't scrawny—each of them around six feet tall, about my size. They could be half a water polo team sponsored by Brooks Brothers. But me, I actually work for a living, and these muscles aren't for show. So I like my odds.

"Coop, stop." Steph pushes me to the side to stand between us. "Forget it. I got this now. Go back to the bar."

"Yeah, *Coop*," Preston taunts. Then, to his buddies, "No piece of townie ass is worth this much trouble."

I look at Steph and shrug. Rich prick should have walked away when I gave him the chance.

While he's still laughing, so smug in his superiority, I reach out, grab a fistful of his Ralph Lauren and drive my fist straight into his face.

He staggers, falling into his friends, who push him at me. Bloody, he lunges like a creature in the third act of a horror film, swinging at me, smearing blood. We crash into the screaming sorority girls until we're against a wall. The old payphone that hasn't operated in fifteen years digs into my back, which gives Preston a chance to land a lucky punch to my jaw. Then I spin us around, pin him against the drywall. I'm about to smash his damn face in when Joe, the owner, along with Daryl and Lenny, hold me back and drag me away.

"You stupid townie trash," he gurgles at me. "You have any idea how dead you are?"

"Enough!" Joe shouts. The grizzled Vietnam vet with a gray hippie beard and ponytail points a fat finger at Preston. "Get on out of here. There's no fighting in my bar."

"I want this psycho fired," Preston orders.

"Kiss my ass."

"Coop, shut it," Joe says. He lets Lenny and Daryl release me. "I'm docking your pay for this."

"It wasn't Coop's fault," Steph tells our boss. "This guy was all over me. Then he followed me to the supply closet and trapped me in the hallway. Cooper was trying to kick him out."

"Do you know who my father is?" Squeezing his leaking nose

shut, Preston seethes. "His bank owns half the buildings on this filthy boardwalk. One word from me and your life gets real complicated."

Joe's lips tighten.

"Your employee put his hands on me," Preston continues angrily. "I don't know how you run this rathole, but if this happened anywhere else, the person who assaulted a customer would no longer be employed." The smirk on his face actually makes my fists tingle. I want to strangle him with my bare hands. "So either you handle this, or I pick up the phone and call my father to do it for you. I know it's late, but don't you worry, he'll be awake. He's a night owl." The smirk deepens. "That's how he made all his billions."

There's a long beat of silence.

Then Joe lets out a sigh, turning to me.

"You can't be serious," I say in amazement.

Joe and I go back a ways. My brother and I used to barback here in the summers during high school. We helped him rebuild after two hurricanes. I took his daughter to homecoming, for chrissake.

Looking resigned, he runs a hand over his beard.

"Joe. Seriously, man. You're gonna let one of them tell you how to run your bar?"

"I'm sorry," Joe finally says. He shakes his head. "I have to think about my business. My family. You went too far this time, Coop. Take what I owe you for the night out of the register. I'll have a check for you in the morning."

Satisfied with himself, Richie Rich sneers at me. "See, townie? That's how the real world works." He tosses a bloody wad of cash at Steph and spits out a thick clump of blood and mucus. "Here. Clean this place up, sweetheart."

"This isn't over," I warn Preston as he and his friends saunter away.

"It was over before it began," he calls snidely over his shoulder. "You're the only one who didn't know that."

Staring at Joe, I see the defeat in his eyes. He doesn't have the strength or desire to fight these battles anymore. That's how they get us. By inches. Breaking us down until we're too tired to hold on any longer. Then they pry our land, our businesses, our dignity from our dying hands.

"You know," I tell Joe, picking up the cash and smacking it in his hand. "Every time one of us gives in to one of them, we make it a little easier for them to screw us the next time."

Except . . . no. Fuck the "next time." These people are never getting a next time from me.

CHAPTER TWO

MACKENZIE

Since leaving my parents' house in Charleston this morning, I've had an itch in the back of my skull, and it only keeps growing more insistent, telling me to turn around. Take off. Run away. Join the proverbial circus and *rage, rage* against the dying of my gap year.

Now, as my taxi drives through the tunnel of bur oaks to Tally Hall on the Garnet College campus, a pure cold panic has set in.

This is really happening.

Beyond the green lawn and lines of cars, swarming freshmen and their parents cart boxes into the redbrick building stretching four stories into the clear blue sky. White trim frames the rows of windows and the roof, a distinct characteristic of one of the five original buildings on the historic campus.

"I'll be right back to grab those boxes," I tell my driver. I sling my duffel over my shoulder, and set my rolling suitcase on the ground. "Just want to make sure I'm in the right place."

"No prob. Take your time." He's unruffled, probably because my parents paid him a huge flat fee to play chauffeur for the day.

As I walk under the massive iron lantern that hangs from the beam above the front doors, I feel like a captured fugitive returning after a year on the lam. It was too good to last. How am I supposed to go back to homework and pop quizzes? My life dictated by TAs and syllabi when I've been my own boss for the last twelve months.

A mother stops me on the stairs to ask if I'm the dorm's resident advisor. Awesome. I feel ancient. A fresh wave of temptation to turn on my heels and split simmers in my gut, but I force myself to ignore it.

I slog up to the fourth floor where the rooms are a little bigger, a little nicer, for those parents willing to leverage the GDP of a small island nation. According to the email on my phone, I'm in room 402.

Inside, a small living room and kitchenette divide the two bedrooms on either side. The room on the left contains an empty bed with a matching wooden desk and dresser. To the right, through the wide-open door, a blonde in a pair of cutoffs and no shirt bounces and sways while putting clothes on hangers.

"Hello?" I say, trying to get her attention. I drop my bags on the floor. "Hi?"

Still she doesn't hear me. Tentative, I walk up and tap her on the shoulder. She jumps out of her sandals and slaps a hand over her mouth to muffle a yelp.

"Ooh, girl, you got me!" she says in a thick Southern accent. Breathing hard, she pulls the wireless earbuds from her ears and shoves them in her pocket. "'Bout peed my pants."

Her boobs are right there in all their bare glory, and she's making no effort to shield herself. I try to look her in the eyes but that proves awkward, so I divert my attention toward the windows.

"Sorry to barge in. I didn't expect . . ." *to find my roommate engaged in the first act of an amateur porno.*

She shrugs, smiling. "Don't sweat it."

"I can, uh, come back in a few minutes, if . . . ?"

"Naw, you're fine," she assures me.

I can't help but glance at her standing with her hands on her hips, pointing the high-beams at me. "Was there a nudist box on the housing form I checked by accident?"

She laughs, then finally reaches for a tank top. "I like to cleanse the energy of a place. A house ain't a home till you spent time in it naked, right?"

"The blinds are open," I point out.

"No tan lines," she answers with a wink. "I'm Bonnie May Beauchamp. Guess we're roomies."

"Mackenzie Cabot."

She smooshes me in a tight hug. Ordinarily I'd consider this a grievous assault on my personal boundaries. But, for some reason, I can't find it in me to be put off by this girl. Maybe she's a witch. Hypnotizing me with her witch tits. Still, I get a good vibe from her.

She has soft, round features and big, brown eyes. A bright white grin that's equally non-threatening to women and approachable to men. Everyone's little sister. But with boobs.

"Where's all your stuff?" she asks upon releasing me.

"My boyfriend's coming by later with most of it. I have a few things in the car downstairs. The driver's waiting on me."

"I'll help you bring it up."

There isn't much, only a couple boxes, but I appreciate the offer and the company. We grab the boxes and toss them in the room, then wander the halls for a bit, checking out the neighborhood.

"You from South Carolina?" Bonnie asks.

"Charleston. You?"

"I'm from Georgia. Daddy wanted me to go to Georgia State, but my momma went to Garnet, so they made a bet on the outcome of a football game and here I am."

Down on the third floor, there's a dude walking around with a backpack cooler of frosé who tries to offer us each a cup in exchange for our phone numbers. His arms, chest, and back are covered in scribbled black permanent marker, with most of the numbers missing a digit or two. Certainly all of them fake.

We pass on the offer and grin to ourselves, leaving him in our wake.

"Did you transfer from somewhere?" Bonnie says as we continue our way through the bazaar of micro communities. "I mean, don't take this the wrong way or nothin', but you don't look like a freshman."

I knew this would happen. I feel like the camp counselor. Two years older than my peers, on account of my gap year and the fact that I started kindergarten a year late, when my parents decided to extend a Mediterranean sailing trip rather than get me home in time for school.

"I took a gap year. Made a deal with my parents that I'd go to whatever school they chose if they let me work on my business first." Though if it were up to me, I'd have skipped this chapter of the coming-of-age story completely.

"You got your own business already?" Bonnie demands, wide-eyed. "I spent all summer watchin' *Vanderpump* reruns and partyin' at the lake."

"I built a website and an app," I admit. "I mean, it's nothing major. Not like I founded Tesla or anything."

"What kind of app?"

"It's a site where people post funny or embarrassing boyfriend stories. It started as a joke for some of my friends from high school, but then it sort of blew up. Last year, I launched another site for people to post about their girlfriends."

What began as me and a blog had ballooned in the past year to include hiring an ad manager, site moderators, and a marketing team. I have payroll and taxes and seven figures in my business checking account. And somewhere on top of all that, I'm supposed to worry about essays and midterms? A deal's a deal, and I'm as good as my word, but this whole college thing seems pointless.

"Oh my God, I know that site." Bonnie smacks my arm excitedly. Girl's got steel rods for fingers. "*BoyfriendFails*! Holy shit. My girls and I probably spent more time readin' those senior year than doin' our homework. What's the one? 'Bout the boyfriend who got food poisoning after a date and the girl's dad was drivin' them home and the guy got massive diarrhea in the backseat!"

She doubles over in absolute hysterics. I crack a smile because I remember that post well. It got over three hundred thousand clicks, thousands of comments, and double the ad revenue of any other post that month.

"Wow," she says, once she's regained her composure. "You really make money off those things?"

"Yeah, from hosting ads. They do pretty well." I shrug modestly.

"That's so cool." Bonnie pouts. "I'm jealous. I got no idea what I'm doin' here, Mac. Can I call you Mac or do you prefer Mackenzie? Mackenzie sounds *so* formal."

"Mac's fine," I assure her, trying not to laugh.

"After high school, college is a thing I'm supposed to do, y'know? 'Cept heck if I got any idea what I'm supposed to major in or what I'm gonna do when I grow up."

"People always say college is where you go to find yourself."

"I thought that was Panama City."

I snicker. I really like this girl.

About an hour later, my boyfriend shows up with the rest of my boxes. It's been weeks since we've seen each other. I had a stupid amount of work to do on the business before I could hand it over to my new full-time staff, so I couldn't take the time off to visit Preston.

This is the longest we've been apart since the summer his family went on vacation to Lake Como.

I had proposed the idea of getting an apartment together off campus, but Preston had roundly scoffed at that. Why slum it in subpar housing when he's got a pool, a personal chef, and a maid at home? I didn't have a good answer that didn't sound condescending. If independence from our parents isn't its own motivation to move in together, I don't know what to say.

Independence has been my sole motivation since high school. Living with my family was like sinking in a pit of quicksand—one that would've swallowed me whole if I hadn't yanked out my own hair to fashion a rope and pull myself out. I wasn't built to be kept. Maybe that's why, when the boyfriend I haven't seen in over a month enters the room with the first load of boxes, I'm not overwhelmed with loin-deep longing or that sudden rush of excitement after time spent apart.

Not that I didn't miss him or that I'm not happy he's here. It's just . . . I can remember crushes I had in middle school where the time between seeing them at lunch and sixth period felt like an eternity that tore at my little, pubescent heart. I've grown up, I suppose. Preston and I are comfortable. Steady. Practically an old married couple.

There's a lot to be said for steady.

"Hey, babe." A little sweaty from four flights of stairs, Pres wraps me in a tight hug and kisses me on the forehead. "Missed you. You look great."

"So do you." Attraction certainly isn't the problem; Preston's about as picture-perfect handsome as it gets. He's tall, with a slim but athletic build. Gorgeous blue eyes that seem impossibly bright when the sun catches them. A classic angular face that collects attention everywhere he goes. He's gotten a haircut since the last time I saw him, his blond hair a little long on top but cut close on the sides.

It's then that he turns his head slightly and I notice his face marked by bruises around his nose and right eye.

"What happened to you?" I ask in alarm.

"Oh, yeah." He touches his eye and shrugs. "Guys and I were playing basketball the other day and I took a ball to the face. No biggie."

"You sure? That looks like it hurt." It's nasty, honestly, like a burnt, runny egg on the side of his face.

"I'm good. Oh, before I forget. I got you this."

He reaches into the back pocket of his khakis and pulls out a plastic card. The words *BIG JAVA* are written across it.

I accept the gift card. "Oh, thanks, babe. Is this for the coffee place on campus?"

He nods earnestly. "Figured it was the most fitting 'welcome to college' gift for a coffee fiend like you. I loaded a couple grand on it, so you're all set."

At the kitchenette, an eavesdropping Bonnie gasps. "A couple *grand?*" she squawks.

Okay, two thousand dollars' worth of coffee is a bit extreme, but one of the things I love about Pres is how thoughtful he is. Driving three hours to my parents' house to pick up my stuff on his own, then all the way back to campus, and he does it with a smile. He doesn't complain or make me out to be a burden. He does it to be nice.

There's a lot to be said for nice.

I glance at my roommate. "Bonnie, this is my boyfriend, Preston. Pres, this is Bonnie."

"Nice to meet you," he says with a genuine smile. "I'm going to grab the rest of Mac's boxes, then how about I take you both out for lunch?"

"I'm in," Bonnie replies. "I'm starved."

"That'd be great," I tell him. "Thank you."

Once he's gone, Bonnie gives me a silly grin and a thumbs-up. "Nice job. How long you been together?"

"Four years." I follow her into the shared bathroom so we can fix our hair and get ready for lunch. "We went to the same prep school. I was a sophomore, he was a senior."

I've known Preston since we were kids, although we weren't exactly friends growing up, given the age difference. I'd see him around the country club when my parents dragged me out with them, at holiday gatherings, fundraisers, and whatnot. When I started school at Spencer Hill, he was nice enough to acknowledge me in the halls and say hi to me at parties—helping me gain some of the clout I needed to survive and thrive in the shark-infested waters of a prep school.

"You must be relieved to finally get to college with him. If that were me, I'da been outta my mind wonderin' what he was gettin' up to out here on his own."

"It's not that way with us," I say, brushing out my hair. "Preston's not the cheating type. He's big on family and the plan, you know?"

"Plan?"

It's never sounded weird until Bonnie looks at me in the mirror with a raised eyebrow.

"Well, our parents have been friends for years, so after we'd been dating a while, it was sort of understood that eventually we were going to graduate, get married, all that. You know, the plan."

She stares at me, her face crinkled. "And you're . . . okay with that plan?"

"Why wouldn't I be?"

That's damn near verbatim how my parents ended up together. And their parents. I know it sounds only a couple steps away from an old-world arranged marriage thing, and to be honest, I suspect Preston got talked into taking me out that first time. He was the upperclassman. I was the awkward sophomore who still hadn't mastered a flat iron. But whether or not it was initially suggested to Pres by his parents, neither of us felt like we were being forced to date. We genuinely enjoyed each other's company, and still do.

"If that was me, I'd be pretty bummed that my whole life was planned before I even started my first day of college. It's like gettin' the movie spoiled when I'm standin' in line for popcorn." Bonnie shrugs, dabbing on some lip gloss. "But, hey, long as you're happy, right?"

CHAPTER THREE

COOPER

Ever since we were dumb, barefoot kids racing each other up and down the dunes, churning up wake in front of million-dollar mansions, and running from the cops, we—the misfit, misspent youth of Avalon Bay—have had a tradition. The last Sunday of summer culminates in a bonfire blowout.

The one rule: locals only.

Tonight, my twin brother and I are hosting the shindig at our place. The two-story, low-country, cottage-style beach house has been in our family for three generations—and it shows. The rambling house is in disrepair and requires a ton of renos, but it makes up for its rough exterior with a hell of a lot of charm. Sort of like its inhabitants, I suppose. Although Evan is definitely the more charming of the two of us. I can be a moody fuck sometimes.

On the back deck, Heidi sidles up beside me, setting a flask on the wooden railing.

"We got liquor downstairs. Tons," I tell her.

"That's not the point of a flask."

She puts her back to the railing, leaning on her elbows. Heidi has this way about her. There's nothing in the world that can satisfy her, her interest so far beyond everyone and everything. When we were kids, it was one of the first things that drew me to her. Heidi's eyes were always looking farther. I wanted to see what she saw.

"Then what's the point?" I ask.

"Feeling a little naughty. A flask is a secret."

She looks over at me, a sly smile pulling at her lips. She's done up tonight, at least as much as one does out here in the Bay. Hair curled. Dark red lipstick. She's wearing my old Rancid T-shirt, which she'd cut into a tank top that now exposes a black lace bra. She put a lot of effort into her look, and yet it's lost on me.

"Not much in the spirit, huh?" she says when I don't take the bait.

I shrug. Because, yeah, I'm not in the mood for a party.

"We can get out of here." Heidi straightens, nods toward *away.* "Go take a drive. Like when we used to steal your mom's keys, remember? Winding up in Tennessee somewhere, spending the night sleeping in the bed of the truck."

"Getting chased out of a national park by a furious ranger at four a.m."

She laughs, nudging my arm. "I miss our adventures."

I take a swig of her flask. "Sorta loses the appeal when you have your own keys and drinking is legal."

"I promise you, there's still all sorts of trouble we can make."

That flirtatious spark in her eyes makes me sad. Because we used to have fun together, and now it feels strained. Awkward.

"Coop!" Down in the yard, my brother shouts at me. "It's a party, dude. Get down here."

Twin telepathy still works. I leave Heidi on the deck, head downstairs, and grab a beer on my way to the beach, where I meet Evan around the bonfire with some of our friends. I drink while they spend the next hour swapping the same stories we've been telling for ten years. Then our buddy Wyatt organizes a game of moonlight football and most of the crowd drifts toward it, leaving only a hand-ful of us by the fire. Evan's in the Adirondack chair next to mine, laughing at something our friend Alana just said, but I can't seem to enjoy myself tonight. There's a bug under my skin. Burrowing. Chewing out holes in my flesh and laying eggs of anger and resent-ment.

"Dude." Evan kicks my foot. "Snap out of it, man."

"I'm fine."

"Yeah," he says sarcastically, "I can tell." He grabs the empty bottle of beer I've been absently holding and tosses me a new one from the cooler. "You've been a moody little bitch for two days. I get you're pissed off, but it ain't cute anymore. Get drunk, smoke some weed. Heidi's here somewhere. Maybe she'll hook up with you again if you ask nicely."

I stifle a groan. There are no secrets in this group. When Heidi and I first slept together, we'd barely dug the crust out of our eyes the next morning before everyone else knew about it. Which is just more proof that it was a bad idea to go there. Hooking up with friends is only inviting trouble.

"Eat me, asshole." Heidi throws a handful of sand at him from across the fire pit. She flashes him the bird.

"Oops," he says, knowing full well she was sitting there. "My bad."

"You know, it's remarkable," Heidi says in that flat tone that is a glaring warning she's about to snip your balls off. "You two are identical twins, and yet I wouldn't touch your dick, Evan, even with Cooper's face."

"Burn," Alana shouts, laughing beside Heidi and Steph. The three of them have been the absolute torment of every boy in the Bay since we were in third grade. An unholy trinity of hotness and terror.

Evan makes a lewd gesture in response because comebacks are not really in his wheelhouse. Then he turns back to me. "I still say we wait till that clone leaves his house and we jump his ass. Word gets around, Coop. People start hearing you let that shit stand, and suddenly they're thinking anyone can mess with us."

"Cooper's lucky that prick didn't press charges," Steph points out. "But if you turn this into a war, he could change his mind."

She's right. There's no good reason why I haven't spent the last two days in a jail cell, other than that Preston guy was satisfied in humiliating me. While I'd never admit defeat, I'm still hot about getting fired. Evan's right—Hartleys can't let that shit stand. We have a reputation in this town. People smell weakness, they start getting ideas. Even when you have nothing, someone's always trying to take it.

"Who was he, anyway?" Heidi asks.

"Preston Kincaid," Steph supplies. "His family owns that massive estate down the coast where they ripped out those two-hundred-year-old oaks last month to put in a third tennis court."

"Ugh, I know that guy," Alana says, her bright red hair glowing in the firelight. "Maddy was running her dad's parasailing boat a few weeks ago, and she took him out on it with some chick. He was trying to talk some game to Maddy right in front of his date. Dude actually asked her out. When she made some excuse, right, because she's still trying to get a tip, he tries to persuade her into a threesome right there on the boat. Maddy said she damn near tossed him overboard."

Steph makes a face. "He's such a creep."

"There you go." Evan pops the cap on a fresh beer and takes a swig. "He's got it coming. We'd be doing a community service to bust him down a peg."

I eye my brother, curious.

"Revenge, dude. He took a pound of flesh from you. We take two from him."

Have to admit, I'm aching for payback. For two days, this chunk of seething anger has sat in my gut, burning. Bartending wasn't my sole source of income, but I needed that money. Everything I've been working toward got a lot farther away when that jackass got me fired.

I think it over. "Can't beat his face in or I'll wind up in jail. Can't take his job because, come on, who are we kidding, dude doesn't have one. He was born with a silver spoon up his ass. So what else is there?"

"Oh, this poor, dumb girl," Alana suddenly says, coming around to our side of the fire to show us her phone. "Just peeped his social media. He's got a girlfriend."

I narrow my eyes at the screen. Interesting. Kincaid posted a story earlier today about moving his girlfriend into her dorm at Garnet. The post includes heart emojis and all the performative, saccharine bullshit that are the telltale signs of a cheater overcompensating.

"Damn," Evan remarks, taking the phone. He flicks through photos of them on Kincaid's obnoxious yacht. "Chick's actually hot."

He's right. The picture Evan zooms in on shows a tall, dark-haired girl with green eyes and tanned skin. She's wearing a white cropped T-shirt that's falling off one shoulder, revealing the strap of a blue bathing suit beneath, and for some reason, that thin strip of fabric is hotter than any pornographic image I've ever seen. It's a tease. An invitation.

A terrible idea forms in the worst part of my mind.

"Take her," Evan says, because for all the ways we're completely different, we're exactly the same.

Alana's eyes light with mischief. "Do it."

"What, steal his girlfriend?" Heidi demands, incredulous. "She's not a toy. That's—"

"A great idea," Evan interjects. "Snipe that clone's girl, rub it in his face, then dump her rich ass."

"Gross, Evan." Heidi gets up and snatches Alana's phone from him as they continue to bicker. "She's a person, you know."

"No, she's a clone."

"You want her to dump Kincaid, right? So why can't we just catch him cheating on her, and send her the proof so she dumps him? Same end result," Heidi points out.

"Not the same," my brother argues.

"How is that not the same thing?"

"Because it isn't." Evan points the mouth of his bottle at Heidi. "It isn't enough for Kincaid to lose. He has to know who beat him. We have to make it hurt."

"Cooper doesn't have to trick her into falling in love with him," Alana tells her. "Seduce her enough that she dumps her boyfriend. A few dates, tops."

"Seduce her? You mean fuck her, then," Heidi says, revealing the real reason she hates this plan. "Again, gross."

Any other day, I might have agreed with her. But not tonight. Tonight, I'm angry and bitter and itching for blood. Besides, I'd be doing this chick a favor rescuing her from Kincaid. Sparing her a life of misery with a cheating bastard who'd only treat her nice enough to get 2.5 kids outta her before shifting all his attention to his mistresses.

I've encountered guys like Preston Kincaid my entire life. One of my earliest memories is of my five-year-old self down at the pier with my father and brother, confused why all those fancy-dressed people were speaking to Dad like he was a piece of dog shit mashed under their deck shoes. Hell, chances are Kincaid's girl is even worse than he is.

Steph brings up a potential snag. "But if he's already cheating on her, then how much does he really care about this girl? Maybe getting dumped won't faze him."

I glance at Evan. "She's got a point."

"I don't know . . ." A contemplative Alana reaches over Heidi's shoulder to look at the phone. "Scrolling through, I think they've been together for a few years. My money's on this one being end-game for him."

The longer the idea tumbles around in my head, the more I'm into it. Mostly for the look on Kincaid's face when he realizes I've won. But also because even if I didn't know she was Kincaid's girl-friend, I'd still try to date her.

"Let's make it interesting," Steph says. She shares a look with Alana, coming around to the possibilities of this idea. "You can't lie. You can't pretend to be all in love with her, or sleep with her unless she initiates it. Kissing is allowed. And you can't tell her to break up with him. It has to be her idea. Otherwise what's the point? We might as well go with Heidi's plan."

"Deal." It's almost unfair how easy this'll be.

"Omissions are lies." Heidi stands in a huff. "What makes you think one of them would step down from their cloud for you any-way?" She doesn't wait for an answer. Just storms toward the house.

"Ignore her," Alana says. "I love this plan."

Evan, meanwhile, gives me a hard look, then nods in the direction Heidi went. "You've got to do something about that."

Yeah, maybe I do. After a handful of hookups, Heidi and I re-verted back to platonic and were cool all summer. But then some-where the tide shifted and suddenly she's bent out of shape more often than not, and it's apparently all my fault.

"She's a big girl," I tell him.

Maybe Heidi's feeling a little territorial, but she'll get over it. We've been friends since first grade. She can't stay mad at me forever.

"Anyway. Final answer about the clone?" Evan eyes me expec-tantly.

I tip the beer bottle to my lips, taking a quick swig. Then I shrug and say, "I'm in."

CHAPTER FOUR

MACKENZIE

On Saturday night, our first week of freshman year behind us, Bonnie pulls me out on the town. *To get the lay of the land*, as she puts it.

So far, we're getting along great as roommates. Better than I expected, actually. I'm an only child and never lived anywhere but my parents' house, so I was a bit wary of the politics of sharing a space with a complete stranger. But Bonnie's easy to live with. She cleans up after herself, and makes me laugh with her endless supply of Southern sass. She's like the little sister I never knew I wanted.

For the past hour since we left campus, she's only reinforced my theory that she's some kind of sorceress. This girl possesses powers a mere mortal could only dream of. The moment we stepped up to the bar in this rowdy hole-in-the-wall place with panties hanging from the rafters and license plates on the wall, three guys practically bulldozed their way through the crowd to buy our drinks. All to get Bonnie to smile at them. Since then, I've watched her charm one guy after the other without even lifting a pinkie. She simply bats her eyelashes at men, gives them a little giggle, a hair twirl, and they're ready to harvest their own mothers for organs.

"You new in town?" One of our latest suitors, a jock-looking type wearing a too-tight T-shirt and too much body spray, shouts in my ear over the blaring music. Even as he chats me up, his eyes drift toward Bonnie as she talks animatedly. I can't imagine any of them can hear her, but it doesn't seem to matter.

"Yeah," I answer, my face glued to the glow of my phone screen as I text with Pres. He's at a friend's place tonight for a poker game.

While I pay the least possible attention to this dude, whose job is to entertain the "friend," his two buddies eat out of Bonnie's hand all the way to the dance floor. I occasionally nod and glance up from my phone as he valiantly attempts conversation that we both must know is useless against the band's set list blasting at full volume.

About forty minutes after the wingman has crept away, an arm catches mine. "I'm bored. Let's ditch these guys," Bonnie says in my ear.

"Yes." I nod emphatically. "Please."

She mimes some excuse to the two guys still clinging to her heels like ducklings, and then we pick up our drinks and take a circuitous route to the stairs. On the second floor, looking down at the live band on the stage, we find a table with a little more breathing room. It's quieter up here. Enough that we can carry on a conversation without shouting or resorting to rudimentary sign language.

"Not doing it for you?" I ask, referring to her latest victims.

"I can get those meatheads a dime a dozen at home. Can't throw a rock without hitting a college football player."

I grin over the rim of my glass. The fruity cocktail isn't exactly my jam, but it's what Bonnie asked her suitors to buy for us. "So what's your type, then?"

"Tattoos. Tall, dark, and damaged. The more emotionally un-available, the better." She beams. "If he's got a juvenile rap sheet and motorcycle, I'm open for business."

I almost choke on my tongue laughing. Fascinating. She doesn't seem like that kind of girl. "Maybe we ought to go find a bar with more Harleys outside. I'm not sure we're going to find what you're looking for in here."

From what I can tell, it's slim pickings. Mostly Garnet students, which skew toward country club types or frat bros, and a few beach rat townies in tank tops. None of whom approach Bonnie's leather-and-studs daydreams.

"Oh, I done my research," she says proudly. "Rumor has it, Avalon Bay's got exactly what I need. The Hartley Twins."

I raise an eyebrow. "Twins, huh?"

"Locals," she says, nodding. "But I'm not greedy. One'll do fine. Figure my odds are improved with a spare."

"And these Hartley twins tick all of your bad boy boxes?"

"Oh yeah. I heard about their exploits from some girls on campus." She licks her lips. "I wanna be one of those exploits tonight."

Humor bubbles in my throat. This girl. "You don't even know these guys. What if they're hideous?"

"They aren't. Their names wouldn't be comin' outta every girl's mouth if they were." She sighs happily. "Besides, that girl down the hall from us—Nina? Dina? Whatever her name is. She showed me a picture of 'em and don't you worry, Miss Mac, they are *fine.*"

My laughter spills over. "Alright. Got it. I'll keep my eye out for a pair of bad boy clones."

"Thank you. Now, what about you?"

"Me?"

"Yes, you."

"I'm not in the market for a bad boy, no." My phone lights up again with a text from Preston telling me his next game is about to start.

Another thing I appreciate about Pres is routine, predictability. I prefer things that act within expected parameters. I'm a planner. An organizer. A boyfriend that's running all over town at all hours wouldn't fit in my life. Then again, I don't get the impression that Bonnie is in the market for a long-term investment. Maybe something more like a microtransaction.

"I'm just sayin'." Bonnie winks. "This is a circle of trust. I'd never snitch on a roomie if she wanted to entertain a little on the side."

"I appreciate it, but I'm good. Pres and I are loyal to each other." I wouldn't have done the whole long-distance thing if I wasn't confident we could be faithful. Now that we're both at Garnet, cheating would be even more pointless.

She looks at me a little cross-eyed then smiles in a way that's a bit patronizing, though I know she doesn't mean it. "So you're really the relationship type?"

"Yeah." I've only been with Preston, but even if it were someone else, monogamy is my thing. "I don't understand the point of cheating. If you want to be with other people, be single. Don't drag someone else along for the ride."

"Well, cheers to knowin' what we want and goin' after it." Bonnie raises her glass. We toast, then suck our cocktails dry. "Come on," she says, "let's get outta here. I got twins to hunt."

She's not joking. For the next two hours, I find myself trailing behind Bonnie as if I've got a dick-sniffing bloodhound on a leash. She drags me from one bar to the next in search of her elusive twins, leaving countless mesmerized victims in her wake. One poor loser after another throwing himself at her feet, slayed by her dimples. I've never had trouble attracting attention from guys, but standing next to Bonnie May Beauchamp, I might as well be a broken barstool. Good thing I have a boyfriend, or else I'd develop a complex.

As much as I want to help Bonnie in her crusade to locate and destroy her townie bad boy, the sidekick routine gets tedious as the night wears on. If she doesn't tire herself out soon, there's a chance I'll need to club her over the head.

"Last one," I warn as we cross the threshold of yet another board-walk bar. This one's called the Rip Tide. "If your twins aren't here, you'll have to settle for any old bad boy."

"Last one," she promises. Then she bats her eyelashes and, like every guy we've encountered tonight, I find myself melting in her presence. It's impossible to stay annoyed with her.

She links her arm through mine and pulls me deeper into the Rip Tide. "C'mon, girl, let's do this. I got a good feeling about this one."

CHAPTER FIVE

COOPER

She's here.

Fate must be on board with the plan, because I'm out with some friends on Saturday night to see a buddy's band at the Rip Tide when I spot *her*. She's alone at a high-top table, placed directly in my path as if by some higher power.

Her face is unmistakable. And holy hell, she was good-looking in photos but a total knockout in person. The kind of girl who sticks out in a crowd. Stunning, with long dark hair and piercing eyes that shine under the lights from the stage. Even at a distance, she's got an effortless cool about her, an aura of confidence. In a white T-shirt knotted at her waist and a pair of jeans, she stands out for not trying too hard.

All that would be enough to capture my attention even if she didn't have a killer body. But she has that too—impossibly long legs, a full rack, a round bottom. She's the girl my daydreams daydream about.

"That her?" Alana leans in to follow my gaze to where Preston Kincaid's girlfriend is sitting. "She's better looking in person."

I know.

"Quick smoke while the next band sets up?" suggests our friend Tate. He rises from the table, dragging a hand through his messy blond hair.

"Nah, we're staying here," Alana answers for us.

He quirks a brow at me. "Coop?"

Once again, Alana is my mouthpiece. "Cooper is cutting back on the cancer sticks." She waves a hand. "You guys go on out."

Shrugging, Tate wanders off, tailed by Wyatt and Wyatt's girlfriend, Ren. The moment they're gone, Alana turns her gaze on me.

"Lemme hear it," she orders.

"Hear what?"

"Your game. Pitch some lines." She flips her hair and props her chin in her hands, giving me sarcastic doe eyes.

"Fuck off." I don't need a pickup coach.

"You need a plan," she insists. Thing about Alana, when she gets her claws into something, she tends to take over. "You can't just go over and drop your dick in her lap."

"Yes, thank you, I'm aware." I drain the last of my beer as I get up from the table.

Alana stops me, pulls the sleeves of my black Henley down and runs her hands through my hair.

"What's that for?" I grumble.

"Best foot forward," she says. "Just in case she's a prude. Tattoos scare off the prudes." Leaning back, she takes a final appraising glance before shooing me with her hand. "You're done. Go forth and conquer."

This is the problem with having girl friends.

Before I approach my mark's table, I take a quick scan of the room to make sure Kincaid isn't lurking somewhere. Not that I have any qualms about a rematch. Getting into a bar fight isn't part of the plan, though. This'll work best if I can swoop in there undetected until it's too late for him to intervene. Win her over before he even knows the enemy is inside the gates.

Satisfied that she's flying sans-boyfriend tonight, I walk up to her table. With her face glued to her phone, she doesn't notice me until I tap her on the arm.

"Hey," I say, bending my head toward her so she can hear me over the music from the loudspeaker. "You using this stool?"

"No." She doesn't lift her attention from the lit screen. "Go ahead." When I sit, her head jerks up. "Oh. Figured you'd just take the stool to another table. But okay."

"Settle a bet for me," I say, leaning in closer. She smells good, like vanilla and citrus. So good I almost forget why I'm here. That she doesn't pull away or throw a drink in my face is a good start.

"Uh . . . what sort of bet?" There's a flicker of hostility in her eyes before her expression softens. When she rakes her gaze over me, I know I've got her intrigued.

"What if I told you, an hour from now, you'd be leaving this bar with me."

"I'd say I admire your hustle, but you'd be better off aiming that arrow at another target."

"So we have a wager then." Holding her gaze, I offer my hand to shake on it. I find the best way to truly know someone is to push and see if they push back. Wind them up and let them go.

"I have a boyfriend," she says flatly, ignoring my hand. "You've already lost."

I meet her eyes. Insolently. "I didn't ask about your boyfriend."

For a moment she's taken aback. Of course she is, because no one talks to her that way. Certainly not her dumbass boyfriend. Chicks like her are used to parents doting on their every desire and servants waiting on them hand and foot. And as the notion of me settles into her mind, I see the moment she decides I'm more interesting than whatever was on her phone.

She puts it to sleep and pushes it away.

So fucking predictable. Every rich girl from a good family wonders what it's like to be with the guy from the wrong side of the gilded gates. It's the closest thing to a thrill they'll ever have.

"Is this a gag?" She looks around. "Did Bonnie put you up to this?"

"I don't know any Bonnie. I'm Cooper."

"Mackenzie," she replies with a furrowed brow, still spinning her wheels wondering what the catch is. "But I really do have a boyfriend."

"You keep saying that."

This time when I lean in, she doesn't back away. The gap between us falls to a few inches, the air between us growing thinner.

"In most of the civilized world," she says slowly, "that matters."

"And here I'm looking around, and I don't see this guy you're so concerned about."

Her face is incredulous, if a bit amused. She knows exactly how hot she is and is used to men chasing after her. Yet I sense her unease. I threw her off-kilter. Which tells me she's thinking about it. I've met countless girls like her, slept with a few of them, and right now, the farfetched fantasies and what-ifs are spiraling through her pretty head.

"I'm with my roommate tonight." There's still fight in her voice, the resolve to hold her ground, or at least appear to do so. This is a woman who's never played the easy target. "It's a girls' thing."

"Yeah, real wild night you're having," I drawl, gesturing at her glass of water. "Someone's got a good girl complex, huh?"

"I'm dying to find out how insulting me is going to win you this bet."

"Stick around and find out."

She holds up her water. "This is called being a good friend. I've already met my alcohol quota of two drinks."

"Whatever you say, princess."

She twirls the straw in her glass. "I'm trying to watch out for my roommate tonight."

"What if I thought you looked lonely?"

She cocks her head, eyes narrowing. I can see the gears working in her mind, analyzing me. "Why would I be lonely?"

"Let's cut the bullshit."

She nods with a smirk. "Yes, let's."

"You're an attractive woman alone in a crowded bar with your face glued to your phone because there's somewhere else you'd rather be. And wherever that place is, there's someone who's having fun without you. Yet you're sitting here wearing your boredom as a badge of loyalty, with some misguided notion that being miserable proves what a good person you are. So, yeah, I think you're lonely. I think you're so desperate for a good time you're secretly glad I walked over here. In the deepest, darkest part of your brain, you want me to give you a reason to misbehave."

Mackenzie doesn't answer. In the crackle of energy building in the tight space between us, I watch the indecision warring behind her eyes. She considers everything I just said, stabbing the straw into her glass of ice water.

If she's going to tell me to get lost, this is it. I've called her out and anything less than shutting me down is an admission that I'm at least a little right. But if she doesn't shut me down, then the path ahead of her is unmarked. There are no rules, and that's dangerous territory for someone whose whole world is mapped out for them from birth. Being rich means never having to think for yourself.

If she chooses to follow me, it only gets less predictable from here.

"Alright," she says finally. "I'll take that bet." I can tell she's still skeptical of my motivations, but she's intrigued. "But if you think this ends with getting me in bed, you might as well pay up now."

"Right. Wouldn't want to tempt you with a good time."

She rolls her eyes, failing to hide a smile.

"I mean, I could feel the bummer energy wafting off of you from way over there," I say, nodding toward the table where Alana and our friends are failing to pretend they aren't watching us. "Honestly, this is a mitigation protocol. If your attitude doesn't improve, we're gonna have to ask you to leave before your bummer spreads."

"Oh," she says, putting on an expression of mock seriousness, "if this is a medical emergency, then, by all means, please."

She's got banter, at least. I was afraid she'd be another stuck-up priss who couldn't string a thought together that wasn't about clothes or nail polish. I assumed going into this I'd have to contend with a typical clone attitude of bitchy entitlement, but this chick seems mostly normal, with none of that pompous pretension.

"So, what *did* drag you out tonight?" I ask. The more she can talk about herself, the more her walls will come down. Gives her the idea she's in control.

"My roommate is hunting a pair of twins," she informs me.

Oh really. "For sport or meat?"

"Bit of both." Her gaze travels the room, presumably searching the crowd for this elusive roommate. "She has a thing for socially unproductive boys who put their personality on their skin, and she's got it in her head that twins are good odds. Personally, I think a bout of herpes isn't worth the morning-after Instagram selfie, but what do I know?"

I struggle to keep a straight face. This is too perfect. I almost feel bad doing this to her, but then she did suggest I have herpes, so not that bad.

"You know these twins?" I paste on an innocent tone.

"No, but if they're so infamous their reputation on campus filtered all the way down to a freshman in the first week of school, their tales must be long and plentiful." Her face scrunches in disgust. If this wasn't so amusing, I might be offended. "Any guy that gets around that much is bound to fill up a petri dish with all manner of genital infestations."

"Obviously," I say solemnly. "Got a name for these twin patient zeros?"

"The Hartleys. They're local." Then her face lights up. "You don't know them, do you? I mean, Bonnie would be excited to pick up a clue on her quest, but if they're friends of yours or something . . ."

I almost can't stand the anticipation anymore.

"Nah, forget those guys." I'm fighting a grin. "Couple dirtbags, those two."

"Mac! I need another drink and then we— Oh." A short blonde walks up and stops short, staring straight through my skull. Her face turns a glowing pink as her big eyes dart to Mackenzie.

A few daunting seconds of mental gymnastics pass wordlessly between the girls before Mackenzie grabs my wrist and yanks one sleeve up my arm to reveal my tattoos.

"Oh fuck off," she says to me, glaring fire. "No. Nope. Not fair." She sits back and crosses her arms in defiance. "You knew I was talking about you and still let me go on like that?"

"I never pass up on free entertainment," I say, my grin springing free.

Her roommate slides onto the stool beside Mackenzie, watching us. It suddenly occurs to me that the roommate situation could be tricky. Either this girl derails my plans by calling dibs and scaring off Mackenzie before I've ever had a shot, or she's my ace in the hole. Get the roommate on my side and coast to the finish line. Luckily, I have a spare me to toss her way.

"You duped me." Emphatic, Mackenzie tells me, "An intentional attempt at deception. That's not allowed. In fact, this entire interaction is now moot. We didn't meet. I don't know you."

"Wow." I push back from the table, smothering a laugh. "You've given me a lot to think about. I'm gonna need another drink to soak that in. Another round?" This time I direct the question to the roommate, whose permanent look of awe has not waned.

"Yes, please," she says. When Mackenzie appears she might object, the roommate shoots her a look. "Thank you."

I head over to the bar and catch a glimpse of Alana, who gets up from our friends' table to follow me. She takes a circuitous route to pass slowly by Mackenzie and her roommate while I order three beers.

"Looks like it went well," Alana says when she finally slides in beside me. The current band's set ends and there's a brief lull before the canned music is pumped into the room as the next band sets up.

"She's cool," I answer, shrugging. "Kinda mouthy, but when has that ever stopped me?"

"Yeah, well, don't get attached." Alana orders a shot for herself.

"I just met the girl. Relax." Besides, attachment's never been my problem. Growing up the way I did, I learned a long time ago that everything is temporary. There's no use investing too much of myself. Easier that way. Clean. Saves everyone all sorts of grief.

"I heard them talking." Alana downs her shot and winces at the burn. "The blonde one was like, *He's yours if you want him*, but our girl was like, *Nah, go for it*. So . . ." She turns around to lean against the bar, looking over at the girls' table. "You've still got a lot of work to do there."

"Long story, but I might have to throw Evan at the blonde one."

"How ever will he manage," Alana says, rolling her eyes at me.

The roommate's hot, no doubt, but she's not really my type. Anyway, she's about half my size, and I hate throwing my back out bending down to kiss a girl.

The bartender comes back with our drinks and I gather them up, returning to the girls as Alana shouts something like *Go get 'em, tiger* at my back. I underestimated how obnoxious turning my sex life into a spectator sport would be.

At the table, I put the drinks down and take a seat. When Mackenzie pushes her water to the side to accept the beer, I know for certain she's along for the ride. If she was going to get spooked and bolt, it would have been before I got back.

"Cooper Hartley." I offer my hand to the roommate, who's studying me not at all discreetly.

She shakes my hand, her small fingers lingering. "Bonnie May Beauchamp," she says with a heavy Southern accent. "Don't suppose your brother is lurkin' around."

"No, he's probably getting into trouble somewhere." Actually, he's hustling rich kids out of their trust fund money at the pool tables a few doors down. It's practically his second job. "Can't take that kid anywhere."

"That's too bad." Bonnie gives a playful pout.

It's clear this Bonnie chick is a tiny bottle of fire. She's got all kinds of mischievous sexual energy bursting out of her.

"We were hoping you had the skinny on the after-party, right, Mac? Somewhere . . . cozier."

Mackenzie shoots a conflicted glance at her roommate. I bite back a grin. Now if she refuses, she's cockblocking her friend. *Tough spot, Mac.* This roommate and I are becoming fast friends. This'll be easier than I hoped.

"Cozy, huh?" I say.

Mackenzie glances back at me, realizing she never stood a chance at winning our little game. I'd feel bad if I were capable of giving a shit. This chick's hot, and not a total nightmare, but I haven't forgotten why I'm here. She's still only a means to an end.

"I know a place." It's too soon to try inviting them back to the house. That's coming on strong, and I know instinctively it's not the right strategy on this one. She needs the measured approach. Build a rapport. Become friends. I can be patient when I need to be; let her come to me. The mission is to break up her and Kincaid. For that to work, she has to be invested.

"That doesn't sound ominous at all." Mackenzie's got some bite to her now.

"I'll text my brother, see if he's interested in getting into some trouble with us instead of whatever he's up to. Yeah?"

"I'm game." Bonnie looks to Mackenzie with *Daddy, can I have a pony* eyes.

"I don't know." Torn, she consults her phone. "It's almost one in the morning. My boyfriend's probably home waiting for me to call him."

"He'll live," Bonnie insists. Her pleading tone grows more urgent. "Please?"

"Come on, princess. Live a little."

Mackenzie wrestles with her better judgment, and there's a split second when I begin to question myself. That perhaps I'd read her wrong, and she's not a bored rich girl who needs to let loose. That she's fully capable of getting up, walking off, and never looking at me twice.

"Fine," she relents. "An hour, tops."

Nah, still got it.

CHAPTER SIX

MACKENZIE

I don't quite know how we got here. I'm with Bonnie, Cooper, and his identical twin Evan, sitting around a glowing bonfire on the sand where the crashing waves and pulsing tide drown out the sounds of the boardwalk. The tiny sparks and embers flicker and float into the warm ocean air. Lights twinkle from behind the sand dunes and reflect off the water.

Clearly I've lost my mind. It's as though someone else hijacked my brain when I agreed to let this stranger drag us into the darkness. Now, as Bonnie cozies up to her bad boy, a growing sense of unease builds inside me. It's coming from the Cooper-sized space across the flames.

"You're so full of it," Bonnie accuses. She's cross-legged beside me, laughing yet skeptical.

"I shit you not." Evan puts his hands up in a show of innocence. "Coop's sitting with this damn goat in the back of the squad car, and it's scared, thrashing around. Kicks him in the forehead, and Coop starts gushing blood everywhere. So he's trying to calm the goat down but everything's all bloody and slippery back there. There's blood all over him and the goat, the windows. And I'm driving this stolen cop car, the sirens are blaring, lights are flashing and shit."

I laugh at his crazy description and animated hand gestures. Evan seems more playful than Cooper, who comes off as a bit intense. Their faces are identical, but it's easy to tell them apart. Evan's dark hair is cut shorter, his arms devoid of ink.

"And we can hear them on the radio," Cooper says, his way too attractive face a dance of light and shadow from the fire between us. "They're all, some damn fool kids stole a goat and a car. Set up a perimeter. Lock down the bridge. So we're thinking, crap, where are we taking this thing?"

I can't peel my gaze off his lips. His hands. Those muscular arms. I'm trying to trace the outlines of his tattoos as he gestures through the air. It's psychological torture. I'm strapped to a chair, my eyes held open, driven mad by images of his dark eyes and crooked smirk. And although Evan literally has the same face, for some reason I'm not responding to *him*. Not even remotely. Just Cooper.

"We're thirteen years old and set off a chase through town," Evan continues, "all because Steph saw this goat chained up in someone's yard and hopped the fence to liberate it just as the owner comes out with a shotgun. And Coop and I are thinking, aw man, she's about to get her crazy ass shot over this goat."

"We jump the fence after her, and I'm smashing the lock with a hammer—"

"You happened to have a hammer with you?" Even my voice sounds strange to me. I'm out of breath because my heart is pumping so fast, though I've been sitting the whole time. Perfectly still. Caught in his spell.

"Yeah." He looks at me like I'm weird for asking. "It's a cheap lock. You smack it good a couple times on the side, and the little parts inside break apart. So Evan grabs the goat and we're dodging buckshot, because the owner is drunk off his ass and can't aim for shit."

"But where'd the cop car come from?" Bonnie asks.

"We're running with this thing on a leash when a cop corners us, right?" Evan becomes animated, gesturing with a bottle of beer that he brought to the beach with him. "He draws his Taser but there's three of us and a goat, so he doesn't know who to aim at. He leaves the door open, so I'm like, screw it, hop in."

"Evan and I dive in," Cooper says. "Steph runs to distract the cop. Anyway, so the goat kicks the hell out of me, and I'm back there getting woozy, about to black out, when Evan says, bro, we gotta ditch this car and run."

"So what happened to the goat?" I demand, now sincerely invested in the fate of this poor animal, but acutely paranoid that everyone notices how out of sorts I am. How hard I'm staring.

"Evan pulls onto this fire road that cuts through the state park and somehow wrestles that thing out of the backseat and takes it into the forest. Leaves me passed out on the ground beside the car so when the cops get there and see me unconscious and covered in blood, looking dead as a doornail, they all start freaking out. They get me in an ambulance, and I wake up in the hospital. In all the confusion, I slip out of there and meet Evan at home like nothing ever happened."

"They never caught you?" Bonnie hoots with laughter.

"Hell no," Evan says. "Got away clean."

"So you left a goat by itself in the woods?" I stare at them, amused yet horrified.

"What the hell else were we supposed to do with it?" Cooper sputters.

"Not that! Oh my God. That poor goat. I'm going to have nightmares about the thing crying alone in the dark forest. Chased down by bobcats or something."

"See?" Evan smacks his brother's arm. "This is why we don't let chicks talk us into playing hero. They're never satisfied."

Still, I laugh despite myself. The image of those two tearing through town, barely able to see over the steering wheel, with a frightened goat kicking and bucking around, is too hilarious.

For a while longer, we trade silly stories. About the time Bonnie and her high school cheerleading squad turned a hotel grand staircase into a Slip 'N Slide at a competition in Florida. Or the time a friend and I met some guys when camping with her family and almost burned down the campground with fireworks.

And then, it finally arrives. The moment Bonnie has eagerly awaited all night.

Evan grabs the blanket he got from his car earlier and asks Bonnie if she wants to take a walk. Those two have been making eyes at each other since we came here. Before they walk off, she glances back at me to make sure I'm cool by myself, and I give her a nod.

Because as terrified as I am to be left alone with Cooper, it's exactly what I want.

"Well, my work here is done," I inform him, trying to act normal.

He pokes the fire with a stick to move the logs around. "Don't worry, she's safe with him. He talks like a delinquent, but Evan's not a creep or anything."

"I'm not worried." I get up and take Evan's spot in the sand beside Cooper. I shouldn't, but I'm a glutton for punishment. And I don't know if it's him or the intoxicating scent of burning driftwood, but I feel drunk despite only having one beer. "Honestly, neither of you are what I expected. In a good way."

Uh-oh. That sounded flirty, I realize. My cheeks heat up, and I hope he doesn't take the comment as a sign of interest.

"Yeah," he says, shaking his head. "I'm kinda still waiting on an apology for that herpes crack."

"I plead the fifth." I bite back a smirk, looking at him from the corner of my eye.

"So that's how it is, huh?" He arches an eyebrow, challenging me with mock bravado.

I shrug. "Don't know what you're talking about."

"Alright. I see. Remember that, Mac. When you had the chance to be the bigger person."

"Ohhh," I taunt. "So it's war now, huh? Sworn enemies to the death?"

"I don't start shit, I finish it." He makes a joking tough guy face and kicks some sand at my feet.

"Yeah, real mature."

"Now about that bet, princess."

That does me in. With that single mocking nickname, I blink and a terrible sinking awareness becomes undeniable.

Cooper's hot.

Insanely hot.

And it's not just his strong, angular face and deep, dark eyes that descend for ages. He also possesses a certain *I don't give a fuck* quality that gets right at the most susceptible parts of me. In the light of the fire, there's something almost ominous about him. A knife when the light glints off the blade. Yet he has a magnetism that's undeniable.

I can't remember the last time I felt such a visceral attraction to a guy. If ever.

I don't like it. Not only because I have a boyfriend, but because my pulse is racing and my cheeks are hot, and I hate feeling like I'm not in control of my own body.

"We never did set the stakes," he muses.

"What do you want, then?" Fair's fair. If nothing else, I'm a woman of my word.

"You wanna make out?"

I play it cool, but my pulse kicks into a new gear. "What else do you want?"

"I mean, I figured a blowjob was a nonstarter, but if we're negotiating. . . ."

Despite myself, I crack a smile. "You're shameless."

Somehow he manages to release the tension from the moment, erasing all awkwardness until I'm no longer hyperaware of myself.

"Alright," he says, a sexy grin tilting his lips. "You drive a hard bargain. I'll go down on you first."

"Yeah, I think we're at an impasse on this one."

"That right?" He watches me under heavy-lidded eyes. It's impossible not to feel he's undressing me in his mind. "Fine. But I'm keeping your marker. You're going to owe me one."

At some point I feel my phone buzz in my pocket. By then Cooper and I are knee-deep in an argument over the socioeconomic implications of pastries. I glance at my phone to make sure it isn't Bonnie asking for a rescue, but it's just Preston saying he's home from his poker game.

"No way," Cooper argues. "Pastries are rich people food. You never see someone making minimum wage popping into a bakery for a box of fucking croissants. We got donuts, cold Pop-Tarts, and maybe a biscuit out of a can or something, but none of that scone shit."

"A donut is absolutely a pastry. And a donut shop is a kind of bakery."

"Horseshit. There are five bakeries in this town, and three of them are only open in the summer. What does that tell you?"

"That the population swells during the tourist season, and the overflow shops open to support that demand. It says nothing about the demographics."

He scoffs, tossing a stick into the fire. "Now you're talking nonsense."

Though it sounds like we're fighting, the subtle turn at the corner of his mouth tells me it's all in good fun. Arguing is practically a pastime in my house, so I'm quite skilled at it. Not sure where Cooper learned to bicker so well, but he definitely keeps me on my toes. And neither of us take well to admitting defeat.

"You're not the most annoying clone I've ever met," he says a while later.

Bonnie and Evan still aren't back. The boardwalk behind us is now mostly quiet in the late hour, and yet I'm not tired. If anything, I feel more energized.

"Clone?" I echo with a wry look. That's a new one on me.

"What we call the rich folks. Because you're all the same." His eyes glint thoughtfully beneath the moonlight. "But maybe you're not exactly like the rest of them."

"Not sure if that's an insulting compliment or a complimentary insult." It's my turn to kick a little sand at him.

"No, I mean, you're not what I expected. You're chill. Real." He continues to study me, all the playfulness and pretense forgotten. On his face I see only sincerity. The real Cooper. "Not one of those stuck-up jackasses who has their head up their ass because they love the smell of their own shit so much."

There's something in his voice, and it's more than the surface annoyance with yuppie tourists and rich jerks. It sounds like real pain.

I give him an elbow jab to lighten the mood. "I get it. I've grown up with those people. You'd think it gets to a point where you hardly notice it, but nope. Still, they're not all bad."

"This boyfriend of yours? What's his story?"

"Preston," I supply. "He's from the area, actually—his family lives down the coast. He goes to Garnet, obviously. Business major."

"You don't say." Cooper dons a sarcastic look.

"He's not that bad. I don't think he's ever even played squash," I say for a laugh, but the joke doesn't land. "He's a good guy. Not the type who's a dick to the waiter or that kind of thing."

Cooper chuckles softly. "You don't think it's telling that your answer is basically, he's nice to the help?"

I sigh. I suppose I don't know how to talk to a guy I just met about my boyfriend. Especially when Cooper is clearly hostile to our entire upbringing.

"You know, this might shock you, but if you gave him a chance, you might actually get along. We're not all jackasses," I point out.

"Nah." Some light returns to his expression, and I take that as a good sign. "I'm pretty sure you're the one exception I've met, and I've lived in the Bay my whole life."

"Then I'm glad I could demonstrate some redeeming qualities of my people."

He smiles, shrugging. "We'll see."

"Oh, yeah? That sounds suspiciously like an invitation. But you wouldn't be caught dead making friends with"—I gasp for effect—"a clone, now would you?"

"Not a chance. Call it an experiment. You can be my test subject."

"And what hypothesis are we testing?"

"Whether a clone can be deprogrammed into a real person."

I can't help but laugh. I've been doing that a lot tonight. Cooper might have those brooding bad boy looks, but he's funnier than I expected. I like him.

"So are we really doing this?" I ask.

His tongue drags over his bottom lip in a positively lewd way. "Going down on each other? Hell yeah. Let's do it."

More laughter sputters out. "Being friends! I'm asking if we're going to be friends! Jeez, Hartley, you are way too focused on oral sex, anyone ever tell you that?"

"Firstly, have you looked in the mirror? Jeez—" He halts, looking over at me. "What's your last name?"

"Cabot," I say helpfully.

"Jeez, Cabot," he mimics. "How can I not think about oral sex when I'm sitting next to the hottest woman on the planet?"

A flush rises in my cheeks. Damn it. That rough honesty is wildly sexy.

Gulping, I force my body not to respond to his crudeness or the compliment. *You have a boyfriend, Mackenzie.* I spell it out for my brain. B-O-Y-F-R-I-E-N-D.

Is it bad that I've had to remind myself an alarming number of times tonight?

"Secondly," Cooper continues, "are you sure we're not gonna hook up?"

"Positive."

He rolls his eyes at me. "Fine, then thirdly—yes, I guess I'll settle for friendship."

"How kind of you."

"Right?"

"Oh God. I'm already reconsidering. I feel like you're going to be a high-maintenance friend."

"Bullshit," he argues. "I'll be the best friend you've ever had. I always go above and beyond what's expected of me. I mean, I've liberated goats for my friends. Can you say the same?"

I snicker. "Goats, plural? You mean it wasn't just the one?"

"Nah, it was only one goat. But one time, I did steal a goldfish for my friend Alana."

"Awesome. I'm friends with a thief." I poke him in the side. "I need to hear the goldfish story, please."

He winks. "Oh, it's a good one."

We talk for so long, the two of us around the dwindling fire, that I don't notice the black night turn to gray early morning until

Evan and Bonnie come strolling toward us looking rather pleased with themselves. By then I realize I have a dozen texts from Preston wondering what the hell happened to me. Oops.

"Take my number," Cooper says in a rough voice. "Text me when you get to campus so I know you made it back safe."

Despite the warning alarms in my head, I punch his number into my phone.

No big deal, I assure that disapproving side of me. It'll just be one text when I get home, then I'll delete the number. Because as fun as it was to joke about our impending friendship, I know it's not a good idea. If I've learned one thing from rom coms, it's that you are not allowed to be friends with someone you're attracted to. The attraction itself is harmless. We're human beings and life can last years. We're bound to feel physical attraction for someone other than our significant other. But anyone who places themselves directly in the path of temptation is only asking for trouble.

So when Bonnie and I stumble out of an Uber and climb up to our dorm, I'm fully prepared to purge Cooper Hartley from my phone. I send a solitary text: *Home safe!* Then I click on his number and hover my finger over the word *DELETE*.

Before I can press it, a message from him pops up.

Cooper: *That was fun. Let's do it again sometime?*

I bite my lip, staring at the invitation. The memory of his dark eyes gleaming in the firelight, of his broad shoulders and muscular arms, jumpstarts my tired brain and tickles that spot between my legs.

Delete him, a strict voice orders.

I click on the chat thread. Maybe a friendship with this guy is a terrible idea, but I can't help myself. I cave.

Me: *I'll bring donuts.*

CHAPTER SEVEN

MACKENZIE

Only two weeks into the semester and I'm already over it. It wouldn't be so bad if I could dig into some business and finance courses. Marketing and mass communications law. Even some basic web coding. Instead, I'm stuck in a lecture hall staring at an illustration of some hairy, naked pre-human ape-man that, frankly, varies little from the current iteration sitting three rows over.

Freshman gen-eds are bullshit. Even psychology or sociology could have had some application to my work, but those courses were full. So I got stuck in anthropology, which so far today has been ten minutes of swarthy protohuman slides and forty minutes of arguments over evolution. None of which benefits my bank account. My parents pushed college on me, but I was hoping I could at least be productive while I was here. Optimizing *BoyfriendFails* and its sister site, targeting keywords, looking at ad impressions. Instead, I'm taking notes because our professor is one of those *an A is perfection, so no one is getting an A in this class* assholes. And if I'm forced to entertain this exhaustive waste of time, I'm not going to walk around with a C average.

It isn't until I step outside into the blazing sunshine that I realize I can't feel my fingertips. The lecture hall was freezing. I head over to the student union for a coffee and sit on a hot concrete bench under a magnolia tree to thaw out. I'm supposed to meet Preston in thirty minutes, so I still have some time to kill.

I sip my coffee and scroll through some business emails, forcing myself not to dwell on the fact that I haven't heard from Cooper yet today.

And I say *yet*, because he's messaged me every day since Saturday night. So I know I'll hear from him at some point today, it's only a matter of when. The first time he texted, I'd hesitated to open the message, afraid a picture of his junk might pop up on the screen. Or maybe hopeful it would? I've never been one for dick pics, but—

But nothing! a sharp voice shouts in my head.

Right. There's no *but*. I don't want to see Cooper Hartley's penis. Period, end of sentence. I mean, why would I want to see the penis of the hot, tattooed bad boy I stayed up an entire night talking to? That's just ludicrous.

Welp, I'm not cold anymore. I'm burning up now.

I need a distraction. ASAP.

When my mom's number lights up the screen, I think about ignoring the call, because that's definitely not the distraction I'd hoped for. But past experience has taught me that ignoring her only encourages her to send increasingly demanding texts to answer her. Then calls to the FBI insisting I've been kidnapped for ransom.

"Hi, Mom," I answer, hoping she can't hear my lack of enthusiasm.

"Mackenzie, sweetheart, hello."

There's a long pause, during which I can't tell if she's distracted or waiting for me to say something. *You called me, Mom.*

"What's up?" I ask to get the ball rolling.

"I wanted to check in. You promised to call after you got settled, but we haven't heard from you."

Ugh. She always does this. Turns everything into a guilt trip. "I called the house last weekend, but Stacey said you were out, or busy or something."

I spend more time on the phone with my mother's personal assistant than I do with anyone in the family.

"Yes, well, I have a lot on my plate at the moment. The historical society is sponsoring a new exhibit at the State House, and we're already planning the fall gala fundraiser for the children's hospital. Still, persistence is everything, Mackenzie. You know that. You should have called again later that day."

Of course. My mother has a personal staff and still can't manage to return a call to her only child, but sure, that's my fault. Ah well. It's something I've learned to live with. Annabeth Cabot simply can't be wrong about anything. I inherited that trait, at least when it comes to pointless arguments about donuts or whatnot. Those, I must always win. But unlike my mom, I'm fully capable of admitting when I've made a mistake.

"How is school?" she inquires. "Do you like your professors? Are you finding your classes challenging?"

"School's great."

Lie.

"My professors are so engaging, and the course content is really interesting so far."

Lie. Lie.

"I love it here."

Lie.

But there's nothing to gain from telling her the truth. That half the professors seem to regard teaching freshmen as an act of spite, and the other half only show up to hand their TAs a thumb drive of PowerPoint slides. That my time would be better spent anywhere else, but especially on my thriving business. She doesn't want to hear it.

The truth is, my parents have never been interested in what I have to say unless it's something they've scripted themselves and forced me to read. In my father's case, the daughter script is typically recited during public events and accompanied by fake, beaming smiles aimed at his constituents.

"I want you to apply yourself, Mackenzie. A lady should be worldly and well educated."

For appearances is the unspoken part. Not for any practical purposes, but so the lady can carry on conversations at cocktail parties.

"Remember to enjoy yourself too. College is a seminal time in a young woman's life. This is where you meet the people who will form your network for years to come. It's important to build those relationships now."

As far as Mom is concerned, I'm supposed to follow in her footsteps. I'm to become a glorified housewife who sits on all the right charity boards and throws parties to support her husband's professional aspirations. I've stopped trying to argue the point with her, but that's not the life I want, and eventually, hopefully, I'll jump on another track and it'll be too late for them to stop me.

For now, I play along.

"I know, Mom."

"What about your roommate? What's her name?"

"Bonnie. She's from Georgia."

"What's her family name? What do they do?"

Because that's what it always boils down to. Are they *someone*?

"Beauchamp. They own car dealerships."

"Oh." Another long, disappointed pause. "I suppose they do well with that."

Meaning that if they can afford to put her in the same dorm room with me, they must not be dirt-poor.

I stifle a sigh. "I have to go, Mom. Got class in a few minutes," I lie.

"Alright. Talk soon, sweetheart."

I hang up and release the breath I was holding. Mom is a lot sometimes. She's been heaping expectations and projecting herself onto me for my entire life. Yes, we have our similarities—our looks, our tendency toward impatience, the work ethic she displays with her charities and I apply to my business and studies. But for as much as we're similar, we're still two different people with totally different priorities. It's a concept she hasn't grabbed onto yet, that she can't mold me in her image.

"Hey, gorgeous." Preston appears with a smile, looking fully healed from his basketball injury and bearing a small bouquet of pink snapdragons, which I suspect are missing from a flowerbed somewhere on campus.

"You're in a good mood," I tease as he pulls me from the bench and tugs me toward him.

Preston kisses me, wrapping me in his arms. "I like getting to see you more now that you're here."

His lips travel to my neck, where he plants a soft peck before playfully nipping my earlobe.

I try not to raise a brow, because normally he shuns all public displays. Most of the time, I'm lucky to get him to hold my hand. But he's never been an overly physical boyfriend, and that's something I've learned to accept about him. If anything, the lack of PDA is a plus, especially when we're around our families. I realized at a young age that masking my emotions and repressing my occasional wild streak were necessary survival tools in our world.

"You ready?" he asks.

"Lead the way."

It's a beautiful day, if a little warm, as Pres guides me on a tour across the campus. Our first stop, of course, is Kincaid Hall, which houses the business school. Preston's family is a legacy at Garnet, going back generations.

Pres laces his fingers through mine and leads us outside again. As we stroll down a tree-lined path toward the art school, I admire the passing scenery. The campus truly is beautiful. Redbrick buildings. A great clock tower over the library. Sprawling green lawns and giant, majestic oak trees. I might not be enthused about college life, but at least everything is pretty to look at.

"What do you think of school so far?"

With Preston, I can be honest, so I sigh. "I'm bored out of my mind."

He chuckles. "I was the same way as a freshman, remember? For the first couple years until you can start upper level courses, it's pretty tedious."

"At least you have a purpose." We walk past the theater department, where students are in the parking lot, painting what looks to be an old-timey street set. "You need a certain level of education to work for your dad's bank. There are expectations and requirements. But I already have my own business. I'm my own boss, and I don't need to get a degree to prove anything to anyone."

Smiling, Pres squeezes my hand. "That's what I love about you, babe. You don't wait for permission. You didn't want to wait to grow up to become a tycoon."

"See?" I say, beaming. "You get it."

"But look, if you really want to keep working on your little tech thing in college, then think of Garnet as your incubator. There's going to be lots of opportunities for you to grow your brand here."

Huh. I hadn't thought about it that way. Although I'm not in love with his phrasing—*my little tech thing?*—I realize he's right.

"You make a good point there, Mr. Kincaid." I stand on my tiptoes and kiss his clean-shaven cheek before ambling forward again.

Another reason Pres and I are well-suited to each other: We're both business-minded people. Neither of us is enchanted by an artist's idealism, or distracted by romantic notions of backpacking across Europe or hiking Machu Picchu. We're products of our upbringing, and our cold blood runs blue. Two formidable, future heads of empires.

There's a lot to be said for compatibility.

After we explore the art building and the small museum where student work is displayed, wander among the sculptures in the botanical gardens, and follow the footpath through the greenhouse and vegetable garden, Preston brings me around to his car.

"Come on, there's something else I want to show you." He opens the door for me, and I slide onto the sleek, leather passenger seat. He puts the top down on the silver Porsche convertible before we drive off.

It's a short ride around the back of the campus, past the sports complex and up a hill, before we eventually reach a tall, circular building with a dome. The astronomy department's telescope. Preston leads me to the side of the building, to a door that's been propped open with a small wooden block.

"Are we supposed to be here?" I ask as we creep inside a narrow hallway that wraps around the circumference of the building.

"I know a guy." Then Preston puts his index finger to his lips. "But no, not really."

We follow the hallway to a metal staircase. On the second floor, we enter a room with computers along the wall and a massive telescope in the center, pointed to the sky through a wide slit in the roof.

"Oh, cool," I say, walking toward the telescope.

Preston stops me. "That's not what we came to see."

Instead, he leads me to a door, then a ladder going up to the roof. We emerge onto a platform. From here, we can see the entire campus. Rolling green hills and white-topped buildings. Practically the whole town, all the way to the blue horizon of Avalon Bay. It's spectacular.

"This is incredible," I say, smiling at his thoughtfulness and ingenuity.

"It's not a VIP tour without a bird's-eye view." Preston stands behind me and wraps his arms around my waist. He kisses the side of my head as we appreciate the landscape together. "I'm really glad you're here," he says softly.

"Me too."

Admittedly, things were slightly strained between us the last couple of years, while he was at college and I was stuck in high school. Doing the long-distance thing, even when we could see each other on weekends, was stressful. It took a lot of the fun out of our relationship. Today, though, I'm remembering how it was when we first started dating. How enamored of him I'd been, feeling like I'd won a prize, being chosen by an upperclassman.

Still, as Pres holds me against him and nuzzles my neck, a thought nudges its way into the back of my mind.

A very traitorous thought.

Of Cooper's chiseled jaw and fathomless eyes. The way my pulse sped when he sat beside me and flashed that arrogant smile. I don't get palpations when Preston walks into a room. My skin doesn't tingle when he touches me. My thighs don't clench, and my mouth doesn't run dry.

Then again, those responses can be overrated. Too many hormones running rampant can cloud your judgment. I mean, look at the statistics—all those people who end up in a dysfunctional relationship because they base it on sex, not compatibility. Pres and I are right for each other. We get along well. We're on the same trajectory. Our parents already approve, and it keeps everyone happy. I could play the field with a dozen Coopers and get my heart broken by every one. Why do that to myself?

There's a lot to be said for knowing a good thing when you've got it.

"Thank you," I tell Pres, turning in his arms to kiss him. "Today was perfect."

But later that night, as I'm half watching Netflix in my room while doing my English Lit reading, a flutter of excitement races through me when Cooper's name pops up on my phone. Then I remind myself to calm the fuck down.

Cooper: *Want to grab dinner?*
Me: *I already ate.*
Cooper: *Me too.*
Me: *Then why'd you ask?*
Cooper: *To see what you'd say.*
Me: *So sneaky.*
Cooper: *What are you doing?*
Me: *Netflix and homework.*
Cooper: *Is that code for something?*
Me: *Busted.*
Cooper: *I can't even imagine what rich people porn is like.*

Those words on the screen make me squeeze my legs together and put terrible ideas in my head. Which I promptly shove in a box labeled *don't you dare.*

Me: *It's mostly eating scones off the pages of* The Wall Street Journal.
Cooper: *You people are fucked up.*

A cackle bursts out of me, and I slap my hand over my mouth before Bonnie hears me and comes rushing in to see what's so funny. She's a doll, that one, but she has no concept of boundaries.

Me: *What are you doing?*
Cooper: *Flirting with some chick I just met.*

I walked right into that one.

Me: *Still have a boyfriend.*
Cooper: *For now.*
Me: *Goodnight, townie.*
Cooper: *Night, princess.*

I know he's just pushing my buttons. Cooper's thing, I'm learning, is trying to get a rise out of me. I can't say I hate it, exactly. It's refreshing to have a friend who gets that part of my personality. And, okay, it's technically flirting, which is technically frowned upon, but it's all in good fun.

No matter how many hormonal reactions Cooper elicits in me, I'm not about to leave Pres for the first tattooed bad boy I meet at college.

CHAPTER EIGHT

MACKENZIE

The next afternoon, I decide to explore the town on my own since my schedule is free. Preston inspired me to try embracing my time at Garnet rather than looking at it like a prison sentence. With that thought in mind, I throw on a flowery summer dress and call a cab.

Avalon Bay is a paradoxical coastal town full of rugged fishermen and multimillionaires. On one side of Main Street are high-end boutiques selling handmade soaps. On the other, pawnshops and tattoo parlors. The boardwalk is quiet on a weekday afternoon. Most of the bars are sparsely populated with sweaty locals propped up on stools watching ESPN with their pals.

I walk farther than the last time I was here and reach a section still devastated by hurricane damage from a couple years ago. Several buildings are under construction. Nearby, a crew works on restoring a restaurant where scaffolding is erected around its exterior. Other businesses have been cordoned off with caution tape and plywood. It's apparent they haven't been touched since the storm tore off their roofs and flooded the interiors.

I stop when I come to a quaint late-Victorian-style hotel. It's white with green trim, and the entire back side of the building had been gutted by storm surge. The hotel's walls were ripped out, its innards exposed. Old furniture and wrinkled carpets still wait for the guests that aren't coming. The weathered sign out front reads *The Beacon Hotel* in gold script font and is broken in two places.

I wonder what happened to the owners that they never rebuilt. And how has no one swooped in to claim the property and restore it to its former glory? This is a prime location.

My phone buzzes a few times with incoming emails, so I stop at an ice cream shop and buy a vanilla cone. Then I settle on the bench out front, scrolling through my inbox one-handed.

The first email is an update from one of my site moderators. She informs me she had to block several users who'd been trolling every post on *GirlfriendFails*, leaving racist and sexist comments. I open the attached screenshots. My jaw drops at the level of vitriol I read in those comments.

I shoot off a quick email: *Good call blocking them.*

The next one is an SOS from the guy I hired to oversee *BoyfriendFails*. Apparently, a user is threatening legal action, claiming one of the posts on the site is libelous. I click on the post in question. The writer of it went out with a guy she calls "Ted," who didn't disclose he had a micropenis and blindsided her during their first intimate encounter.

I return to my email to skim the letter my admin, Alan, received from some DC law firm with a scary letterhead. I guess the user— butterflykisses44—picked an alias too close to her boyfriend's real name. Ted is actually Tad, who is suitably outraged, humiliated, and demanding *BoyfriendFails* not only take down the post, but pay him damages because of the emotional distress it's caused him.

Since the site is a platform and not a publisher, we can't be sued for the content of our users, but I tell Alan to forward the letter to my own lawyer just in case. Then I shut off my phone and slurp down the rest of my melting ice cream. Just another day in the life of Mackenzie Cabot, CEO.

If I'm being honest with myself, though, lately I've been itching for . . . something *more*. I love my apps, but nowadays there's nothing for me to do but say yes or no. Sign here, initial there. Read this email, approve this ad. The real excitement came at the beginning, when I was sitting with my friends and brainstorming features for the apps. Meeting with the developer and programmer and bringing my ideas to life. Creating the marketing campaign to attract users. The launch.

It was challenging and exciting. It was the most fun I'd ever had. *That's* the part I truly enjoyed, I realize now. The creation, not the maintenance. Not that I hate the sites and want to sell them. I don't. They're still mine. Part of my budding empire. But maybe it's time to brainstorm some new business ideas.

As the sun dips low in the sky, I walk onto the beach and sit on the sand, listening to the waves and watching the seagulls glide against the wind. Behind me, a construction crew is winding down for the day. The noise of drills and saws has ceased.

Mostly zoned out, I don't notice someone approaching me until he plops down beside me.

"What's up, princess?"

I jolt in surprise, staring at Cooper, who's in the process of taking off his shirt and work gloves.

He's as potent as the night at the bonfire, and I'm pinned by the sight of him. His hair and jeans are covered in sawdust and dirt. His muscular chest and abs are shiny with sweat. This is the first time I've seen so much of his ink, which runs up both arms and stretches toward his chest. I lick my lips then inwardly wince at myself. At the person I become when he's around. Lustful. Irrational. I take those thoughts and tamp them way down in a box labeled *stay the hell out*.

"Are you stalking me now?" I demand.

"You stroll by my jobsite in"—he gestures, looking me up and down—"some ridiculous ruffle dress thing and all this leg, like, 'Oh, don't mind me, boys, I *hate* attention.'"

"That is so exactly how I sound," I reply, rolling my eyes. "And what's wrong with my dress?" I smooth my hands over the hem of the floral print sundress.

"It's got flowers on it. You're not a flower person, Mac."

"Don't call me Mac."

"Why not?"

"Because it's a nickname reserved for friends."

"We are friends. Best friends." He flashes a crooked smile. "I see you didn't deny the not being a flower person part."

He's right. I'm not usually into girly prints and ruffly sundresses. My style runs toward white tees and worn jeans, or a tank and cutoff shorts when it's hot out. But every now and then, I like feeling cute. Sue me. Anyway, he's not allowed to be so presumptuous about my taste in clothing, so I argue just because.

"I happen to love flowers. Especially on clothes. The flashier, the better."

Cooper rolls his eyes as if he knows I'm lying through my teeth. "You know, you don't have to work this hard." He crosses his arms, pulling his knees close to his chest. "I'm pretty easy."

"I'm sorry, what? Who's working too hard? You've been blowing up my phone talking about scone porn."

"You're kinky," he says, shrugging. "I get it. It's not my thing, but whatever gets you off."

Ha. If he only knew. Preston and I have a perfectly fine sex life, but I'm not even sure we have enough spice to be vanilla. In the beginning, I thought maybe sex was supposed to be that way: functional, quick, a tad boring. I was sixteen when I lost my virginity to Pres, and more than a little naïve about that stuff. It was only when I spoke to girlfriends about my lackluster encounters that I realized sex is supposed to be—imagine this—*fun*.

When I'd very awkwardly broached the subject with Pres, he'd confessed that he hadn't wanted to scare me off by being "too passionate." I told him to feel free to step up his game, and our bedroom activities did get more fun after that. But if I'm being completely honest, it's been four years now and that passion he'd mentioned still hasn't made an appearance.

"I shudder to think what's rattling around in your spank bank," I say.

"If you're trying to get me in bed, you can just ask." Cooper nudges my arm with his elbow. He has this unflappable confidence about him. Arrogant yet charming. Completely self-assured but not overbearing. It's almost a shame he's wasting his natural talents on construction. He'd make a hell of a CEO if he had a mind for business.

"This half-assed reverse psychology routine isn't going to work on me," I inform him. Because I didn't make my first million by being easily manipulated. "I'm not going to be goaded into accidentally winding up in bed with some townie stranger because he dared me to."

Still, his playful smirk and roguish eyes are not lost on me. I'm not immune to broad shoulders and rock-hard abs. Moreover, he's a bit of a conundrum. Everything I learn about him makes me wonder if what he portrays—the tattoos, the attitude—is all clever camouflage. Hiding what, though? My brain loves puzzles.

"I wouldn't be caught dead sleeping around with some Garnet clone. I do have an image to protect."

"Right, of course. Wouldn't want anyone confusing you for a man of taste."

He bites back a smile, and in that fleeting look, I see all sorts of bad intentions. I see blurry nights and wild regrets. Heavy breathing. It's enough to make my pulse spike and my toes go numb.

This guy is dangerous.

"Coop!" someone calls from the jobsite. "You coming to the bar or what?"

He glances over his shoulder. "Go on without me."

Knowing laughter tickles our backs. I'm glad Cooper's co-workers can't see my face because I'm fairly certain I'm blushing.

"Why'd you have to do that?" I grumble.

"Do what? Tell them I'm not going to the bar?"

"Yeah. Now they're going to think you stayed behind to bang me on the beach or something."

He gives a deep chuckle. "I guarantee they weren't thinking that. But now *I* am. Would you like to bang here, or should we go under the pier?"

"Go to the bar with your little friends, *Coop*. You'll have a better shot of getting laid there than here."

"Nah. I'm good where I am." He lifts one hand and rakes it through his dark hair, and I can't help but stare at his flexing biceps.

"So you guys are fixing up that restaurant?" I force myself to stop gawking at his very sexy muscles. "It looks like a huge job."

"It is. And once we're done this one, we have about, oh, half a dozen more buildings to renovate." He waves that sculpted arm toward the boardwalk, highlighting the destruction left by the hurricane.

"Do you like working in construction?"

He nods slowly. "I do, yeah. Evan and I work for our uncle's company, so we don't have to deal with some jackass boss who tries to rip us off or does shoddy work to cut costs. Levi is a good man, fair. And I've always been good with my hands."

I gulp. There's no overt innuendo in his tone, but I'll be damned if my gaze doesn't shift to his hands. They're strong, big, with long fingers and callused palms. No dirt under his nails, even after a day of manual labor.

"What about you, princess?" He tips his head, curious.

"What about me?"

"This is the second time I've walked up to you and seen that look on your face."

"What look?" Apparently, I just repeat everything he says now. But the intensity in his eyes has triggered a rush of anxiety.

"The look that says you want more."

"I want more . . . And what more do I want?"

He continues to study me. "I don't know. Just *more*. It's like . . . a mixture of boredom, dissatisfaction, frustration, and yearning."

"That's a lot of shit packed into one look," I joke, but my heart is beating faster now, because he's pretty much summed it up. That's been my state of mind since I got to college. No, even longer—dare I say, my entire life.

"Am I wrong?" he asks roughly.

Our gazes lock. The urge to confide in him is so strong I have to bite the tip of my tongue to stop myself.

Suddenly, amidst the crashing waves and screeching seagulls, I hear a faint yelping.

"Did you hear that?" I look around for the source of the pained, desperate noise.

Cooper chuckles. "Stop trying to distract me."

"I'm not. Seriously, don't you hear it?"

"Hear what? I don't—"

"Shhh!" I order.

I listen, straining to discern another clue. It's getting darker, with the lights from the boardwalk overtaking the dwindling dusk. Another yelp rings out, this one louder.

I jump to my feet.

"It's nothing," Cooper says, but I ignore him and follow the sound toward the pier. He jogs after me, his voice frazzled as he assures me I'm imagining things.

"I'm not imagining it," I insist.

And then I see it, the source of the yelps. Beyond the pier, on the jetty, I make out a shape stranded on the rocks as the tide comes in.

Heart pounding, I whirl around to face Cooper. "It's a dog!"

CHAPTER NINE

COOPER

Before I can blink, Mackenzie tears her dress off.

As in, this chick is actually getting naked.

No, not naked, I realize when she doesn't remove her bra and underwear. My disappointment over the strip show ending prematurely is dimmed by the fact that she looks pretty goddamn good in a bra and underwear.

But as she runs into the rising tide and is quickly swallowed up to her neck, the rational part of my brain kicks in.

"Mac!" I shout after her. "Get back here, damn it!"

She's already swimming away.

Awesome. She's gonna drown trying to get that mangy stray back to shore.

Grumbling curses under my breath, I strip out of my jeans and shoes and chase after Mackenzie, who has reached the rocks and is now climbing up to the dog. I swim hard against the current, as the waves try to throw me against the pier's pylons or slam me into the rocks. Finally, I grab on to one of the boulders and haul myself out of the water.

"You're crazy, you know that?" I growl.

The shivering dog sits anxiously by Mac, who's attempting to comfort it. "We have to help her," she tells me.

Shit. This filthy, pathetic thing is just a puppy, but there's no way

Mackenzie is swimming with it back to shore. I had a hard time myself fighting off the current, and I probably weigh twice as much as Mac.

"Give her to me," I say with a sigh. When I reach for the dog, she hides behind Mac and almost falls in the water trying to back away from me. "Come on, damn it. It's me or nothing."

"It's okay, little one, he's not as scary as he looks," Mac coos to the mutt. Meanwhile I stand there glaring at them both.

The dog continues to hesitate, so finally Mac picks her up and deposits the unhappy wet bundle into my waiting hands. Almost instantly, the frightened animal is clawing and kicking to get away. This is going to be a goddamn nightmare.

Mackenzie pets the dog's soaked fur in a futile attempt to calm her. "You sure about this?" she asks me. "I can try—"

No chance. The waves would knock the dog right out of her grip and the damn thing would drown while I pulled Mac to shore. Not happening.

"Go," I order. "I'm right behind you."

With a nod, she dives and makes for the shore.

Standing on the rocks, I have a little pep talk with the pup. "I'm trying to help you, okay? Do not bite my face off. Let's get along for the next few minutes. Deal?"

The animal whines and whimpers, which I suppose is the best I'm getting.

As gently as I can, I climb down into the water and hold the dog like a football above the waves as I swim with one arm. The whole time, the damn thing is freaking out thinking I'm trying to kill her or something. She barks and scratches. Tries a few times to wriggle free. With every move she makes, a little more flesh is gouged from my body. As soon as we reach the sand, I let the dog go and it runs straight for Mac, all but diving into her arms. *You're welcome, traitor.*

"You okay?" Mac calls out.

"Yeah, fine."

Both of us are breathing heavy after fighting the waves. It's fully dark now, the only light coming from the boardwalk. Mackenzie isn't much more than a hazy shape in front of me.

My temper gets the best of me, spilling over as I stalk up to her. "What the *hell* was that?"

She plants one hand on her bare hip. Her other hand protectively holds the dog. "Seriously?" she exclaims. "You're mad that I wanted to save a helpless animal? She could have died!"

"*You* could have died! You feel that current, sweetheart? That shit could've sucked you right out to sea. At least once a year someone drowns down here because they're a reckless dumbass."

"I'm not your *sweetheart*," she grumbles. "And did you really just call me a dumbass?"

"Act like a dumbass, get called a dumbass." I angrily shake water out of my hair. Doesn't escape me that the dog is currently doing the same. We're both feral animals, I suppose.

Mackenzie tightens her hold on her new pet. "I will *not* apologize for having a heart. I can't believe you were prepared to let this poor puppy die. Oh my God. I'm friends with a puppy killer."

My jaw falls open.

Christ, this chick is turning into a handful. I've never worked this hard to win over a girl. And yet, despite being mauled half to death for her—and being accused of attempted dog murder—my anger dissolves into a wave of laughter. I double over, dripping seawater onto the sand as I laugh my ass off.

"Why are you laughing?" she demands.

"You called me a puppy killer," I manage to croak between laughs. "You're insane."

After a second, she breaks out in giggles. The dog's gaze shifts uncertainly between us as we stand there laughing like a pair of idiots, soaking wet and half naked.

"Fine," she relents when her giggling fit finally subsides. "I may have been out of line. I know you were just worried for my safety. And thank you for swimming out there to help. I appreciate it."

"You're welcome." I hike up the waistband of my jeans. My wet boxers are plastered to my crotch, making it hard to zip up the jeans. "Come on, let's get our stuff and go back to my place. I need to get changed. You can dry off there and I can give you a ride home."

She doesn't say anything, staring at me.

"Yes," I sigh, "bring the dog."

The house is dark when we arrive. Neither Evan's motorcycle nor Jeep are in the drive, and the front door's locked when Mac and I step onto the wraparound porch. Thankfully, the place isn't a mess inside. With our friends frequently using our house as a party pad and way station between bars, it tends to get tossed around a lot. Evan and I, for our lack of other social graces, try to keep our home clean, though. We're not complete animals.

"You can use my shower," I tell Mac, pointing toward my ground-floor bedroom after I turn on lights and get myself a beer from the fridge. I deserve a drink after my heroic dog-saving efforts. "I'll find some clothes you can borrow."

"Thanks." She carries the dog with her, all cuddled and sleepy in her arms. I told her in the truck that if she wants to leave it here, I'll take it to the shelter in the morning. Though I'm starting to wonder if I'll be able to pry it away from her.

When Mac's in my en suite bathroom, I dig out a clean T-shirt and a pair of jeans Heidi left here ages ago. Or maybe they're Steph's. The girls are always leaving their stuff lying around after a party or a day at the beach, and I've stopped trying to return them.

I leave the clothes in a neat pile on the bed, then strip out of my wet clothes and throw on a T-shirt and a pair of sweatpants.

The steam rolling out from under the bathroom door is unbelievably tempting. I wonder how Mac would react if I stepped into the shower stall, eased up behind her, and reached both hands around to cup her tits.

A groan lodges in my throat. She'd probably saw my balls off with her fingernails, but it might be worth it, just to get to touch her.

"Hello, hello," my brother calls from the front door.

"In here," I answer as I head back to the kitchen.

Evan drops his keys on the splintered wood island. He grabs a beer and stands against the fridge. "What's that smell?"

"Mackenzie and I rescued a stray puppy from the jetty." Poor thing did kind of stink. Guess I do too now. Awesome.

"She's here?" A wicked grin spreads across his face as he looks around.

"Shower."

"Well, that was easy. I'm almost disappointed I didn't get more time to enjoy it."

"Not what you're thinking," I grunt out. "The dog was stuck out on the rocks and we had to get in the water to save it. Told Mackenzie she could come here to clean up, and then I'd take her home."

"Take her home? Dude. This is your chance. Close the deal." He shakes his head impatiently. "You helped her rescue a puppy, for chrissake. She is primed."

"Don't be a dick." Something about the way he says that strikes a nerve with me. This scheme isn't exactly ethical, but we don't have to be sleazy about it.

"What?" Evan can't pretend to hide his glee at how well this plan is working. "I'm just saying."

"Well . . ." I take a swig of my beer. "Keep it to yourself."

"Hey," comes Mac's hesitant voice.

She walks in, and the sight of her—in my shirt, dark wet hair combed back—brings all sorts of sinful thoughts to my head. She didn't put on the jeans, so her legs are bare and tanned and endlessly long.

Fuck.

I want them wrapped around my waist.

"Evan," she greets my brother, nodding at him as if she knows, somehow, he is up to no good. Unsurprisingly, she's still carrying the sleeping puppy.

"Welp." Evan gives her a parting smile as he grabs his beer and pushes off from the fridge. "I'm beat. You kids have fun."

My brother has no appreciation for subtlety.

"Was it something I said?" she asks dryly.

"Nah. He thinks we're gonna hook up." When I lift my arm to run a hand through my damp hair, her eyes grow wide with alarm. My brow furrows. "What?"

"Cooper. You're hurt."

I look down, almost forgetting that her precious little pup damn near filleted me alive not an hour ago. Both my arms are covered in red scratches, and there's a particularly nasty-looking cut on my collarbone.

"Eh. I'm fine," I assure her. I'm no stranger to cuts and scrapes, and these ones are definitely not the worst I've experienced.

"No, you're not. We need to clean those."

With that, she marches me to the bathroom and, despite my protestations, forces my ass down on the closed lid of the toilet. The puppy is promptly deposited in my claw-foot bathtub, where she curls up and sleeps while Mackenzie rifles through my cabinets for the first aid kit.

"I can do this myself," I tell her as she sets out a bottle of alcohol and cotton swabs.

"Are you going to be difficult?" She eyes me with a raised brow. The earnest conviction on her face is cute, in a stubborn *shut up and take your medicine* sort of way.

"Fine."

"Good. Now take off your shirt."

A grin tugs on my lips. "This was your plan all along? To get me naked?"

"Yes, Cooper. I broke into an animal shelter, stole a puppy, placed it in a perilous situation, swam out to rescue it myself—so as to not raise your suspicions that it was I, in fact, who trapped the dog on the jetty—then telepathically ordered the dog to scratch you up. All so I could see your perfect pecs." She finishes with a snort.

"Extreme actions," I agree. "But I get it. My pecs *are* perfect. They're transcendent."

"So's your ego."

I make a slow, deliberate show of removing my shirt. Despite her mocking, my bare chest elicits a response. Her breath hitches, and then she averts her gaze, pretending to focus on opening the rubbing alcohol.

I hide a smile and sit back as she begins to clean the wounds on my arm.

"Is it just the two of you here?" she asks curiously.

"Yeah. Evan and I grew up in this house. My great-grandparents built it after they got married. Grandparents lived here after them and so on."

"It's beautiful."

It was. Now it's falling apart. Roof needs replacing. Foundation is cracking from beach erosion. The siding has seen one too many storms, and the floors are worn and warped. Nothing I couldn't fix if only I had the time and money, but isn't that always the story? Whole damn town full of *if only*s. And just like that, I remember why I'm sitting here letting some clone's girlfriend run her hands all over my bare chest.

"There," she says, touching my arm. "All better."

"Thanks." My voice sounds a bit gravelly.

"No problem." Hers sounds slightly hoarse.

I find myself momentarily caught in her bright green eyes. Taunted by the flashes of her almost-naked body as the hem of my shirt rises on her thighs. Her warm palm against my skin. The thrumming in her neck that tells me she's not indifferent to me either.

I could do it. Take her by the hips, coax her into straddling me. Shove my hand through her hair and pull her mouth to mine in a blistering kiss. I'm not supposed to sleep with her unless she initiates, but if the chemistry sizzling between us is any indication, I suspect she won't stop with a kiss. It'll be a kiss that leads to the bed that leads to getting balls deep inside her. She'll dump Kincaid faster than you can say *game over*. I win. Mission accomplished.

But where's the fun in that?

"Now," I say, "about your friend."

Mackenzie blinks, as if snapping out of the same lust stupor I'd fallen into.

We draw a warm bubble bath for the puppy and put her in. She's a completely different animal all of a sudden. The drowned rat becomes a small golden retriever, splashing around and playing with a bottle of shampoo that falls into the tub. Poor thing is all skin and bones, lost or abandoned by its mother, and she didn't have a collar when we found her. The shelter will have to figure out if she's chipped or not.

After we scrub the dog clean and dry her off, I set out a bowl of water in the kitchen and feed her some cut up turkey franks. Not ideal, but it's the best we have under the circumstances. While the pup eats, I leave the door open and step out to the back deck. The temperature's cooled off, and the ocean breeze is blowing in off the water. Out on the horizon, a tiny blip of a boat's bow lights flickers as it travels.

"You know . . ." Mac comes beside me.

I'm acutely aware of her, every nerve attuned in her direction. This chick barely glances at me and I'm half hard. It's very annoying.

"I shouldn't be here," she finishes.

"And why's that?"

"I think you know why." Her voice is soft, measured. She's testing me as much as herself.

"You don't seem like the kind of girl who does anything she doesn't want to." I turn to meet her eyes. In my limited experience, Mackenzie is stubborn. Not the type to get pushed around. I'm under no illusion that she's here because I'm so damn clever.

"You'd be surprised," she says ruefully.

"Tell me."

She appraises me. Doubtful. Questioning how sincere my interest is.

I raise a brow. "We're friends, aren't we?"

"I'd like to think so," she says, wary.

"Then talk to me. Let me get to know you."

She continues to study me. Christ. When she stares into me like this, I feel her picking me apart, working things out. I've never felt so exposed in front of another person before. For some reason, it doesn't bother me as much as it probably should.

"I thought freedom was being self-sufficient," she finally confesses. "I'm finding out that isn't exactly true. I know this probably sounds stupid coming from me, but I feel trapped. By expectations and promises. Trying to make everyone else happy. I wish I could be selfish for once. Do what I want, when I want, how I want."

"So why don't you?"

"It's not that easy."

"Sure it is." Rich people are always going on about how money is such a burden. That's only because they don't know how to use it. They get so caught up in their bullshit, they forget they don't actually need their dumb friends and stupid country clubs. "Forget 'em.

Someone's making you miserable? Something is holding you back? Forget 'em and move on."

Her teeth dig into her bottom lip. "I can't."

"Then you don't want it bad enough."

"That's not fair."

"Of course not. What's ever been fair? People spend their whole lives complaining about things they're unwilling to change. At a certain point, either pluck up the courage or shut up."

Laughter sputters out of her. "Are you telling me to shut up?"

"No, I'm telling you there are plenty of ways that life and circumstances beyond our control conspire to keep us down. The least we can do is get out of our own way."

"What about you?" She turns on me, pointing the question back in my face. "What do you want right now that you can't have?"

"To kiss you."

She narrows her eyes.

I should regret saying that, but I don't. I mean, what's stopping me from kissing her, from telling her I want to? Gotta pull the trigger on this thing at some point, right? I've clearly got her on the hook. If I don't commit to this plan now, why am I wasting my time?

So I watch her, trying to discern her reaction through the stone-cold façade of indifference. This chick is implacable. But for a split second, I glimpse the flicker of heat in her gaze as she considers it. Gaming it out. One action begetting another, a cascade effect of consequences.

She licks her lips.

I lean closer. Just a little. Tempting myself. The need to touch her is almost unbearable.

"But then I'd screw up a perfectly good friendship," I say, because I've lost all control of my goddamn mouth. "So I behave myself. It's still a choice."

What the hell am I doing? I don't know what spooked me, but

suddenly I'm giving her an out when I'm supposed to be reeling her *in*.

Mac turns back toward the water, resting her arms on the railing. "I admire your honesty."

Frustration rises inside me as I look at her profile from the corner of my eye. This woman is gorgeous, she's wearing my shirt and nothing else, and instead of pulling her into my arms and kissing her senseless, I just friend-zoned myself.

For the first time since we hatched this plan, I'm starting to wonder if I'm in over my head.

CHAPTER TEN

MACKENZIE

I wake up in the morning to a text from Cooper. Only I guess Evan must have taken the photo, because it shows Cooper asleep in bed with the puppy snuggled on his chest, her face buried under his chin. It's fucking adorable. Last night, I thought those two were doomed, but it seems they worked out their differences.

I hope he and Evan decide to keep her. I know the right thing to do is to take the dog to the shelter—I certainly can't keep her—but my heart is breaking a little at the thought of never seeing her again.

I text a reply to Cooper, and by the time I get out of my second class for the day, I still haven't received a response. He's probably working. I tell myself it's just concern for the dog that causes the pang of disappointment. But who am I kidding? I can't ignore what happened on his deck last night. The sexual tension nearly spilling over, his rough admission that he wants to kiss me. If he hadn't pulled back I might have caved in a moment of blind weakness.

I have underestimated Cooper's allure. That's my fault—I know better than to be seduced by handsome, half-naked guys who race in to help rescue animals in distress. I just have to be more cautious going forward and keep reminding myself that we're friends. That's it. No use getting it twisted.

When my phone buzzes, I eagerly yank it out of my pocket, only to find a message from Preston. Not Cooper.

I banish the second wave of disappointment to the very back of my mind and use my thumbprint to open my lock screen.

Preston: *Waiting for you in the parking lot.*

Right. We're having lunch off campus today. I'm glad he reminded me, because I was about five minutes away from scarfing down a chicken fiesta wrap from the sandwich shop near the business school.

I slide into Preston's convertible, and we talk about our classes as he drives us to Avalon Bay. Pres finds some street parking near the boardwalk. My pulse quickens, and I force myself not to look in the direction of the restaurant that Cooper and his uncle are restoring.

I last about 3.5 seconds before I cave. But the jobsite is empty. I guess they're on their lunch break. Or maybe the crew is on another job today.

Once again, I pretend I'm not disappointed.

"You didn't tell me what you ended up doing yesterday." Pres holds my hand as we head toward the sports bar, where we're meeting some of his friends. "Did you come into town or no?"

"Oh, yeah, I did. I explored the boardwalk and walked down the pier, then watched the sunset on the beach. It was really nice."

I make an on-the-spot executive decision to omit the entire puppy encounter. Not that Pres is the jealous type, but I don't want it to turn into a whole discussion, especially when I've only just arrived at Garnet and we're doing so well. There'll be an opportunity to tell him about my friendship with Cooper. At some point. When the time's right.

"How did your poker game go? You didn't text me either, now that I think about it." But I'm also not the jealous type. Having done the whole long-distance thing, Pres and I are used to the occasional forgotten text or unanswered call. If we got worked up every time one of us didn't respond until morning, we'd have broken up a long time ago. That's trust.

"How was the poker game?" echoes Benji Stanton, who over-hears my question as Pres and I approach the group. He snickers loudly. "You better watch out for your man. This kid is shit at cards and doesn't know when to quit."

"So . . . not good?" I ask, shooting a teasing smile at Pres.

"Not good at all," Benji confirms. He's a business major like Pres. They met when they shared a few classes last year.

Benji's parents own property in Hilton Head, and his father runs a hedge fund. All of Preston's friends hail from similar backgrounds. As in disgustingly rich. Finance, real estate, politics—their parents are all members of the billionaires' club. So far, everyone's been friendly and welcoming to me. I was nervous at first that they might look at me sideways because I'm a freshman, but I only get positive vibes from Preston's Garnet friends.

"Don't listen to him, babe." Pres kisses the top of my head. "I'm playing the long game."

A few minutes later, we're climbing up the stairs. Sharkey's Sports Bar has two floors, the upper one consisting of tables over-looking the ocean, the lower level offering game tables, a plethora of TVs, and the bar. As a server seats our group at a long high-top near the railing, the guys continue to rag on Preston for being terrible at cards.

"Lock up your good jewelry, Mac," Seb Marlow advises me. He's from Florida, where his family is a major defense contractor for the government. It's all very serious and secret. *I'd have to kill you*, and all that. Or that's the line he uses at parties, at least. "He was this close to throwing down his Rolex to buy back into the game."

Stifling a laugh, I question Pres. "Please tell me he's joking."

He shrugs, because the money means nothing to him, and he's got more watches than he knows what to do with. "How about you try me at pool?" he scoffs at his friends. "That's a real gentleman's game."

Benji looks at Seb and smirks. "Double or nothing?"

Never one to back down from a challenge, Preston is all too eager. "You're on."

The guys push back from the table as Preston gives me a parting kiss on the cheek.

"One game," he says. "Back in a flash."

"Don't lose your car," I warn. "I need a ride back to campus."

"Don't worry," Benji calls over his shoulder. "I got you."

Pres just rolls his eyes before sauntering after his buddies. Another thing I appreciate about him is that he's a good sport. I've never seen him get bent out of shape over a stupid game, even when his wallet is a little light at the end of the night. Granted, it's easy to get over losing when there's a seemingly endless supply of someone else's money to play with.

"Now that the boys are gone . . ." Melissa, Benji's girlfriend, pushes the collection of water glasses aside to lean in toward me and Seb's girlfriend Chrissy.

I don't know anything about Melissa other than she sails, and I know even less about Chrissy. I wish I had more in common with these girls other than the size of our parents' bank accounts.

Truth be told, I don't have too many female friends. And these past few weeks have confirmed that I still suck at building connections with my female peers. I love Bonnie to bits, but she feels more like a younger sister than a friend. I had girlfriends in high school, but nobody I'd consider a ride-or-die type of friend. The only one who comes closest to being my "best friend" is my old camp friend Sara, who I raised hell with every summer until I turned eighteen. We still text periodically, but she lives in Oregon and it's been a couple years since I've seen her.

My social group now consists of my roommate, my boyfriend, and my boyfriend's friends, who waste no time bending their heads together to gossip.

"So what did you find out about that Snapchat girl?" Melissa demands.

Chrissy takes a deep breath like she's about to dive to the bottom of a pool for a pair of Jimmy Choos. "It was some sophomore chick who's at Garnet on scholarship. I found her roommate's best friend on Instagram and DMed her. She said her friend told her that her roommate said they met at a boat party and made out."

"So they only kissed?" Melissa asks, as though she's disappointed in the answer.

Chrissy shrugs. "Supposedly someone at the boat party walked in on someone getting a BJ. Maybe it was Seb, maybe not. Doesn't really matter."

If I'd known my mother in college, I imagine she'd have been a lot like Chrissy. Prim, put together, and unflappable. Not a hair or eyelash out of place. So the fact that she would entertain something as messy as cheating strikes me as antithetical.

"Wait," I interject, "your boyfriend is cheating on you, and you don't care?"

The girls both stare at me as though I haven't been paying attention.

"Two former presidents of the United States and the crown prince of Saudi Arabia were at his father's birthday party in the Seychelles last year," Chrissy says flatly. "You don't break up with guys like Sebastian over something as trifling as infidelity. He's the man you marry."

I frown at her. "You'd marry someone you know is cheating on you?"

She doesn't answer, just looks at me, blinking. Is an expectation of monogamy so banal and old-fashioned? I thought I was fairly open-minded, but apparently my beliefs about love and romance are scandalous.

"It's hardly even considered cheating," Melissa scoffs, waving a dismissive hand. "Seb hooked up with a scholarship chick? Who cares. Now, if it was a wifey, that's a whole other story. A real reason to worry."

"A wifey?" I echo.

Chrissy gives me a condescending look. "For men like Seb and Benji and Preston, there are two kinds of women. A wifey and a Marilyn. The ones you marry, and the ones you screw."

Can't you screw the one you marry? Or marry the one you screw? I swallow the questions. Because what's the point?

"Don't worry," Melissa says. She reaches across the table to put her hand on mine, in what she must think is a comforting gesture. "You're definitely wifey material. Preston knows that. All you need to worry about is locking that down and getting the ring. Everything else is . . ." She glances at Chrissy for the word. "Extracurricular."

That is the most depressing relationship advice I've ever heard. These women have their own family money and small empires—they don't need strategic marital alliances. So why do they sell themselves into loveless arrangements?

When I marry Preston one day, it won't be for money or family connections. Our vows won't include a caveat that cheating is tolerated as long as the stock price is up.

"I wouldn't want to live that way," I tell them. "If a relationship isn't built on love and mutual respect, what's the point?"

Melissa regards me with a patronizing tilt to her head and a faintly pouting lip. "Oh, sweetie, everyone thinks that way at first. But eventually, we have to start being more realistic."

Chrissy says nothing, but her cold, impassive expression strikes something inside me. It's fleeting and undefined, but it unsettles my stomach.

All I know is, I don't ever want to reach the point where I view infidelity as "extracurricular."

Later, when Preston's driving me back to Tally Hall, I broach the subject. Since Melissa and Chrissy didn't swear me to secrecy, I don't feel bad asking, "Did you know that Melissa and Chrissy think Seb's cheating on Chrissy?"

He doesn't flinch, changing gears as he takes us down the winding roads around the edge of campus. "I had a feeling."

I fight a frown. "Is it true?"

"I haven't asked," he says. Then, after a few seconds, "I wouldn't be surprised."

Whether Preston was at that boat party or knows of the particular incident is irrelevant. He wouldn't throw his friend under the bus if he didn't believe it was possible. Which tells me everything I need to know.

"She isn't even mad about it." I shake my head in disbelief. "Either of them, actually. Cost of doing business, as far as they're concerned."

"I figured." Pres pulls up to the parking lot outside my dorm. He takes off his sunglasses and looks me in the eyes. "There've been whispers for a few weeks. Seb and Chrissy have chosen to ignore it, best that I can tell. Honestly, it's not unusual."

"Cheating isn't unusual?" To me, cheating is so insulting. It says to your partner: I don't love you enough to be faithful, and I don't respect you enough to let you go. It's the worst kind of trap.

He shrugs. "For some people."

"Let's not be those people," I implore him.

"We're not." Preston leans over the center console. He cups the side of my face and kisses me softly. When he pulls back, his pale blue eyes shine with confidence. "I'd be a complete fool to jeopardize our relationship, babe. I know wife material when I see it."

I think he's saying it as a compliment, but the fact that he uses Melissa's exact phrasing brings a queasy feeling to my gut. If I'm the wifey, does that mean he has a Marilyn? Or multiple Marilyns?

Frustration rises in my throat. I hate that Melissa and Chrissy planted this nasty seed of suspicion in my head.

"I'm wife material, huh?" I tease, trying to tamp down my unease. "Why's that?"

"Hmmm, well . . ." His lips travel along my cheek toward my ear, where he gives the lobe a teasing nibble. "Because you're hot. And smart. Good head on your shoulders. Hot, of course. You're loyal. You're hot. Annoying how much you argue sometimes—"

"Hey," I protest.

"—but you don't fight back on the important stuff," he finishes. "We have similar goals about what we want out of life. Oh, and did I mention you're hot?"

His lips brush mine again. I kiss him back, albeit a bit distracted. The list he'd recited was really sweet. So sweet that guilt is prickling at my throat now, because I guess that makes *me* the asshole with this whole Cooper thing.

Friendship isn't cheating, even if the other party is attractive, but maybe it's cheating adjacent?

No. Of course not. Text messages aren't adultery. It's not like we're sending each other nudes and describing our sexual fantasies. And after last night, Cooper and I both have a clear idea where the line is. More than ever, I know better than to cross it.

I'm walking to my dorm when a text pops up from the devil himself. It's accompanied by a picture of Evan and the puppy playing fetch on the beach.

Cooper: *Change of plans. She's moving in.*

CHAPTER ELEVEN

COOPER

"Who's the prettiest girl in the world? Is it you? Because I think it's you! Look at you, you beautiful little angel. I could eat you up, that's how perfect you are, you pretty girl."

The litany of baby talk escaping the mouth of my grown-ass twin brother is shameful.

And the object of his adoration is shame*less*. The newest member of the Hartley household struts around the kitchen like she was just named supreme leader of the pack. Which she basically is. She's got Evan wrapped around her little paw. Me, I'm not going to fall in love with the first cute face I see.

"Dude," I warn. "Dial it down a notch. You're embarrassing yourself."

"Nah. Look how pretty she is now." He scoops the puppy off the floor and thrusts her toward me. "Pet her. Feel how soft and silky."

I dutifully pet her golden fur, which, for the fifty bucks it cost to groom her yesterday, better be soft. Then I swipe the dog from his hands and set her back on the floor.

On which she promptly pees.

"Motherfucker," I grumble.

Evan instantly becomes a mother hen, grabbing paper towels and cooing at his new girlfriend as he sops up her pee puddle. "It's okay, pretty girl. We all have accidents."

We're still working out this whole dog-training thing, learning as we go from vet blogs and pet websites. All I know is, in the past seven days I've cleaned up more piss and dog shit than I ever intended in my life. That thing's lucky she's so cute. Last week, after the vet at the shelter confirmed the dog wasn't chipped and had probably been abandoned for some time, I didn't have the heart to stick her in a cage or abandon her again. I might be a bastard, but I'm not without mercy. So the vet gave us some special food to fatten her up, sent us on our way, and now we have a dog.

And a busy day of manual labor, if Evan would quit fawning over his pretty girl.

This morning, I woke up with a fire under my ass to get stuff done. Evan and I have the day off, so I decided, what the hell, there's never going to be a right time to start getting this house in better shape. It's the only lousy legacy our family has left. So I shook Evan out of bed early, and we headed to the hardware store to figure out what we would need.

First job on the home renovation list: replacing the roof. It's not going to be cheap. Digs into my savings quite a bit, but Evan kicked in half with some convincing. At least doing the work ourselves will save us a few grand.

"Come on, we should get started," I tell my brother. We plan to spend the rest of the day pulling the old roof off, and then tomorrow we'll lay down the new materials. Shouldn't take us more than a couple of days if we work fast.

"Let's go for a quick walk first. It'll tire her out so she'll sleep while we work."

Without awaiting my response, he scoops up the puppy and heads for the back door, where her leash is hanging on a hook.

"Swear to God, if you're not back in ten minutes, I'm returning her to the shelter."

"Fuck off. She's here to stay."

Sighing, I watch him and the dog scamper down the deck steps toward the sand. Our delivery from the hardware store hasn't arrived yet, but we could at least be making ourselves useful by prepping the current roof. Unfortunately, Evan's work ethic isn't as solid as mine. My brother will find any opportunity to procrastinate.

On the deck, I rest my forearms against the railing and grin when I see the golden retriever make a beeline for the water. There goes her newfound softness. Serves Evan right.

As I wait, I pull out my phone and text Mac.

Me: *How about Potato?*

Her response is almost instantaneous. Makes my ego swell a bit, knowing I've got priority in her texting queue.

Mackenzie: *Absolutely not.*
Me: *Mary Pawpins?*
Mackenzie: *Better. I'm saying Daisy.*
Me: *Can you get any more generic?*
Mackenzie: *You're generic.*
Me: *Nah babe, I'm one of a kind.*
Mackenzie: *Not your babe.*
Me: *Whatcha doing right now?*
Mackenzie: *In class.*

She follows that up with a gun emoji next to a girl's head emoji. I snicker at my phone.

Me: *That bad?*

Mackenzie: *Worse. I stupidly chose biology for my required science. Why are all the species names in Latin!!! And I forgot how much I hate cell theory! Did you know the cell is the most basic building block of life?*

Me: *I thought that was sex.*

Mackenzie sends an eye roll emoji, then says she has to go because her professor is starting to call on students to answer questions. I don't envy her.

Even though Garnet has decent scholarship opportunities for locals, I've never had any desire to attend college. I don't see the point. Everything I need to know about construction or woodworking, I can learn from my uncle, online, or in library books. Last year, I took some bookkeeping classes at the community center in town so I could learn to better manage our finances (as meager as they are), but that only cost me a hundred bucks. Why the hell would I ever pay twenty-five grand per *semester* to be told cells are important and that we evolved from apes?

A honk from the front of the house catches my attention. Our order's here.

Out front, I greet Billy and Jay West with fist bumps and good-natured back slaps. They're some of the old crew, grew up in the Bay. Though we don't see much of them these days.

"This ought to be everything you need," Billy says, opening the tailgate of the pickup truck. We had to buy and borrow some specific tools, get an air compressor and whatnot. On the trailer, he's got the new shingles on pallets.

"Looks good," I say, helping him haul things off the truck.

"Dad said there's no charge on the compressor if you can get it back to him by Monday. And he's giving you the underlayment and valley flashing at cost."

"Appreciate it, B," I say, shaking his hand.

Around the Bay, we watch out for each other. We have our own bartering system—*do me a favor today, I help you out tomorrow*. It's the only way most of us have survived the storms over the past couple years. You need to be able to rely on your neighbors to come together, support one another; otherwise, this whole town goes to shit.

Billy, Jay, and I unload the trailer in the blistering heat, all three of us drenched in sweat by the time we lift the last pallet. We're setting it on the ground when Billy's phone rings, and he wanders off to take the call.

"Hey, Coop." Jay wipes his brow with the short sleeve of his shirt. "Got a sec?"

"Sure. Let's grab some water." We walk over to the cooler on the front porch to pull out a couple bottles of water. It's blazing out here. Summer refusing to die. "What's up?"

Jay awkwardly shifts his huge feet. He's the biggest of the five West boys—six five, over two hundred pounds of solid muscle. Steph calls him the "gentle giant," which is an apt description. Jay's a sweet guy, the first person to help someone in need. He doesn't possess a mean bone in his body.

"Wanted to ask you something." His cheeks are slowly reddening, and it's not because of the heat. "You and Heidi . . ."

I wrinkle my forehead. Definitely not what I expected him to say.

"I heard some rumors about you guys this summer, and uh . . ." He shrugs. "Wasn't sure if it's a thing or not."

"It's not."

"Oh. Okay. Cool." He chugs half the bottle before speaking again. "I ran into her at Joe's the other night."

I try not to chuckle at his shy expression. I know where he's going with this now, but he's taking the long way to get there.

"And how'd that go?" I ask. I haven't seen Heidi or the girls in several days.

"Fun. It was fun." He gulps down some more water. "You don't mind if I ask her out, do ya? Since you two aren't a thing?"

Jay West is the epitome of the boy next door, and Heidi will eat him alive. If she even gives him a shot to begin with, which I doubt, since I'm fairly sure I'm the only guy in town she's slept with. She dated some dude for a year in high school, but he didn't live in the Bay. Heidi's always had one foot out the door anyway. I'm honestly surprised she hasn't skipped town yet.

I don't have the heart to tell Jay she'll probably turn him down, so I simply clap him on the shoulder and say, "'Course I don't mind. She's a great girl—make sure you treat her right."

"Scout's honor," he promises, holding up one hand in the Boy Scout gesture. Of course he was a Scout. Probably earned all his badges too. Meanwhile, Evan and I got kicked out of our troop when we were eight because we tried setting our scout leader's gear on fire.

"Hey, didn't realize you boys were here." Evan comes up with the puppy on a leash, ruefully glancing at all the supplies we've unloaded—no thanks to him. "Otherwise I would've given you a hand."

I snort. Yeah right.

"When'd you get a dog?" a delighted Jay asks. He promptly kneels and starts playing with the puppy, who tries to nip his stroking fingers. "What's his name?"

"Her," I correct. "And we don't know yet."

"My vote is for Kitty, but Coop doesn't appreciate irony," Evan pipes up.

"We're still deciding," I say.

Billy wraps up his call and approaches us. He nods at Evan, who nods back and says, "Billy. How's things?"

"Yeah, good."

The two share an uneasy look, while I stand there in discomfort. Gentle giant Jay is oblivious to the tension, thoroughly occupied by the puppy. This is why we don't see Billy and his brothers anymore. It's too damn awkward.

But Evan can't help himself. Always takes it to the next level of awkwardness. "How's Gen?"

Billy grunts a curt "Fine," and can't get his trailer closed up fast enough before he and Jay are practically peeling out of our front yard.

"The hell was that about?" I say to Evan.

"What's what?" He says this as if I don't know exactly what goes on in his damn head.

"Thought you weren't hung up on Genevieve."

"I'm not." He brushes me off and goes to the porch, grabbing some water.

"She blew town with barely a heads up," I remind him. "Trust me, that chick isn't sitting around worrying about you."

"I said it's whatever," Evan insists. "I was just making conversation."

"With her brothers? I wouldn't be surprised if Billy blames you for her running all the way to Charleston. For all I know, he's been waiting to kick your ass."

Evan's ex was the real hellion of our group. We've all experimented with the occasional illicit substance, broken a few laws, but Gen was on another level. If it was stupid and stood a chance to kill her, she wanted seconds. And Evan was right there next to her. Allegedly, she left to get her shit together. New place, new life. Who knows if it's true? If any of the girls still talk to her, they don't bring it up. Which is all the proof Evan should need that Genevieve West doesn't give a crap that she tore his fucking heart out.

"You still in love with her?" I ask him.

He takes off his shirt to wipe the sweat from his face. Then he meets my eyes. "I don't even think about her."

Yeah right. I know that expression. I wore that same expression every day our dad wasn't around. Every time our mom walked out on us for weeks or months at a time. Sometimes he forgets I'm the one person in the world he can't lie to.

My phone vibrates, momentarily distracting me from my brother's bullshit. I check the screen to find a text from Mac.

Mackenzie: *My bio prof just shared with the class that he's got a dog named Mrs. Puddles. I say we steal the name and never look back.*

I can't stop a chuckle, causing Evan to eye me sharply over the lip of his water bottle.

"What about you?" A bite creeps into his voice.

"What about me?"

"Every time I look over, you're texting the clone. You two are getting awfully cute."

"Thought that was the idea, genius. She's not dumping her boyfriend for some asshole she doesn't like."

"What do you text about?" he demands.

"Nothing important." It's not a lie. Mostly we argue about names and how to train *our* dog. Mac has granted herself partial custody and visitation rights. I tell her she's welcome to chip in for puppy pads and dog food. She demands more photos.

"Uh-huh." He reads me with narrow eyes. "You're not catching feelings for the rich bitch, are you?"

"Hey." Evan can throw all the shit he wants at me, but his anger has nothing to do with Mac. "She didn't do anything to you. In fact, she's been perfectly nice. So how about you watch your mouth."

"Since when do you care?" He steps up to me, getting in my face. "She's one of them, remember? A clone. Her entitled shithead boyfriend got you fired. Don't get it twisted which side you're on."

"I'm on our side," I remind him. "Always."

There's nothing stronger than my bond with my brother. Period. A girl doesn't change that. Evan's just got a thorn in his paw about everyone who goes to Garnet. Far as he's concerned, they're the enemy. It's an attitude most kids who've grown up around here share, and I don't blame them. I don't remember the last time a clone did anything but use and abuse us.

When it comes down to it, Mac's a product of where she comes from, the same as me. That doesn't mean if we weren't different people—if we came from similar backgrounds, lived similar lives—I couldn't see myself liking her. She's smart, funny, sexy as hell. I'd be an idiot not to admit that.

But we aren't different people and this isn't some other life.

In the Bay, we play the cards we're dealt.

CHAPTER TWELVE

MACKENZIE

I'm twenty minutes into my Wednesday biology class before I realize it's Friday and I'm actually sitting in my media culture lecture. Now those *Real Housewives* clips on the projection screen make way more sense. I thought maybe they were nervous hallucinations.

Truth is, I haven't been quite right the past few days. School bores me, and my dissatisfaction over my business is growing. It's frustrating how little work there is to do on the apps, now that I've delegated most of my duties to other people. I need a new project, something big and challenging to sink my teeth into.

To make matters worse, I'm battling this constant feeling that someone is looking over my shoulder. Toeing a knife's edge. Every time my phone buzzes, it's a shot of endorphins followed by a rush of adrenaline, guilt, and a pit of nausea in my stomach. I'm an addict, jonesing for the hit despite knowing it's killing me.

Cooper: *How bout Moxie Crimefighter?*
Me: *I like Jimmy Chew.*
Cooper: *She's a girl!*
Me: *I still think she's a Daisy.*
Cooper: *Muttley Crue.*

It's some kind of twisted foreplay. Bickering about puppy names as a form of flirting, every escalation another piece of clothing we're daring the other to remove in a metaphorical game of strip poker. It's gotten to be too much. I can't stop myself, though. Every time he texts me, I say this will be the last time, then I hold my breath, type a reply, hit send, and wait for my next fix.

Why do I do this to myself?

Cooper: *What are you up to now?*
Me: *Class.*
Cooper: *Come over after? We'll take Moon Zappa for a walk on the beach.*

Why do I do it? Because Cooper turns my insides out, gets my head messed up. I wake in cold sweats from unbidden dreams of his sculpted body and his soulful eyes. As much as I want to deny it, I'm starting to like him. Which makes me a terrible person. A rotten, horrible girlfriend. Still, I haven't acted on anything. I'm capable of exerting self-control. Mind over matter and all that.

Me: *Be there in an hour.*

For our dog, I tell myself. *To make sure he's taking good care of her.*
Uh-huh.
Self-control, my butt.

An hour later, I'm at his front door and shit is awkward. I don't know if it's me or him or both, but luckily our puppy serves as a much-needed distraction. She jumps at my knees, and I spend the next few minutes entirely focused on petting her, scratching behind her ear and kissing her cute little nose.

It isn't until we're some ways down the beach from his house that Cooper nudges my arm.

I glance over. "Huh, what?"

"Something up?" he asks. The beach is empty, so Cooper lets the dog off the leash and tosses a small piece of driftwood for her to fetch.

It isn't fair. He has just removed his shirt, and now I'm forced to watch him stroll around bare-chested, a pair of worn jeans hanging off his hips. No matter where else I try to divert my eyes, they return to the yummy V that disappears into his waistband. My mouth actually waters like one of Pavlov's stupid dogs.

"Sorry," I say. I take the stick from the dog when she brings it to me, then toss it for her again. "Distracted with school stuff."

It doesn't take long for us to wear the puppy out and head back to Cooper's house. He puts his shirt on, a faded Billabong tee so thin it molds to each muscle of his perfect chest. It's getting harder and harder not to think very un-friend-like thoughts. Which means it's definitely time for me to go.

Yet when he asks if I want a ride back to my dorm, I find a way to refuse without quite saying no. Instead we end up in his studio, a detached garage on the side of the property that contains table saws, machines, and an array of other tools. There are racks of raw wood on the walls. The floor is covered in sawdust. At the far end of the space, I glimpse several pieces of finished wooden furniture.

"You made these?" I run my hands over a coffee table, a chair, a skinny bookshelf. There's also a chest of drawers and a pair of end tables. Everything is done in varying finishes, but they all have a modern coastal aesthetic. Clean and simple. Elegant.

"Sort of my side hustle," he says with obvious pride. "It's all reclaimed wood. Stuff I find. I break it down to its basic forms, then repurpose it, bring out what it was meant to be."

"I'm impressed."

He shrugs, brushing off the compliment as though I'm merely being polite.

"No, I mean it. Cooper, you have real talent. You could make serious money off this. I know a dozen of my mom's friends who would tear through this place like it was a Saks trunk sale, throwing money at you."

"Yeah, well." He hides his face while putting away tools and rearranging his workbench, as if he needs to keep his hands busy. "Without the capital to quit my day job, I don't have time to churn out the kind of volume I'd need to turn it into any kind of sustainable business. I sell a few things here and there. Make a little extra cash we can use to fix up the house. It's just a hobby."

I plant one hand on my hip. "You have to let me buy something."

Before I can blink, he walks over and throws a drop cloth over the pieces. He won't meet my eyes as he warns, "Don't."

"Don't what?" I say blankly.

"Don't do that. The second you start looking at me as a project, this"—he gestures between us—"stops working. I don't need your help. I didn't show you this to get money out of you."

"I know." I grab his arm, forcing him to look at me. "This isn't charity. You're not a pity case, Cooper. I consider it an investment in an undiscovered talent."

He snorts softly.

"Seriously. When you blow up, I'm going to tell everyone I got there first. Rich girls love being trendsetters."

He studies me, his dark eyes searching. He has an intensity about him, a natural aura that's both magnetic and dangerous. The more I tell myself to keep my distance, the closer I'm drawn in.

Finally, a reluctant smile surfaces. "Fucking clones."

"Good. You think about a fair price for the coffee table and chairs. The furniture we have in the dorm is hideous, anyway. Bonnie and I were going to shop for something but got sidetracked with school."

I hop up to sit on a nearby worktable, swinging my legs beneath me. I know I should go, but I enjoy this guy's company far too much.

It's becoming a real problem.

Cooper's still watching me, his expression indecipherable. His gaze jerks away from mine when he gets a text. He pulls out his phone, and whatever he reads makes him laugh to himself.

"What's so funny?"

"Nothing. My friend Steph just sent a funny post to our group chat. Here, look." He joins me on the table. It takes absolutely no effort for him to haul his big body up and plant his butt beside me.

I lean toward him to look at his phone, trying valiantly not to notice how good he smells. A combination of spice, sawdust, and the ocean—which isn't a scent that springs to mind when you think of aphrodisiacs and pheromones, and yet it makes me light-headed and tingly.

Oddly enough, his open chat thread shows a screenshot of none other than my website. This particular post is from *GirlfriendFails*, an anecdote about a girl who goes home with a guy late one night after meeting at a bar. They sleep together, but after he's fallen asleep, she realizes she's started her period and doesn't have a tampon or pad. So she goes rummaging through his apartment to see if there are any in one of the bathrooms. The first bathroom is devoid of menstrual products, so she has no choice but to creep into the second bedroom and sneak into the en suite bathroom. She finds a box of tampons under the sink just as someone walks in on her. It's the guy's mom, wielding a lamp as a weapon because she thinks she's being robbed. She's screaming like a banshee, demanding to know why this nearly naked girl in a T-shirt and underwear is rifling through her bathroom at four in the morning.

"Can you even imagine?" Cooper grins. "Kinda makes me glad my mom isn't around."

I should probably tell him that I'm the brains behind the site he's laughing over. But I don't have the heart to say, *Yeah, I own this website. Launched it and made my first million while I was still in high school. But tell me more about your struggling furniture business.* What a jerk that would make me.

I don't brag about my success in general, but it feels extra wrong to say something now. So I address his mom comment, asking, "Where is she?"

"No idea." There's a sting in his voice. Hurt and anger.

I'm realizing I've touched a nerve and am scurrying to think of how to change the subject when he releases a ragged breath and keeps talking.

"She was barely around when Evan and I were kids. Coming and going with a different guy every couple of months. She'd take off one day, then show up unexpected looking for money." He shrugs. "Shelley Hartley was never any kind of mother."

The burden he's carried—still carries—is obvious in the drop of his broad shoulders, the crease of his forehead as he picks at frays on his jeans.

"I'm sorry," I say earnestly. "What about your dad?"

"Dead. Died in a drunk driving accident when we were twelve, though not before racking up a mountain of credit card debt that somehow became our problem." Cooper picks up a chisel, handles it a moment, then absently scratches at the plywood surface of the table. "The only things either of our parents ever gave us were liabilities." Then with a sudden ferocity, he stabs the chisel straight into the wood. "But I'll be damned if I end up like them. Rather throw myself off a bridge."

I swallow. He's a bit scary sometimes. Not threatening, exactly. Unpredictable, wired with the kinetic potential of the demons that torment his mind. Cooper Hartley has depths that are dark and treacherous, and that reckless part of me—the impulses I keep buried deep—wants nothing more than to dive in and explore.

It's just one more reason I'm finding myself in over my head.

I wrap my hand over his. "For what it's worth," I tell him, because right now he needs a friend to say they hear him, they understand, "I don't think you're anything like them. You're hardworking, talented, smart. You have ambition. Trust me, that's more than most people have going for them. A guy with a little bit of luck and a lot of initiative can make his life anything he wants."

"Easy for you to say. How many ponies did your parents buy for your birthdays?" He lobs a sarcastic jab my way, and I know it's because I'm the only target in the room.

I offer a rueful smile. "I'm lucky if I can get past my own mother's assistant when I call. My birthday cards are issued by their personal staffs. My report cards and permission slips were signed by employees."

"Fair tradeoff for getting everything you've ever wanted by snapping your fingers."

"Is that really what you think?" I shake my head at him. "Yes, I'm extremely fortunate to have been born into a wealthy family. But money becomes an excuse for everything. It becomes a wall between all of us. Because you've gotten one thing right—we *are* clones. From the day I was born, my parents have groomed me to be like them. They don't think of me as an individual with my own thoughts and opinions. I'm a prop. I swear, sometimes I wonder if I was only born to help my father's political aspirations."

Cooper gives me a questioning look.

"My father is a US Congressman," I explain. "And everyone knows voters prefer candidates with families. At least that's what the pollsters say. So, *poof,* here I am. Born and bred for campaign photo ops. Built to smile pretty for the camera and say nice things about

Daddy at fundraisers. And I did it, all of it, without question or complaint. Because I hoped one day it would make them love me." A bitter laugh pops out. "Honestly, though, I don't think they'd notice if I were replaced with a totally different daughter. Recast in my own life. They're not all that interested in me as a person."

It's the first time I've vented all this out loud. The first time I've let anyone into this part of me. I mean, yeah, I've confided in Preston plenty of times, but not so unfiltered. The two of us come from the same sphere. It's normal to him, and he has no complaints about his lot in life. And why would he? He's a man. He gets to run the family empire someday. Me? I have to keep my aspirations on the down-low so my parents don't realize I have no intention of being a quiet housewife when I finally grow out of "my teenage trifles."

They think my websites are a complete waste of time. "A passing folly," as my mother kept referring to it during the gap year I had to fight tooth and nail for. When I'd proudly told my dad that my bank account had officially reached seven figures, he'd scoffed. Said a million bucks was a drop in the bucket. Compared to the hundreds of millions his company nets every quarter, I suppose my earnings seem pitiful. But he could've at least pretended to be proud of me.

Cooper regards me in silence for several long beats. Then, as if a daydream evaporates in his mind, his intense eyes refocus on me. "Alright. I'll grant you that having emotionally absent parents isn't much better than physically absent ones."

I laugh. "So where does that leave the scorecard in the tournament of childhood trauma?"

"Yeah, I've still got you beat by a mile, but you're on the board."

"Fair."

We exchange knowing grins at the futility of such arguments. It wasn't my intention to turn the discussion into a competition—I'd never make light of the pain Cooper has suffered—but I guess I was holding in a bit more frustration than I'd realized. It all sort of spilled out.

"Hey, you got any plans tonight?" he asks as he gets to his feet.

I hesitate. I should check with Preston, see if he's doing anything with the guys tonight.

Instead, I say, "No."

Because where Cooper's concerned, my better judgment has gone to hell.

His gaze rakes over me in a way that elicits a hot shiver. "Good. I'm taking you out."

CHAPTER THIRTEEN

COOPER

"I've always wanted to do one of these," Mac says, grabbing my arm and tugging me toward some spinning monstrosity a hundred feet in the air.

Is this chick serious? I roll my eyes at her. "If I wanted to get dizzy and choke on my own vomit, I could do that on the ground."

She spins on me, eyes wide and shining in the multicolored lights. "You're not chicken, are you, Hartley?"

"Never," I say, because the inability to back down from a challenge is one of my personality defects.

"Then put your money where your mouth is, chicken man."

"You're gonna regret that." I warn, gesturing for her to lead the way.

The annual boardwalk festival is a highlight of the fall season in Avalon Bay. It's supposed to commemorate the founding of the town or something, but really, it's become an excuse to throw a party. Local restaurants bring out their food trucks and vendor stands, bars sling signature cocktails from carts, and midway games and carnival rides cram the boardwalk.

Evan and I used to smoke a bowl with our friends, get smashed, and jump from one ride to the next to see who lost their lunch first. Last couple of years, though, I guess we've gotten tired of it.

For some reason, I feel compelled to be the one to introduce Mac to the festival.

The boardwalk is crowded. Carnival jingles compete with live bands playing at three stages spread out through Old Town. The aromas of corn dogs and cotton candy, funnel cakes and turkey legs, waft on the breeze. After the Wave Flinger and Moon Shot, we go down the fifty-foot Avalanche slide and tackle the Gravity Well. All the way, Mac is skipping around with a huge grin on her face. Not an ounce of trepidation. She's an adventurer, this one. I dig it.

"What next?" she asks as we're recovering from her latest ride selection. I wouldn't call myself a wimp, but the daredevil beside me is definitely giving me a run for my money.

"Can we do something chill?" I grumble. "Like, give me five seconds to readjust to gravity."

She grins. "Something chill? Gee, Grandpa, like what? Should we sit quietly on the Ferris wheel or board that slow little train that goes through the Tunnel of Love?"

"If you're going into the Tunnel of Love with your grandpa, then you've got a whole new set of problems we need to talk about."

She flips up her middle finger. "How about a cotton candy break, then?"

"Sure." As we amble toward one of the concession stands, I speak in a conversational tone. "I got a BJ in that tunnel once, you know."

Rather than look disgusted, her green eyes twinkle with delight. "Really? Tell me everything."

We stand in line behind a woman who's trying to wrangle three kids under the age of five. They're like a litter of puppies, unable to stay still, bouncing around from the sugar highs they're undoubtedly on.

I drag my tongue over my bottom lip and wink at Mac. "I'll tell you later. In private."

"Tease."

We reach the counter, where I buy us two bags of cotton candy. Mac eagerly snatches one, peels off a huge, fluffy piece, and shoves the pink floss into her mouth.

"Soooo good." Her words are garbled thanks to her completely full mouth.

X-rated images burn a hole in my brain as I watch her suck and slurp on the sugary treat.

My dick thickens against my zipper, making it difficult to concentrate on what she's babbling about.

"Did you know that cotton candy was invented by a dentist?"

I blink back to reality. "Seriously? Talk about a proactive way to ensure a customer base."

"Genius," she agrees.

I reach into the bag and pinch off a piece. The cotton candy melts the moment it touches my tongue, the sweet flavor injecting a rush of nostalgia directly into my blood. I feel like a little kid again. Back when my parents were both around and still somewhat in love. They'd bring me and Evan to the boardwalk, stuff us full of junk food and sugar, and let us go wild. We'd drive home laughing and giddy and feeling like a real family.

By the time Evan and I turned six, their relationship turned combative. Dad started drinking more. Mom looked for attention and validation from other men. They separated, and Evan and I became afterthoughts to booze and sex.

"No," Mac orders.

I blink again. "No what?"

"You have that look on your face. You're brooding."

"I'm not brooding."

"Yes, you are. Your face is totally saying, *I'm lost in my broody thoughts because I'm SUCH a tortured bad boy.*" She gives me a stern look. "Snap out of it, Hartley. We were discussing some pretty insightful stuff."

"We were talking about cotton candy." My tone is dry.

"So? That can be insightful." She raises one eyebrow, smug. "Did you know scientists are trying to use cotton candy to create artificial blood vessels?"

"That sounds like pure and total horseshit," I say cheerfully.

"It's not. I read about it once," she insists. "Cotton candy fibers are, like, super small. They're the same size as our blood vessels. I don't remember the exact process, but the basic premise is—cotton candy equals medical breakthrough."

"Junk science."

"I swear."

"Cite your sources."

"Some magazine."

"Ohhhh, of course! Some magazine—the most reputable of publications."

She glares at me. "Why can't you just accept I'm right?"

"Why can't you accept you might be wrong?"

"I'm never wrong."

I start laughing, which causes her to glower harder at me. "I'm convinced you argue just for the sake of arguing," I inform her.

"I do not."

I laugh harder. "See! You're so damn stubborn."

"Lies!"

A tall blonde holding hands with a small boy frowns as she passes by. Mac's exclamation has brought a flicker of concern to the woman's eyes.

"It's okay," Mac assures her. "We're best friends."

"We're bitter rivals," I correct. "She's always yelling at me, ma'am. Please, help me out of this toxic relationship."

The woman gives us one of those *you're incorrigible* looks anyone over forty sports when they're dealing with immature children. Joke's on her. We're both in our twenties.

We continue down the boardwalk, stopping to watch some sucker boyfriend hurl darts at a wall of balloons to try to win a massive stuffed animal for his girl. Forty bucks later, he still hasn't secured the prized panda, and the girlfriend is now spending more time checking me out than cheering him on.

"Can you believe that chick?" Mac says when we walk off. "I swear she was picturing you naked in her mind while her poor boyfriend was bleeding money for her."

"Jealous?" I flash a grin.

"Nope. Just impressed. You're hot stuff, Hartley. I don't think we've passed a single girl tonight who hasn't stopped to drool over you."

"What can I say? Women like me." I'm not trying to be arrogant. It's just a fact. My twin and I are good-looking, and good-looking guys are popular with the ladies. Anyone who says otherwise is damn naïve. When it comes to our basic animal instincts, who we're sexually drawn to, appearance matters.

"Why don't you have a girlfriend?" Mac asks.

"Don't want one."

"Ah, I get it. Commitmentphobe."

"Nah." I shrug. "I'm just not in the market for one right now. My priorities are elsewhere."

"Interesting."

Our eyes lock for a fleeting, heated moment. I'm seconds away from reexamining the aforementioned priorities when Mac visibly swallows and changes the subject.

"Alright, time for another ride," she announces. "We've been dilly-dallying long enough."

"Please go easy on me," I beg.

She simply snorts in response and dashes off in search of our next death-defying adventure.

I stare after her in amusement. And a touch of bewilderment. This girl is something else. Not at all like the other bored clones at Garnet. She doesn't care how she looks—hair wild, makeup sweating off. She's spontaneous and free, which makes it that much more confounding why she stays with that jackass Kincaid. What the hell does that guy have that makes him so damn great?

"Explain something to me," I say, as we approach some enormous bungee thing that slingshots a small, two-person basket of screaming victims nearly two hundred feet in the air.

"If this is you trying to stall, it won't work." She marches right up to the ride attendant and hands him our tickets.

"Your boyfriend," I start, stepping around her to get into the basket first.

The attendant straps me in and starts his spiel that amounts to: *Keep your hands and feet inside the vehicle, and if this kills you, we're not liable.*

For the first time tonight, Mac looks nervous as she slides in beside me. "What about him?"

I choose my words carefully. "I mean, I hear things. None of them good. And for a girl who insists she doesn't want to be her mommy and daddy's little princess protégé, I'm wondering why you would do the expected thing and settle for another Garnet clone."

The thick bundle of cords, which will in a moment launch us into the night sky, rises up the ride's arms that form an obtuse angle above us.

"That's not really any of your business." Her expression turns flat, her tone adversarial. I'm touching a nerve.

"Come on, if you two have crazy-good sex or something, just say so. That I understand. Get yours, you know? I'd respect it."

She looks straight ahead, as if there's any chance of her ignoring me in this four-foot-wide tin can. "I'm not having this conversation with you."

"I know it's not for the money," I say. "And the fact that you never talk about him tells me your heart's not in it."

"You're way off." Mac snaps her gaze to me, lifting a defiant chin. There's all sorts of fight in her now. "Honestly, I'm embarrassed for you."

"Oh, is that right, princess?" I can't help myself. Getting a rise out of her kind of makes me horny. "When's the last time you touched yourself thinking about him?"

"Fuck off." Her cheeks turn red. I can see her biting the inside of her cheek as she rolls her eyes.

"Tell me I'm wrong. Tell me he gets you hot and bothered just walking into a room."

Her pulse is visibly thrumming in her neck. Mac adjusts in her seat, crossing her ankles. As her gaze flicks to mine, she licks her lips and I know she's thinking the same thing I am.

"There are more important things than chemistry," she says, and I hear the uncertainty in her voice.

"I bet you've been telling yourself that for a long time." I slant my head. "But maybe you're not as sure of that as you used to be."

"And why's that?"

"Okay," the attendant announces, "hang on. Counting down from ten. Ready?"

Oh, fuck it.

"I'm calling in your marker," I tell her.

"My what?"

"*Eight. Seven.*" The attendant counts down.

"The bet we made, remember? The night we met? Well, I won, and I know what I want as repayment."

"*Six. Five.*"

"Cooper . . ."

"*Four. Three.*"

"Kiss me," I say roughly. "Or tell me you still don't want me."

"*Two.*"

"What's it gonna be, Mackenzie?"

"*One.*"

CHAPTER FOURTEEN

COOPER

We're propelled into the air, and for several heart-stopping, stomach-twisting moments, we're sort of frozen in time. Pinned by the force of the ride as the ground disappears beneath us. A brief, spectacular moment of weightlessness lifts us from our seats and then the tension of the cords releases slightly and we bounce, once, twice, past the highest point. I turn my head and that's when Mac's lips find mine.

It's like an electric shock, a sizzle of heat from her lips straight down to my groin.

She grabs me, finding fistfuls of my hair, kissing me wildly. She tastes like sugar and endless summer nights. I'm hungry for both as my tongue slicks over hers and we soar so high it feels like we might never come down.

Her gasp heats my lips.

I drive the kiss deeper, swallowing her soft moan.

The basket bounces again, slowly descending on our return to earth. We part only to suck in a startled breath, and I have to remember where we are to stop myself from tearing her clothes off. I'm hard and hungry.

"We shouldn't have done that." Mac adjusts the straps of her tank top and wipes the smeared lipstick from her lips.

"I'm not sorry," I tell her. Because I'm not. I've wanted to do that for weeks. And it's all on the table now. We set fire to the pretense, and there's nowhere to go but forward.

She's silent when we leave the ride. Maybe I came on too strong. Scared her away.

When I realize she's leading us toward the exit, I swallow a sigh. Yeah.

She's definitely running scared.

"I'll take you home, if you want," I offer, following her toward where we parked the truck.

"I want to say goodnight to Daisy first."

I don't bother to correct her this time. Guess she won that battle.

"I'll catch a cab from your place," she adds.

The entire ride to my house, I'm convinced I'm never going to see her again and I've screwed this whole plan. My head is reeling, trying to think of something to say, some way to mitigate the fallout. All I come up with is a dozen ways I want to screw her brains out. Which isn't helping.

"He grounds me."

Her quiet statement has me glancing over in surprise. "What?"

"Preston. There are many reasons I'm with him, but that's a big one. He keeps me grounded." From the corner of my eye, I see she's wringing her hands. "Reminds me to be more restrained."

"Why do you need to be?" My voice is gruff.

"For one, because my dad is in the public eye."

"So? Your father made that choice. You don't have to turn yourself into a plastic person because of his life decisions." I frown at her. "And you don't have to put up with a boyfriend who keeps you on a leash."

Her eyes flash. "I'm not on a leash."

"What do you think 'restrained' means?" I say sarcastically.

"I said he reminds me to restrain *myself*. He's not the one doing the restraining. Whatever. You don't get it." Lips flattening, she fixes her gaze out the passenger window.

"You're right, I don't get it. I just spent the past couple hours watching you seek out every wild ride at that festival. You get off on the thrill. You get off on life. There's fire in you, Mac."

"Fire," she echoes dubiously.

"Hell yes. Fire. And you choose to be with someone who puts out the fire? Screw that. You need a man to stoke it."

"And, what, that man is you?" A sharp edge to her question.

"Didn't say that. Just saying your current pick is seriously lacking."

The house is dark when we pull up. Evan said he was getting together with our friends, but maybe they hit up the festival after all. Another silence falls over us as Mac and I walk inside.

I flick the light switch. "Look," I start. "I don't regret the kiss—we both wanted it, and you know that. But if this friendship thing is gonna be weird for you now . . ."

I glance back to see her pressed against the door, looking insanely edible. She doesn't speak, just tugs the front of my shirt to draw me to her. Before I can blink, she rises on her toes to kiss me.

"Fuck," I gasp against her greedy mouth.

In response, she lifts her leg around my hip and bites my lip.

My brain stutters for a second before I wake up and go with it. I grab her thigh, pressing myself between her legs as I kiss her deeper. Her fingers find their way under my shirt.

"God, all these muscles. I can't even." Her palms travel to my chest, stroking, then around to my back, nails gently scratching down my spine.

Her eager touch sends all the blood in my body rushing to my groin. I'm gone. Hard. Panting. I want her so badly I can hardly breathe.

A detailed fantasy of bending her over my bed plays behind my clenched eyelids. I'm about to pick her up and throw her over my shoulder when I hear the sliding glass door shut loudly in the kitchen.

Our mouths break apart.

"Oh, sorry, didn't mean to interrupt." Heidi stands in the kitchen doorway, watching us with a sarcastic smile. "Didn't know you were back."

I'm still breathing hard, trying to find my voice.

She walks to the fridge for two handfuls of beers. "Please, as you were. Don't let me interrupt."

Heidi winks at me before leaving the way she came.

Great.

"I should go." Immediately Mac is disentangling herself from me, putting distance between us. The dog hasn't come running, which means Evan has her down at the beach, with Heidi and the rest of the gang.

"That's my friend Heidi," I hurry to explain, not wanting Mac to leave. "I'm sorry about that. I didn't know anyone was here."

"It's all good. I have to go."

"Stay. They're probably all down at the beach. I'll get Daisy for you."

"No, it's fine. I'm going to call a cab."

"I'll drive you," I counter.

She's out the door, slinking away before I can stop her.

Damn it. "At least let me wait with you."

She acquiesces to that much, but the moment's passed. Once again there's a massive crater between us as we wait in silence, and I get nothing more than a wave goodnight as she's pulling away.

I drag a hand through my hair and trudge into the house. Fucking hell. One step forward, two steps back.

Story of my life.

In the kitchen, I grab a beer for myself, twist off the cap, and take a long swig before stepping out onto the deck. Where Heidi is standing. Her arms are free of bottles, so she must have delivered them to the beach and come back to wait for me.

"Hey," I say roughly.

"Hey." She leans against the railing, one hand playing with the frayed ends of her denim skirt. "So. You've got the clone on the hook."

"I guess." I swallow a hasty sip of beer. Truth be told, the plan, the bet, the rules . . . they were the last thing on my mind back there. My entire world had been reduced to Mackenzie and how good she felt pressed up against me.

"You guess? The chick was looking at you with stars in her eyes. She's into you."

Rather than comment, I pivot by saying, "Speaking of people being into other people—Jay West was asking about you."

She narrows her eyes. "When?"

"A few days ago. Said he hung out with you at a bar or something."

"Oh, yeah. We ran into him and Kellan at Joe's."

I flick up one eyebrow. "He's gonna ask you out."

She doesn't say anything. Just watches me warily.

"Will you turn him down?"

"Should I?"

A sigh lodges itself in my throat. I know she wants me to stake my claim, throw myself at her feet, and beg her not to go out with anyone but me. But I'm not going to do that. I told her I didn't want a relationship when we first hooked up. I hoped it would only be a one-night thing, each of us scratching an itch, and then we'd go back to being friends. But I was naïve. One night led to a few more, and now our friendship is more strained than ever.

"Do whatever you want, Heidi," I finally say.

"Got it. Thanks for the advice, Coop." Sarcasm drips from every word. Then, with a frustrated shake of her head, she stomps down the steps.

I release the breath trapped in my lungs. Chug the rest of my beer. The taste of Mackenzie still lingers on my tongue. Sugar and sex, an addictive combo. I step inside to grab another bottle, hoping the alcohol might help erase the flavor of the woman I'm aching to kiss again.

I join everyone on the beach. I'm relieved—and then ashamed of my relief—when I spot Heidi about ten yards away at the water's edge, texting on her phone. Maybe reaching out to Jay? But I doubt it. She's never been attracted to the nice ones. Just the jerks like me.

Around the fire, Steph and Alana are ragging Evan about some girl he hooked up with yesterday, after getting into a fight with her boyfriend. First I'm hearing of either, but Evan's not particularly forthcoming when it comes to his transgressions. From what I gather, he threw down with some Garnet clones who refused to pay up after he schooled them at the pool hall.

"She came in tonight all moon-eyed, asking where she could track you down," Alana is telling him.

He pales. "You didn't give her my number, did you?"

Alana lets him sweat for a few seconds before she and Steph break out in grins. "'Course not. That would go against the friend code."

"Speaking of the friend code, does it say anything about subjecting your friends to a front-row seat to your slobbery make-out session?" Steph pipes up, gesturing to the culprit in question.

At the far edge of the fire pit, our friend Tate is sprawled on one of our old lounge chairs with a curvy dark-haired chick draped over him like a blanket. He's got a hand thrust in her hair and his tongue in her mouth, while she rubs herself against him like a cat in heat. They're oblivious to our presence.

"Shameless," Evan shouts at the couple with feigned outrage. Then he grins, because my brother's an exhibitionist himself.

Tate gives his girl's bottom a playful smack and they stumble to their feet, cheeks flushed and lips swollen. "Coop," he drawls. "Mind if we head inside and watch some TV?"

I roll my eyes. "Sure. But there's no TV in my room, so I'd better not find you in there." I love my friends, but I don't need them banging on my bed. I just changed the sheets this morning too.

After Tate and the brunette disappear, Alana and Steph bend their heads close and start whispering to each other.

"Share with the group," Evan mocks, wagging a finger at the girls.

With a look of evil glee, Steph jerks her thumb toward Alana and says, "This bad girl slept with Tate last weekend."

I lift a brow. "Yeah?"

An unimpressed Evan shrugs. "You finally took a ride on the Tatemobile, huh? Surprised it took you so long."

My brother makes a good point. From the moment Tate's family moved to the Bay when we were in junior high, all the local girls went crazy for him. One cocky smile from Tate and they're hooked.

Alana's expression reveals not an ounce of shame or regret as she offers her own shrug. "Sort of wish I had done it sooner. Man gives good dick. Great kisser too."

"He's not bad," Evan agrees, and I can't help myself—I burst out laughing.

"Shit," I wheeze. "I always forget about that night you guys made out."

He rolls his eyes. "It was just a kiss."

"Dude, it lasted like three full minutes." My mind is now flooded with the vivid images of Evan and Tate sucking each other's faces off at one of Alana's house parties when we were sixteen. The girls cheering them on, the guys catcalling. That was a weird night.

"In Ev's defense, making out with Tate was the only way they were gonna see me and Genevieve take our tops off—" Alana stops abruptly.

Well, hell. She actually did it. Uttered Genevieve's name, the Voldemort of our group. I have to assume the girls are still in touch. Steph, Alana, Heidi, and Gen were the fierce foursome.

Evan and I have a habit of reading each other's minds, but whereas I possess at least some self-restraint, he doesn't know the meaning of it. So he says, "You guys still talk to her?"

Alana hesitates.

Steph opens her mouth, only to be interrupted by Heidi's reappearance.

"What's going on?" she asks, carefully glancing around the group. Then she nods. "Oh. Cooper told you."

Genevieve is all but forgotten as everyone's gazes swivel to me. "Told us what?" Steph demands.

I shrug. So, naturally, Heidi doesn't waste a second filling them in on finding me and Mackenzie wrapped up at the front door.

"Gotta admit, Coop, I didn't think you'd get this far," Alana says, lifting a beer in salute. "I'm impressed."

"I've changed my mind, by the way." Heidi eyes me through the flames. "I'm totally on board with this plan. I cannot wait to see the look on that girl's face when she realizes what you've done."

"How are you gonna do it?" Steph asks excitedly.

This is the most fun these girls have had since they went ham on some clone's car after he ran off with Alana's bikini top while she was sunbathing on the beach.

"Yeah, we have to talk endgame," Evan says. "It'd be a shame to waste an opportunity."

"Yes," Heidi agrees. "You have to get her and Kincaid in the same place, let him see you two together, and then dump her in public. Make it dramatic." Heidi is in a mood tonight. I know I'm to blame for it, but I'm not sure how to fix things between us. "Maybe we can throw a party."

Steph splashes beer on the fire in her eagerness. "Nah, too tame. Has to be on their turf. It's no fun unless Kincaid is humiliated in front of his own kind."

"I know where we can get a couple buckets of pig's blood," Alana says, which gets the rest of them doubled over laughing.

I laugh with them, playing along. Because a few weeks ago, I wouldn't have given a damn what happened to the random clone girlfriend of a rich punk who crossed me.

But now I've gotten to know Mac and . . . I genuinely like her. She doesn't deserve their scorn just because she's connected to a jackass like Kincaid. And after that kiss, I know there's something real between us, even if she's afraid of it. I can't tell these guys I'm having second thoughts, though. They'd tear my ass a new one.

Now that they've gotten a whiff of blood in the water, they won't be satisfied until they've tasted flesh.

CHAPTER FIFTEEN

MACKENZIE

"Three days in a row, this boy lets the door slam in my face at the smoothie place. Not once does he apologize. I'm startin' to think he's doin' it on purpose. I'm old-fashioned, okay? I value manners. Open a door for a lady, will ya? So the fourth day, I see him comin'. I'm ready for him. I'm inside and grab the door before he can open it. I flick the lock. This whole smoothie joint is held captive because I ain't letting this guy in. Over my dead body."

It's Monday morning, and Bonnie and I are both dragging ass. She shouts from the bathroom, putting on makeup, as I make us coffee in the kitchenette. I'm only half paying attention and manage to spill milk on my shirt.

"How long did that go on?" I call from my room while I change shirts. I'm supposed to meet Preston for lunch at his house later, so I have to make sure my outfit is appropriate. Not for him, but for his mother. She likes me fine—I think?—but she's very . . . particular. A tank top and jeans are not going to cut it with Coraline Kincaid.

"Long enough that the manager jumps in demandin' I let people out. And I'm all, I'd love to—as soon as this guy apologizes or leaves. Well, eventually he must realize I'm not playin' around, so he takes off. Next day, he locks me out of the sandwich shop until I agree to go on a date with him. So he's pickin' me up Friday night."

"That's great," I shout, only to turn and realize Bonnie is standing right behind me with our coffee in two travel mugs. "Sorry."

"You seem edgy." She stares at me. "You have a secret."

"No, I don't."

Her eyes burst into wide, blue saucers. "You kissed a boy."

Witch.

"Who is he?" she demands.

There's no use denying it. I'm entirely convinced of Bonnie's otherworldly powers. She'll berate me until I give her what she wants.

"Some townie," I say. Technically, it's true. She doesn't need to know the townie in question is Cooper.

Ugh. Just the thought of his name quickens my heart rate.

What in the *world* have I done? The kiss at the festival? I can blame that one on the sugar high. But the full-on make-out grope session at his house afterward?

There's no excuse.

I'm a horrible person. A horrible, selfish, awful girlfriend who doesn't deserve a stand-up guy like Preston.

There is absolutely no coming back from what I did on Friday night. I know this. And yet despite the whirlpool of guilt currently foaming in my stomach, one stupid little butterfly continues to flutter inside me, flapping around and churning up memories of Cooper's hungry lips and heated gaze.

His tongue in my mouth.

My fingers skimming the defined muscles of his unbelievably ripped chest.

And it's not only the physical stuff that lingers in my mind. It's everything that came before it. Talking about our families in his workshop, running around the boardwalk like a pair of rowdy kids. When I'm with him, I don't need to put on a front. I don't have to pretend to be the proper, well-behaved lady I'm expected to be. I feel like I'm my true self when I'm around Cooper. And that . . . scares me.

"That's it?" Bonnie's voice jerks me from my unsettling thoughts. "Nuh-uh, I don't think so. I require more details."

I shrug awkwardly. "There's not much else to say. It just sort of happened."

"Is it going to just sort of happen again?" Her expression tells me she's hoping the answer might be yes.

"No. Definitely not. I feel terrible. Preston—"

"Doesn't need to know," Bonnie finishes for me. "Nothin' good will come of telling him. If it was a mistake, and even if it wasn't—a girl has a right to her secrets. Trust me."

I know she means well, but I've already kept too much from him. This whole thing with Cooper has gone too far. I'm not a liar, and I never, ever thought myself capable of kissing someone other than my boyfriend. It's a humbling experience, discovering you're not as morally virtuous as you once thought.

Bonnie's wrong. Preston needs to know what I've done to us.

The right thing to do now is tell the truth and accept the consequences.

Later that afternoon, Pres picks me up from class for lunch. All day, I practiced what I would say. How I would tell him. But when he kisses my cheek and wraps his arm around my waist, I lose my nerve and keep my mouth shut.

"You look great," he says, nodding in approval.

Relief flutters through me. Thank God. I went through three outfits before I decided on a silk blouse and navy pixie chinos. My own mother doesn't give me this much anxiety.

"Freddy is preparing lamb shank," Preston adds. "Hope you're hungry."

"Famished," I lie.

He steers his Porsche into the parking lot of Garnet's football facility and pulls into a spot. Like the gentleman he is, he hops out of the convertible and runs over to open my door. Then he extends a hand, I take it, and we walk toward Preston's helicopter.

Yup. His helicopter.

Most days, it's how he commutes to school. His family had the helipad installed behind the football stadium his freshman year. It's a bit ridiculous, even for our circle of society, and the sight of the gleaming, white aircraft makes me wonder what Cooper would say if he saw—

No. Nope. Not going there. Today, I come clean.

It isn't long before we're flying in over the Kincaid estate, a massive piece of gated property on the coast. Endless lawns and oak trees stretch out for acres, the property divided from the ocean by an expansive white mansion. There's a pool, tennis courts, basketball court, and flower garden. All maintained by at least a dozen employees at any given time.

On the back patio, his mother greets us. As always, she's impeccably dressed. Head-to-toe Prada. I'm not sure why she bothers, seeing as how most days she has little reason to leave the house. Like my mom, Coraline doesn't work and employs a personal staff that handles every aspect of the home and her affairs.

"Hey, Mom." Preston leans in to kiss his mother's cheek.

"Hi, darling." Smiling, she shifts her gaze to me. "Mackenzie, honey." She hugs me, but with the light touch of someone who might shatter if you squeezed too hard. She's a slight woman. Fragile, not frail. Just don't make her angry. "You look lovely."

"Thank you, Mrs. Kincaid. Your new roses around the gazebo are gorgeous."

I learned long ago that the easiest way to keep her happy is to find something new on the estate to compliment on every visit. Otherwise, she spends the entire time commenting on my split ends or the size of my pores.

"Oh, thank you, honey. Raúl planted them just this week. He really is an artist."

"Are you joining us for lunch?" I inquire. *Please say no, please say no—*

"I'm afraid not. I'm meeting with my architect soon. He'll be here any minute. Did Preston tell you we're building a new pool house?"

"No, he didn't. How exciting." Really, the only exciting thing about any of this is that she's not having lunch with us.

And it's a good thing she doesn't, because lunch ends up being hella awkward. Not that Preston notices. In the formal dining room among the lamb shank and fine china, he goes on about some professor he insists has it out for him, while I pick at my food and work up the nerve to confess my sins.

"Of course, I could go to the dean and have the whole matter sorted out. He'd be out of a job. Then I thought, well, where's the fun in that, right? I'll come up with something more creative. That's the thing with those people. You give them a little respect, and suddenly they forget their place. It's our job to remind them. Another refill, Martha," he says to the maid. "Thank you."

Finally, I can't stand the pit in my stomach any longer.

"I have something to tell you," I blurt out.

He sets down his fork and pushes his plate away for Martha. "You okay?"

No. Not even a little. It isn't until right now that I realize I do care about Preston. Not only because we've been together so long. Not because of some sense of loyalty.

Cooper might draw out my "true self," whatever the hell that even means, but Preston does exactly what I told Cooper the other night: He keeps me grounded. He's a stable presence in my life. He knows this world, knows how to handle our parents, which is important in maintaining our sanity. Around him, I'm not a ball of anxiety and dread.

And what I've done to him isn't fair.

I wait until Martha leaves the dining room before releasing a shaky breath.

Now or never.

"I kissed someone. A guy."

He waits, watching me, as if I might say more.

I should. I will. This seemed the most expedient way to begin. Except now I'm regretting not waiting until we were somewhere more private. If his mother decides to walk in right now, I might not make it off the estate alive.

"Is that all?" Preston prompts.

"No. I mean, yeah. We only kissed, if that's what you mean." I bite my lip. Hard. "But I cheated on you."

He gets up from his seat at the far end of the table and comes to sit beside me. "Do I know him?"

"No. Some local I met at a bar when I was out with Bonnie. It was a stupid thing to do. We were drinking and I wasn't thinking and . . ." And I can't help myself from softening the blow with another lie. I was going to tell him. Everything. Now, looking in his eyes, I can't hurt him that way. He is taking it better than I expected, though. "I'm so sorry, Pres. You don't deserve this. I was wrong and I have no excuse."

"Babe," he says, squeezing my hand. He smiles, almost amused. "I'm not mad."

I blink. "You're not?"

"Of course not. So you had too much to drink and kissed a townie. Welcome to your freshman year of college. Guess you learned a lesson about handling your liquor."

Chuckling, he kisses the top of my head, then offers his hand to help me up from the table.

"How are you taking this so well?" I'm absolutely dumbfounded. Of all the ways I thought he might react, this wasn't one of them.

He leads me out to the back veranda to sit on the porch swing, where the maid has already put out two glasses of iced tea. "Simple. I can see the big picture. You and I have a future together, Mackenzie. I'm not interested in throwing that away over some minor indiscretion. Are you?"

"Definitely not." But I thought there'd be some groveling involved, at the very least.

"I'm glad you told me the truth. I'm not thrilled about what happened, but I understand, and I forgive you. Water under the bridge." He hands me an iced tea. "Not too much sugar, just the way you like it."

Okay, then.

For the rest of the afternoon, I expect Preston to pull away. To be cold, unhappy, even though he insisted he was fine.

But that isn't the case at all. If anything, he's more affectionate. This whole ordeal has only brought us closer together, which in a way makes me feel worse. I can't say precisely how I would've handled it if the situations were reversed, but I'm fairly sure I wouldn't have shrugged and said, "Water under the bridge." I guess Preston is a better person than I am.

I need to follow his lead. Be better. Focus harder on our relationship. The big picture, as he'd phrased it.

So that night, when Cooper texts me, I'm ready for it. I'd been waiting all day, all evening, for him to reach out. I knew he would, and I know what I have to do.

Cooper: *We should talk.*
Me: *There's nothing to say.*
Cooper: *Let me come get you.*
Me: *I can't. I told Preston about the kiss.*

Cooper: *And?*
Me: *He forgave me. I can't see you anymore.*

There's a very long delay, nearly five minutes, before Cooper
sends another message. By then, I'm on pins and needles, practically
jumping out of my skin.

Cooper: *Is that really what you want?*

I stare miserably at the screen, a lump rising in my throat. Then
I force myself to type.

Me: *Yes. Goodbye, Cooper.*

Part of me hates cutting him off so abruptly. It isn't his fault that
I messed up. But I can't trust myself around him, and this is the
decision I should have made weeks ago. I was stupid. I thought I
could have him as a friend. I thought I could play both sides. Now,
I'm choosing.

I'm choosing Preston.

CHAPTER SIXTEEN

COOPER

On Sunday afternoon, I'm in the garage when my uncle calls to say he's stopping by. Every time my phone buzzes in my pocket, there's a second or two where I think it might be Mackenzie. Then I look at the screen and remember that I blew it. Read her all wrong.

Goodbye, Cooper.

Yeah. It must've been fun for her to slum it with some townie trash, make believe she was living dangerously. And then, the second it got real, she split. I was stupid to think it would end any other way.

But goddamn it, I can't get the taste of her off my tongue. For the past week, I've woken up every morning with a hard-on from imagining her legs wrapped around me. I can't even jerk off without pictures of Mac forcing themselves into my mind. This chick is slow-acting poison. And all I can think about is getting more.

Today, thanks to Evan, I have to build a new coffee table. The one I "sold" to Mackenzie is still sitting under a drop cloth, because it doesn't seem right to take it in case she decides to come back for it. I tell myself it's for the money and leave it at that. Anyway, this one's going to be a quick and dirty piece. Fucking Evan. Last night during a sudden party that broke out at our place, he got into it with some guy we went to high school with. I don't know how it started, only that it ended with one of them slamming the other through the table and leaving a bloody trail out my back door. Evan insists he's fine, but I'm starting to worry about him. Lately, he's been finding more excuses to start fights. Always in a pissy mood. Drinking more. This shit's getting old.

When Levi shows up, he hands me a cup of fresh coffee he picked up on the way and I dust off a couple stools for us.

Levi is our father's brother. Tall, rugged, with a short brown beard and square face. Although he bears a resemblance to my dad, the two of them couldn't be more different. Where Dad never missed a chance to fuck himself up and pass it on to us, Levi actually has his life together.

"Your brother around?" he asks.

"Left a little while ago." Probably picking up a greasy hangover cure from the diner. "So. What's up?"

"Nothing." He shrugs. "Just wanted to stop by and say a quick hello. I haven't been to the house in a few months, so I wanted to check in." Levi eyes the table in progress. "Working on something new?"

"Nothing important."

"When are you going to get serious about that, Coop? I remember you talking about trying to make a go of it sometime back."

"Yeah, I guess that's kind of on the back burner."

"It shouldn't be. You're good enough. Much as I like having you on the jobsite, you could be doing more for yourself."

Levi gave us our first full-time jobs out of high school. He's done well at it too. Not rolling in dough by any means, but he stays busy. Like a lot of people, the storms gave him more work than he knew what to do with.

Shrugging, I take a sip of coffee. "I got a few pieces in some coastal furniture shops in the tri-county area. Maybe about ten grand saved up, but that's still nowhere near enough for all the overhead I'd need to start a real business."

"I'd give ya the money if I had it," he says, and I know he's being entirely sincere. He's always been there for us since our dad died. When our mom was strung out or missing, when the fridge was empty, when our homework was due. "Everything I've got is tied up in the business. I love having the work, but it's expensive to keep up with demand."

"It's no sweat. I can't take your money, anyway. You've done more than enough for Evan and me." I've never in my life asked for a handout, and I'm not about to start now. I make fine money working for Levi. If I keep at it and save up, I'll make my own way. Eventually.

"What about a bank loan?" he suggests.

I've always resisted the idea. Not the least of which because I dealt with the banks after our dad's death—and every one of them are filled with nothing but bloodsucking suits who would sooner grind us into food pellets than help us succeed.

"I don't know," I finally answer. "I don't like the idea of going into more debt. Or having to leverage the house." I know I sound like a whiny bitch. At some point, I'm gonna have to make up my mind. Either get serious about getting my business off the ground or stop moaning about it.

"Well, that's true. It costs money to make money. But give it some thought. If this is really something you want to build a business out of, I can help. Co-sign the loan for you."

It's a generous offer, and one I don't take lightly. Even if I'm not thrilled about the idea now, I'm not about to throw his graciousness in his face, so I nod slowly. "Thanks, Levi. I'll think about it."

Levi doesn't stay more than a few minutes. After we finish our coffee, he's off to meet with a client about another job, and I'm back to measuring a plank of cedar. My head's not in it, though. It's never a good idea to operate power tools when your concentration is shot, so I call it quits and leave my workshop. Whatever. Evan can eat his dinner off the floor tonight like his precious girlfriend Daisy.

Speaking of Daisy, she's nipping at my heels when I stride back in the house. For the next ten minutes, we practice her sit-stays, but my head's not feeling that either.

Goodbye, Cooper.

I feel . . . heavy. Like I'm being dragged under the surface by a hundred-pound steel anchor wrapped around my neck. It's not a foreign feeling for me. My whole life, I've felt weighed down. By my parents' debts, my brother's bullshit, that sense I get sometimes that I'm trapped in my own head.

"Sorry, girl, I gotta get out of here," I tell the dog, reaching down to scratch beneath her silky ear. "I'll be back in a minute. Promise."

That's a lie. It'll take more than a minute to do what I'm itching to do. Daisy'll be fine, though. Evan will shower her with love and attention when he gets home. Same way Mackenzie did every time she was with the dog. I wonder if she'll come back to visit Daisy sometimes.

Doubt it. She's probably already forgotten about the both of us.

Gotta admit, I didn't expect her to be so cold. I guess in the end she is just like all the other Garnet clones. Cold-blooded to the core.

Honestly, it serves me right. I went into this with bad intentions, treated her as a means for revenge against Kincaid.

Karma's a bitch.

I forcibly shove her out of my mind. Ten minutes later, I'm parking my truck near the boardwalk. The tattoo parlor is empty when I enter, save for a frazzled-looking Wyatt sitting at the counter with a sketchpad in front of him.

"Yo," he greets me, his expression brightening.

"Yo. Got time for a walk-in?"

Wyatt's been tattooing me since I was a sixteen-year-old punk requesting a tombstone on my left biceps. 'Course, he was only a year older at the time, with a tattoo gun he picked up from the pawnshop, so my first ink wasn't exactly a masterpiece. If I have kids, first thing I'm telling them is to never let their dumbass teenage friends poke needles into their flesh. Fortunately, it turned out all right in the end. Wyatt honed his craft and now co-runs this joint with another artist, and my shitty tombstone was skillfully camouflaged within a full sleeve featuring a watery graveyard among the crashing waves of Avalon Bay.

"Depends," Wyatt says. "What's the piece?"

"Simple, small. I want an anchor." I rub my fingertips over the back of my neck. "Right here."

"What kind of anchor? Stockless? Admiralty?"

I'm not a boat guy, so I roll my eyes. "How the fuck do I know? A fisherman anchor—you know the one I mean."

He snickers. "Admiralty, then. Come to the back. It'll take less than an hour."

In no time at all, I'm straddling a chair while Wyatt preps his workstation. That's how it works in the Bay. If you're good to your friends, they're good to you. Wyatt probably won't even charge me for this new ink, no matter how much I insist. Instead, he'll show up at my place in a few months or a year from now asking for some random favor, and I'll happily oblige.

"So what were you looking all bothered about when I got here?" I ask.

He releases a frustrated groan. "Ah. Yeah. I was trying to design a piece so fucking sexy that Ren'll have no choice but to take me back."

I smother a laugh. "She dump you again?"

"What else is new, right?"

He's not wrong. Wyatt and Lauren aka Ren break up at least every other month, usually on account of the most random nonsense you can imagine. They're a great source of entertainment, though.

"What happened this time?"

"Lean forward," he orders, nudging me so that I'm bent over the chair, the back of my head at his mercy.

A second later, I feel a cool spray at my nape. Wyatt cleans the area with a soft cloth before reaching for a razor.

"Okay," he says as he starts shaving the short hairs on my neck. "I need you to imagine something. Ready?"

My snicker is muffled against my forearm. "Sure. Ready."

"You're on an island."

"Deserted or, like, a resort island?"

"Deserted. You were in a plane crash. Or your boat capsized. Not important."

"How is it not important?" I object. "If I was on a boat, I'd probably be more familiar with islands and tides and shit, which means I'd have a better shot at survival."

"Oh my God. That's not the point," he grumbles. "Why you gotta complicate it, Hartley? You're on a deserted island. The end."

"Cool story, bro."

"You realize I'm holding a razor near your neck right now?"

I swallow another laugh. "Okay. I'm on a deserted island. Now what?"

"Want me to stencil this out or freehand it?"

"Freehand. I trust you." Besides, if the tat is trash, at least it's somewhere I can't see it.

Wyatt keeps jabbering as he preps the ink. Black only. I'm not fancy. "So you're stuck there. This is your life now, this island. But! Good news. You're about to get some company. Two boats appear—"

"Sweet, so I'm rescued?"

"No!" He sounds aggravated. "I just said you're stuck there forever."

"But there are boats."

"The boats explode in five minutes, okay? There are no boats. Jesus."

It occurs to me that maybe I shouldn't be antagonizing the guy with the needles. But damn, it's fun to annoy Wyatt.

"On the first boat, there's your girlfriend, or partner, or whatever. But just them. Nothing else. The second boat has nobody on it. But it's got all the supplies you need to survive on the island. Fire kits, building materials, food, weapons, I'm talking *everything.*"

My lips twitch. "Did Ren pose this thought experiment to you?"

"Yes," he says glumly.

I twist my head to peer at him. "You stupid bastard. Did you pick the supplies boat instead of her?"

"Like you wouldn't," he accuses.

Laughter rumbles out of my chest.

"It's a matter of life and death, Coop. I need food and shelter! Sure, it'd be great to have Ren there, but we'll die in five seconds flat if we don't have the tools to live. And anyway, with all the stuff at my disposal, I can build a raft and make my way home to her. It's common sense."

"Ren really dumped you because of this?"

"What? No. That's insane. She dumped me because I was an hour late to her sister's birthday dinner. I was out with Tate telling him about her dumb thought experiment and lost track of time."

I stare at him. How are these my friends?

On the other hand, I'm getting a free tattoo out of him, and his nonsense did succeed in helping me forget about Mackenzie.

Goodbye, Cooper.

Or not.

CHAPTER SEVENTEEN

MACKENZIE

I've been on my best behavior. I haven't spoken to Cooper in a couple weeks. Kept my distance from the boardwalk. I figured if I were to accidentally bump into him, it'd be there, so best to remove all temptation. My restraint hasn't stopped the dreams, though. Or the forbidden memories that flood my mind whenever I'm in class.

I catch myself reliving our first kiss during English Lit.

Remembering the way his hands held me firm against his front door during Biology.

In European History, I'm thinking about his hard chest beneath my palms, and suddenly I'm flushed and breathing heavy, wondering if everyone notices.

On the bright side, Preston and I are rock solid, and I finally made a Garnet friend who isn't Bonnie. Her name is Kate, and although she happens to be Melissa's younger sister, the two are not at all alike. Kate's hilarious, sarcastic, and hates sailing—all pluses in my book. We met at a Kappa Nu dinner that Preston urged me to attend because he thinks I should be making more of an effort to connect with Melissa and Chrissy and their sorority friends. Instead, I spent half the night in the corner with Kate debating the artistic merit of *The Bachelor*.

So when she texts on a Thursday night asking if I want to grab drinks with her and some friends in town, I'm totally down. It means risking running into Cooper, but I can't decline my first invite from someone other than Bonnie.

"You wanna come with us?" I ask my roommate as I braid my hair in our shared bathroom.

Bonnie's head appears in the mirror behind me. "I would, but I'm seein' Todd tonight."

I grin at her reflection. "Again? Looks like things are getting serious between you two . . ." I swear she's gone out with the sandwich shop guy a lot lately. So much for her bad boy fetish. I met Todd once and there was neither a piercing nor tattoo in sight.

"Serious? Pfft!" She waves her hand. "He's one of three on my rotation, Mac. Tomorrow night I'm seein' Harry, and Saturday it's dinner with that boy I was telling you about—Jason? The one who looks like Edward?"

"Edward?" I echo blankly.

"From *Twilight*?" She shivers happily. "Oooh, he is *sooo* handsome I wouldn't even care if he ended up being an actual vampire. How wild is that? And blood totally makes me squeamish."

I snort. "I'm pretty sure he's not a vampire." Though I still haven't ruled out the possibility of Bonnie being a witch.

I wish her luck on her date, then leave the dorm and head for the parking lot, where my Uber awaits me. I'm meeting Kate and her friends at the Rip Tide. As the car approaches the beachfront venue, my mind flashes back to the last time I came here, and my heartbeat accelerates. That was the night I met Cooper. The night Bonnie hooked up with his twin while Cooper and I stayed up all night, talking about everything and nothing.

Enough, a stern voice orders. *Forget about him.*

I really need to do that. I'm with Preston. Thinking about Cooper isn't good for my relationship.

I thank the driver and slide out of the car. As I rearrange my side braid, my gaze flicks toward the crumbling hotel I'd first seen over a month ago. It's still standing. Still vacant, from the looks of it. A weird sensation flutters in my belly as I stare at the sprawling hotel, its weathered, white façade gleaming from the glow of a lone streetlight.

It takes surprising effort to tear my gaze away. Great. First my brain gets hung up on Cooper, now it's obsessing over an abandoned hotel? I've got issues.

Inside the bar, I find Kate at a table at the side of the stage. She's with three other girls, two of whom I don't recognize. The third is Melissa. I stifle a sigh, because I hadn't realized Melissa was coming too. I don't have anything against her, but her gossipy nature puts me on guard.

"Hey girl," Kate greets me.

Like her sister, she has pale hair and big, gray eyes, but their styles are completely different. Kate's wearing a tiny blue dress that barely covers her thighs, flip-flops, and chunky bangles on both wrists. Meanwhile, Melissa's knee-length pink dress is buttoned all the way up to the neck, and there are two massive diamonds sparkling in her earlobes.

"Hey." I direct an awkward smile across the table. "Hey, Melissa."

Kate introduces me to her two friends, Alisha and Sutton. We decide to order daiquiris at Melissa's insistence, although when Kate and I head to the bar to place our order, she winks and gets us two vodka shots as well.

"Don't tell my sister," she says, and we sling them back with conspiratorial grins.

Back at the table, the first round of daiquiris is gone in the blink of an eye, so we quickly order more. By the third round, our conversation topics devolve from our classes and future plans to embarrassing stories and men. Kate tells us about the TA who has a massive crush on her and shows his love by stapling a dried flower on the last page of every paper she submits.

I burst out laughing. "No! He doesn't."

"Oh, he does. And if you think the eternal love flame he keeps burning earns me better grades, you're wrong. He gave me a C minus on my last essay." She looks outraged. "Screw your perfectly pressed petunia petals, Christopher. Give me the A."

Alisha beats Kate's story with one about a professor who accidentally emailed her an impassioned love letter that was supposed to go to his estranged wife.

"Her name was Alice so I guess he auto-filled the email with 'Al' and clicked my name instead." She twirls her daiquiri straw as she giggles. "The email was a list of all the reasons she shouldn't go through with their divorce. Basically stating his case of why he's amazing."

Melissa's jaw drops. "Oh my God. What were the reasons?"

"I don't remember them all, but the first one was . . . wait for it . . ." Alisha pauses for dramatic effect. "'Adequate lover.'"

Our entire table hoots with laughter.

"Adequate?" Kate says through giggles. "Oh, that poor wife."

I slurp down the rest of my drink. It occurs to me I haven't had a proper girls' night since high school, triggering the realization that I've been terrible at keeping in touch with my Spencer Hill friends. Granted, they haven't reached out either, so I guess that says a lot about our friendship. I vow to do a better job at nurturing these college friendships.

Our conversation devolves even further, as Sutton suggests we play a game. Well, not so much a game as "let's rate the hotness of every single guy who walks past our table."

"Oooh, how about him?" Alisha asks in a loud whisper.

We all examine a long-haired surfer dude in a red tank top and orange board shorts. "Two out of ten for fashion sense," Melissa says, lifting her nose. "Red and orange? Come on. Have some respect for yourself, sir."

I can't help but snicker. Drunk Melissa is still snooty, but she's also cattier, which I'm loving.

"Butt? Nine out of ten," Kate decides. "It's a great butt."

"I bet I could bounce a quarter off that thing," Alisha agrees.

Yes, we're objectifying these boys. Intoxicated girls have neither shame nor scruples.

"Seven overall," Sutton says.

"Three," Melissa corrects, jutting her chin. "I can't get past the red/orange combo. I just can't."

"Um, guys?" hisses Alisha, who leans forward eagerly. "Six o'clock, far end of the bar—I just found a ten across the board."

We all turn toward the bar. I nearly choke on my tongue.

Alisha's perfect ten is Cooper Hartley.

Kate whistles softly. "Oh yeah. I like."

"I *love*," Alisha corrects, her face taking on a dreamy glow.

I don't blame her. Cooper looks damn good tonight. He's wearing that threadbare T-shirt I like, the one with the Billabong logo that stretches across his broad shoulders and emphasizes his defined chest. Add to that the messy dark hair, the two full-sleeve tattoos, the cargo pants hugging an ass even tauter than the surfer's, and you've got one fine specimen of a man.

As if sensing the female attention, Cooper's head jerks sharply. A second later, he's looking at our table. Heat floods my cheeks when my gaze locks with his. Shit. Am I blushing? I hope I'm not blushing.

His eyes narrow at the sight of me. Lips flatten for a second before twisting in a slight smirk.

Beside me, Alisha gasps. "He's staring at you," she accuses me. "Do you know him?"

"I . . . uh . . ." My mind races in an attempt to come up with a suitable reason why a hot townie might be making prolonged eye contact with me.

"Mackenzie?" Melissa's shrewd gaze burns a hole in the side of my face. "Do you know that guy?"

My throat is completely dry. I wrestle my eyes off Cooper and reach for my drink. Taking a sip provides me with a few extra seconds to panic-think of an excuse. Melissa isn't only nosy—she's smart. If I admit to knowing Cooper, even in a just-friends capacity, it'll absolutely trigger her gossip setting. She'll ask more questions, and if even one of my answers doesn't ring true for her, she might tell Benji, who'll in turn tell Preston, who literally just forgave me for kissing another guy.

So, no. There's no way I can fess up to knowing Cooper in any capacity.

"Evan," I blurt out.

Melissa frowns. "What?"

I set down my plastic daiquiri cup. Relief and satisfaction course through me at my stroke of genius. "That's Evan Hartley. My roommate hooked up with him at the beginning of the semester."

She relaxes slightly, her manicured fingers toying with the diamond in her ear. "Really? Little Bonnie tapped that?"

"Oh yeah." I muster up a laugh and hope nobody hears the tension in it. "She totally abandoned me for a moonlight beach hookup with the guy."

Perfect. Now if Melissa tries to fact-check me, Bonnie can easily corroborate. As long as Cooper stays across the room and doesn't—

Walk over to us.

Son of a bitch, he's walking over here.

My heart beats faster than the canned dance music pouring from the speakers. What is he doing? I told him I couldn't see him anymore. I made it clear, damn it. He can't just come up to my table like nothing happened and—

"Evan!" I exclaim in a too-loud voice with a too-bright smile.

Cooper's gait stutters for a second. Then his long legs resume their easy stride until he's standing in front of me. He shoves his hands in his pockets, donning a lazy pose as he drawls, "Mackenzie."

"Evan, hey. How's it going?" I ask, all friendly and laidback as if we hadn't made out, as if I'd never felt the prominent ridge of his erection pulsing against my belly. "I haven't seen you since that night you stole my roommate away and seduced her."

Kate snickers.

I remain focused on Cooper, hoping my eyes are conveying everything I can't say out loud. *Play along. Please. I can't have these girls gossiping about us and risk it getting back to Pres. Please play along.*

The fact that I'm not acknowledging his true identity sparks guilt in me, but it doesn't compare to how awful I felt about cheating on Preston. Kissing Cooper had been a mistake. But I came clean to my boyfriend, my conscience is clear, and now I just want to move on. Which won't be possible if Melissa decides there's gossip potential here. So I silently implore Cooper, who isn't giving me an inch.

His smirk deepens, dark eyes glittering with something I can't decipher.

By the time he finally speaks, I'm a bundle of nerves and sweating through my tank top.

"I didn't hear Bonnie complaining that night," he says with a wink.

I almost faint with relief. Hopefully no one notices my hand shaking as I reach for my drink. "Well, she's not the one who had to Uber back to campus all alone at two in the morning." I take a hasty sip before making the introductions. "Alisha, Sutton, Kate, Melissa. Guys, this is Evan."

It's funny, I never realized how different Cooper and his twin are until this very moment, when Cooper transforms into Evan. His normally intense, brooding eyes gleam mischievously. His tongue gives his bottom lip a teasing swipe before he flashes a cocky grin at my friends.

"So." Even his voice sounds different now. Lighter, flirtier. "Which one of Mackenzie's friends will I be seducing tonight?"

You'd think a line that sleazy would evoke groans. Instead, the girls all but swoon over it. Even Melissa is affected. Her face turns pink, lips parting slightly.

I don't blame them. This guy is sex personified. Doesn't matter if he's being his broody self or pretending to be his manwhore brother, the sexual energy pours off him in waves.

"Keep it in your pants, *Evan*." My tone is meant to be teasing but sounds like a warning.

His grin widens.

"Alright." Sutton releases an exaggerated sigh and hops off her stool. "I guess I'll take one for the team." Her hazy expression tells me she's already having sex with Cooper in her mind. "How 'bout a dance first, and then we can discuss that seduction offer?"

There's not a single muscle in my body that isn't coiled tight. My fingers curl around my cup, squeezing hard. I'm worried I might crush it. It's a damn good thing it's made of plastic, otherwise there'd be glass shards everywhere.

Cooper's mocking eyes don't miss my response. He's watching me even as he answers Sutton. "A dance sounds great. Lead the way, babe."

Three seconds later, he's wrapped up with Sutton on the dance floor in front of the stage. Her arms loop around his neck, her slender frame pressed against his strong one. Cooper's hands skim the back of her lacy camisole, one palm trailing lower, resting right above the curve of her ass. His other hand glides up her spine and tangles in her dark ponytail before cupping the back of her neck.

Bitter rage coats my throat. I reach for my daiquiri hoping to get rid of the vile taste, only to find my cup is empty.

"Ugh, I can't believe her," Alisha is griping.

Her? I can't believe *him*. What is he doing, dirty dancing with a complete stranger?

Beside me, Kate pats Alisha's arm. "I'm sorry, hon. Next time you gotta be quicker."

"Lord, he is *hot*," Melissa remarks, her attention glued to Cooper and Sutton. "If I wasn't with Benji, I would totally consider slumming it with a townie for the night."

I lift a brow. "I thought extracurricular activities were perfectly acceptable?"

She laughs. "Um, no. Not for us, sweetie. At least not until we've got the *I Do*s locked down. Then you can screw the pool boys and gardeners to your heart's content."

Kate rolls her eyes at her older sister. "You're one classy bitch, Mel."

Melissa shrugs. "What? That's the way it's done."

I tune them out, distracted by the vertical sex display happening ten feet from our table. Sutton is now on her tiptoes, whispering in Cooper's ear.

He chuckles, and I stiffen. What are they giggling about over there?

And he *really* needs to remove his hands from her ass. Like, right now. He's laying it on thick for my expense, and I am not having it. I bite the inside of my cheek. Hard.

"I totally should've staked my claim the second he walked up to us," Alisha moans. She's also obsessively watching the dance floor.

"Early bird gets the dick," Kate says solemnly.

"Ugh. Whatever." Alisha slams her cup on the table and pouts. "She's all talk anyway. Sutton doesn't do casual sex. She's not going to fall into bed with some guy she doesn't even—" Alisha stops abruptly, her jaw dropping.

I follow her gaze just in time to see Cooper and Sutton leaving the bar together.

CHAPTER EIGHTEEN

MACKENZIE

The next morning, my media culture class is canceled. The professor sends a mass email that defies the laws of oversharing, informing us that his bowels had revolted against the meatloaf his wife prepared for dinner last night.

I feel your pain, bud. My stomach's been in knots since I saw Cooper leave the Rip Tide with his arm slung around Sutton.

Did they have sex? I feel queasy at the thought. And a little angry. How could he fall into bed with some chick he'd known for 2.5 seconds? Or maybe they didn't sleep together. Maybe she just blew him.

A red mist overtakes my field of vision at the thought of Sutton going down on Cooper. I want to rip his dick off for letting her touch it.

Hmm. Okay.

Maybe I'm more than a "little" angry.

But I'm not allowed to feel that way. Cooper is not my boyfriend. Preston is. I'm not allowed to have an opinion about who Cooper hooks up with, and I certainly shouldn't be reaching for my phone right now and pulling up our chat thread and—

Me: *You didn't have to do that on my account. And by "do that," I mean Sutton.*

Damn it. What is wrong with me? I regret sending the text the moment it appears on the screen. I frantically tap at the screen in search of an unsend option, but that's not how text messages work.

And now Cooper is typing a response.

Heart beating wildly, I sit up in bed and inwardly curse myself for my lack of self-control.

> Cooper: *Oh we're talking again?*
> Me: *No. We're not.*
> Cooper: *Cool. Later.*

I stare at my phone in frustration. I'm more frustrated with myself than with him, though. I told him we couldn't be friends. I literally said, "Goodbye, Cooper." Last night I called him Evan and all but threw him at my single friends so that Melissa wouldn't suspect anything and tell Benji. This is on me. Of course Cooper doesn't want to talk to me.

And yet my stupid fingers have a mind of their own.

> Me: *I'm just saying. Thanks for playing along when I called you Evan, but you didn't have to go full-on method acting.*
> Cooper: *Hey princess? How about you worry more about your boyfriend's dick and less about mine?*

I want to scream. I wish I'd never met Cooper Hartley. Then I wouldn't be feeling this way. All twisted up inside. Not to mention the jealousy eating at my throat like battery acid thanks to his reply. Is he saying his dick *was* a factor last night, then?

I'm three seconds away from asking Kate for Sutton's number so I can confirm *exactly* what happened last night, when common sense settles in. If my goal last night was to ensure Melissa wouldn't get suspicious, going batshit crazy on Sutton won't help the cause.

Utilizing every iota of willpower I possess, I shove my phone aside and grab my laptop. No class means more time for work, which is always a great distraction.

I check my email, but there's nothing pressing that needs to be addressed. The matter with Tad and his micropenis has blown over, thank God. And my mods and ad managers are reporting that September was our best month yet in term of revenue. It's the kind of news any business owner should be thrilled to hear, and don't get me wrong, I *am* thrilled. But as I spend the next couple hours doing basic business housekeeping, the frustration returns, rising in my throat. I have the sudden urge to get off campus for a walk. Sick of the same old scenery. Sick of my obsessive thoughts about Cooper.

Ten minutes later, I'm in a cab heading for Avalon Bay. I need the fresh air, the sunshine. The car drops me off near the pier, and I walk toward the boardwalk, shoving my hands in the pockets of my cutoff shorts. I can't believe how balmy the temperature is for October, but I'm not complaining. The hot breeze feels like heaven against my face.

When my feet carry me all the way to the hotel, I suddenly realize what motivated me to come here today. The same thrill of possibility surges through my blood upon finding the hotel still sitting empty. Waiting.

It's crazy, but as I stare at the derelict building, my body starts humming. Even my fingers are itching, like a metaphorical need to get my hands moving. Is this the challenge I'd been looking for? This condemned hotel I can't quit fantasizing about?

It's not even for sale, I remind myself. And yet that doesn't seem to matter. The humming refuses to subside.

An idea forms in my mind as I make my way back through town, where I stop at a café for a drink. When the woman behind the counter hands me my juice spritzer, I hesitate for a moment. Avalon Bay is a small town. If we're going by the small towns I've seen on

TV shows like *Gilmore Girls*, that means everyone knows everything about everyone and everything.

So I take a wild guess and ask, "What do you know about the old abandoned hotel on the boardwalk? The Beacon? Any idea why the owner hasn't done anything with it?"

"Ask her yourself."

I blink. "Sorry, what?"

She nods toward a table by the window. "That's the owner."

I follow her gaze and spot an elderly woman wearing a wide-brim hat and huge black sunglasses that obscure most of her face. She's dressed more like a beachcomber than a hotelier.

What are the odds? The humming intensifies, until my entire body feels wired with a live current. This has to mean something.

Carrying my drink, I slowly approach the table by the window. "Excuse me, I'm sorry to bother you. I wondered if I might talk to you about your hotel. May I sit down?"

The woman doesn't look up from her coffee cake and cup of tea. "We're closed."

"Yes, I know." I take a breath. "I hoped I might change that."

She picks at her cake with brittle fingers. Pulls tiny crumbs, placing them slowly, gently, in her mouth.

"Ma'am? Your hotel. Can I ask you a few questions?"

"We're closed."

I can't tell if she's putting me on, or not all there. I don't want to be rude or upset her, so I try one last time.

"I want to buy your hotel. Is that something that would interest you?"

Finally, she lifts her head to look at me. I can't see her eyes because of the sunglasses, but the thoughtful purse of her lips confirms I've captured her interest. She takes a long sip of her tea. Then, setting down the cup, she pushes out a chair for me with her foot.

I sit, hoping I don't appear too eager. "My name is Mackenzie.

Cabot. I'm a student at Garnet College, but I'm sort of an entrepreneur too. I'm really interested in discussing your hotel."

"Lydia Tanner." After a long beat, she removes her sunglasses and places them on the tabletop. A pair of surprisingly shrewd eyes laser into mine. "What do you want to know?"

"Everything," I answer with a smile.

For more than an hour, we discuss the hotel's history. How she built it with her husband after the war. How it was practically demolished and rebuilt three times since then, before her husband died two years ago. Then after the last storm, she was too old and too tired to rebuild again. Her heart wasn't in it, and her kids weren't interested in salvaging the property.

"I've had offers," she tells me, her voice sure and steady. Not at all the timid old lady she might appear. "Some generous. Some not. Developers who want to tear it down and build some hideous high-rise in its place. People have been trying to tear down the boardwalk for years, turn this place into Miami or something. All concrete and shiny glass."

Her derisive sniff reveals exactly how she feels about all this. "This town will never be like Miami. It has too much charm," I assure her.

"The developers don't care about charm. They only see dollar signs." Lydia picks up her teacup. "My only terms are that whoever buys my hotel has to preserve the intent. Maintain the character. I want to move closer to my grandkids, spend whatever time I have left with my family." She sighs. "But I simply can't bear to leave without knowing The Beacon is well cared for."

"I can make you that promise," I say honestly. "It's the charm of the place that made me fall in love with it. I can commit to restoring everything as close to original as possible. Update the wiring and plumbing. Reinforce the bones. Make sure it survives another fifty years."

Lydia examines me, as if gauging whether to take me seriously or write me off as a silly college girl who's wasting her time.

Several seconds tick by before she gives a slow nod. "Well, then, young lady, write down a number."

A number? I know nothing about the hotel real estate market, so I'm completely flying by the seat of my pants as I type a figure into the Notes app on my phone. It's my best estimation of how much a property like this might cost, but also not enough to clean out my entire business account.

I slide the phone over. Lydia studies the screen, one eyebrow jerking up as if she's surprised I have real money to offer.

For the next ten minutes, we go back and forth. It takes some haggling on my part. And I might have been suckered into over-paying by pictures of her grandkids, but eventually we come to a deal.

Just like that, I'm about to be the proud owner of my very own boardwalk hotel.

I feel high after closing my first successful business deal, giddy ex-citement coursing through my veins. *Such* a rush. At the same time, it's insane. I'm twenty years old and I just bought a *hotel*. Despite how crazy it sounds, it feels so right. My mind immediately races with next steps. In an instant I see my future, my empire growing. I promised my parents I would focus on school, and I still plan to— I'll just be focusing on my new role as hotel owner at the same time. I can juggle both.

Maybe.

Hopefully.

Even after Lydia and I shake on it and I call my lawyer to start the paperwork, it doesn't feel real until I coax Preston to see the property the next day.

Rather than share in my excitement, however, he sticks a knife straight through my enthusiasm.

"What's this?" He scowls at the gutted hotel with its crumbling walls and water-damaged furnishings spilling out.

"My new hotel."

Eyes narrowed, Preston slants his head at me. As if to say, *Explain yourself.*

"I know it isn't much now. You have to imagine it after a complete renovation." I almost cringe at the note of desperation I hear in my voice. "I'm going to restore it entirely. Totally vintage. Postwar luxury all the way. Turn this place into a five-star resort."

"You're not serious." His expression falls flat. Mouth presses into a hard line. Not exactly the reception I'd hoped for.

"Okay, I get that I don't know anything about owning a hotel, but I'll learn. I didn't know anything about building a website or running a business either. But that didn't stop me before, right? Maybe I'll change majors to hospitality or something."

He doesn't answer.

Each second of silence slowly sucks away more of my joy.

"Preston. What's wrong?" I ask weakly.

He shakes his head, tosses up his hands. "I'm really at a loss here, Mackenzie. This has got to be the most irresponsible, immature thing you've ever done."

"What?"

"You heard me."

He sounds like my dad, which I don't appreciate in the least. Granted, I didn't put a lot of thought into this venture before pulling the trigger—I tend to act more on gut instinct. Still, I thought he'd be a little happy for me.

"I'm very disappointed in you, frankly. I thought after our talk—after your little mistake—we were on the same page. About the plan. Our future."

"Preston, that's not fair." Throwing the kiss back in my face is a low blow. One has nothing to do with the other.

He ignores me, finishing with, "That plan doesn't include a hotel." His lips twist into a disapproving frown.

"You don't see the potential here? At all?" I ask unhappily.

"Potential? Look at this place. It's a dump. A teardown at best. Maybe you can get something out of the land, but a renovation? You're out of your mind. You don't know the first thing about any of this. Did you even think for two seconds before leveraging your trust fund for this stupid distraction?"

Indignation shoots through me. "I'm more capable than you think. And I didn't use my trust fund. I have the cash on hand, if you must know."

"How?" he demands.

I jut my chin. "From my websites."

Pres looks startled. "Your silly little tech thing?"

Now I'm pissed. I can feel the heat pouring out of my face as my nails dig into my palms. "Yes, my silly little tech thing," I echo bitterly.

I've never elaborated on how much money my sites have generated, and he has never seemed particularly interested beyond poking fun at them. I thought it was a guy thing. Harmless teasing. Sometimes he'd come over when I was working on *BoyfriendFails* and tell me how cute I looked with my face all furrowed in concentration. He'd grin and call me his "sexy tycoon." I thought he was proud of me, proud of all the work I was putting into the venture.

It isn't until this very moment that I realize he wasn't smiling out of pride. He wasn't seeing me as a "tycoon."

He was laughing at me.

"That was supposed to be a hobby," he says flatly. "If I'd known you were earning an income from it, I would have—"

"You would have what?" I challenge. "Forced me to stop?"

"Guided you in the right direction," he corrects, and his patronizing tone makes my blood boil. "We've spoken about this before. Many times. We'd go to college together. You'd have whatever hobbies you wanted during school. I'd graduate first, take over at my dad's bank. You'd graduate, join the boards of your mom's foundations." Preston shakes his head at me. "You agreed I'd be the breadwinner in the relationship, while you focused on charity work and raising our family."

My jaw falls open. Oh my God. Whenever he'd said stuff like that, he'd used a teasing voice. Made it sound like a joke.

He was actually being *serious*?

"You're going to back out of the deal." The finality with which he issues the order shakes something loose inside me. "You're lucky I'm here to stop you before your parents find out. I don't know what's gotten into you lately, Mackenzie, but you need to get ahold of yourself."

I stare at him. Stunned. I never imagined he would hate this idea with such ferocity. At the very, *very* least, I thought he would be supportive of my decision. The fact that he isn't leaves me shaken.

If I could misjudge him on this to such an extent, what else have I been wrong about?

CHAPTER NINETEEN

COOPER

"We're out of booze."

I roll my eyes at Evan, who's sprawled on the living room couch with one arm flung over the edge. The coffee table I built last weekend is already stained with beer and covered with cigarette butts. Someone must've knocked over the overflowing ashtray last night, during another one of Evan's impromptu parties.

"It's noon on Sunday," I tell my brother. "You don't need booze. Chug some water, for fuck's sake."

"I'm not saying I want a drink right now. But someone needs to make a beer run. We're hosting poker night tomorrow."

By "someone," he clearly means me, because he promptly closes his eyes and says, "Take Daisy with you. She likes riding in the truck."

I leave Evan to his beauty sleep and whistle for the dog. I don't normally let my brother order me around, but truth is, I'm feeling stir crazy.

I didn't join in on last night's drunken festivities. Instead, I spent most of the night in my workshop, went to sleep before midnight, and was abruptly awakened at seven a.m. by a disturbing, X-rated dream about Mackenzie. I was in bed with her, on top of her, thrusting deep while she moaned against my lips. Then I lifted my head and Mac's face transformed into that chick Sutton's face, which jolted me right out of slumber.

Swear to God, this girl has wreaked havoc on my brain. Doesn't matter if I'm asleep or awake—thoughts of Mackenzie Cabot poison my consciousness and drum up a whole slew of emotions I'd rather not feel.

Anger, because she'd chosen Kincaid over me.

Frustration, because I know there was something real between us.

Guilt, because my original intentions had been shadier than shady.

And for the past couple days? Disgust. Because, in order to divert her friends' suspicions that we might know each other, she forced me to pretend to be my twin brother—and then had the nerve to bitch about me hooking up with another girl. Not that Sutton and I even hooked up. We went for a walk and then I put her in a cab. But still. Mackenzie had no right to be pissed. She's the one who kissed the hell outta me and then bid me fucking adieu.

"Come on," I mutter to Daisy. "Let's go buy some beer for your boyfriend."

When she sees me reaching for her leash, the golden retriever dances happily at my feet. We head out to my truck, and I open the passenger side door so Daisy can jump up. She only recently learned how to do that. Before, she'd been too little, but now her legs are in that gangly teenager stage, giving her enough leverage to leap higher. She's growing so damn fast.

"Too bad Mac can't see you," I muse to the dog, whose curious, excited gaze is glued out the window. Each time the wind tickles her nose, she releases a high-pitched yip. She derives joy from the simplest pleasures.

In town, I grab a few cases of beer, along with a bottle of tequila and some snacks. As I stow my purchases in the cab, someone calls my name.

I turn to see Tate striding down the sidewalk toward me. He's holding aviator sunglasses in one hand, and his keys and phone in the other.

"Hey," I greet him. "How's it going?"

"Good. I'm meeting Wyatt at Sharkey's for lunch if you want to tag along."

"Yeah, I'm in." The last thing I feel like doing right now is going home and cleaning up the mess Evan left. "Lemme grab Daisy."

"Oh, hell yes," Tate says when he notices the dog's head poking out the passenger window. "Bring the chick magnet."

Most of the bars and restaurants in the Bay are dog friendly—particularly Sharkey's, where the staff brings out water bowls and treats for canine guests. Once Tate and I climb the rickety wood staircase up to the second floor of the bar, Daisy is treated like the queen she thinks she is.

"Oh my goodness!" the waitress up front exclaims, pure delight in her eyes. "Look at this cutie! What's her name?"

"Daisy," Tate answers for me, then takes the leash from my hand as if to claim ownership of the puppy. "And you are?"

"Jessica," chirps the waitress. Now she's all starry-eyed, because she notices Tate's golden-boy looks. Dude has the infallible ability to dazzle every woman he meets.

This isn't to say I don't attract my fair share of attention. It's just a different kind of attention.

When women look at Tate, they're struck with romantic notions of weddings and babies.

With me, they see raw, dirty sex. Joke's on them, though. Tate is the biggest slut in the Bay. Jessica must be new in town, otherwise she'd be well aware of this fact.

"Let me show you to your table," Jessica says, and then she, Tate, and my dog saunter off.

With a grin, I trail after them, silently betting that Tate will have secured her number before we even pick up our menus.

I lose. He doesn't get it until she delivers our waters.

"Good job, partner," Tate tells Daisy, who's sitting at his feet and gazing up at him adoringly.

Wyatt arrives about ten minutes later. Since Ren isn't with him, I assume they're still broken up.

"No Ren?" Tate wrinkles his forehead. "She hasn't taken you back yet?"

"Nope." After greeting Daisy with a pat on the head, Wyatt plops himself on the stool across from me and grabs a menu. Then he sets it down without reading it. "Who am I kidding? We all know I'm getting the fish sandwich."

"What's taking Ren so long to forgive you?" Tate asks, grinning. "Your epic reunions usually happen fairly fast."

"She's dragging it out this time," Wyatt complains. "She went out with some meathead from her gym last night and sent me a selfie of them watching *The Bachelorette* together because she knew it'd piss me off."

I raise an eyebrow. "Why would that piss you off?"

"Because it's our favorite show, dickhead. She's goddamn TV-cheating on me with a guy who wears mesh tank tops."

Tate snickers. "Are you more upset about the fact that Ren's watching a dumb reality show without you, or that she might be banging a gym bro?"

Wyatt waves his hand. "She's not banging him. It's just revenge dating. Like when I went out with that chick who works at the surf school after Ren threw out all my band shirts without asking."

"Didn't you end up screwing the surf school chick?" Tate says in confusion.

Wyatt stares at him. "That was you, dumbass."

After a few seconds of pensive recollection, Tate nods decisively. "Oh yeah. You're right." He grins. "That chick was wild. She convinced me to try Viagra for the first time. Long night."

Laughter sputters from my throat.

"You took Viagra without me, bro?" Wyatt accuses.

I laugh even harder. "Since when is it a team activity?" I howl at Wyatt.

Jessica returns to take our food orders and proceeds to flirt shamelessly with Tate. "Does this cutie like walks?"

He winks. "This cutie *loves* walks."

"I meant the dog."

"So did I," he says innocently.

"I'm off in about an hour. Why don't you and Daisy meet me on the beach once you're done eating and I clock out?"

Before I can remind Tate that Daisy isn't his dog, he flashes his dimples at the waitress and says, "It's a date."

As Jessica saunters off, I roll my eyes. "Are you seriously using my puppy to get laid?"

"Of course. I told you, puppies are chick magnets." He shoves a strand of hair off his forehead. "Just let me borrow her for a few hours, dude. You know I'm good with dogs. I've got three at home."

"Fine. But I'm not hanging around town on your account. Drop her off at my place later. Her dinnertime's at five. Don't be late, asshole."

Tate grins. "Yes, Dad."

"You think if I had Daisy with me when I go to see Ren, I'd have a better shot at winning her back?" Wyatt asks thoughtfully.

"Definitely," Tate says.

Wyatt's head swivels toward me. "Can I borrow her tomorrow?"

My friends are idiots.

Then again, so am I. Because when my phone buzzes and Mac's name flashes on the screen, I don't do the smart thing and ignore the call.

I answer it.

CHAPTER TWENTY

MACKENZIE

The summer after I graduated high school, I traveled alone in Europe. A present from my parents. I had just walked back to the Colosseum from Vatican City when, in a sort of burst of manic impulsiveness, I marched right past my hotel to the train station. I didn't know where I was headed. I simply bought a first-class ticket on the next train, which happened to be going to Florence. From there, Bologna. Milan. Then, through Switzerland, France, and Spain. Two days after leaving Italy, I called my hotel to have them send my luggage to Barcelona.

To this day, I don't know what possessed me. A sudden, urgent need to break free, to get lost. To disrupt the order of my life and prove to myself I was alive and in control of my own destiny. Which is to say I don't remember deciding to call Cooper, only that one day after Preston shot down my hotel fantasy, two weeks since I'd kissed Cooper and told him never to contact me again, and fifteen minutes after we hang up, he's standing beside me on the boardwalk staring at the dilapidated exterior of The Beacon Hotel.

"You just . . . bought it?" Bemused, Cooper rakes a hand through his dark hair.

I'm momentarily distracted by his tanned forearm, his defined biceps. He's wearing a black T-shirt. Jeans that hang low on his hips.

It feels like I'm seeing him for the first time all over again. I hadn't forgotten what the sight of him does to me, but it's more potent now that my tolerance has waned. My heart beats faster than usual, my palms are damper, my mouth drier.

"Well, there's paperwork and due diligence. But if that goes well . . ."

I'm more nervous now than when I made the offer to Lydia. Than when I showed Preston. For some reason, I need Cooper to be happy for me, and I didn't realize how much until this moment.

"Can we look around?"

He gives nothing away. Not boredom or disapproval. Not excitement either. We barely said hello and didn't mention a word about our kisses or our fight. Just *Hey, so, um, I'm buying a hotel. What do you think?* I have no idea why he even showed up to meet me here.

"Sure," I say. "The inspector said the ground level is stable. We shouldn't go upstairs, though."

Together we tour the property, stepping over storm-tossed furniture and moldy carpets. Some interior rooms are in nearly perfect condition, while beach-view rooms are little more than empty carcasses exposed to the elements, where the walls have collapsed and storm surges long ago sucked everything out to sea. The kitchen looks like it could be up and running tomorrow. The ballroom, more like a setting of a ghost ship horror movie. Outside, the front of the hotel facing the street belies the damage inside, still perfectly intact except for missing roof shingles and overgrown foliage.

"What are your plans for it?" he asks as we peek behind the front desk. An old-fashioned guest book, with the words *The Beacon Hotel* embossed on its cover with gold lettering, is still tucked on a shelf with the wall of room keys. Some scattered, others still on their hooks.

"The previous owner had one demand: Don't tear it down and put up an ugly high-rise."

"I came here all the time as a kid. Evan and I would use the pool, hang out in the beach cabanas until we were chased out. Steph worked here a few summers during high school. I remember all the old hardwood, the brass fixtures."

"I want to entirely restore it," I tell him. "Salvage as much as possible. Source vintage antiques for the rest of it."

He lets out a low whistle. "It'd be expensive. We're talking about cherry furniture that'll have to be custom replicated. Handmade light fixtures. There are stone floor tiles and countertops in here they don't even make anymore except in small batches."

I nod. "And I already know the electrical is out of code. All the drywall has to come out."

"But I see it." He wanders through the lobby toward the grand staircase, where he runs his hand over the intricately carved bannister. "With the right touch, and enough money, it's got potential."

"Really?"

"Oh yeah. Teeming with potential."

"I know this sounds dumb," I say, taking a seat at the foot of the stairs, "but when I first set eyes on this place, I had this image in my head. Guests sitting on the veranda in rocking chairs, sipping wine, and watching the tide roll in. I saw it so clearly."

"It's not dumb." Cooper sits beside me.

I feel no animosity from him, as if we're almost friends again. Except for the same magnetic tug begging me to run my fingers through his hair.

"When I put a salvaged piece of wood on my bench, I don't have a plan for what it'll be. I just sit with it. Wait for it to express itself. Then it practically builds itself in my mind, and I'm following along."

I bite my lip. "My parents aren't going to be happy about this."

Lately it doesn't take much to set my father off. Most of it is work stress, but it seems as if he's engaged in constant battle about one thing or another. Probably where I get my combative side. Thing is, when the battles end badly, his frustration tends to manifest in being loudly disappointed in me.

"Who the hell cares?" Cooper scoffs.

"Yeah, easy for you to say."

"I mean it. Since when do you care about what anyone else has to say?"

"You don't understand how hard it is to get out from under their thumb. They run practically every part of my life."

"Because you let them."

"No, but—"

"Look. In the time I've known you, you've mostly been a stubborn, opinionated pain in the ass."

I laugh, admitting to myself that most of our conversations have devolved into stalemate arguments. "It's not my fault you're always wrong."

"Watch it, Cabot," he says with a playfully threatening glare. "Seriously, though. You've got your shit together better than most people I know. To hell with your parents approving. Be your own person."

"You don't know them."

"I don't have to know them. I know you." He turns to face me fully, leveling me with serious eyes. "Mac, you are a force to be reckoned with. You don't take shit, you take names. Don't forget that."

Damn it. Fucking damn it.

"Why do you have to do that?" I mutter, getting to my feet. I can't control my muscles. I have to move, find some air.

"Do what?" He gets up, following me as I pace the room.

"Be so . . ." I gesture incoherently in his direction. "Like that."

"You've lost me."

It's easier when he's being a dick. Flirting, coming on strong. Arguing with me and calling me princess. It's easier to dismiss him as just another hot guy with too much attitude, someone not to be taken seriously. Then he's all sweet and kind and gets my head messed up. Drags my heart into it, kicking and screaming.

"Don't be nice to me," I blurt out in frustration. "It's confusing."

"Yeah, well, I was a little confused when you were scraping your nails down my back, but hey, I went with it."

"Good," I say, spinning to point at him. "Do that. That I can work with. I handle you better when you're a prick."

"So that's what it is? You're afraid to give a damn because then you can't keep lying to yourself about us?"

"There is no us," I shoot back. "We kissed. Big deal."

"Twice, princess."

"And it went so well we didn't talk for two weeks."

"Hey, you called me." Defiant, he stares me down. A dare.

"And I see now it was a mistake."

Gritting my teeth, I stalk forward, my sights set on the arched doorway leading to the exit. But that requires walking past Cooper, who reaches for my waist before I can sidestep him.

In the blink of an eye I'm in his arms, pressed tight against his chest. I feel every warm, solid inch of him against my body. Silence descends as he tips his head to look down at me. My breath catches. I forget who I was before I met him. In this bubble, in this quiet place where no one will find us, we can be entirely ourselves.

"Well . . ." I whisper, waiting for him to say something, do something. Anything. The anticipation is killing me, and I think he knows it.

"You can leave anytime you want," he says roughly.

"I know." Still, my feet don't move. My heart beats a barrage against my rib cage. I'm suffocating, but all I want to do is sink deeper into his arms.

I shiver when his thumb lightly caresses my side over the thin fabric of my loose white shirt. Then the light touch becomes strong fingers curling over my hip, and my knees wobble. I'm smoke in his arms. I don't feel solid.

"What are we doing, Mac?" His deep, dark eyes penetrate me.

"I thought you knew."

Urgently, his lips cover mine. His fingers bite into my hip as mine snake into his hair and pull him toward me. The kiss is hungry, desperate. When his tongue prods at the seam of my lips, seeking entry, I whimper quietly and give him what he wants. Our tongues meet and I nearly keel over again.

"It's okay, I got you," Cooper whispers, and before I know what's happening, I'm off my feet, legs wrapped around him.

He walks us backward until I'm pressed into the exposed concrete of a cracked wall. He's hard against me. I can't fight the wave of insistent arousal that compels me to grind myself against him, seeking the friction that will unleash this knot of repressed longing that's sat taut inside me for weeks. This isn't me. I'm not the girl who loses her mind over a guy, who gets tangled up in midafternoon interludes of semi-public, semi-sexual exploits. And yet here we are, mouths fused, bodies straining to get closer.

"Fuck," he groans. His hands find their way under my shirt, callused fingers dipping beneath the cups of my bra.

The moment he teases my nipples, it's like someone's opened the curtains in a pitch-black room. Startling as blinding sunlight pouring through.

"I can't," I whisper against his lips.

Right away Cooper pulls back and sets me on my feet. "What's wrong?"

His lips are wet, swollen. His hair wild. A dozen fantasies rush through my mind as I struggle to slow my breathing. The wall at my back is the only thing keeping me upright.

"I still have a boyfriend," I say as an apology. Because although I might not be happy with Preston at the moment, we haven't officially broken up.

"Are you serious?" Cooper storms away before turning to stare at me with exasperation. "Wake up, Mackenzie." He throws his hands up. "You're a smart girl. How are you this blind?"

My eyebrows crash together in confusion. "What is that supposed to mean?"

"Your boyfriend is cheating on you," he spits out.

"What?"

"I asked around. For two years, everyone in the Bay has seen that asshole screwing everything that moves."

An angry scowl twists my mouth. "You're lying."

He's picked the wrong girl if he thinks I'm falling for such an obvious ploy. He's only saying this because he wants to get in my pants, to make me furious enough at Preston that I'll give in to the undeniable attraction between us. Well, Cooper doesn't even know Preston. If he did, he'd understand that Pres is the last one who'd be running around with random hookups.

"You'd love it if I was." Cooper approaches me, visibly seething. I'm not sure which one of us is more pissed off at this point. "Face it, princess. Your Prince Charming pulls more ass than a barstool."

Something comes over me.

Blind, hot rage.

I slap him. Hard. So hard my hand stings.

The crack echoes through the empty hotel.

At first he just stares at me. Shocked. Angry.

Then a low, mocking laugh slides out of his throat. "You know what, Mac? Believe me or don't believe me." He chuckles again. A raspy, dark warning. "Either way, I'll be the one watching smugly from the sidelines when you're finally hit with a dose of reality."

CHAPTER TWENTY-ONE

MACKENZIE

Cooper's accusation against Preston torments me for the next twenty-four hours. It clouds my mind, poisons my thoughts. I don't pay a lick of attention during my Monday classes. Instead, I run Cooper's words over and over again in my head, alternating between anger, uneasiness, and doubt.

For two years everyone in the Bay has seen that asshole screwing everything that moves.

Face it, princess. Your Prince Charming pulls more ass than a bar-stool.

Was he telling the truth? I have no reason to trust him. He could have made the allegation merely to get under my skin. It's what he's good at.

Then again, what reason does he have to lie? Even if I dumped Preston, that doesn't mean I'd run straight into Cooper's arms.

Does it?

When I got back to the dorm yesterday after our fight, I had to force myself not to call Preston and lay everything on the line. Ask questions and demand answers. I'm still pissed at him for how he reacted to my hotel. Pissed at the realization that he doesn't take me seriously as a businesswoman, and at the way he flatly laid out a future that robs me of all agency.

I already had plenty of reasons to question my relationship with Preston before Cooper lobbed those accusations. Now, I'm even more of a mess. My mind is mush, my insides twisted into knots.

I leave the lecture hall with my head down, not stopping to make small talk with any of my classmates. Outside, I inhale the fresh air, now crisp and a bit cooler, as fall begins to make its appearance after an extended summer.

My phone buzzes in my canvas shoulder bag. I reach for it, finding a text from Bonnie asking if I want to meet for lunch. My roommate has the uncanny ability to read my mind, so I tell her I have to study, then find an empty bench in the quad and pull out my laptop.

I need a distraction, an escape from my chaotic thoughts. Making plans for the hotel provides that respite.

For the next few hours, I scour the internet for the resources I need to get started on this project. I make a list of contractors, contacting each one to request a site visit, so they can give me hard estimates about how much it'll cost to get the building up to code. I research county ordinances and permit regulations. Watch a couple videos about commercial plumbing and electrical installations. Read up on the latest in hurricane-proof construction and pricing insurance policies.

It's . . . a lot.

My mother calls as I'm sliding the laptop back in my bag and getting up to stretch my legs. Sitting on a wrought iron bench for three hours did a number on my muscles.

"Mom, hey," I greet her.

Skipping the pleasantries, she gets right to the point. "Mackenzie, your father and I would like to take you and Preston to dinner this evening—how is seven o'clock?"

I clench my teeth. Their sense of entitlement is grating as hell. She's acting as if I have a choice in the matter, when we both know that's not the case.

"I don't know if Preston is free," I say tightly. I've been avoiding him for two days, ever since he shot down my dreams and told me I was irresponsible and immature.

The memory of his harsh, condescending words reignites my anger at him. No. No way am I bringing him to dinner tonight and risking a huge fight in front of my parents. I've already slapped one guy. Best to not make it two.

But my mother throws a wrench in that. "Your father already spoke to Preston. He said he's happy to join us."

My mouth falls open in shock. Seriously? They made arrangements with my boyfriend before calling *me*, their own daughter?

Mom gives me no time to object. "We'll see you at seven, sweetheart."

The moment she disconnects, I scramble to call Preston. He answers on the first ring.

"Hey, babe."

Hey, babe? Is he for real right now? I've been ignoring his calls and texts since Saturday afternoon. On Sunday morning, when he threatened to show up at my dorm, I texted that I needed some space and would call him when I was ready.

And now he's *hey, babe*ing me?

Does he not realize how mad I am?

"I'm glad you finally called." His audible remorse confirms he does recognize my unhappiness. "I know you're still sore over our little spat, so I was trying to give you some space like you asked."

"Really?" I say bitterly. "Is that why you agreed to have dinner with my parents without even consulting me?"

"Would you have picked up the phone if I called?" he counters.

Good point.

"Besides, I literally just hung up with your dad. You called before I had a chance to call you first."

"Fine. Whatever. But I don't want to go tonight, Preston. After what happened Saturday at the hotel, I really do need that space."

"I know." The note of regret in his voice sounds sincere. "I reacted poorly, I can't deny that. But you have to understand—you threw me for a total loop. The last thing I expected was being told you'd gone and bought a *hotel*. It was a lot to take in, Mac."

"I get that. But you spoke to me like I was a disobedient child. Do you even realize how humiliating—" I stop, drawing a calming breath. "No. I don't want to rehash this right now. We do need to talk, but not now. And I can't do dinner. I just can't."

There's a brief pause.

"Mackenzie. We both know you're not going to tell your parents you can't go."

Yeah.

He's got me there.

"Pick me up at quarter to seven," I mutter.

Back at Tally Hall, I steam a suitable dress my mom won't side-eye and make myself presentable. I decide on a navy boatneck that's just on the slutty side of modest. My silent protest against having my evening hijacked. As soon as Preston picks me up from my dorm, he suggests I put on a cardigan.

I sit in silence on the drive over to the fancy new steakhouse near campus. Preston is smart enough not to push me to talk.

At the restaurant, we're given a private room, thanks to my dad's assistant calling ahead. On the way in, Dad does his usual grip-and-grin with voters, then poses for a picture with the manager that'll end up framed on the wall and run in the local paper tomorrow. Even dinner becomes a major affair when my father shows up, all because his ego isn't content to anonymously eat out with his family.

Meanwhile, my mother stands to the side, hands clasped politely in front of her, a plastic smile on her face. I can't tell if she still loves this stuff or if the Botox means she feels nothing anymore.

Beside me, Preston has stars in his eyes.

Through cocktails and appetizers, my father goes on about some new spending bill. I can't find it in me to even feign interest as I push my beet salad around my plate. Preston engages him with an eagerness that, for some reason tonight, is getting on my last nerve. I'd always appreciated Preston's ability to chat up my parents, take some of the burden off me at these things. They love him, so bringing him along keeps them in a good mood. But right now, I'm finding him incredibly annoying.

For a fleeting moment I consider plucking up the courage to break the news to my parents—*Guess what! I bought a hotel!* But as Mom starts on how she can't wait until I get more involved with her charities, I'm convinced they won't react any better than Preston did.

"I was hoping you'd let me take Mackenzie along to Europe this summer," Preston says as the entrées arrive. "My father's finally bowed to the pressure and agreed to take my mother shopping for a new vacation home. We're sailing the yacht along the coast from Spain to Greece."

This is news to me. I'm pretty sure there's been no recent discussion of my summer plans, and even if there has been, that was before I had a hotel to restore. Preston knows damn well I can't leave Avalon Bay this summer.

Or maybe he's confident he can talk his immature, irresponsible, wife-material girlfriend into not going through with the purchase.

Bitterness coats my throat. I gulp it down with a bite of my lemon and garlic infused sole.

"Doesn't that sound marvelous," my mom says, with the slightest edge to her voice.

One of her greatest resentments over her husband's career—

not that she hasn't enjoyed the privilege of being a congressman's wife—is her enforced poverty of only two domestic vacation homes when all her friends are always skipping off to their private chalets in Zermatt or villas in Mallorca. Dad says it isn't a good look for them to flaunt their wealth while on the taxpayers' dime—even if the vast majority of the family money comes from inheritance and the corporation my father stepped down from to run for office, though he still sits on the board. But attention invites questions, and Dad hates those.

"She does put up with a lot from him," Preston jokes, grinning at my mother. "So does this one." He nods at me and finds my hand under the table to squeeze.

I shrug his hand off and reach for my water glass instead.

My patience is at an all-time low. I used to be so good at tuning out these conversations. Blowing them off as harmless banter to keep my parents happy. As long as Preston kept them entertained and everyone got along, my life was infinitely easier. Now, it seems the status quo isn't doing it for me anymore.

"What are your plans after graduation next year?" my dad asks Preston. He's barely said two words to me all night. As if I'm an excuse to see their real child.

"My father wants me at his bank's headquarters in Atlanta."

"That'll be quite the change of pace," Dad says, cutting into his bloody steak.

"I'm looking forward to the challenge. I intend to learn everything about the family business from the bottom up. How the mail gets processed to acquisitions and mergers."

"To how the regulations get passed," my father adds. "We should set something up for next term. Have you at the Capitol. There are some important pieces of legislation up for committee—it'd be an invaluable learning experience to sit in on those hearings. See how the sausage gets made, as it were."

"Sounds great," Preston says, beaming. "I'd appreciate that, sir."

Never once has my father offered to have me out to Washington for a take-your-daughter-to-work day. The only time I ever stepped foot inside the Capitol building was for a photo op. When Dad was sworn in, I was ushered into a room with the other freshman families, posed, and was promptly shoved out the door. The other ne'er-do-well congressional kids and I ended up running amok through the bars and clubs of DC, until some senator's kid started roughing up a diplomat brat and it turned into a showdown between Secret Service and foreign security forces.

"It's a shame you and Mackenzie only have one year together at Garnet before you'll be separated again. But I know you'll make it work," Mom chimes in.

"Actually," Preston says, "Mackenzie will be joining me in Atlanta."

I will?

"Garnet offers a full online curriculum to finish her degree so she won't have to transfer schools," he continues. "It's only a short flight from Atlanta if she should need to visit campus for any reason."

What the fuck?

I gawk at Preston, but he either doesn't notice or doesn't care. My parents, too, are oblivious to my rising distress.

"That is an excellent solution," Dad tells Preston.

Mom nods in complete agreement.

Why am I even here if my participation in the conversation, in my life, is entirely superfluous? I'm little more than an ornament, a piece of furniture they move from room to room. These are my parents. My boyfriend. The people who, ostensibly, care the most about me in the world.

Yet I feel completely invisible. And not for the first time.

As they chatter through the main course, oblivious to my existential crisis, I suddenly see the next five, ten, twenty years of my life closing in on me.

Less a future than a threat.

More a sentence than an opportunity.

But then it occurs to me. I'm not a child anymore. I don't have to be here. In fact, there's absolutely nothing holding me in this seat. My mind wanders back to that lunch with Preston's friends, how the girls were so accepting of Seb's apparent forays into extracurricular fellatio. And then later, the way Preston so easily forgave me for my own indiscretion. The clues align themselves and the picture becomes clear.

So fucking clear.

Pushing my plate away, I toss my napkin on the table and scrape my chair back.

My mother looks up, frowning slightly.

"I'm sorry," I announce to the table. "I have to go."

Without a second of hesitation, I bolt for the door before anyone has a chance to protest. Outside the restaurant, I try to camouflage in the shrubbery near the valet stand as I hurriedly call for a cab, but my hiding spot sucks and Preston spots me the moment he stalks outside.

"What the hell was that?" he demands.

I draw a slow breath. "I don't want to argue with you. Go back inside, Pres. I'm done here."

"Keep your voice down." Shushing me, he grabs my elbow and drags me around the corner, out of earshot, like I'm a child getting scolded. "What the *hell* has gotten into you?"

I yank my arm from his grasp. "I can't do this anymore. You, them—all of it. I'm so over it I'm bursting with apathy. That, in there, was me spending my very last fuck."

"Have you completely lost your mind?" Preston stares at me, incensed. "That's what this is—this tantrum, the hotel nonsense. It's stress. The stress of freshman year is getting to you. You're cracking under the pressure." He starts nodding. "I understand. We can get you help, send you to a spa or something. I'm sure we can make arrangements with the dean to finish your semester—"

"A spa?" I can't help it. I erupt, laughing in his face. In this moment, I don't think he's ever known me less.

He narrows his eyes at my mocking laughter.

"This isn't stress. It's clarity." My humor fading, I meet his gaze. "You're cheating on me, Preston."

He frowns. "And who told you that?"

That's his response? If I'd doubted it before, I'm not doubting it now. He can't even be bothered to muster up a denial?

"Are you saying it's not true?" I challenge. "That you aren't just like your buddy Sebastian, sleeping around with girls that aren't 'wife material' while pledging his undying love to Chrissy? Chrissy, who doesn't even care that he's sleeping around." I shake my head incredulously. "Look me in the eye and tell me you're not like that."

"I'm not like that."

But he doesn't look me in the eye.

I bark out a harsh laugh. "That's why you weren't at all disturbed by Seb's actions, right, Preston? Because you're exactly like him. And you know what's funny? I'm not even mad. I should be," I tell him, because there's plenty of anger from all the ways he's disrespected me tonight. "I should be pissed. But I realized tonight that I don't care anymore."

"You can't break up with me," he says sternly, as if he's telling me I can't have candy because it'll rot my teeth.

"I am. I did."

"Forget whatever it is you think I've done. That's just extracurricular bullshit—"

There's that word again.

"It has nothing to do with our relationship. I love you, Mackenzie. And you love me too."

For years, I've confused what we had for love. I do love Preston. Or at least I did, at some point. It started that way. I'm sure of it. But we were never *in love*. I mistook boredom for comfort and comfort for romance. Because I didn't know what true passion was. I didn't know what I was missing, how it's supposed to feel when you can't contain yourself, when desire for another person consumes you so completely, when your appreciation and affection for them is total and unconditional.

"Stop it, Mackenzie." Oops. Now he's pissed. I might be sent to my room with no dessert. "You're throwing a temper tantrum and it isn't cute. Come back inside. Apologize to your parents. We'll forget this whole thing ever happened."

"You don't get it. I've made up my mind. I'm done."

"No, you're not."

I didn't want to resort to the nuclear option, but he's given me no choice. "There's someone else."

"What the fuck? Who?" he snaps, anger reddening his face.

My cab pulls up to the curb. Thank God.

"You don't get to know," I say coolly. "And now I'm leaving. Don't follow me."

For the first time tonight, he listens.

CHAPTER TWENTY-TWO

MACKENZIE

Fifteen minutes later, I'm standing at Cooper's front door. I think I knew when I left the dinner table where I was going to end up. I knew—when I walked away from Cooper yesterday, when I spent hours spinning his words over in my head, remembering our hungry kisses—that if I found my way back here again, it would be with a purpose.

When he opens the door, I almost lose my nerve. He's wearing a T-shirt and ripped jeans. Hair damp as if he just showered. His looks, his body, his tattoos are pure temptation. I hate that he doesn't have to do anything, say anything, to get me all sideways and messed up. It isn't fair.

"Hey." I swallow against the sudden onset of dry mouth.

He stares me down hard without a word. I expected anger. Maybe to be chased off with a warning not to show my face in these parts again.

This is worse.

"Look, I came to apologize."

"That right?" Cooper takes up the whole doorway, strong arms braced on either side.

"I was out of line," I say remorsefully. "I never should have insinuated you have herpes. Perpetuating the stigma of STDs and slut-shaming is wrong, and I'm sorry."

Though he tries his best to hide it, Cooper can't entirely smother the smirk that pulls at the corner of his mouth. He drops his arms.

"Fine, come in."

He leads me through the empty house to the lit back deck that looks out onto the bay. Neither of us is quite sure how to start, so we both lean against the railing, pretending to watch the waves through the darkness.

"I've never slapped anyone before," I confess, because it's my responsibility to break the ice, and for some reason this is harder than I expected.

"You're pretty good at it," he says dryly. "Fucking hurt."

"If it makes you feel any better, my hand was still sore when I woke up today. You have a hard face."

"It does make me feel better," he says with a smile in his voice. "A little."

"I am sorry. I way overreacted and totally lost it. I felt terrible about it. I still feel terrible."

Cooper shrugs. "Don't sweat it. I've had worse."

Part of me wants him to lash out. Tell me I'm a brat and a spoiled bitch. But he's so cool and calm. Unreadable, giving nothing away, which makes all of this nearly impossible. Because for everything I learn about Cooper, I don't know him at all. Sometimes I think we have a connection, then I get to thinking about it until I convince myself I've concocted the entire thing in my head. As if every time we meet, I'm waking up from a dream and I don't remember what's real.

"Want to ask me where I was tonight?" I don't know why I say it except that I want him to know and coming right out with it seems . . . presumptuous?

He cocks an eyebrow.

"Well, first off, I walked out on my parents."

"Is the building still standing?" he asks, not even trying to hide his amusement.

"Uncertain. I sort of ran off in the middle of dinner." I pause. "Know what else I did?"

"What's that?"

"I broke up with my boyfriend."

This gets his attention. He turns to put his back against the railing and folds his arms, attentive.

Cooper chuckles, shaking his head. "There, now it makes sense. You're on the lam and you figured, where better to hide out? No chance anyone will come looking for you here. Am I right?"

"Something like that," I answer sheepishly. That wasn't the explicit thought in mind when I gave the cab driver Cooper's address, but it was certainly an unconscious instinct.

"So how long do you plan on lying low? Not to be a dick about it, but I'm not running a hotel here, princess."

"Touché."

Silence engulfs us, louder than the crashing of the waves against the shore.

This morning, I woke up sweating. As I blinked against the sun, the final frames of Cooper holding me against the wall—my legs wrapped around his hips, his hands burning across my skin— evaporated with the morning dew on my windowsill. What do I do with that? These are new feelings for me. I've never been this wound up over a guy. And yeah, okay, he's shown some interest too, but if he doesn't make the next move, I don't know what any of this means.

"Part of me wishes we never met," he finally says, shadows playing across his face from the deck lights.

"Why's that?" I mean, besides the obvious, I guess. I have been a major pain in the ass to him and probably way more trouble than it's worth.

"Because this is gonna get messy." Arms at his sides, he closes the small space between us until he's got me pinned against the railing with only his eyes.

Something in his expression shifts, and like a subliminal signal to my system, I'm suddenly alert.

"What's going—"

Before I can finish the thought, his lips are on mine.

Caging me against the rail, Cooper kisses me deeply. Urgently. This whole time, for weeks, we've held our breath until this moment. Relief. As his hands find my hips and press me into the splintered wood, I forget myself, consumed by lust. I kiss him back like a starved woman, moaning when he parts my legs with his and I feel his erection.

"Tell me now," he mutters, running his mouth down my neck. "Are you going to tell me to stop?"

I should consider the question. The future implications. All the ways I'm completely unprepared for what happens when I wake up tomorrow and survey the damage of tonight.

But I don't.

"No," I answer. "Don't stop."

Unleashed, Cooper doesn't hesitate. He yanks down the front of my dress just enough to expose my breasts. When he wraps his lips around one budded nipple, the rush of excitement, the adrenaline syringe through my chest, is overwhelming. I'm a different person with him. Unbridled. I grab his hand and push it down until he finds his way under my dress. Then his fingers are pulling away my bikini underwear, sliding across my clit, entering me.

"Ah fuck," he whispers against the feverish skin of my neck. "So wet."

Two fingers move inside me, while his thumb tends to the bundle of nerves that's pulsing with excitement. I hold on to his broad shoulders, biting my lip so hard I taste blood, until my legs are shaking through an orgasm.

"Mmm, that's my girl." A grin appears as he bends to kiss my lips, swallowing my gasped breaths.

His words send a thrill shooting through me. His girl. I know he doesn't mean it that way, just a turn of phrase, but the idea of being his, being entirely owned by him tonight, triggers a fresh wave of desire.

I hurry to undo the front of his jeans and pull him out, stroking. His answering groan is music to my ears. His hands slide down to squeeze my ass, dark eyes glittering with heat.

"Let's go inside," I urge.

"I've got a condom in my pocket." His voice is hoarse as I hold him throbbing in my hand.

"Really, why?"

"Let's not ask those questions."

Fair. Until an hour ago I had a boyfriend. Whatever Cooper was getting up to, or about to get up to, is none of my business.

He tears open the condom and slips it on, then hoists one of my legs up around his hip. Suddenly I'm sitting on the ledge of the railing, clinging to him as he slowly, achingly enters me. If he let me go right now, I'd topple over the rail. But I trust him. I submit completely, trusting his steady grip, welcoming the thick, hard length of him inside me.

"You feel so good, Mac." He's kissing me again. Thrusting deep, making me mindless with need.

A warm breeze sweeps through my hair. I don't care that at any moment we could be caught. That I don't even know if his brother is home. That someone might be watching us from among the silhouettes that circle the house. I don't care about anything but the foreign sensations coursing through my body, this feeling of fullness, rightness. When Cooper's fingers tangle in my hair and tug my head back to kiss my throat, nothing distracts me from his long, deep thrusts and the wild, carnal need that drives us both.

"You gonna come again?" he whispers in my ear.

"Maybe."

"Try."

He withdraws until only his tip remains in me, then plunges back in. Hard, purposeful. Keeping one strong arm wrapped around me, he brings his other hand between my legs and swipes his fingers over my clit. I gasp with pleasure.

"Oh, keep doing that," I plead.

His husky chuckle tickles my mouth as he bends his head to kiss me. His hips continue moving, but slower now, teasing, coaxing me back to the edge. Under his deliberate worshiping of my body, it doesn't take long for the pleasure to rise again, to tighten and knot and then burst in a blinding rush.

"Yes," he hisses, and his tempo speeds up. He thrusts into me with abandon until he's groaning from his own release, shuddering, panting out unsteady breaths.

I swallow, inhaling deeply to try to regulate my erratic heartbeat. "That was . . ." I have no words.

He grunts unintelligibly, also at a loss. "It was . . . yeah."

Laughing weakly, we disentangle from each other. I clumsily slide off the railing. Fix my dress. Cooper takes my hand, leading me inside.

After a shower, I borrow some clothes from him, and we take Daisy out on a walk along the moonlit beach. My fingers are still a little numb, my legs heavy. He was everything I expected and better. Raw, zealous.

Now, I'm struck by how not awkward it is. I'd never been with anyone except Preston, so I didn't know what to expect after a . . .

I don't know what this is. A hookup? A tryst? Something we won't really talk about in the morning? Somehow, I don't care. For now, we're good.

Walking back toward the house, Cooper teases Daisy with a long reed.

"So you wanna spend the night?" he asks me.

"Yeah, okay."

Starting now, I'm not overthinking it. Clean slate. Starting from scratch.

It's time I get to enjoy myself.

CHAPTER TWENTY-THREE

COOPER

My head is wrecked. Waking up with Mac in my bed, my first thought is to make some bad decisions all over again. Then I remember that I'm in deep trouble. I was all about it last night when she practically jumped on my dick. But afterward, something really messed up happened. I didn't want her to leave. I started thinking, well shit, what happens if she goes home and I get another goddamn text like, *Sorry, my bad, I made a mistake and I'm getting back together with my dipshit boyfriend?*

Which is about the point I realized that I'm fully screwed.

"Morning," she mumbles, eyes closed.

When she rolls over and drapes her thigh over my leg, teasing my hard-on, I don't stop myself from grabbing a handful of her ass.

"Morning," I answer.

She responds by kissing my left pec before giving it a little bite.

This chick is something else. It's always the good girls, right? All sweater sets and manners until you get them alone. Then they're shoving your face between their legs and leaving with blood under their fingernails.

We cuddle there for a few minutes, warm and lazy in my bed. Then Mac lifts her head to peek at me. "Can I ask you something?" She's apprehensive.

"Sure."

"It's kind of a nosy question."

"Alright."

"Like, totally none of my business."

"You gonna ask it or should we keep discussing the question-asking process itself?"

She bites me again, a teasing nip at my shoulder. "Fine. Did you have sex with Sutton?"

"No. We took a walk on the pier and then she puked over the railing, so I put her in a cab."

Mackenzie keeps prying. "If she hadn't thrown up, would you have done anything? Kissed? Brought her back here?"

"Maybe. Probably." When I feel her body stiffen beside me, I thread my fingers through her long hair. Other guys might have held back, but I'm not other guys. She asked. I answered. "You wanted to know."

"Yeah, I did. And I'm the one who threw her at you. I guess I'm not allowed to be jealous." Mac growls softly. "But I fucking am."

"Welcome to the club," I growl back. "The thought of anyone but me putting their hands on you makes me homicidal."

She laughs. "Anyone ever tell you you're a bit intense?"

I shrug. "Got a problem with that?"

"Not at all."

I twist a chunk of her hair around my finger. "You know," I say pensively, "as pissed as I was at you that night, I'd forgotten how fun it is to be Evan. It'd been ages since we pulled a twin switch."

She tilts her head curiously. "You two would switch places a lot?"

"All the time. He used to take all my geography tests for me in high school—swear to God, that kid has a weirdly good memory when it comes to state capitals. Sometimes we'd break up with each other's girlfriends."

Mackenzie gasps. "That's awful."

"Not our finest moments," I agree. "We also switched places to mess with our friends, although most of them can tell us apart, even when we make ourselves identical from head to toe. But yeah, sometimes it's nice to take a break from myself and be Evan. Live life with zero regard for consequences. Do what you want, screw who you want, no regrets."

"I don't know . . . I like you just fine." Her palm slowly trails down my bare chest. "More than fine, actually."

"Wait. I want to make you breakfast," I say, stopping her when her hand reaches into my boxers.

"Can't we do this first?" Mac looks up and licks her lips.

Goddamn. Yes, princess, by all means I'd love to see how you look with my cock in your mouth, but I'm trying out this new being-a-gentleman thing, if you'll let me.

Like I said, my head's wrecked.

"You start that," I warn, "and we aren't leaving this bed."

"I don't mind."

Groaning, I push her off me and slide out of bed. "Tempting. And trust me, I'd absolutely smash that, but Evan and I are getting a delivery today for the house renovations. We've gotta get an early start."

Mac pouts, my T-shirt hanging off one tanned shoulder. Her bare legs are begging me to come back to bed. Fucking death of me, right there.

"Fine. I guess breakfast will do. Got any scones?"

"Fuck off," I laugh, heading to the bathroom.

After I grab a spare toothbrush from the cabinet, Mac tears open the packaging. We brush our teeth side by side, but draw the line there. She shoos me out so she can pee, and I go and answer a text from Billy West about today's lumber order. I'm still texting when Mac wanders out of my room toward the kitchen.

By the time I'm done, the aroma of freshly brewed coffee is wafting through the house.

"Sure, honey, help yourself," I hear Evan drawl.

I round the corner to see Mac standing by the coffeemaker with a mug in her hand.

"I thought I'd get a pot going for whoever wants some," she says, noting as I do the sarcasm in his voice. "I hope that's alright."

"Of course it is," I say pointedly at Evan. Because I don't get his sudden attitude. "Have a seat. I'm gonna get some eggs going. You want bacon?"

"Shall I have the maid fetch the good china, or would her majesty prefer to be hand fed?" Evan inquires, grabbing a box of cereal.

"Hey." I shove him as he tries blocking me from the fridge. Fucking child. "Give it a rest, man."

Mac is visibly uncomfortable. "Yeah, you know, I've actually got to get back to the dorm, so I'm going to head out."

"Come on, stay," I urge. "I'll drive you back after breakfast."

But it's too late. Whatever bug's crawled up Evan's ass this morning, he's already scared her off. Mac can't get away from us fast enough, hurrying off to my bedroom, where she calls a cab while changing back into her dress from last night.

"I'm sorry about him," I tell her, catching her around the waist before she walks out the front door. "He's not much of a morning person."

"It's fine. Really."

I study her face. Her makeup's been washed off and her hair's in a loose knot on top of her head. It's the most beautiful she's ever looked. And now I'm thinking we should have gone with her plan of staying in bed all day.

"I'm sure if I had siblings, they'd be a pain in the butt too." Mac lifts up on her toes to kiss me. I take that to mean we're still gonna be on speaking terms.

After she's gone, I find Evan in the garage.

"Hey, what was all that about?" I ask tersely.

"Better ask yourself that question," he retorts, brushing by me with his tool belt over his shoulder. "Since when are you playing butler to the princess? The plan was to get her to break up with Kincaid, not play house."

"Yeah, and it worked." I follow him across the yard and back toward the house, choosing to ignore the way the inflection of hatred in his voice pricks my nerves. "She dumped him last night."

"Great," he says, cracking open a beer from the cooler on the front porch—at seven in the morning. "Then it's time to cut her loose. We get both of them in the same place, let him see you two together, then be done with the clones. End of."

I snatch the beer from his hand and pour it out. "Would you quit it with this shit? I don't want you wasted and shooting a nail gun at me."

"Sure, Dad," he says, flicking me off.

"Hey." I point a stiff finger at his chest because he fucking knows what he just did. "You say that again, we're gonna have problems."

He smacks my hand away. "Yeah, whatever."

Evan's on one today, and I'm about sick of this crap. But I can't worry about what's got him all twisted up, because I need to figure out how the hell I'm going to handle this thing with Mackenzie. There's no way my brother and our friends are going to let me off the hook. All four of them have been circling, waiting for the feeding frenzy. They want blood.

I stew about it all day, but no solutions come to me. By the time we all hit up Joe's later while Steph's there on her shift, I haven't come up with anything better than stalling and hoping they don't mention the plan.

We're on good terms again, Joe and me. I'm still disappointed in how easily he caved in firing me, but I get why he did it. Hard to hold a grudge against a guy who has a mortgage and his kid's college loans to worry about. It wasn't fair to expect him to go to the mat for me when he's got his own family to protect.

We grab a booth near the bar, with Evan sliding next to me, and Heidi and Alana across from us. Steph wanders over with drink menus none of us need or glance at. The chicks order shots. Evan and I stick with beer. We took today off to rebuild our front porch, which means we're pulling a double shift for Levi tomorrow. We've got to wake up at dawn, and I'd rather not do that with a hangover. Evan, I'm sure, doesn't give a shit.

Of course, he wastes no time updating the girls on the latest Mackenzie developments.

"I'm so turned on right now," Alana says, with an evil grin that is honestly disturbing. Chick is scary sometimes. "Look at me." She holds out her arm to us. "I've got goose bumps."

With her phone out, Heidi is scrolling through Kincaid's Instagram. "All we have to do is keep an eye out for where he's going to be one night. Somewhere public. Then you bring his ex, and we humiliate the hell out of him. Shit, we could probably sell tickets."

"Make it soon." Steph groans. "If he doesn't stop coming around here, I'm going to poison his drink with laxatives. I want him afraid to show his face in public."

"Why not this weekend?" Evan suggests, elbowing me as I concentrate on my beer, trying to ignore the rest of them. "Tomorrow. You ask the princess out on a date. Steph, you get Maddy or somebody to invite him out, and we corner him then."

I finally contribute to the conversation. "No."

Evan frowns. "What?"

Hearing him taking shots at Mac again does me in. I'm sick of this whole stupid plot, and I'm sick to death of pretending I'm still on board. I jumped off this train the moment I realized how cool Mac was. How smart and sexy and intriguing. She's unlike any woman I've ever been with.

"It's over," I tell my friends, eyeing them over the rim of my bottle. "Forget about it."

"What do you mean forget about it?" Evan snatches the beer from my hand.

My shoulders stiffen. He'd better be real careful how he comes at me next.

"We had a deal," he snaps.

"No, you have a vendetta, and I want no part of it anymore. I'm the one who got fired, not you. Which means I get the final say about this. And I'm calling it off."

He shakes his head incredulously. "I knew it. She got to you, didn't she? Fucking clone got you wrapped around her prissy little finger."

"Enough." I smack my hand down on the table, rattling our drinks. "That goes for all of you," I tell the girls. "She's off-limits. As far as you're all concerned, she's not to be messed with."

"When did this happen?" Steph looks at me in confusion. I don't blame her. Until this second, I've kept everyone out of the loop.

"This is why we can't have nice things," Alana says.

"I'm serious. Look, I like Mac." I let out a breath. "Didn't expect to, but here we are. I'm into her."

Across the booth, Heidi's lips twist into a scowl. "Men," she mutters under her breath.

I ignore the jab. "I don't know where this is going with us, but I expect you all to be nice to her. Forget we ever hatched this stupid plot. It's not happening anymore. No more rude comments," I say to my brother. To the girls, "And no scheming behind her back. For better or worse, you assholes are my family. I'm asking you to do this for me."

In the silence that follows, each of them gives a curt nod.

Then Evan storms off, because of course he does. Steph shrugs as she goes to check on her tables. Heidi and Alana just stare at me like I'm the biggest dumbass they've ever met. It's not the enthusiastic confirmation I want, but it's honestly better than I hoped for. Still, I'm under no illusions that this'll be painless for any of us.

Heidi shoves a hand through her short hair and continues to eye me. In her expression, I see a flicker of anger. A hint of pity. And a gleam of something else. Something vindictive, alarming.

"No one breathes a word of this to Mac," I warn Heidi. "Ever."

CHAPTER TWENTY-FOUR

MACKENZIE

I spend the next week dodging Preston with such skill it's a shame avoidance isn't an Olympic sport. If it were, Bonnie would also make a worthy competitor. She covers for me at our dorm one night, answering the door topless to scare him off. For whatever lewdness Pres gets up to in his free time, he remains terrified of public embarrassment. So when Bonnie starts shouting at the top of her lungs, and our hallway neighbors poke their heads out their doors to see what all the commotion is about, Preston is quick to retreat.

Ignoring his texts and phone calls is easy. Hiding from him on campus has been trickier. I've taken to ducking out the back entrance of every class a few minutes early or several minutes late to make sure he isn't waiting for me. Getting classmates I've befriended to text me a heads-up when he's spotted nearby. It's a lot of effort, but a hell of a lot less messy than getting cornered.

Seems like everything in my life has been reduced to the act of sneaking around. Avoiding Pres. Going behind my parents' backs to work on the hotel. Slipping around town to meet up with Cooper. I can't risk anyone on campus recognizing him and ratting me out to Preston, and I think Cooper's hiding me from Evan, so our rendezvous have become increasingly creative.

And while we still haven't had The Talk about our dating situation, we can't keep our hands off each other. I'm addicted. Utterly addicted to him. Bonnie calls me dick crazed. I'd argue with her if she hadn't been right about absolutely everything since the moment we met.

On Saturday night, I meet Cooper at one of our usual spots down the beach from his house. This end of the Bay was the hardest hit from the last couple hurricanes and has been pretty much abandoned for years. It's nothing but empty houses and decaying waterfront restaurants. An old fishing pier broken and mostly overtaken by the ocean. We let Daisy off her leash to run around a bit, and she wastes no time terrorizing the tiny sand crabs and chasing birds.

After stopping to sit on a piece of driftwood, Cooper pulls me to straddle his lap, facing him. Both hands cradle my ass as I scratch my fingertips lightly up and down the back of his neck, in the way I know gets him a little hard.

"You keep doing that," he warns, "I'm gonna bang you right here in front of the seagulls."

"Animal," I say, biting his lip.

"Tease." He kisses me. Strong hands slide up my ribs to give my breasts a teasing squeeze before settling around my waist. He eases his mouth away, his gaze finding mine. "I was thinking. There's a party tonight. Come with me."

I lift a brow. "I don't know. We'd be going public. Sure you're ready for that?"

"Why wouldn't I be?"

Our sneaking around hasn't been an explicit topic of conversation, but more an unspoken agreement. Altering that agreement, while inevitable, comes with a whole new net of consequences. That isn't to say I'm unhappy at making this official. Surprised, maybe.

"So . . ." I run my palms down his chest, feeling every hard muscle until my hands meet his waistband. "Like a date."

"*Like* a date, sure." Cooper does this thing where he licks his lips when he thinks he's being charming. It's annoyingly hot.

"Which would mean we're *like* dating."

"Let's put it this way." Cooper brushes my hair off my shoulder. He wraps the length around his fist and tugs. Only a little. It's a subtle, evocative gesture that has become our shorthand for *I want to rip your clothes off.* Like when I bite his lip or tug the front of his jeans, or look at him or breathe. "I'm not fucking anyone else. I don't want you fucking anyone else. If anyone looks at you funny, I'm breaking their face. How's that work?"

It isn't exactly poetry, but that might be the most romantic thing a guy's ever said to me. Cooper might be a bit uncouth and rough around the edges, but I'm kind of into it.

"Works for me."

Grinning, he nudges me off his lap. "Come on, let's take the little monster home. And I want to take a quick shower before we head out. I swear there's always a layer of sawdust on me."

"I like it. It's manly."

He rolls his eyes.

We walk to his house, entering through the back deck. I fill Daisy's water bowl while Cooper goes to his room to shower. I'd join him, but I blow-dried my hair before coming over and I don't want to mess it up, especially now that we're going to a party.

"Hey," grunts Evan, his tall, broad frame appearing in the kitchen doorway. He's barefoot, wearing threadbare jeans and a red T-shirt. "Didn't know you were over."

I slide onto a stool at the counter and watch as Daisy laps noisily at her water. "Yup. Here I am. Cooper's in the shower."

Evan opens a cupboard and grabs a bag of potato chips. He tears it open and shoves some chips in his mouth. As he chews, he watches me suspiciously. "What're you two up to tonight?"

"Cooper says there's a party? I guess we're going to that."

He raises his eyebrows. "He's bringing you to Chase's?"

"Yeah." I pause. "Got a problem with that?"

"Not at all, princess."

"Oh, really."

"It's about time you came out with us," Evan adds, shrugging. "If you're with my brother, you'll need to meet the gang sooner or later. Win 'em over."

Well, hell. Now I'm nervous. Why'd he have to phrase it that way? What if Cooper's friends hate me?

My distress is momentarily forgotten at the sound of Daisy's urgent barking. I glance over at the puppy, only to find she's standing there barking at the wall.

"Daisy," I chide.

"Don't worry," Evan says. "It's probably just the ghost."

I roll my eyes at him.

"Coop didn't tell you about our ghost?" He tips his head. "For real? That's usually the first thing I tell guests. It's like a badge of honor, living in a haunted house."

"Your house is haunted," I say skeptically. Because, come on. I'm not that gullible.

"Sort of? She doesn't really bother us," Evan explains. "So it's not exactly a haunting. But she definitely hangs around."

"She. She who?"

"Patricia something or other. Little girl who drowned out back like a hundred years ago. She was six, seven? I can't remember her age. But when it storms you can hear her screaming, and every now and then, the lights in the house flicker, usually when she's feeling playful—"

He halts abruptly as the light fixture over the kitchen island honest-to-God flickers.

Oh *hell* no.

Evan catches my alarm and grins. "See? She's just teasing us.

Don't worry, princess. Patricia's a nice ghost. Like Casper. If you want more details, I think the town library has some old newspaper articles about it." He walks over to pat Daisy, who's quieted down. "Good dog. You tell that little ghost girl."

I make a mental note to visit the Avalon Bay library. I don't really believe in ghosts, but I do like history, and now that I own a hotel here, I'm even more curious to learn about the history of this town.

"I'm gonna ride with you guys, if that's cool?" Evan says, then wanders out of the kitchen before I can answer. I guess it was a rhetorical question.

Sighing, I stare at the empty doorway. I think there's only one person I really need to "win over" at the moment, and that person is Cooper's twin brother.

Cooper's friend Chase has a split-level house in town with a massive yard backing onto a wooded area. The moment we get there, I'm slightly overwhelmed by the number of people. There's a ton of them here. Inside playing beer pong. Outside around a fire pit. Music blasting. Raucous laughter. We make the rounds as Cooper makes the introductions. It'd be fun if I didn't notice everyone staring at me. Meanwhile, an oblivious Cooper keeps one arm around my waist as he talks with his friends. Everywhere I look are side-eyes, over-the-shoulder glances, and conspicuous whispers. I don't usually get self-conscious in social situations, but it's hard not to when everyone is making it clear with their eyes that they think I don't belong. It's nerve-wracking. Suffocating.

I need more booze if I'm going to survive tonight.

"I'm going to get another drink," I tell Cooper. He'd been chatting with a tattooed guy named Wyatt, who's complaining about how his girlfriend won't take him back. Nearby, a small crowd is watching a game of bikini-and-briefs Twister in the backyard.

"I'll get it for you," he offers. "What do you want?"

"No, it's okay. Stay and chat. I'll be right back."

With that, I slip away before he can argue with me. I wind my way through the house and end up in the kitchen, where I find a lone, unopened bottle of red wine and decide it's the least likely to give me a raging hangover in the morning.

"You're Mackenzie, right?" asks a gorgeous girl with long hair and a dark complexion. She's in a bikini halter top and high-waisted shorts, mixing a drink at the counter. "Cooper's Mackenzie."

"Yep, that's me. Cooper's Mackenzie." It sounds like a '70s cop drama or something.

"Sorry," she says with a friendly smile. She puts a lid on the cocktail shaker and vigorously shakes it over her shoulder. "I just meant I've heard a lot about you from Coop. I'm Steph."

"Oh! The goat girl?"

Her lips twitch. "I'm sorry—what?"

I laugh awkwardly. "Sorry, that was random. Cooper and Evan told me this story about rescuing a goat when they were preteens at the behest of their friend Steph. That was you?"

She bursts out laughing. "Oh my God. Yes. The Great Goat Robbery. Totally my idea." She suddenly shakes her head. "Except did they tell you the part about abandoning the goat in the woods? Like, what the hell!"

"Right?" I exclaim. "That's what I said! That poor thing totally got eaten by mountain lions or something."

She snickers. "Well, we live in a seaside town, so maybe not mountain lions. Definitely got mauled by some predator, though."

I set the wine bottle on the counter and open a drawer in search of a corkscrew.

Steph pours her concoction into two red cups then offers me one. "Leave the wine. That stuff's terrible. Try this." She pushes the drink at me. "Trust me. It's good. Not too strong."

No sense in offending the only person to speak to me all night. I take a sip and am pleasantly surprised by the slightly sweet taste of orange and botanicals.

"This is good. Really good. Thanks."

"No problem. Don't tell anyone where you got it," she says, tapping the side of her nose. As if to say, if the cops raid the party and catch you underage drinking, don't snitch on me. "I was hoping Cooper would decide to share you soon. We've all been anxious to meet you."

"We?"

"Just, you know, the gang."

"Right."

Evan had also used that phrase. I wonder who else comprises this "gang." Cooper and I haven't done much in the getting-to-know-you realm this week. I mean, beyond anatomy.

Speaking of anatomy, an insanely attractive, anatomically perfect guy strides into the kitchen. Tall, fair, and armed with a pair of dimples, he flashes a smile at Steph. "Who's your friend?" he asks, curious blue eyes landing on me.

"Mackenzie," I say, holding out my hand.

"Tate." He shakes my outstretched hand, his fingers lingering.

Steph snorts. "Keep it in your pants, babe. She's with Coop."

"Yeah?" Tate sounds impressed. His gaze rakes over me in slow, deliberate perusal. "Lucky Coop." He grabs a few longnecks from the fridge. "You girls coming outside to the fire?"

"In a bit," Steph answers.

"Cool." He nods and leaves the kitchen.

Once he's gone, Steph is quick to give me the skinny on Tate. Apparently he sleeps around, but his dimples and easygoing charm make it hard to view him as a douchebag. "He's just so darn likeable, you know?" She sighs. "I hate people like that."

"Those likeable pricks," I agree, solemn.

We continue chatting as we drink our cocktails. The more we talk, the more I like her. Turns out we both have a thing for amusement parks and the one-hit wonders of early 2000s pop music.

"I saw them last year in Myrtle Beach. They were opening for . . ." Steph thinks about it then laughs to herself. "Yeah, I can't remember. They're in their fifties now."

"Oh God, I can't believe they're still together."

"It was weird," she says, pouring us another couple of mixed cocktails.

"What was weird?" A girl with platinum hair and dressed in a black cropped T-shirt with the sleeves cut off slides in next to Steph.

"Nothing," Steph says. She's smiling until she clocks the hard glare on the blonde's face. Then all the humor falls. "Heidi, this is Mackenzie."

There's too much emphasis on my name. I can't help wondering what Cooper's told them. It leaves me at a significant disadvantage.

"Nice to meet you," I offer to cut the tension. I'm assuming Heidi is yet another member of this "gang."

"Great," she says, bored the minute she looked at me. "Can we talk, Steph?"

Beside her, a redhead is sporting a smirk that signals I'm not in on the joke, whatever it is.

I get the distinct impression I'm no longer welcome here.

"You know, I should go find Cooper," I tell Steph. "Nice meeting you all."

I don't wait for a reply before shuffling off, leaving my drink behind.

Cooper's still in the backyard, only now he's standing around the bonfire next to a very cute brunette whose ass is trying to climb out of her shorts. When her hand touches Cooper's chest I want to charge her like a bull. Instead, I keep my cool and saunter up to him, grabbing him by his belt loops. That gets his attention. The corner of his mouth lifts wryly.

"Come on," I say, ignoring the irritated look from the brunette. "I want to grope you in the dark."

Cooper doesn't miss a beat. He sets his bottle on the cement blocks lining the bonfire pit. "Yeah, okay."

Together we round the side of the house to the street out front, where Cooper's truck is parked. He lifts me up to sit on the open tailgate. With a dirty grin, he steps between my legs.

"Came to piss on my leg, huh?" He runs his callused fingertips up and down the tops of my exposed thighs. My teeny yellow dress has ridden up almost to my waist, but Cooper's big body shields me from view.

"In not so many words, yeah, I guess so."

"I'm into it," he says, smirking. "You were gone awhile. Everything cool?"

"All good. Just mingling. I met your friend Tate." I wink. "He's cute."

Dark eyes narrow at me. "Did he hit on you?"

"For about a second. Backed off when he learned I came here with you."

"Good. I don't have to kill him. Meet anyone else?"

"A few others," I say vaguely, because I don't want to talk about it.

Truth is, tonight has been a bust and I'm feeling anxious about the prospects of how Cooper and I are going to fit into each other's lives. The longer I'm left to think on the subject, the more the doubt digs its roots into my brain. I don't want to think. I want Cooper to make it all go away. So I tangle my hands in his hair and pull him toward me, kissing him with purpose until I feel the slightest groan from his chest, and he wraps his arms around me, deepening the kiss.

"What's the matter, you two?" I jump when Evan sneaks up behind us, shining the flashlight from his phone in our eyes. "Party run out of Dom Pérignon already?"

"Fuck off," Cooper grumbles, swatting the phone away. "Can't you find someone else to entertain you?"

"I'm good. Came to check on you crazy kids."

Evan flashes a grin and waves at me with a bottle of beer in his hand. The first night we met on the beach, I thought Evan was all right. Since then, I've found him rude and pointedly unfriendly. It isn't enough to be a dick to me; he wants me to know he's *trying* to be a dick. It's the commitment to effort that's been getting to me.

"Now you have." Cooper levels his brother with a look. A whole silent conversation is happening that I can't translate. "Bye."

"Tell me something, Mac."

"Give it a rest, dude." Cooper backs away from me, trying to escort his obviously drunk brother toward the house.

Evan eyes me over the top of his beer. He takes another gulp while pushing his brother away. "I've been dying to ask. Do rich chicks do anal?"

"That's enough, asshole. Leave her alone."

"Or do you pay someone else to do it for you?"

It happens in a blink.

One second Evan is laughing at his own unfunny joke.

Then he's flat on the ground, blood pouring from his mouth.

CHAPTER TWENTY-FIVE

COOPER

I put him on the ground with one punch. Evan was already well on his way to wasted, or else he might have taken the hit better. I feel a small pang of regret when I see the blood leaking onto the asphalt, but all remorse fades when Evan lumbers to his feet and charges at me.

He drives his shoulder into my gut, grabbing me around the waist as we stumble backward against my truck. Somewhere I hear Mac screaming at us, but it's no use. Evan is on one now. And when he lands a couple of hard jabs to my ribs, I don't give a shit who he is anymore. Something in me snaps and my entire world reduces to the sole task of kicking my brother's ass. We trade blows until we're rolling around in the middle of the street, picking up road rash. Suddenly my arms are locked up and people are pulling Evan and me apart.

"Fuck you, man," Evan shouts at me.

"You came asking for it," I growl.

He lunges again.

My fists swing up.

Bodies crowd the space between us as we're forcibly separated.

"What is *wrong* with you two?" Heidi shouts. She and Jay West cage Evan, stepping between us as I shove away the hands of at least three other guys from the party.

"I'm fine," Evan grumbles. "Back off." He wrestles out of their grips and storms down the street on foot.

"I'll get him," Steph offers, sighing softly.

Seeing the fight's over, everyone but my closest friends drifts back to the house.

"Nah, let him cool off," Alana advises.

Heidi side-eyes me before stalking away, Jay trailing after her like a lovesick puppy. I wonder if they came together. I hope so. Maybe then she'll stop hating on me so much.

Steph and Alana wear matching frowns as they study me. Whatever. I don't give a flying fuck what they think right now. Evan deserved every last blow.

Mac grabs my face, inspecting the damage. "You okay?"

I wince when her fingers skim over the rapidly swelling spot beneath my left eye. "I'm fine." I search her face just as intently. "Are we okay?" I don't regret slugging Evan over what he said—nobody gets to talk to Mac like that—but I am sorry she had to see it.

Fuck, if this is the thing that drives her way . . .

She kisses my cheek. "You should go after him."

I hesitate.

"I'll be here when you get back," she promises, as if reading my mind.

I don't have any choice but to believe her. Besides, Evan loaded up on anger and alcohol roaming the streets at night alone is begging for disaster. So I head down the road to find him. I glance over my shoulder once, twice. Sure enough, Mackenzie is still there, standing by my pickup.

Eventually I catch up to Evan, finding him on a bench in a small playground lit only by a couple of dim streetlights.

"Still got all your teeth?" I ask, taking a seat beside him.

"Yeah." He rubs his jaw. "You hit like a ten-year-old."

"Still kicked your ass."

"I had you."

"You had shit," I say, eyeing him with a smirk.

We sit quietly for some time, watching the swings waving in the breeze. It's been years since Evan and I fought this bad. Really going to blows. I'd be lying if I said I hadn't felt it coming. Shit's been building up with him for a long time now. Maybe I'm the asshole for not talking to him about it sooner. Then again, taking his own issues out on Mac is weak, and I'm not about to let him keep that up.

"You were out of line back there."

"Ah, come on. It was a little funny." He slouches on the bench, spreading his legs like he might slip right off the thing in a pool of liquid.

"I'm serious. She hasn't done a goddamn thing to you. You got a problem with me, grow up and say so. The snide comments and passive-aggressive bullshit, it stops now."

"Kind of sounds like you're giving me an ultimatum." Evan tips his head toward me. "That what it's come to?"

"Damn it, dude. You're my brother. We're blood. Nothing changes that." I shake my head, frustrated. "So why are you getting so bent outta shape about her?"

"It's the principle of the thing. She's a clone, Coop. Those people, they've been standing on our necks since we were kids. Or don't you remember? Assholes rolling up in their stupid golf carts, throwing drinks on us, running our bikes off the road."

Evan ended up with a broken arm once. Flipped over his handlebars into a ditch when one of them bumped his tire. We went back a week later and slashed all four of theirs. There are years of that shit. Getting into fights. Tit for tat.

"People," I remind him. "Not her. You can't punish Mac for everything one of them's ever done to you. That's exactly what I was about to do to her if I'd stuck to the plan. And I would've been a bastard for it too." I groan quietly. "Why can't you let me have this?"

His shoulders stiffen.

I mean, hell, all of us lived through the daily soap opera that was the Evan and Genevieve show. Constantly bickering in front of everyone. Making us choose sides in arguments we wanted no part of. Breaking up. Screwing around. Getting back together like nothing happened. I never threw a tantrum about it, and I certainly didn't treat her like crap hoping she'd go away. If Evan was in love with her, that was his own damn problem.

So why now, when I find someone I care about, does he have to be such a jackass about it?

Evan sighs. Scratches his hands through his hair. "I can't help it, man. It gnaws at me. Why'd it have to be one of them? You could point in any direction and land on ten chicks who would fall to their knees for you."

"I don't know what to tell you. She's different. If you gave her even half a chance, you'd see that."

There's no good reason Mac and I should work. I can't give him one. And hell, maybe we won't work. She's a stubborn, opinionated pain in my ass. She's also gorgeous, funny, spontaneous, and ambitious. Turns out, that's my type. She makes me crazy. I've never met a girl that stays on my mind days and weeks after I've seen her. She's under my skin. And for all the ways we're completely different, she gets me in a way few others do.

If I'm kidding myself, if this whole thing's bound to blow up in my face, so be it. At least I tried.

"No talking you outta this, then?" he says, his resolve slowly crumbling.

"I'm asking you, as my brother, to accept it."

He thinks on it. Too long for my taste. For the first time in our lives, we're on opposite sides, and I have to wonder if there's too much bad blood there—too much rage toward the clones—to get him back on mine.

Then he sighs again and rises from the bench. "Yeah, fine. Guess there's no saving you from yourself. I'll back off."

I take what I can get from Evan and we call it squashed. Back at the party, I send him home in Alana's car to make sure he gets there safe while I drive Mac to her dorm.

"I'm sorry about that," I tell her when she hasn't spoken in several minutes. She's staring out the passenger window looking deep in thought, which gets me worried. "It had nothing to do with you. Evan's got a lot of misplaced anger."

"Brothers shouldn't fight."

I wait, uncertain if there's more to that statement. My concern deepens when more doesn't come.

"Talk to me, Mackenzie." My voice comes out a bit husky.

"What if this is a bad idea?"

"It isn't."

"Seriously." Out of the corner of my eye, I find her watching me. "I don't want to be the reason you fall out with him. It's good for no one. You can't be happy because he's upset, and I can't be happy because you're upset. We all lose."

This is exactly why Evan needs to get over his bullshit and let us be. She's not the person he imagines in his head, and if he understood her at all, he'd realize how unfair he's been.

"Evan will get over it."

"But what if he doesn't? These things can fester."

"Don't worry about it, Mac. Seriously." I don't care if my brother wants to be a cranky little brat about it, as long as he's on his best behavior around Mac and keeps his comments to himself. My whole life I've lived for the two of us. Evan and me. This one thing, though, I get to have for myself.

Clearly I'm not doing a good job at easing her unhappiness,

because she lets out a miserable-sounding moan. "I don't want to come between you and your twin, Cooper."

I glance over. Sternly. "I've made my choice. I want us to be together. Evan can deal."

Distress flickers through her eyes. "What does that even mean, being together? I know earlier we said we're dating, and I thought I was cool with that—"

"You *thought*?" I growl.

"But then we went to the party and did you see how everyone was looking at us? No, looking at *me*—like I didn't belong there at all. That one girl? Heidi? Completely froze me out with her gaze. And I overheard a couple chicks calling me a rich snob and saying my dress is ridiculous."

"Why is your dress ridiculous?" From where I'm sitting, her short yellow dress looks ridiculously sexy.

"Because it's Givenchy and I guess nobody wears a thousand-dollar dress to a house party?" Mac's cheeks redden with embarrassment. "My mom's assistant buys most of my clothes. In case you haven't noticed, I don't care about fashion. I live in jeans and T-shirts." She sounds more and more anguished. "I only wore this stupid dress because it's cute and summery and short enough that I knew it'd drive you crazy."

I fight a laugh. I also force myself not to comment on the fact that the scrap of yellow fabric barely covering her delectable body cost a *grand*.

"But maybe it did come off like I was flaunting? I don't know. I wasn't trying to. All I know is that nobody wanted me there tonight."

"I wanted you there."

"You don't count," she grumbles.

I reach over the center console and grab her hand. Forcibly lacing our fingers together. "I'm the only one who counts," I correct.

"They count too," she argues. "You've got an entire group of friends, and you've all known each other forever. I have like two friends, one of whom is my roommate so she's kind of forced to like me."

The laugh slips out.

"I wish I had a huge friend group like yours. I'm jealous," she says frankly. "And I really wanted everyone to like me tonight."

I release her hand and steer the truck to the shoulder of the road. I put it in park and turn to her with a firm stare. "Babe. *I* like you. Okay? And my friends, they'll come around and grow to like you too. I promise you that."

She frowns. "Don't make promises you can't keep."

"I mean it. Give it a little more time," I say gruffly. "Don't bail on me, on this, just because the reception tonight wasn't the warmest, and some girls got all judgmental about your dress—which, just so you know, is the hottest thing ever and I want to rip that thousand-dollar fabric off your body with my teeth."

Mac laughs, albeit weakly.

"Please." I almost cringe at the pleading note I hear in my voice. "Don't bail on me, princess."

The shadows in the truck dance over her pretty face as she sits in silence for a moment. It feels like an eternity before she finally responds.

Green eyes gleaming from the headlights of a passing vehicle, she leans toward me and kisses me. Hard. With a lot of tongue. Then she pulls back breathlessly and whispers, "I won't bail on you."

CHAPTER TWENTY-SIX

MACKENZIE

Give it time, he said.

They'll come around, he said.

Well, I'm calling bullshit on Cooper's bullshit. Since the disaster at the party, I've been on a hearts-and-minds campaign, doing my damnedest to try to win over Cooper's "gang." Though he'd never admit it, I know he's bothered by the fissures where his friends and I are concerned, and I don't want to be the reason he drifts away from the people he cares about. They've been in his life a lot longer than I have. The way I see it, there's no reason we can't all get along.

So I'm trying. I'm really, really trying. Whether it's out at the sports bar playing darts or hanging on the beach at a bonfire, I've been working to make inroads in recent weeks. Most of Cooper's guy friends—Tate, Chase, Wyatt—seem to have completely warmed up to me. We even went out for dinner one night with Chase and his boyfriend, a cute guy named Alec who also goes to Garnet. Except they don't count, because they're not the ones I need to win over. That would be the gang, the inner circle.

Aside from Steph, who continues to be an ally, I can't seem to crack the iron curtain that is the Alana and Heidi blockade. And while Evan hasn't been overtly hostile lately, it seems he's opted for the silent approach where I'm concerned. *If you can't say anything nice*, and all that.

Which is why I thought tonight would be the perfect opportunity for a more intimate get-together. Just *the gang*. S'mores, scary movies, maybe a little Truth or Dare and Never Have I Ever. Bonding stuff and all that jazz.

So of course, by midafternoon the scattered showers predicted for this evening turn into severe thunderstorm and tornado warnings throughout the Carolinas.

Awesome. Even the weather is against me.

An hour ago, Cooper and Evan left to help Levi batten down the hatches at one of his construction sites. So now I'm sitting here at their house with ten pounds of cold buffalo wings and cheesy garlic bread, and beyond the sliding glass doors, the sky grows gray and foreboding over the bay. Without much else to do, and because I happen to love storms—there's something about the fierce, electric anticipation of chaos—I open the back door to let the cool air in and then curl up on the couch with some homework. The TV is on quietly in the background, turned to the local news, where the weather people are standing in front of a radar image awash in red and orange, tossing around words like *hunker down*.

I get my anthropology reading done and am watching some clips on my laptop for my media culture class when a huge crack of lightning flashes outside and the resulting thunder shakes the house. The startling barrage knocks the wind right out of me. Daisy, who was curled up under a blanket at my feet, bolts out of the room for her favorite hiding place under Cooper's bed. Rain begins to pour outside in a sudden deluge that swallows the horizon behind a silver curtain. I jump off the couch and quickly shut the sliding door, then wipe up the water that snuck inside with a dishrag.

It's then I hear it, a faint wailing in the distance.

"Daisy?" I shout, glancing around. Had she run outside when I wasn't looking?

Nope. A quick peek into Cooper's room reveals her lying under the bed, front paws flat on the hardwood, with her little face squished between them.

"Was that you crying, little one?" I ask, only to jump when I hear it again. It's more of a scream than a wail, and it's definitely coming from outside.

When it storms you can hear her screaming . . .

My pulse accelerates as Evan's words buzz around in my head. Was he serious about this place being haunted? What the hell had he called her again—

"Patricia?" I say feebly, my cautious gaze darting around the room. "Is that you?"

The light fixture above my head flickers.

A startled yelp rips out of my throat, causing Daisy to crawl backward and disappear deeper under the bed.

I leave Cooper's room, heart pounding. Candles. I should probably find some candles in case the power goes out. Because nothing sounds less appealing to me than sitting in the dark listening to the shrieks of a century-old dead child.

As if on cue, the shrill noises start up again, a cacophony of sound mingling with the crashes of thunder outside the old beach house.

"Patricia," I call out. Steady voice now. Hands, not so much. "Look, let's be cool, okay? I know it's probably not fun being dead, but that doesn't mean you have to scream your lungs out. If you use your indoor voice, I'm happy to sit down and listen to whatever you—"

Another scream pierces the air.

"Or not," I backpedal. "Fine. You win, Patricia. Just keep scaring the crap out of me, then."

In the kitchen, I start opening lower cabinets in search of candles or flashlights. I find a pack of tea lights and breathe in relief. Good. Now I just need to grab one of the gazillion lighters on the coffee table and I'm all set.

On my way back to the living room, a buzzing noise catches my attention. I think it might be my phone, until I realize it's still in my pocket. I follow the sound to the kitchen counter where Cooper's phone has now stopped vibrating. Shit. He'd forgotten his phone. With the screen still lit, I see he has several missed calls and text messages. I don't look long enough to read them, not wanting to invade Cooper's privacy, but I do note Steph's and Alana's names.

Given the number of calls and texts, it could be urgent. I'd get in touch with Evan to give him the heads-up, but I don't have his number and can't unlock Cooper's phone to get it. If it's important, the girls will try Evan eventually, I reason. So I mind my business and go back to my homework.

But the buzzing continues. For another half hour, about every five minutes, Cooper's phone rattles on the kitchen counter. Fuck it. I grab the phone the next time a call comes in and this time I answer it.

"Hello, Steph?" I say, reading her name on the screen.

"Who's this?"

"Mackenzie. Cooper's out with Evan and Levi. He left his phone at home."

"Damn," she says with a frustrated huff. "I've been trying to get ahold of Evan, but he's not answering either."

"What's going on?"

"There's water coming in through the ceiling of the bathroom. We heard something that sounded like a tree falling on the roof, and then suddenly water's running down the wall."

"You okay?"

"We're fine, but we need to fix this before the entire house is flooded. We've got towels down, but there's too much water and we don't have any way to stop it."

Shit. If they can't reach Evan, it probably means the twins are still wrapped up helping their uncle. The storm is really wailing now, thunder and lightning coming every few minutes and the wind and rain battering the windows. And according to the radar on TV, this thing isn't passing quickly. Which means Steph and Alana are going to need a raft soon.

Pausing for a moment to think, it occurs to me Cooper's truck is still here, and his keys are sitting on the coffee table. I bet he's got all kinds of stuff in the garage—a ladder and tarps.

A plan forms in my head.

"Okay. Write down my phone number and text me your address," I tell Steph. "I'm coming over."

"Uh . . ." There's muted chattering in the background that I assume is Alana. "I'm not sure if that's—"

"I'm going to grab some supplies from Cooper's garage and head over there. Trust me, this'll work."

"Alright," she finally relents. There might even be a hint of relief in her voice.

After we get off the phone, I borrow a rain jacket from Cooper's closet then grab his keys and dash through the rain and mud to his garage. Inside, against the wall, he's got all sorts of building materials stacked up from the renovations he and Evan have been doing on the house. Among them, some black vinyl-type material and rope. Thankfully, Cooper keeps his tools well organized and I find a hammer, nails, and a heavy-duty staple gun with little effort. Good enough.

Ten minutes after hanging up with Steph, I back Cooper's truck up to the door of the garage, get everything loaded into the bed, wrestle with the twelve-foot ladder, and then head to Steph and Alana's house.

Everything looks normal when I pull up to the little blue house. No obvious signs of damage from the front. As soon as I ring the doorbell, Steph flings the door open and pulls me inside with the rain trailing after me and a puddle around my feet.

"It's this way," she says after brief hellos. She takes me to the screened-in rear porch. From there, I see the branches of a tree hanging off the back corner of the house. "We were lucky to make it through the last hurricane with those branches overhanging the house. It was only a matter of time."

"Evan kept saying he'd come trim them back." Alana steps onto the porch with an armful of wet towels. "But of course he forgot."

Steph glances at her. "Maybe toss those in the dryer so we can have something to put down when the others soak through?"

Alana sighs. "Hope no one wanted a shower tonight."

"Give me a hand outside," I say to them. "First thing, we've got to get on the roof and pull those branches off. With the wind and everything, leaving them up there could make it worse."

"What?" Steph looks at me, aghast. "You're not going out there?"

"What'd you expect?" I give a wry laugh. "You weren't calling Cooper for more towels."

"But it's dangerous. There's lightning."

Steph has a point, of course. The alternative is flooding their whole house and ending up with a massive hole in their roof. Anyway, I spent three years of high school on the stagecraft crew with the drama department. I can be pretty handy when I need to be.

"I'm going to get up on the roof and tie a rope around the branches to lower them down to you two. Then I've got some stuff to cover the hole. It'll be quick." I'm lying. It won't be quick. But it's got to be done, and the more Steph keeps us standing around worrying, the worse it'll get.

"Just tell us what to do," Alana says, nodding. This might be the most words she's said to me that weren't accompanied by a sarcastic smirk. That's progress, I suppose.

Together the three of us trudge through the downpour to get all the supplies positioned in the backyard and stand the ladder against the side of the house. RIP their living room carpet. I know I'm taking my life into my own hands climbing a metal ladder in the middle of a thunderstorm, but it's been several minutes since the last flash of lightning, so I take my chances and climb up with the rope over my shoulder.

Wearing a borrowed pair of Steph's hiking boots, I walk across the slanted roof. Every step is like being on ice skates for the first time, except here I can't hug the railing for support. Careful not to make any sudden movements, I manage to tie the rope around the huge, forked branch of the tree, then ball up the slack and make my best Hail Mary pass at throwing it over an exposed limb of the tree to act as a pulley. I succeed on the first attempt. Hell yeah.

On the ground, Steph and Alana take up the weight as best they can as I gingerly help push the branch off the side of the house. As they lower it to the ground, I immediately see where some shingles are missing and a foot-wide dent has been punched through the roof, water pouring inside.

I gingerly make my way down to the ground, where the girls have untied the rope.

"How bad is it?" Steph asks, wiping in vain at the water pouring down her face. We're standing in about four inches of mud at this point. The yard has pretty much turned to liquid and my feet squish inside Steph's boots.

"It's not big, but there's definitely a hole," I report.

We're practically shouting through the deafening wind and rain beating down on the metal porch roof and pelting the trees.

I shove my wet hair off my forehead. "Best we can do is cover it up and hope the rain stops soon."

"What do you need?" Alana eyes me anxiously from under the rim of a baseball cap. Her bright red hair is plastered to her neck.

"I'll take the staple gun, hammer, and nails with me. Then you and Steph tie the tarp to the rope so I can pull it up once I'm up there."

"Be careful," Steph reminds me for the fifth time.

I appreciate the concern, but really, I want to get this done and get dry. My fingers are already turning pruney, I've got a water-logged wedgie riding up my ass, and the chill has soaked into my bones. After they raise the tarp to me and I cut a large-enough piece off with Alana's pocketknife, I tack it down with the staple gun to hold it in place while I put in some sturdier nails. I'm shivering so violently, my teeth chattering, it takes forever to get the nails in.

"You okay?" Steph shouts from the ground.

I get a nail about halfway in, then miss it when the hammer slips, and bend the damn thing. Oh, to hell with it. Good enough.

"Coming down," I shout back.

I scurry my ass down the ladder and we all bolt inside, leaving the rope and tarp in the yard, right as a massive crack of lighting seems to strike right on top of us.

In the laundry room, we strip down to our underwear and toss our wet, muddy clothes in the washing machine.

"That was close." Alana gives me a wide, exhilarated smile that I wholeheartedly return, both of us seemingly aware that we escaped by the skin of our teeth.

"Too close," Steph says with a frazzled look. "What would I tell Cooper if you got electrocuted up there?"

"Yeah, no." From the linen closet, Alana pulls out three blankets for us to warm up in. "We would've had to hide the body and tell Cooper you skipped town." When I raise an eyebrow at her, she shrugs, grinning blithely. "What? You haven't seen Cooper's temper. It's self-preservation at that point."

Alana and I go into the living room. Steph puts on a pot of coffee. I'm shivering, wrapped up in my blanket cocoon on the couch, when Alana gets a phone call.

"Hey," she answers. "Yeah, we figured it out. She's here, actually. Sure. See ya." She sets the phone down and takes a seat beside me. "They're on their way over."

"Think I could borrow some clothes to go home in?" I ask. With my stuff in the wash, I'd rather not leave here in nothing but my underwear and Cooper's rain jacket.

"No problem."

Steph comes back with the coffee. I normally take cream and a mound of sugar, but I'm not picky at the moment, and scalding hot black coffee is exactly the thing to chase the frigid out of my blood.

"Okay, so that was legit badass," Steph admits, squeezing on the couch between Alana and me. "I wouldn't have taken you for the manual labor type." She regards me with a regretful smile when it dawns on her that I might take it as an insult.

"Sophomore year of high school, I had this chemistry teacher whose fetish was dragging down his students' GPAs with impossible pop quizzes. The only way to get extra credit was through volunteer hours, so I helped build sets and stuff for the school plays. It was fun, actually. Except for the time I almost lost a finger when Robbie Fenlowe ran a drill over it." I show Steph the scar on my index finger. "Mangled flesh and everything."

"Eww, that's disgusting."

"For real, though," Alana says, her cheeks turning a shade of crimson not far off from her hair. "Thanks for coming over. We would have been shit out of luck."

"Yeah," Steph laughs, "Alana's a total wuss. She's terrified of heights."

Alana glowers at Steph, flashing her middle finger. "Thanks, bitch."

"What?" Steph shrugs. "It's true."

"I'm being nice, okay? Give me a break."

I don't know Alana well, but I'd call this a breakthrough. All it took was a death-defying act of heroism to break some ground with her. That's two-thirds. Now if I can figure out how to crack Heidi, I'll be golden.

For the next fifteen minutes, the girls and I keep chatting. When I tell them about the hotel I purchased, Steph offers a ton of details about the place, gathered from the three summers she worked there. Realizing her knowledge is invaluable, I make a mental note to invite her to the site once I take possession. Her familiarity with the hotel could be a real asset.

"Help has arrived, ladies!" Evan bursts through the door not long after, shirtless and dripping. "Where's the fire?"

Somewhere, someone has fantasized about exactly this. Which is weird, because even as I'm sleeping with his identical twin, a half-naked Evan does nothing for me.

"You're about two hours too late," Alana says flatly, unimpressed with his grand entrance.

"Oh, I'm sorry." Evan shakes the water from his hair with all the grace of a stray dog and shoots Alana a sarcastic glare. "I guess I didn't get your retainer fee this month to be at your beck and call."

Cooper has to practically push his brother through the door to get inside and out of the storm. He appears a bit perplexed to see me on his friends' couch, wrapped up in a blanket like a soggy corn dog.

"Couldn't help noticing my truck outside," he says with a raised eyebrow. "Went and helped yourself, huh?"

I shrug, meeting his crooked grin. "Stole a bunch of stuff too. I think you're a bad influence on me."

He huffs out a laugh. "That right?"

Something about the gleam in his eyes starts to feel like foreplay. That's how quick it happens when he's around. From zero to *fuck me* in ten seconds flat. I can't help feeling like everyone else can see it, and yet I don't care. Cooper Hartley walks into a room and I lose my whole damn mind. I hate it. I love it.

"We're lucky she came," Steph says as the guys pour themselves a couple cups of coffee in the kitchen.

"This crazy bitch got up on the roof and patched the hole all by herself." Alana holds out her coffee mug for Evan to refill, which he does, rolling his eyes at the sight of the three of us bundled up in our cocoons. "On a related note," she adds, "no one use the guest bathroom. It's an aquarium now."

"I've always hated the wallpaper in there anyway," Steph remarks, and for some reason that gives Alana and me the giggles.

"Hold on." Cooper comes up short, standing in the middle of the living room. His distrustful gaze singles me out. "You got up on the roof?"

"I might have found a new calling," I tell him, sipping my coffee. "I should do the hotel renovation myself like the people on TV."

"Ooh." Steph smacks my arm. "I call dibs on hosting the reality series."

"I still can't believe you bought The Beacon," Alana marvels. "That's so frickin' random."

Cooper slams his coffee cup down on the TV console, liquid splashing out and startling the room silent. "Neither of you even tried to stop her?"

"Coop, it was fine." Steph disregards his outburst. "It was only a little rain."

"It wasn't your ass up there."

The venom in his voice is striking in its severity. I'm not sure where all this sudden anger is coming from. Was it a particularly responsible thing to do? No. But nobody got hurt. Except Cooper's butt, apparently.

I fix a small frown in his direction. "Hey, it's fine. I'm fine. They needed help so I offered to come over. It was my decision."

"I don't give a shit whose dumbass idea it was. You shoulda

known better," he tells me with a condescending tone, not unlike the one I heard from Preston when I showed him the hotel.

And now I'm kind of pissed. Why does every guy I date think he needs to be my dad? I didn't break up with Preston to start letting another guy treat me like a child.

"And you two," he glowers at the girls, "shoulda stopped her."

"Dude, chill." Alana throws her head back with a bored sigh. "She's a big girl. And we're glad she's here." I sense that's about as sincere an apology one gets out of Alana. Our efforts tonight have thawed the cold shoulder she's been giving me, and I think we're on good footing now.

"Shove it, Alana. She only pulled this stunt so you and Heidi would stop freezing her out."

"I don't remember asking you to speak for me," I snap at him, because thanks, asshole. I was making progress here and this isn't helping.

Cooper stalks toward the couch, looming over us. "You could've been killed," he snaps back. "In case you hadn't noticed, we're practically in the middle of a hurricane."

My jaw drops. "Are you kidding me right now? *In case I hadn't noticed?* And *now* you're suddenly worried about my safety? You're the one who left me at your house in the middle of a hurricane. I was all alone there! Just me and Patricia screaming like a banshee!"

He blinks at me as if I'm insane. "Her name is Daisy."

I stumble to my feet, clutching the blanket against myself like a toga. "I'm not talking about the dog! I'm talking about Patricia!"

"I don't know who Patricia is, you lunatic!"

"The little dead girl who drowned outside your house a hundred years ago and—"

I stop, my outraged gaze swinging toward Evan, whose lips are twitching wildly.

"You asshole!" I snarl. "Seriously?"

Evan crosses his arms over his chest. "Mackenzie. Sweetheart. I'm not gonna apologize for you being gullible. This one's on you."

On the couch, Alana and Steph are in hysterics. Steph has tears running down her cheeks as she wheezes out *little dead girl* between giggles.

In front of me, Cooper is clearly trying not to laugh too.

"Don't you dare," I warn, jabbing a finger in the air between us.

"I mean," Cooper trembles as he battles his laughter, "he's not wrong. That one's on you."

I glare at him. "He's a sadist! And you're a jerk."

"I'm a jerk? Remind me, who went out on the roof and almost got struck by lightning?"

"Oh my God, I did not almost get struck by lightning. You're being ridiculous right now." Indignant, I plant my hands on my hips, forgetting about the blanket wrapped around me.

It falls to the wet carpet, leaving me in nothing but a black sports bra and neon-pink bikini panties.

Evan licks his bottom lip. "That's what I'm talkin' about."

Despite the flicker of heat in his expression, Cooper's tone remains cool. "Get your clothes, Mac. We're leaving."

"No," I say stubbornly.

His eyes narrow. "Let's go."

"No. I live here now."

Alana snickers.

"Mackenzie." He takes a menacing step forward. "Let's go."

"No." My throat is suddenly dry. Tension thickens the air. I don't know if Cooper is angry or turned on, but his blazing eyes are sucking up all the oxygen in the room.

Cooper glances at his brother. "Evan, gimme your keys. You can take my truck home."

With a knowing grin, Evan reaches into his pocket then tosses a set of keys at his twin.

I jut my chin. "I don't know what you think is happening right now, but I am *not* going—"

Before I can blink, I'm being flung over Cooper's shoulder. Staring at his wet boots as he marches us to the door.

"Put me down!" I yell, but the downpour that hits us the moment we leave the house drowns out my furious request.

Cooper unceremoniously shoves me into the passenger seat of Evan's Jeep before running to the driver's side. When he starts the engine and turns to look at me, I have the answer to the *angry* versus *turned on* question.

His gaze has turned molten. "I'm going to be inside you the moment we get home." A threat. A promise.

Turned on.

Most definitely turned on.

CHAPTER TWENTY-SEVEN

MACKENZIE

"Shower. Now."

Cooper's growly order sends a shiver skittering through me. We'd just run from the Jeep to his house, getting soaked in the process. I'm still in nothing but my underwear, and my teeth are chattering again. Luckily, I'm not cold for much longer. In his bathroom, Cooper cranks the hot water, and soon there's steam rolling out of the tiled shower stall.

I strip out of the sports bra and panties and step into the shower, moaning happily as the heat suffuses my body. A moment later the temperature spikes another hundred degrees, because a naked Cooper is coming up behind me.

Strong arms encircle me, holding me against him. My back is flush against his broad chest. I can feel the long ridge of his erection pressing against my ass.

"You make me crazy." His hoarse words are muffled in the spray of the shower.

"Really? Seems to me like you're the one making *me* crazy." I shiver in pleasure when his big palms slide up my ribcage to cup my breasts. My nipples pucker.

"You could've gotten hurt up on that roof."

"But I didn't."

"Were you really scared here alone?" He sounds guilty.

"Kind of? I was hearing this shrieking from outside and the lights kept flickering."

He chuckles. "The wind gets pretty loud here. And we need to rewire most of the house. The electrical sucks."

"Stupid Evan," I mutter, pissed that he'd managed to make me question my former disbelief in the existence of ghosts.

"How about we don't talk about my brother when we're both naked?" Cooper suggests.

"Good point." I turn, reaching between us and taking him in my hand.

He shudders. "Yeah. Keep doing that."

"What? This?" I curl my fingers around his shaft and give it a teasing stroke.

"Mmmm."

"Or . . ." I give another pump, another slow glide, before sinking to my knees. "I could do *this*?"

Before he can respond, I wrap my lips around him and suck gently.

Cooper groans, and his hips thrust forward.

A rush of pure power surges through my blood. I could get used to this feeling. The satisfaction of knowing I'm the one who put that needy, desperate look on his rugged face. That right now, in this moment, I have him in the palm of my hand. Or rather, on the tip of my tongue. I give a little lick, and he makes a husky noise that brings a smile to my lips.

"You're teasing," he mutters.

"Uh-huh." I lick him again, a long, wet swipe along the length of him. "It's fun."

His hand comes down, long fingers tangling in my soaked hair. The water beats down on us. Droplets cling to his chest before dripping downward, traveling over muscle and sinew.

I brace one hand on his firm thigh, wrap the other around his erection, and suck him deep. He guides me wordlessly, encouraging me by cupping the back of my head. My entire body is scorching, taut with desire. When I peer up at Cooper, see those tattooed arms, the stubble shadowing his jaw, and feel him throbbing on my tongue, I don't regret a single thing that brought me to this point.

There's fire in you, Mac. He'd told me that the night of the carnival. Said I get off on the thrill, on *life*. He wasn't wrong. Since I broke up with Preston and started dating Cooper, I'd never felt more alive.

"I don't want to come this way," he mumbles, and then he's pulling me to my feet and kissing me hard enough to rob me of breath.

His hands hungrily roam my body as his tongue toys with mine. I'm hot and achy and more than ready for him. But for all my thrill-seeking, unprotected sex isn't on my thrill list, and Cooper and I only just got together.

"Condom." I whisper the reminder against his eager lips.

Without argument, he shuts off the shower and we sprint into his bedroom, dripping water everywhere and laughing at our own urgency.

"On the bed," he orders, devouring my naked body with his eyes.

My wet hair soaks the pillow the moment I lie down, but I'm too turned on to feel bad and Cooper doesn't seem to mind. He's wearing a condom and on top of me before I can blink. He kisses me again, hot, greedy, his tongue sliding into my mouth at the same time he thrusts deep.

I gasp, shaking from the jolt of pleasure that sizzles up my spine. I scrape my nails down his damp back and wrap my legs around him to draw him in deeper.

"You feel so good," he croaks against my lips.

"So do you." I lift my hips to meet his hurried thrusts, rocking against him. Mindless with need. "Faster," I beg.

He moves faster, and it isn't long before I'm seeing stars and trembling with release. He doesn't last much longer than me. Soon he's slamming into me harder, still kissing me, biting my lip as he comes.

Afterward, we lie on our backs and catch our breath. A feeling of pure contentment washes over me. I can't remember the last time I felt so sated after sex. Sated in general.

"I'm still pissed you went up on the roof."

I twist my head to look at him. "Seriously?"

"It was a dumbass move."

"I stand by it," I say haughtily.

"Of course you do." It sounds like he's trying not to laugh. Or maybe he's trying not to strangle me.

Apparently we both suck at backing down from an argument. It isn't in our natures, I suppose. But I can live with that. I wouldn't respect him otherwise. The last thing I want is a doormat.

On the other hand, all that bickering can't be good, can it?

I sigh. "We argue a lot. I feel like that's a second strike against us."

"What's the first strike?" he asks curiously.

"We're total opposites. And yeah, they say opposites attract and fighting can be a healthy release of passion and all that, but our backgrounds are so different." I hesitate, then confess, "Sometimes I have no idea how we're supposed to fit in each other's lives. And then add in the fact that you're an argumentative jackass and I want to punch you half the time, and . . ." Another sigh slips out. "Like I said, two strikes."

"Mac." The mattress shifts as he sits up. Dark eyes peer down at me. Intense, with a hint of amusement. "First of all, *they say*? Who's *they* and who cares? Every relationship is different. Some people fight, some people don't. Some want calm, some want passion. We define our own relationship. And second, I hate to break it to you, but we're *both* argumentative jackasses."

I grin at him.

"The only opposite thing about us is our bank accounts. We're a lot more alike than you and your uptight ex."

"Is that so?"

"Oh, it's fucking so. You know what I think?"

"Please, do tell," I say graciously.

"I think you were with that prick because he was safe. You said it yourself—he helped you stay restrained. And you needed that, because in your world, you can't act out or be yourself or do anything that might bring negative attention to your family, right? Well, you don't need to do that with me. Those two strikes you listed might be strikes in your other world, but here, you and me, we're exactly who and what we need to be."

My heart squeezes. Oh hell. When he says stuff like that, he makes it pretty damn hard to not catch feelings.

* * *

Bonnie: *Won't be home tonight! Try not to miss me too much, k? I know it'll be tough but I have faith in you!*

I grin at the text. Bonnie is the best. Sitting up in bed, I type a quick response.

Me: *Oooh, staying out on a school night, you bad girl. Let me guess, you're having a slumber party with . . . Edward?*
Bonnie: *You mean Jason. He just looks like Edward. And nope.*
Me: *Todd?*
Bonnie: *Out of rotation.*

I scan my brain trying to remember who else she'd been seeing these past few weeks. But I've kind of been distracted by all the wild sex I'm having with Cooper.

Bonnie: *Tell ya what, hun. Gimme the name of your townie, and I'll spill all the beans about my new beau.*

She's like a dog with a bone, this one. Bonnie's been on my case day and night about who I'm dating. I feel bad hiding Cooper from her—she was there when it started, after all—but I also know that knowledge in the wrong hands is a weapon. I'm not sure I'm ready to arm that cannon yet.

Me: *My townie is still my dirty little secret.*
Bonnie: *FINE! Then mine's a secret too.*

Two seconds later, she texts again.

Bonnie: *Who are we kiddin'? We both know I can't hide anything from you. His name is Ben and he is beautiful!*

She follows it up with a screenshot of an Instagram picture featuring a tall boy with the face of a Norse god.

Me: *Niiiiice. Have fun.*
Bonnie: *Oh I will. See you tomorrow!*

I set the phone on the nightstand and pick up my anthropology textbook. It's Monday night, and while I'd rather be naked in Cooper's bed right now, we spent all weekend together. So I'm forcing myself to stay in the dorm tonight. Not just to keep on top of my course work, but because too much time together could lead to burnout and the last thing I want is for Cooper to get sick of me. God knows I'm nowhere close to being sick of *him*. I spend, conservatively, three full hours a day fantasizing about him.

So, like a good girl, I finish all my readings for anthropology and bio, write an outline for my English Lit paper, and go to bed at the very reasonable time of ten forty-five.

Alas, the good night's sleep I'd hoped for doesn't come.

Around two in the morning, I'm rudely awakened by three consecutive phone calls from Evan.

Followed by a text message that reads: *Forget it. Not an emergency.*

If anyone else had been serial calling me in the middle of the night while maintaining it wasn't an emergency, I would've told them to fuck right off. But the fact that it's Evan gives me pause. We only recently exchanged numbers, after the night of the storm when I had no way to reach him. So I'm pretty sure he wouldn't be abusing phone privileges unless it was, indeed, an emergency. Or at least somewhat dire.

I shove my hair out of my eyes and call him back. "You okay?" I demand when he answers.

"Not really." There's a heaviness weighing down those two words.

"Where are you?"

"Outside Sharkey's. Can you come get me?" he mumbles. "I know it's late and I didn't want to call but—"

"Evan," I interrupt. "It's fine. Just stay put. I'm on my way."

CHAPTER TWENTY-EIGHT

MACKENZIE

Fifteen minutes later, I jump out of an Uber and scan the sidewalk in front of Sharkey's Sports Bar. It doesn't take long to spot him. Evan's sitting on the curb, looking like a month's worth of sludge at the bottom of a trash can that's been left in the rain.

"What happened to you?" I ask, noting the blood smeared on the side of his face, his shirt torn at the shoulder, and hands scraped and swollen. I can smell the alcohol on him from two feet away.

With his arms propped up on his bent knees, he looks exhausted. Defeated, even. He barely raises his head to acknowledge me. When he speaks, his voice is strained and weak. "Can you get me out of here?"

It's then I realize I'm his last resort. That turning to me for help is more painful than whatever he's endured tonight and what he needs the most now is grace.

"Yeah." I bend down to gather one of his arms over my shoulder to help bear his weight. "I've got you."

As we're getting up, a trio of guys rounds the corner. Wearing their Greek letters on their shirts, they shout something slurred and incoherent as they approach.

"Oh, hey, baby," one says when his bleary eyes land on me. A slimy grin appears. "What you got there? Find yourself a gutter stray?"

"Piss off, asshole." Evan grumbles a half-hearted insult. He can barely stand up straight, leaning on me for balance, but that isn't enough to deter him from picking a fight apparently. Got to admire his fortitude.

"It's this fucker again?" The tallest of the frat boys staggers closer, peering at Evan before turning to his buddies. "Look who's back, boys."

I level the three guys with a deadly glare. "Leave us alone."

"Haven't you had enough, my man?" The third guy comes closer, ducking to meet Evan's eyes as Evan fights to lift his head. "Thought you were fucking hilarious when you were trying to scam us, huh? Not laughing now, are you? Townie piece of trash."

My eyes become murderous. I'm tired, cranky, and I've got my hands full with Evan. There's not an ounce of patience left for these idiots.

"Hey, I know you," the tall one suddenly says, squinting at me.

"I doubt that," I snap.

"No, I do. I know you. You're Preston Kincaid's girlfriend." He laughs gleefully. "Yeah, you're Kincaid's girl. I'm in his frat. I saw you two at some sorority party a while back."

Strands of unease climb up my throat. Wonderful. The last thing I need is tonight's activities getting back to Preston. I tighten my grip on Evan and say, "I have no idea who you are, dude. Now, please, get out of our way."

"Does Kincaid know you're messing around on him?" His laughter turns maniacal. "And with this piece of shit, no less? Jesus. Women are such trash."

"Trash," one of the other guys echoes drunkenly.

When both of them try advancing closer, I've officially had enough.

"Back off, motherfuckers." My voice cracks like a whip off the brick wall of the bar.

"Or what?" mocks the tall one.

With an angry, impatient growl, I shove my hand in my purse and whip out a can of pepper spray, aiming it at the frat bros until they stagger back. "I promise you, I'm crazier than I look. Please test me."

Somewhere in the distance, a siren blares. It's enough to spook them. "Man, forget this bitch, let's get out of there."

They hurry to pile in a car across the street and flee, tires squealing as they pull a hard U-turn.

"Where the hell did that come from?" Evan manages a faint laugh, still clinging to me with one arm over my shoulder.

"All women are wolverines."

"Clearly."

"I've also done a fair bit of solo traveling, which if nothing else has taught me to be prepared for what lurks in the shadows." With that, I all but drag him to his Jeep and fish his keys out of his pocket. He manages to climb into the passenger seat while I slide behind the wheel.

"I can't go home," he says. Eyes closed, his head lulls against the window. Too heavy for his neck.

I adjust the driver's seat to accommodate my shorter legs. "Okay . . . Steph and Alana's house?"

"No. Please." He speaks in gusts of breath. "Coop can't find out."

I'm not sure why or which part he's referring to, but I understand his desperation. Which leaves me no choice but to bring him back to Tally Hall.

Getting him up to my dorm room on the fourth floor is a challenge, but we make it there in one piece. Once inside, I sit him on the edge of the bathtub to clean him up. A sense of déjà vu hits me. What is it about these Hartley boys, huh?

As I'm wiping the blood from his face with a wet washcloth, I can't ignore his gaze following my every move. He has some bruising and small cuts, but nothing serious. Just need to dab a little ointment and apply a couple bandages.

"Sore losers," he says.

"Huh?"

"Those guys. I beat them at pool, and they didn't take it well. Shouldn't play with money they aren't prepared to lose."

"Do you always shark people outnumbered?"

He breathes out a laugh then winces, holding his side. "I thought I had the home field advantage. Turned out there were a few more people holding a grudge than I figured."

I cock a brow at him. "Don't you townies have a saying about shitting where you eat?"

"Yeah, I might have heard that one."

"You've got to diversify."

"Adapt or die, is that it?"

"Something like that." Once I've got him fixed up, I get him a glass of water and some aspirin and bring him an ice pack. "You can sleep it off in Bonnie's room," I offer. "She's out tonight and I know she won't mind."

"She'd better not. I made her come three times that night."

I choke out a laugh. "How kind of you." Man, it seems like ages ago that Evan and Bonnie had wandered down the beach together. A day later, she was already chasing after her next conquest. No muss, no fuss between those two.

I prop him on the edge of Bonnie's bed and proceed to undress him in the most clinical of manners. I try not to stare at his body and compare it to Cooper's, but it's difficult. His chest is right there, and yes, it's as muscular as his brother's. No tattoos, though. At least until I help him roll over and realize he has a huge one on his back. It's too dark to make out the ink.

"Thank you," he says once he's lying down.

Though he doesn't offer more than that, I know it's sincere. Whatever is going on between him and Cooper, it's enough that turning to me for help was the more attractive option. I take it as a step in the right direction that Evan trusts me this much. Baby steps.

I pat him gently on the head, as if he's a child with a slight fever. "You're welcome."

The next morning, I'm getting ready for class when Evan bursts out of Bonnie's room with his phone to his ear.

"Yeah, I know, I know. I'm on my way. I said I heard you, fuck." He's stumbling around trying to pull his jeans up while rummaging through Bonnie's room for something. "Ten minutes."

When I question him with a look, he holds up his fingers to mime dangling keys. Keys! I still have his Jeep keys in my room. I dash off and grab them, then toss them at him. He snatches them easily from the air.

"No," he says into the phone. "Dude, I'm leaving right now, chill the fuck out."

Cooper? I mouth at him, to which Evan nods his head. I hold my hand out for the phone. He's skeptical at first, then relents.

"Here, the princess wants to talk to you." This time, instead of a sarcastic sneer, there's a smile in his eyes. Maybe a plea.

"Hey," I say, not giving Cooper a chance to cut me off. "I invited Evan out for breakfast but the place was slammed and I lost track of time. I just had to order the soufflé, you know."

"Breakfast, huh?" He's wary, of course. As he should be.

But I stick to the story. "Yeah, I thought it'd be a chance for us to chat, you know? A little family time."

I can practically feel Cooper's eyes rolling through the phone.

"Whatever. Tell him to get his ass to work."

"K, smooches, bye," I sing sweetly, because the more I throw Cooper off balance, the more he'll accept this completely preposterous premise. Ending the call, I hand the phone back to Evan. "I think he bought it."

He gives me a look of confused amusement. "You're a lifesaver."

"I know. Now can I ask why I'm lying to your brother?"

Running his hands through his hair, Evan sighs. He's the type who hates explaining himself. I get that. But fair's fair.

"Coop's already on my case," he says reluctantly. "If he finds out about last night, he'll force an intervention on me or some dumb shit."

"Do you need one?" I know Cooper's been concerned that Evan is spiraling, but he hasn't told me any specifics. Judging by last night, I suspect booze and fighting are possible culprits.

"Definitely not," Evan assures me.

I'm not sure who he's trying to convince, but it doesn't work on either of us.

I let out a breath. "Make me a promise."

He rolls his eyes. It's these times I forget he and Cooper are two different people.

"I'll cover for you as long as you're honest with me. If you won't talk to Cooper, I'll feel better if you at least let me keep an eye on you."

"I don't need a babysitter." He punctuates that with a dark scowl.

Yup. I get why they fight so much. Cooper's overbearing and Evan is an obstinate ass. Together they create a perfect storm.

"I don't want to be one," I tell him. "So how about we settle for friends. Deal?"

He licks his lips to smother a grin. It's almost charming. "Alright, princess. Deal."

We shake hands. I give it about a fifty-fifty chance that he holds up his end of the bargain. Still, it's miles from where we started, and I'm smart enough to take what I can get.

CHAPTER TWENTY-NINE

COOPER

Mac's got yet another inspection at the hotel today, so I take the afternoon off to go there with her. She says it's so I can translate for her, but I think she's nervous about what she's gotten herself into. Can't blame her. Even if I had boatloads of family money, jumping into something as complex as renovating a hotel—not to mention running the damn thing—would make me a whole lot of anxious too. So as the inspector does his thing, Mac and I hang out on the boardwalk waiting for the verdict.

"I'm starting to think one does not simply buy a condemned hotel," she says glumly.

I can't help a smile. "That so?"

"Yup." She bends to pet Daisy, who's sitting at her feet. That dog doesn't leave me alone for a second when we're home, and then as soon as Mac comes around, she doesn't know me.

"You can walk away." From what I understand, the final sale of the property is still pending the completion of this last inspection. Crossing *t*'s and all that.

"No, I'm committed. It's just overwhelming, you know? Thinking about everything there is to do. How much I don't know."

"So you'll figure it out."

She bites her lip. "Right." Then she nods. Swiftly, decisively. "You're right. I will figure it out."

This is what I dig about her. Her confidence. The courage. She had an idea and some gumption and went for it. Most people spend their whole lives talking themselves out of their dreams. Point out all the reasons it's too hard or farfetched. Not Mac.

"When you look at this place, do you still feel the same way as you did when you put the offer in?" I ask.

She smiles, the gleam of ambition fresh in her eyes as she stares at the crumbling building. "Yes."

"Pull the trigger. Can't win if you don't play."

"That's the lottery," she says, nudging my shoulder.

"Same difference."

To be honest, I'm glad she asked me here. Even if only for moral support. There isn't much I can give a girl like Mackenzie Cabot. Nothing she doesn't already have or can't get on her own. We all want to feel useful, though. I don't know when it happened, but somewhere along the way, I started needing her to need me.

After a couple hours, the inspector comes out with his clipboard and runs down the list with Mac. Most of it we expected, some we didn't. All of it carries a price tag.

"What's the bottom line?" Mac asks him after he's gone over every bullet item line by line.

"It'll cost ya," the man says through his overgrown mustache. "That said, there's no reason this place can't be operational again. I wish you luck."

After a handshake, he gives her the paperwork and walks off to his car.

"So?" I prompt, taking Daisy's leash from her.

She hesitates. Only for a second. Then she smiles wryly. "Guess I better call the bank."

Gotta admit, it's kind of hot that she can just call up a few million like placing a bet on the Panthers. She wears it well.

After she gets off the phone, we take a walk on the beach and let Daisy run around a little.

"So listen." Mac sifts through the sand with her toes, picking out shells that catch her eye. She scoops one up, admires it, then drops it back in the sand. "I know I'm out of my depth here. I'm better at writing checks than rewiring a building."

"That's no sweat. I know everyone in ten square miles who does this kind of work."

"That's what I mean. You know the area, the people."

There's an ask coming, and I can't imagine what it could be that has her dancing around the subject.

"Spit it out, Cabot."

She rounds on me, arching an eyebrow. "I want to hire your uncle Levi to do the work."

I furrow my brow. "What part?"

"All of it. As much as he can handle. Whatever he can't, I want him to sub-contract out to people he trusts. The guys he'd get to do his mother's house. Keep it in the family, so to speak."

"Wow. Okay . . ." I mean, I'd expected her to pick his brain, maybe. Get some references. Maybe toss him a project or two.

This is . . . a lot.

"You seem unsure," Mac observes.

"No, no. I'm not. It's, uhh . . ."

"A big commitment?" She's smiling. Grinning, actually. I think this chick is laughing at me.

"I'm not afraid of commitment, if that's what you're suggesting."

"Uh-huh," she says.

"I'll commit the shit out of you."

"Good." Thinking she's already won, she spins on her toes and resumes walking. "Then we have a deal. You'll set up a meeting with Levi so we can discuss scope and an equitable price."

"Hang on, princess. He's got other jobs on the books already. I don't know what kind of time he has. Don't get ahead of yourself."

"Details." She waves her hand at me. "All can be negotiated. Where there's a will, there's a way."

"Okay, I'll put the offer to him if you keep the cheesy platitudes to yourself."

Mac picks up a piece of driftwood and tosses it for Daisy. "I make no promises."

I roll my eyes at her back. This woman is kind of insufferable, but I love it. Somehow, she got under my skin. Even when she's being obnoxious, I'm still into it.

"Be honest," I say before I can stop myself. "Does this whole thing even put a dent in the trust fund?"

I hesitate to even guess at a number. At a certain point, all the zeros start to run together. The difference between a hundred million and five hundred million is the difference between swimming to China and New Zealand to a drowning man.

She goes quiet for a second. Then another. An apparent unease steals the humor from her face. "Actually, I can't touch my trust fund until I'm twenty-five."

That gives me pause, because how did she buy a hotel, then? I know her parents aren't giving her the money. She's been vocal about their lack of approval for her ambitions.

"Unless you've been a drug kingpin this whole time—I'd be totally sympathetic if you were—where the hell does a twenty-year-old get that kind of cash?"

"You're going to think it's silly," she says, stopping to stare at the ground.

I'm getting a little nervous. Suddenly, I'm wondering if I'd be okay if she told me she was a camgirl or something. Or worse, if she asked me to join her essential oils pyramid scheme.

Fortunately, she works up the nerve to spit it out before my imagination really takes off.

"You remember that time you showed me the funny boyfriend story? The one where the girl was looking for tampons in her date's mom's bathroom?"

My eyebrows fly up. What does that have to do with anything?

"Yeah . . ."

"I built that website. *BoyfriendFails*. Which spun off to *GirlfriendFails*."

"Wait, for real?"

She shrugs. "Yeah."

Holy shit. "And you made all this money from that?"

Another embarrassed shrug. It confuses me, because what is she so shy about?

"Mackenzie, that's badass," I inform her.

"You don't think it's stupid?" She looks at me with these big, hopeful green eyes. I'm not sure if I should feel like a dick that she thought I'd judge her for this.

"Hell no. I'm impressed. When I was twenty, I was still burning mac and cheese." I mean, I'm *still* burning mac and cheese.

"My parents hate it." Her voice grows sour. As it does every time the subject comes up, but more so lately. "You'd think I got a tattoo on my forehead or something. They keep waiting for me to 'grow out of it.'" She makes angry air quotes, kicking sand. "They don't get it."

"What's not to get? Their daughter can't even rent a car yet but she's already a self-made millionaire."

"They're embarrassed. They think it's crass and silly high school nonsense. And, whatever, maybe it is. But what's so wrong with that if it makes people laugh, you know? Far as they're concerned, my business is a distraction. All they want for me is to frame a respectable degree and marry rich, so I can be like Mom and sit on charity boards. It's about appearances. It's all fashion to them."

"See, that sounds dumb as hell." I shake my head, because I truly don't get it. Rich people buying status symbols to impress other rich people who bought the same status symbols to impress them. A vicious cycle of waste and pretension. "Hundreds of thousands of dollars to a university just for looks? Fuck that noise."

"I didn't even want to go to Garnet—it was the only way they'd support my gap year so I could have the time to build my apps and expand the business. But since I got here, all I've been thinking about is tackling a new challenge, finding a new business venture that excites me as much as my websites did when I was first launching them."

"Well, you know what I think? Do you, and to hell what everyone else thinks."

"Easier said than done," she says with that familiar tone of trepidation.

Daisy brings us a small hermit crab hiding in its shell, which Mac takes and sets back in the sand before finding another stick to throw instead.

"Yeah, so what?" Where she's concerned, her parents have always been a daunting obstacle to realizing what she really wants out of life. For someone with every advantage, that's bullshit. She's stronger than that. "If you want it bad enough, fight for it. Take the bruises. What's the worst they can do, cut you off? If you're honest with them about how much this all means to you and they still don't support your dreams, how much are you really going to miss them?"

She lets out a soft sigh. "Honestly, sometimes I wonder if they love me at all. Most of the time, I'm a prop or a piece on a board in their larger game of strategy. I'm plastic to them."

"I could bore the hell out of you with crappy family stories," I tell her. "So I get that. It's not the same, but trust me, I get feeling alone and unloved. Always trying to fill that void with something, anything else. I can almost forgive my dad for being a mean bastard, you know? He had an addiction. It turned everything he touched to shit. Eventually killed him. I wasn't even that sad about it, except then all we had left was our mom. For a while, anyway, but then she split too. The two of them couldn't get away from us fast enough." My throat closes up. "I've spent so much time scared that I'll turn into one of them. Afraid no matter what I do, I'm fighting against the current and I'll end up dead or a deadbeat."

Fuck.

I've never said those words out loud before.

It's terrifying how much Mac brings out of me. How much I want her to know me. It's terrifying how I don't feel in control of my heart that's racing to catch her. To keep her. Worried that at any moment she might come to her senses and ditch my ass.

"Hey." Then she takes my hand, and all I can think is that I'd stand in traffic for this girl. "Let's make a pact: We won't let each other become our parents. The buddy system never fails."

"Deal." It's so corny I half manage a laugh. "Seriously, though. Don't waste this moment. If your heart's telling you to follow something—go for it. Don't let anyone hold you back, because life is too damn short. Build your empire. Slay dragons."

"You should put that on a T-shirt."

Daisy comes back, curling around Mac's feet. Guess she finally ran herself ragged. I put her on the leash as Mac and I sit in the sand. A comfortable silence falls between us. I don't understand how she manages to instill equal parts chaos and peace inside me. When we're arguing, sometimes I want to throttle her. She drives me mad. She does crazy shit like climbing metal ladders during lightning storms. And then suddenly we have moments like this, where we're sitting side by side, quiet, lost in our own thoughts yet completely in tune. Connected. I don't know what it means. Why we can yell at each other one second, and be totally at peace the next. Maybe it just means we're both nuts.

Or maybe it means I'm falling for her.

CHAPTER THIRTY

MACKENZIE

A few days after my hotel inspection, I meet up with Steph and Alana at a sandwich shop in town. Seems strange that a couple of weeks ago we were barely on speaking terms, and now we chat almost every day. It started when Steph looped me into a group text with Alana to share some pictures of Evan on their roof fixing the hole from the storm. His jeans had ridden down, revealing half his ass, and she'd captioned the pics with: *Someone's doing a half-ass job.* Then Alana shared a funny screenshot from *BoyfriendFails*, and—although I was worried it might sound like a brag or serve as another glaring allusion to the topic of money—I confessed to the girls that I'm the one who created those sites. Luckily, it only made them like me more.

"Settle something for us," Alana says, gesturing across the table with a pickle spear. "True or false—Cooper has his dick tattooed."

I almost cough up a french fry. "What?"

"A few years back, there was this story about some chick who got banged on the roof of the police station on Fourth of July weekend," Steph says beside me. "And there was a picture going around of a dude with a tattoo on his dick, but we never nailed down who it was."

"You didn't ask Heidi this question?"

The girls stare at me with apprehension.

"What, was I not supposed to know about that?" My tone is glib. I'd thought it was obvious those two had been hooking up at some point in the recent past.

Steph and Alana exchange a look, silently debating how to respond.

I offer a shrug. "It's fine. I get it, she's your best friend."

"They didn't date or anything," Steph says as a consolation. "It was, you know, friends with benefits."

For Cooper, maybe. But when it comes to those types of arrangements, I know that one person, without fail, is always more invested than the other.

"Heidi's still got a thing," Alana adds flatly, never one to mince words.

I'd already suspected that unrequited feelings or maybe a breakup was the source of Heidi's irrational hatred of me. My instincts are rarely wrong about these things, so Alana's confirmation is almost vindicating.

"I figured," I tell them. "But maybe she'll be ready to move on one of these days. Cooper said there's some guy interested in her? Jay something?"

That earns me two groans.

"Don't get me started on that one," Alana gripes. "Yeah, I want her to get over this Coop thing so life can go back to normal—but Genevieve's brother, of all people?"

"Who's Genevieve?"

"Evan's ex," Steph answers. "Gen lives in Charleston now."

"I miss her," Alana says, visibly glum.

Steph snorts. "So does Evan. Otherwise he wouldn't be trying to bang her out of his system. Or rather, bang everyone else." She flips her ponytail over one shoulder and turns to grin at me. "It's all super incestuous here in the Bay. Evan and Genevieve. Heidi and

Cooper—although thank God that's over. Friends shouldn't hook up, it's just asking for trouble." Her gaze pointedly shifts to Alana. "And then we've got this bitch here who keeps going back for seconds with Tate? Or are we on thirds now? Fourths?"

"Tate?" I echo with a grin. "Oh, he's hot."

Alana waves her hand. "Nah, that's done now. I don't like the friends with bennies thing either."

"I've never done it." I give a self-deprecating shrug. "My hookup history consists of Cooper, and a four-year relationship with a guy who was apparently sleeping with anything that moves."

Steph grimaces. "Honestly, I can't even believe you were dating that creep."

I feel a groove dig into my forehead. "Do you know Preston?" There'd been a troubling sense of familiarity in her statement.

"What? Oh, no, I don't. I mean, I know *of* him. Cooper told us he was cheating on you—I just assume all cheaters are creeps." Steph reaches for her coffee, sips it, turning her face away from me for a second before glancing over with a reassuring smile. "And look, don't worry about Heidi. Cooper's crazy about you."

"And Heidi's been sufficiently threatened to behave herself," Alana finishes, then reacts with a knitted brow when Steph gives her the facial equivalent of a kick under the table. They're about as subtle as a jackhammer.

It's not the first time I've caught a similar exchange between the two of them, as if they're having an entire unspoken conversation I'm not a part of. My relationship with Steph and Alana has warmed significantly—and I have no doubts about Cooper's sincerity where the two of us are concerned—but I get the distinct impression there's a lot more I don't know about this tight-knit group. Obviously, I can't expect to fully penetrate the circle of trust so quickly.

But why does it feel like their secrets are at my expense?

I don't get the chance to ponder that question, as my phone

vibrates in my pocket. It's my mother. Again. I woke up this morning to several missed text messages from her, picking up mid-rant
from the several missed text messages from the night before. I've
taken to periodically blocking her number just to get some peace
from her blowing up my phone. It's one tirade after another over my
breakup with Preston. There's nothing left to say on the subject. For
me, anyway.

But it seems my mother is determined to force me to talk about
it. I glance at my phone to find she's abandoned texting and is now
calling me. I send the call to voicemail just as a 911 text from Bonnie
pops up to alert me that judgment day has arrived.

"What's wrong?" Steph leans over my shoulder, apparently
alarmed at the blood draining from my face.

"My parents are here."

Well, not here. At my dorm. Poor Bonnie's in lockdown mode
awaiting further instructions.

Bonnie: *What do I do with them?*
Me: *Send them to the coffee shop. I'll meet them there.*

I knew this was coming. I've been dodging calls and texts, making myself scarce. But it was only a matter of time before they came
for my reckoning.

No one walks out on my father.

I bail on lunch with an apology and haul ass back to campus
with my blood pressure spiking. After a short phone call, the best I
could do was lure them to a public venue. My parents wouldn't dare
make a scene. Here, I have the strategic advantage—and an escape
route.

Still, when I walk in the café to see them seated by the window,
awaiting their rogue daughter, I struggle to put one foot in front of
the other. No matter how old I get, I'm still six years old, standing in

our living room as my father berates me for spilling fruit punch on my dress before the Christmas card photo shoot, after he specifically told me I could only have water, while my mother stands fraught in the corner by the bar cart.

"Hey," I greet them, draping my purse strap over the chair. "Sorry if I kept you waiting. I was having lunch with some friends in town—"

I halt when I read the expression of impatience on my father's face. He's dressed in a suit, one sleeve pushed up to expose his watch. I get the message. Loud and clear. He's missing meetings and who knows what other world-altering events to tend to his errant offspring. How dare I make him deign to parent.

Then there's Mother Dearest, who's tapping her manicured nails on her leather Chanel clutch as if I'm also holding her up. Honestly, I couldn't say what the hell she does all day. I'm sure there's a call with a caterer somewhere in her schedule. Her weeks are an endless haze of decisions like chicken or fish.

For a split second, as the two of them glare at me with annoyance and disdain, I see the template of their lives superimposed on my future, and it stitches up my side. My throat closes. A full-blown panic explodes through my nervous system. I imagine this is how drowning must feel.

I can't live this way anymore.

"I'm glad you're here," I start, only for Dad to hold up his hand. *Kindly shut up*, the hand says. Okay then.

"I believe you owe us an apology, young lady." Sometimes I wonder if my father uses the term because, for a moment, he's forgotten my name.

"Really, you've gone too far this time," my mother agrees. "Have you any idea the embarrassment you've caused?"

"Here is what's going to happen." Dad doesn't look at me, instead scrolling through emails on his phone. All of this is a prepared speech that doesn't include my participation. "You will apologize to Preston and to his parents for this episode. After which they've agreed to the resumption of your relationship. Then you're coming home for the weekend while we evaluate how to proceed. I'm afraid we've allowed you too much latitude lately."

I stare at him.

When I realize he's being serious, I cough out an incredulous laugh. "Um, no. I can't do that."

"Excuse me." My mother adjusts her scarf, a sort of nervous tic she gets when she's acutely aware she can't snap at me in front of quite so many witnesses. "Your father isn't giving you a choice, Mackenzie."

Well, at least one of them knows my name. I try to imagine them picking out baby names. If ever there was a moment in time they looked forward to a child, it was then, right?

"I won't get back together with Preston." My tone invites no argument.

So, of course, I get one.

"Why not?" Mom wails in exasperation. "Don't be a fool, sweetheart. That boy will make a loyal, upstanding husband."

"Loyal?" I snort loud enough to draw gazes from a few neighboring tables.

Dad frowns at me. "Keep your voice down. You're attracting attention."

"Trust me when I say Preston is *not* loyal to anyone but himself. I'll spare you the details." Like how he was a cheating prick who was probably messing around since the moment we got together. How in some ways he saved us both, because I was no saint either. "But suffice it to say we don't have a connection anymore." I hesitate. Then I think, fuck it. "Besides, I'm seeing someone else."

"Who?" Mom asks blankly, as if Preston were the last man on earth.

"A townie," I reply, because I know it will drive her nuts.

"Enough."

I jump when my father smacks his phone down on the table. Ha. Who's attracting attention now?

Realizing what he did, Dad lowers his voice. He speaks through clenched teeth. "This disobedience stops now. I will not entertain your provocations any further. You will apologize. You will take the boy back. And you will fall in line. Or you can kiss your allowance and credit cards goodbye." His shoulders shake with restrained rage as I now have his complete attention. "So help me, I will cut you off and you can see exactly how cold and dark this path can get."

I don't doubt him for a second. I've always known he was ruthless where I'm concerned. No coddling. No special treatment. That used to scare me.

"Tell you what," I say, pulling my purse off the back of my chair, "here's my counteroffer: no."

His eyes, the same dark shade of green as my own, gleam with disapproval. "Mackenzie," he warns.

I reach into my bag. "Do what you must, but I'm tired of living in fear of disappointing you both. I'm sick of never living up to your ideal. I have had my absolute fill of killing myself to make you happy and constantly falling short. I'm not ever going to be the daughter you want, and I'm done trying."

I find what I'm looking for in my purse. For the first time my life, my parents are speechless as they watch me fill out a check.

I slide it across the table to my father. "Here. This ought to cover what you spent for the first semester. I've decided my interests lie elsewhere."

With nothing left to say—and certain this burst of madness and courage will not last—I hold my breath as I get up from the table and walk out, not sparing a glance behind me.

Just like that, I'm a college dropout.

CHAPTER THIRTY-ONE

MACKENZIE

I'm waiting on Cooper's doorstep when he gets home from work that evening.

After leaving my parents, I had all this pent-up energy and nowhere to release it, so I walked the boardwalk for a while, then strolled down the beach until I wound up at his place. A while later, I'm still sitting on the porch when Cooper's truck parks in their driveway and both brothers get out.

"What's up, princess?" Sauntering up to the front door, Evan gives me a wink as he lets himself inside. We're old pals now, me and the Bad Twin.

"How long have you been out here?" Cooper looks surprised to see me as he comes up the steps.

I momentarily forget what he asks, because I'm too busy gawking. He puts me on my ass every time I see him. His dark eyes and windswept hair. The suggestion of his body under his T-shirt and faded jeans flirts with my memory. There's something wildly masculine about him. He's spent all day on the jobsite, dusty remnants still coating his skin, his clothes. The smell of sawdust. It gets me positively reckless. Reduces my entire being to *want want want*.

"Mac?" he prompts. A knowing smile curves his lips.

"Oh. Sorry. An hour, maybe?"

"Something wrong?"

"Not at all." I take the hand he extends and let him help me to my feet. We go inside. Once we kick off our shoes, I lead him straight to his bedroom.

"I have news," I announce.

"Yeah?"

I close his door and lock it. Because more than once lately, Evan has gotten his kicks by jiggling the handle when he knows we're getting up to something, just to scare the shit out of me. Guy needs a hobby.

"I dropped out of school." I can barely contain my excitement. And maybe there's some fear too. It all feels the same, bubbling inside.

"Holy shit, that's big. How'd that happen?"

"My parents ambushed me on campus and kind of forced my hand."

Cooper peels out of his shirt and tosses it in his hamper. When he starts to unbuckle his belt, I cross the room and pull his hands away, taking over. As I undo his zipper, I feel him watching the top of my head and his abdomen clenches.

"How'd that go?" He sounds a bit distracted now.

Leaving his jeans on, I reach inside his boxers and begin to stroke him. He's already half hard when I do. Quickly, he's fully erect and his breathing is shallow.

"I told them to get bent." I swipe my thumb over the drop of moisture at his tip. He hisses in a sharp breath. "Not in so many words."

"Feeling pretty fucking full of yourself, huh?" His hands comb through my hair and tighten at my scalp.

I lean closer and kiss him under the corner of his jaw. "Just a bit."

Then I walk us backward until his legs hit the bed and he sits on the edge.

Hunger darkens his gaze. "What brought this on?"

"Mostly me." From his nightstand I grab a condom and toss it to him. Then I pull my dress over my head. "A little you."

My bra and underwear drop to the floor.

"Independence looks good on you," he says roughly, running his fist up and down his shaft as he watches my every move.

Slowly, I climb onto his lap. He curses in my ear, grabbing my ass with both hands. With my palms flat against his chest, I ride him. Gently at first, as a flurry of shivers race through me. It's always a shock to my system, being with Cooper. Everything about him feels right, and yet I'm still not used to this. I don't think I want to be. I'm still finding surprises. Still shaken every time his lips travel along my skin.

I rock back and forth. Shamelessly. I can't get him deep enough, close enough. My head falls to his shoulder and I bite down to keep from making a sound as I grind on him.

"Oh hell, I'm not gonna last," he mumbles.

"Good," I breathe.

He groans and gives an upward thrust, his arms tightening around me.

I smile as I watch the haze of bliss fill his expression, as I listen to the husky noises he makes when he comes. After he tosses the condom, he lays me on the bed and kisses his way from my breasts to my stomach, and then lower, until he settles between my legs and opens me to his tongue. Cooper licks me until I'm tugging at his hair and moaning with pleasure. He's too good with his mouth. It's addictive.

Later, after a shower and another round of orgasms, we sit on the front porch with Daisy while a frozen pizza bakes in the oven.

"I don't know if I would've gone through with it if I hadn't met you," I tell Cooper, as our puppy sleeps in his lap. "Dropping out, I mean."

"Yeah, you would have. Eventually. I'm the excuse that gave you a nudge."

"Maybe," I admit. "But you inspired me."

He rolls his eyes.

"Shut up. I mean it." Something I've learned about Cooper: He's terrible at taking compliments. It's one of his more endearing qualities. "You're not afraid of anything or anyone. You make your own rules. Everyone else be damned."

"It comes easy when you don't have shit to start with."

"You believed in me," I say. "You're the only one who ever has. That means a lot. I won't forget that."

But even as I bask in my newfound independence, I'm not naïve enough to believe my parents will take my decision lying down. They'll figure out a way to make it hurt. No one crosses my father and gets away with it. So there will definitely be fallout from this sudden outburst of disobedience. It's only a question of *how bad*.

It doesn't take long for the consequences of my actions to make themselves known. Exactly six days after dropping out, I receive an email from the dean of students. It's short and concise. A polite *Get your ass in here*.

I'm a few minutes late for the meeting, and I'm ushered into a cherry wood–trimmed office by the secretary. The dean is otherwise engaged and will be with me in a moment. Would I care for some water?

I guess my parents made a few calls hoping a neutral third party can lobby me on their behalf to not drop out of school. Though as far as I'm concerned, all that's left are the formalities of paperwork. Admittedly, I've made little progress on finalizing my withdrawal from Garnet. Between the hotel and my websites occupying most of my attention, I've enjoyed what counts for me as slacking off.

"So sorry about that." Dean Freitag, a petite woman whose leather skin clings in brittle ripples to her bones, enters the room. She comes around her desk, breathless, fluffing the humidity out of her shoulder-length helmet of blonde hair. She adjusts the jacket of her cranberry suit ensemble and pulls the silk scarf from her neck. "Hotter than the devil's bathtub out there."

The dean flicks on a small desk fan and aims it at herself, basking for a moment in the breeze before turning her attention back to me.

"Now, Ms. Cabot." Her demeanor shifts. "I understand you've not attended a single class in the last week."

"No, ma'am. I've come to the decision to withdraw from the semester."

"Oh? If I recall, you've already delayed your freshman year by twelve months." One pencil-thin eyebrow props up. "What's so pressing that your education must wait?"

Something about her friendly ignorance unnerves me. As if I'm walking into a trap.

"Actually, I'm withdrawing from Garnet entirely. I won't be back next semester."

She regards me, impassive, for several seconds. So long that I'm almost moved to elaborate to get her going again. When she finally speaks, I can't help but interpret some vengeance in her voice.

"And I suppose you've given this a fair bit of thought?"

"I have. Yes, ma'am."

A brief *suit yourself* smile crosses her lips before she rattles her computer mouse to wake the screen. She trains her attention on it as she speaks.

"Well, then we can certainly help you with that. I'll have my secretary pull the necessary forms." She glances at me with a look that falls short of reassurance. "Don't worry, it's just a signature or two." Clicking her mouse around. "Of course you'll need to vacate your dorm at Tally Hall within twenty-four hours of submitting notice to the Office of Student Housing." She hits me with the Miss Melon Pageant smile. "Which—here we are!—I've just submitted it for you."

And there it is. Total setup.

A big *screw you* from Daddy.

She's right, of course. I have no business squatting in a dorm room if I'm not a student here. A minor detail that seemed to slip my mind. No doubt my parents spent the last week waiting for me to come crawling back home for a place to stay.

"Will there be anything else?" The dean grins at me as if I've done this to her. A personal slight.

I don't waste a second agonizing over it, however. For better or worse, we're broken up.

"No, ma'am." I offer a saccharine smile and rise to my feet. "I'll just be on my way."

An hour later, I'm in my dorm, boxing up my belongings. A little over three months. That's how long my college career lasted, and yet . . . I'm not sad to see it end.

I'm pulling clothes off hangers when I hear the buzz of an incoming text. I grab the phone from my desk. It's a message from Kate, who I haven't seen in weeks. I asked her to hang out a couple times—I didn't want to be one of those girls who ditches her friends the moment she starts dating a new guy—but she's been busy rehearsing with some band she joined last month. She plays the bass guitar, apparently.

Kate: *Hey girl! Sooo, heads up—I spoke to my sister on the phone earlier and your name came up. Mel said your ex is asking around, trying to find out who you're dating. I guess someone saw you in town with some local?*

I curse out loud. Damn Evan. I knew that night would come back to haunt us.

> Me: *Ugh. Awesome.*
> Kate: *Yeah. Preston's on a mission now. You've been warned.*
> Me: *Thanks for letting me know.*
> Kate: *Np. Btw—our first gig is next Friday, open mic thing at the Rip Tide in town. Come!*
> Me: *Text me the deets!*

Before I can get back to packing, the phone vibrates again in my hand. Speak of the devil. This time it's Preston, and he's not happy.

> Preston: *You dropped out of Garnet? WTF is wrong with you, Mackenzie. Why are you throwing your life away?*

My jaw tightens. I'm so sick of his high and mighty bullshit. The judgmental, patronizing way he treats me, acting as if I'm incapable of living my own life.

> Me: *Out of curiosity, are you spying on me personally or are you paying other people to keep tabs on me?*
> Preston: *Your father called me. He thinks you've gone off the rails.*
> Me: *I don't give a shit what he thinks.*
> Me: *I also don't give a shit what you think.*
> Me: *Stop texting me.*

When I see him typing, I switch on Do Not Disturb mode. I can't bring myself to block his number yet. A concession to our history, I guess. But I have a feeling I'll need to, sooner or later.

When Bonnie returns to the dorm following her afternoon class,

I'm completely done packing. The little blonde stops short in our common area and stares at the half dozen boxes lined up against the wall.

"You goin' on the run?" She tosses down her backpack and grabs a water from the mini fridge, then stands there with the door open, cooling her legs.

"Got kicked out," I answer with a shrug. "It was bound to happen."

"Well, shit." She pushes the fridge closed with her foot. "You think I'll get to keep the place to myself now?"

I smile at her. Bonnie isn't an especially sentimental girl, but I know she cares. "I'll miss you too."

"What are you going to do with all your stuff?" She nods toward the boxes. Then she gives a catty smile. "I suppose we can ask our cheatin' ex to borrow his Porsche?"

I snicker. "I'm sure that would go over well." Walking toward my former bedroom, I fish my phone from my pocket. "It's fine, I know someone with a truck. Let me see if he can come get me."

"Oooh, is it the townie with the magic dick?"

"Maybe." Laughing, I duck into the bedroom to make my call.

"Hey babe. What's up?" Cooper's rough voice tickles my ear and sends a shiver up my spine. He even sounds sexy.

"Hey. So. I have a big ask."

"Shoot." The banging of hammers and whir of saws fade in the background, like he's stepping away from his jobsite.

"I have to vacate my dorm. Was tossed out, basically. I guess I'm not allowed to live in student housing when I'm not a student."

"You realize that's a completely reasonable decision on the school's part, right?"

"They gave me twenty-four hours' notice," I argue. "How reasonable is that?"

He chuckles. "Need help packing?"

"Nope, but I'm hoping you can pick me up after you're done working so I can load some boxes in your truck? I'll put most of it in a storage unit in town until I find an apartment." I hesitate. "And, um, I could use a place to crash until I find something more permanent. If it's not too much to ask."

I mean, it is a lot to ask. We've barely started dating. Moving in, even on a temporary basis, is no small favor. Yes, Evan and I are on good terms now, which eases the possible tension, but they didn't exactly sign up for a third roommate.

"No, you know what," I interject when he starts to answer, "I'll get a hotel. That'd make way more sense."

Because seriously, what was I thinking? This was a stupid idea. How did I think my first option should be to force my way into Cooper's house, as if I've known him for longer than a few months? That's insane.

"There's that motel at the north side of the beach. I bet they rent rooms weekly—"

"Mac?"

"Yeah?"

"Shut up."

I bite back a laugh. "Rude."

"You're not staying at a shithole motel on the north side. You're staying with me. The end."

"You're sure? I didn't really think this through before I called, I just—"

"I'm done at six. I'll come grab you from campus afterward."

A lump of emotion rises in my throat. "Thanks. I, uh . . . damn it, Cooper, I really appreciate it."

"I got you, princess." Then he hangs up with a harried goodbye, leaving me to smile at the phone. Not that I expected Cooper to be a dick about it, but he's taking the whole thing remarkably well.

"I'm sorry, do my ears deceive me?" a highly excited voice bubbles

from my open doorway. "Or did I just hear you refer to our mysterious caller as *Cooper*?"

I meet her wide eyes. Sheepish.

"As in Cooper Hartley?"

I nod.

Bonnie gasps loud enough startle me, even though she's right in
front of me. "Oh sweet little baby Jesus! *That's* who you been hidin'
from me?" She barrels into the room, blonde curls flying around her
shoulders. "You are not leavin' this dormitory till you provide me
with every last detail. I need *everything*."

CHAPTER THIRTY-TWO

COOPER

This chick is out of her mind.

"What is the peanut butter doing in the refrigerator?" I shout from the kitchen.

I swear to God, having three people in this house has turned the place into a circus. I used to know where Evan was by the creaks and groans the house made around him. Now there's two of them and it's like this old place is haunted—constant noises coming from every direction at once. Hell, at this point, you could probably convince *me* that Patricia exists.

"Hey!" I shout again into the void. "The hell did you go?"

"Right here, dipshit." Evan appears beside me, shouldering me out of the way as he grabs the two six-packs of beers from the fridge and throws them in the cooler.

"Not you. The other one."

He shrugs in response and leaves the kitchen with the cooler.

"What's up?" Mac pops in from fuck knows where in a tiny bikini. Her tits are pouring out of the top, and the little strip of fabric between her legs is begging me to rip it off with my teeth. Damn.

"Did you do this?" I hold up the jar of some peanut butter brand I've never heard of. It was sitting in the door of the fridge the whole time I was emptying every cabinet in the kitchen looking for a jar of Jif.

She scrunches her face at me. "Do what?"

"Who puts peanut butter in the fridge?"

"Uh . . ." She comes over and takes the jar from me, turns it around in her hand. "It says so right on the label."

"But then it gets all hard. It's gross." I open the jar to see an inch-thick layer of oil on top of the solid butter. "What's all this shit?"

"It's organic," she tells me like I'm stupid for asking. "It separates. You have to stir it up a little."

"Why on earth would anyone want to *stir* their peanut butter? You actually eat this?"

"Yes. It's delicious. And you know what? You could do with laying off the added sugar. You seem a little wound up."

Am I having a stroke? I feel like I'm losing my mind. "What does that have to do with anything?"

Mac rolls her eyes and kisses my cheek. "There's regular peanut butter in the pantry." Then she walks out onto the deck after Evan, shaking her ass at me.

"What pantry?" I yell after her.

When she ignores me, I turn to examine my surroundings until my gaze finally lands on the broom closet. A sinking feeling settles in my gut.

I open the closet door to discover she's moved out the tools, emergency hurricane supplies, and other shit I'd neatly organized in there. It's been replaced by all the real food that had mysteriously gone missing after she moved in and started filling our cabinets with non-GMO certified fair-trade flax seed crackers and whatever the fuck.

"Let's go." Evan pokes his head inside.

"You see this?" I ask him, pointing at the "pantry."

"Yeah, it's better, right?" Then he slips outside again, calling over his shoulder, "Meet you out front."

Traitor.

It's only been a week since Mac moved in, and already she's turned the dynamic of the house upside down. Evan's in a weirdly good mood lately, which I don't trust in the slightest. All the counter space in my bathroom has been annexed. The food's weird. The toilet paper's different. And every time I turn around, Mac's moving stuff around the house.

But then something like this happens. I lock the front door and step onto the porch to find Mac and Evan laughing their asses off about who knows what as they wait for me. They seem happy. Carrying on as if they've known each other forever.

I still don't know how or when things changed. One day, Evan stopped leaving the room when she walked in and muttering under his breath. She'd been inducted into the brotherhood. One of us. Practically family. A scary thought, if only because I hadn't dared hope for as much. I figured to some extent we'd be fighting the blood feud, townies versus clones, till we were all sick of each other. I'm happy to be wrong. Though some part of me doesn't trust it, because nothing comes this easy for long.

Evan and I carry the cooler to the truck, setting it in the bed of the pickup. My brother hops up too, using his backpack for a pillow as he stretches out like a lazy asshole.

"Wake me when we get there," he says smugly, and I vow to hit as many potholes as possible on the drive to the boardwalk, where we're meeting some friends. Earlier, Wyatt called everyone to organize a volleyball tournament. Nearly all of us were down, wanting to make the most of the good weather while it lasts.

"Hey," Mac says as I slide into the driver's seat. "I grabbed a book off your shelf in case you wanted something to read between games."

She's rummaging through the oversized beach bag at her feet. To my disappointment, she's slipped a tank top and a pair of shorts on, covering up that insanely hot bikini.

"Thanks. Which one?"

She holds up the paperback—*Rags to Riches: 10 Billionaires That Came from Nothing and Made Everything.* The title is corny as hell, but the content is pure gold.

"Nice." I nod. "That's a good one."

"Your bookshelf is fascinating," she says matter-of-factly. "I don't think I've ever met anyone who reads so many biographies."

I shrug. "I like them."

I steer the truck down the dusty, sand-covered drive to the stop sign at the end of the road. I signal left and when I twist my body to ensure the way is clear, I suddenly feel Mac's fingertips graze the nape of my neck.

Heat instantly travels to the southern region of my body. A common reaction to her touch.

"I just noticed this," she says in surprise. Her fingers trace my most recent tattoo. "Did you always have this anchor?"

"Nah. Got it done a couple months ago."

When she removes her hand, I feel a sense of loss. If it were up to me, this girl's hands would be on me twenty-four seven.

"I like it. It's simple, clean." She smiles at me. "You're really into all the nautical stuff, huh?"

I grin. "I mean, I do live on the beach. Although, to be honest, it's just a coincidence that a lot of my ink involves water. And the anchor was a spur of the moment tat when I was in a bad mood." I give her the side-eye. "It was after you told me you were picking your ex over me."

"Dumbest mistake I ever made."

"Damn right." I wink at her.

"Luckily, I rectified it." She smirks and plants her palm over my thigh. "So the anchor represents what? You being pissed at me?"

"Feeling weighed down. I'd just been rejected by the coolest, smartest, funniest girl I've ever known. And she didn't want me."

I shrug. "I felt like I've been dragged down my entire life. By this town. The memory of my parents. Dad was a loser. Mom is a loser." Another shrug, this one accompanied by a dry smile. "I have a bad habit of getting very straightforward, un-metaphorical tattoos. No subtext at all on this body."

That gets me a laugh. "I happen to like this body very much." She squeezes my thigh, not at all subtly. "And you're not a loser."

"Certainly trying not to be." I gesture to the book in her lap. "I read stuff like that—biographies, memoirs by these men and women who crawled out of poverty or bad circumstances and made something of themselves—because they inspire me. One of the dudes in that book? Mother was widowed, left with five kids she couldn't take care of, so she sends him to an orphanage. He's poor, alone, goes to work at a factory when he's still young, making auto part molds, eyeglass frames. When he's twenty-three, he opens up his own molding shop." I tip my head toward Mac. "And that shop ends up creating the Ray-Ban brand."

Mackenzie's hand travels to my knee, giving it a squeeze, before seeking out my hand on the gearshift. She laces our fingers.

"You inspire me," she says simply. "And I have no doubt, by the way, that your name will end up in a book like this someday."

"Maybe."

At the beach, Wyatt and the rest of the crew have already claimed one of the volleyball nets. Nearby, the girls are set up on the sand with an umbrella. Steph reads a book, Heidi tans on her stomach, and Alana looks characteristically bored with all of it while she sips a concealed cocktail from a water bottle.

Evan and I greet the guys with fist bumps. We've barely finished saying our hellos before Wyatt starts shouting at everyone to break up into teams.

"Getting dumped turned him into a real dictator, eh?" Tate mutters as we watch our buddy order us around like a drill sergeant.

I chuckle. "She still hasn't taken him back?"

"Nope. I think it might actually be over this time—" Tate stops, narrowing his eyes.

I look over to see Wyatt tugging Alana out of her beach chair. She sighs and takes his hand. I guess she's on his team. Although what's up with the way he's whispering in her ear?

"What's that about?" I ask Tate.

"No clue." His jaw is tight.

Okay, then.

The volleyball tournament gets under way. And since we're all a competitive bunch here in the Bay, it turns intense fast. Mac's on my team, and I'm pleasantly surprised to discover she has a killer serve. Thanks to her, we take an early lead that has us winning the first game. Wyatt's crew wins the second. For the tiebreaker, Mac tags Steph in and walks down to the water.

"I'll sub back in," she calls to me. "Just cooling off for a bit."

I nod and return to the task of crushing Wyatt and Evan's team into the sand. It isn't until an hour passes that I realize Steph's still playing in Mackenzie's place.

"Dude!" Tate grouses when I miss a spike.

But my focus is now on finding Mac. My gaze roams up and down the beach until finally I spot her. She's at the water's edge talking to someone.

Despite the sun beating down on my head and bare chest, my entire body runs cold when I recognize who she's with.

Kincaid.

CHAPTER THIRTY-THREE

COOPER

"Coop, it's your serve," Steph says expectantly.

"I'm out," I tell the group, throwing up my hands. I seek out my brother's eyes on the other side of the net.

"Evan" is all I have to say for him to jog to my side. When I nod in Mac's direction, his expression darkens.

"Fuck," he curses.

"I know."

Trying to look like we're not in too much of a hurry, we make our way over there to protests from our teams for walking off the game. Screw the game. My ass is about to be in deep shit if this goes sideways.

"How are we playing this?" Evan murmurs.

"Not sure. Follow my lead." As we approach the water's edge, it occurs to me that it might've been better if I'd pretended not to notice Kincaid and kept my distance, camouflaged myself in the group of volleyball players. But there's no way in hell I'm leaving Mac hanging with that asshole around.

"There a problem here?" Putting my arm around Mac's shoulder, I square up to Kincaid, who is conspicuously alone.

A moment of confusion crosses his face as he recognizes me. It was probably too much to hope he had forgotten all about me.

His eyes narrow as he does the math in his head.

"Hang on, this is the guy?" he demands, his head swiveling back to Mackenzie.

Mac shoots me a frustrated glare. She notices Evan lingering nearby and lets out a sigh. "Yes, this is the guy. And now we're leaving. Enjoy the rest of your afternoon, Pres."

"Hang on a minute." He sounds incensed as we start to walk away. "This is goddamn convenient. I *know* this loser."

I feel Mac stiffen slightly. She stops, turning toward her ex. "What are you talking about?"

Kincaid meets my eyes with a pompous smirk. "She has no idea, does she?"

I have a split second to decide. Deep down, though, I know there's no choice, at least not with Kincaid here providing an audience.

So I say, "Am I supposed to know you?"

No one plays dumb better than a kid who pulled the twin swap on damn near every algebra test in school.

"Yeah, nice try, bro." He returns his attention to Mac. "Let me guess, this guy showed up right after you got to town? Some friendly townie you happened to run into on a night out with the girls. Stop me if this sounds familiar."

A frown touches her lips. "Cooper, what is he talking about?"

The second she fixes her concerned green eyes at me, my mouth turns to sand. Acid rises in my stomach.

"No idea," I lie.

I scare myself with how easily I can lie to her. How convincingly the words slide out of my mouth. Not the slightest flinch.

"Mackenzie, babe, listen to me." Kincaid reaches out to touch her, and it takes a hell of an effort to not break his hand as I step between them. Mouth flattening, he drops his arm. "The weekend before school started, this guy picked a fight with me in a bar and

I got him fired on the spot. Remember? I had a black eye when I helped you move into the dorm?"

"You told me you got it playing basketball," she accuses with no small amount of venom in her voice.

"Yeah, okay, I lied." He concedes the point grudgingly, hurrying to make his case as Mac's crossed arms and lack of eye contact say he's losing her interest quickly. "But I'm not lying now."

"How am I supposed to tell the difference?" Nobody matches up to Mac in a battle of attrition. She'd argue all day about the number of clouds in the sky just to be right.

"Isn't it obvious?" He's losing his patience, tossing his hands in the air. "He's only fucking you to get back at me."

"Alright, that's enough." If I can't put his face in the sand and end this here, I'm not sticking around to let him blow up my life. "You need to get outta here, man. Leave her alone."

"Mackenzie, come on," he pleads. "You're not seriously falling for his BS, right? I know you're young, but you can't be this stupid."

That does it. The thick accents of condescension trigger Mac's last nerve, and her expression grows stormy.

"The dumbest thing I ever did was dating you for so long," she retorts. "Fortunately, that's not a decision I have to live with."

She tears off toward our group, brushing past Evan. As the two of us fall in line behind her, I have a vivid flashback to the many times we got marched to the principal's office by our teachers. I feel rather than see Evan asking me if we're good, but I don't have an answer until we reach our patch of sand and Mac spins on me.

"Out with it," she orders.

"With what?"

Even as I stonewall her, I wonder if this is the moment I should come clean. Admit I had less than honorable intentions at first, but that things changed after we met.

She'd understand. Maybe even get a kick out of it. We'd have a good laugh and it'd become a funny story we tell at parties.

Or she'd never talk to me again, until I come home one day to my house on fire and a sign stuck in the ground with *We should see other people* written on it in ash.

"Don't mess with me." Mac sticks a finger in my chest. "What was he talking about? You two know each other?"

Once again, we have an audience, and once again, feeling our friends' eyes on us, my courage abandons me. If I tell her the truth in private, there's a chance I'll lose her. If I tell her the truth in front of a dozen other people, losing her is a guarantee. She'd be humiliated in front of everyone. She'd never forgive me.

This time, the lies burn my tongue. "Everything I know about him I heard around town, or from you. Couldn't have picked that guy out of a lineup."

She becomes eerily still, barely breathing as she stares at me.

Panic churns in my gut, but on the outside I maintain a neutral expression. I stick to my story. I learned a long time ago, those who get caught are the ones who break. The key to a successful lie is to believe it. Then deny, deny, deny.

"Was there a fight?" Mac cocks her head as if she's trapped me.

"Mac, they could fill football stadiums with the number of idiots who get drunk and start shit. If he was one of them, I honestly wouldn't remember."

Visibly frustrated, she turns to Evan. "Did Cooper really get fired?"

For a split second, I worry their new platonic romance might end me.

"He had a summer job at Steph's bar." With a shrug, Evan even has me convinced. Guess we're still on the same side when it counts. "It was temporary."

She looks past Evan to where Steph has resettled in her chair and picked up her book. "Steph?" Mac says. "Is that true?"

Without looking up from her book, Steph nods behind her thick black sunglasses. "It was a summer gig."

Relief trickles into me, then dissolves when I notice Heidi edging closer to the group. There's indecision in her expression.

Fuck.

I know that look. Mischief for mischief's sake. Heidi's the girl who's never missed an opportunity to set a fire just to hear the screams. Add to this the fact that she's been mad at me more often than not lately, and that she's not a fan of this arrangement or Mac. But when our gazes briefly meet, I silently plead with her to give me this one thing.

"Seriously, guys, I'm starved," she says with a bored whine. "Can we get the hell out of here already?"

By the skin of my teeth, I make it out alive.

Every day after that, I'm holding my breath, waiting for the other shoe to drop. Looking over my shoulder for Kincaid to sneak up on us again. Mac seems to let the matter go, and Evan and I have been avoiding the subject by miles. But it was a close call. Too close. A reminder how fragile our relationship is and how easily it can all be ripped from my hands. That realization hits me harder than I thought possible. She's under my skin and getting deeper.

The night of our run-in with Kincaid, after Mac had gone to bed, I ended up in my workshop sucking on a cigarette like a madman, hoping the nicotine would ease the guilt, the stress, the fear. Usually, I only smoke when I'm drinking, and even that isn't a hard and fast rule. But lying to Mackenzie had wrecked me.

Evan found me there at one in the morning, nearly half a pack's worth of cigarette butts in the ashtray on my worktable.

"I need to tell her the truth," I'd said miserably.

He'd balked. "Are you fucked? What's that gonna achieve, man? The plan was aborted. You're with her because you like her."

"But it started as a way to get back at Kincaid. Me and her, this whole relationship, was founded on bad intentions."

In the end, Evan convinced me to stay quiet. Though who am I kidding, it didn't take much convincing. The thought of losing Mackenzie rips my insides to shreds. I can't lose her. And Evan was wrong—I'm not with her because I like her.

I'm in love with her.

And so I banish the guilt to the furthest recesses of my mind. I work hard to be the kind of man Mac needs, deserves. And then, one morning, we're lying in bed and I take my first deep breath in almost a month. She's barely awake when she rolls over and drapes her leg over my hip. An overwhelming sense of calm I've never known before envelopes me as she cuddles into my chest.

"Morning," she whispers. "What time is it?"

"Dunno. Ten, maybe?"

"Ten?" She sits abruptly. "Shoot. Your uncle will be here soon. We gotta clean this place up."

It's cute she thinks Levi gives a shit.

She leaves me alone in bed to take a shower, reappearing ten minutes later with wet hair and a flushed face.

"Ugh. I can't find my blue dress," she grumbles from the closet, half of which now contains her clothes.

It's been weeks since she came to stay with us, and yet nobody's brought up the prospect of her moving out. I'm happy to ignore the subject. Sure, having another person in the house has been an adjustment. And maybe we're still learning how to respect each other's quirks. But she makes the place feel warm again, like a home rather than a house. She gives the place some life after years of bad memories and empty rooms.

She just fits.

"So wear something else. Or don't and come back to bed."

"It's my *take me seriously* dress," she calls from under what sounds like a mountain of hangers.

She's got no reason to be nervous about meeting with Levi. He might look intimidating, but he's the friendliest guy you'd ever meet. And yes, there's a lot to be said for not mixing business with pleasure, but I'm choosing to look at this possible endeavor of them working on the hotel together from an optimistic perspective.

"How about this one?" She comes out modeling a green top that matches her eyes and a pair of navy pants that hug her ass in a way that is not helping my semi.

"You look great."

Her answering smile. The way her head tilts and eyes shine. Those looks that are only for me. They get me right in the fucking chest.

I've absolutely lost my head over this chick.

"What?" she asks, lingering at the foot of the bed and wrapping her hair in a knot atop her head.

"Nothing." All I can do is smile at her and hope I don't screw this up. "I think I'm happy, is all."

Mac comes over and plants a kiss on my cheek. "Me too."

"Yeah? Even with, you know, your parents basically disowning you?"

Shrugging, she walks into the bathroom. I get dressed and watch her in the mirror as she puts on her makeup.

"I don't love not being on speaking terms with them," she admits. "But they're the ones being stubborn. Choosing to live my own life is hardly grounds for excommunication."

I've been worried that the longer this dispute with her parents rages on in silent conflict, the more she'll come to regret her decision to leave school. To buy the hotel. To be with me. But so far, there's been no sign of remorse on her part.

"They're going to have to get over it eventually," she says, turning to look at me. "I'm not stressing over it, you know? Rather not give them the satisfaction."

I search her face for any traces of dishonesty and find none. As far as I can tell, she *is* happy. I'm trying not to let myself sink into that paranoid place. I have a way of spiraling with anticipation of catastrophe. But that's always been the rhythm of my life. Things start looking too good and a house falls out of the sky.

This time, I'm hoping she's broken the curse.

CHAPTER THIRTY-FOUR

MACKENZIE

Well, it's not winter in Jackson Hole or Aspen—the weather's been in the seventies all weekend like Carolina's stuck in autumn—but shopping for a Christmas tree with Cooper and Evan has thus far been an adventure. Already we've been chased out of three tree lots because these ruffians are incapable of behaving themselves in public. Between challenging each other to see who can bench press the biggest tree and holding a jousting contest in the middle of a grocery store parking lot, we're running out of options to find a tree without crossing state lines.

"What about this one?" Evan says from somewhere in the artificial forest.

To be fair, one of the lots we got kicked out of was for Cooper and I getting caught making out behind the Douglas firs. Proving he hasn't learned his lesson, Cooper sneaks up on me and smacks my ass while I try to navigate my way toward his brother.

"Looks like your eighth-grade girlfriend," Cooper remarks when we find Evan standing next to a round spruce that's big on the top and bottom but noticeably naked in the middle.

Evan smirks. "Jealous."

"This one's nice." I point to another tree. It's full and fluffy, with plenty of evenly spaced branches for ornaments. No gaping holes or apparent brown spots.

Cooper sizes up the tree. "Think we can get it through the door?"

"Can bring it in through the back," Evan answers. "Pretty tall, though. We might have to poke a hole in the ceiling."

I grin. "Worth it."

I've always been a big-tree girl, though I was never allowed to pick out my own. My parents had people for that. Every December a box truck would show up and unload a mall's worth of decorations. A huge, perfect tree for the living room, and smaller ones for nearly every other living area in the house. Garlands, lights, candles, and the whole lot. Then an interior decorator and a small army of help would transform the house. Not once did my family get together to decorate the trees; we never looked for the perfect branch for each keepsake ornament like other families seemed to do. All we had was a bunch of expensive, rented junk to accomplish whatever motif my mother was interested in that year. Another set dressing for their life of parties and entertaining influential people or campaign donors. A completely sterile holiday season.

And yet despite that, I find myself a bit emotional at the idea of not seeing my parents for the holidays. We're still barely speaking, although my father did courier over a stack of Christmas cards and order me to sign my name under his and my mother's. Apparently the cards are being delivered to hospitals and charities in my father's congressional district, courtesy of the perfect Cabot family who cares so much about humanity.

That evening after dinner, the three of us scrounge for decorations and lights in the attic, buried under years of dust.

"I don't think we've decorated for Christmas in, what?" Cooper questions his brother as we carry the boxes to the living room. "Three, four years?"

"Seriously?" I set my box on the hardwood floor and sit in front of the tree.

Evan opens a box of tangled lights. "Something like that. Not since high school, at least."

"That's so sad." Even a plastic Christmas is better than nothing.

"We've never been big on holidays in this family." Cooper shrugs. "Sometimes we do stuff at Levi's house. Usually Thanksgivings, because every other year for Christmas they go see Tim's family in Maine."

"Tim?" I ask blankly.

"Levi's husband," Evan supplies.

"Partner," Cooper corrects. "I don't think they're actually married."

"Levi's gay? How come this is the first I'm hearing of it?"

The twins give identical shrugs, and for a second I understand why their teachers had a tough time telling them apart. "It's not really something he talks about," Cooper says. "They've been together for, like, twenty years or something, but they don't flaunt their relationship. They're both really private people."

"Most folks in town know," Evan adds. "Or suspect. Everyone else just assumes they're roommates."

"We should've had a dinner here and invited them." I feel glum at the lost opportunity. If I'm going to be living in Avalon Bay and staying with the twins, it might be nice to form deeper connections.

It's strange. Although we grew up in two opposite worlds, Cooper and I aren't that different. In many ways, we've had parallel experiences. The more I come to understand him, the more I realize that our shared language is deeply influenced by the ways we've felt neglected.

"Dude, I think some of these ornaments are from Grandma and Grandpop." Evan drags a box closer to the tree. The guys dig into it, pulling out little, handmade ornaments with photos inside. Dates from '53, '61. Souvenirs from trips all over the country. Evan holds up a little cradle that must have belonged to a manger set at one point. "What the ever-loving fuck is this?"

He shows us a swaddled baby Jesus that more closely resembles a little baked potato in tinfoil with two black dots for eyes and a pink line for a mouth.

I blanch. "That's disturbing."

"Didn't even know these were here." Cooper admires a picture I can only guess is his dad as a boy. Then he tucks it back in the bottom of the box.

Once again, a lump of emotion clogs my throat. "I wish I had boxes like these at home, full of old pictures and knickknacks, with interesting stories behind them that my parents could tell me about."

Cooper gets up to heave one of the larger boxes back to the hallway. "I don't know . . . Having a bunch of servants to do the heavy lifting can't have been all that bad," he calls over his shoulder.

"Not to mention waking up to a ton of presents," Evan pipes up.

"Sure," I say, picking out the ornaments that are still in good shape and appear the least emotionally detrimental. "It *sounds* great. It was like waking up in Santa's workshop. Until you get old enough to realize all the cards on your presents aren't written in your parents' handwriting. And instead of elves, they're actually people your parents pay to keep as much distance as possible between them and anything approaching sentimentality."

"Bet they were sick presents, though," Evan says with a wink. We've moved well past the *how many ponies did you get for your birthday* jokes, but he can't always resist getting in a jab.

I shrug sadly. "I'd give them all back if it meant my parents would want to spend time together, even just once. To act like we were a family rather than a business venture. My dad was always working, and Mom was more worried about her charity functions—

which, yeah, I know, she wasn't boiling puppies or something. There are worse things than raising money for a children's hospital. But I was a child too. Couldn't I have gotten some of that holiday spirit?"

"Aww, come here, you little shit." Evan throws his arm around my neck and kisses the top of my head. "I'm messing with you. Parents fucking blow. Even rich ones. We're all screwed up, one way or another."

"All I mean is, doing this, the three of us, means a lot to me," I tell them, surprised at myself when my eyes start stinging. If I cried in front of these guys, I'd never hear the end of it. "It's my first real Christmas."

Cooper pulls me on his lap and wraps his arms around me. "We're glad you're here."

Evan disappears for second, then returns with a small box. "Okay. So I was going to sneak this in your stocking later, but I think you should have it now."

I stare at the box. He's done an absolutely awful job of wrapping it, the corners all uneven and held down with way more tape than anything the size of my palm should require.

"Don't worry," he says, "it's not stolen."

I crack a smile as I tear into the present with all the grace of a petulant preschooler. Inside, I find a plastic figure of a girl in a pink dress. Her hair is colored black with a permanent marker and a tiny, yellow crown cut from paper is glued to her head.

"I swear I looked in six different stores for a princess ornament. You have no idea how fucking hard it is to find one." He grins. "So I made my own."

My eyes water. Another lump lodges in my throat.

"I wanted to get you something. To celebrate."

My hands shake.

"I mean, it's supposed to be funny. I promise I wasn't trying to be a dick or anything."

Doubling over, I start laughing hysterically. So hard my ribs hurt. Cooper can't hold me, and I tumble to the floor.

"Is she laughing or crying?" Evan asks his twin.

It's honestly the sweetest thing anyone's ever done for me. All the more meaningful that Evan put so much effort into the perfect gift. His brother's going to have to step up his game if he wants to compete.

Once I've collected myself, I get up and hug Evan, who seems relieved that I'm not kicking his ass. I guess there was always the chance the gift would backfire, but I think Evan and I have reached an understanding.

"If you two are done, can we get this damn tree finished?" Apparently feeling left out, Cooper pouts behind us.

"Keep that attitude up and you're not getting your present tonight," I warn him.

"Please," Evan says, hushing us with his finger over his mouth. "Baby Potato Jesus can hear you."

A few days later, after the most low-key—and best—holiday I've ever had, I'm with Cooper in his workshop, helping him dust, polish, and wrap some furniture. I think watching me manage the hotel renovation gave him a kick in the butt to push himself harder with his own business venture. He's been pounding the pavement and making inquiries, and this week, he received a couple calls from boutique stores that want to sell a few of his pieces. This morning, we sent off new photographs for their websites, and now we're getting everything ready for transport.

"You're not selling my set, right?" I ask anxiously.

"The one you never paid for?" He winks, coming up to me covered in the sawdust that clings to everything in here.

"Things got a little hectic. But you're right, I owe you a check."

"Forget it. I can't take your money." He shrugs adorably. "Those pieces were always yours whether you bought them or not. Once you laid hands on them, it would have felt wrong to let them go anywhere else."

My heart somersaults in my chest. "First of all, that's one of the sweetest things you've ever said. And second of all, you can totally take my money. That's the thing about money. It works everywhere."

"Spoken like a true clone."

For that, I smack him with my polishing rag.

"Hands, Cabot."

"Yeah, I'll show you hands, Hartley."

"Oh yeah?" With a smirk, he tugs me toward him, his mouth covering mine in a possessive kiss.

His tongue is just slicking over mine when an unfamiliar female voice chirps from the open garage door.

"Knock, knock!"

CHAPTER THIRTY-FIVE

COOPER

I freeze at the sound of that voice behind me. My blood stings ice cold. I hope as I grudgingly turn around that the sound was a vivid hallucination.

No such luck.

At the entrance, Shelley Hartley stands waving at me.

Goddamn it.

I don't how long it's been since the last time she blew into town. Months. A year, maybe. The image of her in my mind is distorted and constantly shifting. She looks the same, I guess. Bad blonde dye job. Too much makeup. Dressed like a woman half her age who wandered into a Jimmy Buffet concert and never left. It's the smile, though, as she waltzes into the workshop, that gets my back up. She hasn't earned it.

My brain is reeling. Someone's pulled the pin and handed me a live grenade, and I've got seconds to figure out how not to let it blow up in my face.

"Hey, baby," she says, throwing her arms around me. The stench of gin, cigarettes, and lilac-scented perfume brings hot bile rising to the back of my throat. Few smells send me so violently back to childhood. "Momma missed you."

Yeah, I bet.

It takes her about six seconds to catch her eyes on Mac and the diamond bracelet she wears that belonged to her great-grandmother. Shelley all but shoves me out of the way to grab Mac's wrist under the pretense of a handshake.

"Who's this pretty girl?" she asks me, beaming.

"Mackenzie. My girlfriend," I tell her flatly. Mac flicks her eyes to me in confusion. "Mac, this is Shelley. My mom."

"Oh." Mac blinks, recovering quickly. "It's, ah, nice to meet you."

"Well, come on and help me inside," Shelley says, still holding onto Mac. "I've got groceries for dinner. Hope everyone's hungry."

There's no car in the driveway. Just a bunch of paper bags sitting on the front porch steps. No telling how she got here or what dreadful wind blew her back into town. She was probably kicked out by another pathetic sap who she drained for every last dime. Or she ran out on him in the middle of the night before he discovered she'd robbed him blind. I know this for certain: It won't end well. Shelley is a walking catastrophe. She leaves only ruin in her wake, most of it laid at the feet of her sons. I learned a long time ago that nothing with her is ever as it seems. If she's breathing, she's lying. If she's smiling at you, guard your wallet.

"Evan, baby, Momma's home," she calls when we get inside.

He comes out of the kitchen at the sound of her voice. His face blanches at realizing, as I did, it isn't a trick of his imagination. He stands dead still, almost as if expecting her to evaporate. Indecision plays behind his eyes, wondering if it's safe, or if he'll get bitten.

Story of our lives.

"Come here." Shelley coaxes him with open arms. "Gimme a hug."

Tentative at first, keeping one eye on me for an explanation I don't have, he embraces her. Unlike me, he actually returns the hug.

Disapproval flares inside me. Evan's got an endless supply of forgiveness for this woman that I will never understand. He's never wanted to see the truth. He expects that every time our mom walks back through our door, she's here to stay, that this time we'll be a family, despite the years of disappointment and hurt she's put us through.

"What's going on?" he asks.

"Dinner." She picks up a couple of the grocery bags and hands them off to him. "Lasagna. Your favorite."

Mac offers to help because she's too polite for her own damn good. I want to tell her not to bother. She doesn't have to impress anyone. Instead, I bite my tongue and stick close by, because there's no way I'm leaving Mac alone with that woman. Shelley'd probably shave Mac's head for the price her hair would fetch with a black-market wig maker.

Later, when Shelley and Evan are in the kitchen, I take the opportunity to pull Mac aside under the pretense of setting the table.

"Do me a favor," I say. "Don't talk about your family when she asks."

Her forehead wrinkles. "What do you mean? Why not?"

"Please." My voice is low. Urgent. "Don't mention money or what your dad does. Anything that suggests they're well off. Or you, for that matter."

"I'd never try to make your mom uncomfortable, if that's what you mean."

Mac's good about not rubbing her fortune in everyone's face, but that's not what I'm getting at.

"It's not that, babe. I don't care what you have to say. Lie. Trust me on this." Then, remembering her bracelet, I hold her wrist and undo the latch, sticking it in the pocket of her jeans.

"What are you doing?" She looks alarmed.

"Please. Until she's gone. Don't wear it in front of her."

I have no idea how long Shelley's planning to stick around or where she intends to stay. Her room is exactly how she left it. We don't go in there. If past experience is any indication, however, she'll be out trawling for a new man before midnight.

We're all painfully well-behaved during dinner. Evan, poor guy, even seems happy to have Shelley home. They chat about what she's been up to. Turns out she's living in Atlanta with some guy she met at a casino.

"We fought over a slot machine," she gushes with a giggle, "and ended up falling right in love!"

Uh-huh. I'm sure they'll live happily ever after. Given that she's here, they've probably already broken up.

"How long are you staying?" I interrupt her love story, my brusque tone causing Mac to find my hand under the table. She gives it a comforting squeeze.

Shelley looks offended that I would dare ask her that question.

Evan shoots me a dark look. "Dude. Chill. She just got here."

Yes, and I want to know when she's leaving, I want to snap. It takes superhuman effort to keep my mouth shut.

"So, Mackenzie," Shelley says after the strained, prolonged silence that falls over the dinner table. "How did you end up dating my son? How did you two meet? Tell me everything."

For the next fifteen minutes, Mac dodges dozens of prying questions where she can and spits some Grade-A bullshit for the rest.

I get a surreptitious *what the fuck* glance from Evan, who manages to keep his damn mouth shut and go with it. My brother might be a pushover where Shelley's concerned, but he's not an idiot. For my part, I speak as little as possible. Afraid at any moment my filter will malfunction, and I'll be unable to stop the tirade that will inevitably follow. Few people get me worked up like Shelley Hartley.

After dinner, I'm at the sink rinsing plates when she corners me alone.

"You were awfully quiet," she says, taking a plate from me to put in the dishwasher.

"Tired," I grunt.

"Oh, my sweet boy. You work too hard. You need to get more rest."

I make a noncommittal noise. My skin crawls every time she tries playing the maternal role. It doesn't suit her.

"Mackenzie seems sweet." There are all sorts of euphemisms in that statement, none of them nice.

I do my best to ignore her as I rinse and pass, keeping my head down. "Yeah. She's cool."

"Noticed that bracelet. And the purse in the living room."

My shoulders tense.

"Very pricey. Nice job, baby."

I taste blood from the inside of my cheek when she flashes a knowing smile. It's blatantly obvious what she thinks—that I've found myself a meal ticket. She's been running the same con so long, I'm not sure she remembers any other way to live.

"So, listen, baby . . ."

Here it comes. Of fucking course. There's always an ask. An angle.

"You know, I almost didn't make it here in one piece," she continues, oblivious to the anger bubbling up in my gut. "That old car of mine started spewing smoke on the highway. Had to get it towed from a truck stop. Turns out some little plastic box in the engine went and blew up." She laughs sheepishly. "Now I talked the guy down, but I'm gonna come up a little short on the repair cost."

"What's up?" Evan enters the kitchen in time to overhear the end of her bullshit story. Fucking perfect. "Your car broke down?"

"It's always something with that piece of junk, wouldn't you know?" she says, playing the damsel because Evan can never resist a chance to be a hero. "Anyway, I was working this job, but I got laid off after the holidays. It's been tough finding something new. This'll wipe out everything I had saved up."

"We're tapped out," I inform her, glancing at Evan. "We've been putting everything into fixing the house."

"And the place looks great." She won't meet my eyes. Not when she's got such an easy target with Evan. "I need a couple hundred to get the car back. Then I can get around to look for a new job around here. I'll pay you back."

"You're staying?" Evan says.

Poor, dumb bastard. The hopefulness in his voice is pitiful. I want to slap him upside the head.

Shelley goes to him, hugging his side as she buries her head under his chin. "If you'll let me. I miss my boys."

Evan reaches right into his pocket and pulls out several twenties. Probably everything that was left from his last paycheck. "Here's one-fifty." He shrugs. "I'll hit up the ATM for the rest." Meaning his savings account.

"Thanks, baby." She kisses his cheek and immediately extricates herself from his arms. "Who wants milkshakes? Like we used to get from the boardwalk? I'm gonna run out real quick for smokes and I'll bring some milkshakes back for us."

I'll be shocked if she's back before sunrise.

Later in bed, I can't sleep. I'm racked with tension, still stewing about Shelley. I didn't bother waiting around to see if she'd materialize with the milkshakes. As soon as she left, Mac and I went to hide in my room. Or rather, I did, and she came to keep me company. Now, she rolls over, and flicks on the bedside lamp.

"I can feel you thinking," she murmurs, finding me staring at the ceiling fan.

"Yeah. I just . . . I'm sorry I asked you to do that earlier. My mother took one look at you, your bracelet, your purse, and figured you were loaded." Resentment tightens my throat. "Shelley never met anyone she couldn't use. I didn't want her to know your family has money because, sure as shit, she'd find a way to help herself to some of it."

"Okay, but that has nothing to do with us." Mac runs her hand over my chest and rests her head on my arm. "I wouldn't want you to judge me by my parents, either."

"She thinks I'm only with you because you're rich."

"Yeah? Well, she's wrong. I know that isn't true. I mean, hell, you should probably be referring me to collections for that furniture I keep forgetting to pay you for."

"I'll put the interest on your bill." I kiss the top of her head and pull her closer. Having her in my arms does take the edge off. "Seriously, though. I'd never use you that way. I'm nothing like that woman."

"Cooper." Her voice is gentle, reassuring. "You don't have to convince me."

Maybe. Seems I've never stopped having to convince myself.

Mac snuggles closer to me. "How long do you think she'll stick around for?"

"I give it twenty-four hours. Maybe forty-eight."

"That's really sad."

I chuckle softly. "It's really not. Maybe it was sad, once upon a time, but these days I wish she'd just stay away for good. Every time she comes back, she toys with Evan's emotions. She stresses me out, and I end up snapping at everyone around me. I spend the entire time holding my breath, waiting for her to leave, praying that this time it'll be forever."

"But she keeps coming back. That has to mean something, right?" Mac, bless her heart, is clearly trying to equate Shelley's visits with some sort of loving, maternal need to reunite with her sons.

"It means her latest relationship blew up in her face, or she's broke, or both," I say simply. "Trust me, princess. We've done this same old song and dance since I was fourteen years old. Shelley isn't here for us. She's here for herself."

I feel Mac's warm breath on my collarbone as she rises on her elbow to kiss the side of my jaw. "I'm sorry, Cooper. You don't deserve that."

"It is what it is."

"Stop," she chides. "Just accept my sorry and now let me help you forget for a little while." She kisses her way down my body, reaching inside my boxers.

I close my eyes, moan quietly, and let myself forget.

Forty-eight hours.

I would've wagered on twenty-four, but hey, I still called it. Exactly two days after her sudden arrival, I catch Shelley making for the back door with a duffel bag over her shoulder.

It's barely seven a.m. and I'm the first one up. I'd just put on a pot of coffee after letting Daisy out when Shelley came creeping into the kitchen.

"Sneaking off already?" I inquire from the counter.

She turns around, startled, but covers it with a laugh. "Baby. You scared me. I was trying not to wake anybody."

"Weren't even going to say goodbye?" Personally, I don't give a damn. But taking off on Evan is a heartbreak he doesn't deserve.

"Why don't I throw on some pancakes?" She drops her bag by the door and prances over with her typical misdirecting smile. "We can enjoy a nice breakfast together."

Fine. Guess we're doing one last song and dance. I can play along if it means her departure is the end result.

Mac and Evan are up shortly after, entering the kitchen in time for Shelley to serve them breakfast. I shove some pancake in my mouth and chew slowly, then lean back in my chair, waiting for the bullshit to start spewing. But Shelley is studiously avoiding my expectant gaze, regaling Mackenzie with some dumb story about our childhood. We're almost done eating when it becomes clear that Shelley won't get on with it without a little prodding.

"So where you off to now?" I ask dead-faced, interrupting yet another story of Evan and me growing up, which I'm sure is entirely fabricated to make her out to be less of a bad mom.

Shelley pulls up short and barely covers the glare of annoyance. She wipes her mouth then drains the last of her orange juice. "It's been so good seeing you boys," she says to Evan, putting on a sad voice. "I really wish I could stay longer, but I'm afraid I'm heading out this morning."

A frown mars his lips. "Why?"

"Thing is, you know, there ain't any jobs around here for me right now. I know this fella, though. Met him back in Baton Rouge. He's got some work. I mean he practically begged me to come back and run the place." Her bottom lip sticks out. "You know I don't want to leave my boys, but I gotta make some money. I want to help you two fix this place up."

She goes on like that for a bit longer. Blowing smoke. Convincing herself there's some noble end to her perpetual abandonment and broken promises. She's full of shit—yesterday I saw at least five HELP WANTED signs around the Bay. And I'm pretty sure this *fella* is her ex, who she probably sweet-talked into a second chance. Or maybe it's just been long enough that she could hit him up for round two. Doesn't matter. If it wasn't one excuse, it'd be another. She'd leave us for a bologna sandwich as long as it was away from here.

"Once I get settled in, you should come visit me," Shelley says fifteen minutes later when she's hugging Evan goodbye. "I'm gonna have to get a new phone. Last one got shut off. I'll call you soon as I have it."

She won't. There won't be any calls or texts. No family vacations. It's routine at this point, the bullshit farewells and insincere placations. It doesn't faze me anymore, but fuck her for putting Evan through this again.

"Yeah, make sure you give us the new number when you get it," Evan says, nodding seriously. "We need to have a way to contact you."

Why? I almost ask, but tamp down the urge. If Evan wants to live in some delusional world where his mother loves him, who am I to judge?

"Bye, baby." Shelley pulls me in for a hug despite my visible reluctance. She even plants a kiss on my cheek. Someone give her a *Mom of the Year* award, quick. "See you soon, I promise."

And then, as quickly as she blew in, Shelley's gone. Inflicting minimum damage, fortunately.

Or so I think.

It isn't until about a week later, one evening after work, when I discover the true extent of the damage done by my mother's visit. Mac's birthday is coming up—turns out it's the day before mine—and although she told me not to get her anything, I'm determined to buy her something awesome. Mac gives me so few chances to spoil her, I made the executive decision to ignore her and do whatever the hell I want instead.

In my room, beneath a loose floorboard under my dresser, I pull out the old toffee tin where I've kept my cash and contraband since I was eleven years old. I open the lid, expecting to find the money I've stashed there, all the under-the-table cash I'd earned from side gigs, kept hidden from the bank and tax authorities' grubby hands.

Twelve grand held together by two rubber bands. The *if all else fails* fund.

But the money's not there.

Every last dime.

Gone.

CHAPTER THIRTY-SIX

MACKENZIE

From the living room, I hear a commotion in Cooper's bedroom. A sharp snap off the wall and something clattering to the wooden floor. Suddenly, Cooper barrels down the hall.

Daisy, barking her head off because she gets rambunctious about an hour before it's time to feed her, chases after him as he tramples through the living room.

"Hey, you okay?" I jump up from the couch.

"Fine," he says, growling the words through gritted teeth. He doesn't pause to even look at me.

"What's wrong?"

Rather than get a reply, I watch him fling open the sliding glass door and stomp outside. He slams the door shut in Daisy's face, barely missing her, though she seems only disappointed that he's going outside without her.

To appease her, I put out her food, then grab my shoes to go hunting for Cooper. I find him a hundred yards down the beach throwing small pieces of driftwood at the waves. By the time I reach him, I'm regretting not grabbing a sweater first or at least putting on some long pants, rather than running out in shorts and a T-shirt. It's nearly dark and a steady breeze turns my skin bumpy in minutes.

"What happened?" I ask him.

"Go home." His voice is eerily flat, a stark contradiction of his angry, violent movements.

"Okay, no. So let's move on to the part where you just tell me."

"Damn it, Mac, not now, alright? Let it be." He kicks up sand, searching for something else to throw and growing more frustrated at the lack of options.

"I want to. I would, if I thought it would help. But I don't think it will, so . . ."

He drags his hands through his hair. He'd throw his own head at the tide if he could get it off his neck. "Why do you have to be so damn . . ." The rest comes out only as grunts.

"Born this way, I guess." Disregarding his frustration, I sit and invite him to join me.

Several seconds of silence eventually break his will and he plops down on the sand.

"What's up?" I ask quietly.

"She stole it."

"What?"

Cooper refuses to look at me, his gaze glued to the water. "My emergency fund. Every last dollar."

"Wait, your mom?" Dismay ripples through me. "You're sure?"

He huffs out a humorless laugh. "Positive. Not even Evan knows where I keep my stash."

Damn. That's harsh.

"I should have hidden it the second she showed up," he says, groaning. "She found my pot when I was thirteen and smoked it all when I was at school. I forgot about that until tonight, forgot she knew about the hiding spot. Or maybe I just gave her too much credit not to steal from her own kids."

"I'm sorry." It sounds inadequate under the circumstances. How do I apologize to someone for a lifetime of pain? "How much did she take?"

"Twelve grand," he mutters.

Jeez. Okay. My brain kicks into solution mode, because that's how I operate. Whenever there's a problem with one of my websites, an unwelcome snag in the hotel renos, I become analytical. I assess the problem and try to find a way to fix it.

"That sucks, it really does. I know you're pissed off and feel betrayed, and you have every right to feel that way." I link my arm through his and lean my head on his shoulder. For support. And because I'm freezing. Cooper always runs warm, a perpetual source of heat. "But at least it's only money, right? I can help you. I can replace it."

"Seriously?" He rips his arm from me. "Why would you—" Cooper can't finish the sentence. He jumps to his feet. "What the fuck, Mac? Why is that always where your head goes? Throw money at the problem."

"I thought money was the problem," I protest.

The thunderous look on his face pricks my nerves. Why is it every time I offer to do something nice for him, I get sand kicked in my eye?

"How many different ways do I have to say it?" he shouts at me. "I don't want your goddamn money. Do you even grasp how infantilizing it is to have your girlfriend constantly following you around with her purse open?"

"That's not what I do," I answer, my jaw tight. This guy is pushing the limits of my patience. He wants to be mad at his mom, fine. He wants to vent, good. But I'm not the bad guy here. "I'm only trying to help. You need money, I have more than enough. Why is that wrong? The money doesn't mean anything to me."

"We know." The words come out as a long, sullen sigh. "That's the whole fucking point. You clones throw it around like party favors and expect the rest of us to be grateful for the invitation. I'm not another servant groveling at your feet for tips, goddamn it."

So it's like that. I'm back to being a "clone." Fine.

"You know what, Coop? How about you deal with your own hang-ups instead of heaving all your insecurities on me? I'm getting real fucking sick of withstanding the worst of everyone's little townie microaggressions. Get over it. Because let me tell you something from experience: Rich or poor, bad parents are just bad parents. Your mom sucks. Welcome to the club. Having money wouldn't have made her stay."

I regret the words the second they fly out of my mouth.

Both of us stand there astonished at what we've witnessed. How quickly we went for blood. Every pent-up feeling I've had since my parents cut me off came rushing back to the surface, and I threw it all in Cooper's face as if it were his fault—exactly what I accused him of doing seconds ago.

Overwrought with remorse, I scramble to apologize. But he's already storming off, shouting over his shoulder not to follow him unless this is the last conversation we ever want to have. This time, I take his word for it.

Hours later, though, when he hasn't returned and Evan asks if I know why Cooper's phone is going straight to voicemail, I start to worry. If he were only mad at me, fine, I'd accept that. But the way he tore out of here . . . the rage in his eyes . . . There are a thousand ways a guy like Cooper can get himself into trouble.

It only takes one.

CHAPTER THIRTY-SEVEN

COOPER

There's a dive about an hour west of Avalon Bay. A shack, if you can even call it that, off a two-lane county road that cuts through nothing but empty swamps and small farms. You can usually hear the rumble of motorcycle engines idling in the dirt parking lot from half a mile away. I pull my truck in and cut the engine, then duck inside to find the place is dead, save for a few mean-looking bikers by the pool table and some old guys spread out at the bar. I take a seat on a stool and order a couple fingers of Jack. By the second glass, a guy a couple seats down starts jawing at no one in particular. He's going on about football, responding to everything the ESPN talking heads are saying on the lone television above us. I try to ignore him until he leans toward me, smacking the bar with his flat palm. I get flashbacks to being a bartender and have to restrain myself from snapping at him.

"Who ya got?" he demands to know with slurred urgency. When I ignore him, he repeats himself louder and slower. "The Super Bowl. Who ya got, kid?"

I spare him a look. "I'll buy you a drink to get lost."

"Ohhh." He laughs, mocking me. "Get a load of him, huh? Shhh . . ." He holds his finger over his mouth and shows it to everyone.

"Y'all quiet the hell down. The kid wants some damn peace and quiet, ya got that?"

I came here to get lost, to be left alone. There's no chance Mac would find me here, and this was the only place I could think of that Evan doesn't know about. While he was still clinging to Shelley after our dad's death, my uncle brought me here to blow off some steam at the dartboards. I want to be alone, but I'll embarrass the shit out of this asshole if he wants to make a thing of it. Hell, maybe I should channel Evan and start a bar fight, let off some steam. I mean, why the hell not, right?

Just as I'm talking myself into the idea, a hand slaps down on my shoulder from behind.

"Let me get two beers," a familiar voice tells the bartender.

I glance over to find my uncle taking the stool beside me. Fucking hell.

"Gary," he says to the drunk who was getting in my face. "Why don't you get on home to the missus?"

"Super Bowl's on," a belligerent Gary slurs, jerking a hand toward the TV. "Can't expect me to leave during the Super Bowl."

"That's a rerun of last year's game," Levi replies with the patience of a saint. "Super Bowl's next month, Gary. Now you better go home to Mimi, yeah? Sure she's about to send the dogs after you."

"That damn woman." Gary grumbles his way to opening his wallet and throwing down a few bills on the bar. He mutters something about *can't let a man drink* then teeters his way outside.

Despite wanting to knock his teeth in mere seconds ago, I can't help but stare with a bit of concern after the stumbling man.

"Don't worry. He'll get about a quarter mile on foot before she finds him passed out in the weeds," Levi says. "He's fine."

I look at my uncle in suspicion. "Mac send you?"

"Evan texted me. Said you left in a hurry."

Of course he did. Because Mac would've run right to her new

best friend so they could talk shit about me. I've had it up to my fucking eyeballs with those two ganging up.

"I don't want to talk about it," I mutter, leaving no room for argument.

"Good," he shrugs, "I came here to drink."

Levi tosses back his beer and trains his eyes on the TV, never once sliding a glance my way. It's a relief. At first. Then an hour goes by. And another. And soon, I'm as drunk as Gary was when he left, and my mind is torturing me with all the shit that went down tonight, from finding my life savings stolen to the fight with Mac on the beach. Replaying broken bits of the conversation in my head, I can't quite remember what I said to her, but I'm certain it wasn't good.

"Shelley came back," I finally say, the alcohol loosening my tongue. "For two days. Then made off with my life savings."

Levi makes a full quarter turn to stare at the side of my face.

"Twelve grand." I draw circles in the condensation ring on the bar with my cardboard coaster. "Poof. All gone. Right out from under my nose."

"Jesus. Got any idea where she ran off to?"

"Nope. Baton Rouge, maybe. But that was probably bullshit. A lot of difference it makes. She's not coming back this time. No way."

"I'm sorry, Coop, but that woman is no good." Levi drains his beer and plunks it down. "I got tired of apologizing for my brother a long time ago. I make no excuses for him. He left you boys in a bad way with all those debts. But that goddamn Shelley ain't lifted a finger to help in all these years." Bitterness colors his tone. "You and Evan have worked so hard to dig yourselves out. Now she struts in and rips all that out from under you? Hell no. Not on my watch." His hand comes down hard on the splintered wood bar, jarring my whiskey glass.

I've never seen my uncle this upset. He's a quiet guy. Steady.

For years, he bit his tongue while Shelley popped in and out as she pleased. After he eventually became our guardian, he never once made us feel like a burden for it. Hearing him talk this way is about as close to spitting mad as I've heard him get. For all the good it does us.

"What is there to do?" I feel as bitter as he looks. "There's no catching up to her now. If she doesn't want to be found, she won't be."

My gut still twists with anger. For the money, sure, but more so for the humiliation. The betrayal. For all the ways this woman has made a fool of us over the years. And we've taken it. How Evan still thinks, maybe—even when he knows better—maybe this time it's real. Goddamn Shelley.

"We ain't licked yet," Levi tells me. "And we're done enabling that woman's bad behavior, you hear me?"

Before I can answer, he signals someone at the opposite end of the bar. "Steve, hey, got a question for ya," Levi hollers.

Following my uncle's gaze, I spot the off-duty cop whose uniform shirt is open to expose a sweat-stained white undershirt.

"What do you need, Levi?" Steve hollers back, because in the Bay, everyone knows everyone.

"How might we go about pressing charges against someone who skipped town?"

What? My startled gaze flies to my uncle, but he's focused on the cop.

Shaking the glaze out of his eyes, Steve sits up straighter. "What we talking about?"

Levi's tone is grim. Deadly, even. "Grand larceny."

CHAPTER THIRTY-EIGHT

MACKENZIE

Even Daisy has given up on me. At first, she scampered around my feet as I paced the house, typing then deleting texts to Cooper. Next she sat with her chew rope beside the refrigerator when I compulsively cleaned the kitchen. Which is fucked up, because I've never been a stress cleaner. How could I? I grew up in a house full of maids. When the vacuum comes out, Daisy bolts. I don't blame her. I'm terrible company at the moment anyway. But when spotless floors fail to ease my anxious mind, I end up in Evan's room, where Daisy is curled up at his feet as he plays a video game.

"Hey," I say, knocking on his open door.

He pauses the game. "What's up?"

"Nothing."

Evan answers the unspoken question in the air. "He hasn't texted me back either."

"Yeah, I figured." Hugging the doorframe, I don't know what I came here for, but I was bored of stewing alone. I'm a doer, not a waiter. I hate sitting still. If Cooper wanted to punish me for our fight, this is doing the trick.

"Come here." Evan jerks his head and picks up the second controller for his console. It's several iterations old and running on a flat screen that looks like it was pawned after getting tossed out on someone's lawn. There are dead spots on the picture and a crack in the frame held together by black tape.

My first instinct is that Evan needs a new one. As if he senses the thought, he gives me a knowing smirk that says not to bother.

Right. Boundaries. I need to work on that. Not everyone wants my help.

"You're going to be this guy," he informs me, then provides a rapid explanation of the game as we sit on the edge of his bed. "Got it?"

"Yep." I grasp the gist of it, I think. I mean, my objective and how to move around. Basically. Sort of.

"Follow me," he instructs, leaning forward.

It does not go well. We're ambushed, and instead of shooting at the bad guys, I set off a grenade and kill us both.

Evan snorts loudly.

"I like the racing games better," I confess with an apologetic shrug. "I'm good at those."

"Yeah, princess. I've seen you drive."

"Bullshit. I'm a great driver. I just prefer to go with a sense of urgency."

"If that's what you want to call it."

I nudge him with my elbow as the level resets for another try. This time, I attempt to focus. We make it a little further before I get blown up again.

"This isn't helping, is it?"

I bite my lip. "Not really."

I don't know why I thought sitting next to the spitting image of Cooper would take my mind off him. It's weird, but I almost never see Evan and Cooper as remotely similar, their personalities diverging in so many ways. Yet if I'm being honest, there are times where I imagine how everything might have been different if not for the whimsy of Bonnie's indiscriminate libido.

Whatever he reads on my face, Evan exits out of the game

and sets our controllers aside. "Let's have it, then. What's on your mind?"

Though our rapport has evolved over the past couple months, Evan's hardly the first person I'd turn to for a heart-to-heart. Most of the time he displays the emotional depth of Daisy's water bowl. At this moment, though, he's the next best thing to his brother.

"What if he doesn't come back?" I ask in a small voice.

"He has to come back. He lives here."

I let out a breath. "I mean, to *me*. What if he doesn't come back to me?" My pulse quickens at that horrible notion. "I just . . . I can't shake the feeling that it's over this time. One fight too many and there's no getting past it. What if Cooper's fed up with me?"

"Okay." Evan seems to ponder that for a second. It's still eerie after all this time how his mannerisms exactly match Cooper's, yet they're like a recording where the audio doesn't quite sync with the video. Everything's a half second off. "So not to be a dick or anything, but that's dumb."

"Which part?"

"All of it. You remember my brother almost knocked my teeth out because I was an ass to you once, right?"

"Once?" I echo with a raised eyebrow.

Evan grins. "Yeah, well. Point is, it'll take a lot more than a few arguments to run him off you. There was one summer Coop and I were at each other's throats over I don't know what, and we were beating the tar out of each other about every other day." He shrugs. "Doesn't mean shit. Fighting is how we worked things out."

"But you're brothers," I remind him. "That's a huge difference."

"And what I'm saying is, Coop cares that much about you. You're not staying here for the rent money or because he likes your cooking."

He has a point. I don't cook. At all. Ever. Not once. As for rent, every month I've been here I've left what I thought was a fair market value of a rent check on Cooper's dresser, but he keeps refusing to cash them. So I always leave a backup with Evan.

"But . . ." My teeth worry my bottom lip again. "You didn't see the look on his face when he stormed off."

"Um. I've seen every look on his face." He mugs for me, seeking a laugh.

Fine. That was sort of funny.

"Look," he says, "at some point, Cooper's going to stumble in piss drunk and grovel for you to forgive him once he's come to his senses. He's got a process. You just gotta let him work through the steps."

I want to believe him. That despite all the ways we have absolutely nothing in common, Cooper and I somehow developed a connection stronger than what separates us, deeper than the scars that keep him up at night. The alternative is too painful. Because I can't change where I come from any more than he can. If this is the distance our relationship can't span, I'm not ready to consider what my new life would be without him.

Evan throws his arm around my shoulder. "I know Coop better than anyone. Trust me when I say he's crazy about you. And I've got no reason to lie."

Evan's pep talk digs my mood out of the gutter at least marginally. Enough that when a yawn slams into me, I'm motivated to get ready for bed.

"Promise you'll wake me up if he calls you?" I fret.

"I promise." Evan's voice is surprisingly gentle. "Don't stress too hard, Mac. He'll be home in no time, okay?"

I give a weak nod. "Okay."

"No time" ends up being a quarter past midnight, as I'm woken from a restless sleep when the bed dips beside me. I feel Cooper slide under the covers. He's still warm from a shower and smells of toothpaste and shampoo.

"You awake?" he asks in a whisper.

I roll over to lie on my back, rubbing my eyes. It's pitch black in the bedroom but for the pale glow of the floodlight on the side of the house, filtering in through the blinds.

"Yeah."

Cooper lets out a long breath through his nose. "I talked to Levi."

That's what he's leading with? I'm not sure what relevance it has to our situation or our fight, and part of me wants him to stop stalling and tell me if we're going to be all right. But I keep my impatience at bay. Evan said his brother has a process. Maybe this is part of it.

So I say, "Yeah?"

"Yeah." A long beat. "I'm going to press charges against Shelley. For stealing the money."

"Wow." It hadn't occurred to me that would even be an option. But it makes sense. Mother or not, she stole more than ten thousand dollars from him. "How do you feel about it?"

"Honestly? Fucked up. She's my mom, you know?" I'm startled to hear his voice crack. "I don't want to think about her getting thrown in jail. At the same time, what kind of person steals from their own kid? If I didn't need the money, I'd say whatever. To hell with it. But that was every cent I had saved up. Took me years."

He's talking to me. That's a good sign.

Except then, he falls silent, and the two of us lie there, not touching, both seemingly afraid to disturb the air too much. After several seconds tick by, I realize there's nothing stopping me from going first.

"I'm sorry," I tell him. "I was out of line earlier. I got defensive and lashed out. It was mean and you didn't deserve that."

"Well . . ." he says, and I think I detect a hint of a smile in his voice. "I had it coming a little. Shelley gets under my skin, you know? I just want to throw shit when she's around. And then she goes and steals my money . . ." I can feel the tension building up in him, the effort it's taking to stay calm. Then on a deep breath, he relaxes again. "A lot of what I said came out at you because I was mad at her. You were right. I've got some bullshit that was there way before you came along."

"I get it." Turning on my side, I find his silhouette in the dark. "I thought offering you the money was helpful, but I see now how in that moment it hit a nerve. I wasn't trying to throw money at the problem or emasculate you, I promise you that. It's just . . . that's how my brain works. I go into problem-solving mode—*Money stolen? Here's money.* You know? It wasn't meant to be a statement about our respective bank accounts." I swallow a rush of guilt. "In the future, when it comes to that kind of thing—family stuff, money stuff—I'm here if you need me. Otherwise, I'll butt out."

"I'm not saying I don't want you involved." He shifts, rolling over to face me too. "I don't want all these lines and rules and shit." Cooper finds my hand in the dark and brings it against his chest. He's shirtless, in only his boxers. His skin is warm to the touch. "The money thing is always going to be there, and I've gotta stop getting bent outta shape about it. I know you're not trying to make me feel any sort of way."

"I was afraid you weren't coming back." I swallow again. Harder. "As long as I was here, I mean."

"Gonna take more than that to get rid of me." He tangles his fingers in my hair, rubbing his thumb against the back of my neck. It's a sweet, soothing gesture, practically putting me right back to sleep. "I figured something out tonight."

"What's that?"

"I was sitting in this grimy little bar with Levi and a bunch of sad old bastards hiding from their wives or avoiding their sad old houses. Guys only twice my age but who've already done everything that's ever going to happen to them. And I thought, fuck me, man, I've got this crazy hot girl at home and our biggest problem is she's always trying to buy me shit."

I smile against my pillow. When he puts it that way, we sound like a couple of dumbasses.

"And this jolt kind of hit me suddenly. I thought, what if she isn't there when I get back? I was glaring into the bottom of a glass feeling sorry for myself. What if I'd run off the best thing that ever happened to me?"

"That's sweet, but I wouldn't go that far."

"I'm serious." His voice is soft yet insistent. "Mac, things around here were never good. Then my dad died, and it was confirmation that nothing would get any better. Shelley split. We made do. Never complained. And then you showed up and I started getting ideas. Maybe I didn't have to settle for slightly better than nothing. Maybe I could even be happy."

He breaks my heart. Living without joy, without anticipation that tomorrow can still be extraordinary, will suck the soul right out of a person. It's the cold, dark, strangling infinity of nothingness, of being swallowed up by despair. Nothing can grow in the empty places where we resign ourselves to the numbness. Never really alive. It's the same long tunnel into complacency that I saw closing in around me the harder I looked at the future Preston and my parents imagined for me.

Cooper saved me from that. Not because he whisked me away, but because meeting him finally revealed the possibilities I'd been missing. The exhilaration of uncertainty. Passion and curiosity.

I was half asleep until I met him.

"I thought I was happy," I tell him, gliding my fingers up and down his ribs. "For a long time. What was there to complain about, right? I'd been given everything I could ever ask for—except purpose. A choice. The potential to fail, to get hurt. To ever love something so much the thought of losing it tears me open. Tonight, when I thought you and I might really be over, all sorts of things ran through my head. I was making myself crazy."

Cooper tilts my chin toward him and presses his lips to mine with the lightest touch. Enough to make me seek him out for another taste.

His breath is a warm whisper against my lips. "I might just be falling in love with you, Cabot."

My heart jumps. "Uh-oh."

"You have no idea."

He drags his fingers down my spine, setting every nerve alight. I bite his bottom lip, tug a little, in our wordless language that says I need him. Now. Take this ache away. But he's methodically, frustratingly patient in removing my tank top before he palms one breast while licking at the other. He pushes his boxers down. I wiggle out of my underwear as he puts on a condom. A shiver of anticipation skitters through me when he drags the hot length of him over my core.

He holds me tight as he moves inside me. Unhurried. Slow, languid strokes. I cling to him, muffling my moans against his shoulder.

"I love you too," I say, shaking in his arms while I come.

CHAPTER THIRTY-NINE

COOPER

A few days after filing charges against Shelley, I receive a call to come to the police station. On the phone with the sheriff, I learn that the cops picked her up in Louisiana, where she must have forgotten about all the unpaid parking tickets she'd left behind after her "fella" kicked her to the curb. When the South Carolina warrant popped up, the sheriff in Baton Rouge had her transferred back up to the Bay.

Mac and my brother come to the station with me, but I make Evan wait outside while we go in to speak to Sheriff Nixon. Evan was equally furious to learn that Shelley robbed me blind, but I know my brother—he'll always have a soft spot for that woman. And right now I need to keep a clear head, not allow anything to cloud my judgment.

"Cooper, have a seat." Sheriff Nixon shakes my hand, then settles behind his desk and gets right down to business. "Your mother had about ten grand in cash on her when the Baton Rouge boys brought her in."

Relief slams into me like a gust of wind. Ten grand. It's a couple thousand short of what she stole, but it's better than nothing. Hell, it's more than I expected. She was gone four days. Shelley is more than capable of blowing twelve grand in that amount of time.

316 • ELLE KENNEDY

"However, it could be a while before you get the money back," Nixon adds.

I frown at him. "Why's that?"

He starts rambling on about evidence procedures and what not, as my brain tries to keep up with all the information he's spitting out. First things first, Shelley will be arraigned in front of a judge. Mac asks a lot of questions because I'm kind of in a stupor about the whole thing now. All I keep thinking about is Shelley in an orange jumpsuit, her wrists shackled. I despise everything that woman's ever done to us, but the thought of her behind bars doesn't sit right. What kind of son sends his own mother to jail?

"She's here now?" I ask Nixon.

"In holding, yes." He rubs a hand over his thick mustache, looking every inch the part of a small-town sheriff. He's new to town, so I doubt he knows much about me and my family. His predecessor, Sheriff Stone, hated our guts. Spent his afternoons tailing Evan and me around the Bay all summer, looking for a reason to glare at us from his unmarked cruiser.

"What would happen if I changed my mind?"

Beside me, Mac looks startled.

"You want to withdraw the charges?" he says, eyeing me closely.

I hesitate. "Will I get my money back today?"

"There'd be no reason to hold it in evidence. So, yes."

Which is all I wanted in the first place.

"What would happen to her after that?"

"It's your prerogative as the victim. If you're not interested in prosecuting, she'll be released. Mrs. Hartley was only held in Louisiana at the request of this department. Whatever fines she faces there are a separate matter. We aren't aware of another warrant for her at this time."

I glance at Mac, knowing it isn't a decision she would make for me one way or the other, but wanting the confirmation that I'm doing the right thing. I guess in this situation, it's all degrees of shitty either way.

She studies my face, then offers a slight nod. "Do what you feel is right," she murmurs.

I shift my gaze back to the sheriff. "Yeah, I want to drop the charges. Let's get this over with."

It still takes about an hour to sign the paperwork and wait around for an officer to appear with a plastic bag of my cash. He counts out every bill, then has me sign some more papers. Another huge wave of relief hits me when I hand Mac the cash to stuff in her purse. The very next thing I'm doing is sucking it up and depositing the money in the bank, the taxman be damned.

Outside, Evan's waiting for us by the truck. "All good?" he says.

I nod. "All good."

We're about to leave when Shelley walks out of the building rubbing her wrists.

Shit.

She lights up a cigarette. As she exhales, her gaze lands on us, catching our attempted escape.

"I'll get rid of her," Mac offers, squeezing my hand.

"It's fine," I say. "Wait in the truck."

In typical Shelley fashion, my mother strides over with a cheerful smile. "Well, what a day, huh? Someone sure screwed up, didn't they? I don't know where they got their wires crossed. I told them, I said, call my boys. They'll tell you I didn't take anything that didn't belong to me."

"Jesus, give it a rest, would you?" I snap.

She blinks. "Baby—"

"No, don't *baby* me." I can't take another second of her bullshit, her smiley evasions. I've been choking on them since I was five, and I'm fucking full. "You found my stash and stole from me, and *that's* why you skipped town. Hope it was worth it." I stare at her. "*Mom.*"

"Baby, no." She reaches for my arm. I take a step back. "I was only borrowing a little to get set up. I was going to send it right back after I got on my feet. You know that. I didn't think you'd mind, right?"

Amazed laughter trickles out of my mouth. "Sure. Whatever. I don't want to hear it anymore. This is the last time we're gonna do this. I don't want to see you anymore. Far as I'm concerned, you don't ever need to come back here. You have no sons, Shelley."

She flinches. "Now, Cooper, I get you're upset, but I'm still your mother. You're still my boys. You don't turn your back on family." She looks at Evan, who has remained silent, lingering behind me. "Right, baby?"

"Not this time," he says, gazing off at the passing traffic. Emphatic. Stoic. "I'm with Coop. I think it's better if you didn't come around anymore."

I fight the urge to throw my arm around my brother. Not here. Not in front of her. But I know the pain he's feeling. The loneliness. Evan lost his mom today.

I lost mine a long time ago.

Shelley makes one last attempt to get us in line until she realizes we aren't budging. Then the act falls apart. Her smile recedes to flat indifference. Her eyes grow dull and mean. Voice bitter. In the end, she has little in the way of parting words. Barely a glance as she blows smoke in our faces and walks to a waiting cab that carries her off to be someone else's problem. We're all better for it.

Even if it doesn't feel that way right now.

Later, as Mac orders us a pizza for dinner, Evan and I take Daisy for a walk. We don't talk about Shelley. Hell, we don't talk much at all. We're in somber spirits. Each of us is lost in our own thoughts, and yet I know we're thinking the exact same things.

When we return to the house, we find Levi on the back deck, sipping a beer. "Hey," he calls at our approach. "I came by to see how it went at the police station."

Evan heads inside to grab two beers for us, while I stand at the railing and fill our uncle in. When I reach the part where Shelley disappeared in a taxi without so much as a goodbye, Levi nods in grim satisfaction.

"Think she got the message this time?" he asks.

"Maybe? She looked pretty defeated."

"Can't say I'm sorry for her." Levi never got along with Shelley, even when she was around. I don't blame him. The only redeeming quality about either of my parents was giving us a decent uncle.

"We're orphans now," Evan remarks, staring at the waves.

"Shit, guys, I know this ain't easy. But you're not alone in this. If you ever need anything . . ."

He trails off. But he doesn't need to finish the sentence. Levi's tried his damnedest to make us feel like a family despite all the missing pieces, and he's done a pretty good job considering what he had to work with.

"Hey, I know we don't say it enough," I tell our uncle, "but we're only standing here because you were there for us. You always are. If it weren't for you, we would've ended up in the system. Shipped off to foster care. Probably separated."

"We love you," Evan adds, his voice lined with emotion.

It gets Levi a little choked up. He coughs, his way of covering it up. "You're good boys," is his gruff response. He's not a man of sentiment or many words. Still, we know how he feels about us.

Maybe we never got the family we deserved, but we ended up with the one we needed.

CHAPTER FORTY

MACKENZIE

He's being utterly unreasonable.

"You said you were going to pick up ice on your way home," I shout from the backyard, where I'm standing with six coolers of warm beer and soda.

With February came a sudden ferocious winter, so while I'm freezing my butt off out here, the drinks are still hot to the touch because Evan left the cases sitting too close to the firepit. Now he's taking a load off, and I'm left to wrestle with a folding table that is refusing to budge as I try prying the legs open. These folding tables must've been designed by a sadist, because I cannot for the life of me get them open.

"The freezer at the liquor store was broken," Cooper responds from the deck. "Heidi said she's going to swing by Publix on the way here and get some."

"But the drinks won't have time to chill before everyone else arrives. That's the whole reason I sent you out early!" I'm about to rip my damn hair out. This is the third time I've tried explaining this to him, and still it's like arguing with an ornery sand crab.

"I would have stopped, but it was out of the way and I wanted to get home to help set up. You'd rather I left you here to do everything by yourself?" he shouts back, throwing his hands up.

"I was here to help her," Evan says from his chair. Where he's been sitting on his ass drinking the last cold beer, instead of helping me set up. "She's got a point, Coop," he adds, nodding graciously at me, as if to say *See, I'm on your side.*

"Stay out of it," Cooper tells him.

I glare at them both.

There have got to be few worse hells than sharing a birthday one day apart with a couple of barely housetrained twins. Last night, they had this brilliant idea to throw a massive last-minute party instead of the dinner I was planning, so now we're rushing to put something together, except Evan is lazy and Cooper has all the logistical abilities of a herring.

"Forget it." I didn't even want this stupid party, but they insisted that since it's my twenty-first, we had to go big. So, of course, I'm stuck doing most of the work. "I'll go get the food from one end of town, the cake from the other, then double back for ice and try to make it back before dark. Wish me luck."

Cooper lets out an exasperated groan. "I'll call Heidi and ask her to come sooner. Okay? Happy?"

I kick over the folding table, because fuck it, and rush up the steps toward the sliding door, which is currently being blocked by Cooper. "Don't bother. For my birthday, all I really want is one less minute of her snide comments and sneering looks. Is that too much to ask?"

"I've talked to her, okay? I can't control how she acts. Just give it time. She'll get over it."

"You know, I'm not even mad at Heidi. If I'd been led on for an entire summer, I'd be pretty cranky too."

"That's not what happened," he growls.

"It's what she thinks, and that's all that matters. Maybe that's the talk you should be having."

"Fuck, Mac. Could you get off my case for ten minutes?"

322 • ELLE KENNEDY

"Hey dumbass," Evan yells from the yard. "She's right."

Cooper flips his brother off and follows me into the house as I hurry to grab my purse and find his keys. Not seeing them in the kitchen or living room, I make my way to his bedroom. He trails after me, looking as frazzled as I feel.

"You know what?" I turn to look at him. "I don't think this is working anymore."

Our bickering is draining. And annoying, because it's usually about stupid stuff. We dig in and refuse to relent until we exhaust all our energy fighting and forget what started the argument in the first place.

"What the hell does that mean?" He snatches his keys from his dresser before I can reach for them.

I grit my teeth, then let out a harried breath. "Crashing here was supposed to be a temporary thing. And seeing as how we're constantly at each other's throats, I've clearly overstayed my welcome."

Like a gust of wind knocks him sideways, Cooper deflates. He places the keys in my upturned hand. When he speaks, his voice is gentle.

"That's not what I want. If you're ready to get your own place, I understand. But don't think you have to move out for me. I like having you here."

"You sure?" I've noticed complaints about my invasion of his space have grown exponentially since I shacked up here. "I'd rather you tell me the truth. Not what you think I want to hear."

"I swear."

His gaze locks with mine. I search his face, and he searches mine, and something passes between us. It's what always happens. When all our anger and frustration subsides, when the storm passes and I notice him again. The way his tattoos carve along the muscles of his arms. The broad plane of his chest. The way he always smells of shampoo and sawdust.

Cooper places his hands on my hips. Looking down at me with heavy-lidded eyes, he walks me backward and closes his bedroom door to press me against it.

"I like having you close," he says roughly. "Going to bed with you. Waking up to you. Making love to you."

His hands capture the hem of my dress and move upward, pulling the fabric up with him until I'm exposed from the waist down. My pulse thrums so fervently in my neck I can feel the frantic little thumps. I've been conditioned to him. He touches me and my body squirms in anticipation.

"I'm not cramping your style?" I tease. My palms splay against the door, fingers digging into the grooves.

His answer is a dismissive flicking of his eyes. He steps closer until only a sliver of air stands between us. Then, licking his lips, he says, "Tell me to kiss you."

My brain doesn't have a response for that, but everything clenches and my toes grab at the floor.

He presses his forehead to mine, gripping my ribs. "If we're done fighting, tell me to kiss you."

I hate fighting with him. But this. The making up. Well, it's the undiluted syrup at the bottom of the chocolate milk. My favorite part.

"Kiss me," I whisper.

His lips brush mine in a featherlight caress. Then he pulls back slightly. "This . . ." he mutters, his breath tickling my nose.

He doesn't finish that sentence. But he doesn't have to. I know exactly what he means. This.

Just . . . *this*.

As it turns out, I own at drinking games. In fact, the more I drink, the better I get. I'd never played flip cup before tonight, but after a couple rounds, I couldn't lose. One challenger after another left slayed at my feet. After that, I destroyed three beer pong opponents, then managed to embarrass the hell out of some dude with neck tattoos at the dartboard. Apparently, once I've consumed a bottle of wine, I can't *not* hit a bull's eye.

Now, I'm standing by the fire, listening to Tate lay out some thought experiment that's hurting my tipsy brain.

"Wait. I don't get it. If there are boats coming to the island, why can't I get on one and sail home to safety?"

"Because that's not the point!" Tate's blue eyes convey pure exasperation.

"But I've essentially been rescued," I argue. "So why can't I get on a boat? I'd way rather do that than pick between Cooper and a bunch of supplies without having access to either boat."

"But that's the actual dilemma! Not how you're going to get off the island. You have to choose."

"I choose the boats!"

Tate looks like he wants to murder me, which is confusing, because I think the answer to this deserted island thing is stupidly simple.

"You know what?" He lets out a breath, then grins, his dimples making an appearance. "You're lucky you're cute, Mac. Because you suck at thought experiments."

"Aww." I pat his arm. "You're cute too, Tater-Tot."

"I hate you," he sighs.

Nah, he doesn't. It's taken time, but I think I've finally settled into my place in Cooper's life. No longer the square peg. Not just his life—ours.

"I'm cold," I announce.

"Seriously?" Tate points to the raging bonfire in front of us.

"Just because there's a fire doesn't mean it's not February," I say stubbornly.

I leave him at the firepit and make my way toward the house to get a sweater. Just as I reach the back steps, I catch my name and turn to answer before realizing it's Heidi talking to someone on the upstairs deck. I tilt my head back. Through the gaps in the slats, I make out Heidi's blonde head and Alana's red one, along with the faces of a few other girls I don't know. I'm about to climb the first step when Heidi's next words stop me.

"I can forgive her for being dumb, but she's so painfully boring," Heidi says, laughing. "And Cooper's no fun at all anymore. All he wants to do is pretend they're married. He hardly ever comes out anymore."

Little waves of anger ripple through me. This shit. Every time. Not once have I stopped Cooper from hanging out with Heidi or asked him not to invite her somewhere, because I can at least tolerate her for his sake. Why she's so committed to not giving me the same courtesy, I don't understand. Instead, it's always dirty looks and passive-aggressive bullshit. And, apparently, trash-talking behind my back.

"I still don't know how she bought Cooper acting like he never met that guy." Heidi laughs again, smug now. "I mean, wake up and smell the conspiracy, right?"

Wait, what?

Is she talking about Preston?

"I'd feel sorry for her if she wasn't so gullible."

Screw Heidi. She doesn't know what she's talking about. Still, I'd rather know what other bile she's been spewing behind my back, so I hug the shadows as I creep up the steps, keeping bodies between myself and Heidi, hiding among the other people lingering on the stairs talking.

"Okay, but it's been long enough," another girl says. "He must be into her, don't you think?"

"What does it matter?" Heidi offers that dismissive shrug she does. "Eventually she's got to figure out he's been lying to her from the start. That he only got with her as a means for revenge."

"Leave them alone," Alana says. "You promised to let it go."

I stop dead. Did I hear her right? Because that sounded suspiciously like confirmation.

What else could it mean?

"What?" There's a coy note in Heidi's tone.

I'm barely three feet away now. So close I'm shaking.

"I didn't say I was going to tell her. Not on purpose, anyway."

My heart thumps erratically against my ribs. Alana is standing right there, mouth shut. Not disputing Heidi's version of events.

Which means, if I've read it right, Cooper has been lying to me since the moment we met.

Worse, he lied when I confronted him directly. He lied to my face. And he made all his friends—*our* friends, I thought—go along with the lies. Evan. Steph. Alana.

I feel small, like I could fall right through the space between the deck boards. Utterly humiliated. Who else knew about it? Have they all been laughing at me behind my back this entire time? Poor, dumb clone.

"Go on, then," I say, charging forward to confront the group. "Don't wait for word to get around, for something to slip—why don't you tell me to my face, Heidi?"

Alana has the decency to look contrite. Heidi, however, doesn't even pretend to hide her smirk.

Seriously, this girl makes me want to boob-punch her. I've tried with her. I really have. Make conversation. Be civil. Give her time. But no matter how much or how little I give, she's flatly refused to budge from her total contempt. Now I understand why—she and I weren't in an uneasy truce, but a cold war to which I was oblivious. That was my mistake.

"I get it, you hate my guts," I say testily. "Find a new hobby."

She narrows her eyes.

I dismiss her from my gaze, turning to Alana instead. "Is it true? This was some sort of revenge plan against my ex? Cooper lied?"

Saying it out loud makes me queasy. All the alcohol I consumed tonight churns dangerously in my belly as I replay the events of the last six months. My memory flips through a dozen early conversations with Cooper, wondering what obvious clues I ignored. How many times was the answer right in front of me, but I was too enamored of his fathomless eyes and crooked smile?

Ever enigmatic, Alana reveals no emotion. Only hesitation. I thought we'd grown close, gotten past the rough patches to actually become friends. Yet here she is, silent, her expression shuttered, while Heidi makes me the butt of her jokes. Guess I really am dumb. They all had me fooled.

"Alana," I press, almost cringing at the helplessness I hear in my voice.

After an interminably long pause, her aloof expression slips, just enough for me to glimpse a flicker of regret.

"Yes," she admits. "It's true. Cooper lied."

CHAPTER FORTY-ONE

COOPER

I catch a glimpse of Mac through the flames of the bonfire, a glowing fleeting glimpse, before a wave of beer smacks me in the face.

"Asshole."

Confusion jolts through me. Staggering backward from the firepit, I wipe my eyes with sandy fingers. I blink a few times, using my forearm to mop beer off my face. I blink again, and Mac is directly in front of me, holding an empty red cup in her hand. As our friends all stand there staring at us, I struggle to understand what the hell is happening.

"Lying asshole," she repeats with seething ferocity.

Evan tries to approach her. "Whoa, what was that for?"

"No. Fuck you too." She points a warning finger at him. "You lied to me. Both of you."

Beyond her slender shoulder, I spot Alana weaving her way through the crowd, trailed by Heidi. Alana looks guilty. Heidi's expression is one of pure apathy.

Mac's expression? Sheer betrayal.

And now I get it. Reading her face, I feel like I'm falling. It's like that second when our brains jerk inside our skulls and we experience a frozen moment of terror before the descent, because we know: *This is going to hurt.* There's nothing to grab on to now. She's got me dead to rights.

"Mac, let me explain," I start hoarsely.

"You *used* me," she shouts.

Her arm thrusts forward and the empty cup bounces off my chest. A stunned audience stands silent, retreating to the opposite side of the pit.

"It was all about revenge this whole time." She shakes her head repeatedly, the emotions in her eyes running the gamut from embarrassed to incensed to disappointed.

I think about the first night I approached her, how irritated I was at having to feign interest in some stuck-up clone. How she snuck up on me with her smile and wit.

What the hell did she ever see in me to make it this far?

"It started that way," I admit. I've got seconds, maybe, to get this out before she runs off and never speaks to me again, so I drop the bullshit and lay it all on the table. "Yes, I found you because I wanted to get back at him. I was stupid and pissed off. And then I met you and it blew up my whole life, Mac. I fell for you. It's been the best six months of my life."

Some of the hardest months too. All of which she's endured with me. Despite me. I've thrown more shit at this girl than she had any reason to withstand, and still she found her way to love me regardless. Of course I was gonna mess that up. How could I ever think otherwise?

But holy fucking shit, it hurts worse than I ever could've imagined, the thought of losing Mackenzie. My heart feels like it's being crushed in a vise.

"And, yeah, I should have come clean a long time ago. But goddamn it, okay, I was scared." My throat starts closing in on me, cutting off my airway. I suck in a ragged breath. "I was scared of this moment right here. I made a terrible mistake, and I thought if you didn't find out, it wouldn't hurt you. I wanted to protect you."

"You humiliated me," she spits out through tears and rage. I want to throw my arms around her and take her pain away, but I'm the one doing this to her, and every second she levels me with that look of devastation rips me apart. "You made me look like an idiot."

"Please, Mac. I'll do anything." I grab her hands, squeezing when she tries to turn away. Because I know the second she takes that first step, she's gonna keep walking forever. "I love you. Let me prove it. Give me a chance."

"You had a chance." Tears stream down her cheeks. "You could have told me the truth months ago. You had a million opportunities, including the day I asked you point-blank if you knew Preston, if he got you fired. But you didn't tell me the truth. Instead you let everyone laugh at me behind my back." Mac pulls her hands from mine to wipe her eyes. "I might have been able to forgive you for everything else if you hadn't lied right to my face. Got to hand it to you, Cooper. You did it so well. And then you got everyone I thought was my friend to lie too. Put me in this perfect little glass house of bullshit for your own amusement."

"Mackenzie." I'm grasping at a rope as it's sliding through my fingers. With every breath I take, she's slipping further away. "Let me fix it."

"There's nothing left to fix." Her expression flattens to an eerie dullness. "I'm going into the house and I'm packing up my stuff and I'm leaving. Because that's the only thing left for me to do. Don't try to stop me."

Then she turns her back and disappears beyond the glow of the fire.

There's silence in her wake.

"Forget what she said," Evan blurts out, shoving my shoulder. "Go after her."

I stare out at nothingness. "She doesn't want me to."

I know Mac well enough to see when she's made up her mind. Anything I do now will only chase her off faster, hardening the hatred. Because she's right. I was a shit person when I met her.

Nothing I've done since has proven different.

"Then I'll go," Evan growls, throwing off my attempt to stop him.

Whatever. He won't succeed in changing her mind. She's leaving.

She's gone.

Everyone else slowly wanders away until I'm left alone on the beach. I sink down to the sand. I sit there for I don't know how long—so long the bonfire is reduced to cold embers. Evan doesn't return. No point telling me what I already know. The sun peeks above the waves by the time I trudge back to the house through the remnants of the aborted party.

Daisy doesn't come running to be let out when I walk inside. Her water bowl isn't in the kitchen.

Half the closet is empty in my room.

I throw myself on the bed and stare up at the ceiling. I feel numb. Empty.

I wish I'd known then how hard it would be now to miss Mackenzie Cabot.

CHAPTER FORTY-TWO

MACKENZIE

I lived my whole life without Cooper Hartley. Then, six months together and I've forgotten what it was not to know him. Six months, and only minutes to shred it to hell.

One overheard conversation.

A single devastating admission.

Quick as blowing out a match, my heart went numb.

After leaving Cooper's house in a despondent haze, I sat in the back of a cab with Daisy and paid the guy to drive through town for nearly two hours. At some point, the cab dropped me off at Tally Hall. I showed up at Bonnie's door with my bag in one hand and Daisy's leash in the other, and with a sympathetic pout, she welcomed us home. Lucky for me, her new roommate sleeps out most nights. Less lucky, the moment people started getting up for class and trudging through the halls in the morning, Daisy began barking at the unfamiliar foot traffic. In an instant, the resident advisor was on us, demanding that we vacate.

For Bonnie's sake, I told him we'd only popped in for a few minutes to say hello, though I'm not sure he bought it. By the afternoon, Daisy and I were in the backseat of another cab, searching for a plan B. Turns out there isn't a hotel in the Bay that allows pets. Something about a dog show years back that went horribly awry.

So that's how I find myself at Steph and Alana's house. Daisy, the little traitor, hops right onto the couch and into Steph's lap. I'm a bit more reluctant as I sit down next to Steph, while Alana pleads their case. They'd sent a dozen or so text messages after I'd stormed out of the party. It wasn't so much the content but the persistence that convinced me of their sincerity.

"In our defense," Alana says, standing with her arms crossed, "we didn't know you'd end up being cool."

I have to hand it to her, she's unapologetically herself. Even in admitting that she had no small part in crafting the revenge plot, she doesn't have it in her to mince words.

"For real, though," she continues. "By the time Cooper told us you two were really a thing, it seemed meaner to tell you the truth."

"No," I say simply. "It was meaner to lie."

Because while the truth hurts you, the lie degrades you. When I realized Preston had slept around on me, I understood what it was to be That Girl. For years, our friends had smiled in my face, knowing all along I was his patsy, while I remained oblivious to his "extracurriculars"—his parade of Marilyns. It never occurred to me that Cooper would turn around and lie to me as well. Or that, yet again, the people I called friends would play accomplices to my ignorance. Some lessons we have to learn twice.

Nevertheless, I'm not entirely without mercy. The mathematics of loyalty are tricky, after all. They were Cooper's friends first. I can't not factor that into the equation. It would be well within my rights to hate them both for their part in this charade, but I also see where they got caught in the middle. They should have told me the truth, yes. It was Cooper, though, who swore them to secrecy. It was his ass they were covering.

If anyone deserves the brunt of the blame, it's him.

"We feel awful about it," Steph says. "It was a crappy thing to do to someone."

"Yep," I agree.

"We're sorry, Mac. *I'm* sorry." Tentative, she reaches over to squeeze my arm. "And if you need a place to crash, you're welcome to stay in our spare room, okay? Not just because we owe you, but because you really are cool, and I, we"—she glances at Alana—"consider you a good friend."

Despite the awkward implications, staying here is the most attractive option until I find a more permanent solution. Besides, Daisy already seems quite at home.

"And we won't discuss Cooper unless you want to," Alana promises. "Although for what it's worth, he's pretty torn up about everything. Evan says he sat on the beach all night in the cold, just staring at the bay."

"Am I supposed to feel sorry for him?" I ask with a raised brow.

Steph laughs awkwardly. "Well, no, and we're not saying you don't deserve to be pissed. I'd have complete sympathy if you wanted to torch his truck."

"The whole revenge plan was juvenile bullshit," adds Alana. "But he wasn't faking liking you. We told him he wasn't allowed to pretend to fall for you, so that part was completely real."

"And he is sorry," Steph says. "He knows he messed up."

I wait a few seconds, but it seems they've wrapped up their pitch. Good. Now we can set some boundaries.

"I get that you two are stuck in the middle of this and that sucks," I tell the girls. "So how about we set a house rule: I won't get weird every time someone mentions his name or bitch about him in front of you, and you guys agree not to campaign for him. Deal?"

Steph gives me a sad smile. "Deal."

That night, I allow myself to cry alone in the dark. To feel the pain and anger. Let it rip me open. And then I put it away, bury it deep. I wake up in the morning and I remind myself that there's a lot more to my life than Cooper Hartley. For the last year, I've complained about all the things keeping me from concentrating on my business. Well, there's nothing stopping me now. I've got time in the day and more than enough work between my websites and the hotel to fill it. Time to wipe up my smudged mascara and be a bad bitch.

Fuck love. Build the empire.

CHAPTER FORTY-THREE

COOPER

"Hey, Coop, you in here?"

"Back here."

Heidi finds me in my workshop, where I've been holed up for the past six hours. Orders keep pouring in for new furniture pieces via the website Mac had set up for me. She'd asked someone who worked on her apps to design it, and one of her marketing people created an advertising account for my Facebook business page too. Just another way she'd changed my life for the better. The orders are coming almost faster than I can fill them, so every second I'm not on one of Levi's jobsites, I'm in here busting my ass to push out new work. Can't say I mind the distraction. It's either keep myself occupied, or wallow in self-destructive misery.

My head jerks up in a quick nod of greeting. I have a raw piece of oak from a fallen tree that I'm chiseling into a chair leg. The repetitive motions—long, smooth strokes—are all that keep me sane these days.

"Why does your porch look like a funeral home?" Heidi says as she hops on my worktable.

"Mac. She keeps sending my gifts back."

For two weeks now, I've tried sending flowers, baskets. All kinds of shit. Every day, they end up on my front porch instead.

Initially, I was sending them to the hotel, knowing she was out there daily checking on the work Levi has one of his crews starting on. But then I wore Steph down and she told me Mac is staying with her and Alana. I thought for sure I'd at least get one of them to accept delivery. No such luck.

The intensity with which this chick refuses to let me apologize is fucking ridiculous. She even took our dog. I still wake up in the middle of the night thinking I hear Daisy barking. I'll roll over and ask Mac if she's taken her out, only to realize neither of them are there.

I miss my girls, damn it. I'm losing my mind.

"Guess that answers the question of where you two stand." Heidi draws a sad face in the fine yellow dust. "Not for nothing, but I told—"

"I swear to God, Heidi, you finish that sentence and I better never see your face here again."

"Whoa, what the hell, Coop?"

I put too much force behind the chisel and crack the wood. A huge gash opens down the middle of the chair leg. Dammit. The chisel flies out of my hand and pings off the floor somewhere across the garage.

"You got exactly what you wanted, right, Heidi? Mac won't talk to me. And now, what, you've come to gloat? Fucking spare me."

"You think I did this to you?"

"I know you did."

"God, Cooper, you are such an ass." Cheeks stained red with anger, Heidi throws a handful of sawdust in my face.

"Motherfucker," I curse. There's sawdust in my mouth and up my nose.

Muttering under my breath, I douse my head with a bottle of water and spit up tiny splinters on the concrete floor. My wary gaze tracks Heidi's pissed off movements as she starts pacing the garage.

"I warned you this was a bad idea," she fumes. "I said it was cruel to play with someone like that. But you didn't listen because *Oh that Heidi, she's just jealous.* Right? Isn't that what you thought?"

A sliver of guilt pricks my chest, because, yeah, it's precisely what I thought when she'd protested Evan's revenge scheme.

"Well, I'm sorry it blew up in your face exactly how I knew it would." She jabs her index finger in the air. "Don't put that on me."

I jab my finger right back. "No, you only made Mac miserable every second she was around until you finally got your chance to drive her away."

"She was eavesdropping. Play stupid games, win stupid prizes."

I'm so goddamn over Heidi and her attitude. For six months, I've made myself grin and bear it, but there's a limit.

"You made it pretty clear you hated her from the second we got together. I asked you, as a friend, to do me this one favor. Instead you stabbed me in the back. Honest to God, I thought we were tighter than that."

Heidi launches forward and chucks a sanding block at my head, which I manage to catch before it wallops me in the face. "Don't pull that loyalty card nonsense on me. All you've done since the summer is act like I'm the heartsick psycho who can't get off your dick, but it was you who showed up at my door drunk and horny one day, and the next you're treating me like a stalker."

"Where did this come from?"

"You, jackass." Heidi paces around the table. Too close to my chisels and mallets for my liking. "Yes, okay, sorry, I made the unforgiveable mistake of catching feelings for you. Fucking crucify me. I don't remember you telling me our shit was over. I don't recall a conversation where you said, *Hey, it's only sex and we're cool, right?* One day I'm getting the brush-off and that's it."

I falter, forcing myself to look back to last summer. My memory is a bit fuzzy on the details. I'm not even sure how we ended up in bed the first time. Can't say I remember having a meeting about the particulars either. There'd been no *what are we* talk. No discussion where we laid out some ground rules. I just . . . assumed.

And that's when I realize, as I feel the color drain from my face and guilt twist up my insides, that maybe I was the asshole.

"I didn't realize that's how you felt," I admit, keeping my distance because another violent outburst is not out of the question. "I thought we were on the same page. And then, yeah, I guess I felt kind of cornered and took the easy way out. I didn't want to make it awkward."

Heidi stops. She sighs, slumping down on a stool. "You made me feel like some random hookup. Like, even as a friend, I didn't mean anything to you. That really hurt, Coop. Then I was so mad at you."

Fuck. Heidi's always had my back. I was so up my own ass I didn't think for a second how I did her wrong.

"Come here," I say gruffly, holding out my arms.

After a second, she comes forward and lets me hug her. Though she does slug me in the ribs before wrapping her arms behind my back.

"I'm sorry," I tell her. "I didn't mean to hurt you. If I'd seen someone else treat you that way, I'd have beaten him senseless. It wasn't cool at all."

She peers up at me, and there's moisture clinging to her lashes. She hastily wipes her eyes. "I guess I'm sorry too. I should have put on my big girl pants and cut your brake lines like an adult instead of taking it out on your girlfriend."

Ah, fucking Heidi. Never can tell with this one. I wouldn't for a second put it past her.

I give her another squeeze before releasing her. "Are we good?"

She shrugs. "Eh. We will be."

"If you need me to grovel some more, say the word." I flash a self-deprecating grin. "I've gotten damn good at groveling these past couple weeks."

Her lips twitch with humor. "The flowers on your porch say otherwise. But sure, I'll take some groveling. You can't act like a fuckboy and expect to get away with it."

I wince. "God. No. Definitely don't let me get away with it." A groan slips out. "I just realized something. I'm Evan. I fucking Evan'd you."

Heidi starts to laugh uncontrollably, bending over to clutch her side. "Oh my God, you did," she howls. When she regains her composure, her cheeks are flushed and stained with tears of laughter rather than pain. She grins at me and says, "I almost feel like that's punishment enough."

I know Heidi well enough to be sure we'll work our stuff out, and it's especially promising after our talk in the garage. The harder mission right now is Mac, whose determination to ignore me has surpassed even my most pessimistic estimations. Two weeks becomes three, and the stubborn woman continues to act as if I don't exist.

I've taken to texting her as I get off work, a reward to myself for making it all day without leaving her a dozen voicemails. Not that she ever replies, but I'm holding on to hope that one day she will.

I've just hit send on my latest *Please please call me* when Levi signals me and Evan as we're getting into my truck and asks us to meet him down at his lawyer's office on Main Street. He mentioned something recently about amending his will, so I figure it's about that. But when we get there, he drops a bomb on us.

After we're ushered into a small conference room and take our seats, Levi slides a small stack of documents across the table.

"For you boys," he says.

"What's this?" I ask.

"Have a quick read."

Confused, I scan the documents. My eyes widen when they land on the words *Hartley & Sons*. "Levi. What is this?" I repeat.

Evan pulls the papers toward him to take a better look.

"I'm restructuring the company," Levi explains, pushing two pens toward us. "And, if you're interested, Coop, bringing your furniture business under the new H & S umbrella."

"Wait." Evan pops his head up after a careful reading of the contract. "You want to make us owners?"

Levi nods with a reserved smile. "Equal partners."

"I . . ." Am lost for words. Dumbstruck. I didn't see this coming whatsoever. "I don't understand. What brought this on?"

Levi clears his throat and gives his lawyer a look that gets the older man peeling out of his big leather chair to give us some privacy. "The day Shelley left town for good, when I came by the house to check on you," he starts. Then stops, clearing his throat again. "What you boys said really got to me. About being all alone now. Feeling like orphans. And, well, if I'm being honest, I always thought of you two as my sons."

Levi's never been married or had kids of his own. It wasn't until we were in high school that Evan and I caught on that his friend and roommate Tim was his boyfriend. They've been together as long as I can remember, though they try not to be obvious about it. The Bay that Levi grew up in is of another time, so I get it. He prefers to keep his personal life private, and we've always tried to respect that.

"I figured, well, let's make it official." He gulps, shifting awkwardly in his chair. "If you're good with it, that is." Another gulp. "I want to make sure you boys have a legacy you're proud of in this town."

All I can do is stare at him. Because . . . wow. No one has ever invested anything in us before. Growing up, most people wrote us off as a lost cause. Bound to end up like our parents. Drunks.

Deadbeats. Drop-outs. All waiting for the day they could wag their fingers and say, *See, I knew it.* But not Levi. Maybe because he's family, but mostly because he's a decent guy. He saw us as worth protecting. He knew, if given a chance, an ounce of help, we'd turn out okay. A little frayed, maybe, but still in one piece.

"So, what do you say?" he prompts.

My brother wastes no time grabbing one of the pens. "Hell yes," he says, the crack in his voice revealing he's as affected by this as I am.

I always knew our uncle cared, that he'd never let us down, but this is more than I ever expected. It's a real future. Something to build on. It's the feeling that Evan and I finally have some firm footing in this world. One thing that isn't crumbling around our heads.

Evan scribbles his signature on the bottom of the page. He jumps to his feet, meeting Levi first with a handshake and then a back-slapping hug. "Thanks, Uncle Levi," he says in a very serious un-Evan-like tone. "We won't let you down. I promise."

My hand shakes slightly as I add my own signature to the page. I get up and embrace our new business partner. "I can't thank you enough," I tell our uncle. "This means so much to us."

"Don't thank me yet," he says with a smirk. "You're owners now. That means early mornings and late nights. I've got a lot to teach you."

"I look forward to it," I answer, and I mean every word.

"Good. I'm thinking first thing we do is get one of you boys to head up the demolition crew at Mackenzie's hotel. Frees me up to focus on the Sanderson restaurant."

I flinch. Just hearing someone say her name stirs up a world of pain. "Yeah. Maybe Evan'll handle that. I don't think Mac is ready to have me around on the site every day."

Levi's brow furrows. "You two are still on the outs?"

I nod miserably. "She won't answer my calls or accept my gifts."

"Gifts?" he echoes in amusement.

My brother speaks up, taking great delight in describing to our uncle the field's worth of flowers I'd sent, the numerous heart-shaped chocolate boxes, the overstuffed baskets. "So many baskets," Evan stresses. "It's disgusting."

"And futile," Levi says after a bout of gentle laughter. "Boy, you're not winning back a girl like that with candy and flowers."

"No?" Frustration jams in my throat. "Then what do I do? How do I get her to talk to me?"

My uncle claps a hand over my shoulder. "Easy. You need to think bigger."

CHAPTER FORTY-FOUR

MACKENZIE

On my way back to Steph and Alana's house from the hotel, I stop to grab takeout from their favorite Chinese food place. It's only been a few weeks since Levi's guys started work on ripping out all the old carpet and drywall, tossing the damaged furniture and fixtures and anything too far gone to salvage, yet the place is almost unrecognizable on the inside.

A blank canvas.

Already I'm rethinking much of the interior design aesthetic. I still intend to preserve the original look as much as possible, but with an eye toward editing. I want to open the place up more, bring the outside in. Brighten it with natural light and greenery. Reflect a sense of luxurious relaxation. My architect is about sick of me with all my phone calls and emails tweaking the plans. I'm sure I'll calm down once the new construction begins. I just want it to be perfect. This is my legacy I'm building, after all. With any luck, it'll be standing for another fifty years.

I pull into the driveway in the used SUV I purchased from the local dealership last week. I finally caved and got a car after realizing I can't spend the rest of my life in this town in the backseats of taxis and Ubers.

I'm killing the engine when I receive a text message from my mother.

Mom: *Mackenzie, I'm forwarding you the name of my designer, as promised. If you insist on continuing on with this little project, then you must do it right.*

My snicker echoes loudly in the vehicle. That's the closest thing to a stamp of approval my mother is currently capable of providing. After months of playing the silent treatment game with my parents, I ended up contacting them a week after I moved out of Cooper's. I blame it on my highly emotional state. But honestly, despite their overbearing, condescending personalities, they're still my parents. The only family I have. So I bit the bullet and extended the olive branch, and to my surprise, they accepted it.

A few days ago they even made it out to the hotel—for about ten minutes. Long enough for my dad to grimace a lot and my mom to give me an earful about linen patterns. I can't say they were entirely enthused about the project, but they made the effort anyway. A small step toward normalizing relations.

I send back a quick text.

Me: *Thanks, Mom. I'll give her a call tomorrow.*
Mom: *If you need another set of eyes once you enter the interior design phase, contact Stacey and she'll add you to my calendar if I have the time.*

I roll my eyes at the screen. Classic Annabeth Cabot. But nothing I can do about that.

I'm barely in the door of the house before my roommates pounce and tear the takeout bags from my hands. We set the table and start digging in while Steph turns on her nightly paranormal investigations marathon on TV. Six straight hours of grown men in night vision goggles, running through an abandoned mall and screaming about a rat kicking around an errant food court cup or something. But whatever. It's her thing.

"So what were you saying about some shit that happened at work?" Alana says, picking all the pork out of the lo mein before anyone else has gotten their hands on the carton.

"Oh, right." Steph talks with her chopsticks like she's conducting an orchestra. "So Caitlynn tells Manny that his ex blasted him on *BoyfriendFails*. Everyone's on it now at the bar," she tells me with a grin.

"How'd they know it was about him?" Alana demands.

"Oh, 'cause we were all there when the original incident happened. Long story short: Manny met some girl at a bar last month and took her home. Few days later, he sees her again and asks her out. They're dating for a few weeks when a group of us are out bowling, and he apparently calls her by the wrong name. I don't know how he'd managed to go all that time never calling her by name, but turns out he'd slept with her older sister that first night, then met the younger sister and confused the two."

"Ouch." Every time I think I've heard it all, there's a new twist on an old favorite.

"Anyway, fast forward to tonight. Caitlynn's showing Manny the *BoyfriendFails* post when this teenage kid walks in. He marches right up to the bar. And it's the middle of the lunch rush so we're pretty slammed. The kid shouts something at Manny in Spanish, then grabs some dude's drink, splashes it on the bar, and throws a match."

I gasp loudly. "Oh my God, is he okay?"

Steph waves away my concern. "Oh, yeah, he's fine. Joe's been watering down the wells for decades."

And this is why one of the first things I did after the money started coming in was get a lawyer to write up a liability disclaimer for the website.

"When the bar doesn't ignite, he's furious and jumps over it," Steph continues. "Kid isn't more than five-foot-nothing and can't be older than fifteen. Must not be the first time Manny's been chased because I'd never seen him move so fast."

Alana snickers.

"He ducks out from behind the bar and hauls ass. The kid's diving over tables. Takes a swing at him with a chair until Daryl picks him up and tosses him outside. Daryl has to barricade the doors until the kid finally gives up and leaves. Manny sneaks out the back." Steph starts cracking up. "Turns out it was those girls' little brother come to beat Manny's ass. It was adorable."

"You know," I say, trying not to choke on my food, "good for the kid."

"Right?"

I swallow my lemon chicken and reach for a can of Diet Coke. "Speaking of bitter exes, I ran into Preston today when I was having lunch with Bonnie on campus."

Steph lifts a brow. "How'd that go?"

"Not terrible," I admit. "He was with his new girlfriend. Cute, typical Garnet girl whose father is some hedge fund guy and mother is an heir to an electric fan fortune or something. They've been together for a couple months now."

Alana makes a face. "Poor girl."

I shrug. "I don't know, far as I can tell, she worships Preston. Which is all he really wants, I guess. Someone to smile and thank him for making the decisions." I pop another piece of chicken into my mouth, talking while chewing. "If it makes them both happy, then who am I to judge?"

"Oh, hey, did you see this?" Alana shoves the last bite of an eggroll in her mouth, then wipes duck sauce from her fingers before handing me her phone. "From today."

I glance at the screen to find a new post from *BoyfriendFails*. Except it starts with a caveat. This isn't from a disgruntled girlfriend anonymously blasting her ex—it's from the boyfriend confessing his misdeeds to the world.

I'm the #BoyfriendFail

You read the title right. I'm the boyfriend fail. As in, I failed. Big-time. I failed the woman I love, I failed our relationship, and I failed myself.

I raise my head to shoot a suspicious look at Alana. She pretends to be overly focused on her food.

I messed up the best thing that ever happened to me. Let my perfect girl slip through my fingers because I was a selfish asshole. The night I met her, I had revenge on the brain. I had a beef with her boyfriend. I wanted to punish him for getting me fired, for stirring up all my insecurities about being a loser townie, being stuck here without prospects for anything better. Anything more.

But then I got to know her, and something happened. She inspired me. She showed me there's more to me than this anchor around my neck weighing me down. She made me believe I'm capable of greatness.

She was right. But also wrong. Because I don't want greatness, I don't want a bright sunny future—if she's not by my side to enjoy it.

A pit grows in my stomach as I read on. It's sweet and sincere. My fingers go numb and my eyes sting.

> She doesn't owe me a second chance, I know that. She doesn't owe me anything. But I'm still going to ask.
>
> Give me a second chance, princess. And if you do, I promise you this—I will never lie to you again. I will never take you for granted. I will never, for the rest of my life, forget the goddamn treasure you are.

I almost can't see by the time I finish reading, my vision completely blurred by tears. The post closes with a plea to meet him at six o'clock this Saturday at the place where we rescued our dog.

"Damn it," I mumble when I put the phone down on the table. "I thought we had a deal."

Alana hands me a napkin to wipe my face. "We did. But he's a mess. You're miserable. Neither of you are coping. I'm sorry I resorted to a sneak attack, but come on. What's the harm in hearing him out?"

"I'm not miserable," I say in my defense. "I'm moving on."

Steph gives me a look that begs to differ.

"You're in denial," Alana corrects. "Spending ten hours a day at the hotel and another five holed up in your room on your websites is not the sign of someone who's moved on."

So it's been difficult. Fine. When everything else is spinning out of control, work is where I find my center. It's a distraction, and the most effective way I've found to keep my mind off Cooper.

Truth is, he's a hard man to get over. Hardly a day passes without me waking up and expecting to feel his arm around me in bed. Ten times a day I almost text him some funny joke or exciting update about the hotel—until I remember he isn't mine anymore. Daisy still searches for him. Picking up his scent here and there. Lying at the foot of his side of the bed. Waiting at the door for someone who never comes.

Nothing about being in this town feels right without him.

And none of that changes the fact that he lied to me. Repeatedly. He took away my power to make my own decisions. He tricked me, and I can't so easily disregard that. If I can't have respect for myself, no one will.

"Meet him," Alana urges. "Listen to what he has to say. Then go with your heart. What's the harm in doing that much?"

Irrevocable damage. A small crack in the levee that gives way to insurmountable anguish. When I left Cooper, I built my walls sturdy, made to last. I wasn't designed to open and shut at will. More than anything, I fear that if I let myself see him, I won't ever stop feeling this terrible ache. That if I forgive him, I'm setting myself up to be ruined again. Because I don't know how to walk away from Cooper Hartley twice.

I might not survive it again.

CHAPTER FORTY-FIVE

COOPER

It's seven o'clock.

I feel like a moron. I should have dressed better. Brought her some flowers. I was knocking around my house all afternoon trying to not get worked up about this that I drove myself fucking batshit. I walked out of the house in my cargo shorts and a T-shirt, looking like a goddamn bum asking this amazing woman to forgive him for being a complete bastard since the day she met him.

What the fuck am I doing here?

My eye twitches. It's been doing that for two days. Alana told me she'd shown Mac the post I'd written, but wouldn't elaborate much on her reaction, except to say she didn't chuck the phone into the street. It's been an hour since the time I'd asked to meet, though, and with each passing second my hope evaporates. Somehow, I'd gotten into my head this plan was foolproof. Mac would see my sincerity and thoughtfulness, and of course she'd forgive me.

This was a stupid plan. Why did I think pouring my heart out on a website she built to drag dumbasses like me would be romantic? I'm a joke. Maybe if I'd gone after her that night at the party, I wouldn't be standing here with the seagulls, which are circling as if they're mobilizing for an assault. I kick a mound of sand in the air to remind them of their place in the food chain.

Seven fifteen.

She's not coming.

Maybe I shouldn't have expected to win her over with one grand gesture, but I never thought she'd blow me off entirely. It knocks the wind out of me like a punch right to the center of my chest. The boardwalk lights flicker on as the sun dips behind the town.

She's really not coming.

Accepting my fate, I slowly turn back toward the way I came, and that's when I see a lone figure walking toward me.

I careen into a full-blown panic at the sight of Mac approaching. She's only ten yards away now. Five. She looks stunning, her tall, slender body wrapped up in an ankle-length blue dress with a low V neckline. I haven't forgotten a single freckle or the way her eyes have little flecks of blue in their green depths. The crease of her lips when she says my name. Seeing her again, though, it's wiping the dust off the window.

"I didn't think you were coming," I tell her, trying to keep my composure. I got her here. Last thing I want to do is scare her off, even if every ounce of me wants to hold her one more time.

"I almost didn't."

She comes to a stop, keeping a few feet of distance between us. Those three feet feel insurmountable. It's strange how I can read her less now than the first time we met. She's impenetrable. Not giving anything away.

Too much time passes where I'm lost, remembering what it was like to feel her hair between my fingers, and she gets impatient.

"So . . . what's up?" she asks.

For days, all I've done is rehearse how I'd do this. Now I'm here and everything I'd planned to say sounds like some corny bullshit. I'm dying here.

"Look, the truth is I'm gonna be bad at this no matter how I say it, so I'm just gonna say it." I take a deep breath. *Now or never, asshole.* "I've regretted every day I was too chickenshit to tell you the truth. I was selfish and stupid, and you have every right to hate me. I've had nothing but time to think about how to convince you I'm sorry and why you should take me back. Honestly, I don't have a good reason."

Mac looks away, and I know I'm losing her because this is all coming out wrong, but I can't seem to stop the words from tearing out of my mouth.

"What I mean to say is, I know what I did was wrong. I know I destroyed your trust in me. That I betrayed you. I was careless with something very precious. But, damn it, Mac, I'm so in love with you and it's killing me that you're still out here, out of reach, when I know in my soul I can make you happy again if you let me. I've been a bastard and want you to love me back anyway. It's not fair. I should have to suffer for how I hurt you. I fucking am suffering. But I'm begging you to put me out of my misery. I don't know how to be without you anymore."

I'm out of breath by the time my jaw snaps shut, the delayed message finally making its way to my brain, saying *Shut the hell up.* Mac wipes at her eyes and I have to lock myself down to stop from reaching for her. Seconds pass as I wait for her to respond. Then the cold, dead silence when she doesn't.

"I want to show you something," I blurt out when I sense she's ready to bail. "Will you take a walk with me?"

She doesn't budge. "What is it?"

"It's not far. Please. It'll only take a minute."

She ponders my offer for almost longer than my nerves can tolerate. Then her head jerks in agreement.

I hold my hand out for hers. Instead, she walks ahead of me.

We go a little ways down the beach, where I coax her up to the boardwalk in front of her hotel. It's still a gutted shell, though the debris has been hauled away. On what's left of the veranda, two matching rocking chairs sit looking out on the water. Flickering candles line the railing.

Mac's breath hitches. Slowly, she turns to meet my earnest gaze. "What's this?" she whispers.

"First time you brought me here, you told me that you pictured guests sitting out here in rocking chairs, sipping wine, watching the waves roll in."

She looks up at me with the thousands of tiny lights of the boardwalk shining in her eyes. "I can't believe you remembered."

"I remember every word you've ever said to me."

Her gaze returns to the veranda. I can feel her softening, the stiffness of her body melting away.

"Mac, when I picture my future, I see myself old and gray, sitting in a rocking chair on a porch. With you beside me. That's my dream."

Before her, I didn't bother looking ahead even five years. The image was never a pretty one. I figured I'd spend my days scraping by, getting the bare minimum out of life. I never considered the possibility that someone might be crazy enough to love me. But Mac *did* love me, and I'd gone and run her off.

"I can't say I won't ever mess up again," I choke out through the gravel lining my throat. "I don't have a great frame of reference for functioning relationships. Sometimes I get too far up my own ass, or too stuck in my own brooding thoughts. But I can promise to try to be a man you deserve. To be someone you're proud of. And I will never lie to you again." My voice grows hoarser by the second. "Please, Mac. Come home. I don't know what I am if I can't love you."

She stares down at her feet, twisting her hands together. I'm bracing for the worst the longer she doesn't speak, but finally she takes a breath.

"You broke my heart," she says, so softly a slight breeze could blow the words right out of the air. "I've never been so hurt by anyone in my life. That's not an easy thing to let go, Cooper."

"I understand." My heart is racing and I'm thinking I might drop to my knees if she doesn't say yes.

"You'd have to promise me something else."

"Name it." I'd freeze a kidney for her if she asked for it.

A slight smirk curves her lips. "You have to start cashing my rent checks."

My brain stutters to catch up. Then her smile widens and she grabs the front of my shirt, pulling my lips to hers. Overcome with relief, I hoist her up and wrap her legs around my hips, kissing her until we're both gasping for air. I've never kissed anyone with more conviction or intent. Never needed anything the way I've needed to feel her in my arms again.

"I love you," I mumble against her lips. It doesn't seem enough to say it, and yet I can't get the words out fast enough. "So much." As far as close calls go, this one was razor thin. I almost lost her, lost this.

She clings to me, kissing me back with urgency. And my chest fills to the brim with the kind of naked, honest love I never thought myself capable of feeling. Of finding. I've learned a lot about myself over the last several months. Not the least of which is learning to take better care of the people I love.

Mac pulls back slightly, her gorgeous eyes seeking mine. "I love you too," she breathes.

And in that moment I vow, even if it takes me the rest of my life, to show this girl she didn't waste her heart on me.

ACKNOWLEDGMENTS

As anyone who knows me can attest, I've been obsessed with quaint beach towns for ages. Avalon Bay might be a fictional town, but it's an amalgamation of all my favorite parts of various coastal towns I've visited over the years, and it was an absolute joy to lose myself in this world. Of course, I couldn't have done that without the support and general awesomeness of the following people: my agent, Kimberly Brower, and editor, Eileen Rothschild, for their contagious enthusiasm for this story; Lisa Bonvissuto, Christa Desir, and the rest of the terrific staff at SMP, and Jonathan Bush for the incredible cover!

Early readers and author friends who provided feedback and amazing blurbs; Natasha and Nicole for being the most efficient human beings on the planet; every single reviewer, blogger, Instagrammer, Booktokker, and reader who has shared, supported, and loved this book.

And as always, my family and friends for putting up with me whenever I'm in deadline mode. Love you all.

Bad Girl Reputation

Available Fall 2022

GENEVIEVE

The guy's got some nerve walking in here looking like he does. Those haunting dark eyes that still lurk in the deepest parts of my memory. Brown, nearly black hair I still feel between my fingers. He's as heart-stabbingly gorgeous as the pictures that still flicker behind my eyes. It's been a year since I last saw him, yet my response to him is the same. He walks into a room and my body notices him before I do. It's a disturbance of static in the air that dances across my skin.

It's obnoxious, is what it is. And that my body has the audacity to react to him, *now*, at my mother's funeral, is even more disturbing.

Evan stands with his twin brother Cooper, scanning the room until he notices me. The guys are identical except for occasional variances in their haircuts, but most people tell them apart by their tattoos. Cooper's got two full sleeves, while most of Evan's ink is on his back. Me, I know it from his eyes. Whether they're gleaming with mischief or flickering with joy, need, frustration . . . I always know when it's Evan's eyes on me.

Our gazes meet. He nods. I nod back, my pulse quickening. Literally three seconds later, Evan and I convene down the hall where there are no witnesses.

It's strange how familiar we are with some people, no matter how much time has passed. Memories of the two of us wash over me like a balmy breeze. Walking through this house with him like we're back in high school. Sneaking in and out at all hours. Stumbling with hands against the wall to stay upright. Laughing in hysterical whispers to not wake up the whole house.

"Hey," he says, holding out his arms in a hesitant offer, which I accept because it feels more awkward not to.

He always did give good hugs.

I force myself not to linger in his arms, not to inhale his scent. His body is warm and muscular and as familiar to me as my own. I know every inch of that tall, delicious frame.

I take a hasty step backward.

"Yeah, so, I heard. Obviously. Wanted to pay my respects." Evan is bashful, almost coy, with his hands in his pockets and his head bowed to look at me under thick lashes. I can't imagine the pep talk it took to get him here.

"Thanks."

"And, well, yeah." From one pocket, he pulls out a blue Blow Pop. "I got you this."

I haven't cried once since finding out Mom was sick. Yet accepting this stupid token from Evan makes my throat tighten and my eyes sting.

I'm suddenly transported back to the first time a Blow Pop ever exchanged hands between us. Another funeral. Another dead parent. It was after Evan's dad, Walt, died in a car accident. Drunk driving, because that's the kind of reckless, self-destructive man Walt Hartley had been. Fortunately, nobody else had been hurt, but Walt's life ended on the dark road that night when he'd lost control and smashed into a tree.

I was twelve at the time and had no clue what to bring to a wake. My parents brought flowers, but Evan was a kid like me. What was he going to do with flowers? All I knew was that my best friend and the boy I'd always had a huge crush on was hurting badly, and all I had to my name was one measly dollar. The fanciest thing I could afford at the general store was a lollipop.

Evan had cried when I quietly sat beside him on the back deck of his house and clasped the Blow Pop in his shaking hand. He'd whispered, "Thanks, Gen," and then we sat there in silence for more than an hour, staring at the waves lapping at the shore.

"Shut up," I mutter to myself, clenching the lollipop in my palm. "You're so dumb." Despite my words, we both know I'm deeply affected.

Evan cracks a knowing smile and smooths one hand over his tie, straightening it. He cleans up nice, but not too nice. Something about a suit on this guy still feels dangerous.

"You're lucky I found you first," I tell him once I can speak again. "Not sure my brothers would be as friendly."

With an unconcerned smirk, he shrugs. "Kellan hits like a girl."

Typical. "I'll make sure to tell him you said so."

Some wandering cousins glimpse us around the corner and look as though they might find a reason to come talk to me, so I grab Evan by the lapel and shove him toward the laundry room. I press myself up against the door frame, then check to make sure the coast is clear.

"I can't get hijacked into another conversation about how much I remind people of my mom," I groan. "Like, dude, the last time you saw me, I still wasn't eating solid food."

Evan adjusts his tie again. "They think they're helping."

"Well, they're not."

Everyone wants to tell me what a great lady Mom was and how important family was to her. It's almost creepy, hearing people talk about a woman who bears no resemblance to the person I knew.

"How you holding up?" he asks roughly. "Like, really?"

I shrug in return. Because that's the question, isn't it? I've been asked it a dozen different ways over the past couple days, and I still don't have a proper answer. Or at least, not the one people want to hear.

"I'm not sure I feel anything. I don't know. Maybe I'm still in shock or something. You always expect these things to happen in a split second, or over months and months. This, though. It was like just the wrong amount of warning. I came home and a week later she was dead."

"I get that," he says. "Barely time to get your bearings before it's over."

"I haven't known which way is up for days." I bite my lip. "I'm starting to wonder if there's something wrong with me?"

He fixes me with a disbelieving scowl. "It's death, Fred. There's nothing wrong with you."

I snort a laugh at his nickname for me. Been so long since I've heard it, I'd almost forgotten what it sounded like. There was a time when I answered to it more than my own name.

"Seriously, though. I keep waiting for the grief to hit, but it doesn't come."

"It's hard to find a lot of emotion for a person who didn't have a lot for you. Even if it's your mom." He pauses. "Maybe especially moms."

"True."

Evan gets it. He always has. One of the things we have in common is an unorthodox relationship with our mothers. In that there isn't much relationship to speak of. While his mom is an impermanent idea in his life—absent except for the few times a year she breezes into town to sleep off a bender or ask for money—mine was absent in spirit if not in body. Mine was so cold and detached, even in my earliest memories, that she hardly seemed to exist at all. I grew up jealous of the flowerbeds she tended in the front yard.

"I'm almost relieved she's gone." A lump rises in my throat. "No, more than almost. That's terrible to say, I know that. But it's like . . . now I can stop trying, you know? Trying and then feeling like shit when it doesn't change."

My whole life I made efforts to connect with her. To figure out why my mother didn't seem to like me much. I'd never gotten an answer. Maybe now I can stop asking.

"It's not terrible," Evan says. "Some people make shit parents. It's not our fault they don't know how to love us."

Except for Craig—Mom certainly knew how to love him. After five failed attempts, she'd finally gotten the recipe right with him. Her one perfect son she could pour a lifetime of mothering into. We might as well have been raised by two different people. He's the only one of us walking around here with red, swollen eyes.

"Can I tell you something?" Evan says with a grin that makes me suspicious. "But you have to promise not to hit me."

"Yeah, I can't do that."

He laughs to himself and licks his lips. An involuntary habit that always drove me crazy, because I know what that mouth is capable of.

"I missed you," he confesses. "Am I an asshole if I'm sort of glad someone died?"

I punch him in the shoulder, to which he feigns injury. He doesn't mean it. Not really. But in a weird way I appreciate the sentiment, if only because it gives me permission to smile for a second or two. To breathe.

I toy with the thin silver bracelet circling my wrist. Not quite meeting his eyes. "I missed you, too. A little."

"A little?" He's mocking me.

"Just a little."

"Mm-hmm. So you thought about me, what, once, twice a day when you were gone?"

"More like once or twice *total*."

He chuckles.

Truthfully, after I left the Bay I spent months doing my best to push away the thoughts of him when they insisted their way forward. Refusing the images that came when I closed my eyes at night or went on a date. Eventually it got easier. I'd almost managed to forget him. Almost.

Amanda Nicole White

A *New York Times, USA Today,* and *Wall Street Journal* bestselling author, ELLE KENNEDY grew up in the suburbs of Toronto, Ontario, and is the author of more than forty romantic suspense and contemporary romance novels, including the international bestselling Off-Campus and Briar U series.